THE REDW

—————————— BOOK

MW00806025

KING'S GAMBIT

SHARON K. GILBERT

KING'S GAMBIT
BOOK SEVEN OF THE REDWING SAGA
BY SHARON K. GILBERT
WWW.THEREDWINGSAGA.COM

Published by Rose Avenue Fiction, LLC
514 Rose Avenue, Crane, MO 65633

First Print Edition - December, 2020
Kindle Edition - December, 2020
All Content and Characters © Sharon K. Gilbert
All global and domestic rights reserved.

ISBN-13: 978-0-9980967-9-7

AVENUE FICTION
514 ROSE AVENUE, CRANE, MO 65633

Published by Rose Avenue Fiction, LLC
514 Rose Avenue, Crane, MO 65633

TABLE OF CONTENTS

FROM THE AUTHOR

It's been a challenging year, hasn't it? But no matter what happens in our lives—as Christians—we *know* that God works all things together for good, according to his purposes. But have you really considered what that verse means? If not, you're about to; for Romans 8:28 forms the central theme of this installment of *The Redwing Saga*. No matter how challenging the task, God remains with us till the very end.

King's Gambit finds Charles Sinclair running through his own challenges, and when he finishes this journey, he'll discover his destiny. I've hinted at this in previous books, but now, it's made clear that the Sinclair family play a central role in prophecy. Yes, the series is fiction, but many of the historical references and even some of the characters are real. More importantly, the series reveals the role that each one of us plays in God's prophetic timeline.

YOU are just as important as anyone else.

Remember that.

This book has taken longer than the others, and I've tried to reduce the manuscript by removing some of the scenes. Originally, the manuscript came in at over 200,000 words, which is far too long. But never fear. All those deleted words and scenes, all those plot points, will go into *Two Knights Defence*.

You'll remember that I use British spelling throughout. If you wish to check, I refer you to the *Oxford English Dictionary*.

This book's title is taken from a chess opening that's fallen out of favour (yep, British spelling). The *Two Knights Defence* (British spelling again) sometimes follows the *King's Gambit* opening and is alternately referred to as the Chigorin Counterattack.

Therefore, in the next book, our two knights, Charles and Paul, will go on the attack against Redwing and Blackstone; but also, against a new opponent, rising up from the West.

I hope you enjoy this installment as much as I've enjoyed writing it. God bless you all, dear readers. May our Lord be with you, no matter what labyrinths now challenge you.

Sharon K. Gilbert
December, 2020
- Romans 8:28
- Eph. 6:12

www.sharonkgilbert.com

"It doesn't require much for misfortune to strike in the King's Gambit. One incautious move, and Black can be on the edge of THE ABYSS."
- Anatoly Karpov, Russian chess champion

LABYRINTH:
Based on Latin <u>laborintus</u>, a great maze or building with many doors, corridors, and turns.
Traditionally connected to the Lydian word <u>labrys</u>, meaning 'double-edged axe'. A maze if therefore a symbol of royal power.

For now we see through a glass, darkly; but then face to face: now I know in part; but then shall I know even as also I am known.
- I Corinthians 13:12

And we know that all things work together for good to them that love God, to them who are the called according to his purpose.
- Romans 8:28

For Derek.
My knight.
My inspiration.
My wonderful husband.

PROLOGUE – PART ONE

11ᵗʰ August, 1889 – A Meeting in Heaven

God's ways are not our ways. He takes all our choices, all our mistakes, then weaves in the dark plots of fallen angels, demons, and devils, and he works *all of it* together for good, according to HIS plans and purposes. Because God is omniscient, seeing the end from the beginning, this great and mighty Lord of Armies faithfully prepares his angels and his human children, for every battle and every war.

On the eleventh day of August in 1899, an event occurred in the city of London, that would lead one particular human into a test of his mind, his will, and even his faith. That man is Charles Robert Arthur Sinclair, 1st Duke of Haimsbury; and the event would occur just after the christening of his twin children, Robert and Georgianna Sinclair, at Drummond Chapel. On that day, two unsuspecting dupes of fallen-realm schemers would attempt to slay Sinclair and all his family.

The human dupes were Baron William Wychwright, a crack shot who'd served with the British Army in Egypt and Afghanistan, along with his dim-witted friend, Mr. Cecil Brandon, a profligate gambler and penniless lay-about.

The attempt would fail, of course, but the resulting chaos would provide a perfect diversion for the REAL PLOT that day: the abduction of the duke and his adopted daughter, Adele Stuart Sinclair.

We might worry about our duke and his beloved daughter, but God, being omniscient, omnipresent, and omnipotent, and also *all-loving*, had already devised a way to work this devious fallen-realm plot into something good and wonderful. In chess terminology, he'd placed his 'king' in jeopardy by offering up the king's pawn as bait. Now, lest we worry about this offered pawn, remember that God chose Adele Sinclair for her strength of mind and heart, just as he chose Charles to become her adoptive father. And these two Sinclairs form the opening gambit of a long, supernatural match that would eventually lead to the fulfilment of a very special prophecy.

Despite the subtle plots created by Araqiel, Eluna, and their Watcher brethren, the Lord is never once surprised, indeed he prepared a trap for them—and part of that preparation commenced at precisely seventy-seven minutes and forty-nine seconds *before* Adele Sinclair was lured into Araqiel's coach, when a very special meeting took place in the heavenly realms.

That bright day in the sacred land, an elohim soldier passed beneath a grand arcade of luminescent pearl and entered into a broad and airy expanse with dimensions beyond any human's ability to imagine or comprehend. And yet, to those living within the Golden Halls of Eden, to those who enjoy the shade of the King's garden and walk beside the still waters of the clearest river imaginable; to such as these, the space felt intimate, familiar, and eternally serene. For these blessed corridors of Eden were free of the taint and twisting trickery of the fallen brethren, to whom the Golden Halls were shut and barred.

On that memorable day, the valiant soldier took the form of a typical human male: auburn hair, hazel eyes, a pleasant face with a smooth, firm jaw. His clothing echoed the human form, with dark trousers, a white cotton shirt, dark waistcoat and overcoat, made of wool.

"You called me, sir?" the soldier asked. "Forgive the attire, my lord, I was just about to leave for Earth. The moment is almost upon us."

The being to whom the soldier spoke was dressed in heavenly robes of pale blue, wrapped round a trailing sheath of glittering starlight. The glorious raiment glowed with the shimmer of feldspar. His keen almond-shaped eyes were a clear, cerulean blue and set within an ageless countenance filled with compassion and wisdom.

The soldier knelt down, his head bowed. "How may I serve, sir?"

"Arise, Hadraniel, trusted and faithful warrior of the One. These are your new orders."

"New orders, sir?"

The heavenly commander handed the soldier a small scroll. "You're no longer to rescue the duke and his daughter. Instead, you must stand aside and let the plot unfold, according to the enemy's plans."

The soldier gasped. "And let the enemy win? Prince Shelumiel, you are my trusted commander, leader of many battles, and so I beg you to forgive my question. It comes not from any doubt, but from love, sir. I've watched Charles Sinclair since the day of his birth. Yea, even before! You know what terrible trials the rebels have planned, my lord Prince. How can you ask me to stand aside and allow his capture, when they'll mislead, entice, and force him to pass through seasons and times and even confront the one from the..."

"Enough, Hadra, enough!" ordered the commander. "All this is known. The One has foreseen it all, and we must trust in his plan."

"And what about the girl? Surely, I may rescue her?"

Prince Shelumiel's eyes shone like perfect sapphires as he replied. "Hadraniel, you are my dear friend, an honoured and beloved brother. Your eagerness to intervene is admirable, but this battle must be fought to the end. Hadraniel, do you trust in the One, who is, and was, and always will be? Do you trust the great I AM?"

The soldier bowed his head. "I do. I trust in him with all my being and all my heart, sir. He is the ONE, the Father, the Son, and the Spirit. He is the King of Kings and Lord of All. Are you saying he *wants* Adele captured?"

"Adele is not your task, Hadra. Another looks after her."

"But Charles Sinclair loves Adele, which makes her important to my mission," the soldier argued. "The duke adopted the girl because he loves her as his own. Her capture will cause him very great distress."

"That is precisely why Araqiel will take her, Hadra," Shelumiel explained patiently. "The One has foreseen every choice Charles Sinclair will make, every path he will walk, and every mountain he must climb. He knows the dark devices the rebels will employ to lure the duke into joining them. If he's to achieve his ultimate destiny, then Charles Sinclair must face this challenge. Without the test, his wonderful future might never take place."

The kneeling angel's head jerked up, a smile setting his eyes aglow. "Then, the trial is part of his preparation?"

"It is the bedrock upon which all Sinclair's future actions must build. Do you not yet realise, Hadra, that the One uses the enemy's own devices against them, working all things together for good?"

"Yes, of course, sir. I know and believe it."

"Then, will you follow the One's commands, even though you cannot see their end?"

The angelic soldier nodded solemnly. "I shall do whatever the One commands. I shall fight for his people, his plans, and his purpose. But if I'm no longer to prevent the abduction, what are my new orders?"

"Every detail is written in the scroll," Shelumiel answered. "And as this challenge includes actions beyond the veil, you will not go alone, Hadraniel."

"No? Then who will accompany me?"

The commander clapped his hands. Immediately, a side door opened to the vast audience hall, revealing a brilliantly clad being, much taller than either of the other two. His raiment was so bright it pulsed with its own silvery light. His hair was black as midnight and fell along a muscled back like a river. He was dressed as a soldier. A great broadsword hung from the wide belt, and starlight covered the scabbard with a thousand names. This fierce newcomer approached the kneeling soldier and placed a hand upon his shoulder.

"Hadraniel, my friend and brother, you are not alone in this battle. Once again, we shall face the enemy as one."

The soldier's face radiated with joy. "My dearest friend! Prince Samael, is it really you? But you serve and spy within the enemy camps, do you not?"

"I go where I am needed; through all the Earth, keeping watch upon the deeds of men as well as the fallen," replied the being that London's inner circle knew as Prince Anatole Romanov. "Charles Sinclair is my task, also, Hadra. The future is already past. The One and his Son, who is the Name above all names, have seen the end from the beginning and made preparation. The war is won, but the battles play out. Sinclair will prevail, but first he must endure the great trial."

"The trial is so very difficult. May we fight with him?" asked Hadraniel.

"Yes, but our form of warfare is accomplished more subtly. To begin, you must take on two earthly guises with very different occupations."

"Yes?" asked Hadraniel. "Then, you and I shall act as spies again, as we did long ago?"

"Indeed, we will. Now, my friend, come. Let us return to Earth and protect all that must be."

PROLOGUE – PART TWO
17ᵗʰ October, 1889 – Kent, England

It was a glorious day. The fierce reds and mellow golds of autumn coloured the thick woods with sheaves of splendour. It was a magnificent time of year, when musky florals set sail upon crisp breezes, and the heavens dropped silvery rain upon green meadows. In fallow fields, wildflowers sprang up like volunteer soldiers, each fresh face filled with eagerness and joy, oblivious to the frosts and freezes to come.

Branham Hall gardeners were cutting back rose bushes, whilst teams of footmen with shirtsleeves rolled up, laughed and told tales of older times, as they stowed away wicker tables and willow chairs. Four miles away, the shepherds of Anjou Farm sheared plump sheep in the barns. The thick wool would be dyed, spun, carded, and wound into balls of yarn to make clothing and blankets. Beyond the hedgerows sunburnt farmers harvested acres of golden wheat, yellow squash, and bright orange pumpkins; then stored them in cribs, silos, and granaries as food for the winter. Branham's chittering, chirping birds had moulted their summer raiment in favour of winter's darker hues; whilst in the woodlands, bears and badgers gorged themselves to put on fat, in preparation for a long winter's sleep.

During that long sultry summer, the county seat of the powerful Dukes and Duchesses of Branham had undergone a series of planned alterations. Once the Spring Fête finished, the carpenters tore down all the pavilions and cloth palaces. They dismantled the famous tiltyard, where Duke Charles had thrown a miraculously aimed and supernaturally vaulted lance to bring down an assassin's balloon. Once all this was done, the duke ordered the groundsmen and carpenters to begin razing the Hall's peculiar and quite possibly haunted 'second east' wing, where Sir William Trent once lodged. All leftover stones would be used as fencing or cottage foundations for the Anjou Sheep Farm expansion.

A second project commenced in early July with the arrival of Kent ragstone. Twenty dozen trainloads of the county's beautiful limestone were loaded onto waggons, then delivered to masons and carpenters for use in a new Dower House, to be situated twixt Queen's Lake and Faery's Copse.

The third project involved an infamous pagan site known as 'Herne's Crown'. Just before his disappearance in August, Duke Charles had signed an order for the destruction of the stone circle, a group of sarsen and bluestones, that stood two miles beyond the second-east wing. Once, the henge was used in pagan rituals. Locals claimed the largest bluestone, known as the King's Stone, marked the rising of the summer sun on the solstice. Preliminary excavation of the henge revealed a central tumulus with buried animal remains, and footings that reached deep into the earth.

To pacify the London Society of Antiquarians, the duchess hired an archaeological team, led by Dr. Seth Holloway and his father, Lord Salter, to inspect the henge and determine its age. The initial survey indicated the site pre-dated Stonehenge by a thousand years. Lord Salter recommended a thorough geological survey and a preliminary dig, and the duchess ordered all activity stopped until her husband returned.

The morning following the twenty-first of September, the night of the Autumnal Equinox, a young man called on Branham Village's Police Constable Tower to report seeing a great disturbance at the henge. The witness claimed he'd seen "heathen witches, wearin' nary a stitch upon their young bodies and dancin' round a great fire." The constable dutifully investigated the entire area round the ancient henge, finding evidence of a recent and very hot fire. He also discovered streaks and splashes of dried blood upon the King's Crown stone, as well as on a nearby altar stone, known as Herne's Table.

The crime would be difficult to solve, for the only witness admitted to drinking heavily that night; but also because, he boarded a train for London the following day, leaving no family and no trail to follow. Assuming Duke Charles would find the report of interest, Tower dutifully stored the report and all his photographs in a large and somewhat crowded box, marked 'Occult Activities at the Hall'.

Little did the constable realise how important this box would prove to be in years to come.

As to the reason for the duke's long absence, very few outside the family knew the truth. The official story was that Haimsbury had sailed away on Crown business, but Stephen Blinkmire knew the truth, and since that fateful day, the Irish giant suffered from constant nightmares. Stephen dreamt of dragons, snatching infants from their cots, or flying through the air and disgorging flames upon crowds during the Branham fête. Sometimes, he relived that terrifying moment when he, Count Viktor Riga, Cornelius Baxter, and David Anderson rushed to the centre of the Branham hedge maze to rescue their regal friend. On that Boxing Day, the duke had faced a hideous dragon. Stephen believed the dreadful worm intended to abduct the duke then and there, and he wondered what the brave duke might be facing now.

On that day in mid-October, Stephen had a mind to revisit the maze. The idea came to him suddenly, as if whispered. After setting off from the main house, he ran into Chief Gardener Tom Powers, who was stacking up blighted rose canes for burning.

"Are they decayed?" asked Stephen as he reached the gardener.

"Aye, sir. Most are. It's rust disease, I'm afraid. Shame to cut 'em back, but if we don't, the canker could spoil all the plants. Sometimes, cuts are kindness, sir. What brings you out today, Mr. Blinkmire?"

"Just a walk along the maze."

"Beautiful day for it. Keep watch on the time, sir. The sun sets early now."

"I will, thank you. Mr. Powers, I wonder if you heard anything about a group of witches at Herne's Henge a few weeks ago? The night of the equinox."

"Aye, sir, I heard 'bout it, but such as that happens now an' again. Most likely gypsy children howlin' at the moon, or villagers with naught to do. Happens every year come harvest time. My men and I have to clean up the mess, assumin' the police don't come out."

"And did they?" asked Stephen.

"Did they what, sir?"

"The police. Did someone come to investigate the report of witches?"

"That young constable over to the village, he come out, sir, but there weren't too much to be found."

"I heard there was blood on the King's Stone, as though a sacrifice was made."

"Aye, sir, there's been rabbits and such killed over there. Me an' my men have even found horse's leg bones and goat skulls. Some folks still keep the old ways, sir. They sing on Sundays and pray to the Lord, then go out to Herne's Oak and hang up strips o' cloth to catch a blessing."

"Herne's Oak?" asked Stephen.

"Aye, sir. About forty paces or so east of King's Stone, there's an old well with a tree beside. The women still hang their cloths on the oak, thinkin' Herne or his faery wife'll bring them a babe come spring."

"Do you mean these are fertility rites?"

"Aye, sir. Like I said, there's some folks still pray to the old gods. Branham's got many stories, sir. Take care through the maze, Mr. Blinkmire. We've not gone through there yet to trim. And keep watch for adders. We seen a couple of 'em this mornin' under the roses, makin' little adders."

"Do you mean they were mating?" asked Blinkmire in amazement. "Do females lay eggs during hibernation season?"

"Can't say, sir, but it don't seem likely. Just mind your way. Adder bites are right painful."

"Yes, I shall, Mr. Powers. Thank you."

The eight-foot-tall Irishman left the busy gardener to his work and headed towards the statuary entrance to the infamous hedge maze. He walked through a double row of dukes and duchess, their haughty faces and perfect forms carved from Carrara marble. The vacant eyes watched the giant, as though some spirit inhabited each figure.

As he entered the living puzzle, Stephen could just make out the orange-coloured rays of the afternoon sun as it descended like a sleepy-eyed god into the west. Towards the east, stood the upper regions of Lion Hall's broken battlements. Beneath the ruins, lay the secret tunnels explored one year earlier by Seth Holloway and his Cambridge friends. Further on to the east, stood the haunted bell tower of St. Arilda's Abbey, where Carthusian monks once worshipped demons and sacrificed children to their hungry pagan god.

Despite these many disturbing scenes, the afternoon seemed altogether glorious. The fresh and heady smell of sea salt floated high upon an easterly breeze, whilst above, he spied the soaring flight of grey herons as they darted in and out of tufted white clouds. Joining the herons, were white-winged gulls, performing dazzling displays of aerial acrobatics. The brightness of the afternoon sky, the crispness of the autumn air, the majestic and gambolling birds overhead, conspired together as if to say, "All is right with the world, Stephen Blinkmire. No matter what may come, God Almighty is still in control."

The Irish giant had first entered Branham's famous, evergreen puzzle during last year's Boxing Day festivities. Even now, the memory haunted him a little. He and Riga referred to it as *The Day of the Dragon*, though few who'd seen the monster wished to talk about it. On that fateful day, Stephen joined Inspector Cornelius Baxter, David Anderson, and the indomitable Count Viktor Riga, to battle a dragon of the pit, whose only aim was to inflict mortal injury upon the most magnificent and remarkable gentleman Blinkmire had ever known: none other than His Grace, Charles Robert Arthur Sinclair III, 1st Duke of Haimsbury and England's Shadow Sovereign.

Since that day, the duke had become father to twins and adoptive father to Adele Stuart Sinclair, one of the most endearing young ladies ever to grace the Earth. But with his disappearance, the duke had become the tantalising topic of newspapers round the globe, whose headlines asked in large type:

WHERE IS ENGLAND'S UNCROWNED KING,
DUKE CHARLES OF HAIMSBURY?

As misdirection, Paul Stuart and his inner circle agents fed each ravenous reporter a feast of tantalising possibilities. Some were told the duke was abroad, pursuing a ring of criminals behind the assassination attempt. Others, that he'd sailed for Egypt to negotiate a new canal treaty on behalf of the Crown. One reporter invented a tale, claiming the duke was leading an expedition to claim Jerusalem for England!

Such was the state of media in 1889.

In the first few weeks after the christening, Blinkmire and Riga attended every inner circle meeting, jointly led by Duke James Stuart and Prince Anatole Romanov. The prince advised discretion, caution, and a united front, but some members disagreed with the prince's directions, and the circle began to fracture. Blinkmire and Riga warned their Russian friend about possible sedition, but Romanov responded with his typical ease, "Fear not, my dear friends. These members have always had darkness in their hearts, and remain only because the One allows it—for now. Even Judas walked, talked, and planned with the Son, did he not?"

Days had passed, then a week, then two weeks, with no word of the duke's whereabouts. Then, on the 12th of September, Adele Sinclair was found not far from Montmore House, unconscious, shivering, and with no memory of where she'd been. The girl's sudden return ignited a fresh fire within their hearts, and Lord Aubrey planned to go out and search for the duke, but Romanov advised caution, saying, "The enemy seeks to divide you, my friends. Keep close to one another, and watch for adders beneath all roses."

Fearing for his cousin, Paul Stuart had asked Romanov, "Shall we sit on our hands and do nothing?"

The prince responded by admonishing the circle to sharpen their spiritual weapons, using prayer to undergird their friend's current task. "Charles is following God's plan, Lord Aubrey. You must do likewise. Do not allow this to divide you. That is what the enemy wants."

All circle members voiced open agreement; but secretly, the seed of deceit had taken root, and soon, two members would heed the dragon's whispers.

Paul Stuart wasn't designed to sit and wait. He preferred action and open combat. Still, the young earl submitted to Romanov's admonition and pulled back all of his agents and brought them home.

With Charles missing, it fell to Aubrey to keep watch over Elizabeth and Adele, along with his heavily pregnant wife. To make the task easier, Paul moved Cordelia and her staff to Haimsbury House. By day, he dealt with ICI administrative issues and filled in for Charles as shadow sovereign; by night, he paced upstairs, or poured out his heart to his Cousin Elizabeth, whilst Cordelia slept in a nearby apartment.

Thankfully, Adele's overall condition was quite good. She had suffered minor physical injuries, but sustained the heaviest damage to her mind. She retained no memory of the ordeal, but suffered from nightmares and daytime visions. And so for the present, she remained at Montmore House with Dr. Henry MacAlpin.

As for Blinkmire and Riga, Romanov suggested the two men return to Branham in the event that word of the duke arrived there first. The two friends had asked permission to remain in London, but Romanov insisted. Leaving circle friends like Cornelius Baxter and Martin Kepelheim, but also Duchess Elizabeth and Cordelia Stuart, was a very great blow to both men. However, they knew the prince well, and so trusted in his commands.

Once back at Branham, Stephen and Riga made themselves useful by scanning through newspapers in every language they could read, searching for information. They discovered tales of missing dead in several major cities, but also a sudden rise of paganism in Christian enclaves. A third commonality involved mental illnesses. Count Riga noticed that more and more titled and wealthy individuals were listed as 'taking the cure' at famous spas. The count explained to his friend that 'taking the cure' was a polite euphemism for admission to a private mental hospital like Montmore.

That crisp October day, after a late night spent reading through French newspapers, Blinkmire awoke with an unsettling malaise about his heart; a growing sense of doom, like the premonitions sailors experience just before a great storm erupts at sea. The feeling remained with him all that day, and so once he and Riga finished their four-o'clock tea, Stephen left his friend to an afternoon nap, whilst he toured the gardens and revisited the place where they'd fought the infamous *Dragon*.

The Irishman possessed a remarkable memory and used that mental map to chart a course through the maze, readily avoiding most of the blinds and dead-ends that so often confounded Branham Hall's guests, including Martin Kepelheim on a warm summer day several years earlier. The bed of white pea gravel offered reassuring, tactile pressure beneath his large feet, and the music of warbling birds and croaking toads soothed the malaise of his weary heart.

The giant's emerald green eyes delighted in the maze's many rest areas, where pleasant treats awaited the traveller: comfortable ragstone benches; multi-coloured beds of shade-loving hydrangeas, geraniums, cyclamen, and clematis; mythologically-themed fountains that effervesced with crystal clear water; well-worn statues of tranquil angels, posed in conversation with kings and dukes; and a grand menagerie of carved-oak animals that scampered beneath bent-willow arcades. Such attention to design and detail made Branham's hedge maze the finest and most copied labyrinth in all the kingdom.

Tom Powers had warned the giant that the maze needed cutting back, and indeed the shaggy yews that formed the corridors seemed to plead for their annual trim. The Latin term for the yew was *Taxus baccata*, meaning toxic berries, but yews were known throughout history as the tree of death.

"The death tree," Stephen said aloud as he examined one of the tender green needles. "'Tis a very strange name for something so very beautiful." Each and every bough was laden with bright red berries, and the supple limbs moved and swayed, as though the death trees were alive with demonic spirits. Blinkmire shivered at such a dark thought and began to doubt himself. Perhaps, this journey was ill-conceived. He'd felt certain he should walk the maze today, but why did he think of death? He should concentrate on the beauty of life, not hideous death; but no matter how he tried, Stephen couldn't shake the feeling he was being watched.

Were the trees inhabited? Did they have eyes? Had the equinox witches opened some treacherous pagan portal?

Stephen recalled Irish legends of a woodland spirit known as the Green Man and Herne the Hunter. Since Branham villagers and local farmers worshipped a tree called Herne's Oak, these disturbing legends must perpetuate here as well. Herne's seductive fertility consort was called the Mother Goddess of Nature, most likely a Celtic version of Rhea or Demeter. Idols and stone memorials to these hungry, silvan deities could be found throughout the English countryside; and their leaf-adorned faces decorated gravestones, fertility pillars, and even the altars of some churches.

"It's wrong," Stephen declared as he continued to walk. "It's all so very wrong!" The very idea of idol worship and the elevation of a pagan deity inside *a church* made him angry, particularly as All Hallow's Eve was but a fortnight away. As a boy in Ireland, he dreaded the high pagan holiday with its tales of witches, warlocks, and primeval princes. Samhain brought out the worst in some children. They called him Hell's Spawn, Six-Fingered Freak, Stephen the Troll, and Bran the Cursed: a reversal of Bran the Blessed, a famous Welsh giant, beheaded by King Maltholwch.

But there was another reason Stephen dreaded the devilish season. Long ago, on All Hallow's Eve, he tried to end his own life by hanging from a yew tree.

The Death Tree.

He didn't die that day, of course; for a most unlooked for individual strolled up to the tree and began to talk. Prince Anatole Romanov placed his hand on the fifteen-year-old giant's shoulder saying, "Stephen, why do you want to end your life, when it is just beginning? Come down from there and rejoice, my friend! God loves you and has a great plan for your life. The darkness is now over. Your future is bright."

The prince's intervention had changed everything for him that day. *No,* thought Stephen. *God changed it.* What was it St. Paul wrote to the Philippians? Something about thinking on good things?

"Think on the good things. That's what I'll do," Blinkmire declared aloud. "I'll stop letting this darkness overwhelm my heart. God does have a plan for my life. And I'm here, because he wills it. My unusual strength helped save Duke Charles, didn't it? Yes, I'll think on that!"

At the very instant he spoke these happy words, a large brown hare appeared on the path ahead. The animal's velvety ears pointed straight up, and the sharp eyes were fixed with steely purpose upon Stephen's boat-like feet. The surprised human remained perfectly still, trying not to frighten the magnificent hare.

The Lepus europaeus, thought Stephen. *It's so very beautiful, but why doesn't it run away?*

The large-eared rabbit was a wonderful example of God's rich handiwork. The engineering and musculature of the legs allowed the furry animal to sit or stand upright with ease, whilst providing options for locomotion: a loping, leisurely hop when feeding, a bounding leap to hide from strangers, and a long-strided sprint if pursued, so swift that even most dogs would fail to catch it.

Dogs! the giant thought with alarm. The kennels of Branham contained over two-hundred, working canines, including the prize-winning Labradors, Briar and Bella; but also their newest litter of puppies. These five playful pups had grown to such a degree now, that any one of them could easily catch and devour a precious animal such as this.

Stephen began to fear one might have followed him. Aramis loved to shadow the giant's footsteps. In fact, the mischievous white Labrador had caused Blinkmire to fall headlong into Queen's Lake in early May. Since then, the five precocious pups had matured into large, lean hunting dogs, and their favourite prey was rabbit.

What if Aramis followed me?

"Shoo!" Stephen called to the hare. "Run, please! Find a deep hole to hide in! You're in danger, if you wander these grounds for long. Go now! *Go!*"

But despite the shrill shouts and constant cries, the stubborn animal refused to move even one muscle. Instead, it stared up at the giant, the brown nose twitching as if signalling to him in some unknown rabbit code. The round, amber eyes had fixed upon the human's large face with singular fascination. Despite the giant's frantic pleas, the brown hare remained perfectly calm—as if nothing in the world could ever harm him.

Hoping to frighten it into fleeing, Blinkmire ran towards the hare, his massive boots scattering the gravel in all directions. Any other animal would have bolted for cover, but to his utter dismay, this animal not only failed to run, it actually hopped *closer*.

"Oh, why don't you run?" he asked the rabbit plaintively. "Has someone made a pet of you? Is that it? Did Lady Della once keep you in a cage, and now you wander about, hoping to find her? She's very far from here, I'm afraid. In London in a very nice home, overseen by a fine doctor."

The thought of Adele Sinclair brought a pang of anguish to the soft-hearted giant. He offered up a silent prayer, petitioning the Lord for his tender mercies and adding a plea that God might send his angels to protect the Duke of Haimsbury and bring him home.

"Whatever has happened to him, wherever he might be," Stephen whispered in supplication, "please, dear God, keep him safe and bring our duke back to us. Lady Della would surely recover, if she could see her father again, Lord. Bring him home to us. Please!"

As if in defiance of the giant's prayer, a dense shadow fell across the path, and the pleasant calls of gulls and herons vanished amidst a multitude of harsh avian battle cries. The abrupt aural shift drew Stephen's eyes upwards, and he cringed at what he saw. High above the maze, descending in a spiral of utter darkness, flew a great congregation of ravens.

For a moment, Stephen considered running back to the safety of the Hall. He paced back and forth in the growing darkness, his mind filling with fear. *If I die here, will they find me? Shall I be listed as missing like our beloved Duke?*

As Stephen began to pray again, the brown rabbit inched closer to his feet. Perhaps, it wanted to listen to the prayer, or sought shelter beneath the human's massive body. Or perhaps, and decidedly worse, the hare perceived a more dangerous foe. Might something be hiding inside the centre of the maze?

Might it be the *Dragon?*

Blinkmire swallowed hard, gulping down bitter fear and dread. Again, he thought of running away, of returning to the maze's north entrance and back into the Hall. But the hare inched closer still. Stephen looked down at the animal, perceiving the impossible.

Its amber eyes had transformed to an *icy blue.*

Run, Stephen! a voice told him. *Run!*

A sudden surge of courage replaced the human's fear. Lightning coursed through Stephen's long limbs, and every nerve tingled with fiery purpose. Without one other thought, the Irish giant's feet dug into the gravel and propelled him forward with all speed; and he had but one thought: *Get to the centre! No matter what, I must reach the centre!*

A terrible tempest, like something from the throne of an angry storm god, formed over the maze's centre. Stephen could hear the percussive peals of thunder and see the bright lightning flashes. The cyclone of ravens had brought down a raging torrent of anger. Hot blood pumped through his circulatory system, and Stephen's great heart hammered against his inner chest wall.

But he refused to slow. He kept on running.

There's no time for fear! the voice told him. *Whatever awaits, God will help you! Just run, Stephen, RUN!*

Then a second, slippery voice whispered into his deepest thoughts; a seductive sound like that of a hissing serpent:

'Tis the Dragon, Stephen. He's come to exact revenge for that torn claw. Nothing but a rope awaits you, Bran the Cursed. A thick noose, wound about the Death Tree!

The serpent's words were very hard to ignore, but Stephen prayed as he ran, and the first voice spoke words of scripture that drowned out the snake's lies.

Fear not, Stephen. Even in the valley of the Shadow of Death, the Lord is with you. The Shepherd's rod and staff will smite and crush the enemy! Fear not, Stephen. RUN!

These powerful words circulated through the giant's spirit just as the blood pumped through his veins, and the brave Irishman hurled himself forward, ready to meet whatever dangers lay ahead—even a Dragon.

The brown hare with the impossible blue eyes followed after, matching its long strides to those of the giant, and together these two—human and hare—raced towards the unknown. Above their heads, the hellish maelstrom of supernatural ravens had darkened the sky into a semblance of bare midnight, as though the goddess Nyx had taken control of all the world. But Stephen raced onward, through the walls of bitter darkness, towards the tumult at the maze's darkening centre.

As he ran, the grating voice of the serpent hissed and screamed into his thoughts: *HELL'S DEMON! STEPHEN THE TROLL! Heaven's gates are shut to misshapen creatures like you, Stephen. You're not worthy of God's love. I am your destiny and master, and I shall hang you on a tree and bring you down to my lowest dungeon, where I shall TEAR OUT YOUR CLAWS and let rats feed upon them!*

This horrid voice berated, rebuked, and shrieked at poor Stephen until the human very nearly stopped. But then, as his courage began to wane, that first bright voice softly whispered into the giant's mind, and a peace beyond all imagination filled his soul.

Fear not, brave warrior. You are Stephen the Blessed! Be strong and of good courage, child of God. The Lord Himself fights for you this day, and your future is bright!

A bright future? These were very words Prince Anatole had spoken on that pivotal day in his youth. Stephen had never felt such peace in all his life. And he sensed a mysterious but reassuring presence, running beside him, as if some brightly-armoured warrior angel rushed to battle as his companion. But he could see no one. Was this angel invisible? The only creature Stephen saw could hardly be an armoured warrior: just the ever-faithful, brown hare.

A rabbit with ice-blue eyes.

They had reached the final section, and his animal escort leapt ahead, its quick strides outpacing the human to lead him through the trickiest part of the dark and twisting maze. They formed an unlikely pair, these two: an Irish giant and a brown English hare, but together they crashed through the final wall of Night and burst into the labyrinth's heart, ready to confront whatever Evil lurked within it.

But Stephen met no Dragon.

He met no hissing Serpent within the maze's heart, no utter darkness, not a Storm God's fury.

Instead, stretched out before the marble fountain, lay a living miracle.

At that very instant, the last beams of the setting sun pierced through the dense blackness of the raven tempest and cast a shaft of golden light upon the upper reaches of the deadly yews, as though all of heaven sang for joy!

For you see, the miracle within the maze was none other than His Grace, Charles Sinclair, 1st Duke of Haimsbury. Once again, the Irish giant had come to the duke's rescue.

Blinkmire bent low and spoke softly to the unconscious peer. "Your Grace? Sir? Can you hear me?" The duke gave no reply. His eyes remained shut, but he breathed regularly, at least. *Praise God, he's alive,* thought Stephen. He whispered a prayer of thanksgiving and then lifted the duke into his tree-trunk arms and carried his friend through the maze as quickly as his long legs could manage.

Busy with his gallant errand, the giant failed to notice that his companion, the brave brown English hare remained beside the infamous fountain. And once the human departed, the animal's rich brown fur shimmered and shifted into a cloud of white feathers. The twitching brown nose flattened, the mouth became a beak, and the paws formed pinions and talons.

But the impossible eyes remained as blue as polar ice.

Satisfied with his new form, the magnificent white owl stretched out its long wings and rose up, up, and up!—flying into the very eye of the demonic maelstrom above the maze. The owl's attack scattered the raven horde, and the formation dispersed and vanished into a swirling spiral of black. With the serpent and ravens vanquished, the skies returned to normal, and the pinks and oranges of the setting sun filled the horizon once again.

Then, the white bird descended back towards the estate; turning and turning and turning, in a slow, circular pattern until it found the perfect perch on Branham Hall's tallest chimney. Settled there, the vigilant bird of prey fixed his ice-blue eyes upon the world beyond human sight and watched.

And whilst he did, all the inner circle telegraph wires sang out the good news to each and every member. By nightfall, the duke's very grateful wife would arrive at Branham, via the *Captain Nemo Special*. And then, the next battle of a very long war would commence.

Ah, but Stephen's unexpected discovery occurs at *the end* of our current tale. To understand what happened *before* the duke's serendipitous appearance in the Branham maze; and how his journey through a twisting and tortuous Time Maze would lead Charles and his children through two Great Wars and the fulfillment of prophecy—to understand all of this, we begin our tale with a girl's strange dream.

CHAPTER ONE

Early September – Somewhere Beyond Human Reality

"Wake up," a voice whispered into Adele Sinclair's dream. The voice sounded a little like her father's rich baritone, but with accented notes that evoked images of foreign lands and ancient kings. "Really, Adele," asked the voice, "do you plan to sleep all day?"

The girl's chestnut lashes fluttered then parted, revealing large blue irises with dark pupils. *Where am I?* she thought.

"You're close to me; that's where you are," the voice answered. "I trust you slept well. You certainly slept very long. Somewhat like the princess in that story you read recently. *Little Briar Rose*, no?"

That much was true. Adele had read the story in a collection by the Brothers Grimm, but how could the speaker know about a book she'd only just read? Adele saw no one nearby.

Where is he?

"I must have slept too long and too well," she told the invisible gentleman. "I might still be dreaming, for I'm unable to see you. Where are you hiding? Are you outside? Why don't you knock and come in?"

The surroundings of the bedchamber were luxurious and inviting, perfect in every way, as if designed for her alone. There were lots of bookcases, each shelf crowded with adventure stories and faery tales. A cheerful fire crackled and popped in the firebox of a marble mantelpiece, decorated with carved bluebirds and painted roses. There were four chairs nearby, covered in blue-and-yellow chintz and dotted with plump, striped cushions in the same palette. There was even a furnished dollhouse, set inside an ebony-and-tortoise shell Flemish cabinet.

It was Adele's dream bedchamber come to life, the very one she'd designed with her father that summer, when they'd discussed a future project, intended as a surprise for her new mother Duchess Elizabeth.

But when was that? A week ago? A month?

Adele had no idea.

Though the room pleased, her head was filled with worrying memories of a terrifying coach ride through a thick cloud of darkness; armour-plated horses and ghostly gatekeepers, but also flying machines as they drove through the dark veil. Worst of all, Adele had a dreadful, gnawing, aching sort of dread that her father was in grave danger.

Had something happened after the twins' christening? There'd been gunfire, coming from the organ loft. She remembered that much clearly. Her father's agents helped everyone from the chapel, and then two men were arrested. She'd asked if she might walk to Drummond House. And as she left the chapel, Adele had seen an expensive black coach with curtained windows. The coach sat by itself, near the far end of the gravel drive. Had someone called her name?

No, she'd heard a puppy yelp.

She had mental pictures of a thin man with cruel black eyes, and then her father had come to help—but what came after? Had someone assaulted him? Was her father dragged into the mysterious coach? Why would anyone try to harm her father?

No, she'd had a nightmare; that's all.

But was it a nightmare?

"I need your help, please," she asked the disembodied speaker. "Please, sir, where are you? Where am I? Why can't I see you?"

"You see only what you want to see," the voice answered.

"That makes no sense."

"But it does. Come, find me."

"Was it you who took me?" she asked the invisible speaker. "I demand to see my father! Now, this very minute, or I shall scream and scream!"

"I shouldn't do that, Lady Adele," the voice answered calmly. "It would only bring trouble to your door. If you seek answers, come find me. I am close. Come, and we shall discover the answers together. I have made Russian tea, and there are lots of cakes."

He's Russian! Adele began to smile, for she knew a very kind man with the same voice, and he was a Russian prince.

The adolescent tumbled out of the four-poster bed and landed with a graceful bounce on the cool, black-and-white tile floor. She wore a fashionable night dress made of lace and silk. Della wondered who had dressed her.

Next to the Flemish cabinet, stood an oval mirror, framed in ropes of chased silver, embellished with ivory figures. Adele stopped, surprised by the reflection. She studied herself in the looking-glass. *Am I taller?* The exquisite night dress was fashioned from rose-coloured silk with ribboned shoulders that puffed like pink clouds. The empire bodice was overwrought with Genovese bobbin lace, and the skirt fell to the floor in soft pleats with a little train behind. Della's chestnut hair had lightened over the summer months, and the unbound waves cascaded down the gown's shoulders as glimmering strands of amber gold.

"Do you mirror gaze, my lady?" asked the Russian. "The tea grows cold. Come! We have much to discuss."

Adele knew the speaker well; a unique and very helpful gentleman, whom her father considered a trusted friend. She followed the voice through a connected hallway, decorated in watercolour birds and graceful flowers, then into a warm drawing room. It looked just like her father's study, with a piano near the corner, an oak desk, walls of bookshelves, and leather chairs waiting beside the fire. A low mahogany table was set with cups, saucers, sugar, lemon, a steaming china teapot, and lots of tempting cakes atop a silver tray.

Where was the prince?

Adele drew close to the fire, noticing a skillfully wrought painting just over the mantelpiece. The painting was of her, and she stood before the northeast entrance to the Branham hedge maze. Her painted self wore a gauzy summer dress of cream muslin and a broad-brimmed hat with a wide pink ribbon. A black-and-white dog stood by her side. It had to be Lady Napper, the Cavalier King Charles Spaniel, given to her by Queen Victoria last Christmas.

The artist had placed Adele beside an alabaster statue of a tall woman in Greco-Roman dress. The statue's chiseled marble features were regal and flawless, with a straight nose, large eyes, and full lips. A bird perched upon the woman's left shoulder, its head turned backwards, as if it stared into the maze's entrance.

Just inside the painted labyrinth's northeast gate, stood a tall figure, dressed in shining medieval armour. There was no doubting the handsome knight's identity, for it was Duke Charles Sinclair, Adele's father, clad in the same armour he'd worn for the Branham Fête that May. But why would the artist paint a powerful peer in such a minor role, as if Charles Sinclair were incidental? And why was he wearing armour?

"You're right, of course. That is indeed your good father."

Adele spun round. Before her, stood a tall, well-proportioned man with pale blue eyes. His raven hair was longer than the last time she'd seen him, flowing all the way to his narrow waist.

"Oh, it is you!" she cried out happily, throwing her arms round the Russian aristocrat's middle and giving him a fond hug. This was followed by a litany of questions, asked in a single breath.

"Is this your home, Prince Anatole? How did I get here? Why am I here? What happened to my father? Why is he in your painting? Why am I there?"

"You certainly ask a great many questions, dear lady," the handsome Russian laughed. "I shall try to answer them all, though not necessarily in the order you've asked them. I pray you had a restorative rest?"

"Oh, yes. I feel as if I've slept for years, actually."

"Like the young woman from your book? Briar Rose?"

She nodded. "I feel as though I've slept for a hundred years!"

"Indeed? This particular night has been very long, when measured in human time; but prolonged hours beneath closed eyelids do not guarantee recuperation. After all, you had a most trying flight."

"Did you say flight, Your Highness?" she asked. "Flying is for birds and insects. Or perhaps for aeronauts like Inspector Reid in his balloon."

"In this case, you required no balloon to fly. You do not recall passing through a dark veil?" he asked gently.

Della's smile vanished. "A veil? I thought I'd dreamt it."

"What do you remember?"

"I remember falling through a deep black hole filled with hatred and liars and... And *monsters*."

"Yes, dear Adele," he said, taking her hand. "There are monsters within that veil. You have travelled from the human realm into the mirror world of Sen-Sen, but there are no monsters here. Not

31

in this place. This is a perfectly nice place with Russian tea, and cakes, and honest answers. Come now. Sit and share the tea with me. You'll find it healing to your spirit. And you shall need it, for I fear this conversation may be quite perplexing, even to someone as perceptive as you."

"Yes, all right." Adele took one of the smaller chairs, and then offered to pour the tea, but the otherworldly prince insisted he do the honours, for she was his guest. He filled a pair of delicately painted cups, added milk and two sugars to each. "Lemon?"

She shook her head. "Not generally, no, but thank you. May I have a third cube of sugar, though?"

"Taste it first," he said, passing the cup to his guest. "The tea is blended with cinnamon, clove, bergamot oranges, and lemon. It is naturally sweet."

Adele took a sip, her petite mouth forming an appreciative smile. "Oh, yes. It's exactly right, and it's so very good. Is this Russian tea, Your Highness? My mother said you introduced her to it, when she stayed at your castle last year."

"It is. The cakes are of several varieties. You should try them all."

"Thank you," she said, taking a rich confection topped with candied fruit and placing it on her plate. "If you please, sir, why am I here? It's a very beautiful apartment, and I am grateful, but I mustn't stay too long. I need to find my father, you see. I believe he came through the veil, too, and I'm sure he's in danger."

"You remember your father's abduction?"

"Yes," she whispered. "Is that why this conversation will cause me perplexity?"

"You remind me of your father," he answered as he stirred his tea. "Charles stayed with me for two years of human time, but we often walked outside such chronological limitations. As to this conversation, it may not perplex one as astute as you. Do you remember anything that happened before you awoke? You spoke of seeing monsters as you passed through the veil."

"I had some very peculiar dreams, if that's what you mean," she said. "But are you saying they weren't really dreams?"

He remained silent, allowing her to work through the puzzle in her own time. Romanov's glacial eyes gleamed with the light of ancient shores and long-forgotten wisdom, an ethereal beauty unmatched by anything Della had ever seen.

"Are you saying they weren't dreams, Your Highness?" she asked again.

"What do you think?"

Della sighed. "I'd hoped they might have been. After all, you've already asked about passing through the veil and seeing those awful monsters. You couldn't know about them if they were in my dreams, could you?"

He smiled. "You might be surprised at what I know, Lady Adele."

"Would I? Can you see into my dreams? Are you able to see into my mind as I sleep? Your Highness, am I awake now, or do I dream still?"

"Ah!" he exclaimed with a knowing tilt of the head. The movement caused his unbound hair to part at the jawline, revealing a softly pointed ear.

Della looked closer. She'd never noticed such a peculiar shape in anyone's ears before. *Is he an elf or a faery? No, he cannot be either. Can he?*

Romanov touched the ear, smiling. "No, my lady, I am neither elf nor faery, though both do exist. You are a rarity amongst Eve's daughters, Adele Marie. And yes, I am able to see into some of your dreams, providing the One allows it. In this case, reality has blurred into a dreamscape."

"A dreamscape?" she asked breathlessly. "Are you saying I'm still dreaming? That you're not real? That I'm really asleep and all alone?"

Her voice grew fearful, and the angel reached for her hand, his long fingers wrapping round hers with great respect. "Have no fear, gentle lady. All will be well. Trust in the One, for twas he, who sent me to you."

Adele's grip tightened in his, and she bit her lower lip anxiously. "When you say the One, do you mean Jesus?"

His lean face widened into an infectious smile that brightened the room and cheered her spirit. "Indeed, I do! My brothers and I call him the *Anointed One, The Name*, and *The Word,* but he has many, many other titles. He is the only begotten Son of the One, who is called Yahweh and Adonai in the Bible. In English, most call him God. The One created you, my lady; and he looks after you, even now, even within a dream. There is nowhere the enemy might take you, that the One cannot follow."

"But why did God allow us to be taken through the veil?"

"It is not for your sake, young Della, but for the sake of your father that this happened. Do you remember the christening? The sinister black coach drawn by four horses?"

She nodded. "That's Prince Araqiel's coach, and I ran to see him, because he'd found an injured puppy. The prince said the animal needed my help, and perhaps I might take him to the house. The prince lied to me, didn't he?"

"Yes. He lied."

"Is he the Devil?"

"Araqiel is subservient to a far greater evil. Many ages ago, this evil prince seduced Araqiel into joining him in rebellion."

"But why me? What have I done to him, Your Highness?"

"My dear friend, you have done nothing to him. He used you as bait to catch a bigger fish."

"My father?" she asked in a whisper.

"Yes. You see, this enemy knew that Charles Sinclair would do anything to save you, even at the cost of his life."

"No! I don't want Father to give his life for me!"

"Yet, he would still give it, little Della. But have no fear. The One has always known this would happen. He knows the end from the beginning. And so, he sent me to help you."

"But you should help my father, not me!" she pleaded. "Go to him, please, Your Highness!"

"How brave you are," the angel marvelled. "Though fear claws at your heart, you put your father's life before your own."

"I'm not afraid," the girl insisted.

"But you are, Adele Marie, and I understand your fears."

"How can you understand them? When have you ever been afraid?"

He grew quiet, his icy eyes fixed upon the fire. "Battle causes many emotions, including great fear, my child. Endless wars and crushing defeats can wear upon one's heart. Do you think the life of an angel is easy? No, darling girl, it is not, but it is endlessly rewarding. We appear powerful, almost omnipotent to humans, but when we fight, the battle is often against our own kind. Such an enemy matches us in every way—but one. And it is *that* difference which writes the end of the story."

"What difference is that, sir?"

"The One fights on *our* side, Adele. He is our general and has foreseen every possibility play out. He has watched every free-will choice that I will make, every choice that the enemy will make, and every choice that you will make. Then, the One works all of it together for good. That is my strength, Lady Della. Not greed. Not lust. Not desire for power or rule. But *trust*. Trust is a mighty weapon, Lady Adele. A mighty weapon indeed!"

"Can trust be a real weapon, though? Like swords and pistols?"

"Indeed, it is much greater. Trusting in the One releases his infinite power. Charles Sinclair is never alone, Adele. Nor are you."

"You're certain of that?"

"I know this as well as I know the One created all the worlds and everything in them. Now, tell me about your dream."

She took a sip of the tea, her left brow arching as she set down the cup. "Which dream do you mean, Your Highness? The one I had whilst sleeping, or the dream I'm presently in?"

Romanov laughed, his face shining as though lit from within. "You are very clever, Lady Adele. Much like your father. Charles and I shared many such conversations, when he lived with me."

"You mentioned that earlier. When did my father live with you?"

"Long ago, when he was quite young, but that is a tale for another day."

"You promise to tell me?" she said, the brow arching again.

"I promise," he laughed. "Now, let us consider this dream you are in. Tell me about it."

She pointed to the portrait above the fireplace. "I think that might be a clue, Your Highness. I never posed for any such painting, and no artist would ever depict my father as little more than an afterthought. Did you paint it?"

"No. I would never consider your father an afterthought, Lady Della. Charles Sinclair was placed into my care long before he was born."

"Are you his guardian angel?"

"Think of me as the captain of his guardians," he answered after a long drink of tea.

"You must be very important to be their captain," she said.

"Your father is the important one, Lady Della. As are you, and all your family. You have a great purpose."

"What purpose?" she asked, wide-eyed.

"That will become clear to you soon, and it is why the enemy seeks to lure you away. Regarding the painting, I can tell you the artist's name and why the picture hangs in this room."

"Please, do."

"The painting sends a message, and the artist is you," he answered, his icy eyes fixed upon her face.

Della shook her head defiantly. "No, you're very wrong. I'm sure I didn't paint it. I couldn't have. Why ever would you say I did?"

"You cannot guess?"

She concentrated on the oil painting, examining every colour and shading. Her cheeks flushed with roses, and the chestnut brows pinched together over the freckled nose as she tried to work it out. The beautiful brushwork seemed almost three-dimensional, as though, the elements might spring to life at any moment. The statues of Branham's long-deceased dukes and duchesses formed a wide corridor of the dead. That corridor led to an evergreen arcade, just as it looked in reality. But as Adele gazed at the painting, the statues' faces altered, and their countenances became fierce and defiant, as though each long-dead peer conspired with some great evil to bring an end to every human on Earth.

Then, above their carved marble heads, there arose swirling rows of ominous black clouds, invading the landscape like pirate ships. The sun hid its face, defeated by the ominous black ships, and the silvery blue sky retreated in shame. Then, the storm clouds transformed, undulating round and round as though driven by fierce easterly winds.

But the painting's truth grew stranger yet.

The black clouds weren't pirate ships at all; nor were they even clouds.

They were birds.

Lots of birds.

An army of birds. Thousands upon thousands of black-winged demons that swirled downward in a cyclone of terror; down, down, down, into the centre of the Branham maze. Adele could hear them cawing, crying, talking. *Screaming.*

"That's impossible!" she cried, leaping to her feet. "Those clouds weren't even there, and now they've become birds!"

"Yes?" the prince asked calmly.

She stared, replying in a whisper. "They're like the monsters I saw, but paint cannot move, can it? Please, tell me this won't happen. My father's in there!"

"I'm afraid it will happen," he told her. "The birds are harbingers of a very real, very difficult trial, now facing your father."

"Then, we must find him and help!"

"Your father must face this challenge without your help, little Della. He will tread within corridors of everchanging perplexity, but it is a path he *must* walk. The One has ordained it. This journey will strengthen your father, and he will emerge from the crucible with a singular vision and purpose."

"But if I'm not allowed to help, why do I see the birds?"

"A very good question. You see them, because your Sinclair blood calls to his."

"You mean, because my mother was really a Sinclair?" she whispered, her heart aching.

"Yes. Charlotte Sinclair was torn from her family as a baby. Because of this blood tie, your father's trial invades your dreams, and you long to help. That is why you stand in the painting's foreground as the key figure. But Charles will never consent to the ordeal until you are free. That is why you must escape."

She backed away, trying to distance herself from the landscape of oil and terror. "No, I'm not leaving. If what you say is true, then my father's in danger, and I must go to him. Tell me where he is, and we'll escape together."

"Your courage is most admirable," the prince said, rising to his feet, "but you cannot go to your father. Charles must walk this path alone. The One has decreed it, and I will not disobey that decree."

"But if I cannot help, may I not at least talk to him? Tell him I love him? May I do that, at least?" she asked, agony wetting her cheeks with tears.

Anatole embraced her as he might a younger sister. "Your heart does credit to all the daughters of Eve, Adele Marie. I promise you this: your father will come through the test a stronger, fiercer warrior for Christ the King, and he'll even be a better Holmes to your most impressive Dr. Watson."

He wiped her tears, and Adele managed a wan smile. "Then, you've come to take me home?"

"No. I am here, yes, but only inside your dreams."

"I'm still dreaming?"

"Indeed, you are."

"Then where am I?" she asked, her voice trembling.

"You sleep as a prisoner within a dark castle, in the mirror world of Sen-Sen. I mustn't enter that world, for it is against the One's command."

"Why? Doesn't God want you to rescue me?"

Anatole touched her face, and for a moment, a thousand thousand thoughts rushed through Della's mind. And she saw Anatole in his true form: magnificent and massive, holding a fiery sword, covered from hilt to tip with strange symbols. He rode upon a stallion, fighting battle after battle against terrors with cruel shapes and unimaginable weapons. The warrior angel shouted commands to a million others. It was a terrifying warscape, filled with lightning and thunder and blood and death.

The vision made her tremble.

"Do you understand?" he asked gently.

"That was you, wasn't it? On the horse, carrying a sword that looked like lightning?"

"It was and is. I take many forms and have used many names. Long ago, I left one of these swords with a Sinclair ancestor. He called it *Lain Lassair*."

"Lain Lassair. That's beautiful. What does it mean?"

"It is Gaelic for 'fire sword'. The weapon was made during the first great war, for another time, another land. One day, your father will find it."

"The sword is real? Will he use it in this test you mentioned?" she asked.

"No, Charles must use other weapons for the test."

"Like *trust?*" she asked, smiling at last.

"Yes, Lady Della. Like trust."

"Is my father in this castle? Is he with me?"

"No. He was taken to a vast fortress, far beneath the earth, but Charles is looked after and watched by another of my kind. Your father is never alone, remember that."

"Will you help me escape?"

"Not directly. As I said, I must not enter this place, for to do so would break an ancient accord from the First War. Your captor was once defeated by me, you see. Twas I who helped imprison him."

"I don't understand."

"I know, child, but fear not. Though I may not enter, the One has despatched two of my loyal brethren. They may enter without breaking the treaty and will take you home."

"Where beneath the earth is my father being held? Once I'm home, I can tell Paul, and he'll find Father. Is it inside the Branham tunnels? There are lots of old caverns underneath the abbey. Or is it under London? Scotland? Tell me, and Paul and I can search together."

"It is not for you to find your father, little Della. I have already explained this."

"I will not leave without him!" she shouted, stamping her feet.

The prince showed no sign of irritation. "Adele, even if I told you where to find him, you would not remember it."

"I would. I have a very fine memory."

He smiled. "Yes, and you have the heart of a lioness. I have seen such courage before, you know. In a girl with dark eyes and raven curls. Elizabeth was also taken as a child, but those terrible memories were shut away, for they were too heavy a burden for a child to carry."

"What do you mean?"

"Your mother suffered greatly as a child, but the One allowed the trials to strengthen her, and one day—when the time is right—she will remember everything. For now, to protect her, I have stored all such darkness in a safe place."

"How could you do that?"

"The same way I shall remove your memories and store them."

"No, please! Please! I must remember what happened. I want to remember all of it!"

"It is too heavy a burden, Adele Marie. The dark memories will become dreams. These dreams will very slowly open the memory closet where I store them, allowing you to reconcile each with safety and avoid permanent harm to your young mind." Then a slight smile crossed his face. "If you wish, I could arrange for Henry to help. But only if you wish it."

"Dr. MacAlpin?" she asked, her eyes brightening. "He's very nice. Henry rode after me last Boxing Day. My horse had bolted into the woods."

"You like Henry, I think," he observed, his eyes twinkling.

"Of course, I do. But he's just a friend," she answered with a modest blush.

"A very good friend, no? You and Lord Salperton share a future, though I cannot reveal more to you yet."

"Is Henry here, Prince Anatole? Did the kidnappers take him, too?"

"No, dear child, the viscount is well. I shall have my brethren take you to Henry, and he will help restore your hidden memories. But slowly, to prevent injury, as I have said."

She looked at the painting. "Father's in terrible trouble, I'm sure of it. You're sure that he'll be all right?"

"I promise. Many of my brethren are charged to look after Charles. He is always protected."

Adele began to weep again, and even Anatole's eyes grew moist. This surprised Della, and she wiped his face.

"That is kind of you," he said. "I have learnt much from tears. They express joy, sorrow, and sometimes pain, but weep not, little one. I and my fellow guardians keep watch upon you; just as we have have watched you from the moment of your birth. You are a remarkable young woman, destined for greatness. Your strong mind and insight are revealed in this very painting! You see your father as a warrior, capable of any feat. A brave knight! That is why he wears armour. And though dark clouds threaten, the duke will prevail, and soon the sun will rise again. The One has foreseen all this. Even before Time began, he had prepared for it."

He touched her forehead, the smooth fingertips tracing the sign of the Cross. "Now, forget all these troubles, little one. Forget the abduction, forget the trip through the veil of Sen-Sen. Forget the monsters. Forget all your fears and close your eyes. Remember only that your father loves you, and that he will come home very soon. Go to sleep, little one. Go to sleep."

Della collapsed into his arms, and Romanov carried her back into the dream's bedchamber. "Now, listen to me, Della Marie," he whispered as he walked. "Hear my words and remember. Soon, a clock will chime the hour of ten. When you hear the tenth bell, you will awaken. A woman will knock upon your door. Her name is Mrs. Grey, and her words will confuse and even frighten you, but remember that *rescue is coming*. My brothers ride to you upon the swiftest of horses! Look for them as the clock strikes eleven!"

He placed her on the dream bed, drew the silk coverlet up to her chin, and kissed her forehead.

Satisfied that she was safe and secure, the warrior angel raised his right arm, and a blinding light filled the chamber. Then, with a rush of wind, the mysterious prince vanished like a rainbow-hued vapour.

Then, a clock began to chime.
One, two, three, four, five.
Six, seven, eight, nine.
Ten!

Della's eyes popped open, their sea-blue irises staring up at the underside of a painted canopy, that looked old and worn. The room smelled of must and damp.

Someone knocked on a nearby door.

"Time to wake up, little miss!" a woman called from the other side. "Breakfast hour's long since gone. You must wake up!" More pounding. "Wake up!"

Adele sat upright, alert and ready. Something was about to happen, though she couldn't remember what. She hastened out of the bed and found a pair of slippers. Upon a nearby chair, lay a bathrobe of blue velvet. She pulled her arms through, tied the belt, and crossed to a tall, six-panelled door.

"Wait a moment," Della called.

"I have your breakfast and need to bring it in, little miss."

Della opened the door.

The woman had a haggard face and wore a charcoal dress with a stained white pinafore. Her large hands held a silver tray, laden with hot food.

"Yes?" asked Della. "Who are you, please?"

"You still don't remember me after all this time?" laughed the servant as she pushed into the room with the tray. "Now, I got rashers, poached eggs, scones, sliced peaches, and a pot o' tea. I hope you're hungry this mornin'. Cook's outdone 'erself."

The woman carried the tray to the sitting area and while her back was turned, Adele peered into the corridor to scan for signs of anyone else. Where was Prince Anatole? The details of the dream were already fading, but she thought he'd promised to send help. Surely, he didn't mean this woman.

"Are you alone?" she asked the servant.

"What might you mean, little miss? Am I alone up here with you, or alone in the house?"

"Alone in the house, I suppose. No, wait, you mentioned a cook, didn't you?"

"Like I've told you many times now, there's the cook, that's Mrs. Black, you know. Black runs the kitchen with the help of two scullery maids—don't know their names, cause they come and go. I'm Mrs. Grey. My husband, Mr. Grey, runs the downstairs. And there's Miss White. She lives in the north tower, but that woman's nothin' but trouble, little miss, so stay clear o' her. Mr. Scarlet's in the west tower, though I got no idea what he does. Some kind o' scientist, I reckon. And we all work for the Master. I've told you all this before, miss. Many times."

"I'm sorry to make you repeat yourself, Mrs. Grey, but who is the Master?" Adele asked.

Grey laughed again. It was a piggy sort of snort that exploded through her nose as though emitted from an off-key wind instrument. "You sure are a funny one, little miss! Dr. Brown says we're not to worry you about it, though. Says your head's a bit broke. If you ask a hundred times, we're to answer like it's the first. But don't you worry. He'll mend your head soon enough. You'll see, little miss. You'll see."

Della felt certain the woman was lying, but decided to go along in hopes of learning more. "I suppose my head is a bit broken, which means I cannot help asking over and over again, can I? Would you remind me of the Master's name, Mrs. Grey?"

"Why it's Prince Araqiel, o' course! Nicest, handsomest man in all the realms, as you've told me more'n once, little miss. I reckon the Master's got a soft spot for you. Else you'd not be livin' in this nice apartment. It overlooks the sea cliff. Such a nice view. Eat up, now."

"And this is a house?"

"It's a castle, my lady. A right nice old castle by the sea. Him an' his sister own it together. The Princess..."

"Eluna," Della answered. "See? My memory's already mending. No need for any doctors."

"I reckon that's for Dr. Brown to decide," the woman said carefully, her rheumy eyes narrowing.

"Forgive me. Yes, of course, it is," answered Adele, praying the look on her face didn't betray her heart. It seemed she'd been imprisoned by Prince Araqiel and his sister, but why? Her father had said the prince was evil, and his sister Princess Eluna had cast very seductive looks towards her father on more than one occasion.

However did she get here? Where was her father?

"I wonder, Mrs. Grey, might there be another guest staying in the castle? A man with very dark hair, somewhat long and curling?"

"Might be," the woman said. "Why?"

"No reason. Is there a garden or courtyard? I thought I might take a walk, if that's allowed. Perhaps, I could walk with His Highness, if he's available. I should like to offer my thanks for his generosity."

"You want to walk with the prince?" the woman mocked, her pale eyes turned cruel. "My girl, no one with a bit o' clear headedness would make such a statement as that! Be sensible now. Stay here, eat your breakfast, then go back to sleep, like Dr. Brown ordered."

"I've slept long enough, thank you," Adele answered, restraining an impulse to hit the woman on the head and rush out the door. "I'm sure Prince Araqiel wonders about me. After all, I am his guest, correct? Not a prisoner? I may leave at any time?"

The woman laughed again, another piggy snort. "You are a funny one, little miss. Askin' if you're a prisoner! Such an imagination. Eat up now. I'll come back in an hour to collect the tray and make sure you're asleep. Mr. Grey's men will be just outside, in case, you need anything."

"His men are outside my door? That's—yes, that's very reassuring," Della said carefully. "Mrs. Grey, why do you work for someone you so clearly fear? Can't you get a position with someone who's kind?"

The woman stared, her heavily lined face sprouting a dozen new creases around the eyes and mouth. "Now, why would you think I fear the Master?"

"Because you refuse to deliver my message. Surely, you think the prince would scold you for doing so, but I'm sure he wonders why I've not come down to visit him, if as you say I've really been here for many days."

The woman's wiry brows arched into harsh lines above the cold eyes. "You should take care what words you speak round here, little miss. You think yourself brave, I reckon, but the bravest o' men drops to his knees in naked terror when the prince and his brothers look in their eyes. Such looks might *burn you to ash*. Eat your breakfast now, while you still got a mouth."

The servant slammed the door, leaving Adele to consider her plight. She sat next to the tray of food and poured a cup of tea, praying it wasn't poisoned or laced with some sleeping potion. The tea tasted flat, weak, and utterly flavourless. Della added more sugar and milk, but nothing helped. Sitting back in the chair, the girl tried to remember how she got here. The brass hands on the ebony clock above her head moved rhythmically, accompanied by a pleasant ticking sound. The bedchamber was dusty with a dismal sort of decor, just as flat and flavourless as the tea. Dull walls, dull paint, and dull furnishings. The bed coverings looked expensive, but there was no charm or personality to the damask. Dull, dull, dull.

Adele longed for her own apartment back at Haimsbury House. She missed her baby brother and sister, little Robby and Georgianna Sinclair. She missed her mother, the Duchess Elizabeth, and her elder brother, Paul Stuart. Were they well? Had Araqiel taken all her family captive? Might they, too, be in a distant tower of this horrid castle?

Never let the enemy know your thoughts, Della, Paul once told her. *Keep them guessing and on their toes. Otherwise, they'll crush yours, the moment you're not looking.*

With a plaintive sigh, Adele Marie summoned up all the courage she could muster. The world felt very unfriendly.

CHAPTER TWO
Real World - St. Rosaline's Abbey, Goussainville, France

As Adele Sinclair sipped flavourless tea in an unfriendly castle in the mirror world of Sen-Sen, at the very same moment in the real world, Lionel Archibald Wentworth was talking to the dead. He'd spent more than seven months as Prince Araqiel's human slave, and the former Cambridge student had grown decidedly gaunt and just a bit insane.

He missed his Neville's Court room at Trinity College, that *sanctum sanctorum*, where a man could waste entire days at Wren Library or visit Isaac Newton's famous tree. There, Lionel had enjoyed long nights at his favourite pubs: the Angel, the Devil, the Magdalene, and the Green Man. He imagined loitering about the tables and bars, pinching pints, talking nonsense, and chatting up girls from Girton College. But instead of chin-wags with luscious brunettes, he wagged his chin alone, living like a scraggly rat in a damp and utterly desolate tower, where nary a pub nor female voice could cheer him. His was a Biblical fall indeed!

On that crisp, September morn, Lionel leaned out the ancient turret's arched windows, wistfully watching the free men toiling below. The disheveled and utterly broken prisoner gazed down upon the abbey's busy courtyard, where the prince's day labourers continued repairs to the abbey's kitchens and storage buildings.

Lionel contemplated the pleasant golds and russets of Goussainville's ripening grain fields beyond. And five miles further, his thirsty spirit drank in the colourful stucco façades of the village houses and blue-tiled steeple of the three-hundred-year-old church. He longed to walk free amongst that rural beauty, if only for a day! To breathe clean, pure air and hear songs of real birds; not live amongst putrid filth, listening to bats and rats, squeaking and scratching.

Last December, he'd sustained serious injury in the tunnels under Branham's Lion Hall, but these had healed, though he would forever walk with a limping gait. Wentworth considered the injury a fair trade, for at least, he was alive, unlike his late friend. Peter Patterson hadn't fared well at all. He was slain in a most ghastly way, with eyes gouged out and skin flayed by the beaks of supernatural ravens. Albus Flint's demonic birds had enjoyed their grim nightwork and taken their time, eagerly sharing the disgusting spoils. Why, they'd even ripped away poor Patterson's manhood.

After witnessing the unholy slaughter, Lionel Wentworth made a devil's bargain with Albus Flint: in return for his life, he pledged eternal loyalty and service to the Blackstone Society, or else die like Patterson.

His first assignment was to dispose of Pitt's body in a place where local authorities were sure to find it. Hoping to avoid the grisly task, Lionel complained to Flint that he'd no idea how to escape the lower tunnels, much less where to leave Patterson's mangled remains. The cadaverous lawyer reassured his new slave, that he knew the way out and where best to leave the body. Then, the hellish solicitor waved his pale hands like a stage magician, and each of the ravens transformed back into shards of black mirror. On command, the shards reassembled, as if by magic.

"Your future lies this way, Mr. Wentworth," Flint had told him. "Follow me."

With no other choice, Lionel hoisted his friend's bloody corpse across one shoulder and followed the demon through the reassembled looking glass. They'd emerged into a clearing on the outskirts of Branham Village. Seeing several rail sheds marked 'Branham Hall' within walking distance, Lionel left his dead friend in the first shed. And since prayer seemed out of place, particularly as he'd just pledged his life to the Devil, Lionel spoke a few words from Shelley's *Adonais* instead:

> He will awake no more, oh, never more!
>   Within the twilight chamber spreads apace
>   The shadow of white Death, and at the door
>   Invisible Corruption waits to trace

His extreme way to her dim dwelling-place.

After finishing the brief recitation, he turned to Flint and asked, "What now?"

The lawyer snapped his bony fingers and instantly, as if newly created from the air, there appeared a black coach, drawn by a quartet of equally black horses. He and the lawyer boarded, and the coach sped away to Dover; and from there, they sailed for Calais.

Had that been just eight months ago? It felt like eight centuries.

"Black mirrors, vampires, bats, and a bed full of bugs and lice! That's what I got for my bargain, Pitt," he muttered to his invisible companion. "Not eternal life. *Eternal hell.* You may be dead, old chum, but it's a sight lot better than you left me. Why did I ever sign that contract, eh? Why did I even apply? What madness possessed me, Pitt?"

The apparition laughed. "Why, money, of course. The glint of gold, the shine of shillings. Worthy, you've lacked sufficient funds to fuel your exotic passions since the day I first met you at Eton. Even then, you were a wicked spender. When were you ever content with your allowance, eh? Your dad gave you thirty pounds a month, and you spread it about like a farmer spreads horse manure. And still, you complain. If you think your lot's so bad, try being dead."

"If only I could be," moaned the human.

"Oh, dying is easy," the ghost replied. "Tie a slip-knot in a length of hemp and step in. Or leap out a window."

"That would hurt."

"Not for long. But if you want something less painful, then break the window glass and use a shard to slice through your wrists. Cut deep, though. Otherwise, the cuts might heal, and we wouldn't want that, now would we?"

The prisoner pushed to his callused feet, the stiff left knee creaking. The movement caused a scrawny mouse to scuttle from its napping spot beneath Wentworth's straw mattress. The starving human eyed the creature hungrily. Seeing the huge predator, the quick brown mouse raced across the flagstone floor towards the door.

Lionel licked his dry lips. A thick stream of saliva drooled down his scaly chin as he considered chasing the mouse and pouncing upon it, like a cat.

"Go on, take it," the phantom urged him sardonically. "Mouse flesh is a delicacy to tribes in the Argentine. And though small, the veins are full of hot, red blood. *Blood is the life*, after all. Isn't it, old chum?"

"I prefer a steak-and-kidney pie, thank you," answered Lionel proudly, his face turned to the wall.

"Or perhaps, just the kidneys, eh? Raw and dripping with fat and energy!"

"Someone will bring up supper soon. You wait."

"Really?" the phantom smirked. "If you think one of Araqiel's servants is going to bring you a bowl of day-old stew or a few table scraps, think again. It isn't on the cards, my friend. Araqiel's gone, and what few servants remain have forgotten you're up here."

"Go away!"

"Take it, Worthy. Devour that warm, wriggling mouse before someone else gets it. A mouse in the hand is worth two in the straw, so to speak. I'm paraphrasing, of course."

Suddenly, Lionel scrambled to the locked door, but the mouse had already escaped beneath it. "Gone!" the human wailed. "Gone and down the tower steps to the outside world. Oh, to be a happy mouse, Pitt! To slip beneath the door and scamper away to freedom, unseen, unobserved, unhindered!"

"And *unclean*," the ghost added. "Not the mouse, Wentworth. You."

"Oh, leave me alone!"

"The window's still available," the ghost countered. "Or else, you could... But no, you'd never want to use that way. It's out of the question."

"What?" the prisoner begged. "Do you know of some other way of escape? Not death, though. I prefer to remain alive."

"It's quite dangerous. How strong are your feet and legs?"

Lionel gazed down at his swollen knee. "If you mean I should clamber down the tower's sides, forget it, Pitt. My leg, remember? I'd surely fall to my death."

"True. Very true. But falling is still escape. Who knows? You might even survive. Or not."

"Woe is me! Abandon all hope, ye who enter here," the human sighed.

"Are we quoting Dante now?" asked the ghost.

"Yes. I used to laugh at that foolish poem, Pitt, but I laugh no longer. Hell is a very real place, and I'm in it."

"Have you thought of talking? To *him*, I mean?"

"What? To Dante? He's long gone to that place of utter hopelessness. Or else to a better place. If heaven exists, that is."

"I don't mean Dante," said the cruel apparition. "Poetry and poets are useless, though *Adonais* does have some lovely lines. You quoted it over my body, remember? But what about these lines? '*Sad Urania scann'd the stranger's mien, and murmur'd: Who art thou? He answer'd not, but with a sudden hand, made bare his branded and ensanguin'd brow, which was like Cain's or Christ's—oh! that it should be so!*' Lovely words. Is your brow stained with the mark of Cain or with that of Christ, Lionel? Which is it?"

"Cain's curse is nothing compared to mine!"

"And what of mine?" shouted the ghost, its transparent hands thrown upwards. "What of my lost eyes, my skin, my—well, my other parts? I do still have my brain, though, Lionel. And I'm not suggesting you discourse with the Devil. No, you should talk to *HIM*."

Wentworth glared at Patterson's shimmering shadow, his heart filling with hatred. "Do you suggest that I should pray to GOD? *Bah!* Even if I believed in him, why would he listen to me?"

"I didn't mean God either, Lionel. Do be reasonable."

"Who, then? What *him* could you possibly mean?"

"Praying doesn't always involve invoking God with the capital 'g'. But there is a god without that capital letter, who could and *would* help you escape. You only need to ask him, Lionel. He's very close..."

Lionel's face reddened with anger. "No. Not ever! Not again. The god you speak of is fiendishly cruel, Pitt. He and his brothers devour humans, for nothing more than a moment's pleasure. Death is not beautiful. Shelley is wrong! There is no glory in joining Adonais."

"'*Tis Adonais calls*," quoted the ghost. "*Oh, hasten hither! No more let Life divide what Death can join together!*"

"SHUT UP!" Lionel screamed. "All that prattle is nothing but lies. Death is the true king, and we are pawns in his game. Why would anyone with a brain believe in heaven or God, when he allows that horrid king to devour us like dust? God claims to love us *so much* that he died for us, but it's all a lie, Pitt. A lie! Oh, how I wish I'd never met Albus Flint or heard of the Blackstone Society! If Araqiel's name were unknown to me, and his mad sister a mystery, a happier man I'd be! THEY are the true gods of this earth, Pitt, and I'm doomed to serve them forever. I am not a mouse. There is no escape for me. I'm truly and eternally damned!"

Lionel began to weep, his thin hands clapped against the temples of his head and over his eyes.

Patterson's vapourous ghost responded with a dispassionate shrug. "So you're damned. No hope. Not even a sliver. I suppose it's useless for me to offer my own help. The abbey has a very special visitor. Did you know that? He's been here for weeks."

Wentworth's head bobbed up, the swollen eyes round as grey buttons. "Visitor? No, no, this is a lie. No one is visiting. If someone were, the prince would have told me. Who do you think procures their horrid blood feasts? None of the farmers or bricklayers. No, I'm the one who patrols the streets of local villages, the back alleys of Paris, and who steals away life!"

"I speak the truth, Lionel. There is a visitor, and he requires no blood feast. No revels. He comes and goes as he pleases. Don't you know what season it is?"

"One is the same as another. Time has lost all meaning."

The ghost walked closer, and Lionel could see the damp stones of the chamber walls through Pitt's empty eye sockets. The unearthly body was covered in black flies and stripes of congealed blood, long ago dried and oxidised from months of ageing. A circle of scarlet stained the groin of his trousers, where the living Patterson's manhood had once existed.

"Time is *all* that matters, Lionel. Time is the real enemy."

"Leave me alone, Pitt. I just want to sleep."

The cruel apparition laughed as it drew near and asked, "Do you mean eternal sleep?"

The ghost's mocking smile evoked nothing of the gentle-hearted Cambridge student once known as Peter Patterson; the cheerful, trusting lad, whom the ravens had pecked to death in England. The horrid, black mouth elongated into an impossibly wide oval, the cavity filled with flies and blood and running pus.

Lionel shrank back in revulsion. "Go away! Leave me in peace, please!"

"Does my face frighten you, Worthy?" asked the entity. "What if I told you the visitor I mentioned is me? Your long-dead friend, who still loves you. What then?"

"I'd say you're lying."

"But *I am* that visitor. And if I help you escape, would you think better of me? Would you embrace your poor, dead friend the way you did the night we pledged ourselves to the Silver Spoons Society? Would you kiss me, Lionel?"

The terrified human wanted to vomit, but did he dare pass up any possibility to escape?

"How? How could I leave this place, without dying, that is? Adonais, Apollo, and Shelley be damned, I've no desire to leave here by way of the grave!"

"No grave. No death. If I tell you, would you love me?"

"I..." the human started to answer, but he dreaded the apparition's power. Signing Albus Flint's contract had brought him here. Would another bargain lead to a far worse condition?

Peter Patterson's spirit had first appeared four weeks earlier. At first, Lionel welcomed the ghost as a gruesome kind of comfort, but lately, the wraith brought only heartache and terror. And now it wanted a kiss?

"No," he answered at last. "I could never kiss you, Pitt. Not for anything."

The phantom stared at the human, and within the empty ocular orbits, glittered the diamonds of a thousand tiny eyes, like a thousand demons watched.

What if he's telling me the truth?

"How can you help me?" Lionel asked.

"Simple. You just take my hand," the other promised. "If you trust me, I'll lead you to a far better world, filled with wine and women and wantonness."

"Women?" Wentworth asked, not daring to think it possible.

"Yes, my friend. Women! Plump and pretty beauties, filled with sugary sweetness. Take my hand, Worthy. Take it and kiss me. That is my price."

Wentworth's emaciated face twisted into a mask of revulsion. "May I not pay with something else?"

"You must prove your love to me, if you wish to leave here. After all, I am *dead*, because of you."

51

"But why now, Pitt? Why wait all these weeks to offer it?"

"Because the season matters, Lionel. It is almost the equinox. The day when the veil twixt worlds thins."

"Araqiel will stop us," Lionel said, looking about as though his cruel master might appear at any moment.

"No, Lionel. He won't. That's why the season matters. Araqiel and Eluna are occupied with matters elsewhere. But if we're to escape unnoticed, we must go now," the wraith explained. "Tomorrow could be too late. You needn't kiss me yet; but if you'll trust me enough to take my hand and say you believe in me, then I'll take you home."

"And what will Prince Araqiel do when he finds me gone?" asked Wentworth in terror. "He'll send Flint to hunt me down, that's what he'll do! And I'll become a neutered corpse with no eyes and no heart—just like you!"

"None of that need happen, Lionel, but you must believe in me to make it so," whispered the phantom, extending its left hand. "Make your choice. Remain here, eating worms and rats, or follow me to freedom, Lionel Wentworth. Take my hand. This is the only time I shall offer it."

The strange conversation at St. Rosaline's abbey had lasted for just six hours, but to the half-mad human, it seemed like six weeks. The sun's rays had now set beyond the village, bringing the rising of a full moon. Lionel had grown to hate that moon, just as he hated himself.

I cannot bear spending one more night in this hell!

"All right!" he declared, his voice quivering. "If I die, then at least I escape."

He reached out to take Pitt's wispy hand, shocked at its strength and firmness. The walls of the room began to spin, as if they stood inside a dizzying, whirligig zoetrope toy. The human heard a deafening clap of thunder, mixed with high-pitched laughter inside the rush of swirling pictures. He heard a voice cry, *"Wir und die Todten reiten schnell!"* – We and the Dead travel fast!

And then...

...in a flash...

...they were gone!

One second later, Lionel opened his eyes to a cobbled street, filled with human voices and the clatter of carriage wheels. The stench of sweat and horse droppings crept into his nostrils. That stench was like heaven, for he knew it at once: London's East End.

"Need a girl?" asked a middle-aged woman with intermittent teeth and a bruised cheek.

"Sure," he smiled in return. *Where was Pitt?*

Any worries about his dead friend soon vanished in the realisation that he was really, actually in London!

But at what price?

"How much?" he asked, partly to the girl and partly to his vanished deliverer.

"Two bob," she laughed. "One if it's quick."

He took her into the nearest alley, wondering how he'd pay when he had no money. But two bob was nothing compared to the real debt he'd just incurred. Wentworth would soon learn the truth of the bargain he'd struck, as well as the real identity of his dead 'friend'.

Not Peter Patterson at all.

Not even close.

CHAPTER THREE
Real World - Westminster, London

Exactly thirteen hours and thirteen minutes before a fallen, six-winged pretender flew Lionel Wentworth from a tower in France to a backstreet rookery in Whitechapel, a middle-aged woman was dressing for breakfast. Margaret Hansen closed the topmost pearl button of the blue Paisley jacket, amazed at the altered face in the looking glass. Since coming to live with Dr. Lorena MacKey and Violet Stuart (the former Susanna Morgan, a.k.a. Cassandra Calabrese), the retired whoremonger's life, health, and even her appearance had changed for the better. She no longer powdered her face or cinched her waist with painful bands of steel and whalebone. Clean eating, fresh air, and just one glass of wine at supper had whittled her body by twenty pounds and coloured her cheeks with a natural pink, courtesy of daily walks in Prince Anatole's spacious courtyard.

Meg first met the mysterious Anatole Romanov in 1876, when Sir William Trent introduced her to an organisation called Redwing. She never quite understood why Trent called his elite club The Round Table, but the group's thirteen members met at her establishment every Saturday night. Back then, Hansen thought the Russian prince exceedingly handsome, though snobbishly distant; a man who smiled at fallen women, but never took them to bed. Two years later, Romanov came to visit her during the day and confessed he was actually a spy, telling Hansen that war was coming and she must choose which side to serve: either the fallen realm, or God Almighty and his loyal angels. He'd whispered to Margaret of her secret sins; those past mistakes, known only to herself. His knowledge left her terrified, and she begged him to leave her in peace. But then Romanov did something extraordinary. Instead of threatening her, the prince vowed to protect her on behalf of a being he called 'the One'. She need only follow his instructions from that moment onwards.

At first, Hansen doubted his promises, for experience had taught her that most men lied. But then, in 1879, Meg met Lorena MacKey, a student at the London Medical School for Women in Whitechapel. As part of her studies, nineteen-year-old Lorena called weekly at the Empress to patch up the brothel's prostitutes, who'd suffered beatings or botched abortions. Over time, Meg came to trust this new friend. MacKey implied Romanov was more than human, and said anything he vowed to do, he would fulfill without reservation. And though MacKey's path diverged soon after, following Sir William Trent, Margaret remained a faithful spy for Romanov; placing her life at risk every time Trent came to call.

Oh, how difficult those first tentative steps had been; yet how sweet the ground now felt beneath her timid feet! The prince had told the truth. Meg remained loyal, and God watched after her. Slowly, she'd even come to trust in the Bible and Christ, and now had the promise of heaven and an earthly path filled with inconceivable brightness to light the way.

Sadly, Lorena had fallen into a deep dark hole, dug and maintained by Sir William Trent. But a kind word from an unlikely source pulled her out. In Scotland, the man known then as Superintendent Charles St. Clair brought her out of the darkness and showed her God's true light. He'd told Lorena about forgiveness. That moment of compassion formed the doorway that led Lorena to Christ. Later, she spoke to Susanna, and then reminded Margaret of God's boundless love. These three women, who'd once wallowed in the Devil's mud, were now washed clean of their sins.

Oh, how life had changed!

Margaret checked all the hairpins in her greying chignon one last time, making certain the style was secure, and then left the apartment. Romanov owned a dozen or more homes in London and used this one for government business and as guest quarters for diplomats and friends. Margaret lived on the first floor in spacious rooms once used by kings, queens, and archdukes. God's bright path had led her from artificial elegance and debauched nights to honesty, charity, and truth.

Fully dressed and ready for the day, she descended a broad, marble and ironwork staircase that wound its way throughout the four-storey home like an elegant Jacob's ladder. It was ten o'clock, and she'd not yet broken her fast. Arriving in the red-and-gold breakfast room, the hungry houseguest was pleased to find hot food waiting on a carved-oak sideboard and her longtime friend Dr. MacKey still eating.

The physician glanced up from a plate, hand-painted in the Old Imari pattern and filled with peppered eggs, sliced tomato, and half a slice of rye toast. She'd been reading the newspapers.

"Good morning," she said to Hansen, offering her friend a bright smile. "Mrs. Pushkina made those cherry *vatrushkas* again. You'll find a few warm ones beneath the silver dome on the right. And there's plenty of tea left in the large samovar, but also coffee in the smaller one."

"Is it that tea with the cinnamon stick added?" asked Hansen as she surveyed the bounty on the sideboard.

"Of course," laughed MacKey. "The tea here's always made with cinnamon. Mrs. Pushkina sometimes adds bits of dried strawberry or apple, but it's always delicious."

"Has Violet eaten yet?"

"Long ago. She took the prince's new clarence to Fulham. Anatole gave her permission before he left last week. Did you sleep well? There was some noise overnight along York Street. A carriage accident, I think."

"I guess I didn't hear it," said Meg. "I always sleep better here than anywhere else, don't you? It was lovely getting to spend time at Inspector Stanley's home, but with Ida's baby coming in February, they're converting the guest room to a nursery. It was kind of the prince to invite me to live here."

"I'm glad you've joined us, Margaret. So is Violet."

Lorena MacKey was a very different woman from the Redwing operative that once tried to lure Paul Stuart into her bed. Her bright auburn hair was arranged into a chic French knot, and her face scrubbed and devoid of artifice. She wore wire-rimmed spectacles, and the lenses magnified her intensely green eyes.

"You should read this," she said, pointing to a copy of *The Pall Mall Gazette*. "It's a bit odd, but enlightening. I'm not really sure what to make of it."

After filling her plate, Margaret sat across from the physician. She took the newspaper, stirring a cube of sugar into the hot tea as she read. Her eyes widened. "This cannot be true."

"Of course it isn't, but none of the paper's readers would dare question it," replied MacKey. "*The Gazette*'s circulation includes Whitehall, the Palace, Westminster, Mayfair, Belgravia, Hanover Square, and every noble house. By now, that writer's opinion has become fact."

"But it's a bunch of lies, isn't it? Surely the duke's family didn't announce any of this. I thought Charles was—well, that he was *missing.*" Her voice hushed to a mere whisper as she pronounced the final word.

The headline was set in Brim Narrow typeface, that stretched across the entire front page, just beneath the paper's masthead. The six-column report was written by Sir John Fellowes, Q.C.:

HAIMSBURY MYSTERY CONTINUES:
HAS OUR DUKE LEFT ENGLAND
FOR OTHER SHORES?

FOR WEEKS NOW, we have received thousands of your letters, posted from all parts of the Empire, asking this paper for news—any news at all—regarding the whereabouts of His Most Royal Grace, Charles Sinclair, 1st Duke of Haimsbury. As we reported to you last week, His Grace is *not* in England; for surely, if true, he would release us all from our bondage of worry, would he not?

And so, because of your concerns—indeed all our concerns—we approached the family multiple times, but as you may surmise, Duchess Elizabeth adamantly maintains that her husband is away on Crown business. We then approached that most elusive of England's spies, Paul Stuart, 12th Lord Aubrey. For some reason, the gracious duchess's former fiancé, has moved his entire household and maintains lodgings at Haimsbury House, where he serves as a formidable wall to all our enquiries. His delightful bride, Lady Cordelia Stuart, is expecting the couple's first child in a few weeks, but even she has moved to Haimsbury House for her confinement. Entering this fortress is difficult indeed, but we stubbornly tried, yet even the most innocent attempt to ascertain facts from the duke's family and staff met with fierce, yet polite, resistance.

Your vigilant servant endeavoured to speak to His Grace, Duke James of Drummond, but was informed the duke is away, ostensibly in France. We wonder, might the two dukes be working together? Enquiries to Paris revealed tantalising rumours that Duke James and his sister Lady Victoria Stuart have taken rooms at the Hotel du Louvre, due to a fire and housebreak at Château Rothesay, his sister's home in Goussainville. Few details are forthcoming regarding this strange development, but this reporter continues to cable Paris authorities for information.

No one in Paris admits to seeing Duke Charles anywhere. So, where is he? Gentle readers, we have worn out several pairs of shoe leather in our pursuit of truth, if only to allay all your fears and warm your true English hearts.

But now, with information gleaned just yesterday afternoon, we may joyfully report that the mystery is solved and our wonderful duke's whereabouts are revealed!

According to Mr. Gerald Pennyweather, His Grace's personal secretary and notable scion of an old and much revered Mayfair family, the reason for Haimsbury's long absence from Whitehall and his apparent neglect of governmental duties, was kept secret, due to international treaties and diplomatic promises made through the War Office. Of course, those missed duties include the Dock Strike in Whitechapel, two meetings of the Privy Council, the formal reception for the King of Prussia, and the Lords vote on Ireland (certainly a waste of time), but several cabinet meetings as well. We all commiserate with our duke, who must shoulder the burden of so many, dull gatherings.

But now, all restrictions and embargoes are removed, and this writer may report that on 12 August, Duke Charles sailed from Dover to a port in Lisbon, where he conducted two weeks of treaty talks on behalf of England.

In early September, the duke left Lisbon for Port Said in Cairo, where he spent three days as the guest of Consul-General Lord Cromer, where it is highly probable they discussed the ongoing Mahdist crisis in the Sudan.

Mr. Pennyweather explained that His Grace left Cairo in good humour and from there sailed to New York City. We may also reveal that every leg of His Grace's sea journey was enjoyed aboard the newly christened, and very well-appointed, royal navy ship, the HMS *Duchess of Branham*. A photograph of the ship is included with this article. The ship features a triple-screw drive and the very latest in steam technology. We're told the *Duchess* could break all speed records and give Mr. Ismay's White Star Line a run for its money. Are we surprised? No! Our royal duke deserves nothing less!

When contacted for comment, a representative of the New York City Mayor's Office confirmed via cable that His Grace disembarked the *Duchess of Branham* JUST ONE DAY AGO and was immediately conveyed, via unmarked brougham, to the world-renowned Astor Mansion on Fifth Avenue. There, the duke is expected to attend a round of meetings with President Benjamin Harrison, newly commissioned British Ambassador Sir Julian Pauncefote, U.S. Secretary of State Thomas F. Bayard, and New York's Governor David B. Hill, as well as New York City Mayor, Hugh John Grant.

It is also said our duke may attend several of New York City's high-society balls, with at least one to be hosted by Governor Hill. These grand masques and dances are attended by all the greatest names in *crème de la crème* families, like that of John D. Rockefeller, George Vanderbilt, Andrew Carnegie, Henry Clay Frick, William Backhouse Astor, Jr., and Francis Appleton, to name but a few. Whilst there is no guarantee that our duke will attend any balls (as he is *sans* his beautiful duchess), it is always the custom for foreign dignitaries, such as 'kings', to be fêted at many 'royal' celebrations.

The tours of Spain, Portugal, and Egypt do make diplomatic sense, but one wonders why our duke might wish to form social and political relationships with America's political leaders and *nouveau riche?*

Here is what this reporter has uncovered, and we have to thank a source who wishes to remain anonymous: It seems His Grace hopes to arrange a favourable marriage for a certain eligible young lady, whom the duke recently adopted. Though the unnamed (and dare we call her elegantly lovely?) ingenue isn't yet thirteen, everyone knows that 'royal' marriages are contracted quite early, often before a child has gained majority. Our duke may also be negotiating future marriages for his newly born twins: HRH Prince Charles Robert Arthur Sinclair IV, Marquess of Anjou; and HRH Princess Elizabeth Georgianna Victoria Regina Sinclair, the recently elevated Marchioness of Loudain.

We may also report that, whilst pursuing the topic of the Duke of Haimsbury's royal associations, your faithful correspondent spent countless hours unravelling a thread regarding our duke's heritage.

We commenced our search with certain startling reports, that blazed across morning editions throughout the metropolis last year. These implied the duke's very royal heritage and multi-branched kingly lineage. We scoured every book, every scroll, every patent, and every diary available, and may now happily confirm that all the rumours are true, and that we may anticipate the eventual emergence of a Sinclair Dynasty.

In fact, our digging revealed that Duke Charles, descends from FAR MORE monarchs than previously listed. Therefore, with so heady a mix of thrones and dominions in His Grace's VERY BLUE BLOOD, one wonders if there might also be a new 'House' established one day at Buckingham Palace? We shall explore that idea in next week's Royal Report.

For now, to our seafaring ROYAL DUKE, we say, 'Come home, soon, sir! Your people await!'

Margaret looked up from the article. "What sort of nonsense is this? Lorena, is any of it true? I thought the duke was missing, not sailing the Atlantic!"

Lorena cautioned Hansen to lower her voice. "Be careful, Meg. Whilst the prince's staff are fiercely loyal, I'm not as sure of the Whitehall people, who come and go here. This residence is used for government business, and you can never tell when some secretary or ambassador's clerk might be lurking about the foyer. Whether inside or outside this house, we're to repeat this sort of nonsense, anytime someone asks about Charles."

"Of course, I know, but it is nonsense, isn't it? And you needn't hush me. I just came through the foyer, and no one else is in the house. Lorena, do you know more than you're telling? Has Charles written to you since the christening?"

"Charles seldom returns my letters, and I only started writing, because Anatole insisted. I suppose, Charles and I've formed an odd sort of friendship through them." MacKey's attitude surprised her friend.

"A friendship? Do be honest, Lorena. If not with me, then with yourself. Are you in love with him?" Meg asked. "If you are, I understand. I fell for Charles as well, when he moved across from the Empress all those years ago."

Lorena sighed and set down her teacup. "If a person presumes emotions based on words, then that reporter for *The Gazette*'s in love with him, too. But no, I'm not. Not any longer."

"Rena, I don't mean to pry, but you once thought you loved William Trent, then you took a fancy to Lord Aubrey. Can a true heart be so changeable?"

"Ask any woman, Meg. You of all people should know the answer. But our pasts are forgiven, and I choose to think of today. Paul and I are friends, just as Charles and I are friends. What my heart once felt has become something far better."

Margaret salted her eggs. "Is that so? What happened to that, Lorena? And what do you mean by 'once felt'? My dear I understand the attraction to both men. Really, I do! I'm not made of stone, though I've been accused of it. How do you fall out of love? If love is real, then it simply isn't possible."

"Perhaps, not, but God helped me to put it aside," the physician replied with conviction. "He changed my hopeless infatuation into a deep and abiding affection. We really are friends, Meg. If anything, Charles sees me as a sort of sister, nothing more."

Hansen laughed. "I've seen friendly affection become quite physical, given the right situation. I used to run whores, Lorena. I know men, and I know women."

"It isn't physical, nor ever will be," Lorena insisted. "I really do love him as a sister loves a brother. And I pray for Charles every day. God will return him to all of us. I know it, Meg! Not because Anatole has said so, but because our Lord always keeps his promises. God has something special for Charles to do. I don't know what, exactly, but..."

"But?"

"Nothing."

Margaret took a deep breath, waiting a moment. "Did Trent tell you something about Charles?"

"No more than he ever told you," said the physician.

"Hmm," said Hansen. "Very well. Keep your secrets."

"You think me foolish, don't you?" asked MacKey.

"No, I speak from love, Lorena. I've no children of my own, and I suppose it's my mothering instinct. I worry that this sisterly affection, as you call it, is consolation, because of his happy marriage. You feel as if you've lost him to the duchess, but you cannot lose what you've never possessed. Charles has always belonged to Elizabeth."

"I never said he was mine," the doctor told her. "And I admire the duchess, if you must know. She's considerate and generous—and oh, let us talk of something else! My heart needs a distraction!"

Margaret ignored her friend's 'heart' reference and took a small bite of the Russian pastry instead. "This is very good. I shall gain back those twenty pounds, if the cook continues baking like this." She took a second bite and after swallowing, offered a suggestion. "Look, we've been cooped-up here for weeks. When Violet returns, why don't we all take a drive to Whitechapel and visit the Stanleys?"

"That sounds lovely, but I'm seeing patients today. At St. Mary's," replied the doctor.

"I'd forgotten you'd started your new position. Do you like working with Dr. Emerson?"

"He's become Lord Braxton, now that his father's died. It's why I started in the first place, remember? Michael and Andrea had to spend a fortnight in Edinburgh for the funeral and legal matters."

"Well, Lord Braxton's blessed to have you as a partner. You're a very fine physician, Lorena. I take it, he and Andrea are back?"

MacKey started to reply, but the ladies were interrupted by male voices. One was instantly recognisable. The women turned towards the sunlit breakfast room's main doors. Two very tall men entered: one with raven hair that fell past his shoulders, the other's hair short, brushed with the rich carnelian shades of autumn leaves.

"Good morning, ladies," Prince Anatole greeted his guests. "I see you're enjoying Madam Pushkina's delicious *vatrushkas*. I confess to having a sweet tooth, when it comes to Russian pastries, and our cook has a way with them, does she not?"

"Oh, yes, Your Highness. They're delicious," agreed Hansen. "We weren't aware you'd be coming home today, sir. Vasily thought you'd be away for another week. Was the trip successful?"

"Indeed, very," he answered. "Whilst there, I met an old friend. Ladies, allow me to introduce my cousin, Lord Daniel Porter, Earl of Ailesleigh."

The auburn-haired earl was dressed in a dark woolen suit and tweed waistcoat. He stood almost as tall as Romanov, and had laughing, golden brown eyes.

The earl bowed low, saying, "It is my very great honour to meet you both." His voice was melodious and deep. "You are Madam Hansen and Dr. MacKey?"

The women nodded.

"As I thought," Ailesleigh smiled. "Tolya's told me a great deal about you both. I hope we'll become friends."

"Tolya?" asked Lorena.

"You've never called him that? I've known this Russian for aeons, and he has many names, including Tolya."

"As we're both commoners, we've always called him Prince Anatole, my lord," said Lorena.

"Your lord? No, no," said the earl. "Call me Daniel. You're Tolya's friends, and I hope you'll become mine, too. And neither of you is common, dear lady. I see through to the true beauty of the heart," he said, touching his chest. "And it pleases me that you're here on such a beautiful September morn. I'm honoured to meet you both."

Anatole laughed at the other's manners. "Ladies, you can see that, of all my many cousins, Daniel has all the charm. Sadly, he's come on business that cannot wait, so forgive us, please. We came only to change from our travelling clothes."

Romanov turned to Ailesleigh, speaking quickly in another language; the ladies assumed it was Russian. When finished, Anatole returned to English. "Your rooms are upstairs. Just follow André, he will carry your luggage and other items."

"I can get them," the earl replied. "And I'll be back down soon. There's much to discuss before I leave for my assignment. Disturbing news, Tolya. Not the least is those visitors from America."

"America?" asked MacKey, daring to interrupt. "Are these visitors from Chicago, by any chance?"

"Why, yes, they are," answered Ailesleigh. "Two men and a young woman arrived three days ago. Their ship docked in Liverpool. Are you familiar with Chicago, Dr. MacKey?"

"No, neither of us has ever been there, but there's a third woman living here, who grew up in Chicago. Prince Anatole, is this bad news?"

"Perhaps. There is a sticky web that grows and stretches from America to England's shores, and some of the web begins in Chicago. We must wait and see what spiders cross it."

"Spiders?" she asked warily.

"Or perhaps, it is better to call them birds," replied the prince. "There is a saying in St. Petersburg, *the bird is known by its flight.*

Let us see what feathers sprout from these spidery visitors. That will determine their loyalties."

"Do you think they could be *red feathers*, Your Highness?" asked Meg fearfully.

"I know that they are red," Romanov told her plainly, "but what other colours help them fly is yet to be seen. Worry not, Mrs. Hansen. All is in hand. Has our Miss Stuart already left?"

"Not long ago," MacKey answered. "If we'd known of your return, she'd have waited."

"She and I will talk later, I'm sure. I am pleased to be home. Or rather to be *here*," he added, smiling. "My true home is far away, as is Lord Ailesleigh's." They bowed and left. Romanov spoke quickly to André as he and Ailesleigh headed towards the staircase.

Margaret pushed away the empty teacup, her appetite suddenly vanished. "Romanov is so vague sometimes."

"He's always been that way," replied MacKey, glancing at the clock. "I have to go. My first appointment's in thirty minutes. If you still want to visit the Stanleys, perhaps we can go tomorrow evening."

"Yes, I'd like that. With the house empty, I may try my hand at the piano again. Or paint."

"The prince talked of missing home, but you're still finding yours, aren't you, Meg?"

Hansen reached for Lorena's hand, as a mother might to a daughter. "I've already found my home. Here, with you and Violet. Strange, isn't it? My life is so radically different. Perhaps, I'll write to Father Lambelet and ask him to join us for dinner one night soon. I love listening to his teachings on the gospels."

"As does our prince. He and Father Lambelet have been friends for a long time."

"What do you think Prince Anatole meant by another home?" asked Meg. "Does he refer to St. Petersburg?"

"Of course, not," MacKey answered. "Anatole's home is in another realm."

"Another realm? Where?"

MacKey sighed wistfully. "It's a place for which we all yearn, Meg, though neither you nor I have been there yet. Anatole was born there. Perhaps, one day, he'll tell us what it's like."

CHAPTER FOUR

The Mirror World of Sen-Sen - Adele is rescued

Nearly an hour had passed since she'd awoken, and in that hour, Della had done all that Mrs. Grey had asked, trusting in Prince Anatole's promise that her rescuers would arrive at eleven. She sipped the flavourless tea, not caring that it had gone cold. She didn't shout or scream. Adele even pretended to sleep, though she peeked now and then, to see where the clocks hands stood; and all the while, wondering about her father and praying for his safety.

The clock hands seemed frozen at two minutes till eleven. Della deliberately pinched herself, happy to feel the pain. "I'm awake and I'm alive," she whispered. "And soon I shall be home. Then, Paul will help me rescue my father."

Finally, the minute hand moved, and Adele exhaled. *One minute more*, she thought. *Just one until my rescue!*

But wait. What if she was wrong? What if the promise of rescue was nothing but a story she'd made up whilst dreaming? Was her hope futile? Would the evil Mrs. Grey return before anyone came? And what of Prince Araqiel? Would he hurt her, if he caught her trying to escape? Was her father nearby? Should she try to find him? What was true and what false?

The agonisingly long minute finally passed, and the clock's hand moved up to the hour. Then, the chimes began. *One, two, three*, she counted in her mind. *Four, five, six*—oh, please, let them come! *Seven, eight...*

On the sounding of the ninth, Adele heard a dull rustling against the shuttered window. She'd already inspected this window, right after Mrs. Grey had left. Della had hoped to find an escape route, but the room overlooked a deep, precipitous chasm, making escape impossible.

Hearing the peculiar rustling, she rushed to the window, wondering what sort of person could find secure footing without trees or ladders for support. Della threw back the shutters just as the eleventh chime sounded and discovered a complete impossibility.

Precariously perched and gripping the outer edge of one of the shutters with the talons of its right foot, was a small brown owl.

"Oh, my!" Adele exclaimed. "However did you get here? Here, let me help you come in!"

At Della's invitation, the tiny owl flapped its fluttery brown wings and flew into the apartment, where it transformed into a gentleman Adele knew well: the endearing, if somewhat forgetful, Professor Archibald Cherubino; linguist, historian, antiquarian, and the most charming of guardians. She'd first met Professor Archie in May, when Prince Anatole sent him to Paris with orders to watch after her welfare. Since then, he'd become a very special friend.

Cherubino stood the same height as Adele and had a most unprepossessing appearance: sad eyes, bulbous nose, flat cheeks, and large ears. He looked for all the world like a disappointed French Artesian Basset. After changing form, the diminutive professor offered his customary bow, which sent his eyeglasses tumbling down the bulbous nose. Cherubino caught them in a singularly deft sweep of the right hand and then settled the spectacles more securely against his somewhat flat bridge.

"Forgive the unusual entry, Lady Adele," he began as he smoothed tufts of thinning hair back into place. "I'd not intended to enter your apartment in such a clumsy manner, but there are very strong wards surrounding this castle that prohibit entry by any other means—for me, at least. Prince Anatole told you I was coming, I hope? You look surprised."

And so she was. The very last thing in all the world Della expected was Archibald Cherubino, but hadn't he just been an owl?

"Yes, he did tell me, or at least, I think he did. In a dream, sort of. It's a bit unclear, actually. Am I still dreaming?" she asked, poking his shoulder and then pinching her hand. "That hurt, so I must be awake, oh, but never mind! I'm so very glad you're here!" she exclaimed, throwing her arms round his short neck. "Forgive me, if

I look surprised, Mr. Archie. It's because you were an owl a moment ago. Or I think you were. Were you?"

He nodded. "I was, indeed, Lady Della."

"Then, are you an angel? Or something else?"

"Actually, I'm an elohim, which is a more precise term, but you may think of me as an angel, if you wish. I've come to offer my assistance."

"If I remember the dream correctly, there should be two helpers. Was Prince Anatole mistaken, or am I?"

"Neither, dear lady. Prince Anatole, as you call him, is never mistaken, and your memory is remarkably accurate, as always."

"That's very kind of you, but why did you say as you call him? Isn't Prince Anatole his name? It's the only name I was ever told."

"The prince has many, *many* names—as do most of us—and by that I mean the elohim who serve here, in the human realm. And though I find the topic of great interest, discoursing on the nature of names and elohim postings isn't my present mission, Lady Adele. Might we speak of it another time? Would you like that?"

"Very much, and I'd prefer doing it elsewhere. I don't like this place at all, Mr. Archie, and I need to find my father."

The plump professor's pale eyes turned even more sad. "I am sorry to tell you, my lady, but rescuing Duke Charles is not my mission. Another of my kind looks after your good father. Oh, but look! My friend is arriving—*and, oh!*—he is breaking through the wards! Hold on to something, Della! This will cause quite a shaking!"

Cherubino grabbed the girl's hands firmly, and together they fled to a far corner of the bedchamber. A great thundering sounded, rattling all the books, the teacups, and every stick of furniture. Archie's thick glasses fell off his nose again, but Della caught them.

"What's happening?" she shouted over the great noise. "Is it an earthquake? Should we hide beneath the bed?"

Archibald's sparse hair puffed into a feathery spike as a tempest tore through the bedchamber. The winds were so fierce that even the massive tester bed began to rattle upon its heavy legs. After three minutes of this unsettling tumult, the shaking stopped, and everything grew eerily still. It was a palpable sort of silence. The professor's large ears perked up as he listened, and then his flat cheeks rose into a wide smile.

"Marvellous! That is so much better. All is well, Lady Della," he declared. "I'd worried for a moment it might be Araqiel or another of his brothers, but everything's all right. Truly, I'd no idea my friend had such *power!* And here he comes at last."

The stillness was broken again, this time by a gentle breeze, and the softest of voices spoke in a whispered tone.

"You called me?"

Archie took the round spectacles from Adele and settled them back onto his face. The thick lenses made the irises look like a pair of pale robin's eggs. "Why, it's Prince Uriel! Yes, yes, I did call, but I was told to expect Prince Hadraniel, sir. Not you."

The newcomer's cloak shimmered in brilliant hues of gold and silver over a tunic of radiant pearl. His hair fell in brass-coloured waves, the long locks ending at a belted waist; and his eyes were black mirrors filled with ancient fire. A long sword hung from the belt, its crimson scabbard covered in gemstones that shone like a constellation of stars. Adele thought him both beautiful and terrifying, all at once.

"Lord Hadraniel is occupied elsewhere presently," the visitor told Archie. "If you prefer to work alone, I can..."

"No, no!" the little professor blurted out. "Prince Uriel, I hope you've come to help, not to engage in any *battle?* I shouldn't wish to expose our Della to any fighting twixt you and Prince Araqiel."

Uriel stood so very tall that his head nearly touched the ceiling. He bent low to whisper into Archie's right ear. Della could hear a little of their conversation, but the words sounded completely foreign; like no language on Earth. As the brown-owl messenger listened to his fellow elohim, a series of puzzling expressions, ranging from surprise to shock, tumbled through his plump features until, at last, Archie nodded.

"Yes. Yes, of course! I understand the situation completely now. Prince Samael is right to do so."

"I'm glad you agree, Raguel," said Uriel.

"Raguel?" asked Adele. "Who's that? And who is Samael?"

"Raguel is one of *my* other names," said Archie. "As I said, we all have numerous names and titles, for each represents a part of our history."

"Like words and pages in a book?" asked Adele. "I like Archie better. And this other one? Prince Samael?"

"It is one of Prince Anatole's names," answered Uriel.

"Oh," said Della, still wondering if she dreamt. "Then, Prince Uriel, you've come to help me escape? Why does Mr. Archie—I mean Raguel—need another to help him? Am I too heavy for him to carry? No one need carry me, you know. I'm happy to walk."

"Legs will not take you through the veil, Lady Della," said Uriel. "That is my task. Unless Raguel prefers to try. The veil winds are howling with demon soldiers, for the Shadows sense a disturbance."

"The Shadows!" exclaimed Raguel. "If they're awake, then we must hurry! But you must promise to take good care of her, Lord Uriel. Lady Adele is very important, you see. Not just to mankind's future, but—well, she's become quite important to me," he admitted. "If you cannot guarantee her safety, then I shall call upon another for aid."

Uriel touched the jewelled hilt of his bright sword, as if in warning. "Do you challenge my authority, Raguel?"

This alarmed Adele, and the girl responded by placing herself in front of her brown-owl friend. With hands raised protectively, her eyes fixed upon the tall stranger, she warned him, saying, "See here, Mr. Uriel! If you intend to use that sword against my friend, then you must come through me. He is a very fine man, or perhaps an owl, but he is a good friend, and I shan't allow anyone to hurt him. Is that clear?"

Uriel's hand relaxed and he bowed deeply. "I meant no harm to you or to my brother."

"If he's your brother, then why threaten him?"

"It was a test, my lady."

"A test? Why would you test someone from heaven?"

"The test was not for Raguel, but for you, Lady Adele. And I'm pleased to say you passed."

"I don't understand," she answered.

"Your bravery is legendary amongst my brethren, Lady Della. Both now and in the future. That bravery will serve you and your offspring well in the coming years. Forgive me for testing its merit."

"Very well, but don't do it again," Adele answered.

The imposing angel smiled at this. "As you wish, my lady. Now, we must go before Araqiel discovers I've broken through his wards."

"I'm sure he already knows. In fact, I'm sure everyone knows!" Della said. "All that shaking and tempest. It's a wonder no one's come to see about it."

"No one will come, Lady Della," Uriel assured her. "Only you and Raguel could feel it."

"I doubt that," she argued. "You shook every part of the room!"

"They did not feel it, because I have suspended time," he explained, "but it will not hold much longer. We must go."

"No. Not until you rescue my father."

The great elohim's brows rose up. "You're very particular for a girl who is locked inside a prison, Lady Adele."

"Perhaps I am, but my father would do the same for me."

"That is true," the rescuer answered, "but have no fear for Charles Sinclair. Lord Hadraniel looks after him. The duke is in good and capable hands."

She stamped her right foot and shook her head stubbornly. "No. No! I won't have it! If you're so very sure of my father's welfare, then take me to him. Let me see for myself."

Uriel's radiant face widened into a handsome smile, and his fierce eyes softened. "I've heard tales of your loyalty and great passion, Lady Adele, but it is quite different to meet your formidable nature head-on. However, I cannot comply with your demands. Taking you to the duke is quite impossible. You must trust me. The passage of time will soon resume, and the guards outside your door will perceive the change in the wards. If you're to escape unnoticed, then you must come with me now."

"Mr. Uriel, you don't understand. My father needs me. Let me go to him, please," she begged.

The tall warrior knelt before her, his black eyes transforming to a warm blue. "You are exceedingly brave, my lady, but my orders are to protect you first and foremost. Your friend Mr. Archie serves as your guardian and would gladly endanger himself for you, but his abilities are no match for Araqiel. Mine are, which is why I've been sent to lead you both to safety. Come with me, please. Your father would wish it, and the One commands it. I must not fail in my assignment."

Adele's face grew still as she considered his words. She knew the angel was right. Her father would want her to leave. "Prince Anatole says the One is another name for God."

71

"Yes, that's true," Archie told her. "The Creator has many names."

She sighed. "Very well, then. If it's God's wish, then I shall go, but you must promise to see to my father's safety. Will you promise me?"

Uriel bowed deeply, his hand over his heart. "It is my vow to you, dear lady. After your rescue, I shall go directly to Hadraniel and make certain the duke is safe."

Archie heaved a great sigh of relief, but then the clock began to tick once more. Hastily, Cherubino grabbed Della's shoes and handed them to her. "Go, Uriel! Go! Take her quickly, dearest friend and brother. Time has returned, and I hear the guards rousing outside the door!"

The warrior angel lifted Adele into his arms and in less than a blink, the pair had vanished. The clock's ticking grew louder, and the men guarding the bedchamber began to shout and pound on the door. Its wood bowed inward as the men threw themselves against it over and over. Finally, the door splintered, and the enraged men tumbled into the bedchamber.

When they scrambled to their feet, all they saw was a small brown owl, perched atop the bookcase.

"Get it!" shouted one of the men. "Don't let it get away!"

Both men ran towards the bird, but the brown owl's wings stretched outward, and he escaped through the open window, vanishing into a misty cloud.

The guards stared at the empty room, raw terror paling their rough faces. Adele Sinclair had escaped.

CHAPTER FIVE
Real World - Montmore House Private Asylum

For three days, Dr. Henry MacAlpin had been treating a trouble-some new patient with an *idee fixe* regarding an imagined personal relationship with Queen Victoria. Ewan MacNee was just twenty years old, the eldest son of the Earl of Redcliffe, a prominent mem-ber of the House of Lords. The young man tried twice to enter Her Majesty's private chambers, and a judge had ordered him examined by a professional. Thus, Ewan entered Henry's tender care.

For three nights, the young man howled and shouted to get out, as though a fever took control of him. And on each of those nights, Henry visited the lad, speaking in soft tones until Ewan fell asleep again, leaving his doctor wide-eyed and weary. That September morning, Henry was using a new Volta Dictaphone to record his thoughts on the case, when his butler knocked on the library door.

"You've a caller, sir," Elias Saunders told him.

"A caller?" asked the alienist as the needle continued scratching into the wax cylinder. "What time is it?"

"Half ten, sir. And you should probably stop the recorder."

"Oh, yes, of course," said the bleary-eyed viscount. "I'm still getting used to it. Marvellous machine! Half ten, you say? No won-der I'm hungry. Wait, is it Duchess Elizabeth who's called? She mentioned stopping by, but I've no idea what time she intended. Though perhaps, not today. I believe the duchess has a meeting else-where today. In Whitechapel, or she might have said Whitehall."

"My lord, it isn't the duchess, though she is a lady of your ac-quaintance."

Henry searched his coffee-drenched brain for names. "A lady of my acquaintance? Is it my cousin? I shouldn't think Lady Ellen would drop by without writing first. Wales to London is a ten-hour drive down some miserable roads."

"Shall I make an end of the mystery and bring the lady in, sir?" asked Saunders, smiling. "She is waiting, after all."

"Yes, yes, of course! Oh, but wait, Saunders. Am I presentable? I shouldn't wish to entertain morning callers, particularly lady callers, in a state of ill-preparedness. My morning rounds didn't leave any *traces*, I hope? Mrs. Crossfield suffered a dreadful nosebleed earlier, and I've no idea if there might be blood on my waistcoat, or even in my hair," he added, combing the thatch of dark curls with his fingers. "It was a veritable fountain, you see. I'm sure I washed my hands right away, but it's just the sort of habit, that one easily forgets. Wait, I see you're smiling. Saunders, am I that amusing?"

"Quite often, my lord."

Henry took the comment with good grace. "Yes, I suppose you're right. I'm turning into my scatterbrained grandmother made over again, aren't I? Very well, send in this lady of my previous acquaintance. And do wipe that grin off your face."

"As you wish, sir," bowed the servant, the grin remaining intact.

Whilst waiting, Henry straightened the papers on his desk. The surface was ever and endlessly messy, no matter how tidy he endeavoured to be. He'd just picked up two empty coffee cups and was about to place them on a nearby cabinet, when the caller entered. His back was turned, and so Henry hadn't heard her footstep. His attention remained on the cups as he tried to decide whether to set them down or return them to the desk.

"I hope you're not drinking two coffees at once now, Henry," spoke an American voice.

MacAlpin spun about, and a ripple of shock, mixed with relief and joy ran through the viscount's facial musculature.

"Violet!" he exclaimed, nearly dropping both cups. "I mean—of course, I mean Miss Stuart." He set the cups back on the desk and crossed to the door, his hands outstretched in friendship. "My very dear friend, wherever have you been? I've looked for you everywhere!"

Overcome by surprise, Henry impulsively started to draw her into an embrace, but stopped short, fearing impropriety. "Do forgive me, Miss Stuart. It's just.. Well, it's so very *good* to see you at long last!"

Violet Stuart's soft brown eyes sparkled, and a hint of pink coloured her cheeks. The woman once known to London society as Susanna Morgan, the late Sir Clive Urquhart's mistress, laughed and offered a hug to the bashful bachelor. He held the embrace a little too long, and Violet found herself enjoying it a little too much.

"It's good to see you, Henry," she said, once they'd parted. "I'm sorry to keep you wondering about me, but I've been well cared for and now live with a kind gentleman who watches over me. So I'm quite safe."

Henry's smile vanished. "I see. I suppose congratulations are in order then. Do I know this kind gentleman?"

She noticed his eyes glanced down at her hands, as though wondering if a wedding ring were concealed beneath the lavender gloves.

"I believe you do know him," she answered, removing the gloves to show she wore no rings. "I imagine he's very well known to the inner circle by now. He's been consulting with all of you since mid-August."

Henry mentally sorted through a list of possible names. The Stuart-Sinclair family rarely admitted anyone new to the circle meetings, but when they did, it was usually a relative or son of a previous member. Might she refer to Sir Thomas Galton's younger brother? He'd recently joined and was unmarried. Sir Thomas was now engaged to Lady Vera Comstock, a third cousin, and so he could be ruled out. Sir Percy Smythe-Daniels returned from Ireland the previous week and remained unmarried, though rumour had it Percy was courting a wealthy Frenchwoman. Then again, might she refer to Malcolm Risling? Another bachelor.

"That's actually quite odd," Henry noted, desperately trying to sound nonchalant and failing miserably. "Your name comes up at the meetings from time to time, though not as a houseguest. Paul's mentioned you, in the context of wondering after your welfare, of course. You and he have a *past*, I understand," the viscount added, instantly wishing he'd avoided any mention of the handsome earl. "Forgive me. Your relationship with Lord Aubrey is none of my business. You're no longer my patient, and your life is your own, Miss Stuart. I am just your former doctor."

She touched his cheek fondly. "But not a former friend, I hope? And do stop calling me Miss Stuart. You used to call me Violet." She glanced at the empty chairs near the fireplace. "May we sit?"

Realising his rudeness, Henry blurted out, "Do forgive my manners, yes, yes, of course! Do sit, Miss Stuart—I mean, Violet. I'm sure Saunders is already preparing tea. Or rather Mrs. Merchant is. She's new, but quite good at protocol and all that. She used to cook for the queen, you see. Protocol's the order of the day there, and I'm talking too much, aren't I?"

"A little," answered the American as she took one of the chairs near the fire. "I find it charming, actually. Henry, must I sit alone? Or do you prefer to continue straightening the papers on your desk?"

"Do they need straightening?" he worried. "I'm terrible about such things, you know. I should probably interview for a secretary. Pennyweather might know a good man. Or I could..."

"Henry, sit!" she exclaimed, laughing.

On command, the viscount plopped into the companion chair, grinning at his beautiful guest like a lovestruck schoolboy. "See how I obey your commands, dear lady? I could do with someone to order me about. Although, perhaps, not someone so very pretty as you. Now, tell me what brings you to Montmore today?"

"Confession, I suppose."

"Confession? As one tells a priest?"

"No, Henry. A confession to you, for running away last year. It wasn't my intent to deceive you, but my memory returned without any warning, and it frightened me. Since then, a lot's happened. To begin, the gentleman watching me isn't a suitor. It's Prince Anatole Romanov."

"Romanov?" he repeated. "Surely, you and he aren't romantically involved?"

"No," she laughed. "Not in the slightest. He's my protector, but not a romantic one. Did you know I'm from Chicago?"

"Lord Aubrey told me, yes."

"I'd thought he might. Paul knows all about my true life. I'm American, of course, but my heritage is Sicilian through my father, and Irish through my late mother. Recently, my father came to England, and disappeared shortly after. I'd planned to come visit you today anyway, but this morning, before I left, I received a note from the earl. He's learned that my brothers have come to England with a young woman who's unrelated. I'm sure they're looking for our father."

"But surely, your brothers' arrival is a good thing? Families are a vital part of our mental health and well-being, Violet. My father and I don't always get on, but if he were missing, I'd certainly go look for him, no matter how far I had to travel."

"I'm sure most children would, but this isn't about family, Henry. It's about power and control. My brothers don't give a fig for our father. They've come to make sure he's dead, so they can inherit his money. However, if someone has murdered him, they'll want retribution. Sicilian style. And if they find me, they'll force me back to Chicago. Henry, I need your advice. Will you allow me to lean on you?"

He reached for her hand, his nut-brown eyes alight with deep affection. "Miss Stuart, my shoulders and my life are yours, should you need them."

She smiled through tears. "It's Violet, remember?"

"Yes, of course," he said, blushing. "Sweet Violet."

She was the one blushing now, and her honey-brown eyes lowered a little. "You're far too kind to me, Henry."

MacAlpin smoothed over the embarrassing moment by returning to a more familiar and comfortable topic. "You've regained your memories? All of them?"

"Yes, all of them," she answered, wiping a tear. "I'd thought Dr. Gehlen might have told you."

"No, he's never said anything. How do you two know one another?"

"We met years ago in Paris. It's a long story from my old life. While staying here, I noticed him through my window, and thought he looked familiar. I'm ashamed to admit this, Henry, but I sneaked down to the gardener's cottage to talk to him. You see, he looked so very familiar, and I thought he might tell me who I was."

"I take it, he did?"

"Not directly, but seeing Anthony stirred up all the old memories of my former life, and it frightened me."

"Why? Were the memories troubling? I always felt your amnesia was rooted in trauma."

"Actually, the memories made me feel shame. Abject shame at who I really was. You've always seen me as pure sweet Violet

Stuart, but I'm not pure. Or I didn't used to be. I've worked through most of the old heartaches now and confessed my many sins to a wonderful old priest. His name's Father Georgio Lambelet. He's Greek Orthodox, but their ways are close to my own Catholic up-bringing, so it's familiar. He's a genuine believer, and he's taught me a great deal about being a Christian."

"Then, you've found Christ? You've asked him to be your Saviour?"

She smiled nervously. "I have, but it was Christ that found me, and since then, my life has changed along with my heart. I'll tell you about all of it another time, if I may. My family's the worry right now. My brothers are cold-blooded killers, Henry. And I've no idea who the woman is that's come with them, but she'll be trouble, I'm sure. If they learn I'm still alive, then..."

Her hands trembled, and Henry reached over and took them in his. "Take heart, sweet Violet. The circle members are accustomed to dealing with dangerous men like your brothers. We'll protect you." He gazed into her eyes hopefully. "And if you'll allow it, I'd protect you for all my days."

She nearly pulled back the hands, fearing the sudden intimacy, but the idea of a life with the endearing viscount seemed so very pleasant and restful that she wanted to say yes. Did she dare to draw such a gentle man into the black maelstrom of the Calabrese family and their connexions to Redwing's American branch?

"I hope you don't misunderstand, Henry, but may we speak of that another time?" was all she could say, praying he'd not take it as a rebuff. "I should be going. I've another call to make, and then I need to return the prince's new coach. Vasily's waiting."

"Vasily? Oh, yes, that's Romanov's butler, isn't it? Odd sort of man, but intimidating. I'm glad you didn't come alone. Look here, Violet, I understand that you're afraid, but would you consider re-siding here until the danger passes? It would be a great help to me. I could use someone to look after my paperwork and empty all my coffee cups. And Mrs. Winstead's planning to retire in another year. I'm sure she'd be happy to train a new nurse."

"Me? A nurse?" she asked in amazement. "Henry, I'm not sure I could do it. I'm not the sort of woman who'd make a good nurse."

"Why not?"

"Because my whole life is a lie. Yes, I've found a new life through Christ, but my American past will always be with me."

"But as a Stuart, you're one of my cousins, right?"

"Henry, I'm not really a Stuart, and you know it. That new name was Paul's idea. It's one of the last things he said to me before I lost my memory. I guess it stuck in my head. I'm really Cassandra Calabrese from Chicago."

"Nonsense! I see Stuart sinews in your face and eyes. I'm sure we're related," he said with a wink. "But to make it real, I could have a specialist create heritage papers, if you like. I could even ask my father to adopt you, as a ward. Or there might be other ways to change your name."

"I can't ask you to do that."

"It's no imposition, and I want to help. Christ changed your soul, why not change your name?"

"Is that really possible?" she asked, fearing to hope.

"Anything's possible, if you have faith, Violet. Let me talk to Paul about it. I'm sure he and Kepelheim could produce a very official looking set of heritage papers."

"Like a family tree?"

"Yes, only the kind that peers use to prove they're entitled to inherit titles and the like. All the peerage houses keep them, and they're filed at the Royal Archives. You know, Reggie Parsons might even lend a hand. He's been keeping company with Kepelheim of late. Never fear, sweet Violet! We'll get it done before you can sing God Save the Queen!"

"Do you really think I could become Violet Stuart? Legally? It isn't just a dream?"

"I hope it's a pleasant dream? I promise, Violet, we'll make your dreams come true. And if Romanov agrees, then you can move in here whilst we prepare the papers. You could study nursing, if you wish."

"I'm not sure about that. Let me speak to Prince Anatole first." She had grown fearful again. "I really should go."

"Violet, if you're worried about your brothers, let me protect you."

She pulled on the gloves again, covering her hands as though closing her heart. "I need to discuss it with Lorena and Margaret."

"Lorena? Margaret?"

"My friends, but they've become more like sisters. The prince rescued them as well. Lorena's a doctor, and Margaret is a former businesswoman."

"I know a doctor named Lorena. Might her surname be MacKey?"

"Yes, do you know her?"

"I do, though I've not see her in several years," Henry answered. "I teach a course on the brain at the Women's Medical School in Whitechapel. Lorena was a fine student, and I tried to convince her to become an alienist. She seemed interested at first, but suddenly decided on another specialty. Herbalism and women's health, I think."

"Lorena and I've been friends for a long time. She, Margaret, and I used to belong to Redwing, remember?"

"Yes, so you did," he whispered. "Did the prince rescue all of you? Our Russian is certainly busy. He's been advising the circle since the duke... Well, since August. Come to think of it, I've not seen Romanov for over a week."

"He's been away, but Vasily and several other men keep watch on us. And Father Lambelet visits for supper now and then. Henry, are you sure about my moving in? I don't want to be a bother."

Henry pulled her into a warm embrace and sweetly kissed her forehead, his lips lingering. "Dear lady, you could never be a bother to me. Say you'll come back. For my sake as well as yours."

He kissed her hands and then, without stopping to think, moved his lips to hers.

Once the kiss ended, Violet answered in a hoarse whisper, mixed with tears. "I can think of nowhere else I'd rather live, Henry. But it could bring you a great deal of trouble."

"If trouble comes, then we'll meet it together." He stroked her soft cheek, his eyes glistening. A question rose to his lips, the most important question a man ever asks a lady, but before he could ask it, the door opened.

It was Elias Saunders, and he wasn't bringing tea.

"Forgive me, sir, but there's a man at the door who claims to know you. He's quite frantic and will not desist."

MacAlpin sighed, the opportunity lost. "Does this inconveniently frantic gentleman have a name?"

"It's Lord de Margravene, sir. He's the viscount who lives nearby."

"Yes, yes, I know who he is. Bert's a distant cousin, but what of it? Why is he so frantic, as you say?" Henry wanted the world to leave him alone, so he could voice the unvoiced words. *Violet, would you consent to becoming my wife?*

But the butler wouldn't go away, nor would the inconvenient caller. "What does the man want, Saunders? Is he ill?"

"No, sir. He's brought a young girl."

"A girl? Bert has a son. Who's the girl? Is she ill?"

"She's unconscious, sir," the butler answered. "And you know her, sir. I believe it's the Lady Adele Sinclair."

CHAPTER SIX
How Lady Adele was found at Margravene Manor

Two days before Elias Saunders interrupted his employer's unvoiced marriage proposal and announced the arrival of a most improbable visitor, the missing and much missed Lady Adele Sinclair; another young woman, wife to Lord Bertram de Margravene had taken her final breath on Earth.

After a day of funeral preparations, a small procession of mourners fell in behind a flower-strewn waggon, bearing the slender casket to its final place of rest. The dreadful day began with sunshine; but by afternoon, a grey and ghostly mist whispered into the homes and churches and made itself at home as if the Druids of old had sent a shroud of tears to cover the dead. The intemperate weather kissed and caressed the graveyard's old stones, chilling and choking the grass, along with all who walked upon it. Even the the air quivered in anticipation of a great pagan shift to come. Eleven days until the equinox, when sun and moon shared control of the heavens, and the veil twixt worlds thinned to paper.

Woe to the weeping man and his sad-eyed son, for twas Death that shepherded them that mid-September day. And though the equinox wouldn't come for over a week, that thinning veil could still allow angry faes and furious phantasms to steal through and snatch away life. Certainly, it seemed to all, that some unwholesome spirit's breath surrounded the mourners: a small boy and his thirty-four-year-old father, who'd come to lock away his mad wife, one last time.

Exactly eight years prior to her death, the sensitive and increasingly unstable Lady Vera Elizabeth Cotterfield de Margravene shocked her party guests, when she drew a fish knife across both her wrists. The viscountess survived, but the suicide attempt forced her husband to place Vera into a series of very private, very expensive asylums, ending at last with Pollux Institute of Fulham. Lady Vera's confused and equally sensitive husband, unwilling to believe his wife's condition hopeless, spent most of his inheritance in an attempt to cure her, but to no avail. Finally, it was the godlike Dr. Alphonse Theseus, head alienist at Pollux, who brought Lady Vera a sense of calm, stability, and dignity.

Vera remained at Pollux until her death.

Not wishing to court publicity, and upon the advice of the family's cheerless solicitor, the aptly named Sir Jeremiah Albatross, the lady's sudden passing wasn't announced, meaning the mourners were few. The procession began at Margravene Chapel and ended at Margravene Mausoleum, a cheerless pavilion built in 1745, used only for viscounts and their wives. Twelve coffins would keep her company, making Lady Vera number thirteen. Two gardeners conveyed the lady's brass and mahogany mantle, placing the coffin upon a ragstone plinth in the centre of the mausoleum's main chamber. Once settled there, the boy's governess covered the coffin in white lilies, picked from the estate's ample gardens.

The widower's son stood beside the flowered casket, his face pale as milk, hazel eyes swollen from weeping. He knew very little of his mother. The first indication of Lady Vera's madness appeared just five months after the birth of her son, and the attending physician declared it hysterical neurosis, caused by postpartum sadness. He recommended rest, isolation, and ample amounts of laudanum.

Three months after, Lady Vera began to suffer from night terrors and persistent dreams, even demonic visitations. Her longsuffering husband, the Viscount Bertram de Margravene, would have kept his deranged wife isolated in an upper apartment of their home, but Lady Vera's attempt at self-slaughter made such a solution an impossibility. Bertram was advised to place the lady into professional care, if only for the child's sake. This 'care' usually consisted of morphine, high-pressure water therapy, and hot steam baths. Nothing worked, until Dr. Theseus took the case and admitted her to Pollux, allowing Vera to spend her final two years in comfort, dignity, and elegant surroundings.

As he stood beside his wife's coffin, Bertram's stoic demeanor broke down completely. Albatross, the corpulent lawyer, placed a kid-gloved hand on his client's shoulder. "No tears, sir. It's not a fit example for the boy."

The viscount nodded and wiped his swollen eyes. "Yes. You're right." He looked down at his ten-year-old son. "Your mother loved you, Thomas. She gave all her strength to you, I think, and kept none for herself. But she's with God now. Free from all the darkness that haunted her."

A thin man with stooped shoulders, dressed in a priestly black cassock, white surplice and white stole, entered the house of cold death. He carried the *Book of Common Prayer* in his hand. "If I may continue, Your Lordship?" the clergyman asked the viscount.

"Yes, yes, of course," muttered the widower. "But we mustn't be here after dusk, Bishop Blighton."

Blighton opened the book and read aloud: "I am the resurrection and the life, saith the Lord: he that believeth in me, though he were dead, yet shall he live: and whosoever liveth and believeth in me shall never die."

The bishop's nasal voice droned on and on about life after death, quoting familiar passages from Job and the Psalms, before he ended with the lesson from I Corinthians 15, with words of hope to a hopeless man: "Now is Christ risen from the dead and become the first-fruits of them that slept. For since by man came death, by man came also the resurrection of the dead. For as in Adam all die, even so in Christ shall all be made alive. But every man in his own order: Christ the first-fruits; afterward they that are Christ's, at his coming."

"That's enough," said the viscount, placing a hand on the clergyman's wrist. "Offer the rest tomorrow, please. I cannot bear it!"

"And dusk is nearing. We should go, my lord," Albatross warned de Margravene. "The light is fading. Mr. Greene must latch the entry before nightfall. You know the rules, sir."

Outside the mausoleum, the retreating sun hovered over a crooked line of yews that bordered a neighbouring property, an old castle known locally as Geist—Gaelic for 'Ghost'. The ruins grew active at night, and the family had learnt to stay indoors when darkness fell, particularly during seasonal changes.

The dying sun's final glory painted the bank of cold clouds with a blood-red hue, as if old Sol had given his last drop of life and yielded to pale Luna and her army of stars.

A gardener entered the darkening chamber, ducking his head as he passed beneath the low doorway. Bowing, he said, "I'm sorry, my lord, but Pierce and I need to close up. It's nearly nightfall."

"Yes, yes, I know, Greene. I'm aware of the rules. But how can I leave her like this?" the husband murmured in a vacant tone. "This chamber must get very dark when night comes, and there are no windows or torches. She'll be cold, and Vera has a great fear of closed, dark places."

The lawyer drew the peer from his reverie. "Keep your voice measured, sir. Remember the boy."

"Boy?"

"Your son, my lord. Master Thomas."

"Oh, yes. Tom." Bertram looked up at the ceiling of the mausoleum, painted with scenes of angels escorting the dead to heaven. It did nothing to soothe his broken heart. The fingers of his gloved hands clasped his face, and Bertram shuddered, visibly shaking off the strange mood like discarding a ghostly garment.

"Very well. Do as you must, Greene," the viscount ordered as he turned towards the doorway.

The fair-haired boy had said little during the long service, but now reached for one of the fragrant lilies, thinking how his mother's body would be sealed here forever. "Must we go, Father? She'll be getting cold."

"Your mother's dressed quite warmly, Thomas. Mrs. Meadows chose the blue dress and the yellow overcoat—your mother's favourites. They're both quite warm."

"Might I stay a few minutes more, Father?"

The lines of Sir Jeremiah Albatross's plump mouth grimaced into a frown. "Rules are rules, Master Thomas. Supper is waiting, and there's hot cocoa."

"Yes, I know, sir, but the doctors never let me speak to Mother without a nurse present. May I say goodbye, please? On my own?"

The boy's governess had been standing by quietly, close to the mausoleum entrance. She cleared her throat. "What harm is there, my lord? Greene and I can see the boy's out by nightfall."

The soft female voice startled the introspective widower, and de Margravene shuddered, thinking his dead wife had risen to speak. "Vera?"

"No, sir," the governess answered gently. "It's just Poole."

"Oh, yes, Mrs. Poole. Forgive me. My mind is elsewhere."

"Of course it is, sir. And Thomas?"

"What about him?"

"The boy asked if he might remain to say goodbye. I shall be with him. We shan't stay past dusk."

"Yes, yes, of course," the viscount muttered. "Very well. It allows me time to discuss other matters with Sir Jeremiah."

Thomas knew what those 'other matters' surely were, for as his mother's only child, he would inherit the income from the vast Cotterfield estate. This fact, and probably only this fact, made him important to the covetous solicitor. The de Margravene viscountancy included two large houses, a hundred acres of woodland, a sheep farm, and a mercantile, but very little money. Marriage to Lady Vera Cotterfield allowed Bertram to keep his family's businesses afloat and repair the crumbling manor houses. Nearly all his friends assumed the viscount's actions were entirely mercenary, but Bertram had loved his wife deeply and would have married her, even without the ample dowry. Now, his son would inherit the entailed portion of the funds, becoming a very wealthy boy.

"Don't be too long, Mrs. Poole," called the viscount as he stepped through the doorway with the bishop and lawyer. "Five minutes only. Nightfall is upon us."

Albatross started to object, worried the boy might disobey, but a stern glance from the viscount froze the remonstration before it left the corpulent lawyer's lips.

"Very good, sir," said Albatross, casting an angry look at the governess before departing.

Greene saw them out, turning to say, "I'll come back in five minutes, Mrs. Poole. Master Thomas, I'm real sorry."

Alone with his dead mother and the governess, Thomas Cottingham de Margravene knelt beside the coffin, tears staining his freckled cheeks. "Does madness come from sin, Mrs. Poole?"

The governess stared at the youth. "Of course not. Why would you think that?"

"Mr. Blighton said it did."

"The bishop said such a foolish thing? Surely not."

"He did," the boy replied. "I overheard him telling my father that madness comes from unconfessed sins, and that it can be passed to children. I do see strange things sometimes, like mother did."

The woman knelt beside the boy, her voice tender. "We all see things sometimes, Tom. It doesn't make us mad."

"But do you see what I do?"

"I don't know. What do you see?"

He paused, taking a deep breath. "Monsters."

She daubed at his cheeks with a lace-edged handkerchief. "What monsters is it you see?"

"Ugly, awful things. But mostly shadow monsters," he said quietly. "I see them walking back and forth, over by the old castle."

"Geist Castle?"

"Yes. Just beyond the gates. And sometimes, they fly."

"I can't speak to anything flying, but I'm sure it's just real people walking there, Thomas. Folks round here say the castle's haunted, but it's just tramps and travellers, making their bed for the night near the ruins, that's all," Poole assured him. She buttoned the boy's overcoat and pulled down his wool cap. "Come now, it's getting dark. Tell your mother goodbye."

Thomas kissed the casket and ran a hand along its brass handles. "I'll pray for you, Mother. I'm sorry you died."

"Well done, dear," said Poole. She pulled away one of the flowers and gave it to him. "Press this into your Bible, to remember her by. She loved you, Tom. Don't forget that."

They left the mausoleum and passed by Greene and his assistant, who bade them goodnight with a tip of their cloth caps. The pathway back to the house took them through rows of crooked stone markers that leaned this way and that; past an older mausoleum, filled with de Margravene viscounts and barons, who'd died in battle, of sickness, or of old age. The name *Braithwaite*, an older family surname, was etched over the door. Braithwaite Tomb, as the family called it, stood closer to Geist Castle than anything else in the cemetery. Wealthy markers and obelisks dominated the area, and a hundred yards to the west, guarding the entrance to the castle ruins, stood a great angel, whose sixteen-foot wingspan marked the border of the de Margravene property. The angel's marble eyes gazed up towards heaven, as if reminding the sleepers of their ultimate destiny.

"Who's that?" asked Thomas, pointing in the direction of the angel.

"One of Greene's other men, I should think," the woman replied nervously, her mind filled with Tom's tale of shadows and monsters.

"No, it can't be, Mrs. Poole. It's not a man at all," the boy said, tugging on the woman's hand. "Come on, please!"

Poole peered into the gloomy mist. "Come where?"

"Over there! Don't you see it? The bright light and the small figure! By the angel!"

Was the bishop right? Could madness be inherited? thought the woman. "Come now, Tom. We mustn't dawdle. Sugden will have the food prepared. There's cocoa, and we can warm up."

"Don't you see her?" he insisted, tugging at her hand with greater force. "There! By the angel! Don't you see her, Mrs. Poole? The angel! The angel!"

Helen Poole had served as Thomas's nurse and governess since the day of his birth; more than ten lovely years, and during all that time, she'd learnt to be patient with the boy's vivid imagination. "It's just more fog coming up, Tom," she declared. "It's settling round the trees and statues. Fog can take very strange shapes."

"No, Mrs. Poole. Look! *The angel!*"

The boy pulled free of her grip and ran towards the statue. Poole shouted, but he refused to heed, and so she ran after, fearing Tom might fall in the thick fog. She'd read of strange dangers, rising up on such nights. The newspapers were filled with awful stories. Tales of wolves that walked like men; even a ghostly woman in white, that lured children to their deaths in the river. What if he'd seen this siren woman? The family had one strict rule about the graveyard. No one stayed here after dark. Not for any reason. Geist Castle was dangerous at all times, but especially after dark.

"Tom! Wait!"

The boy criss-crossed through the graveyard, past rows of engraved granite headstones, round etched obelisks, thick stands of yews, towards Geist Castle and the tall angel.

Poole's left shoe caught on the hem of her skirt, and she stumbled, losing the boy in the unnatural fog. Up ahead, she could make out a faint light near the gates to the castle, and Melissa Poole called for the child, as if he were her own.

"Tom! Tom, wait! It isn't safe! Please, wait!!"

"Hurry!" he called. "Over here! Help me, Mrs. Poole! She's shivering!"

"Stay where you are!" the governess answered as she picked herself up. She could barely see in the thick fog, but followed Tom's voice. "Where are you?"

"Over here! By the angel!"

She ran towards the sound, finding him near the great angel statue, kneeling beside a pale figure: a girl, dressed only in night clothes and satin shoes. The shimmering light Poole noticed earlier still hovered nearby, beside the castle gates. She thought it must be a policeman's lantern, but as she looked closer, the light became a tall figure—it was *a man with wings*. The magnificent angel looked her way and smiled; then he flew silently upwards into the night air and vanished into the heavens.

Poole stared, her mouth open.

"She's cold," Tom was saying. "We have to take her home."

Hearing the boy's voice, Poole snapped back to reality. "Yes, of course, we will." The governess placed her own woolen cloak over the shivering stranger. "Do you know this girl, Master Thomas?"

"No, Missus, I don't, but she's ever so cold. She isn't a ghost, is she? You see her, too, don't you?"

"Of course, I see her. Greene!" she called to the gardener. "Help us!"

Thomas held the girl's hand, trying to warm it as they waited. "I think the angel left her here. Do you think the same angel took Mother to heaven?"

"I don't know, dear," Poole answered.

It took several minutes for the gardener to reach them. He and his assistant arrived, huffing and puffing from running.

"Who's this then, Mrs. Poole?" asked Greene.

"A poor, sick girl. If you'll carry her to the house, we can take her to Montmore tomorrow. Dr. MacAlpin will know what to do with her."

Thomas kept hold of the unconscious girl's cold hand as Greene carried her back along the pathway to the house. "Is she very sick, Mrs. Poole? Will Dr. MacAlpin be able to help her?"

"Yes, assuming he's in residence. If not, Mrs. Winstead will look after her. Poor little thing! She's half frozen. Why isn't she dressed properly?"

The strange discovery sent the de Margravene household into a tizzy, with the lawyer insisting they call the police, the bishop saying she belonged with the church, and the governess demanding MacAlpin's professional opinion before making any other decision. Had her employer not been in mourning, he'd have conceded to Blighton or Albatross, but the girl's pale cheeks and fair hair reminded him of his dead wife.

"The police would put her into some God-forsaken hospital, and you've no caretaker for children at your church, Bishop Blighton. No, Poole is right. Montmore House is best. Henry will know what to do. We'll take her to Henry."

The girl remained with them overnight, sleeping in Poole's apartment, and the following morning at eleven sharp, Lord Bertram de Margravene's unexpected guest was wrapped in a fine woolen blanket, carried to his lordship's finest coach, and conveyed speedily to Montmore House, accompanied by Thomas and his father.

Neither the lawyer nor the bishop was invited.

Henry MacAlpin was indeed in residence that morning, talking with a friend. And as fate—or more accurately, God's mercy—would have it, Henry recognised the girl at once and sent a telegram to Haimsbury House. By evening, the Stuart-Sinclair family had rallied round the unconscious girl with the fair hair and blue eyes that hinted of the sea.

Lady Adele Sinclair was home at last.

CHAPTER SEVEN
Charles Sinclair Awakens to a Strange World

Many days after a the angel Uriel left Adele Sinclair near a ghostly castle near Fulham; far away, beyond the Stone Realms, within a subterranean castle made of iron and volcanic rock, Adele's missing father had just awakened.

In mid-August, he'd seen Della taken and rushed to her aid, only to be chloroformed and forced into a black coach with her. After passing through a veil into the mirror realm, father and daughter were separated. Ever since, the duke had slept; his body placed into a deep slumber, whilst his mind wandered into depths of oblivion. The twentieth of September had come round, one day before the all-important equinox, and Charles's consciousness finally returned.

His head throbbed, his hands felt cold, and there was a dry, acidic taste to the back of his mouth, rather like desiccated oak leaves, mixed with miry clay. If the sickening sensations ended there, he might have assumed it fair recompense paid after a long night, spent talking over crime with his whisky-loving uncle, but these unsettling sensations were entirely different, yet oddly familiar.

He'd experienced them before, when he'd recovered from a coma. *Am I dreaming? Where is this? When is this?*

Charles opened his eyes to darkness.

Is this home? No. It can't be. Beth's scent is missing, and the sounds are wrong. James's house? Paul's?

The duke blinked to clear his head, using every sense to determine his condition and whereabouts. Each fingertip tingled with a mixture of fire and ice, and the swirls and whorls of the distal phalanges grasped at the slick surface beneath their unique patterns.

Silk? Satin? Cotton? Hardly the third. The texture felt cool and smooth, finely woven.

Expensive.

What about sound? His sharp ears detected ticking and hushed whispers from somewhere nearby, the words were muffled and mixed, as though each sound were baffled within the constraining boxes of a coffered ceiling. The murmurs were confusing, like a forest of chittering animals discussing an intruder.

No. The voices were discussing him.

Out of the darkness, came a clear, clarion ringing. A bell. That singular sound dredged up unsettling memories of his childhood. Charles knew it well. It was without a doubt the chiming of King Arthur's clock. Either Arthur's victorious cry of triumph, or fiery doom for the defeated king.

The bell sounded six times, followed by a dead hush.

Am I dreaming about Rose House?

Charles swallowed. The sour, oak-leaf taste transformed into something more familiar. He'd smelled it before. He pictured hospital rooms, white-gowned surgeons, thick cotton wool, and infirmaries. It was the taste and smell of chloroform, but mixed with something else. Laudanum?

"Hush, now, all of you! He awakens!" ordered a woman from somewhere to the right.

Footsteps approached, dull and rhythmic, as though upon a braided carpet. "So he is," a deep voice spoke from the bedside. Charles could make out hints of movement, but little else. "We know you can hear us," the male speaker prompted. "Your ears and mouth should function, unless someone has interfered. Eluna, did you cast one of your enchantments?"

"Must you always be so suspicious of me, Alphonse?" the woman asked petulantly.

A match was struck. Charles saw a bright flash and smelled sulphur. The wicks of candles ignited. A skeletal face intruded into the candlelit area near the bed, and a bony hand jostled his right arm. Fingers poked at the duke's chest, and he felt pressure against the right side of his throat.

"Do stop prodding the poor man!" the woman ordered. "Uriens, I swear by the Ancients, if you injure him, I shall tear out your crooked beak by its treacherous roots!"

"Treacherous?" the corvine lawyer screeched. "You play a dangerous game, Eluna. And must you call me by that name?"
"I shall call you what I like, little bird."
"I'm sick of your mocking superiority!"
"Quiet, both of you!" the deep voice commanded. "You'll frighten our guest."

Charles sensed shapes moving within the room, but very little else. "Who are you?" he asked hoarsely. "I smell candles and hear a crackling fire, but perceive only shadows."

"Is that so?" the deep voice asked. "I hadn't realised." The man's accent was foreign. Romanian? Russian? "Forgive us, Your Highness. This is an unexpected side effect. If you'll allow me to touch your face, I can help." Warm fingers brushed the duke's forehead, temples, and eyes. "There now. Your senses should function correctly."

The room and its environs clarified in an instant, and Charles could see his surroundings without difficulty. He lay against two plump pillows within a gilded tester bed, its corners softened by pleated curtains. The bed was dressed with silk sheets and velvet quilts, and at the foot lay a fur blanket of rich sable. A gold-and-crimson crest was stitched into all the fabrics and painted beneath the canopy. Even his black silk pyjamas bore the unusual crest, embroidered on the pocket and each cuff.

It took a moment to comprehend the monogram's meaning. Charles had seen similar decorations before, but where? He searched the crowded library of his mind, wandering through the cascading shelves like a man half-asleep. Was it Buckingham Palace? He crawled through the section marked 'Palace', finding an ennobled drawer filled to overflowing with imagery, emblems, and crests.

And here it was! A royal cipher, like those used for centuries by every English monarch. Queen Victoria's was a scrolled and entwined V-R for Victoria Regina. The cipher in this place, wherever 'this place' was, displayed an entwined C-R, topped by a gem-studded crown. He noticed the cipher everywhere; sewn, carved, or painted in shimmering gold and deepest red.

The man who'd restored his sight spoke again. "We took great pains to prepare these rooms, Your Grace. I hope you approve of the design and all its symbols."

"Why should I approve the design of a prison?" he answered, his voice cracking from disuse. The vocal cords felt irritated and scratchy. Charles swallowed, and his throat ached as he added, "I've no wish to use a royal monogram."

"Bring water for our king," the man told a servant.

Charles accepted the glass and drank deeply. The clear liquid tasted like warm honey on his parched throat.

"Better?" asked the deep-voiced man.

"Yes, thank you."

"Regarding these symbols," his host continued, "you've every right to use them. We created the design to honour you. The entwined C and R stand for *Charles Rex*, of course, as I'm sure you've guessed. We considered using an 'A' for Arthur, for you have the right to use it as your regnal name. Not only because you descend from that great and very real king, but because you bear his name. Your Grace, you are King Arthur reborn."

Sinclair ignored the flattery. "If I'm your king, then bring me my daughter!"

"Ah, the lovely Lady Adele," a second man remarked from nearer the fireplace. "I said you'd ask about her upon awakening. You owe me a thousand pounds, dear sister."

"I can't say I'm surprised to see you, Araqiel," Charles grumbled, purposely ignoring the fallen angel's title.

"Like an adder beneath the rose, I am ever and always in your shadow," the dragon smirked.

The main door opened, and two servants entered to light additional candles: a set of ornate candelabra near the fireplace and two more near the bed. The additional lighting offered Charles a better look at the deep-voiced stranger. He wore a dark, snugly fitted double-breasted coat, cut to the knees. The broad collar was trimmed in scarlet satin. The crimson waistcoat had pearl buttons, and this sanguine background was set off a delicate sheath of white silk shirting, that unfurled its ruffles beneath the wearer's firm, smooth chin. His hair was midnight brown and long, ending several inches below the shoulders. The shirt-sleeves formed ruffles at the cuffs and fell loosely across tapering fingers. He wore no rings, not even a signet. The face was sensitively handsome. A firm jaw led upwards to a sensuous mouth, rosy with blood, and above the mouth, a straight and regal nose divided a pair of sable brown eyes. Something in those dark orbs warned of danger, mixed with hints of something Charles hadn't expected: kindness and mercy.

"Nonsense, Ara," said the man in black. "You find it amusing that our guest asks after his daughter, but I think it a mark of his kingly character. Unlike any of you, he considers others before himself. Your Grace, you possess a strong parental passion, and I'm pleased to relieve your mind. Lady Adele is quite unharmed. We find the child most pleasant and would never injure or frighten her."

"You're a liar."

"She is well," the man objected.

"Why should I believe you? You abducted us, you terrified my daughter! I dare not imagine what else you've done!"

"Ah, so you remember the coach ride," said Araqiel, moving closer.

"Of course, he doesn't," Flint interrupted. "I made sure of that. His mind is wiped."

"If you're relying on the chloroform, you've failed," the duke interrupted.

"How do you know about that?" asked Flint.

"I can taste it. I'm familiar with chloroform from my work as a policeman. Hospitals and laboratories are full of such smells. But there's something else. Something I still taste."

"Nonsense. He's bluffing!" cried the lawyer. "And he calls *us* liars!"

"Why should we lie?" asked Princess Eluna. "Flint poured some of that horrid chemical on a cloth and put it over your mouth. How else could we get you into the coach? You're quite strong for a human."

"You might have asked me," Charles told her.

"And you'd have said no," Araqiel stated flatly. "Let's get on with this, shall we? I've things to do."

"I want to see my daughter!" the duke ordered his keepers. "If she's unharmed, then bring her to me!"

"Now, why would we do that?" asked the dragon prince.

The duke's anger erupted into a volcano, and he threw off the quilts to leave the bed. But the forward momentum and surge of blood proved more than the sluggish circulatory system could handle. To compensate, blood rushed from his brain and extremities to protect the heart, and Charles nearly lost consciousness.

"Catch him, you fools!" cried the man in black. The two footmen rushed over and helped the peer to a nearby chair, close to the warm fire.

Slowly, his senses returned. Charles stared up at his captors with teeth clenched. "Where is my daughter?"

The haughty Eluna von Siebenbürgen drew near and knelt before him, taking his hands. Bright tongues of fire danced upon the duke's pale face, highlighting the intense turquoise and cobalt blue irises. The princess kissed each trembling hand, offering the duke a warm smile, certain it would please him. "Such beautiful eyes you have, my king."

Not the least bit pleased, the duke snatched back the hands and shouted, "I am neither your king nor anyone else's! For the last time, where is my daughter!" Again, Charles attempted to stand, but the disused legs had no strength to support the effort.

"Be still! Rest, my darling. Rest," cooed Eluna, unfazed by his rebuff. "You've spent many long days in the realms of twilight. You need time to regain your strength."

Charles swallowed the hot anger with a single, dry-throated gulp. Eluna leaned closer, and this time dared to kiss his mouth. The duke pushed her away in disgust.

The willful princess laughed at his reaction. "Make your pretence of rejection, my love, but one day, you will admit your true feelings to me. And do not object to the title, Charles. Those who run London's government already recognise you as their shadow sovereign, do they not? And the Royal Archives list all of your many birthrights. Did you know that, my darling? You are called His Royal Highness, Prince Charles Robert Arthur Sinclair III, 1st Duke of Haimsbury, the Prince du Sang de Valois et Capet, 8th Earl of Loudain—now raised to 1st Marquess of Loudain, of course. Also, the 12th Earl of Goughton, 23rd Earl Randeau, 16th Marquis du St. Clair, 21st Duc du Louvois, Count of this, Lord of that, etc. etc.. The list runs on and on for many, many pages, my darling. And then there are the German, Dutch, and Austrian Houses from which you descend. And even Romanian and Russian. Ah, but you see my point. You may object all you wish, *mon cher,* but you cannot deny that your veins carry a great and powerful heritage of royal blood."

"If you consider me so royal, then why abduct me? Why am I here? For what dark purpose?"

"No dark purpose, my darling. You are simply here to learn and to teach," she answered.

"To learn and teach what?" Charles asked his keepers.

"I promise, you will understand everything quite soon, my love. But we have bothered you enough, I think. We shall leave, so that you may gather your thoughts and dress for dinner," she said with a parting kiss.

The man in the black coat snapped his fingers, and the servants departed through a hidden panel near the bath chamber door. He turned to the duke, speaking in soft accented tones. "Dinner is served in two hours, Your Grace. Join us, and I promise to explain everything."

The arrogant Prince Araqiel offered the duke a mocking bow. "Oh, yes, do join us. You can dazzle us with your royal presence, Your Highness."

"Stop calling me that!"

"Why? You ignite such *a fire* in us!" the dragon added, his eyes glinting red. After another mocking bow, Araqiel took Eluna's arm. At first she resisted, but then he whispered something. Charles had no idea what he said, but the princess grudgingly agreed.

"Don't pout, Lunetta," teased her brother/husband. "If this one won't offer you love, another will. We have two hours to fill, my darling. Allow me to provide what our guest refuses. My ancient blood may not be quite so royal, but I can satisfy you in other ways."

He and Eluna left, followed by the grimacing lawyer. Albus Flint turned to scowl one last time before exiting. "Be prompt, human. We cannot eat until you arrive, and we are all so very—*hungry.*"

"Enough, Crow!" the man in black shouted. "Leave, now before I serve *you* for dinner!"

The lawyer responded by slamming the door.

The man in black sighed and then turned to Charles. "That crow has no proper manners, Your Grace. Believe me, when I say, that I am most pleased you are here. In two hours, then."

The door closed softly with a precise click, and Charles was alone at last.

As any good detective might, his first order of business was to survey his surroundings and look for a means of escape. His jailors had spared neither expense nor royal flourishes in the decor. Acorns, oaks, and roses in both red and white decorated every surface, proclaiming his Stuart, Plantagenet, and Sinclair lineage. Other heraldry emblems included lions (some displayed as rampant, others *couchant*), the French *fleur de lis*, rampant dragons, leaping unicorns, and double-headed eagles. The oil landscapes were familiar: Cumbria, Kent, and Scotland. A large painting of Rose House and its hedge maze hung over the fireplace, depicted as it might look on a bright day in autumn.

Why go to such trouble for a prisoner? he wondered.

The elaborately scrolled C-R cipher was repeated in every textile, drapery, and furnishing. It even perched atop the door lintels, proclaiming him as *Prince du Sang*, a prince of royal blood, with all rights of inheritance and rule. He wondered what kingdom his captors expected him to claim; England, or something more?

Charles sighed. Though every surface gleamed and glittered, though the rooms were beautiful and regal, no crown or kingdom could satisfy without the most important gem of all: his beloved wife, Elizabeth Stuart Sinclair. Every king requires a queen, and his precious little one made all others pale by comparison. Sinclair missed his wife so much it hurt, but he mustn't think of Beth, not now. Not whilst Della was in danger. Promises of his daughter's safety meant nothing, when spoken by the lying lips of Eluna and Araqiel von Siebenbürgen. No matter what it took, he would find his daughter. He may be only her adoptive father to the law, but Charles loved Della just as much as he loved Robby and Georgianna. If it took his life, he would see Adele rescued.

Thinking of his family and his responsibility as a father, sent a lightning surge of protective fury through Sinclair's muscles, and he pushed to his feet, determined to discover where he was imprisoned. London? Paris? Eluna mentioned German, Austrian, and Dutch blood lines. Was she hinting he was in one of those countries? She'd also mentioned Russia. Was she throwing suspicion on Romanov?

No, Anatole had helped them many times. Charles trusted the enigmatic Russian. But why hadn't Anatole come to help? With his abilities to travel anywhere at anytime, surely he could have come. *Find out later. For now, learn all you can and escape!*

He examined the tester bed. On either side, were medieval windows with diamond-shaped mullions. He slowly crossed the room, but each shutter was locked from the outside with not a hint of sunlight entering through the boards. Assuming the sun existed in this world, it had long since set. He pushed against the shutter's iron latch, but couldn't force it open.

He would find no escape here.

Charles tried the main door. Also, locked.

The servants had left through a concealed panel. He tried to locate the panel's hidden spring or latch, but failed. All other apartment doors opened with ease. Most were cedar-lined closets, containing stylish clothing in his exact size and taste: shoes, jackets, shirts, ties, even personal linen and jewellery, all embellished with the C-R cipher.

"How long do they plan to keep me here?" he asked aloud as he glanced through the expensive wardrobe.

"That I cannot say, sir," replied a male voice.

Charles wheeled about in surprise. "Who—who are you?"

"Do forgive me, my lord," the newcomer answered with a formal bow. "I assumed you'd heard me enter. It must be the carpet. The thick braid dampens sound. The name is Fenwick, sir," he said, pronouncing it 'fennick'. "I'm your valet."

"Pfennig?"

"No, sir. Not Pfennig. I'm hardly a penny, nor am I German. F-e-n-w-i-c-k. The 'w' is silent. I'm Scottish, as I'm sure you've already guessed by the accent. My name is a habitational one. Referring to fens. Marshes, I mean. I see you're stroking your chin, sir. The beard's grown a bit during your long recovery. Shall I trim it for you, or do you prefer we shave it off completely?"

Charles had been absentmindedly rubbing his jawline, an old habit when working on mental problems. What was it about the beard? It felt wrong, longer than it should. He reached up to feel his hair, which was seldom cut now; originally because of a head wound received on the night of his wedding, and now because his wife liked it.

But the hair, also, felt longer than it should.

"What do you mean by my long recovery?"

"You've been quite ill, sir. Tended by the doctor, of course. I'm very pleased you've awoken. And may I say, your colour is remarkably bright!"

"Nonsense."

"Oh, but it is, sir," Fenwick argued.

"What? No, I don't mean my colour. I mean I've not been ill. I was taken."

"Taken, sir?"

"Yes, I'm sure they told you. Surely..." He paused, considering what Eluna and the others had said. Somewhere, Adele was their prisoner. He had to assume this servant spied for the others. He'd need to play their game, if he hoped to find Adele. "What I meant to say is, I don't remember an illness."

"Yes, I see, sir. It's my understanding, protracted states of unconsciousness can sometimes lead to memory loss," the servant replied with a handsome smile. "I'm sure everything will come back to you soon, sir."

"I'm sure it will. Have you a mirror, Mr. Fenwick?" he asked, deciding to play along.

"It's just Fenwick, sir. And yes, there are several mirrors in the apartment. There's one in the bath, just beyond the robing room. It's a splendid cheval mirror with a lovely old frame, made in Paris for Louis XII, I believe. Also, the drawing room has a finely crafted oval mirror, hung above the fireplace. It's Venetian. Or I could fetch you a hand glass, if you prefer?"

Deciding on the floor mirror, Sinclair crossed into the bath. The room had silk-covered walls and a muralled ceiling with frescoes of Roman baths and lush gardens. The porcelain tub was large enough for even his tall frame, painted in grape vines and pomegranates. There was a deep wash bowl, set upon a mahogany dressing table and a gold-trimmed water closet with a porcelain stool. Every element, no matter how small, was painted and trimmed with red and gold flourishes. It was a royal bath, fit for a king.

In the far corner, to the right of two shuttered, rectangular windows, stood the Louis XII mirror. The figure reflected in the sparkling surface stared back, and for the tiniest second, Charles imagined another man stood within; not himself at all, but a stranger in black silk pyjamas. The mirror man's curling black hair fell two inches beyond his shoulders, and the beard's upper line demanded a barber's attention.

Fenwick moved close. "Is my lord upset? Angry?"

"Confused," Charles admitted. "Tell me, Fenwick, where am I?"

"In your apartment, sir."

"Yes, I know, but is this a house?"

"It is a castle, my lord. Shall I fetch the shaving kit?"

"Shave?"

"Or I could offer the beard a trim, if you prefer. Dinner here is quite formal, sir. A gentleman should look his best."

"Ah, I see what you mean. I hadn't expected my beard to be so unkempt. Or so long. It doesn't look right."

"A full beard suits you, if I may say so, sir. You've a noble chin that looks well with a beard. But perhaps, a slight trim?"

"Yes, a bit shorter," muttered Sinclair, still trying to work out why the reflection bothered him so.

The servant left to assemble items for the task: a copper bowl, kettle of steaming hot water, scented soap, linen towels, scissors, and a sharp razor. The duke took a chair near the robing room fire, and Fenwick set to the task. In less than twenty minutes, the duke's wiry black beard was tamed to hug its owner's chiseled jawline, and the wild edges along the upper cheeks were now straight and neat. Even the curling hair was cut to a manageable length, ending just above the duke's broad shoulders.

Charles left the chair to admire Fenwick's work in the cheval mirror. "I'm not sure my own barber could have managed so well, Fenwick. You seem to know my face and head better than I do."

The servant bowed and then offered a satisfied smile. "I am gratified by your kind words, sir. Now, might I suggest a hot bath before changing for dinner? There is appropriate evening attire in your closet. Have you a preference in tie? We have the traditional English style, of course, but also the French. White is the preferred colour, as is customary, though there's a pale gold that would look quite splendid on you, sir."

"Whatever you think, and the bath sounds very relaxing, thank you."

Fenwick ran the hot water, and Charles walked about the apartment, studying the layout. He could find no other windows, but discovered an office and a darkened library. He took a small candlestick from the bedchamber to inspect the stacks. The shelves were lined with books on mathematics, science, history, and geography, but also collections of sheet music, bound into volumes by composer. And to go along with the music, he discovered an ornately decorated, Streicher grand piano.

"How do they know I play?" he called to Fenwick. "And someone knows my taste in books, too. Some of these editions are quite rare." He found several copies of Malory's *Morte d'Arthur*. "Fenwick, why are there so many books on King Arthur?"

"Did you call me, sir?" asked the valet as he appeared in the library doorway. The bedchamber, with its bright chandelier and multiple candelabra, stood behind him, casting the servant in silhouette. For a moment, Charles imagined a blur on either side of the valet's broad shoulders, as though another form were trying to emerge.

"I think my eyes are playing tricks," he muttered.

"Did you mention something about King Arthur, sir? I believe it's one of Princess Eluna's favourite stories. She added several books on the topic, so I understand. You would need to speak with her to learn more, my lord. I'm ready for you, sir."

"Thank you. I'm on my way."

Returning to the bath, Charles removed the pyjamas and slipped into the steaming water. As he soaked, he took advantage of the time and interviewed his servant. "Fenwick, why do they call me king?"

The Scotsman chose a loofah sponge and lathered it with a bar of goat-milk soap, scented with lavender and citrus. He scrubbed the duke's shoulders as he answered. "Well, sir, I'm told it's your true title. King Charles. Does it anger you? Shall I call you something else?"

"No, if that's what you've been told, it's all right. I don't think of myself as a king."

"Duke Charles, then, sir?"

"Yes, that's better. Fenwick, what have they told you about me?"

"*They*, sir? I take it you mean Prince Araqiel and Dr. Theseus."

"Is Theseus the man in black?"

"Indeed, sir. The doctor always wears some combination of black, grey, or silvery blue. When he wishes to impress, he chooses scarlet accents. Today, I noticed he wears a coat with scarlet trim and a crimson waistcoat with gold buttons. I'm sure it's in your honour, sir."

"My honour?"

"You're Dr. Theseus's guest. Aren't your family colours red and gold, my lord?"

"Yes. You say he's called *Doctor* Theseus?"

"That's right, sir."

"Is he a professor or a physician?"

"I believe he is both, my lord. The doctor holds multiple degrees, but also peerage titles from a variety of lands. But he prefers to be addressed as Doctor."

"He seems a peculiar man. There's a coolness about him. Ladies might call him elegantly enigmatic, I suppose."

Fennick laughed, and Charles noticed a musical quality to the servant's voice, as though angelic bells rang softly within the Scottish accent. "Elegantly enigmatic. I do like that, sir. But surely such a description applies to you as well? I hope that isn't too personal an observation."

"Not at all," the duke answered, his muscles relaxing in the warm water. He lifted both hands, and the hot water splashed and dripped down the agile fingers. A gold wedding ring gleamed from the fourth finger of the left hand. Charles smiled as he remembered what the ring represented. *Little one, though you're not even here, you still give me strength.* "Have you any idea of my daughter's whereabouts?"

"The Lady Adele? I cannot say precisely, sir, for I'm constrained, but I *can* say she is not here. In fact, it's my understanding the young lady has been rescued."

"Rescued? By whom? How do you know?" he asked, turning round and splashing water on the tiles as well as the servant.

The valet blinked a few times and wiped the water from his eyes.

"Sorry, Fenwick."

"Not to worry, sir. I appreciate your excitement. As to the Lady Adele, I'm unable to reveal that information."

"Have they threatened you?"

"Oh, no, sir! But the others mustn't know what I know."

"Others? Theseus and Araqiel?"

He went quiet for a moment, his eyes shut as though internalising or considering the question. "I've been given permission to say this much, sir. That the *white owl* has sent others to rescue her. And that same white owl sent me."

"The white owl? Who's the... Wait, just who or *what* are you, Fenwick?"

"I am your servant, sir. My sole task is to look after you."

"No, no, you're more. This white owl, he's..."

"He is a friend, sir. You might say he and I keep watch together."

"Keep watch? On me?"

"On you and on your family, sir."

"Even here?" asked Charles.

"Even here, sir. No matter where you go, one of us goes, too."

"Us?"

"Us, sir."

"And where is *here?*" asked the duke.

"That, sir, is difficult to explain. The castle is well hidden and quite difficult to find, though I managed, of course. Despite what locks the lower realms might devise, I have ways to overcome them."

"I imagine you do. Lower realms? Are you saying the castle isn't in England?"

"In a way, sir, it is."

"That's a very odd answer."

"This is a very odd castle, sir. Lean forward, if you please, whilst I rinse your hair."

Charles obliged, closing his eyes, as pitcher after pitcher of warm water ran through his thick hair. "Do you know why I'm being held prisoner, Fenwick?" he asked, wiping water from his face.

"I cannot say, sir. I've not spoken to the castle's other inhabitants. Dr. Theseus has looked in on you with regularity, to make sure of your health, of course. The others have paid call once or twice, particularly the princess."

"That doesn't surprise me. Eluna's devious, if not a bit mad. You say Theseus came regularly? As my doctor?"

"One might say that."

"That's a rather vague answer, Fenwick. Let's try another question. How long have I been here?" asked the peer, turning to look at the servant.

"You were already here when I arrived six weeks ago."

"Six weeks! My wife must be frantic!" he exclaimed.

"Ah, the Duchess Elizabeth. I have heard the others speak her name often, sir. Princess Eluna mentions the name with regularity, though her remarks are couched in somewhat unfavourable terms. However, Prince Araqiel speaks highly of the duchess. His comments are far too personal, in my opinion. I hope I'm not speaking out of turn, sir, but your hosts are very *different*, if you get my meaning."

"Araqiel and Eluna are more different than you might imagine, Fenwick. What more can you tell me about this Theseus? He looks familiar, yet I can't recall where we met."

"I cannot say why he might be familiar to you, sir, but it's my understanding the doctor treats mental patients in the West End of London. Princess Eluna makes great sport of his career, saying it is beneath his station—being a doctor to the mad, I mean. Her words, not mine, my lord. My, but your hair does curl, sir! I imagine the ladies find it quite romantic."

"I care for only one lady, Mr. Fenwick. Duchess Elizabeth, and she often remarks on it, now that it's grown longer. Our son has the same curling hair, but then so does Beth. My wife, I mean. I suppose it's a family trait."

"How very pleasant for you, sir. Now, if you'll allow me to offer a soft towel and a steadying hand as you step from the tub? The marble floor might prove slippery to wet feet."

Charles left the bath and dried himself. Fenwick offered a velvet dressing gown, which also bore the royal cipher on its pocket. Feeling relaxed, the duke sat by the bedchamber fire, watching the valet present a series of options for that evening's dinner. There were several, including a copy of a suit Martin Kepelheim had tailored for the midsummer ball at Kensington Palace. The black tailcoat featured French lapels, trimmed in black satin. The white silk waistcoat had the usual rolled lapels, and the rich fabric was cut low with a double row of covered buttons. Fenwick suggested garnet shirt studs, edged in jet to contrast with the white silk, and he wrapped a tie of pale gold silk round the duke's neck twice before fashioning the ends into a soft, poetic twist.

Charles gazed at himself in the cheval mirror; startled at his own reflection. He looked more like Paul Stuart than ever; the long hair, trimmed beard, and romantic twist to the tie enhanced the familial resemblance.

"I hope I've not made a mistake with the tie, sir," the valet said, noticing the duke's expression. "Perhaps, I should have used a more English style. You've a decidedly dissatisfied look upon your face. Your Grace, have I done something wrong?"

"Not at all," he told the man, offering a smile. "It's just, for a moment there, I saw someone else looking back at me. My cousin and I are a great deal alike in our facial contours, but it's still a surprise, whenever he looks back at me."

"Ah," laughed the valet as he used a boar-hair brush to remove a bit of lint from the coat's sleeve. "I'm glad it's nothing more than that, sir. And I think I understand. My brothers and I share many characteristics in common. So much so, that outsiders often mistake us for one another. Is it the same with you and your cousin?"

"It is much the same, yes. Have you a large family?"

"Very large, sir, with many brothers. It's almost eight o'clock, sir. They'll be expecting you."

"Already? Where is this meal to be served, and what should I know before I attend?"

The servant set the clothes brush aside, and his eyes grew thoughtful. Fenwick had expressive features, but the eyes possessed chameleon qualities and alternated from subtle blues, to browns, even green, depending on the light. Based on his thick hair and lack of any age lines, Charles guessed him at no more than twenty, but the young man had a very mature manner about him. "Is there a problem, Mr. Fenwick? You look puzzled."

The valet sighed. "Not puzzled, sir. Concerned. I'm sure the dinner will be pleasant, but you must be on your guard at all times, my lord."

Charles tilted his head, his left brow arching. "That's an odd comment for a servant to make about his employer. Why must I be on guard?"

"I shouldn't wish to say anything out of turn, but Prince Araqiel is most unpredictable, sir. Since I arrived, I've spent all the time in this apartment, and so my opinion derives only from seeing how the others have treated you."

"You've never been out of the apartment?" asked the duke, taking a seat in the closest chair.

"I need be nowhere else. My sole purpose is to serve you, my lord. But in the course of that duty, I've had opportunities to notice many things about the others. It's quite easy, for they never see me."

"Why don't they see you?"

Fenwick smiled. "No one notices a servant, sir. Not really. I've found this prince and his sister quite unsettling, if you don't mind my saying."

"You came here just to serve me?" asked Sinclair. "You didn't work here before my arrival?"

"No, sir. I am here only to protect and look after you. I hope I've succeeded."

"Indeed, you have, considering how I arrived."

Fenwick's eyes glittered, and Charles noticed their colour had altered yet again—changing from a light grey to an iridescent shade of verdigris.

Is it the light that causes it, or his mood?

"Was there something unusual about your arrival, sir?"

"You might say that," Charles answered off-handedly. "But forget I mentioned it. Look, before you walk me down, could you tell me where you served before? There's something strangely familiar about you, Mr. Fenwick. Perhaps, we met at one of your former employers' homes."

The valet smiled, the eyes gleaming into grey again. "Usually, my place is beside a Russian prince of your acquaintance. I've heard his good name mentioned here with considerable disrespect, so please say nothing of it, sir. I fear such information might cause difficulties and could even lose me this position, and we cannot have that, now can we? It is *vital* that I remain at your side."

Charles stared at the valet. Fenwick's eyes had changed again, and for a brief moment, their colour shifted from the greyish hue to the palest, *icy blue.*

The duke gasped.

"Ah! I see you understand, sir," Fenwick continued, his eyes returning to a greenish grey. "Now, if you'll permit me, I shall lead you to the upper landing. From there, a house servant will guide you to the dining hall. And please, say nothing of my presence. For my part, I shall keep watch on you from here, my lord. No matter what happens, remember, you are never alone. The One is always near."

"The One? Then, I'm right. You are..." Charles began, but Fenwick just smiled, his eyes gleaming that same icy blue.

"I am simply your guardian, sir. That is all." The enigmatic servant stepped round the duke with the grace of a dancer and then led the surprised peer out of the apartment.

The buzzing that always preceded spiritual danger commenced along the duke's skin, and he braced himself for whatever may come. So long as Adele and his family were safe, Charles could endure anything that God might allow.

CHAPTER EIGHT

20ᵗʰ September – Montmore House

Eight days had passed since Adele Sinclair arrived at Henry MacAlpin's resident hospital. In that time, the adolescent had offered very little information regarding her adoptive father's location or his condition. It was a Friday morning; Henry had just completed morning rounds and retired to the library office to make notes and read the morning papers. He noticed several dozen letters and a telegram on his desk.

The viscount opened the telegram first.

It was from the offices of the *Corpo dei Carabinieri Reali* in Rome and written entirely in Italian. The viscount sighed and set the inscrutable message aside for later. He spoke only the tiniest smattering of Italian, which meant he recognised the language and could decipher a few words—mostly to do with ordering luncheon or asking directions—but little else. The letters included a long missive from his cousin, Lady Ellen Foxworthy, complaining about her husband and how very lonely she'd become. Her husband was the 2nd Earl of Claymore, with an estate in Wales near Swansea. His country house was comfortable and newer than most, built in 1834, and overlooked the bay. Henry visited when Lady Ellen married five years earlier; in fact, he'd met one of his two fiancées at Ellen's wedding.

He grew reflective as he read his cousin's mournful, four-page letter. How might his life have altered if he'd married Ellen's friend? He reached the final page, finding to his surprise, that his cousin mentioned that very woman:

And finally, my very dear Henry, I must include some sad news regarding Lady Charpentier, the former Miss Iris Varden of Beaufort. As you may remember, Iris and her husband, the Viscount Charpentier, moved to Lisbon as part of his work for the Foreign Office. I now must report that the viscount has been killed—in a duel of all things! I fear Iris's wandering eye continued its travels after she spurned you for Charpentier. She has written, begging me to intercede with her father for help, for she is destitute. Her late husband left her nothing, and his title and property have passed to a nephew. Iris's lover gives no comfort, for he fled Portugal in the wake of the duel.

She is all alone now.

I promised that we'd look after her—you and I. You were never a man to hold grudges, my beloved cousin. Iris needs a refuge for just a little while. My own husband may not be the most affectionate, but he never beats me, and in the end, I know he loves me as much as his rigid heart allows.

I hope to see you soon, as I'm coming to London in late November to shop for Christmas. My sister Rachel is coming, too, and we shall reside at Claymore House. Until then, you are in my prayers and always in my heart, Henry.

With great affection, I am ever your loving cousin,

- Ellen.

"So Iris is on her own yet again," he said aloud, his eyes on his cousin's letter.

"Who's Iris?" asked Seth Holloway, a book beneath his right arm as he entered the library. "It's a very pretty name. Is she a new patient?"

Henry glanced up, a smile slowly forming. "Do you ever knock?"

"Not usually. Aubrey's teaching me to creep up on people and spy upon them, but I fear your activities hardly warrant such talents, old man. So, who's Iris?"

"Sit down, and I'll tell you. There's coffee on the table. Breakfast was an hour ago."

"Any scones left?"

"None in here, but there may be downstairs. Seth, have you come to visit Adele or to eat?"

"Both, if I can manage it. I'm early for the one and late for the other, apparently," said his friend. "I knocked on her apartment door, but that new nurse, what's her name again?"

"Shelton."

"Yes. Well, Mrs. Shelton said Della's still dressing."

"Then, as you must wait, I'll ask Saunders to see if the new cook has any leftover pastries," he said ringing a handbell.

"New cook? What happened to the old cook?"

"She's retired. You'll like Mrs. Merchant's cooking, Seth. I've not had better since Scotland."

"Is she Scottish?"

"By half yes. The other half is German. Odd isn't it?"

"So long as the scones aren't filled with bratwurst."

Salperton laughed. "I'm glad you've come, Seth. We could use a bit of merriment, and our Della always brightens whenever you visit."

Seth James Edward Holloway, 9th Viscount Paynton, had an easy way about him that disarmed male and female alike; something in the keen blue eyes and boyish face, perhaps, or the wide, infectious smile. Despite a youthful appearance and nearly constant good humour, the twenty-nine-year-old antiquities professor had endured years of hardship and rough living on archaeological digs. He taught ancient languages and approached problems with the tenacity of a terrier after a black rat. Such, too, was his tenacious loyalty to friends. Once formed, relationships ended only when the other broke fellowship; they were never ended by Seth, for he was as true as truth itself.

"So, who is Iris?" asked the freckled Holloway.

The butler interrupted. "You called, sir?"

"Do you know someone named Iris, Saunders?" the copper-haired visitor probed.

"I cannot say, sir. Might she be a patient?"

"Ignore him, Saunders," said Salperton. "Have we any scones or pastries remaining from breakfast?"

"I fear not, sir. Lady Adele was sent the last of them half an hour ago, but there are a few slices of buttercream torte from last night's supper."

"Too sweet," said Holloway. "Thanks anyway."

"Yes, thank you, Saunders. That'll be all for now."

The butler closed the door.

"Iris? Henry, if you're not offering any scones, the least you can do is tell me about her."

Henry MacAlpin couldn't match his friend regarding a truly 'handsome' nature, but his looks were actually quite pleasing. Six feet tall, acorn-coloured eyes, dark curling hair, an easy smile, and an ear that could listen for hours and hours. However, most ladies of his acquaintance preferred rogues and rebels to open ears and an easy smile, and so he'd been twice jilted by fiancées.

The lovelorn bachelor sighed. "Seth, if you must know, Iris is an old friend to my Cousin Ellen. I've just been reading Ellen's letter, you see, and she mentions her."

"And why would she do that?" asked Seth as he poured a cup of coffee and then sat opposite the desk. "Wait, didn't you once mention being engaged to someone named Iris?"

"I fear I was, yes," the viscount muttered. "And I'd rather not discuss it. It's no longer painful, you understand, but my cousin wants me to help her, and I'm not sure about it."

"Because you want to avoid any fresh pain? Is that it?"

"I knew you'd understand. I'll think about it later. Tell me, is there any chance you read Italian?"

"Of course, I do. Why?"

Henry returned his cousin's letter to the envelope and then placed it into a wooden box marked with the label 'To Do'. "I really should hire a secretary. I meant to talk with Pennyweather about that, but it keeps slipping my mind."

"Perhaps, it slips because you want it to slip," suggested his friend. "I imagine you still hope Violet Stuart might assume that role, if not another."

"Yes, I suppose I do."

"Have you heard from her since that first visit?" asked Paynton.

"Not a line, nor a word. I talked with Romanov about her after the circle meeting last week. You may have noticed he and I remained in the duke's library afterward."

"I noticed, and so did Kepelheim. You'll be happy to hear Martin skillfully kept everyone else from interrupting by drawing attention to his latest translation of the puzzle chamber. It wasn't actually new, but it held their attention."

"That was kind of Martin," said Henry.

"He's a romantic. So what did Romanov say?"

"Oh, just that Violet's left England. Honestly, Seth, I feel completely lost. Why would she do that? Why is it every time I pour out my heart to a woman, she runs away from me?"

"Give her time, Henry. Romanov probably knows where she is. Ask him to deliver a message. And I don't think she's running from you. Why would she? Yours is the gentlest heart I've ever known."

"Yes, well, women apparently prefer a cruel heart. As for me, I prefer to let the topic rest." Henry reached for the telegram. "Since you read Italian, see if you can decipher this. It's very official looking."

Seth took the telegram and read through it quickly. "Oh," he said. "Henry, this may answer your question about Violet."

"What? Has she gone to Italy?"

"No, but it seems the Italians want to talk to her. Here's what it says:

> 'Dr. Henry MacAlpin, Lord Salperton –
> My lord, we seek your help. The Antonio Calabrese Family are wanted for multiple murders in Sicily. We understand the Calabrese daughter once stayed at your hospital under another name. Please, be advised that Inspector Umberto Genovese is on his way to England, to arrive in one fortnight. Please, offer him your full cooperation. Your life may depend on this.
> – Regards, Commandant Marco Fretelli'"

Seth handed the message back to Salperton. "Who's Calabrese?"

"That's Violet's birth name," Henry replied with a sigh. "But she wants to put those years behind her."

"If her family's wanted by the Italian Police, then I can see why she would."

"No, there's something amiss here. This commandant must be mistaken. She cannot be mixed up with any crime."

"Ask Romanov about it."

"I will. Oh, I miss Charles, Seth! If he were here, I could ask him to intervene with the Italians."

"Perhaps, Paul could do the same," suggested his friend. "He has contacts in most major cities and knows how to talk to police. And he's taken over for Charles at the ICI, so has the authority of that office. More coffee?"

"No, I've had enough. My stomach's already sprouting little coffee beans, I think. Or perhaps, I'm just worried."

"God will work it out." Seth smiled, his blue eyes glinting as he began to laugh. "I never thought to hear myself say something like that."

"Like what?"

"Invoking God's help. I always considered myself a staunch humanist with no room for any deity and no belief in anything but almighty science. Look how things have changed! That's why you mustn't give up, Henry. The Lord helped Violet to leave Redwing, and he's protected her ever since. He'll help her through this as well."

"I pray you're right," Henry sighed. "And I'm very glad God brought you out of the darkness, Seth. You're a good friend. Yes, I'll talk to Paul about this Italian mystery."

Seth held up the book he'd brought along. "You can deal with Italian constabularies all you like, but I've Jane Austen to muddle through."

"Austen? Whatever for?"

"Adele and I are reading one of her books together," Seth explained. "*Pride and Prejudice*. I take all the men's parts, and she takes the ladies'."

"That's very good of you," Henry replied. "Della's mind needs distraction from discussions of her father."

"Has she remembered anything?"

"No, nothing, but talk of the duke always causes a glimmer of sadness and anxiety to appear. She needs time to untie this knot on her own."

"Then keep the newspapers from her. Every edition contains stories about her father's supposed exploits," said Holloway.

"I think Paul plants those stories with the press. The earl's clever as a cat. As you're going up, might I come along? I've not yet talked with Della today. She was sleeping when I passed by earlier. I need to evaluate her current state of mind."

"Why? Is it changeable?"

"I'm afraid it is highly changeable. Some days, she's quite cheerful; others, entirely despondent and asks after her father again and again. Something's preying on her mind, Seth. I asked Romanov about it, and he said Adele's memories are locked away for now, but they may sometimes seep into her dreams. My grandmother had a saying, 'Dark dreams cause waking worries.' She was right. Grandmother was always right. Here, now, let's go upstairs. I'll explain more as we walk."

They left the library and climbed the back staircase to the first floor. As they neared the entrance to Adele's apartment, Henry paused. "Look here, Seth. Paul wants me to do something quite radical with Della's therapy."

"What?" asked Holloway. "And why is it radical?"

"Promise to say nothing to Adele, but Paul's asked me to place her under hypnosis. Honestly, I hesitate to do it. After talking with Romanov, I've come to believe her memory loss is by design, not due to any brain misfire. I admit, my profession's still crawling in its developmental knowledge about the brain. In truth, the science of alienism is scarcely out of the womb, and we've no idea why or how hypnosis actually works, or what damage it might cause."

"But you used it with me last year," Seth argued, "and I've suffered no ill effects, except for the odd nightmare. I'd probably have suffered far worse dreams, if you hadn't helped me to remember what happened in those tunnels."

"Yes, perhaps, but you've a very strong mind, Seth. Besides, you're a man."

Holloway grinned. "So I've been told."

Salperton's smooth cheeks blushed. "I'm sure you have been, and quite often, I should think. But that isn't the point."

"Henry, I know what you mean. Della's quite strong, and it could yield information to find Charles."

"Yes, that's true," muttered Salperton, absentmindedly. "I'll consider it." They left the landing area and continued to the apartment. It was situated close to Henry's own, on the north side of the house. He knocked, and the door was opened by a stout woman in an indigo-blue dress.

"Ah, Mrs. Shelton," said the viscount. "How is our favourite guest this morning?"

"Having her hair braided, sir."

"I see. Might we come in and wait? I'd like to examine the young lady, and I believe Lord Paynton has a reading appointment regarding Miss Jane Austen."

The woman smiled, softening her wrinkles a little. "Miss Austen's books are a favourite o' mine as well, sirs. Come into the parlour, then. I'll go see if Lady Della's ready."

"You don't leave her alone, I hope?" asked Henry.

"No, Doctor, we never would. If I or Mrs. Winstead cannot remain, we look to Miss Adelaide to fill in the gap."

"Is that the lady's maid Lord Aubrey sent over?"

"Oh, yes, sir. Miss Adelaide's quite nice and trustworthy. She's Mr. Pennyweather's younger sister. She's well educated and has done some nursing, too. I'll go look in now, sir. Oh, and there's tea on the little seashell table."

Salperton led his friend into the cheerful parlour, where they settled into a pair of chintz-upholstered chairs. The nurse had lingered in the parlour, her eyes on Lord Paynton's boyishly handsome face. "Shall I pour, sir?"

"Pour?" asked Henry.

"Tea, my lord. Lord Paynton looks as though he could use a hot cup."

"And so I could, dear lady," said the handsome viscount, "but I shouldn't wish to delay your return to our Della. My mother taught me the ways of a tea table. I can manage for us both. Thank you for asking." He winked and offered the nurse a bright smile.

The middle-aged woman's cheeks rounded into rosy apples. "You are a scamp, my lord," she giggled. "I'll just see to Lady Della."

Henry sighed. "I see you've even charmed Mrs. Shelton. Shall I let Mr. Shelton know he has a rival?"

"Probably not," laughed Seth. "Back to this idea of hypnosis. If it would help, why not do it? Surely, it's been used with women before."

"Women, yes, but Adele's not a woman."

"I think she is," the other argued. "She'll be thirteen next June, and twelve is the legal age for women to marry in Scotland. If you wanted, you could take her there today and make her Lady Salperton. Assuming, I don't make her Lady Paynton first."

Henry stared at his friend. "What the devil are you talking about?"

"I know you care for her, Henry, but then so do I. More than I thought I could. Here's the truth, my friend. As peers, you and I have a duty to marry and produce an heir. I was talking with Elizabeth about it yesterday. Our duchess is observant and speaks directly. She asked if I considered Adele a possible wife."

"And do you?" the doctor asked.

"I'm not sure. I'm still reconciling my old feelings for Beth, if you must know, but I'm in no rush to wed. Adele will be sixteen in three and a half years. I'm told she'll spend most of those years in France, studying with a tutor the way Beth did. Whilst she's there, I plan to visit her now and then, to see where our friendship might lead."

Henry said nothing, for the idea of Adele as a wife had never occurred to him—not even once. "And if Charles wants her to wait until she's twenty-one?"

"If our love is real, then we'll wait."

Salperton sighed. "Before she can marry, she must get well."

Seth put a hand on his friend's arm. "And she will get well, Henry, because you are a fine doctor and a fine man. Marriage thoughts aside, I know you love Adele, just as I do. To know her is to love her, as they say."

Henry nodded, his smile slowly returning. "So it is. Ah, wait, I hear the lady coming. Say nothing of this other therapy. Not until I can discuss it at length with Elizabeth."

"Dr. MacAlpin?" a young voice called from the apartment's bedchamber. "Is that you I hear?"

The bedchamber door had opened, and Adele entered the parlour. The two men stood politely.

"You look lovely this morning, Lady Della," Henry told his patient. "Have you changed your hair?"

"Yes," she answered with a sweet smile. "Adelaide thought a new style might be nice. She's very good at plaiting hair."

The adolescent had grown taller during the summer months, surpassing her adoptive mother's five-foot-two by a full inch. Now, fresh from the bath, Adele Marie's graceful figure was sheathed in a blue velvet robe, trimmed at the hem, throat, and cuffs with white Battenberg lace. The pubescent curves of approaching womanhood were becoming obvious, both above and below the robe's satin belt. Adelaide Pennyweather had braided Della's hair so that it curved into a heart-shape at the nape of her neck. There was no denying it. Adele Marie Sinclair was maturing into a startlingly beautiful young woman.

Seth offered his arm and led Adele to a soft chair near the the fire. "Shall we continue our book?"

Henry drew his chair close. "I'd like a moment first, if you don't mind, Seth. I need to ask my boring list of questions. Is that all right with you, Lady Della?"

"Of course, it is, but I hope you're not going to add any more medicines."

"No, I don't think that's necessary. Mrs. Shelton, if you and Miss Adelaide would go with Dr. Holloway? Perhaps, one of you could order a tray of fruit and biscuits for our special guest."

Holloway took the nurse's arm. "Come with me, Mrs. Shelton. Adelaide!" he called into the bedchamber.

A slender twenty-year-old with flaming red hair and freckles emerged from the next room. She curtsied sweetly. "You called, sir?"

"Come with us, Adelaide. Let's see if there are any fresh biscuits to be found downstairs. See you shortly, Della, and we'll continue our story," he added with a low bow.

As the door shut behind them, Adele began by saying, "Seth has been very kind to visit me so often."

"You call him Seth? Not Lord Paynton?"

"I know Lord Paynton is the proper etiquette, but he asked me to call him Seth. Is that wrong? Should I call him Lord Paynton regardless of his preference?"

"No, not at all," said Henry with ease. "And he is very kind. Now, how did you sleep last night? Remember, you're to be honest with me about everything. If there's any reason why sleep evades you, you're to tell me. Are we agreed?"

She laughed and reached for Henry's hand. "Oh, my dear Dr. MacAlpin, you are so very sweet and considerate, but am I not always honest with you?"

"Yes, I suppose you are," he blushed, "but most of my patients find honesty somewhat difficult to achieve. Young Mr. MacNee, for example. He seldom sleeps, but when he does he's somnambulistic."

"Is that another word for sleepwalking?" she asked.

"Yes, and it's common in people of a restless nature."

"Do you think Mr. MacNee's restless? I know his father, Lord Redcliffe. I don't like him very much."

"Don't you? Why not?"

"He's too sickeningly sweet to my mother."

"What relations has the earl with Duchess Elizabeth?"

"Lord Redcliffe wants to sit on the new hospital's board of governors, but Mother said no. He writes to her a lot. She's told me about it. Should I tell Father when he returns?"

"I'm sure it's all just business, Della. So, did Mr. MacNee's poor night affect you as well?"

"I thought I heard a woman scream once."

"That would be Mrs. Crossfield. Another night terror, I'm afraid. That scream woke me as well, and it took an hour to calm her."

"I was already awake," she told him. "I could hear strange noises from the house next door."

"The one to the west or the north?"

"The north. Just the other side of the hedges."

"Ah," said Henry. "That would be Hemsworth House, but I doubt any noises came from there. It's been empty since Lord Hemsfield's death last year. Might the noises have been a dream?"

"I don't think so. Are you sure the house is empty?" she asked, her smooth face pinching into a slight frown.

"I'm told it is. Apparently, Hemsworth died without issue. Sir Reginald Parsons tells me there's a Parliamentary investigation to find possible heirs. I doubt Lord Hemsworth ever stayed in the house, though. It's been empty for as long as I can remember."

Her left brow arched into doubt, causing Henry to smile. Sometimes, the Sinclair lines of inheritance shone with great intensity in Adele's fair face. He'd seen Charles wearing the very same expression many times.

Della seemed not to notice, for she'd turned to look into the crackling fire. "I'm really not sure it's empty, Dr. MacAlpin. There was an awful lot of activity in the house last night. Have you never visited it?"

"Not for a very long time, and it was just the once, when I was a boy. I've not been inside since. What sort of activity did you notice?"

"The moon was high last night, and I could see long shadows, moving back and forth on the top floor. And lights were flickering, passing from window to window, as though someone carried a candle back and forth."

"I suppose it might be cleaners," mused the physician. "The estate managers recently repaired the broken windows. I've heard the house will go up for sale, if no heirs are found. If it does, I might look into buying it. The attached land includes twenty acres of woods, and there's a lovely pond with a riding path going round it. I think our residents might enjoy horseback riding, don't you?"

"Yes, I suppose so, but Henry—I mean, Dr. MacAlpin—would you do something for me?"

He took her hand, enjoying its warmth. "Anything. And I like hearing you call me Henry. Feel free to do so anytime you wish."

"Henry, then," she whispered, her fair cheeks flushed. "It isn't much. Would you consider visiting the house, just to make sure it's really and truly empty? If you find no one, then, if I awaken again in the night, I shall close my drapes and read a book. I promise."

He kissed her hand and stood. "I shall be honoured to act on your behalf, dear lady. Oh, before I forget, your mother and brother are coming by again this evening. And I think they're bringing your dog."

"Paul is bringing Napper?" she sang back, joyfully. "Oh, that is wonderful! Napper will love the gardens here, Henry. She doesn't dig, you understand. She just likes chasing birds and bees. And Paul might bring news of my father. I'd love to know if he's sent any letters about his trip," she added, referring to the official story regarding the duke's absence from London. "I've read several of the articles in *The Gazette* about him. Most are quite absurd, claiming Father's negotiating marriage contracts. I doubt he is."

"Della, who brought you the newspapers?" asked Henry, for he'd left strict orders to keep all news away from her.

"Gillian. I mean Miss Bunting. She also brought me copies of two New York newspapers and one from Chicago. They're a few days old, but there's nothing about Father's visit in any of them. Don't you find that strange? If he's meeting with important Americans, why wouldn't their own press write about it?"

Henry's brain scrambled to find a reasonable reply. Of course, those papers said nothing. Charles Sinclair wasn't in America at all. His abductors hadn't yet returned him, and Paul Stuart had concocted the cover story to play for time.

"It's because your father's in America on a secret mission," he told her. "As head of the ICI, I imagine he works *incognito*, as they say. Disguised and all that. The way your brother operates when he's spying for England."

"I'm sure you're right," she agreed, apparently satisfied by the answer. "Father will return to England very soon, though, won't he? Travel twixt here and America is much faster than it used to be. Gillian said that some ships can make the crossing in a week. Isn't that marvellous? Do you think the *Duchess of Branham* can make it as quickly?"

"The *Duchess of Branham?*"

"Father's new ship. *The Gazette* has photographs of it, and their writer mentions the ship often. It has a triple screw, whatever that is. "

"Oh, yes that ship! I suppose it could be equipped with a triple screw. That's the drive mechanism," replied the alienist, deciding to have a talk with Bunting about the newspapers. "We'll ask your mother and Paul if they've received any news, when they visit this evening. Now, Adelaide will bring you up a fruit tray. Eat everything, for the nutrition gives you energy."

"And that energy makes me grow?"

"Yes," he said, colour rising to his cheeks. "I imagine it will. Finish breakfast, and then whilst you read Jane Austen with Lord Paynton, I'll call at the house next door. How is that?"

She smiled, and the lines of her oval face became quite grown-up for a moment. The change startled Salperton. *Dear me, she's quite beautiful, when she does that.*

"I'll come back later," he said. Henry left the apartment and headed downstairs to his library office.

His butler met him at the door, along with a middle-aged commissionaire. Saunders had been polishing silver when the bell rang, and wore a leather apron over his livery.

"This gentleman has a message for you, my lord."

"Oh?" asked the viscount. "And you are?"

"Beecham, sir. I used to work at the War Office, but I serve at Queen Anne House now. I run errands for Lord Aubrey. His lordship asked me to bring this to you right away." The short man handed Henry a sealed white envelope.

Salperton opened the message and read it to himself. "I see. Saunders, the earl asks me to meet him in Whitechapel. Is Lord Paynton still downstairs?"

"Yes, sir. He's talking with Mrs. Merchant and eating a slice of last night's torte."

"No surprise there," smiled the alienist. "Well, once he's eaten his fill, ask Lord Paynton if he'd be kind enough to remain here whilst I'm away, will you? Have my coach brought round. Oh, and let the Lady Adele know I'll stop by Hemsworth House on my way."

He gave the messenger ten shillings, bundled up against the cold in a woolen greatcoat, and before the clocks struck half past eleven, Henry's driver had delivered his employer to the gravel park next door. Salperton assumed the call would be quick and uneventful, but that visit would begin a runaway snowball effect that would continue to roll for another eighteen months.

Hemsfield House was not empty.

It was, in fact, filled with *the Dead*.

CHAPTER NINE

Another World - Charles Dines with His Host

Far away, in a realm beyond the veil, within a castle, deep beneath the earth, Charles Sinclair was about to learn the reason for his abduction. After leaving the mysterious Mr. Fenwick, he'd been met at the first-floor landing by a liveried footman, who silently guided him to the main level, where an elegant butler took charge of the unwilling guest. The butler offered a low bow and introduced himself as Voithos. He looked more like a West-End magician than a butler, with oiled hair, sleepy black eyes, and startlingly pale skin.

"If Your Grace would remain here whilst I announce you?" he said in a thick accent.

The duke nodded, and the servant slipped quietly into the next room. He left one of the tall doors slightly ajar, and Sinclair could hear a short conversation within. He recognised one voice as that of the mysterious Dr. Theseus. A moment later, the butler returned and bowed again. He opened wide both doors and announced, "His Majesty, Charles of England." The magician butler then departed for the kitchens.

The duke remained in the doorway, assessing the room and its inhabitants.

"Don't just stand there. Come in!" called Araqiel from a gilded, high-back chair. "Really, Charles, we don't bite. Not usually. Come, sit with us."

Sinclair took a deep breath and imagined himself diving into the deep end of a cloudy pool of water. If he drowned, then it was only because the Lord allowed it.

I am in God's wonderful hands, he reminded himself. *And I am never alone.*

"Come here, darling Charles," Eluna purred as he neared her chair. "Sit by me."

"No, Eluna," said the mysterious Dr. Theseus, who left his own chair at the table's head. "Our king must sit here. I insist."

The vacated chair was the largest of them all, with gilded carved arms, ending in lion's paws. The tall carved back was formed like a two-headed eagle with outstretched wings. It looked very much like a throne.

"I couldn't," Charles answered. "It's your chair."

"The chair should be yours. I insist you take it," countered Theseus. "Besides, it is nearer the fire, and therefore warmer."

"That's kind of you. Thank you," answered the prisoner carefully. "The castle is somewhat cold, I've noticed."

"It is always so, I'm afraid," said his host. "I hope your rooms are agreeable."

"Prisons seldom please those locked within them, not even prisons with velvet bars," Sinclair replied. "Isn't that so, Mr. Flint? If I'm not mistaken, you've escaped from a much colder cell. One with seven gates."

Flint's waxwork face twisted into simulated amusement. "You're clever for a human, Duke Charles."

"Odd. You once said I was quite stupid and untutored," the human told the lawyer.

"Then, it must be true, for I am never wrong about such things."

"You were wrong about me," said Charles.

"No, I only told you the truth."

"How is trying to steal my watch truthful?" asked the human.

"Steal? Steal! I've never stolen anything in my life, you stupid, worthless man!"

"Silence!" shouted Theseus. "That's quite enough of your insolence, little crow. We'll have none of your insults here."

"But he began it!" cried the lawyer.

"Did I?" teased Charles. "I believe it began with you, when I awoke in the Stone Realms. What did you call it? Sebet Babi?"

"That is a lie!"

"It isn't called Sebet Babi?" countered Charles.

Flint's black eyes bulged, and he nearly choked with rage. "You ungrateful wretch! I welcomed you with sincerity and congeniality, human. Was it my fault you refused to recognise it?"

"Yet despite your so-called congeniality, I escaped your prison, without giving up this," Charles volleyed in return, showing the group his pocket watch. "Strange the Lord allows me to keep this, no matter the circumstances."

"Bah! That watch is useless here," the lawyer crowed.

"Then, why would God let me keep it? You've taken all my other clothing, I've noticed. Yet I've retained my wedding ring and this watch. The Lord must think I require them."

"We'll see just how much that dictator lets you keep once the test begins!" shouted Flint.

"Albus, that is enough!" ordered Theseus again. "This is my home, not yours, and the duke is my guest. You and the others are here, only because I allow it. If you wish to remain, then I insist you and everyone show the duke respect, otherwise, you will leave and never receive another invitation. Am I clear?"

The cadaverous lawyer started to offer an angry retort, but the loud clang of a gong drowned out his words. There were five clangs in all, and with each deep sounding of the gong, a new door opened, admitting a total of five footmen. All the servants were dressed in black trousers and red damask waistcoats, trimmed in gold buttons, and their coats were embellished with the C-R royal cipher.

The gong sounded a sixth time, and Voithos, the black-haired butler magician, entered through yet another door and delivered a calligraphed menu to his master.

"As you requested, Lord Theseus. We've prepared selections from your home, as well as that of His Grace. Eight courses in all, from Greece and Scotland."

"Scotland? Now, wait. Wasn't the duke born in Carlisle?" asked Araqiel. "I'm sure, I'm right. I'd remember if I'd met him first in Scotland. Tis a dismal, sad sort of wilderness. Full of black-faced sheep and those wooly red cattle."

Charles stared at the prince, his dark brows furrowing. "Are you saying you met me at Rose House?"

"Is that what it's called?" laughed Ara. "I'd quite forgotten. But that house is new by my reckoning. Aeons ago, a marvellous temple sat on that spot, on a hill overlooking a serpentine river. The Eden, I think it's called. Such lovely ground for *hunting*."

"Hunting? Do you imply that I am prey, Your Highness?" asked the duke boldly.

"I imply nothing. I merely state *fact*."

Ignoring Araqiel, Theseus handed the menu back to the butler. "The choices are fine, Voithos. Serve everyone's wine and then bring the first course."

Voithos bowed and then clapped his gloved hands. The footmen positioned themselves, one beside each guest, and poured from five different bottles. Charles noticed his was a sparkling white with a hint of amber to it.

"Champagne?"

"Not exactly," answered Theseus. "A charming little Prosecco from the Cinqueterra region. I came across it two centuries ago, whilst living with a most enchanting countess."

"I don't suppose her name was di Specchio?" asked the duke as he gazed at the wine and wondered if it might be poisoned.

"No, not Serena. Not that time," the doctor answered with a mischievous smile. "Serena is beautiful but quite devious, Charles. You must be on your guard with her at all times. Do you mind if I call you Charles? It is informal, I know, but as you've been our guest these many weeks, I feel as if I know you."

"Weeks?" asked the duke, feigning ignorance.

"Yes, I'm afraid Araqiel brought you here somewhat early, but—well, I can explain it all later."

"And you are?" asked the prisoner, pretending ignorance to avoid any mention of Fenwick.

"Oh, forgive me! It's a serious and impolite oversight, is it not?" his host exclaimed. "I am Alphonse Poseideou Theseus. Doctor of the arts, medicine, chemistry, linguistics, and many other disciplines. Presently, I've turned my abilities to matters of the mind. I own a clinic in London. Perhaps, you've heard of it? The Pollux. We're currently treating a practitioner friend of mine. Dr. Alexander Collins. Pitiful case. I see you react, Charles. Do you know him?"

"I'm sure you're already aware that I arrested the man last year," Charles answered without blinking.

"Ah, so you did!" laughed Theseus, raising his glass to propose a toast. "Everyone, if you would stand, let us drink to our honoured guest, a man who will very soon reveal much of himself to us all; his mind, his mettle, and also his blood."

"A noticeable lack of alliteration at the last," Araqiel observed, "but I'm always happy to drink blood—I mean, drink *to blood*, of course. And so I drink to our guest, the most useful human prince to walk this earth in a very long time."

All at the table raised their glasses, and each sipped his or her own special wine: white, red, or 'other', clearly enjoying the bespoke libations. Charles decided to trust in the Lord's protection and drank deeply of the Prosecco. *I've probably not eaten much,* he realised. Since awakening, his stomach ached, and his throat itched from dryness. He could still taste laudanum and perhaps other soporifics as well, but the cool wine left a whisper of bubbles on his parched tongue, easing the discomfort and drowning the aftertaste of the medicine.

"You say that I've been here for weeks, Dr. Theseus. How many weeks, and why have I been asleep?"

"It is the twentieth day of September, 1889, according to human reckoning. That makes it almost six weeks since your arrival here, Charles. Though you've slept almost the entire time, I've awakened you periodically to check your health. I fear that, you arrived too early, and I apologise for the inconvenience," said Theseus as he finished one glass and motioned for another.

"And you kept me unconscious?"

"Yes, but only to avoid causing you further distress," answered Theseus. "Begin the first course, now, Voithos."

The butler responded by signalling to the five footmen, who then served a charcuterie of pungent goat cheeses, salted cashews, wafer thin slices of dried salmon, salty prosciutto, ripe pears, and an orange-raspberry compote laced with Frangelico liqueur, that added hints of vanilla and chocolate. Charles ate sparingly, not wishing to overwhelm his sluggish system.

"You do not care for the food?" asked Eluna, who'd gobbled down her own with unladylike gusto.

"I fear my stomach cannot awaken as easily as my mind," answered the duke. "And there's a strange aftertaste on my tongue."

Hearing this, Theseus glared at his table companions, his dark eyes flaming with anger. "The duke should have no aftertaste at all. I used no medicinals that should do so. Who has done this thing? Is there something one of you needs to confess?"

Araqiel ignored the doctor's outrage and even laughed as he nudged his sister. "Honestly, Theseus, I did nothing. Not a single thing. Perhaps, Eluna acted as the duke's secret nurse?"

"I acted as a *what?*" the wounded sister shouted.

"That's so very typical of you, Ara," replied Theseus. "Lacking all chivalry as usual, but it's clear that one of you has interfered with my therapy. Confess now, or else I shall toss you both into a gutter of ravenous gargoyles, where you belong!"

"I may have placed a tiny spell on him," the princess admitted. "But only because..."

Eluna had no opportunity to finish. The doctor jumped to his feet and began to overturn every plate within his reach. "Out! Out, both of you, or by all the Archons, I shall have you roasted on Cain's spit!"

"Really, Alphonse, you're making such a fuss," Luna argued. "I meant well. It was only so the duke might rest. Your methods caused his heart to beat so very slowly, that I feared his breathing might cease altogether. I did it to save his life. Was I wrong to show such tenderness towards our king?"

Theseus slammed his fist on the table, and every footman jumped. The magician butler remained motionless, as though the mercurial behaviour were quite ordinary.

"You have no right to make such decisions in my home! A spell might pollute the test. Have you no sense at all? Did I spend all that time in your company to be fooled?"

Eluna purred as she whispered, "Forgive me, sweet Theseus. I am but a weak female; a foolish woman who desires that which men deny her. I see it now. I was wrong. This is your home, and I submit to your authority."

Araqiel stared at his sister/wife as though she'd sprouted horns and a tail—or worse, that she hadn't. Where had his mischievous siren gone? Where was the mother of evil? The silvery moon of daring and desire? Had she really just crawled in conciliatory obeisance to a halfling? But fearing words to the contrary might reveal his mind to Theseus, the dragon pretended to admonish his sister.

"You should know better, Lunetta. I am quite ashamed of you."

Albus Flint found the tension twixt his superiors amusing, and signalled for more wine. "Another glass is needed, I think. This dinner is certainly enlightening thus far. And it's only the first course," he cackled, and his black eyes blinked yellow for a moment.

Charles sat still, watching the strange play and wondering if he'd fallen down Alice's rabbit hole and joined the Mad Hatter for tea. Or perhaps, *he* was the Hatter. *No, this isn't a dream, and I have to keep my wits about me,* he thought. *I must keep them talking. Divide them, if I can.*

"Then you're saying my prolonged sleep was due to this spell you cast, Princess?" he asked. "Might I ask the nature of the spell?"

She leaned in close, happy to converse with the handsome human. "Just a simple somnolence spell. Most anyone could do it, but I made sure your beautiful body neither languished nor lacked sustenance as you slept. That, too, can be woven into the spell, my darling Charles. I do so admire you," she continued with a kiss to his right hand. "I am your willing servant, my king. To deny your needs would be a crime."

Araqiel huffed, finding the display tiresome. "Humans always have needs, Lunetta. It's a fault of their weak design."

Theseus wasn't the least bit amused. "Take all of this away, Voithos. Perhaps, our guest will find the next course more to his taste. And remove the princess's wine glass. She's had enough to drink."

The servants did as commanded and in less than a minute, the table was cleared and the diners left alone. Silence fell upon the gathering, and Charles noticed a soft, ticking sound. He turned to look in the sound's direction.

His throne-like chair sat eight feet or so from an enormous stone hearth, that rose all the way up to the ceiling beams. Its broad chimney passed through the underground castle's four storeys, and from there, the smoke diverted into the pipes of a complex exhaust system, which vented up to the ruins of an abandoned abbey on the surface.

The dining hall's design and furnishings struck Charles as familiar, in the same way his apartment felt familiar; as though he'd slept here before. But surely, he hadn't. More likely, he'd seen this room, when Araqiel brought him here in August.

But wait. Did I dream of this place as a boy?

The ticking sound grew louder, yet Charles could find no clock anywhere within the dining hall. He shut his eyes to listen, concentrating on the rhythmic sound.

"You hear it, too, don't you?" asked Theseus.

"Hear what?" Flint cawed. "The woman's finally stopped talking, and the room is silent as the grave. I should know. The grave is my domain."

"You don't hear the ticking?" asked Charles.

Eluna touched the duke's right temple and stroked the cool skin. "There is no ticking, my love. Only a long, lovely silence."

"He is not your love!" shouted Araqiel. "And he's clearly suffering some side effect of your secret spell. The man's hearing things. Why would any of us keep a clock? Time is our enemy. We want no reminders of its dreadful power."

"Reminders of its what?" asked the duke.

"Nothing. I said nothing," Ara muttered. "When are the footmen coming back? I'm starved, and my glass is empty."

"Time has power?" Charles asked. "How so? Time is just the progression of nature and the heavens, isn't it? Are you saying God's creation has some power over you?"

"No. Voithos! A drink!" shouted the dragon.

"Let there be light," Charles quoted. "God's first recorded command. One could say that's when Time began, but are you saying *time* became your prison?"

"Let there be DARKNESS!" shouted Araqiel, his eyes turning red. "I am sick to death of this!"

Theseus stood. "Then you may leave us, Araqiel. In fact, all of you may go."

"Go?" Araqiel asked, his crimson eyes glaring at Theseus. "You dare to command me, halfling? Why, I could devour you in a single bite. Gobble you up and have done with all of this!"

"That bite would be your last," Theseus answered in a low, deep voice. "Leave now, foolish dragon, before I remind you just who is in charge here."

"You'll do what?" Araqiel countered.

"I said LEAVE!" Theseus shouted, his voice so much like booming peals of thunder, that Flint transformed into a raven out of shock.

"Do you mean that *we* should leave, or that the human should? I vote for the human," countered Araqiel, his eyes returned to normal. "But aren't we having a meeting afterwards? Shall I come back? Not Luna, though. Who needs a woman? Am I right?"

"This woman could tear out your heart," she threatened.

"We'll meet tomorrow," Theseus decided, his voice growing soft again. He gazed down at his hands, the long fingers curled into the palms over and over, as though the brain that worked the muscles struggled with some horrid thought. "Just go. I wish to speak to our guest alone."

The footmen began to clear the table. Voithos exchanged whispers with Theseus, who ordered food be delivered to everyone's private apartments. Araqiel muttered something about making sure they sent him 'proper wine, with corpuscles in it', and then he left with Eluna. Albus Flint purloined two decanters of cognac from a nearby sideboard then exited quietly, via a side door.

Once they were alone, Theseus took several moments to gather his thoughts. Finally, the doctor raised his head, saying, "You must be quite confused by all of this, Charles."

"One might say so," replied the duke carefully. "And yet I still hear the ticking. You hear it as well, don't you?"

"Yes," admitted his host. "It never ceases. Not for me. Come, my friend. I've ordered Voithos to take food and drink to my private drawing room. It's a bit of a walk from here, but after so long a slumber, the exercise will be good for you."

They left the banquet hall, turning here and there, through a puzzling series of wide corridors, then descended a flight of winding stairs. "The castle isn't built on a single plan," explained Theseus. "Its foundations were laid aeons ago, and since then, others have added to it, meaning the layout is somewhat haphazard. You'll appreciate what I mean soon."

They'd reached a grand gallery, hung with portraits of human-like men, their physiques perfect, each clad in magnificent armour and seated on a great throne. The stern physiognomies of their painted faces held much in common with the fallen angels he'd come to know: Raziel, Saraqael, and now the dragon that called himself Prince Araqiel von Siebenbürgen. All had similar appearances of face and form, as though entering the human realm constrained these rebels to similar patterns. Even Theseus had the same dark hair, though his deep brown eyes held little in common with the icy orbs of the elohim princes. And though the doctor's height was beyond that of most Englishmen, he was no taller than Charles. Hadn't Araqiel called Theseus a halfling at dinner? What might that mean?

"We climb up again, I'm afraid," Theseus said, his accented voice pleasing to the ear. "There are a hundred questions you wish to ask, I know, but have patience, Charles. I shall answer them all, but first, I must make certain we are truly alone."

"We appear to be alone now," Sinclair observed as they neared a broad landing of flagstone and oak timber.

"I'm sure it seems that way, but looks can deceive."

"If this castle is yours, then surely you know whether or not you're being watched?"

Theseus laughed, the deep tone hauntingly familiar. "It's true, the castle is mine, but I did not design it, nor do I control every room of it. Its former owners still hear and see all that happens within these walls, you understand. It's the stones, Charles. They act as spies."

They had reached the final turn, which took them through an arcaded hallway that reminded Charles of the cloisters in old Catholic churches and abbeys. At the end of this passage, Theseus waved his left hand before a set of twin doors, and then across the arched lintel. In response, a series of carved symbols glowed in non-linear order, as though lit by an inner fire. Once all had brightened, both doors opened of their own accord.

"I shall enter first," explained the physician. "I must make certain all is as it should be."

As Charles waited outside, he heard Theseus whispering into each corner of the octagonal room. The interior was dark as pitch to begin, but brightened suddenly as two great fires sprang up on either side. The flames startled the duke, and he stepped backwards instinctively.

"Theseus, are you all right?"

"Yes, of course. I have lit the hearths. We shall be quite warm soon. Please, Charles, join me. We have a great deal to discuss."

CHAPTER TEN
Real World - Paul Stuart's Journal

QUEEN ANNE HOUSE, 20th September, 1889 - Another day with no news of Charles. The press continue to hound all family members regarding his whereabouts. We present a united front, of course. Galton and his team release bits of information, like strips of tender meat to satisfy the pack's hunger. *The Pall Mall Gazette* has run a series of reports, containing meaty portions, but the writer, a conceited Q.C., adds trimmings of his own. Parliamentarians and paupers alike now believe my cousin is in America, being wined and dined by the *nouveau riche* of New York and Washington. Honestly, Sir Thomas Galton is a genius!

The inner circle meets often, and I visit the palace each morning. The Queen is resolved that Charles will follow her to the throne, but I know my cousin well, and he will refuse it. This position as 'shadow sovereign' is far more than he wants, and he does it only because it is the Lord God's will. Drina remains in good health, but she cannot help ageing, for it is our human design. I dearly love that old lady, but she rules one-fifth of the world's population and one-fourth of its land. And that political landscape is changing. I fear that England will be thrust into war soon. North Africa grows restless, and the Sudan's Mahdists demand we supply them with weapons. If we refuse, the French will happily comply. Recently, a group of Mahdists were captured with British armaments in their possession, including two Maxim guns. Who is supplying these? I've sent orders to our men in Egypt to discover the wellspring of these treasonous acts. Africa is a powder keg that will explode in our faces soon, if we do not act. All of Europe awaits that final crack in the Ottoman defence wall, and each country hopes to steal and reuse the fallen stones to build their own castles and walls.

It is a dangerous time to be a king or queen.

Despite the dangers and dreads, my beautiful Cousin Beth bears it all with dignity. What a Queen she would make. What an Empress! No matter how persistent the barrage of reporters at her door, no matter how insolent, she greets them all with patience and sweetness. But I know her well and see the strain upon her dear face. Most of the vermin happily repeat our official story, that my cousin meets in secret with other leaders regarding the North Africa situation. As Commissioner for the Home Office's Intelligence Branch, such activities lie within his purview, but the story confirms the popular notion that Charles is being groomed as England's next King. *The Star*, *The Gazette* and even *The Times* call Beth the next Queen Elizabeth and her husband is the Bonny Prince, Charles III, and even King Arthur. We allow the rumours to gain momentum for they serve as distraction from the awful truth, that Charles was abducted from Drummond Chapel six weeks ago.

There is some good news, though. Adele is home and improves daily at Henry's hospital. Beth and I visit as often as possible and plan to go again this evening and take Napper with us. The sweet dog has missed Della so much, that she refuses to eat. Henry thinks Napper's presence could help Della regain her memories and recover sooner. If she does remember, the account might help us to find Charles.

Now, to other matters.

Tomorrow, William Wychwright is to be released from London Hospital and transferred to a secure cell, owned by the ICI. It's our position that Wychwright's prosecution is an Intelligence Branch matter, and thus far, Commissioner Monro is happy to agree. The only fly in the ointment is Patrick MacAllen (who loudly proclaims he is to be called Lord Granddach). He now serves as Scotland Yard's Special Branch head. Granddach has applied for a separate judgement from Secretary Matthews. I'm pleased to write that, after meeting privately with my Uncle James, Matthews has seen reason. Wychwright will remain in ICI hands.

The inner circle members meet each Monday and Thursday at Haimsbury House. Kepelheim and Holloway have made some headway on the strange puzzle chamber inside that home, and Martin promised a report on it next Monday.

James has gone to France with Victoria. A fortnight ago, someone broke into Chateau Rothesay's stables, stabbed two grooms, and set fire to the building. Both men are in hospital and expected to recover. Four of Victoria's prize horses are dead, drained of blood. The fire was intended to cover this truth, but the necropsy revealed all. As James owns the castle, he's gone to Paris with Tory and they're working together with the police. All Paris circle members are on alert, and the Sûreté have placed men on the château grounds.

We've now implemented wartime rules, meaning every household is guarded in triple numbers, and no one travels without an escort. If Rothesay is under attack, then no home is safe. We will not allow another abduction or assassination attempt to occur.

On a happier note, the Haimsbury-Branham Hospital, called the HBH, is to open soon. Beth's kept her mind off Charles by devoting her energies to this endeavour, and the effort has paid well. I'm proud of our little duchess. How she's changed from the bashful child I once held on my lap! To think that I foolishly thought myself her only champion and assumed she'd always be helpless and dependent on me. Charles has helped our Beth to shine, and I thank God for both of them each and every day.

Beth has a meeting with the management of the HBH this morning. I plan to join her there, though she's unaware of it. I've insisted she take guardians and avoid any crested carriages. My real reason for going is troubling. I've told very few circle members of my plans to go this morning. You might say I'm laying a trap, but I pray no one falls into it. Treason is a very dirty word.

On a very happy note, my wife is in the final weeks of her pregnancy. To keep watch over both Delia and Beth, we have moved to Haimsbury House. Beth's allowed me to install all the necessary medical equipment and furnishings in the east-wing master apartment. And whilst Aubrey House is unoccupied, I'm having it redecorated in all my wife's favourite colours. Beth enjoys hosting us, she says, and visits with Delia every morning, which is a mercy, for I spend most of my days here, at Queen Anne, fighting despair and filling in for my absent cousin. Twice daily, large stacks of red boxes arrive, each one filled with new laws, treaties, and other government business. I'm expected to offer an opinion on all. Please, Lord, I pray never to wear a crown!

Today, a box from the Home Office conveyed warnings of a malady now circulating through our citizenry. It's being called the Russian Influenza (named for its origin), and it's already left thousands dead across Europe. It strikes swiftly and suddenly, leaving victims weak as kittens for weeks and many succumb. I shall add two more, experienced nurses to Beth's staff, just in case.

Another happy development is this: The malicious female cuckoo that so afflicted my household and my marriage has found a nest of her own to infect. Poor old Brackamore! The earl's given Connie a wedding ring and a great London house to command. I know it is unchivalrous of me, but I'm delighted to be rid of my mother-in-law. I pray with all sincerity, that her marriage is fulfilling to the extent that it keeps her working there, and not here.

The new Countess of Brackamore and her unwitting husband have taken a wedding trip to the Continent. Cordelia receives the odd postcard now and then, written hastily and bragging of their fine hotels and indulgent dinners. If I sound bitter, it's because my wife despairs often, and these letters only worsen these dark moods. Delia constantly worries she'll make a poor mother, for she's had no loving example. But I tell her she'll be a wonderful mother—for I believe it.

She suffers from nightmares still, usually of her late father, but sometimes of Charles. My wife has a tender spirit. Henry visits with her before each of our meetings. He believes the nightmares will cease once the baby's born in a few weeks.

A few weeks! I missed Adele's birth and earliest years. I shall make up for that with this baby. The angel told me we'd have a son. A son. What a miracle that will be!

There, I've said enough. Forgive me, Lord, for my unkind thoughts and words. Help my short temper to find patience for all, even for Connie, for she is my unborn son's grandmother, after all.

Lord Almighty, please bring us some sign of Charles's welfare! My dearest friend in all the world is in peril, and I am utterly helpless!

CHAPTER ELEVEN
The Real World - Haimsbury House

Three hours before Henry MacAlpin rang the bell at Hemsfield House and two hours before Paul Stuart composed his diary entry, Duchess Elizabeth Stuart Sinclair, was about to meet a mysterious stranger.

Unable to sleep because of dark dreams, Beth spent several hours reading a preview copy of Bram Stoker's first novel *The Snake's Pass*. The clock had just stuck eight, when the butler knocked on her apartment door.

"Yes?" she called.

"It's Miles, my lady."

She set aside the book. "Come in, Mr. Miles."

The butler entered and bowed. "You've a caller, Your Grace. I explained the hour is far too early to expect you to receive him, but he's most insistent."

"Is he someone I know?"

John Eric Miles was far more than a butler. As a former boxer and circle agent, he also protected the duchess, and early morning strangers often equated to trouble.

"No, my lady, he appears to be a gentleman of quality, however if you prefer not to receive him, you need only ask. I know how much is on your mind at present. I could ask the gentleman to call another time. Or I could ask Inspector Baxter to meet with him."

"I'm sure the inspector and Mrs. Baxter are still enjoying morning coffee in the dower house. I shouldn't wish to disturb them."

"Actually, my lady, the inspector arrived half an hour ago with Mrs. Baxter. Both are in the nursery, I believe."

Beth smiled. "Baxter likes to hold Lord Anjou on his lap and tell him stories. And Mrs. Baxter helps Mary Wilsham to supervise the wet nurses. Despite our trials, this is a happy household, and I thank God for the Baxters."

"I'll suggest the gentleman make an appointment."

"No, I'll come down. Besides, I've been awake for hours with a headache."

"Shall I ask Partridge or Anderson to bring you something for it?" asked the man protectively. "I'm told this new influenza can begin with headache."

"I'm sure it's just our current situation, Mr. Miles, but you're kind to suggest it. What is the gentleman's name?"

Before the butler could answer, a new face appeared in the parlour doorway; the aforementioned Detective Inspector Baxter. "Good morning, my lady," said the inspector, standing tall and proud in a new suit.

"How very smart you look today, Inspector! Your attire is splendid, but you wear a somewhat sullen face. Has it to do with the caller Miles has mentioned to me?"

"It does indeed," the great man answered. "I'm sure he's a reporter using a gentleman's guise as a ruse, my lady. I chanced upon him in the foyer as I was coming up from below stairs. Mrs. Baxter wanted to take some fresh biscuits up to the nursery for little Lord Anjou. She believes the lad is teething already. That gentleman is exceedingly rude to call so early in the day, which marks him as a reporter in my book. Allow me to take care of the matter for you."

"If he's come in disguise, then he's a fool," Beth replied smiling proudly. "For I've two gallant knights to keep watch in the earl's absence, and my husband would..." she added, her smile vanishing.

Baxter stepped closer. "My lady, if you wish, once I've despatched this miscreant, I'll return to keep you company. With Lady Victoria gone, you've no one to assist with hospital business. Perhaps, I might help? If not, then at least, permit me to serve as your somewhat aged guardian."

Beth's smile returned, though her dark eyes remained solemn. "Shall I waste an important detective's time by employing him as a secretary, Inspector? No, not at all. However, if you'd serve as my guardian today, that is entirely different. My husband would be pleased to know you're looking after my welfare, but even if the man is a reporter, shouldn't I receive him? The earl insists we maintain our official story to all members of the press."

"If you must, then I shall sit in—as your guardian."

"Thank you, Inspector. Miles, you were about to give me his name. Did this mysterious gentleman have a card?"

"Yes, my lady."

Miles produced a cream calling card, trimmed in silver. Beth glanced at the card, which read:

Lord Daniel Randolph Porter
17th Earl of Ailesleigh
Ailesleigh House, Westminster

"Lord Ailesleigh? If he's in disguise, it's easy enough to discover it. Miles, please, tell the gentleman I'll be down in a few minutes."

By 8:25, the duchess had settled into the Haimsbury House morning room called 'the Queen Anne' for its splendid view of Queen Anne Park. She'd brought her new book and a file box of hospital papers, intending to work half an hour before breakfast. Afterward, she'd quickly eat and then dress for the eleven o'clock hospital meeting. Baxter took a seat opposite the duchess at a small round table.

Mile arrived, leading the mysterious caller.

Lord Ailesleigh stood a little over six feet tall and had a muscular build, auburn hair, golden brown eyes, arched brows, and a lean jaw. The hair was cut in a modern style, and the bespoke attire revealed a strong sense of style. A watch chain of bright silver was draped across the striped vest. The earl waited for his hostess to speak.

Beth often took her time with unknown visitors, even those from the peerage class. Prolonged silence took the measure of a man's breeding and willingness to wait for a higher ranking peer to speak first. Ailesleigh breathed slowly, and his eyes seemed kind, even thoughtful. A soft smile played at his well-formed mouth, but he remained silent.

After thirty long seconds, the duchess finally spoke. "Welcome to Haimsbury House, Lord Ailesleigh. Forgive me for keeping you waiting," she began, extending her hand to him.

He bowed and offered a polite and perfectly proper kiss to the back of her hand. "You're kind to receive me at such an early hour, Your Grace. May I?" he asked, pointing to a nearby chair.

"Yes, of course. Sit, please."

"Thank you," he said, sitting down.

"Allow me to introduce one of my husband's finest officers. Lord Ailesleigh, this is Detective Inspector Cornelius Baxter. He serves with the ICI and the Home Office Intelligence Branch."

"It's a pleasure, Inspector Baxter," the earl said, rising once more to shake the detective's hand firmly. "I'm actually glad you're here, Inspector. You may have some ideas about my mystery."

"What mystery is that, sir?" asked Baxter.

"It's why I've come at such an early hour, actually. I'm on the clock, you might say. My aunt's business has become my mystery. When I speak of my aunt, I mean my great aunt. She was the Lady Annabelle Dalyrimple of Dinsmore."

"I know the Dinsmore area. Beautiful country, but it's in Ireland, isn't it?" asked Beth. "Is Ailesleigh an Irish earldom?"

"No, the family seat's in Cornwall, Your Grace. Several miles south of Tintagel. It's a rocky, forlorn sort of place, overlooking the sea cliff. I imagine the Brontë sisters would find it quite inspirational."

Elizabeth smiled. Something about the handsome visitor struck her as honest and true, as though a light shone from his golden eyes. "Most of my family are from Scotland, as I'm sure you know. My grandfather's moors might also serve as a setting for a Brontë book. Do you enjoy reading, Lord Ailesleigh?"

"Oh, yes!" he exclaimed, his eyes sparkling with glints of sunshine. "My cousins call me the Ailesleigh bookworm, actually. Is that Stoker's new effort? I've been an admirer ever since his short story collection a few years ago."

"Really? I'm happy to say Mr. Stoker has become a family friend," she said. "He was kind enough to let me read this before its official release next month. When I'm finished, you may borrow it."

"That's very kind of you, Your Grace."

"How may I help you today, Lord Ailesleigh?"

"Well, my lady, it isn't quite how you might help me, so much as how I might be helpful to you. I've recently come into an inheritance, you see, left me by that widowed aunt I mentioned. The Lady

Annabelle Dalyrimple. I just called her Auntie Belle. She lived to be ninety-nine, if you can imagine it. A fit and feisty woman right up to the last. She left me a lovely old terraced home on the northeast side of Regent's Park. Her late husband, Sir Richard Dalrymple, bought the house forty-six years ago. It's four storeys tall. The largest house in the row, and as my great aunt required very little space in her final years, she allowed a gentleman to lease it. I tell you this roundabout tale to explain why I've only just discovered the trunks."

"The trunks, Lord Ailesleigh?"

"Yes. My great aunt's solicitor delivered the keys to me two days ago, but when I took a look at the place yesterday evening, I discovered a great many mysterious items. Some valuable. Amongst them, were dresses, jewels, photographs and the like, all obviously property of my late aunt, but others may have belonged to the previous tenant. Now, you must wonder why I've bothered you so early on such a lovely morning with my dilemma. It's because of these trunks I mentioned. A clause in my aunt's will requires that all materials in the house be removed no later than one week after her death. That's tomorrow, when these trunks will be taken away by her legal representatives for sorting."

"Perhaps, that's a good thing, Lord Ailesleigh. Mightn't the trunks be your late aunt's property?" she asked.

"No, I'm sure they are not. Three are steamer trunks, and there are several wooden crates, as well, old sea cans. As none have markings of any kind, my servant and I prised them open last night, only to discover ourselves quite perplexed."

"I take it the contents didn't belong to your aunt, then?" she suggested. "Forgive my manners, may I offer you tea, Lord Ailesleigh?"

"Uh, no. That's kind of you, Your Grace, but as I say, I'm intruding."

"I was about to have some myself."

He smiled, and the effect brought more sunshine to the room. Beth smiled in return, but Baxter remained unmoved.

"That is most kind," said Ailesleigh. "If you're indulging, I'd love to have some tea. In truth, I'm parched. I stayed at the Regent's house last night, and we've no supplies laid in yet."

Beth looked to Baxter. "Inspector, would you be a dear and ring for Miles?"

"Of course." The ICI inspector was about to pull on the velvet rope near the fireplace, when Miles returned to the morning room.

"You've anticipated us, Mr. Miles. I wonder if we might have some tea? Branham Blend, please."

"Very good, Your Grace. I came, because two gentlemen have called and ask for an interview. They've no card."

"Shall I speak with them for you?" asked Baxter.

"Are these men reporters, Miles?" asked Elizabeth.

"They deny representing any newspapers, and they're accents are American."

"Oh, I see," she answered, setting the book to one side and standing. "Do forgive me, Lord Ailesleigh, but as my husband's away, I should see if this is about an international matter. Inspector, would you accompany me?"

Baxter and Miles left with the duchess. Ailesleigh remained on his own. He sat quietly, observing the paintings and various photographs set about the sunlit space. It was the Queen Anne room, he'd been told, the largest of the house's morning parlours with two panoramic windows that overlooked the magnificent park beyond.

On his own, the visitor decided to explore, and he picked up a prominently displayed photograph of Duke Charles. It was hand-coloured, showing the peer in a bold Stuart tartan kilt and all the necessary accompaniments: short black coat, *sporran*, flashes, hose, and *sgian dubh*. The duke stood at the bottom of the main Haimsbury staircase, his right hand on the westernmost newel post. The ornate ironwork case had marble steps and risers. A pair of winged lion statues stood guard from atop each post. Haimsbury's hand was upon the lion's paw.

"You are very regal, sir," he said aloud, knowing no one would overhear him. "Have no fear regarding the coming trials, sir. You will never be alone, the One has promised it, and I shall keep watch, along with many others."

Footsteps approached, but the disguised angel had heard them long before the owner of those small shoes arrived. He turned to find the duchess returning on her own.

"The inspector's still talking with our American visitors. I apologise for abandoning you, Lord Ailesleigh."

"Not at all, my lady," he answered. "I hope I didn't overstep. I've been looking at this photograph. It's Duke Charles, I presume?"

"Oh, yes. It was taken shortly after he returned last year to claim his inheritance. My husband is my grandfather's nephew and his heir, and so he wears our family tartan. That kilt originally belonged to my late father."

The earl held the photograph, his eyes sweeping across the image. "Strange."

"Strange?" she asked, stepping closer.

"Yes, there's a distortion on the steps behind your husband. Is it intentional? Might it be a new development style, perhaps?"

Beth stared at the photograph. The print was exceptionally large, special-ordered to fit the ornate silver frame. "I don't see a distortion. Where do you mean?"

"Here," he said, indicating a cloudy portion of the image, just behind and several steps above the duke. "I thought you'd asked the photographer to create it intentionally."

"I've no idea what you..." she began, her dark eyes rounding. "Oh! That looks like..."

"You see it as well? A distorted image?"

"I'd never noticed it before, but you're right! Why has no one ever seen this, I wonder? Surely, it's some defect in the man's camera. Our friend, Martin Kepelheim, was there that morning. I'll ask him about it."

"Yes, I'm sure it's just a defect. But it is strange for the artist to hand-colour the distortion, don't you think? One might assume he'd try to disguise it. It reminds me of the spirit photographs that have become so popular. Oh, but wait! Here now," he said, seeing her reaction. "I've upset you. Sit, Your Grace. Please."

In his Ailesleigh disguise, the angel Hadraniel helped the duchess to a small sofa and sat beside her. "Shall I ring for someone?"

"No, I'm fine, really. But you'd begun to explain about the trunks at your late aunt's home. How is this connected to me?"

Baxter returned and assumed his former spot, two feet from the duchess. "The Americans have left, my lady. They're here on ICI matters, and so I asked them to call on Pennyweather at Queen Anne and arrange an interview with Lord Aubrey for tomorrow."

"Ah, yes, thank you," said Beth, who then turned to the visitor. "Lord Ailesleigh, I've known dear Mr. Baxter my entire life, and with my husband away, he's good enough to keep watch on business matters in the duke's absence. The American gentlemen are detectives with the Chicago Police."

"Has this anything to do with the duke's diplomatic mission?"

"I'm not sure, for my husband's visit is intentionally obscured. Some government matters require secrecy."

"Yet, *The Gazette* prints daily reports on the duke's itinerary."

"We've asked them to refrain, but the press seldom listen."

He smiled, bringing another ray of sunshine. "I appreciate the need for discretion regarding diplomatic missions, Your Grace. I've worked in those gilded corridors, as well as in the field, as some call it. Public service invariably leads to public scrutiny and endless curiosity. With so many articles regarding the duke's right of royal inheritance, it's a wonder you're not inundated with reporters every minute."

"They do pop round, when we least expect it," Beth told him.

"And I'm sure it's a great comfort to your husband, knowing that men such as Inspector Baxter keep watch on you. I noticed several men patrolling the grounds as my coach entered the park. Is that to fend off reporters? I pray nothing's amiss."

"Actually, the guards are normal for our household, Lord Ailesleigh. You might remember, I was abducted on my wedding night, and since then, our twin children, have been threatened. I refer to the shooting incident at their christening service last month, of course."

"Yes, I read about that," he answered. "I've a good friend who continues to talk about it. She was there that day and still suffers nightmares. Maisie Churchill. Do you know her?"

"Aunt Maisie?" Beth said happily. "I should hope so. Maisie is one of my Aunt Victoria's oldest friends, and she's also one of my godmothers. Her real name is Florence, but she's been called Maisie since she was a girl."

"Yes, I know. She and my late mother were dear friends," he answered as a footman entered. He pushed a rolling cart that held tea, coffee, and several selections of cakes, and crustless sandwiches. The servant placed the food on a low table near the duchess, who offered to pour. The doors shut again, leaving Beth and Inspector Baxter to interview the intriguing guest, completely unaware he was an angel.

"Do you take sugar, Lord Ailesleigh?" she asked. "Inspector, may I make you a cup as well?"

"Allow me to pour, my lady," the former butler replied.

"That's very good of you, Inspector."

The earl watched as Baxter expertly prepared the cups of tea. "Lemon, sir?"

"No, thank you, and just one cube of sugar. No milk. You know, my mother insisted I learn to prepare tea properly. Not just to pour it and add all the sugar and milk, but to boil the water and brew the tea. She died last year of pneumonia. I'm on my own now, but I think of her every time I make tea."

Baxter poured the steaming, caramel-coloured liquid into a pair of white cups, painted with red roses surrounding a filigree 'H&B' in gold. "Two sugars, my lady?" he asked as he reached for the tongs.

"Yes, please," Beth replied. "And milk."

Baxter handed a cup to the duchess, and then one to her guest. "One cube, no milk, no lemon, sir."

"Thank you, Inspector. My mother used nothing at all in hers. Quite mad, if you ask me. How can you live without a touch of sweetness?"

"Then, surely you'll have a slice of cake," said Elizabeth.

"Oh, no. I have an appointment shortly. Luncheon with a colleague, and his cook will be disappointed if I don't bring a hearty appetite. She's new and quite proud, you see."

"As are our cooks," the duchess said, as she stirred her tea. "Do I know this friend?"

"I doubt it. He's Russian."

"Russian? Might you mean Prince Anatole Romanov?"

The disguised angel smiled, his golden brown eyes glittering. "Why, yes! How did you guess? He's not well known to the peerage set, primarily to Whitehall denizens and the odd Cornish bookworm."

"The prince is a family friend," she told him. "And he's on the board of governors for our charity hospital."

"Charity hospital?" asked the disguised angel. "Do you mean the one on Whitechapel Road? The London?"

"No, this is new, though it's also in Whitechapel. We've renovated three warehouses on Mansell."

"When is it opening?"

"Very soon. In fact, we're meeting this morning to discuss the details."

"Your Grace, if you require additional funding, I'd be pleased to contribute."

"Would you?" she asked. "We're always looking for contributors. I'll send you a packet of information. Now, as you need to make a decision regarding these trunks, perhaps we should learn more about them. How are they of interest to me, Lord Ailesleigh?"

"Ah, yes, of course," he said. "They had no labels as I mentioned, so we broke the padlocks to open them. We discovered a collection of men's clothing. The apparel was bespoke and expensive, but a decade or more behind current fashion. There were personal items, too; pipes, tobacco, a few books, that sort of thing. One trunk had a leather box, filled with very fine men's jewellery. Several watches, a ring, stickpin. I'd assumed all these belonged to my aunt's late husband or perhaps his brother, but then I found a receipt from a jeweller inside one of the crates, near the bottom. It was made out to Lord Kesson."

Elizabeth nearly dropped her teacup in shock.

"Oh, my lady, do forgive me!" said the angel, seeing her reaction. "What a foolish thing to do. Lord Kesson was your father, of course, and he passed away when you were quite young. I am thoughtless. Do forgive me, my lady. I really should have softened that blow, but it's why I've come to you. I believe the trunks and crates all belonged to your late father."

"No, no," she managed to answer, trying her best to recover. "How can my father's belongings turn up in your late aunt's home? I don't understand. He never leased any property. Why would he? He owned three beautiful houses."

"No, he wouldn't have, obviously. But you see, I found other items that belonged to your late father. There is no doubt that all the items were his. Your Grace, I'd be happy to bring them all here for your inspection. With your permission, I can send word to my servant to forward them immediately."

"Yes, I think you should," she managed to say. "Is it possible for you to delay these lawyers from implementing your late aunt's will for another week? I should like to make sure nothing of my father's is missed, and today's quite impossible for me."

"I've tried, Your Grace. They are quite adamant. The removal men come first thing tomorrow morning."

"What firm is it?" she asked.

Baxter took pen and paper, ready to write.

"Simon and Albatross," the disguised angel answered. "Sir Edmund Simon is retired. Sir Jeremiah Albatross manages all the clients now."

"Albatross?" she asked. "A most unfortunate name."

Baxter had written down the information and glanced up from the paper. "I've seen a sign with that name, my lady. Is the firm in Fulham, Lord Ailesleigh?"

"Yes, Inspector, it is."

Baxter stood. "If I may, Your Grace, I shall take care of this. If you'd allow me to speak on your behalf, I'll make sure nothing is removed from the house before you approve. What is the address of your property, my lord?"

"Number 12, Gloucester Terrace."

Beth wrote out a quick letter and gave it to Baxter. "Tell Sir Jeremiah how grateful I can be in return for his help, Inspector," she told him. "But impress upon him that refusal would give me cause for legal action."

"Very good, my lady," said Baxter, smiling. "I'll leave right away."

"Thank you, Inspector," she said as he left. She turned back to the disguised angel. "I should like to ask Lord Aubrey to see your aunt's home as well, when it's convenient to you both. Would that be all right with you, Lord Ailesleigh? The earl is my cousin and knew my father well. He might recognise items I would not."

"Of course. Though I work in Whitehall's maze of buildings and corridors, I've yet to meet Lord Aubrey. I should enjoy that. His reputation in my branch is legendary."

"Are you with the Foreign Office?"

"Yes, and I'm honoured to occupy the same office once used by Lord Aubrey's late father. At that time, Robert Stuart was head of Consular Services. The late earl was somewhat of an inspiration to me, if you must know. He left very big shoes."

"Dear Uncle Robert," she sighed. "I miss him so very much, especially now."

"Why especially now?"

"Oh—well, it's because of my cousin's wife," Beth managed to answer, covering the slip. "Lady Aubrey is close to confinement with their first child, you see. The countess and I share the same physicians, and she's become like a sister. Cordelia is a lovely young woman."

"Do you mean Cordelia Wychwright? I had the honour to meet her once, long ago, at Covent Garden." He finished the tea and set the cup on the table. "You've been very kind to me, Your Grace, and I'd love to stay, but I've taken far too much of your time."

"Must you go?" she heard herself ask. Beth had no idea why, but something about this man reminded her of Charles. He looked nothing like her husband, and yet she felt drawn to him, as if the man had only just touched her husband's arm or hand, or spoken to him. She wanted to ask about it, but didn't dare. Surely, Ailesleigh would think her mad. It was a nonsensical, supernatural idea, like one might find in a Brontë or Stoker novel.

"I needn't leave immediately," he said, happy to be of service. "Finally meeting you in person is more enjoyable than I imagined. Oh, and by that I refer to your reputation, of course, Your Grace. I didn't mean to be so personal."

"You needn't apologise, Lord Ailesleigh, and you're very thoughtful to come by. I'm sure most people would have thrown out the trunks without caring who owned them. Once the house is empty, do you plan to reside at Regent's Park?"

"Oh, not at all," he answered, part of his mind listening to the duchess, another keeping watch on activities in Theseus's castle, whilst still another part spoke silently to Romanov. "I've no need for it. Ailesleigh House and our Cornwall castle are plenty enough," he said. "Actually, I thought I might sell the Regency place. Or lease it, I suppose. I certainly don't need two London homes."

Elizabeth laughed. "Nor do I, yet I have a great many. My husband's turned Queen Anne into headquarters for Inner Circle Intelligence, but we own other homes. Loudain House, Branham Castle, Anjou Court, and Kesson House."

"Queen Anne is well known as a former royal palace, but Branham and Anjou are also palaces, aren't they?" he asked.

"You surprise me, Lord Ailesleigh. Very few know that. Yes, Anjou was used as a palace by Henry II and his son Richard. Branham Castle and Branham Hall in Kent are also listed as palaces, though unofficially."

"And Haimsbury?" he asked, the disguised angel's mind still multitasking. "I understand this house might also be listed as a palace soon."

"So the newspapers claim," she answered tactfully. "My husband is planning to build a new house, though he thinks it a surprise. We own all of King's Meadow and the deer park beyond. It's just the other side of Haimsbury Drive. Charles wants to put a house on the meadow and leave this home to our son."

"Oh, now that would make a splendid setting! And as it's to be a surprise, I promise to say nothing, Your Grace. And at the risk of sounding impertinent, I've a very good friend who's an architect. He's looking for commissions. He read engineering at Cambridge and took an entire litany of drawing courses. He's discreet and very reliable. If you're considering applicants, I'd be pleased to put forward his name."

"Ask your friend to write us a letter, and I'll see that Charles reads it, when he returns."

"I'm sure the duke will return very soon," he said. "Whatever mission he's on, I'm certain God watches over him, my lady, and that Christ is his Shepherd."

Suddenly, Beth began to weep, her eyes filling with tears. This stranger couldn't possibly know how difficult talking of Charles was for her, and yet he seemed to know exactly what to say.

"Thank you," she said, wiping her eyes. "Forgive the tears. I think the mould on the falling leaves is causing my eyes to water."

"Yes, I'm sure that's it."

He stood. "I really must go, but I'm serious about contributing to this hospital."

"Are you?"

"Oh, yes. You say it's on Mansell? I've noticed construction there. With your permission, I should like to stop by and tour it."

"There's a tour this morning," she said. "At eleven. I've a short meeting after with the management, and then I may have luncheon with a friend of mine, if she's available. Her name's Ida Stanley, and she's studying nursing in our school."

"Your school?" he asked.

"The hospital is a teaching institution, and we offer free tuition for any qualified nursing or medical applicant who cannot pay. Those who can pay, help to defray the costs."

"That is quite exciting!" Ailesleigh exclaimed. "I shall definitely stop by there. Perhaps, I can convince Prince Anatole to let me reschedule my meeting with him."

"Then, you must ride with me," she heard herself offer. *Why would I do this?* "That is, if you wish to see it today."

"That's kind of you, but I shouldn't wish to intrude."

"It would be a help," Beth replied. "We could talk about the trunks on the way there, and you can tell me about your inspirational castle in Cornwall."

"What time do you leave? I daresay you've probably not had your breakfast yet, though the food on the cart would be plenty for me."

"Probably not before half ten, but I must change first. Would you stay for breakfast?"

"I'd be honoured," said the angel. His job this morning was simple. Whilst the duke had dinner in the mirror world of Sen-Sen, Hadraniel assumed his London guise as Ailesleigh to keep an eye on the duchess and her cousin; for unbeknownst to either, death awaited them in Whitechapel, and it was the angel's job to stop it.

CHAPTER TWELVE

Real World – The Hospital Meeting in Whitechapel

Hadraniel enjoyed the beautiful churches, the colourful gardens, and even the sounds of London, but the poverty and depravity reminded him why the One sent the Son to die for mankind's sins. What a marvel that sacrifice was! What a miracle! Indeed, the Cross was so miraculous, so utterly magnanimous that Hadraniel found it difficult to understand why any human would refuse the Son's free gift of salvation and eternal life. Why would anyone choose to serve Darkness, when Light is so beautiful? But then some of his own brethren had made such a foolish choice, when they rebelled. Now some lingered in strong chains, far beneath the Earth; whilst others plotted and planned on Earth, to undo the Son's sacrifice and find their own way to raise the dead.

Hadraniel had enjoyed eating breakfast with the family and, as he waited for Elizabeth to dress, he talked with Mrs. Baxter and Mary Wilsham in the nursery, and even got to hold the twin infants, Robby and Georgianna Sinclair. Doing so brought back wonderful memories, for Hadra had also held an infant Charles Sinclair many years earlier, whilst dressed in the guise of a Presbyterian minister named Dr. Jedediah Winslow.

Now, he sat beside Charles Sinclair's wife, sharing a coach ride with two of Elizabeth's guardians, a burly man named Hamish Granger and a former Texas Ranger named Captain Crenshaw. These two capable ICI men had become Elizabeth's personal guards when she travelled, ordered by Lord Aubrey, and she'd come to enjoy their company.

Their driver was Calvin O'Connell, a man of Irish descent, who'd spent his entire life working at Branham Hall and recently transferred to London. O'Connell was a stern-faced, thirty-year-old with wild red hair, pockmarked face, and small black eyes; tall and sturdy, with looks that shouted of danger mixed with even more danger. At six-foot-seven, O'Connell stood two inches taller than Hamish Granger, with an additional twenty-five pounds of muscle. The men of Haimsbury Mews staged weekly boxing matches inside the Queen Anne equestrian arena, and servants from both houses and even their families attended. Of the forty-two grooms, seven drivers, and sixty groundsmen who participated in the bouts, each a fine specimen of manhood, O'Connell was unbeaten. Beth's human protectors formed a formidable team, but today she'd need more.

She'd need something that only *an angel could offer.*

They arrived at three minutes before the hour, greeted by several well-dressed men and one very tall woman. All the men bowed their heads and the woman curtsied as they were introduced by their leader, a man with an American accent.

"Welcome to the Haimsbury-Branham Hospital, Your Grace. We've corresponded for many weeks, but I've not had the honour to meet you. I'm Dr. Nathan Kessler from Johns Hopkins."

"Oh, yes!" Elizabeth answered, smiling. "You're Lord Braxton's friend. I'm very glad to meet you at last, Dr. Kessler."

"Lord Braxton?" asked Kessler.

"Oh, well that's Dr. Michael Emerson. He's only just become the earl, you see. His father passed away very recently. Surely, you'd heard?"

"Ah, no, but I'm sorry to hear it," muttered the American.

"Michael mentioned that your work on germ theory is considered groundbreaking, Dr. Kessler. Allow me to introduce Lord Daniel Porter, the Earl of Ailesleigh. Lord Ailesleigh wishes to tour our facility as a possible donor."

"Excellent. It's an honour to meet you, Lord Ailesleigh."

"The honour's mine, sir," said the angel. "You have an unusual American accent. Do I hear a hint of Maine mixed with Texas? Perhaps, a dash of something else? Austrian or German?"

A shadow passed through the American's features, but he recovered quickly. "Why, yes, I travel a great deal, you see. All over the world, and so my accent varies. Now, if you'll allow me, I'd like to introduce our team, beginning with Mrs. Gwendolyn Howard, our head nursing instructor."

"Mrs. Howard, I'm very happy to meet you," said the duchess to the tall woman. "Mr. Treves at the London speaks very highly of your teaching skills, with glowing tribute and admiration. We're delighted you agreed to teach here."

"It's my honour, Your Grace," the woman answered, her broad accent hinting of Yorkshire. "I've a few ideas I'd be pleased to discuss with you, when you've the time."

"I'd like that, Mrs. Howard. Perhaps, once we're finished, you and I might arrange a time to do just that. You could come to our home for tea."

"That would be a great honour and pleasure, my lady. Thank you. And it's an honour to meet you as well, Lord Ailesleigh."

"That's kind of you, Mrs. Howard, but I'm just here to observe," said the disguised angel.

"I'd be pleased to show you our nursing classroom, sir. We've enrolled twelve women. All are married with one exception. And not one could afford tuition elsewhere. The duchess has accomplished a very great thing here, my lord."

Hadraniel knew Howard's background. Gwendolyn was physically abused by her father and her first husband, Lester Ryan, who'd died of drink six years ago. She had three children by Ryan and two from her current husband, Abe Howard. Abe was nearing sixty, but treated his wife with kindness and was generous with all their children. In Howard, Gwen had found a fine man who loved God. She wanted the same for every young woman, hence her enthusiasm for the project.

Hadraniel wished he could spend hours, even days talking with the human woman, but his task lay elsewhere this day. He also knew that other angels watched over Mrs. Howard, and so he answered her with these words, "The duchess and her husband want nothing less than a new paradigm of society in this quarter, Mrs. Howard. A goal, which you clearly share. You are an exceptional woman, and this hospital is blessed by your presence."

The previous shadow crept back into Nathan Kessler's features, and he cast a scolding glance at Howard before continuing the introductions. The American had a low opinion of women and introduced those he felt mattered far more, the well-dressed men: Dr. Jeremiah Pennington, Professor of Chemistry; Dr. Laurence Mallory, Head of Patient Care; Dr. Richard Stone, Head of the Out-Patient Infirmary; and Dr. Jules Boucher, a visiting professor from the Sorbonne, who'd come to instruct staff and students on proper use of sterilisation equipment and the new autoclave rooms.

Elizabeth smiled patiently as Kessler went on to give a long speech regarding the proper role of charity hospitals and medical schools. The harangue revealed the American's bias and paternalistic attitude, and the duchess tolerated condescending remarks, such as 'I'm sure these medical terms are new to you' or 'sterilisation means cleaning germs, my lady', or worse 'a man would understand, but when I say incision, I refer to the act of cutting into a patient's flesh'.

Finally, when the long-winded speech at last ended, Beth responded magnanimously. "Thank you, Dr. Kessler. It is a great pleasure to meet each one of you today and to learn such new and very interesting medical terms, too! I only wish Duke Charles could have been here, but as he's travelling, I'm afraid you'll have to make do with me and my woman's brain."

Kessler and the other men chuckled at this, and Beth offered Mrs. Howard an understanding wink. "The duke and I pray this hospital will bring healing and life to those with no ability to pay, as well as opportunities for careers as nurses and doctors. And unlike other schools, the HBH will accept any qualified student, regardless of his or her financial situation."

Again, the group applauded, and a few exchanged knowing glances, for the last phrase implied scholarship students. Hadraniel knew Nathan Kessler well. Kessler frowned on such arrangements, believing the best physicians were men from *better* families; meaning they had lots of money. The angel saw beyond Kessler's pretence at charity and suspected the shadow that crept into his face went deep into a rotten soul. He'd have to keep an eye on the so-called American.

Beth continued. "The dream that built this hospital is less than a year old, yet here we stand, inside a shining new facility built to strict specifications, and in record time. I congratulate the builders and all the men and women who've made this dream a reality. And I look forward to this tour. But where are Dr. Emerson and Dr. Gehlen? I understood they'd both be with us this morning. Have you any knowledge of their whereabouts?"

Kessler cleared his throat. "Forgive me, Your Grace, Dr. Emerson planned to join us this morning but is delayed by an emergency at St. Mary's. I believe Dr. Gehlen is interviewing a candidate for the medical school. I'm sure he'll meet us somewhere along the tour. If you're ready?"

"Yes, of course," she said. "I've not seen the facilities for nearly two months, and I'm eager to see the improvements made since."

"A great deal's changed since then, my lady. A great deal. Now, I've taken the liberty of arranging the tour in linear fashion, beginning with the operating theatres and autoclave rooms. Then, we'll explore several of the nicer patient wards, view one of the isolation areas for highly infectious cases, and then end with refreshments in the public lounge."

"It sounds as though you've arranged an interesting tour, but I'd like to begin with the lower levels, Dr. Kessler," the duchess told him.

"But my lady, those areas haven't yet been cleared."

"Cleared of what? Surely, there are no impediments."

Kessler looked exceedingly uncomfortable and tried to protest. He pulled the duchess to one side and began a whispered conversation. Hadraniel remained with the main group, but his supernatural ears meant he heard every word.

"They've not been cleared of possible intruders," whispered Kessler. "Lord Aubrey's instructions were quite clear. We're not to lead you into areas that might allow concealment."

Beth's left brow curved into a sharp question mark. "My cousin gave you such an order? I very much doubt that, Dr. Kessler. Even if he did, I am countermanding it. I appreciate your concern, but I wish to begin with the lower levels. Shall we proceed?"

"Your Grace, the tour has been planned for maximum time and safety. It could be dangerous to alter it."

"Dangerous?" she asked him, her dark eyes boring into his. "Why would anywhere in this hospital prove dangerous to me?

"What I mean to say, Duchess, is I've had the tour planned for days and cleared everything with the earl's people."

"His people? And who are they?"

"His men, my lady. The agents working under his supervision. Please, may we just follow the original tour? I'm sure, if your husband were here, he would understand."

"I understand perfectly well, Dr. Kessler, and I wish to begin with the lower levels. The blueprints for those areas were changed recently, and I want to make sure the changes were followed according to *my* wishes."

"And when Lord Aubrey arrives? How shall I answer him, when he asks why the tour plan has changed? He was quite firm in his orders."

"Dr. Kessler, does it say Aubrey Hospital on the sign outside?"

"No, my lady, but the earl looks after your welfare in your husband's absence, does he not? As I say, his instructions were very clear. I shouldn't wish to disregard them."

"Why?" she asked, putting the American on the spot.

"Well, because he's an important, influential peer, and..."

"I see," she said, her voice lowering. "You really don't know anything about me, do you, Dr. Kessler? It's true, we've corresponded, but have you ever actually asked about me? About my position?"

He sighed, wishing the stubborn woman would do as she was told. "I know that you're the wife of an important duke, and that duke influences a great deal in London. I know the duke is rumoured to be a possible royal heir, and as his wife, it's important to maintain charitable institutions. And as the duke's wife, your influence might..."

The American's foolishness was mercifully cut off, for just then, Anthony Gehlen arrived and overheard every babbling word. "Nathan, you might want to stop talking now, whilst that foot you're chewing on still has a few toes left."

"What?" asked Kessler.

Gehlen went on. "Are you aware you're talking to the wealthiest woman in the entire European continent? Not because of her husband's money. She's the richest all on her own. Nor does she receive power from her husband. Beth didn't become a duchess by marrying a duke. She's been a duchess since she was, what was it, Beth? Ten years old?"

"Eleven," she answered. "Apparently, Dr. Kessler isn't aware that the Branham duchy goes to the first child, be that child a boy or girl."

"Elizabeth's duchess in her own right, Nathan, and she's got more power in that pretty little finger than your President Harrison has in his entire body; and he's got a sizeable girth!" Anthony kissed

Beth's cheek. "Sorry to be late. Here now, since Charles can't be with you, let me take your arm. Where do you want to start?"

Ailesleigh had made his way over and answered for her, "I think she wants to begin with the lower levels. Correct, Duchess?"

"Correct," she said. "Shall we proceed, gentlemen?"

Kessler had no choice, but his angry expression said far more than his mouth did. He motioned to a uniformed porter. "Mr. Stern, it looks like we're going below first. Run down and make certain no one is lurking, that doesn't belong. Take Mr. Cooper with you. Pay special heed to areas four and five. See everything there is stowed away. And lock rooms nine and ten. Quickly now!"

The porters left the main area, and Elizabeth signalled to Hamish Granger and Captain Crenshaw, standing nearby. The burly guardians joined her. Beth turned to the director.

"Dr. Kessler, allow me to introduce two very fine gentlemen, who are ever at my side. Mr. Granger served with the Scots Guards and can hit a white hare in a snow storm with his eyes shut. Our Captain Crenshaw is from Texas. He's a former Ranger who, according to Lord Aubrey, can hit a scorpion from the saddle whilst at full gallop. Both these men are armed."

The men drew back their coats, revealing concealed handguns. Granger's Webley rested inside a black leather shoulder holster. Crenshaw wore a hand-tooled hip holster, containing a pair of pearl-handled, double-action Colt Thunderers.

Though the shadow remained on his face, Kessler forced a smile. "Gentlemen, you are welcome on our tour. Shall we, Your Grace?"

Flanked by Lord Pencaitland (Gehlen's new title) and Lord Ailesleigh, Elizabeth followed Kessler. The group of medical professionals walked alongside, and the entourage made its way through the reception lobby towards a large white door.

"This leads to one of our six lifts," said Kessler. "There are two in each of the three buildings." He pressed a button, and a drive shaft automatically moved the door to one side, revealing a metal grating, which Kessler opened. "If everyone would enter?"

"I'm sorry to be late, Beth," Gehlen whispered as they entered with Ailesleigh. "I'll explain later, but there's a problem with a new applicant. Kessler's not happy about it, but I think the young man would make a brilliant physician. I can't say more now, but I promise to explain later." He looked at the disguised angel, saying, "I'm Gehlen, by the way. And you are?"

"Daniel Porter," replied the angel.

"He's also the Earl of Ailesleigh," Beth added. "And Dr. Gehlen is also the Earl of Pencaitland. Oh, hello, Mrs. Howard."

The tall nurse had found her way to the corner near the duchess. She bent down and whispered, "Thank you for all your efforts, Your Grace. And thank you for speaking up! It's nice to see a woman take charge sometimes."

"Given enough time, our little duchess could own all of London," said Gehlen.

"I think, the duchess is going to change the world," added Ailesleigh knowingly.

The company assembled inside the spacious car. Kessler closed the grating and threw the switch to LL2. The car descended in smooth fashion.

"You'll notice there's very little jostling," the American told them proudly. "The mechanism is electric, and the installation was overseen by Werner von Siemens himself. You'll also notice, that the car has electric lighting in the ceiling."

He pointed upwards, and Beth's eyes followed. "I'm glad to see how well it works," she said. "I insisted there be lifts and electricity in all three buildings. I presume they'll be used to transfer patients?"

"For those unable to climb, yes, but if they're able, I shall encourage taking the stairs. All stairs are well-lit and designed for easy climbing. I prefer patients to participate in regular exercise, whenever possible, Your Grace. For those who cannot climb, the lift readily accommodates wheeled chairs and cots."

The motion stopped, and Kessler drew the grating aside. The lower level hallway was brightly lit, and the sounds of hammers, saws, and men's voices echoed within it.

"I apologise for the noise," said Kessler. "It's one reason I didn't wish to bring you down. The men are still finishing out the last of the storage areas. Watch your step. The workmen sometimes leave things lying about. We'll all go to the right."

The group exited the lift, but Elizabeth turned left and walked six or seven steps towards the sound of construction.

Annoyed by her unwillingness to follow instructions, Kessler repeated himself. "We'll all go right and inspect the storage areas first."

"But isn't the morgue in that direction?" she asked, pointing down the other hallway.

"The morgue is not on the tour."

Beth looked puzzled. "Why isn't it? I receive daily reports from the contractor, and he told me last week, that all the lower level areas were finished. Why may I not see the morgue? More importantly, if the construction is complete, then what are these men doing?"

Kessler looked like a rat in a trap. "They're making a small repair to the boiler room, and the morgue is hardly the sort of place a woman of breeding would want to visit. Now, if you'll follow me to the right, we'll view the storage areas and staff housing facilities. This way, please." Again, he walked right, but Elizabeth took the left path, accompanied by Gehlen and Ailesleigh. Granger and Crenshaw obediently followed the duchess.

"Your Grace, that is the wrong way!" shouted Kessler impatiently.

"No, it is the right way," she told him. "The morgue is down this corridor, and I..."

"No, you're wrong," he interrupted. "The morgue is not even in this portion of the lower level. To reach it, you'll need to pass through the connecting tunnel, which is locked.

Elizabeth stared at Kessler. "Then, the morgue's location has miraculously moved from its position on the blueprints."

"I'm sure you're remembering wrong, Duchess."

Gehlen smiled. "Beth never remembers wrongly, not when it comes to recalling blueprints, books, newspapers, even sounds. She has an eidetic memory, Dr. Kessler. If she says the morgue is this way, then you can bet the crown jewels it is."

"Is there something down here you don't want me to see, Dr. Kessler?" asked Elizabeth.

"No, Duchess. And you're right. The morgue is down this corridor, but it remains locked, and I haven't the key."

"Not to worry," she replied sweetly. "Mr. Granger has keys with him. I do own these buildings, you know."

"Yes, I'm sure, but I had the door re-keyed two days ago. That's why the morgue isn't on the tour."

Elizabeth gazed at the man with a mixture of anger and curiosity. Was it Kessler's American upbringing that led him to make such a faux pas, or was he just an arrogant fool? His letters had been cordial and conciliatory, perfectly respectful and proper. Perhaps, the typewritten letters were composed by a secretary? Kessler may not have read them before signing. No matter, he was here and had management authority, but that was about to change. Beth had no intention of letting a misogynistic fool manage her hospital.

"Why were the locks changed, Dr. Kessler?" she asked.

"Due to a break-in. I sent a letter to Lord Aubrey about it, but never received a reply. Perhaps, the letter failed to reach him. Duchess, this facility is filled with expensive equipment and pharmaceuticals. Would you have thieves gain access to them?"

"Dr. Gehlen, were you aware of this break-in?"

"There was an minor incident," Anthony told her, "but hardly a reason for changing locks down here. Someone broke into a medical school office. Mine, actually."

"Yours? Was anything taken?" she asked him.

"Not that I could discover. Edmund Reid came by and we talked about it. I also discussed it with Lord Aubrey, and he saw no reason for changing any of the locks."

The strange shadow drifted into Kessler's features again and caused them to form a sinister smile. Beth shuddered. She'd seen that sort of smile before: on Sir William Trent.

"What's done is done," the American told them flatly. "Shall we continue this way?"

Granger looked to his mistress. "Your Grace, we can fetch one of the new keys, if you wish to see the morgue."

"No, Mr. Granger, that isn't necessary. We'll leave it for later."

Kessler's eerie smile widened. "This way, everyone. We'll take a look at the housing for the guards."

"Guards?" asked Dr. Boucher. "Why you guard a place of healing? Is it this breaking-in that happen?"

"In part," said Kessler. "Inspector Reid of H-Division not only spoke to Dr. Gehlen, he's talked with me often since I took command. He thinks thieves might find our medicines tempting and could enter through open windows on warm nights. Therefore, guards will watch the entire facility."

"Mr. Reid's a fine man, and he knows the East End very well," the duchess noted. "I shall speak with him about it, when next we meet."

"Do know him, my lady?" asked Mrs. Howard.

"The inspector is a very dear friend," Beth replied. "Very dear. Tell me, Dr. Kessler, will these guards be armed?"

"No, Your Grace. I shall hire police constables. They're trained to disarm a lawbreaker without the use of firearms. All will be competent with truncheons."

Beth turned to Granger for advice. "How would you provide security for such a large building with many hundreds of inhabitants, Mr. Granger?"

Hamish answered firmly and quickly. "You train them yourself, my lady, just as we do at all the estates. Police constables are fine men, but underpaid and overworked, meaning they take extra jobs to make up the lack. They often fall asleep on duty. Lax security is the enemy of rest, my lady. And, I should think, the enemy of healing as well."

"Lax?" asked Kessler. "I hadn't considered hiring policemen lax, Mr. Granger, but if you prefer another model for the problem, I'm happy to comply. I serve only as the interim director. Whoever is hired for the permanent position will settle the issue in his own way."

"Or hers," noted the nurse. Kessler did not smile.

Beth liked this man less and less. "My family have a great deal of experience in security matters. Mr. Granger will take charge of hiring and training all the guards. Now, may we continue?"

The muscles in Kessler's jaw tensed. He detested this pampered peeress's assertive nature, but responded with sugary charm. "As you wish, Your Grace."

They completed the tour of the sub-basement and basement areas, avoiding both morgues. They did view an autopsy theatre, where medical students would observe and learn forensics and dissection methods.

Once upstairs, they toured a few of the wards, with Kessler droning on and on in his peculiar accent. Ailesleigh kept pace with Gehlen, who held Beth's arm. The disguised angel marvelled at Elizabeth's depth of knowledge. She addressed many of her questions to Mrs. Howard, asking about furnishings and equipment, how patient beds would be cleaned, operating theatres staffed, and whether patients and their families would receive education on home hygiene. Kessler had a habit of correcting the nurse, further irritating his benefactress. It soon became obvious to everyone that he was carrying an ever-expanding chip on his shoulder regarding the peeress.

During the tour of the autoclave closets, Elizabeth surprised Boucher by asking insightful questions about germ theory and Listerism. She spoke to him in French, asking if he might consider remaining through Christmas, or even beyond. She asked if she could speak with Boucher privately about the current management situation. Kessler's letters claimed he spoke French fluently; yet he took no note of it.

"This will change medicine, Dr. Boucher. Steam sterilisation is a wonder! And it should help to reduce our nosocomial infection rate," she told him in English.

"You know this word, Duchess? Nosocomial? Is not a layperson's word, my lady."

"Her Grace knows entire libraries of medical terms, Dr. Boucher," said Gehlen proudly. "She reads and retains. You'll find Duchess Elizabeth is exceedingly bright."

"*Mais oui!* So I am seeing," Boucher replied.

"That's kind of you both," she told them. "With regard to general infections, where do you stand on Dr. Lister's use of carbolic acid?"

"Carbolic is good, but scratch the skin and eye, my lady."

"Yes, but he's now diluting it and uses it successfully for surgery. He's developed it into a spray, which has seen great success. I've asked him to come here in a few months and teach germ theory."

"You invited Dr. Lister to come here?" Kessler asked.

"Yes," she told him. "Dr. Lister and my grandfather are good friends. I've known Joseph and his wife Agnes since I was a girl. Twas Dr. Lister, who encouraged my love of science."

Kessler smiled, another rising of that peculiar shadow—as if some other entity lurked behind the mask. "That explains your surface knowledge, but books do not provide comprehensive learning, Duchess. You need experience to understand the secret workings of man. Shall we continue?"

"What sort of comment is that?" asked Gehlen. "I believe you owe our founder an apology, Kessler."

"No, he's right. I'm merely an armchair student," Beth insisted, deciding to let the insult drop for the moment. "Let's continue."

She walked with Gehlen and Ailesleigh as they followed Kessler to the student dormitories. After touring the men's and women's sides, they entered the glassed gardens that formed walk-throughs from one building to the next. Here, sunshine and fresh water enlivened flowers, birds, and bees whilst providing healing to the senses and the weary soul. The group gathered near a high wooden table, filled with an assortment of herbaceous plants.

"Who's acting as our gardener?" asked the duchess. "I see many healing plants here. Have you hired a herbologist?"

Kessler joined her near the table. "It's my wife, Duchess. She has a green thumb, and gardening keeps her mind occupied. I imagine you have a large staff to keep your plants green and happy, but as these areas are somewhat small, my wife looks after them."

Beth touched several of the colourful herbs. "Mrs. Kessler's brought a wide selection of herbs. I see St. John's wort, feverfew, milk thistle, valerian, and..." she paused. "Dr. Kessler, why would your wife raise pennyroyal?"

"Why wouldn't she? Pennyroyal is used for liver ailments, fever, cough, and some say it's effective against this new influenza. Isn't that so, Dr. Boucher?"

The Frenchman touched the purple flowers on the plant. "Oui, it is so, but there are other uses, too, no?"

"There are," said the duchess coolly, her eyes on Kessler, "which is why I ask. Abortion is illegal and immoral. I will not have anyone performing it in this hospital. Is that clear?"

Kessler's shadowy smile returned, a smug indifferent and superior sort of grin that sent a chill down her spine. "I assure you, Duchess, I would never break the law."

"And God's word?" asked Ailesleigh. "Do you consider breaking his laws, sir?"

Kessler stared into the angel's face, as if trying to see past the disguise. Unable to do so, he shook his shoulders, shaking off a guise of his own. "A hospital is hardly the place for theology. It's a place of science. Am I right?" he asked his colleagues. "Now, shall we all proceed to the lounge and enjoy some light refreshments?"

Gehlen pulled Beth close, and Ailesleigh took her other side as the entourage made its way to the public lounge. It was a great space, anchored by a brick fireplace, where patients and visitors could read, talk, enjoy games, or eat a small meal. Today, a group of student nurses served tea, cider, crumpets, cheese, fruit compote, and iced ginger cakes. One of these students was Ida Ross Stanley, who stopped to talk with the duchess and Dr. Gehlen. Ida wore the dark blue uniform of a nursing student, topped by a pinafore embroidered with 'HBH' in red-and-gold thread. Her strawberry blonde hair was tucked up beneath a white muslin bonnet.

Beth offered introductions. "Lord Ailesleigh, allow me to introduce Mrs. Ida Stanley, a very dear friend to both my husband and myself. Ida, you look wonderful."

"Thank you, Your Grace. And it's an honour to meet you, Lord Ailesleigh."

"My pleasure, Mrs. Stanley," said the disguised angel. He'd been observing the humans in the room, all the while keeping close to the duchess. Elizabeth Sinclair was in danger, but he'd not been told the source of that danger. Even angels were sometimes kept in the dark regarding the One's plans. Hadraniel believed this Kessler person had a very dark secret.

"Have you begun your classes yet?" Beth asked Ida.

"I have, my lady," she replied. "There are twelve of us in all. Mrs. Howard and Mrs. Staunton are instructors. Both are very kind to us." She pointed to her slightly rounded stomach and added, "Mrs. Howard promised I could study from home once the baby is born."

"When is your confinement?" asked Beth.

"Not for another four months. I'm happy to say the morning sickness is past now."

"I'm glad to hear that, Ida," said Gehlen. "If you need anything, I keep regular office hours in the dispensary, and I see your husband almost daily at Leman Street."

"Yes, sir, he talks of you often, Lord Pencaitland."

Hearing the woman use his peerage title made Anthony laugh. "That's a title I never imagined having, Ida. My father hated my choice of careers. It would have irked him terribly to know a physician is called by his precious title. Just call me Dr. Gehlen."

Stanley blushed sweetly. "You're very kind, sir. My Elbert thinks the world of you. Being part of the ICI and using his mind again pleases him more than he could ever say. He said Prince Anatole might come today. Have you seen him lately, my lady?"

"Not for over a week," Elizabeth replied. "But Lord Ailesleigh works with the prince, perhaps he knows more."

The disguised angel had been watching Kessler. The American was in deep conversation with several men that Hadraniel knew were foreigners. But something about the growing number of visitors near the lounge doors caused his senses to tingle. Most were reporters, but at least one of them wasn't. Nor was he human.

Despite this, Hadraniel's compartmentalised brain heard the question regarding Romanov. "Ah, Prince Anatole has been visiting Paris and Vienna," he told the women. "He and I met up there, in fact. I've been posted to Paris for the past few months, but word of my aunt's death brought me home. The prince and I shared a steamer back from Calais."

"Will he be attending this morning?" asked Beth.

"No, I'm afraid he's meeting with the Russian ambassador. His Highness hoped to avoid Baron de Stahl, but sometimes a small cog threatens to stop the whole machine."

Elizabeth laughed. "I take it the baron is the small cog?"

"He sees himself as the entire machine, Your Grace," replied the angel.

"Diplomats aren't the only ones who reach beyond their position, Lord Ailesleigh," said Elizabeth as she took Ida Stanley's hand. "Do sit, Ida. You've gone pale. You're carrying an extra person now. Sit down and rest your feet."

"I shouldn't, my lady," said Ida nervously, her eyes on Kessler.

Beth noticed the glance. "Surely, nursing students may sit now and then?"

"We're to keep working, Your Grace. If we finish a task, then we're to report to Mrs. Staunton for instruction."

"Surely, she'd allow you to sit for a moment."

"I'd better not."

Beth pushed back her own chair and stood. "Very well. If you may not sit, then neither shall I."

Gehlen and Ailesleigh stood as well. Seeing this, Kessler excused himself from the intense conversation. Gehlen noticed the two men with whom he'd discoursed began talking to one another, and a moment later, both left; each to a different direction.

Kessler approached the duchess and boldly took her arm. "I hope you're not leaving?"

"Not at all," Beth replied, pulling back the arm. "I've just been speaking with my friend, and she's refused to sit because she fears breaking your regulation. Therefore, I've decided to stand."

Kessler shook his head. "If she's completed her task, then she should talk to a supervisor and get further instructions."

"Surely, a moment off her feet is permitted?"

"Even if it were, all the chairs are occupied, Duchess. We would need to send for more from the stores."

"There's no need for that," said Ailesleigh. "Please, Mrs. Stanley, take my chair. I'm happy to stand."

"Your gallantry cheers my heart, Lord Ailesleigh," said the duchess. "Do sit, Ida."

Kessler waved to one of the porters. "Bring two more chairs, Mr. Lowell!"

Shortly, the man returned with a pair of wooden chairs. Ailesleigh took one, and Kessler the other.

"I wonder, have you met my good friend, Mrs. Stanley?" Beth asked the interim director. "Ida's husband is an agent with my husband's intelligence organisation, the ICI."

Kessler's tone became conciliatory. "Mrs. Stanley, I apologise, if my previous instructions made you think an invitation from the duchess should be refused. Of course, a lady who's carrying new life must rest her feet. Forgive me, all of you. Sometimes, I become so engrossed in my work that I fail to see past my own nose. I hope you'll overlook my American ways."

"That's kind of you, Dr. Kessler," said Ida. "I understand how a man can love his work. My husband's the ICI liaison to H-Division and often becomes engrossed in work. Happily, Elbert leaves work long enough to take lunch with me."

"As it should be," said Gehlen.

That same slithering shadow crossed Kessler's face as he looked at Gehlen. Beth could see that some unspoken enmity existed twixt them, and she decided to talk with Anthony about it later.

As if reading her thoughts, Kessler turned to the duchess and whispered, "Your Grace, if you have time before you go, I should like to discuss the medical college. I realise you've put Dr. Gehlen in charge, but there are a few unresolved matters that overlap with mine, and I hope to clarify them."

Gehlen overheard this and interrupted. "Clarification on what? The admission of a highly qualified student from Persia? The lad is brilliant and has ample funds to pay, which saves another spot for a scholarship student. I don't understand your objection."

"The man's an instigator," said Kessler. "Duchess, do you want to provide a toehold for Islamic proselytism?"

"Mr. al-Din is a Christian, Dr. Kessler. He's the son of a high-ranking noble, and the family are Greek Orthodox. They do not follow Islam," said Gehlen. "Beth, do I have autonomy regarding admissions, or not?"

Beth started to answer, but a great commotion arose near the lounge doors, causing every eye to turn. The nursing students left their stations to peer into the main receiving lobby nearby. Kessler stood. "If you'll excuse me, Duchess, I should see what's going on."

"That man is rude, Beth," said Gehlen, once Kessler left. "Do Americans no longer learn manners?"

"I imagine Dr. Kessler's stems from something other than poor education," said Ailesleigh as he stood. Every fibre of his being signalled warning, and he moved behind the duchess. A non-human entity was somewhere nearby.

Nathan Kessler crossed the freshly scrubbed, black-and-white tiles and passed through the broad doorway. Gehlen whispered to the duchess. "Nathan Kessler thinks he's the sole rooster in a coop filled with adoring hens. Why on earth did you appoint him?"

"He wrote and asked for the appointment, actually," she answered. "It all happened about the time the twins were born. His application included letters of recommendation from Professor Koch at Berlin University and our own Michael Emerson. I wish now I'd investigated him more thoroughly. Should I ask Lord Aubrey to look into his credentials?"

"At the very least, but I doubt Emerson endorsed that man. He detests Kessler's heavy-handed administration policies and his elitist approach to medicine."

Hamish Granger repositioned himself closer to the doors and quietly signalled to Crenshaw. The former Ranger nodded and followed Kessler. The two men were preparing themselves for possible danger.

The source of the commotion near the doors was a great gaggle of hungry reporters, who'd received word the duchess was touring the hospital. Kessler gathered them into a tight group and took control, as if *he* were the reason they'd come.

"Good morning, good morning! May we have quiet? Now, I appreciate your curiosity, gentlemen, but this is a hospital. Though we've not yet opened to the public, our staff appreciate decorum and obedience. If you'd ask your questions one at a time, I'll be pleased to answer them," he said.

"Who are you?" asked a man in the front. "We've come to see the duchess. Is she here?"

"My name is Dr. Nathan Kessler from Johns Hopkins," the American told him. "I'm in charge of the hospital at present. Therefore, I can answer any of your questions."

"John what?" asked another man.

"Johns, with an 's'. Hopkins. It's in Baltimore."

"Where's that?" asked a young man in the middle of the pack. "Up north by York?"

"No, it's in Maryland. The United States."

"I reckon that explains your accent," came the reply.

The journalists peppered Kessler with a barrage of pointed questions, whilst a photographer wormed his way close to the lounge windows and tried to snap photos of the duchess, using a Kodak One film camera.

Then, a murmur ran through the group, like a sudden shudder running through a pride of lions on the hunt. A second collection of jabbering voices drowned out the first. This second group had broken into the lobby area, trailing like ducklings behind two elegantly attired gentlemen: Dr. Michael Emerson, now 15th Earl of Braxton, and a man who was instantly recognisable to all of England and Scotland, Paul Stuart, the 12th Earl of Aubrey.

Every reporter rushed towards Aubrey as though drawn by a magnet. The earl ignored their questions and passed through the dense cloud of sycophants like mighty Zeus through the heavens. He walked straight to his cousin, kissed her cheek, and said, "Hello, Princess. Sorry I'm late."

"Late? I hadn't expected you at all," she said, "but I'm always pleased to see you. And you've brought Dr. Emerson. Hello, Michael. I'm very sorry we didn't come up for your father's funeral."

"That's all right, Duchess. It was a small affair," replied the Scotsman. "Good to see you, Gehlen. I take it Kessler's still running the roost?"

"Like a Yankee cockerel," said Anthony. "And he keeps invoking your name, Paul. Like it has some mystical quality to hush your cousin's objections."

"My name? Why?"

"Never mind," said Elizabeth, who'd begun to tire. "Paul, do you know Lord Ailesleigh?"

"Ailesleigh?" Paul repeated, looking at the disguised angel. "Are you from Cornwall?"

"Why, yes," said Hadraniel through his human facade. "It's a pleasure to meet you at last, Lord Aubrey. I've read of your many exploits from the safety of my desk."

"That's right. You work from my father's old office, don't you?"

"Indeed, I do, sir. There are initials carved into the topmost drawer. PS. "

Paul laughed. "Yes, I did that. Father scolded me about those initials. How is it you came with the duchess this morning?"

"It's a long tale, to do with a house I've inherited. The duchess will explain, I'm sure."

"Lord Ailesleigh's discovered my father's missing trunks in that house," Beth told him.

"What?" Paul asked. "The ones Trent removed from Queen Anne?"

"Yes, but we can discuss it later. Paul, I hope you didn't come all this way just to watch over me. Granger and Crenshaw are quite sufficient. And our Mr. O'Connell drove. Knowing his cautious nature, he's probably by the outer doors even now, keeping watch on the crowd."

"Michael and I passed O'Connell as we came in, but I'm not here to spy on you, Princess. I've called a circle meeting for one o'clock at the London. Perhaps, you'd like to come?"

"I thought the next meeting wasn't until Monday? Has something happened?" she asked. Then, leaning close, she added in a whisper, "Has there been news of Charles?"

"No, dear," Paul whispered back. "Mr. Treves sent word of crimes that Charles and I've been following. That's why we're meeting there. Will you come with me?"

"Yes, of course. Shall we invite Lord Ailesleigh?"

With his supernatural hearing, the angel had been listening to the reporters talking amongst themselves, whilst also listening to Charles Sinclair speak to Theseus in the Sen-Sen castle. Hadraniel wished he could tell Elizabeth that her husband was well and would soon begin a great test, but doing so would be disobedience.

Just then, several reporters pushed past Kessler, shouting questions at the duchess. Hearing the demands, Elizabeth rose to her feet. Aubrey, Gehlen, and the disguised angel, formed round her, like a ring of steel.

Beth looked up at her guardians, a mischievous glint in her eye. "Gentlemen, it looks as though Dr. Kessler's answers no longer satisfy the reporters. Shall we see how the rooster behaves when a hen takes over?"

Beth crossed to the doorway, surrounded by the protective ring. She raised her hands to call for silence, and a hush fell upon the reporters.

"Gentlemen," she began in a loud voice, "it's a pleasure to see the best and brightest of our city's press assembled here this morning. I wish all of you had toured the hospital with us earlier. I've been very favourably impressed with the high quality of each ward and room. The Haimsbury-Branham Hospital is, without a doubt, the most modern medical facility in all of England. You've been speaking to our interim director, Dr. Nathan Kessler," she stated, looking towards the American. "For those who don't know, Dr. Kessler resumé lists training in the most prestigious hospitals in the world. The Johns Hopkins in Baltimore, the Sorbonne in Paris, the Pavia in Italy, the University of Basel, and the Royal Infirmary at Edinburgh, where I'm sure he learnt the principles of germ theory from the resident expert, Mr. Joseph Lister."

Gehlen noticed the careful phrasing, 'Kessler's *resumé lists*', as though she'd come to doubt the director's word. Kessler glared at the peeress, the shadow behind the eyes no longer hiding.

The duchess continued. "Dr. Kessler's full resumé will be made available to all of you for review, of course. You'll see it includes experience with cholera, a disease known all too well in this quarter."

The older reporters nodded and murmured amongst themselves. The deadly disease had killed more than a million people in Europe and Russia during the 1850s. Most physicians still believed cholera passed through a miasma in the air and required masks for anyone entering a choleroid region. More modern thinkers followed the writings of Dr. John Snow, who deduced that cholera arose from a bacterial infection spread through feces, vomit, and infected water sources.

Beth had read a great deal about the outbreak over the past year and trusted Snow's research. "Cholera is a deadly disease," she told the reporters, "but this hospital is committed to finding treatment and prevention for cholera and many other diseases that plague our city, including this new type of influenza that's coursing its way through parts of Russia and the Balkans, as well as Paris. At such a time, we rely upon men like these two fine men beside me, Dr. Anthony Gehlen and Dr. Michael Emerson. Dr. Gehlen is our Medical School Director, and Dr. Emerson is our Chief Surgeon. Because of them, Whitechapel, Spitalfields, and all of East London have a healthier and happier future. The Haimsbury-Branham Hospital, or the HBH as so many now call it, will provide education at no cost to those with aptitude but are unable to pay. Now, I should be pleased to answer any of your questions."

As the duchess replied to dozens of questions, Hadraniel in his Ailesleigh guise kept a close watch on a man near the back of the pack. He had an odd sort of gait, and he was well dressed, in expensive silks and rich wools. But the clothing looked odd. It was bespoke, yet didn't really fit him—as if he'd borrowed it from another. The limping man's hat shaded his face, making it difficult to see the eyes; those windows of the soul. He limped slowly and surely towards them, and the angel's senses began to shout *danger*.

The voice of his commander whispered: *Get ready.*

"Might I ask a question, Your Grace?" called a thin man in a tweed suit.

The man in the hat continued his subtle progress, and he'd just reached the tweed-suited questioner.

Beth responded gently, unaware of the man in the hat. "Of course. What is your question, sir?"

Paul's heightened senses tingled, too. He didn't like this crowd and put a hand on her arm. "Beth, we need to go. No more questions after this."

The duchess nodded to her cousin, "Yes, all right." Then to the reporter said, "Your question, sir?"

The limping man in the hat stumbled slightly as he passed the tweed-suited reporter. Noticing Ailesleigh's glance, he pulled his hat down and stepped back several paces.

The thin reporter asked, "Yer Grace, is it true the duke's in New York makin' deals with President Harrison?"

"I cannot reveal the nature of the duke's activities, but I can tell you he travels in a private capacity."

"Aye, but doesn't His Grace represent the Queen's Empire? Some say he's ta be the next king," the tweed man continued in an accented voice.

"Tell me, sir," she asked, "how do my husband's travels affect the people of Ireland?"

The Irish reporter laughed, but the crowd grew suspicious, fearing the man might be a Republican Brotherhood spy.

The man in the hat used the tense moment to switch direction and approach the duchess from a new angle.

"I suppose me accent give me away, Yer Grace," said the man in tweed. "Aye, ma'am. The name's O'Donnell, an' I come from County Donegal. Árainn Uí Dhomhnaill, t' be exact. Tis a fair small place, m'lady, an' we don' believe in violence. I ain't with any troublesome group. I'm just here t' work, ma'am."

"Damn the Irish!" shouted someone from the rear of the group. "Go home, Fenian! England is for the English!"

Stuart stepped in front of his cousin, fearing arguments twixt Irish and English could lead to a major fist-fight or knives being drawn. His intuition screamed that something was coming.

"Come with me now, Princess."

"I'm not afraid of an Irishman, Paul. I can manage this," Beth insisted, unaware that a deadly adder slithered amongst the throng. "Gentlemen, whether you come from England, Scotland, Ireland, America, or anywhere in the world, let me explain our position. My husband is responsible for the prosecution of international crime and espionage activities on behalf of the Imperial Crown. Specifically, anarchists and even *spies*."

Beth placed great emphasis on the last word, causing a murmur to ripple amongst the reporters. Every pencil began to scratch against paper. The limping adder in the ill-fitting bespoke suit and hat took advantage of the distraction and made his way towards his prey.

"As Commissioner of Intelligence, my husband now works abroad, following such criminal elements to their wellspring, wherever that may be."

"What elements are those?" shouted a tall man near the back. "Is it the Irish, Your Grace? The Brotherhood?"

"No, my husband leaves the Irish problem to others," she answered, "but if Scotland Yard's Special Branch detectives require his help, I'm sure the duke would be happy to offer assistance. Why, he might even have ICI men, hidden in place there already. Other organisations certainly do."

Everyone laughed at this. Since taking over, Patrick MacAllen had made a mess of Scotland Yard's Special Branch, and Irish Brotherhood and Russian activities in England had skyrocketed because of it. Newspapers claimed spies had infiltrated MacAllen's staff and subverted every attempt to investigate.

"Long live our next queen!" shouted a tall man at the back.

Hadraniel's head instantly turned to look at the speaker. *No, it can't be,* he thought. *He's in Paris! At least, he was.*

Noticing Hadraniel's glance, the tall man moved to a new position.

Elizabeth responded with humility. "Thank you, sir, but I say long live Queen Victoria, our Empress and glorious sovereign!"

Shouts of 'God save our Duchess!' rolled through the crowd, and every reporter pressed close.

Just then, a strange sensation ran through Beth's spirit, like a vision that warned of impending doom. A few of the faces took on inhuman proportions, with snouts instead of noses, and claws instead of nails. Their teeth grew long, and their eyes turned red. An oppressive shadow fell upon her, as though something evil formed ranks against her.

The very tall gentleman now stood beside the man in the hat and whispered into his left ear.

In the guise of Lord Ailesleigh, Hadraniel began to pray.

Paul raised his hands for silence. "Thank you all, but I fear the duchess and I must end this very pleasant gathering. We've other duties to perform. Should anyone have further questions, you may call on me at ICI headquarters, Queen Anne House."

The tall man's human guise began to shimmer.

Hadraniel's prayer finished. He now knew exactly who the tall man was, and he warned the disguised Watcher, saying, *I see you, Saraqael ben Chosek! You have no authority here. Leave now, before I remove you by force!*

A voice hissed into Hadraniel's left ear, *You dare to threaten me, boy? I've placed adders throughout this city, Hadraniel ben 'Owr. Run away now, before I eat your heart!*

Ailesleigh reached for the duchess's hand and placed it in Aubrey's. "Go now, both of you. Please, do not object. There is danger nearby." His tone was commanding, and the earl obeyed without question.

Paul guided the duchess through the dense group of onlookers, well-wishers, and journalists. Most just wanted to touch her arm or ask her to bless them. It was like passing through a friendly but ever-narrowing gauntlet of flesh and clothing. Granger walked in front, and Crenshaw behind. O'Connell stood beside the coach door, his hand on a pistol.

Suddenly, someone cried out in German, *"Wir und die Todten reiten schnell!"*

It was the limping man. He ran up to the duchess and shoved the barrel of a prototype Mannlicher pistol into the tiny space twixt her and the earl.

He pulled the trigger.

The breechblock grew warm as eight 7.63 mm projectiles spun through it in rapid succession, each aimed at Elizabeth Sinclair's heart.

Half a millisecond before the Mannlicher's trigger was pulled, Ailesleigh transformed into an invisible protector and threw angelic arms round the two cousins. Elizabeth imagined the fluttering of wings and a strange sense of peace overwhelmed her heart. For a tiny moment, she thought she heard distant voices, as though warfare were being waged in the heavenlies.

At that same moment, a flash of bright, laser-focused light seared into the shooter's eyes, and a white owl appeared from nowhere, as if entering through a hidden door. The predator's sharp talons tore at the shooter's gloved hand, causing his aim to vary wildly.

Hadraniel shouted for joy at seeing his commander's graceful, surprise attack.

One second later, the duchess was overwhelmed by a wave of concerned hands and arms. A sea of angry faces formed up, with men hurling canes, books, anything they could find, at the limping man in the hat.

Cries of "Get him!", "Break his wrist!", and "German scum!" bubbled up from people's throats until, in the third or fourth second after the gunshots, the looming shadow of Calvin O'Connell, darkened the shooter's fine coat, and a sledgehammer punch bloodied the man's face.

Hadraniel transformed back to Ailesleigh and ordered Crenshaw to lead the duchess back up the steps and into the hospital. The disguised angel kept watch for signs of Saraqael as Aubrey placed a knee on the shooter's chest.

"Who are you?" Aubrey demanded, his heart pumping wildly with anger.

"Nobody," the fallen man answered as blood gurgled from his nose and mouth. "Leave me alone! I don't know anything!"

"Then allow me to help with your memory," shouted Aubrey. "Granger, help me take this filth to Leman Street, where Reid can put him in a dark cell, where I can speak to him with no one watching."

"God have mercy, they tried to kill our next queen!" wailed a middle-aged man. "Lord, help us!"

He dropped to his knees to pray for the duchess, and soon, others joined him, forming an organic congregation of penitent petitioners.

Policemen from the nearby station house rushed in and dispersed the shocked citizenry, asking each if he'd seen the shooter's face. A few followed the Lord Aubrey and the shooter to Leman Street with rage and vengeance in their hearts.

Inside the hospital, Kessler tried to take command, but the duchess resisted, looking to Gehlen and Emerson instead. "Michael, help me to to sit, please. The world begins to tilt."

Emerson led Beth into an examination room. He set her into a chair and checked her clothing. "There's blood on your dress. Beth, are are you injured? Are you in pain?"

"No, I..." she managed to say. "Blood? Was Paul shot? Where's Lord Ailesleigh? Was he shot?"

Anthony Gehlen closed the door to keep out the rabble. "Ailesleigh's gone with Paul to the police station. The man that fired the pistol's been arrested. It's madness out there."

"Is Paul all right?" she asked, somewhat breathless.

"I believe so. He was shouting orders to everyone. Did you know that man?"

"No, I don't think so. Where's Lord Ailesleigh?"

"He's with Paul, remember? Beth, you look faint."

Emerson began unhooking her jacket to inspect the area beneath the blood stain. The door opened again, admitting a rush of sound. Someone was trying to get in.

"Anthony, see to that door!" shouted Emerson. "We don't want anyone seeing this, let alone taking photographs!"

Elizabeth could sense movement in the room, like the fluttering of wings overshadowing her eyes. She thought she heard sweet whispers, *God watches over you, Elizabeth Sinclair, never fear.* She imagined the softest touch against her hand, as though an angel kissed it, and then the voice added, *Take care, daughter of Eve. A new life is growing inside you. A son.*

"A son," she whispered. "Charles..."

As Elizabeth fainted, her last thought was to ask God to protect Paul, her husband, and all her children.

Then...

...everything went dark.

CHAPTER THIRTEEN
Real World - Montmore House

Luncheon had come and gone. The new cook, Mrs. Merchant, prepared a delicious quiche, peppered parsnips, roasted chicken, and a creamed potato soup. The food was extraordinarily fine, and the raspberry torte even better; but despite her love of sweets, Adele ate sparingly. She'd begun to think of dress sizes, waistlines, and all the grown-up considerations typical of adolescent females. Seth Holloway sat beside Della, and they played a silly game, deciding which member of Parliament looked most like a parsnip and which like a potato.

Afterwards, she and the viscount continued their Austen reading until half past two, when Seth was called downstairs to speak to a gentleman from Cambridge, regarding the next academic session. Whilst waiting, Adele abandoned the Austen book in favour of a journal Henry had given her to record her thoughts and dreams.

She opened the leather-bound book and gazed at the blank page. What should she write? Dr. MacAlpin called it a dream diary, instructing Della to write whatever ideas or impressions she wished to record, including all her nightly dreams. He warned her, that he'd read it from time to time, for the journal was part of her therapy.

Adele chose one of the Waterman fountain pens her mother had brought and filled it from a bottle of India ink.

A dream diary, she thought. *Very well, let's give it a start*:

> My very dear Dr. MacAlpin—and dare I say, my
> very good friend Henry—I dedicate this diary to you,
> knowing your eyes will look upon each page, as if to
> behold the secrets of my heart and mind. Therefore,

first of all, I wish to thank you for giving me the book and for allowing me to remain at Montmore whilst I work through this 'mind puzzle', as you call it, that currently worries me.

To begin, let me write down all I can remember of last night's dream. I cannot give you a great deal of information, for my remembrances are inconsistent and sparse; more a line drawing than a fully formed painting.

Strange, writing that word caused a tiny thought to jump through my head. The word painting, I mean. It makes me think of Branham, for some reason, but also my father. Now, why would I link Father to danger and a painting? Strange images jump through my head as I write this. They are:

A teapot.

My dog Napper.

Last May's fête.

Medieval knights in armour.

And ravens.

A strange grouping, isn't it? I do pray your insights regarding these images will see their connexion, for I cannot. Ah, but there's more to last night's wanderings, my dear friend, for the dream had two parts.

In the first, I was in Whitechapel, standing at the entrance to the H-Division police station. My father took me there in late July and showed me the various departments and rooms. He even let me sit in his old office chair, and we pretended to be Holmes and Watson (naturally, Father is Holmes), and he suggested I might become a police surgeon one day and solve crimes through evidence obtained by examining the victim's body. Most ladies would be horrified at that, but I find the idea fascinating.

Now, in the dream, it was night, but none of the street lamps were lit. The moon was full and large, and I could see quite well. On the station's second floor, I saw my father. He was leaning out of the open window of his old office, shouting at me and ordering me to run. Only then did I notice the station was filled with horrible, ugly monsters. I tried to run into the station to help my father, but the door slammed in my face and wouldn't open again, no matter how hard I pushed.

Then, as dreams often do, the location changed in a blink. London was gone, and I stood in a woodland. I heard the sound of someone chopping wood, and so I followed it. The woods were thick with brambles and nettles, and I noticed black spiders in the bushes and a slithering adder beneath one of the brambles. The place reminded me of the Bois du Fée near my aunt's home in Paris. It's said the woodland is a faerie domain. These faeries sometimes kidnap humans and keep them prisoner. Ask Auntie Tory about it sometimes, or Dolly Patterson-Smythe.

In the dream, I walked and walked and walked, following the chopping sound. It took ages to reach the woodcutter, and when I saw him at last, I grew very angry. You see, he was cutting the roots of the tallest of the great oaks. I shouted at him and ordered him to stop, but he just smiled. I pleaded with him, crying and weeping until I thought my eyes might swell shut, but he laughed.

Six shorter oaks and two willows stood nearby, each one banded in a black ribbon. I asked the woodsman, "What of these?" He said, "These are future wood that must be destroyed. Kill the tall oak, and the other trees die."

What might it mean? Do I choose imagery to express something hidden within my mind, or might it be that I know—

"You've a caller!" a voice cried.

Della's pen stopped moving. It was Gillian Bunting, who enjoyed sneaking into other residents' rooms and causing them to jump.

"Didn't you hear me? You've a caller," Bunting said again.

"Of course, I heard you. You mustn't do that, Gilly, it's very rude," young Sinclair answered.

"What are you doing?" asked Bunting. "Are you writing a book?"

"No," Della replied, placing the diary into the desk drawer. "Who's the caller? My brother isn't due for hours."

"It isn't your brother," replied the twenty-four-year-old. "Shall I send her up?"

"Is it my mother?"

"No."

"Stop playing games, Gilly. If it isn't my mother, then I can't imagine who it might be, and I'm not to see visitors outside of family."

"Nonsense. Lord Paynton reads with you almost every hour of the day. He is so very handsome, don't you think? In that boyish, Chopin sort of way? Such sensitive eyes and a lovely mouth that you want to kiss and kiss and..."

"Gillian, stop!" Adele shouted. "Who is the visitor?"

Like Ewan MacNee, Gillian Helen Bunting also suffered from an *'idee fixe'* or fixed ideation; in her case, the object of the delusion was Frédéric Chopin. She considered the deceased composer the ideal specimen of manhood. Consequently, since no real man could compare to the fantasy, she'd turned down four offers of marriage. The obstinate behaviour caused her father to cloister her at Montmore, and Gillian became a madhouse version of a Carmelite nun.

"Your visitor's a woman, and she's with child," said Gillian, gleefully pantomiming a rounded stomach with her hands. "She is so very large, Della. I was quite amazed, for I know her, you see. She and I went to finishing school together in Switzerland. She was fourteen, and I was nineteen. It was a disastrous time. Did she ever tell you about it?"

"I've no idea, Gilly, until you tell me who *she* is."

"Didn't I say?"

"Obviously not."

"She knows Seth as well, but I doubt she'd try to take him from you. As she's with child and all."

"Gilly!"

"Oh, very well," Bunting relented. "It's your handsome brother's somewhat plain wife."

179

"Cordelia? That's wonderful, but she isn't plain," Adele told her friend. "I think Cordelia's quite lovely, and so does my brother, if you must know. He calls her his *fear bréagha*. That's Scots for beautiful one. And she's a bit swollen, because the baby's caused her to retain water in her face and hands, but she's still very beautiful. Is she downstairs? I'm sure she's not to climb."

"No. She's playing my piano."

"It isn't your piano," Adele corrected, as she buckled her shoes. "Run down and tell her I'm on my way, please."

"Why? You're nearly ready," Gillian said in a dreamy voice, "and until you came, I was the only one to play the piano, so it's practically mine."

"The piano belongs to Dr. MacAlpin," Adele answered as she checked her face and hair.

"It belongs to Henry, you mean," Gillian bounced back as she followed Della round the apartment. "Dreamy Henry. Isn't he sweet? I do love that crooked little smile of his. And his chin is firm and those warm brown eyes are very pleasant. He sings a bit, though not as well as Lord Paynton."

"Both men are kind and thoughtful," Adele replied.

"I think Lord Paynton likes you," said Gillian. "I do wish he'd look at me. Perhaps, I'll ask if he might read with me."

"I'm sure he'd be happy to," Adele said as she left the apartment.

"And dreamy Henry? What would he say, I wonder?" asked the older girl as she followed Adele out.

"I don't think we should call him dreamy, Gilly," Adele replied as they reached the staircase. "Henry's our physician, and this is his home. We are guests."

"Are alienists real physicians? Could he set a bone or deliver a baby? I hope so, for Cordelia looks like she might need a doctor soon. She is so very big!" Bunting said.

"Dr. MacAlpin can do the same things as other physicians. He helped deliver Robby and Georgianna, if you must know, and Mother said he did a splendid job."

"Alienism is a peculiar word, isn't it?" said Gillian as they descended. "Father says so. He calls Henry a brain explorer. Can you just picture him in the jungle?"

"I'm sure he'd be very brave, if he were," Della told her.

Accommodations at Montmore House included eight large apartments, ten smaller guest rooms, and a comfortably furnished servants' floor. The main staircase reached the first and second floors; but a back staircase, used mainly by servants and staff, ran from the lower level kitchens and cellars, up to the servant floor and attics. At that moment, the young ladies used the main staircase, a long stretch of inlaid maple with carpeted risers to reduce foot noise.

They reached the ground floor, where the air was filled with piano music and the sweet cinnamon aroma of Mrs. Merchant's *Dresdner stollen* and *schneckenkuchen* baking. Adele noticed Dr. Holloway in the foyer, no longer speaking with his Cambridge friend, but discussing something quite serious with two uniformed men. Their conversation was in Italian.

"Who's that?" she asked Gillian as they neared the music room.

"The handsome Italians? Dreamy, aren't they?"

"Every man is dreamy to you, Gilly."

"Not all. Just most," the other said. "But no one is like Chopin."

Adele bit her tongue, for she wanted to remind her friend that Frédéric Chopin was long dead, though his music lived on. As they neared the music room, a black-and-white dog suddenly bolted into view, its feathered tail wagging furiously.

"Napper!" cried Della as the dog ran into her open arms. She knelt to stroke the animal's neck and ears. "Oh, my dear, dear Lady Napper, how big you've gotten, and so very lovely. But you look a bit skinny. Haven't you been eating? Oh, I've missed you, pretty doggy!"

The piano music stopped, and twenty or so seconds later, a heavily pregnant woman appeared in the corridor at the end of the foyer. Cordelia's figure had rounded so much beneath her bosom, that many of the older servants wondered if she carried two children, instead of one. The staff of Haimsbury House had even begun a raffle, betting on boy versus girl; and if there were two, would both be girls, boys, or a mix.

Lady Delia Wychwright Stuart had a Titianesque quality about her looks, with thick mounds of strawberry blonde hair, large blue eyes, and pleasingly plump cheeks, set off by a rosebud mouth. Her figure had expanded with approaching motherhood, and she waddled a bit as she approached Adele.

"Oh, Delia, I hadn't expected to see you!" Adele cried out happily. She left the dog and crossed to give her sister-in-law a fond hug and kiss. "You look so very wonderful, Dee. So healthy and happy. I hope my brother's treating you to all sorts of presents and such. And lots of lovely cakes, too."

Cordelia Jane, whom Adele had nicknamed 'Dee', kissed her in return. "Paul told me I should send Napper with a servant, but I needed to get out of the house, you see. Don't ever get pregnant, Della. It makes your back ache, and your legs become stumps of fleshy lead. Being confined is really quite boring."

"But doesn't confinement imply a lack of mobility, Dee? Hence the word *confined*," said Adele. "Why did you bring Napper? Are Paul and my mother still coming this evening?"

"I cannot say," answered Delia. "May we sit?"

"Of course," Della said, taking Cordelia's arm. "Here now, let's return to the music room as it's closest. Come, Napper!"

The trio of women and one female dog assembled in the music room, and Cordelia chose a sturdy couch. "It's becoming difficult to walk," said the countess, "but I have to do it. My nurse says exercise is good for me. I just have to be careful about it. Oh, and Paul's visit is rescheduled until tomorrow, Della. He sent a telegram. It seems something happened at the hospital this morning, though the telegram didn't explain it much. How are you?"

"Keeping busy, reading books and such. Gillian tells me you and she went to finishing school together."

"Yes, but only for half a year," Cordelia said. "Mother made me come back to England before I'd completed the course. Lucerne is very beautiful, though. The school was at Meggenhorn Castle with splendid views of the Alps and the lake. Della, you really must go there for your schooling. I long to go back one day. Paul says he'll take me there once the baby's born."

"Or the babies, as in plural," said Bunting. "Delia, you are so very huge! It's a good thing we have two nurses here, for it looks as though you might pop any minute!"

Cordelia had known Bunting for years and was accustomed to her strange sense of humour. "Yes, I suppose it does," she replied. "But it isn't twins. The doctors say so."

"Here you all are!" called a man's voice from the doorway. "A cloud of beauties on a starry night, though I suppose it's still day,"

"With apologies to Byron, I suppose," laughed Adele.

"Byron surely dreads it whenever I read his poems, Della. And my dear Lady Aubrey, you walked right past me without even saying hello."

"Only because you were busy, Dr. Holloway," replied the young woman with a bright smile. "Are you working here now? Have you taken up medicine?"

"Hardly," the archaeologist answered with a boyish grin. "No, I'm that maddening gadfly that keeps annoying you at picnic. You brush me away with your hand, yet here I am, returning again and again."

"You're hardly a gadfly, Lord Paynton," Gillian Bunting insisted. "You're Della's favourite reading companion."

"'Tis I who benefit from that arrangement," said Holloway. "I've learnt a great deal about young ladies and their innermost thoughts by reading Jane Austen. Cordelia, your middle name's Jane, did you ever read Austen?"

"My mother always said Miss Austen's writing is absurd and would fill my head with silly ideas, so no, I didn't."

Seth smiled, saying, "I'm sure the only thoughts in your pretty head are of your husband. Everyone admires our Lord Aubrey."

"And everyone loves our Lord Paynton," said Gillian. "And you speak Italian very well. Who were those two men? Might they be detectives? I heard you say *investigatore*, but they weren't in uniform."

"I'm not sure what they are, actually. They claimed to be with the Italian police, but their actions deny that. If either man returns in my absence, you must tell me, Miss Bunting. The same goes for you, Lady Della. They spoke with a far different accent than any Italians I know, and their use of procedural language was filled with errors."

"What's procedural language?" asked Cordelia. "Do you mean detective words? The kind Duke Charles uses with Inspector Reid?"

"That's right, but these men talked about laws and legal requirements that don't exist in Italy. I lived there for over a year, when I was seventeen, and numbered policeman amongst my friends."

"Were you a scoundrel?" asked Gillian, her eyelashes fluttering.

"I was decidedly boring," Seth answered. "The policemen I knew shared a flat with me. I spent a great deal of time in their company, so I'm familiar with their way of talking and their dialects. These two are pretenders, and I intend to talk to Paul about them."

"What did they want?" Della asked her friend. "And why would they pretend to be policemen?"

"To elicit information, I should think," Seth replied. "They claim they're looking for a band of smugglers, who are hiding in London and they followed a line of bread crumbs to this house."

"Bread crumbs? Like the ones left by Hansel and Gretel?" asked Cordelia. "Do thieves really do that?"

Seth laughed and took a seat at the piano, plink-plunking on the keys now and then and shuffling through the music on the stand. "I've only studied the habits of ancient thieves, so I've no idea. My dear Lady Cordelia, shouldn't you be at Haimsbury House with your feet up? You look very flushed."

"Yes, I probably should be, but I needed fresh air and so used this errand to find some," answered the young woman. "I brought Napper. Paul intended to bring her this evening, but as he and Beth postponed, I decided to do it. See how happy she is to be with her owner?"

"Indeed, she is! And I'm sure Mrs. Winstead will *love* looking after a dog," laughed the viscount. "But why aren't Paul and Beth coming tonight? Henry was hoping to ask the earl to join him in an expedition next door."

"An expedition to Hemsfield House?" asked Adele. "I'm sure someone's living over there. Perhaps, it's those thieves the Italians are following."

"Or it's ghosts," said Gillian gleefully. "Shadowy spectres and all manner of horrible dead things!"

"Perhaps, we should talk of the living, Miss Bunting," suggested Seth.

At that moment, the aforementioned Emily Winstead entered, and all eyes turned towards the door, including those of the dog.

"Just what is this, and will it be staying?" asked the nurse.

"This is Lady Cordelia Jane Stuart, beloved Countess of Aubrey," Seth answered mischievously. "And no, dear Mrs. Winstead, the lady hasn't come to stay, although she might want a cup of tea."

"I meant the dog, Lord Paynton," Winstead clarified with a voiced 'harrumph'. She turned to the guest. "Lady Aubrey, it's a pleasure to meet you at last. Lord Aubrey talks about you every time he visits, saying what a pretty mother you'll make. And I see he's right in every aspect. I'm Mrs. Winstead, Dr. MacAlpin's head nurse. Are you feeling all right, my lady? Your face is flushed."

"I fear my face is always flushed, Mrs. Winstead," said Cordelia. "It is a constant state these days. No one warned me of the challenges one endures in the last weeks. I wonder, might you have any water?"

Winstead walked over and felt the young woman's cheek and forehead. "You're very warm, my lady. Would you like to lie down for a bit? We've a vacant apartment that has a fine bed with a comfortable mattress."

Cordelia sighed. "I shouldn't say yes, but that sounds so very nice, Mrs. Winstead. Lord Paynton, I wonder if you'd speak to my driver and let him know I'll be here a little while longer? If he wishes to return here in an hour or so—*oh!*"

"Oh?" asked Seth as he jumped up from the piano and crossed the room. He took Delia's hand. "Contractions?"

"I don't know," Cordelia confessed. "I've never had them before. I do feel strangely, though."

"Strangely? How?" asked Winstead.

"My back aches, and I feel a sort of pressure, as if the baby's pushing on all my bones."

"How long have you felt like that, Lady Aubrey?"

"I don't know. Not long. It started on the drive here."

"Lord Paynton, you must help me," said Winstead. "We'll take her ladyship upstairs to the apartment I mentioned, and I'll start preparations." The nurse put her head into the corridor and called, "Shelton! Mrs. Shelton, we need you!"

A chamber maid answered, dressed in a dark dress and white pinafore. "Mrs. Shelton's below stairs, Missus, talking with Mrs. Merchant about tomorrow's menu."

"Go and fetch her now, and tell Mrs. Merchant that we may need hot water, so be ready with a large pot. Go now." She turned to the pregnant countess. "Lady Aubrey, we'll do this together. Lord Paynton will take one arm, and I'll take the other. Lady Della, if you'd mind your dog? We don't want it to get tangled up with our feet."

"Her name is Napper."

"Well, let's keep Napper from causing any mischief, shall we? Miss Bunting, you run ahead to the Mayfair apartment and turn down the sheets, please. Go now!"

Bunting ran up the steps to a large apartment on the northeast corner of the first floor of the house. Seth took most of Delia's weight as they left the music room and began the climb to the upper floor. "Steady on, now, Delia," he told her. "No rush. One step at at time. You can do this."

It took nearly four minutes, stopping every third step, but they made the climb successfully. The Mayfair was last used by Henry's sick grandmother. Because of that, he seldom put patients in here, using it only in emergencies. The suite was large, with a lovely little parlour that included a writing desk and a pair of wingback chairs. They passed through this to one of two bedchambers, where they found a Tudor-style bed, made with turned walnut posts and a coffered canopy. The bed curtains were damask in a pleasant silver-blue. But like most Tudor beds, the mattress was high and accessed using a step-stool. Seth helped Cordelia to climb up.

"I shan't ever be able to get out on my own," Cordelia moaned as she clutched at her abdomen.

"Someone will be here with you at all times, my lady, and I'm used to taking care of women confined to bed. Never fear now." She turned to Holloway. "Let me see to things now, sir, and if you'd be good enough to send a telegram to Lord Aubrey and Dr. MacAlpin? Do you know where they might be? I remember hearing Saunders say something about a circle meeting."

"Yes, Henry said they'd be at the London, but I should probably wire Dr. Gehlen, too," he said. "I could send to St. Mary's and ask for Emerson, though I'm not sure he's back from Edinburgh yet. Cordelia, dear, have you seen any other doctors? One of Emerson's partners from St. Mary's?"

"St. Mary's?" the girl asked, her face tensing. "I don't kn— *oh!*" Cordelia's eyelids squeezed together as a fierce contraction ran through her abdomen.

"Never mind," Seth replied, kissing her hand. "I'll go fetch a doctor and send the telegrams from St. Mary's."

He met Adele in the hallway as he shut the door. "I think you're about to become an aunt, Lady Della. Now listen to me. We need a doctor, so I have to leave. I hate going, for I promised Henry I'd look after you. Will you be all right?"

"Paul's men are still watching the house, aren't they?"

"Yes, dear, they are," he said, touching her cheek affectionately. "They've been staying in the gardener's cottage, so send a maid out to let them know where I'm going and what's happening. I promise, I shan't be long."

He kissed her forehead and left, calling to the butler as he gathered up a cloak and hat. "Saunders, it looks as though Lady Aubrey may be delivering her baby early. I'm off to find a doctor."

"I can go, sir," Saunders offered.

"No, I need to send telegrams, too, and I plan to drive by Haimsbury House and collect Lady Aubrey's nurse and lady's maid once the doctor's on his way. Let's just pray you don't end up acting as midwife!"

Seth left the house and found the Haimsbury driver talking to two of the ICI men. "Mr. Jones, Mr. Lowell," he called as he reached the coach. "Look to Lady Adele and Lady Aubrey. Go inside and keep watch from the house now. Lady Aubrey's in labour."

Kit Jones and Fred Lowell were both married with two children apiece. "That'll be a blessing, won't it, Lord Paynton?" said Lowell, elder of the two. "We'll keep watch, sir. Never fear."

"You're fine men," said the viscount as he jumped into the coach. "St. Mary's, driver! And hurry!"

The Haimsbury brougham's team of Friesian mares dug their hooves into the gravel and in less than a quarter hour, Holloway was entering the main doors of St. Mary's Hospital. He discovered Michael Emerson was at the meeting in Whitechapel, so it fell to his partner to respond to the call.

Such is the way with the Lord.

Sometimes, he works things together in ways a human might never imagine.

And in this case, a former Redwing member, who'd once tried to ensnare Paul Stuart, was sent by God Almighty to assist with Lady Aubrey's troubles, and in doing so, would save the lives of Paul's wife and his unborn son.

CHAPTER FOURTEEN
Sen-Sen - Charles Learns More About His Host

Whilst this seemingly random series of spiritually interconnected events took place in the real world, Paul Stuart's cousin was trapped in a *demi-monde*, sharing a bewildering conversation with a demigod.

Alphonse Theseus had proven to be a loquacious host. He sat opposite his unwilling guest, near the larger of the drawing room's twin fireplaces. The yellow flames danced upon the halfling's lean face in stripes of flickering light, making him seem like some compound, mythological creature from a bygone age.

Charles Sinclair just wanted to go home.

"Why am I here?" he asked after a sip of brandy.

"To test your blood, " replied the demigod.

"Nonsense. My blood's no different from any other man's."

"Oh, but it is, Charles! It is! There's an element to it that only the Maze can awaken."

"Impossible. Blood is blood."

"Yours has a special quality beyond the physical."

"Do you speak of something metaphysical? Like some sanguineous ghost?"

The demigod smiled. "A delicious idea, but no, Charles. You're neither possessed nor controlled by a bloodthirsty apparition."

"Am I supposed to be flattered by these claims?"

Theseus poured himself another snifter of brandy. "Most men would be flattered. The fact that you are not speaks to your unique nature."

"And so I ask again, why am I here?"

"Shall I speak plainly?"

"Please."

"Very well, you're here to walk the Maze."

"*The* Maze? As if it's some master labyrinth?"

"Even the word master is a limiting adjective, for this is unlike no other. It stands alone by design. It is the Time Maze."

"Time? Do you speak of the hours it takes to traverse it?" asked Sinclair.

"No, of course not. You'll comprehend once you're inside."

Sighing, the duke tried to approach the problem laterally. "You've said this castle is beneath the earth. Is it connected to this Maze?"

"Of course. The Maze and castle are inextricably conjoined. They are one with the netherworld."

"Are you saying I'm in Hell?" Charles asked flatly.

"Not at all! Hell is a very different place, Duke Charles. We are in Sen-Sen. The realm of mirrored reality."

"Sen-Sen? I've heard others speak of it. Is Sebet Babi nearby?"

"The Seven Gates? You may access it from here, but that realm lies elsewhere. Think of Sen-Sen as the darkling glass the Apostle Paul mentions in the New Testament. It is a pool of calm water, clear and fine. The water may show you visions, or lead you to unseen realms. You need only pass through it to achieve your goal. The Scots call such a realm *Elphyne.* The Land of the Fae, where the sprites and faeries live."

"And this castle exists in *Elphyne?*"

"Oh, yes!"

"In an old castle?"

"Not just any castle, Charles. The foundations are deep and old. Far older than your inner circle antiquarians might imagine."

"Older than the pyramids?"

He laughed. "Much, much older. The castle's foundations were laid in the beginning of days. It's called the *E-Buzur.* The House of the God that Solves Secrets."

"And you know these secrets?" asked Sinclair.

"I've learnt a great deal, as will you. The journey through the Maze is difficult, but the reward is sublime."

"Let me see if I understand," Charles said, his keen mind creating a sort of 'thought equation'. "The castle sits in a half-world called Sen-Sen, which the Scots call Elphyne. The castle was built during the earliest age, to house a particular god that solves secrets."

"Not only for a particular god, Charles. Also, for a particular purpose."

"Which is?"

"To test those deemed worthy to enter the god's domain."

"And so we circle back to that. Why am I worthy?"

"Charles, your blood is unique. And before you object again, hear me out. Human science cannot discern animal blood from human, nor can it describe the smallest particles within that blood. How, then, can you expect to comprehend the metaphysical truths within that same blood?"

"My uncle's scientists can differentiate animal from human blood, and their microscopes distinguish one type of bacteria from another and even reveal the structures of their cells."

"Ah, but Drummond's men cannot see the smaller particles that make up those intracellular structures! Nor can they open up the mysteries of the mind. Your friend Lord Salperton is a talented alienist, yet he lacks the knowledge to explain man's deepest pathologies. However, there *is* a science that reveals that and more! I've seen it! If scientists could view the infinitesimally small particles in nerves and bone; if they could perceive the structure of sperm and ova, the components of a hydrogen atom, perceive the truth of light and darkness and the magnificent design of it all, I tell you, they would abandon all their Darwinian models. My friend, our blood—yours and mine—is charged with great purpose. It is *active*. That is why you and I can see and even visit other realms."

Having finished the brandy, the duke set the glass aside. "I agree that Darwinism is a false paradigm, but I needn't see these hidden structures to draw that conclusion, because I believe in a Creator. I believe in God Almighty. It is his Spirit within me, HIS blood, that makes me special, not your metaphysical nonsense. The search for divinity through mind journeys or occult knowledge is pointless. Mankind was created to act as God's imagers on Earth. Sin changed us. But Christ's blood redeems us and restores us to that purpose."

"And you will become a co-ruler in heaven, no? Fine, but what if God has a purpose for you here, now?"

"He leads me upon his path."

"Which means, he has led you here," reasoned Theseus. "God allowed us to bring you here, so that you might walk this special path. Charles, all humans will be blessed by your journey, assuming you are brave enough to accept."

"Do not you *dare* to mock God, Theseus," Charles answered angrily. "He will exact payment for such abuse, and his fee is steep!"

"No, no, you misunderstand me, Charles. I do not mock God, but state fact. He did allow you to come, because he wants you to make this journey. And once through, you'll see the value in becoming king."

"If completing the journey makes a man fit to rule, then, why aren't you king?" the human asked. "If passing through the Time Maze brings a deified nature, then why haven't you taken the crown?"

Theseus sat back and took a deep breath, his hands steepled as he offered a reply. "You try to turn me, Charles, but my destiny lies beside you, not in your place. As with all sovereigns, you must sacrifice your own desires for the betterment of your fellow man. Sacrifice is all important. Did not Christ accept the cross for that purpose?"

"Take care, Theseus, if you suggest you've carried a cross, as Christ did."

"No, I'm not saying that, Charles. The cross served a purpose. It appeased God's wrath, but it failed to stop the true evil of this world. Sin still exists."

"It stopped death," Charles declared. "*O death, where is thy sting? O, grave, where is thy victory?* First Corinthians, Chapter fifteen. You claim to know scripture, yet you haven't believed it."

His host smiled. "I know it far better than you think, my friend. In all the original languages. Do you really believe death is over? Your parents are dead. Where are they? Your sister is dead. Where is she? My mother died long, long ago and awaits her final liberation. And my father... Well, my father is another story entirely."

Charles sighed. He'd come to like Theseus, oddly enough, but the halfling's blind spot regarding God might never see light. "What about your father?"

"That tale is too long for now, but he understood the Maze. He helped build this castle to act as its guardian and gate. Once I completed my journey, he left me in charge."

"And does the castle become mine once I've completed my own journey?"

"No, and be glad of it, Charles. You would never wish such a burden. This place is far from those you love. Far from the realm of your birth. Even I seldom come here. It is not an enviable position, my friend."

"Tell me about this Maze, then."

Theseus sat back, his dark eyes gazing into the fire. "Many aeons ago, in the beginning of days, when the hidden realms shimmered with new life and pure light, the Maze was created to connect all of Time. Its name then was *ana harrani sa alaktasa la tarat*. It is Sumerian for the road which does not turn back."

"Doesn't turn back? Do you speak of death?"

"In a way, but not as an ending to life. A beginning."

"You want me to walk into Death's domain?"

"Yes, but I conquered its corridors, Charles, as will you! And once you've passed through its heart and returned, you become the *engurra*, the lord whose return is triumphant!"

"I don't want such a title," Charles said with confidence.

"Nonetheless, it will be yours. The only alternative is to fail and remain inside."

"And if I refuse to enter?"

"Then, when he is twelve or thirteen, your son will be brought here and put to the test. Is that what you want?"

The duke thought of his infant son. In a little more than ten years, Robby Sinclair would bravely guide his mother through the Stone Realms. To imagine him captured and brought here; forced to enter the realm of death? What father would heap such horrors upon his child?

Lord, you are my Shepherd. Where you lead, I follow.

"When do I begin?" Charles said, resigned to his fate.

"Excellent!" Theseus exclaimed, refilling both their snifters. "The challenge cannot commence until the first rays of the equinox moon strike the gate's lintel. Only then, will the doors open."

"How soon will this light arrive?"

"Tomorrow evening. Again, I apologise for bringing you here weeks before the time. Blame Araqiel. He is an impatient and brainless young dragon. Most of his kind are, actually, regardless of age. Tis a dangerous combination, isn't it? A fiery temperament with no real intellect to guide it. That fool of a dragon will probably try to kill you tonight. He's convinced that only death will awaken your blood to its purpose. I've tried to convince him otherwise, but he is stubborn."

"Why would death awaken my blood?"

"Actually, his idea is to awaken your blood by drinking it. Dragons drink blood to take the another's spirit and power. He smells your blood, Charles, and finds it exceedingly sweet. That brainless dragon would drink every last drop, if given the chance. He believes it would make him king."

"Perhaps, it's best I didn't send him an invitation to the christening, then," replied Charles, a smile playing at his lips.

"Yes, he and Eluna complained of that obvious slight. But I ask you, would two fallen angels really want to sit inside a Christian chapel and watch human infants dedicated to the God that ejected them from heaven? Of course, not."

"And you? How might you have felt at such a ceremony?" asked the human.

"I? Why, I find chapels and cathedrals instructive, even beautiful in their way. Most are architectural marvels. Also, the humans that inhabit them make for grand studies. I enjoy watching the nuns at prayer. I do not say this to mock them. I admire their devotion. It's misguided, but I appreciate their ideals. Churches are quite soothing, don't you think? As a place for reflection and solace."

"Reflection?" asked Charles, in amazement.

"Oh yes," said Theseus, his features softening with great, even tender emotion. "Churches remind me of what *might* have been."

"But surely, you're not welcome in churches?" the duke dared to ask.

"Why wouldn't I be? I've not been barred, if that's what you imply. I may come and go as I please. Even Satan is permitted access to the heavenly realms when called; though a final ejection is bound to happen one day, and soon, I expect. This world rushes forward to its ultimate conclusion, and one side or the other will win."

"God has already won."

"Has he? I do admire your courage, Charles. You're a kindred spirit, I think. A true brother. I feel a kinship with you as with no other."

"How can I be kin to you? I presume you're Greek. My family lines have no such connexion."

"Do they not? It's true, I am Greek. Or more accurately, I am Athenian. I am that nation's founding hero. Ask any historian or antiquarian, any classical scholar; they'll tell you. In those days, the country of Greece did not exist. When I was born, the islands of the Aegean and Mediterranean seas were separate kingdoms, ruled over by tribal kings. Then, Attica ruled most of the fertile peninsula of the Aegean. You may recall from your Cambridge studies that Attica was an ally to Delos against the hated Persians. Have you ever met the Prince of Persia? He is a very old and dreadful dragon, much more powerful than Araqiel, and with a far superior brain."

The duke shook his head. "According to the Bible, the Prince of Persia is a fallen angel."

"He is indeed, and he still controls a vast area of the world."

"And do you claim to be the Prince of Greece?"

"No. Why should I want to be? Being a mere dragon is a position of weakness, as far as I'm concerned."

"How is being a spirit ruler of an entire nation a position of weakness to one such as you?"

"Fallen elohim are limited by design. True, they have more freedom than the unfallen, but each must pledge fealty to whatever Archduke, Prince, or High King is presently in charge."

"Presently in charge?"

"Oh, yes. Do not presume to think these thrones are secure. As with humans, warfare, deceit, and endless betrayal define spirit-realm politics. Becoming the ruler of any region or tribe is a position of uncertainty, for the nature to rebel never changes. Much of human warfare is directed by spirits who lay claim to a rival's territory. However, if one represents both realms, the human and the elohim, then he could rule them *both*. Such a man would have final authority over all."

"And you are such a man, I take it?"

"As are you, Charles! Once you've completed your journey through the Maze, you will become my true brother. Those with twin natures may walk in both worlds—the human and elohim. I am slave to no king. I bow to no ruler. And I am stronger because of it. You see, truth lies at the heart of this challenge, Charles. If the walker is truthful and his actions honourable, then he is rewarded by finding the ultimate truth. You are a man of great principle, my friend, which is why I know that you will succeed."

"I've already found the ultimate Truth in Christ."

"So you think, but the Maze will open your eyes, my friend. I guarantee it."

"I disagree, Christ can walk in all places, all worlds. There's no need for another man to duplicate his work. He became fully human, but remained fully God. You are half and half."

"If your God is so powerful, then why did he abandon you to us?" asked Theseus slyly.

Charles leaned forward to make his point. "Do you really think he sent me here without help?"

"You are alone, my friend. I am your only help."

"Not true."

"Who else is here to watch after you? I can see into the spirit realm, Charles. You are utterly alone."

"No, there's..." He stopped. He'd very nearly told Theseus about Fenwick. God sent someone to help, yet none of God's enemies sensed it. "I may appear to be alone, but God is with me. Always."

"As you say," replied Theseus dismissively. "Very soon, you'll wonder why you ever relied on the Hebrew God. You know, at dinner, Araqiel called me halfling, thinking me insulted, but I glory in that name, Charles. It means I stand on the bridge twixt elohim and human. As Poseidon's son, I am half-human and half-god. You do know what I mean by elohim?"

"Yes."

"Most humans know only angel and devil. Or demon. Who told you of the elohim? The one who calls himself Prince Anatole?"

Charles nodded.

"He must have recognised your unique nature. Romanov is one of the strongest warriors ever to open his eyes. Samael is his primary name, but he has hundreds. Perhaps, even thousands, for he is very old and has seen endless battles. The Sumerians knew him as *Melammu*, the Bright One. Or *Buidu Ilu*, the Ghost God, because of his ability to blend into any surrounding like a chameleon. *Sarzamani*, the King of Lightning, because of the sword he wields. Samael is feared by every dragon, for he has the power to imprison them."

"Can he kill the dragons?"

Theseus smiled. "Of course! Samael is one of the Slayer Class. He can take any life with ease, but he does it only when the One commands."

"Then, Samael could kill you, I suppose?"

"Of course, but only if your God ordered it. The dragons have tried again and again to lure Samael to their side, and for half a millennia, they thought him a fellow rebel, but it turned out Samael was a spy. I'd always suspected him of subterfuge, because I can see both sides. Elohim and human. And sight is not our only ability. Halflings can cross back and forth twixt worlds. We can enter Sen-Sen or any of the lower realms at will, and we may live amongst humans as a true member of their society. Unlike dragons, we needn't change our appearance to blend in."

"Then, this is your real body?" asked the duke.

"Yes, actually, it is. And because I am half elohim, I do not age."

"Is that why Serena di Specchio doesn't age?"

"Serena? She is a lovely little liar. Her youth comes from a baser source. Human blood. She's a vampire. Saraqael turned her long ago."

"And the late Sir William Trent? Who turned him?"

His host took a deep breath. "Strange that you should ask me about Trent. He asked many times to try the Maze, but I refused him. I'd known him for, oh, two hundred years or more when someone finally put an end to him."

"Two hundred years? That's impossible."

"Quite possible, Charles. Trent was just one of many pseudonyms, but his birth name was Leopold Rákóczi, son of a Romanian prince. The Carpathians are a breeding ground for that type. Leopold was disinherited by his father for summoning forth a high-ranking demon duke of the netherworld named Satanachia. It's said Rákóczy sacrificed six-hundred sixty-six infants, children, and adolescents— all female—to gain power and an extended life from the demon. He quite literally sold his soul."

"All of them female? Children? Infants? That monster had control of my wife, when she was very young and would control her still, if he could! I pray he's rotting in the deepest level of Hell," said Charles bitterly.

"I'm certain his soul is, but the demon that inhabited and used the human form can return. And if that demon wants your wife, he's not easily stopped."

"You mean, he could come back?"

"Not the soul of Trent, not the Romanian who made the pact. It's the demon duke called Satanachia who'd come back, and he could imitate Trent's appearance. I'd be wary of that, if I were you."

"And what of your extended life, Theseus? Have you sold your soul?" Charles asked.

"Not at all. My cells renew themselves naturally, as Adam's once did. I am eternally young, but I can alter my appearance, if I wish. Whenever I work in London, I intentionally imagine my dark hair to be salted with strands of silver and add age lines to my face and hands. Looking older makes me seem more trustworthy and wise, you understand. It is strange that humans believe wisdom resides within a lack of pigmentation."

"You just imagine your hair is silver?" Sinclair asked, puzzled by the comment. "Is that all it takes to alter your physicality?"

"It's also how the elohim alter their appearance. This Trent you mentioned, or rather the demon that inhabited him, could feign almost any shape, which is why your Ripper had so many appearances. Trent and his demon-possessed friends committed those crimes and more," he said, rising to add several logs to the fire. "It grows late, and you begin to stifle yawns, I've noticed. Let me quickly finish my story. Have you heard of the Minotaur?"

"Every classics scholar knows the account. He was either Aegeus's son or else a monster that consumed the son. The labyrinth is his domain."

"Old Aegeus believed he was my father, but my mother had lain with Poseidon the night before. When I came of age, she told me to approach King Aegeus and claim his throne on behalf of my own kingdom. And so, when my grandfather died, I went Aegeus and announced myself as Prince Theseus of Troezen. I also declared myself heir to Aegeus's throne. Rather than deny me, the king welcomed me as a true son, but ordered me to perform one small task to prove my worth."

"You had to face the Minotaur?" asked his guest.

"Actually, no," said Theseus. "The tale of the Minotaur is a literary blind to keep people from learning the truth. The fallen realm have no wish for unworthy humans to attempt the Maze."

"The monster's a lie, yet the labyrinth is real?"

"Oh, yes. We're sitting above the entrance."

Charles looked at the flagstone floor, imagining a vast domain beneath his feet. "It's below this room?"

"It is."

"You've said the castle is underground. If so, how can the equinox moon shine on the gate's lintel, if that gate is deeper yet?"

"An excellent question, my friend, and the answer is Eluna," the hybrid replied.

"Eluna?"

"Yes. She's a goddess of the moon. Didn't you know that?"

"That's why she's here?"

"We certainly don't need Araqiel, but where Eluna goes, he follows. Dragons can be so very needy. At least, this one is."

"How does a woman, even a goddess, shine moonlight? Are you telling me she really *is* the moon?"

"Oh, no, not at all! That would be quite absurd, wouldn't it? Historically, she's claimed to represent the moon, or to be the moon's daughter. That moon was called Nanna. Her brother was thought to be the sun god, Shamash."

"Does that make Araqiel the sun?"

"I'm sure he thinks of himself in such grandiose terms, but no. Ara is just a young dragon with great aspirations."

"And what are Eluna's aspirations?" asked Sinclair.

"Ah, now, that is different. Worshipping Eluna requires a sacrifice. Usually, this is a blood offering, either your own or that of a victim. In return, she gives her magical light."

"Her light? If she isn't the moon, then what light is it?"

"Another excellent question, Charles. Now, you mustn't tell Araqiel, but I've bribed Eluna with a *small* offering, and she's given me a vial of that silvery essence. It's an incandescent fluid that imitates lunar light."

"And what small offering did you make to her? What did you give in return for the moonlight?" the duke asked, fearing the answer.

The halfling took a deep breath. "She wanted only one thing. A night with you."

Sinclair jumped to his feet and started for the door, waving his arms angrily as he went. "That will never happen! Not ever!"

"Charles, wait," Theseus begged as he followed the duke. "Robby Sinclair will become a formidable young man one day, but would you leave him an orphan?"

"Are you threatening me?"

"I am being honest with you," Theseus said, grasping Sinclair's wrists. "I am your true friend, Charles. You may not realise it yet, but I am. Please, come back to the fire."

"Not until you explain why my son would be an orphan!" shouted the duke, throwing off the halfling's grip.

Theseus lifted both hands in the air, resigned to the other's wishes. "Very well. I didn't want to coerce you, but if you refuse, the others will kill you. Now, I know you believe the One watches after you and will protect you, but where was he, when Araqiel covered your mouth with chloroform and threw you into his coach? Where was he, when Flint grabbed Adele?"

"My Saviour was with us both, just as he is here with me now, Theseus, so be careful of your blasphemous words."

"I speak only truth," the hybrid answered. "The One is not here. No power exists that can pierce this room. Do you see the runes upon the stonework? They form unbreakable wards that prevent anyone or anything from entering. We are in a chamber of profound silence, Charles. Nothing gets in, and nothing gets out. Now, please, come back to the fire."

Reluctantly, Charles resumed his chair. "You're wrong about your wards, Theseus. My Lord is here, no matter what you might think."

"If that brings you comfort, fine," the other murmured. "You must still face the Maze. That is a fact."

His host opened a glass-doored cabinet and removed two crystal decanters. Holding one aloft, he asked, "Mastika?"

"I've had enough wine, thank you."

Theseus returned, carrying both decanters: one filled with an amber fluid, the other clear as glass. He poured the clear liqueur into a pair of tall flutes and handed one to Charles.

"It's not wine. Mastika is a Greek digestive, made from the mastic tree, an evergreen that grows in my home country. The resin of the tree lends a tart, wonderfully woodsy sort of flavour to the drink. We call it the Tears of Chios. The island of Chios is part of Greece now, but in my youth, it was called Ophioússa. It means snake island."

"This was made on a snake island?" asked Charles, staring at the mysterious liqueur. "How does that help with digestion?"

"Poison and healing form two sides of the same coin. Many plants called poisonous have medicinal uses. And the name is a little misleading. The snakes were really a type of dragon that looked more like a sphinx. They were called the Ophidia, but they no longer inhabit Chios. The ophidia were considered healers. Mastika always settles my stomach after a distasteful night."

Charles took a sip, the rich notes of evergreen reminded him of cool forests and autumn nights. "Has my company caused you poor digestion, Dr. Theseus?"

"Please, call me Alphonse, and no, spending time with you is enjoyable and energising. The distaste to the evening came from our dinner companions. Truthfully, if I never saw Araqiel and his lunatic sister again, it would not displease me!"

"Why invite them? Is it only for Eluna's light?"

"Primarily, yes, but truth be told, I could probably open the gates without the light. However, that alternative is so very distasteful, even an ocean of mastika couldn't heal the acidic pangs in my stomach."

"What alternative is that?"

Theseus remained silent for several minutes, gazing thoughtfully into the clear liqueur.

"Well?" the duke prompted.

"I don't like to speak his name, but the alternative is my father."

"King Aegeus?"

"No. I refer to my true father. Trust me when I say you do not want to dine with him, Charles. He makes Araqiel seem like a taste of heaven!"

Charles set his glass aside. "You mean Poseidon, don't you?"

"Yes," Theseus whispered. "His epithet 'the earth shaker' is well-earned. He pets you one minute, then skewers you with his trident the next."

"Not much of a father," observed the human.

"No, but then he still hates his own father. Never ask him about Kronos. You'll be there for decades whilst he drones on and on about his grandfather's castration and Kronos's insatiable appetite for his own children. Truly, these gods are wretched parents, and yet they procreate again and again and again. And so, I avoid my father. That is why I love this room. The ancient runes predate Kronos and prevent even him from spying on me."

"How do fallen angels give birth to other elohim?"

"Another insightful question. They don't actually. It's all play-acting. They pretend to be this or that, as though assigned by some overarching director or playwright, but even playacting as parents is distasteful. No one wants to assume the subservient 'son' or 'daughter' role, which means those who play them often rebel. In truth, they all rebel over and over. It is not a fellowship of gentlemen. And so I avoid them all, if I can."

Both men grew quiet, their thoughts on fathers and sons. After some time, Theseus gulped down his mastika and changed the subject. "Did you ever study Perseus?"

"The founder of Mycenae?"

Theseus smiled. "I thought you might know him. Perseus is a kindred spirit. Another hybrid, I mean; born of the Princess Danae of Argos and the Olympian Zeus."

"Your Uncle Zeus?"

Theseus laughed. "Yes, I suppose so. The elohim aren't able to procreate with one another, but they can do so with humans. Like Poseidon, Zeus failed at parenting. All the Olympians are cruel and self-absorbed. Perseus and I share many characteristics, but he's never walked the Maze. Of all the demigods, I alone have dared to navigate its hallways. The Maze changed me, Charles. Just as it will change you. Fulfilling such a task is a privilege. It will awaken your blood. Tell me, Charles, have you begun to dream of dragons yet?"

Charles stared at the other. "I sometimes dream of dragons and dark mirrors. Was Araqiel the dragon from my childhood?"

"I doubt it. Araqiel was imprisoned until very recently, but there are other dragons that walk the earth freely; denizens of realms beyond human perception, though, some humans can see beyond the veil."

"Like Henry MacAlpin."

"Yes, but also your wife. And your children, for they've inherited your blood, along with that of the duchess. They are doubly blessed. Charles, I cannot force you into the Maze. It must be your choice to go, but your blood calls to it. That is why you dream."

"I keep telling you, I've no blood that isn't human, Theseus. I am the son of two humans, who themselves descended from long, branching lines of human men and women, reaching back to Adam."

The physician refilled their flutes with more mastika. "Adam was once a citizen of the divine realm. Have you never considered how his blood might have changed after his ejection from the Mount of Eden?"

"The Mount? Eden was a garden."

"The Divine Assembly sit upon a great mountain, Charles. The King's Garden is but one small part of the vast realm. After his sin and expulsion, Adam's very essence began to change, but the *potential* remained. A divine spark that, once ignited, can return a man to greatness. There are certain activities which ignite that divine spark within us, Charles. The former glory can be restored."

"You talk of witchcraft and magic," the duke countered. "Mankind's inheritance is restored through Christ's blood, not through twisted rituals. And if you're trying to tell me that any of my ancestors behaved in such a manner, you're wrong."

Theseus took a sip of mastika, his dark eyes shining. "Some of your distant forebears did, Charles. And not all your ancestors were strictly human. Richard the Lionheart boasted of his descent from the river goddess Melusine."

Sinclair stood. "I've heard enough of this blasphemous rubbish. How do I return to my prison?"

"It is not a prison, my friend. Your apartments are finer than my own."

"If I'm not a prisoner, then I may leave, correct?"

"Sadly, no," Theseus admitted.

"Then, I'm a prisoner, and if you won't show me, then I'll find my own way back." Sinclair started towards the door, but the ticking he'd heard inside his bedchamber and in the dining hall commenced anew, and a wave of nausea overwhelmed him.

Theseus offered his arm as support. "It's the ticking, isn't it? There are no clocks anywhere in the castle, Charles. The ticking arises from the Time Maze. It calls to you."

"I'm tired, nothing more," the human lied, wanting only to leave the accursed castle and return to his family. *But I can't. I'm trapped here, and the only way out is through that horrid Maze.*

Theseus opened the doors. "I could talk with you for years, my friend, but you should get some rest. Eluna's sleep spells may have interfered with the soporifics I administered. I promise you, that witch will pay for her actions."

"We've enjoyed drinks, but my stomach needs real food. Might you send a tray to my rooms?" asked Sinclair.

"Of course. Voithos brought us plenty of food, but we've been so busy talking, we've let it go cold."

They left the private drawing room and re-entered the castle's dimly lit corridors and stone galleries. The two men walked and walked and walked, upstairs and down, until, at long last, they reached the apartment door.

Two mountainous men stood guard on either side.

Theseus placed a friendly hand on the duke's shoulder and offered a pleasant smile. "I know this is difficult, but you are up to the task. I can sense it. Tomorrow evening, the test begins. For tonight, keep your apartment door locked. Do not invite anyone to enter. Nights here can be very dangerous, as I'm sure you know. I've placed these men here for your protection."

With that final word, the enigmatic halfling, Dr. Alphonse Theseus, bowed and left his guest alone.

CHAPTER FIFTEEN
Maze World - Charles has a visitor

One of the guards unlocked the door, and Charles entered the dimly lit drawing room, noticing a familiar scent.

Raspberry and vanilla.

The fragrance hit him quite hard, and the nausea returned with a vengeance. The duke gripped the nearest chair to steady himself. How cruel these captors were! Had they used his wife's signature scent as some new means of torture?

The room began to spin and tilt, but just as a spiralling cone of blackness began to envelop his vision, a pair of strong hands took Sinclair by the shoulders and guided him to a sturdy chair.

"Thank you," he whispered to the invisible helper.

"You're most welcome, sir," Fenwick replied. "Here, sir, drink this."

Charles felt a glass being pressed into his hands, and he opened his eyes. "Is this water?"

"Just water, sir. You're dehydrated and in need of food."

The duke drained the glass. The water tasted like honey, as though drawn from a wellspring of pure nectar. "Are you certain this isn't some sleeping concoction?"

"Only water, my lord. It's from my own home. I brought it with me."

"Then, thank you, Mr. Fenwick. I'm much better now. I believe Theseus is sending up a tray of food."

"Yes, I know, sir."

Haimsbury's brows furrowed in puzzlement. "How could you know? I've just returned from dinner—or at least, that was the original plan."

"But the others irritated Dr. Theseus so much that he threw them out? Isn't that what happened?"

"How can you know that?" Charles muttered in shock.

Fenwick's pleasant features widened into an endearing grin. "I know many things, my lord. I know Dr. Theseus escorted you to the castle's inner sanctum, as he calls it. The warded chamber. There are runes upon the rocks, to prevent being overheard or watched."

"Did he tell you about it?"

"No, sir. As I've already said, I haven't actually met anyone from the castle."

"But surely, you met Theseus when he hired you?"

Fenwick's chameleon eyes lightened into the same icy orbs Charles had noticed previously. His facial features changed from pleasant to perfection, and the hair lightened from auburn to a lustrous golden colour that flowed down his shoulders like molten metal.

"Forgive me, Fenwick. I'd quite forgotten your true nature."

"You need never apologise to me, sir. Not ever. However, make no mention of me to the others." The servant's former face and hair returned, and he knelt down to remove the duke's shoes and socks.

"An angel shouldn't be serving me," the duke objected.

"What else should I be doing, sir?"

"Praising God, I suppose. Isn't that what angels do?"

Fenwick smiled patiently. "Praise is much more than singing. It may also be accomplished through obedience. I am a soldier, my lord, and go where I'm sent."

The duke smiled in return. "Forgive me."

"You have a kind and tender heart, Duke Charles. It's my honour to watch over you."

A hand knocked on the outer door, and Fenwick stepped to one side. "They've no idea I'm here, sir. If you would...?"

Charles answered the knock. "Yes?"

"A tray for you, Your Grace," one of the guards told him. "May I carry it in for you?"

"No, I can take it. Thank you, uh, Mister...?"

"I'm just called Macon, sir," said the mountainous guard.

"Mr. Macon, thank you. Did the princess touch or interfere with any of the food on this tray?"

"No, sir. I've not seen the princess for hours."

"Very good. Thank you."

Charles carried the tray into the apartment, and the guard shut the exterior door. There was a loud *click!* as the guard turned the key.

Fenwick took the tray and arranged the dishes on a large oval table near the pleasant fire. He passed his hand across each item, offering up a whispered prayer in a language Charles sometimes heard Anatole Romanov use.

"All is safe now, sir. You may enjoy the meal."

Sinclair took a seat near the table. "Did you do something to the food?"

"I merely asked the One to make it safe, sir. The guard was lying, of course. Nothing can harm you now."

"What language was that?" asked Charles as he removed a silver dome from one of the plates.

"It is the language of my class, sir. A dialect spoken by soldiers, I mean. The one you call Prince Anatole is my superior officer."

"The prince once told me that he's an investigator. Rather like a Scotland Yard detective."

"That's true, sir. We're trained to act covertly and investigate the enemy's plots. One stratagem is to embed ourselves into the enemy's camp. Prince Anatole is a master at that. Please, eat, sir. Your body requires nourishment, and then you must rest." The servant handed Haimsbury a small glass filled with amber liquid. "To remind you of home, sir."

Charles sniffed the spirit. "This cannot be. It smells like Drummond Reserve! How on earth did you find this, Fenwick? I doubt Theseus keeps any here. Wherever *here* is."

"No, Dr. Theseus doesn't have anything like it. I brought the whisky with me, sir."

"I don't suppose you also brought the scent?

"Raspberry and vanilla?" the valet asked as he drew a footstool up close to the chair. He placed the duke's bare feet onto the richly embroidered surface and answered, "Whilst you had dinner, I travelled to the human realm for a short mission. Before I returned, I stopped by your home and took a small decanter of the whisky and two bars of the duchess's soap—to help you sleep."

"That scent hit me very hard as I entered, but now, it..." Tears formed on his lashes, and Charles gripped the whisky glass with both hands. "Now I just want to be home, Fenwick. I miss my wife and children with all my being."

"I know, sir, but the One allows this test. You must walk the Maze."

Sinclair wiped the tears away. "Is Adele safe?"

"Yes, sir. I checked myself. Even now, that dear lady is resting in a lovely apartment at Montmore House. Lord Salperton will care for Lady Adele until her mind is healed."

"What's wrong with her mind?" asked Charles, his tone changing to suspicion. "What did Araqiel do to her?"

"Be calm, my lord," said the servant. "The dragon prince did all he could to frighten the young lady, but the truth of those dark days is concealed, deep within the recesses of Lady Adele's memory. There they'll remain, emerging only in dreams until they may be safely recovered."

"The way my wife's memories are hidden? She still dreams about Trent and wolves."

"Yes, sir, but I'm told the duchess will soon recall all her forgotten memories. At a time, when they are most needed."

"And Della? Who helped her escape? Was it you?"

"No, sir. Two of my brethren had that honour. My task is to look after you. Have no fear for your daughter, sir. We know what we're doing, and we would never harm that dear lady. Trust us to look after her, sir. Trust in the One."

"Are you really from God, or is this a trick? I have to know, Fenwick."

The servant stood and then stepped back a little. He raised his arms high, and his entire form began to shimmer and brighten. His six-foot height lengthened until his head reached the chandelier, which hung at least twenty-five feet above Sinclair. The auburn hair transformed again, and the strands tumbled down the broad shoulders like a river of gold. The servant's livery became a long robe of the palest sky blue, and a scarlet sash encircled his waist. A broadsword hung from a leather belt, its black scabbard covered in strange letters made from starlight.

Charles fell to his knees and began to tremble, for the warrior's countenance glowed as bright as a thousand lamps.

"Fear not, Charles Sinclair," he said, touching the human's hand. "In the great council, I am called Hadraniel, a name that praises the One for his great majesty and honour. The One's love for humanity is inscribed upon my heart. Only HE is worthy, Charles. Only the blood of *Ha Shem* the Name, known to you as Christ the Son, washes away sins."

"But why reveal yourself to me? Why bring me here? I don't understand. Why does the fallen realm want me as their king?"

"Because you have a mission that the fallen seek to circumvent. The One has placed you in government and made you a secret king for his reasons. Your influence will change the world. And though you will never be publicly crowned, your opinion and power will equal that of any prince. This future will become clear to you once you finish the Maze. It is your destiny to traverse its passages."

"But why Della? Why was she thrown into this, if it's my mission?" Sinclair dared to ask.

"Adele also has a great mission, and her memories will help to guide her future steps. The One has sent me to protect you, son of Adam. And he has sent you a token, to help in your quest."

Hadraniel removed the scarlet ribbon from his waist and passed it to Charles. "This red thread was formed before the world began. Keep it with you at all times; close to your heart. Whenever you are in need, think of Elizabeth, and she will hear you."

"What? How? I don't understand. Please, I'm but a human, and I'm so very tired."

"Then allow me to offer restoration, son of Adam."

Hadraniel touched the duke's head. A surge of energetic fire ran through the human's bones and blood. "Your destiny lies within the Maze. To help you, the One designed this ribbon. It is the visible manifestation of that which is invisible; a thread more powerful than any steel, that runs from your heart to Elizabeth's. Think of her when you are lost. Now, you must eat and rest, Charles Robert Arthur. Tomorrow, at the setting of the sun, your task will commence. Stay true to the One, and all will be well!"

The servant vanished, and the human fell on his face, asking the One, God Almighty, for guidance.

CHAPTER SIXTEEN
Real World - Haimsbury-Branham Hospital

Three hours before Cordelia Stuart experienced intense contractions at Montmore, those living in Whitechapel, were dealing with the aftermath of a shooting. Elizabeth's ears still rang from the pistol shots. She'd been taken to an examination room inside the hospital's main building, looked after by Anthony Gehlen and Michael Emerson

Beth had fainted from shock, and her first thoughts upon opening her eyes were of her cousin. "Paul? Where am I? Where's Paul?"

"Lord Aubrey's dealing with the shooter," answered Emerson. "There's blood on your dress. Are you hurt?"

"Hurt? What?"

"Beth, are you in pain?"

"No, I don't think so," she said. "What happened? Where's Lord Ailesleigh?"

"Who?" asked Emerson. "That fellow with auburn hair?"

"I believe he's gone to Leman Street as well," said Gehlen. "Now, let us do our job."

A crowd of nurses, doctors, and students milled about in the corridor outside her room. Beth could hear them talking. "Who's out there? Have the reporters left?" she asked.

"Most ran over to Leman Street, but a few are waiting to hear about your condition. Your pulse is quite rapid, but fear would do that anyone. We need to move you elsewhere. Can you walk?" Gehlen opened the door slightly and called to the charge nurse. "Sister! In here, please!"

A woman wriggled her way through the waiting crowd and slipped into the room. It was Mrs. Howard. "Yes, sir?"

"Dr. Emerson and I want to move the duchess to the nearest private room."

"Anthony, I'm fine," the duchess objected. "I'm not in pain."

"I could carry her," suggested Emerson.

"If there are reporters out there, that's the last thing we need, Michael," said Gehlen. "No, if she can walk, then it's better. Sister, lead the way, and we'll follow."

The duchess and her medical entourage left the examination room, and Captain Crenshaw joined them. Ida Stanley stood nearby, and Elizabeth took her hand. "Come with us, Ida."

Michael O'Brien and Harry Dam from *The Star* shadowed the group, keeping their distance to avoid being noticed.

They entered the lift, and Mrs. Howard led them to a lovely suite, one floor up. The new corridor was much quieter, and Elizabeth was taken to a private room with yellow walls and black-and-white floors. Captain Crenshaw remained in the hallway to guard the door.

Emerson and Gehlen met together in a small sitting area connected to the suite. In the main room, Ida helped Mrs. Howard remove the duchess's clothing down to the chemise, then placed the duchess upon the bed.

"It's very strange, my lady," Howard told the duchess. "Your dress is stained quite badly, but the blood doesn't go beyond your second petticoat. I see no injuries, which is a great mercy." The nurse grew quiet, her hand touching Beth's abdomen. "Have you felt any nausea recently, my lady?"

"Some. Does it matter? Mrs. Howard, if I'm not wounded, then the blood came from someone else. Has anyone else been admitted? Did Lord Aubrey appear to be hurt? Or Lord Ailesleigh? Ida, would you ask Captain Crenshaw to come in, please?"

Beth drew the bed coverings up close to her chin and sat up a little. She felt nauseous and very worried.

Crenshaw entered. "Yes, Your Grace?"

"Please, go to Leman Street at once, Captain. The blood on my dress must be Lord Aubrey's, or perhaps, Lord Ailesleigh's. Go and find them, please!"

The Texan bowed, his hand on his heart. "I'll go right now, ma'am."

The ICI agent rushed back into the corridor. Beth could hear him barking orders to reporters to clear a path. As Captain Crenshaw exited the lift on the main floor, he passed by Nathan Kessler.

"Is the duchess injured?" asked Kessler.

"Cain't say, sir. I gotta go."

"Yes, of course," the other replied. "But she's being seen by one or more of my doctors. Is that right?"

Crenshaw kept walking, aiming for the entry doors. "Like I said, sir. I cain't say."

As Crenshaw left, Kessler sighed and returned to a conversation with several *Gazette* reporters. But sensing a story, all of them ran after the departing ICI agent like a pack of hungry dogs. They peppered Crenshaw with questions, 'Is the duchess hurt?' 'Who's the shooter?' 'Has this to do with the duke's mission to America?' 'Are we at war with Germany?'

Crenshaw gave no reply other than 'no comment', but the tiresome pack continued to yap behind the Texan, hoping for a bite of tasty news. Alone and without an audience, Kessler decided the real story was taking place one floor up, so he pressed the button for the lift.

Upstairs, inside the private hospital suite, Emerson and Gehlen began the examination.

"I'm perfectly fine," Beth insisted as Nathan Kessler's face appeared in the doorway.

"Are you sure about that?" the mysterious American asked, shutting the door. "Perhaps, you should let a professional decide that."

Michael and Anthony exchanged glances. Michael spoke first. "Nathan, it might be better to have fewer people in here just now. I'm sure the reporters would like to receive a briefing."

"Most have left for Leman Street. Besides, there's ample room in here," Kessler objected. "As director, it's my prerogative to be present."

"Not if I do not wish it," Beth told him angrily. "These two gentlemen are my personal physicians. You are not."

"It's imperative that I know everything that happens under this roof," Kessler dared argue. "I will not leave."

"Continue along this path, Dr. Kessler, and I shall dismiss you immediately!" Beth shouted, her eyes wide. "I will not have you overseeing my own doctors. Get out!"

Kessler left, slamming the door behind him.

"I thought he'd never leave," said Emerson. "Oh, this came for you," he told his colleague. "Mrs. Howard brought it up. Now, let's see what's happened here, Beth. Anthony, do you wish to begin, or shall I?"

Gehlen was still reading the message. He folded the note into his pocket. "Actually, I have to see Treves. There's a minor problem at the London, but I can stay if you want."

"Treves? Why?" asked Elizabeth.

"It's to do with the inner circle meeting, but I promised Fred I'd offer an opinion on another medical matter first. Beth, do you want me to remain?"

"No, not if you have another calling."

He kissed her cheek. "You're the most important calling in all the world, Elizabeth. I can stay."

"Go," she whispered, "but stop and find out about Paul, if you don't mind."

"I will."

He left and Michael shut the door. "I probably shouldn't be telling you this, Beth, but the reason Anthony left was because there's been a shooting at the London as well. It's quite likely Paul's already gone there. And if he is injured, Treves and Gehlen will look after him. Don't worry. God's still in control."

He washed his hands in the nearby sink, dried them on a fringed cotton towel, embroidered with the HBH monogram, and then brought a chair up to the bed.

"Beth, that earlier exchange aside, what do you think of Dr. Kessler now that you've met him?"

"He's not at all likeable, is he? Still, he has no equal when it comes to communicable diseases."

"Yes, so he keeps saying," Emerson replied.

"You don't agree?" she asked.

"I'd like to see proof of his claims. Regardless, the man's overbearing and authoritarian, especially with the nurses. Does this hurt?" he asked, pressing her upper abdomen.

"No."

He passed his right hand across her entire abdominal area, palpating carefully. "Beth, how long since your menstrual cycle returned?"

"Should it have returned? I assumed it could take some time after giving birth."

"Most mothers' courses start up again in two months, some sooner. You gave birth in mid-June?"

"The ninth for Robby. The tenth for Georgie, just after midnight."

"And you bled quite badly. A torn placenta?"

"Yes, so you told me at the time, but I'm much better now. Anthony's been to see me quite often since. Michael, why are you asking me these questions?"

"You've had some worries, of course," the physician continued as he pressed down on her midsection. "Worry can lead to physical and emotional issues. With Charles gone, I'm sure your emotions are erratic."

"I'd not call them erratic, exactly, but I can't help thinking about it," she said, her tone becoming irritated. "I keep busy to avoid thinking about Charles. Paul's been my support, and Della's return gives me hope."

"Have you noticed anything else?" he asked, returning her silk chemise to its proper place and covering her with the sheet.

"Michael, am I injured or not?"

"Any nausea? Lack of energy?"

"Yes, of course! It's been quite awful, if you must know. What is all this?" she asked growing angry and trying to sit.

Emerson answered gently as he pushed her back against the mattress. "Don't sit up yet, Beth, and please, let me do my job, all right? I know you've been under a great strain, but have you felt overly tired? A weariness that hangs about you? Any dizzy spells?"

Beth sighed. "No dizzy spells, but yes, I'm exceedingly tired, if you must know. Isn't that to be expected under the circumstances?"

"Fever? Chills?"

Her anger vanished. "Michael, do you think I have this influenza that's going round?"

"Possibly."

"We had a neighbour who had the illness, but I've not been around anyone from there, nor has any of my staff. Mrs. Reston is my children's nurse, and she's cautioned all of us to avoid homes with colds or ague, so we don't pass anything to the children or to

Cordelia. Michael, you've been my doctor all this time. Surely, you know me as well as anyone."

"Yes, and I examined you before I left for Edinburgh, which is why I'm asking all this. Since that time, your abdomen has swollen, yet your face looks thinner. Is your digestion changed?"

She sighed. "A little."

"Vomiting?"

"Once or twice. My emotions are all over the place, Michael, but I cannot allow anyone to see I'm under strain. I mustn't show pain or hurt or despair. I only tell Paul what's in my heart. If he's been shot, I don't know what I'll do!"

He held her hand, his light grey eyes filled with compassion. "It's been my great honour to be your family physician, Elizabeth, and I know how much Charles's absence grieves your heart. If he were here, he'd insist I look after you."

She nodded, and a tear crossed down her flushed cheek.

"Your cheeks and forehead are warm," he said. "Let me measure that."

Emerson found a thermometer and placed it beneath her tongue. Whilst she couldn't speak to answer questions, he listened to Beth's heart. A moment later, he removed the thermometer. "One hundred degrees. Beth, it might be best for you to avoid the twins until the fever is down. And may I ask one other, somewhat personal question?"

"If you must."

"Had you and Charles resumed your marriage bed prior to the christening?"

She stared at her friend, eyes grown wide as she finally realised what was in Emerson's mind. "That's not possible."

"Not possible to resume marital relations?"

"No, I mean. Well, yes, we did, but we'd slept together no more than two weeks before Charles was taken," she told him. "Michael, I cannot be with child. It's impossible."

"It is quite possible, and it happens all the time. That's why there are so many Irish twins in the world."

"Irish twins?"

"Children born less than a year apart. But it could also be influenza. Go home and put your feet up and avoid seeing the twins or Cordelia for now. Try to stay as calm as possible. Sleep, if you need it, even if it means you sleep through the day. I've a telephone installed at my home now, so ring me if you need anything. No matter the hour. If you develop a high fever or abdominal pain, you must ring me at once. Do you understand?"

"Yes, of course," she whispered, tears staining her face. "Oh, Michael, I cannot be with child. Not without Charles. I need him with me!"

"He'll be home soon, Beth. The Lord has more for the duke to accomplish. Now, consider this a warning for your health. The hospital is practically finished. Let the staff take over now."

"If that staff includes Dr. Kessler, then I'll require more information about the man."

"Stop worrying," said Emerson.

"Yes," she answered somewhat distractedly "Would you send in Mrs. Howard to help me dress?"

"Of course," he said, offering a brotherly kiss to the forehead. "Andrea sends her love, by the way. When I left this morning, she made me promise to tell you."

"And is she well?"

"Very well. We're expecting our first child in about seven months. My mother's on cloud nine. I just wish my father were still here to know."

"I'm sure he's telling everyone in heaven about it, Michael. Congratulations," Beth told him, drying her eyes. "Please, forgive my mercurial temperament. It's been a trying morning, and I'm very worried about Paul."

"No need to explain. I understand." Emerson crossed to the door but added one last thing before he left. "In occurs to me that seven months could be your date as well, Duchess. Another child in late April or early May."

"I'm sure you're wrong," the duchess answered.

Emerson left, but whilst alone, Elizabeth whispered a quick prayer. "Father God, please look after Paul. I pray he's not injured, but if so, please, let it be minor. And bring my husband home! I need Charles with me! And if there is a child growing inside me, he'll need his father here. We all do."

Several blocks away on Leman Street, as the shooter was led to H-Division Police Station, a curious thing happened. The crowd that followed Lord Aubrey began to grow increasingly agitated, as though some foul spirit ran through them. Paul held the limping man by the right arm, whilst a police sergeant held the other; then someone, or rather *something*, struck the sergeant on back of the head, knocking him unconscious. This led to an outbreak of utter chaos, for as the shooter's free arm dangled in the air, every citizen and reporter rushed in to restrain it.

Improbably, at the very same second, a runaway horse and hansom appeared out of the aether and came barreling like a demon up Leman Street. The horse was a black stallion, and witnesses would later claim the animal's nostrils exhaled fire, and his eyes were crimson red. With such terror rushing down upon them, the panicked crowd dispersed into streams of screaming as EVERYONE scrambled to escape the demonic horse's sharp hooves and the hellish hansom's fiery wheels.

With no thought for himself, Paul Stuart instinctively tried to rescue the fallen police sergeant. He grabbed at the sergeant's limp hand to pull both him and the shooter to safety. The pure physics of the situation meant there would be no escaping for any of them, but adding to the danger, a black cloud of ravens flew out of the hansom's windows, enveloping the shooter, the sergeant, and the earl. The black birds formed a swirling cyclone that actually sucked the shooter from this realm into another and almost killed the earl.

Only two people saw it.

Or rather one human and one angel saw it.

Aubrey saw the horse and hansom, he saw the dense twister of cawing demons, heard the rushing of their black wings, smelled fire and sulphur.

Paul was certain Death had come to take him.

But the angel disguised as Lord Ailesleigh had remained with Stuart and threw a spiritual shield round the earl and the unconscious sergeant, that enfolded them both into a supernatural embrace and protected them from any harm. Ailesleigh, Aubrey, and the sergeant actually winked out of existence, just long enough for the hansom, horse, and ravens to *pass through* them.

From his perspective, Stuart believed with all his heart and soul he was about to die. Paul thought of his wife first, his beautiful Cordelia, and he wished he'd spent more time with her. He thought next of his unborn son and prayed God would watch after him. He wondered if Charles were dead, and if he'd soon see his closest friend in heaven.

But then, as the melee of birds and beast passed through him, at the last tick of that half second, came the sweet scent of raspberry and vanilla. Paul smiled.

The scent came from two bars of Elizabeth's signature soap, hidden inside the angel Hadraniel's pocket.

CHAPTER SEVENTEEN
Haimsbury-Branham Hospital

Half an hour later, Paul awoke with a start. During the half second of time when he'd disappeared to allow the coach, horse, and raven horde to pass through him, the earl stood talking to his rescuer. The bright angel explained to Paul that Charles Sinclair was being held prisoner deep inside a dark labyrinth. The shocked human asked the beautiful being to take him to his cousin so he might speak to him, but the angel answered no. He promised that Charles would be home soon.

Awakening to the real world, felt out of sync and flat to Aubrey, for this human realm seemed less real than the dream realm.

But was it a dream?

"Paul?" asked a sweet voice.

Is that an angel?

Almost. His beloved Cousin Elizabeth, asked again, her voice more plaintive. "Paul, talk to me, please!" Her fingers were tight round his hand. She was crying.

"What happened?" he asked. "Where is this?"

Relief and joy replaced the worry in her eyes. "Praise God! Paul, I thought I'd lost you!" she said, kissing his hand.

"No, darling. I'd never leave you. Where am I?"

"At our hospital. You've lost some blood. Paul, why did you leave? Didn't you know you'd been shot?"

"Shot?"

"Yes, darling, shot. You should have let the constables or Granger take that man to Leman Street. You should have stayed here."

"Man? What man? Leman Street?"

Paul's mind was all tangled up. Was this the dream or another reality? Had he just spoken to an angel?

His brain was filled with moving pictures: a speeding hansom, a flock of ravens. Fire. Smoke. Then nothing, followed by peace. Bright light and colours deeper and truer than anything on Earth.

"Paul? Darling, look at me."

"Sorry. Did you say I'd been shot?" he asked, only now realising he lay in a bed. "Did you say I lost blood?" He tried to sit up, but a heavy bandage bound his midsection. He felt stiff and weak. "What did you say?"

Didn't this happen before? Last year? We'd gone to Branham. Saucy Jack. Am I reliving that? How was I shot?

"Where's the train?" he asked, immediately realising his mistake. "No, not train, sorry. Someone shot at us, didn't they?"

"Yes, darling, someone did," she said, squeezing his hand again. "You took a bullet to your side. Dr. Emerson called it a flesh wound, but it bled a great deal. Paul, I..." her voice choked, and she began to weep. "When Granger and Lord Ailesleigh brought you in, I thought you might be dead. I thought I'd lost you."

"Ailesleigh?"

"Yes, he and Granger brought you here. Michael said the bullet was quite a large caliber, whatever that means. But you're all right now. Praise God!"

Beth's head lowered as she wept, and she clutched at his hands tightly. Paul tried to think rationally, clearly, but he kept seeing Charles inside a labyrinth. Had an angel told him that?

"Beth, I think someone talked to me," he whispered. "An angel."

"An angel?"

"Yes, but how could that have happened? It makes no sense. Or does it?" He tried to sort through the thick wool inside his brain. He kept seeing images of words, as though looking at a list. Charles. Maze. Castle. Beth. Raspberry and vanilla.

Cordelia. Baby. Son.

"Where's Delia?" he asked. "Is she here?"

"No, dear, you're in hospital. Lord Ailesleigh's promised to send her a telegram, so she won't worry if she hears of the shooting. Daniel's been very helpful."

"Shooting? Daniel?"

"Yes, Paul, you were shot. And Daniel Porter is Lord Ailesleigh's given name. Perhaps, your blood loss has caused some memory issue."

"Ailesleigh? Oh, yes, sorry. You said that before. Do I know him?" *Why can't I think? Did she say blood loss?*

Angel. I talked to an angel.

Charles is in a labyrinth.

"Ailesleigh's the man you met this morning, remember? He works at the Foreign Office in your father's old position."

He tried again to sit up. This time more successfully. Beth placed two pillows behind his back to help.

"Thank you, Princess," he said, sounding more like himself. "I remember meeting him now. Seems like a good man." *Why am I thinking of an angel? Charles is in a labyrinth.* "It's strange. My last thought as I fell was that you were there with me. I could smell your soap."

She smiled and traced his cheek. Paul hadn't shaved for several days, and her fingers brushed through short, wiry hairs. "The mind is a strange kingdom, isn't it? Filled with all sorts of castles, with gates that can open and close without prompting. I'm glad you thought of me. I think of you often. Sir Paul, my warrior knight. Though I'm grown up and married, you'll always be my knight, darling." She squeezed his hand again. "Granger said you probably saved my life. He and Lord Ailesleigh both think I was the target. I suppose Ailesleigh's another knight, then. I remember how closely the two of you stood to me, just before the shooting began—as though you sensed danger."

He kissed her hand. "I'd die for you, Beth, if God ever asked it. Really, I would."

She took a deep breath; the slow, stuttered, childlike sort of breath that happens when you try not to cry. "Please, don't say that. I can't lose you, too. With Charles gone, you're all I have."

The earl smiled, and it seemed to Elizabeth that sunshine filled the room. She'd always loved her cousin's dimpled smile, and how the blue of his eyes glimmered whenever he was happy. For a tiny moment, she felt like a little girl again, placing all her fears and worries on the shoulders of her brave Scottish knight.

"Don't worry, Princess," he promised, kissing her hand again. "I'll always be here for you. Always. And Charles isn't gone, Beth.

He's coming back. Remember that. Believe in that. Now, could you ask Granger or Inspector Reid to come in?"

She nodded, stifling that childlike stutter. "Yes, of course. They're both outside with Sir Thomas, but you need to rest."

The door opened, admitting Michael Emerson, who wore a bright smile. "Now, this is a rare day. I'm back from Scotland less than a day, and I've already seen two Stuart patients. I suppose, this means we've officially opened the hospital, then?"

"It's not the opening I envisioned," the duchess said as she wiped tears from her face.

"Nor mine," said Aubrey. "What time is it?"

"Half past twelve," replied Emerson. "But don't even think of getting up. You're to stay in this bed for at least an hour. Lord Ailesleigh's sent telegrams to both your houses, letting everyone know that you're fine. That's a stretch in your case, Paul, but I didn't want to alarm your wife."

"Beth, are you all right?" asked the patient, his mind finally sharpening. "I hadn't thought to ask. Were you injured?"

"No, darling, I wasn't. Michael, are the reporters still hanging about? Did any of them see the earl brought in?"

"All of them, I'm afraid. There was no getting round it," he said. "I expect all the afternoon editions will carry the story. One or two even snapped photographs with one of those new film cameras."

"Someone must keep Adele and my wife from reading the papers," Paul announced. "Beth, I'd send you home, but I prefer you to keep close to me today. Just in case."

"You should both go home," Emerson argued.

"Not yet," Paul argued. "I've no idea who's behind this, and other shooters may be waiting to follow us home. Beth, are you brave enough to stay with me? I don't wish to alarm you, but this might be a new Redwing plot."

"Redwing? Are you sure? He shouted in German, Paul," said Beth. "Might it be Blackstone?"

Paul searched his mind, but found only memories of ravens and an angel. "Do you remember the exact words?"

"Of course," she told him. "*Wir und die Todten reiten schnell.* It's a line from a poem. *Lenore*, by Gottfried Bürger."

"A poem? Are you sure about that?"

221

"Yes, darling, I'm very sure. When the man said it, I remember thinking it strange. You see, when I was a girl, Father read the poem to me, during one of my German lessons. He asked me what it meant. The poem's about a maiden who's taken on horseback by someone she believes is her lover. The horseman rides exceedingly fast, and she asks him why. His answer is..."

"We and the dead travel fast," Paul finished for her. "She'd been taken by Death."

"Yes. Why would this man shout so obscure a verse?"

"I cannot say, Princess, but I intend to find out. Michael, would you help me dress?"

"Paul, you mustn't get up yet. Rest for an hour, please."

"I have an important meeting at the London, Beth. Fetch Granger for me, please."

"Sir Thomas can chair the meeting."

"No, Beth, someone hired this shooter. Whoever is behind it must see us in public. Do you understand me, Princess? We cannot hide at home."

"Yes, of course, I do. I'm a Stuart, aren't I? And it's just what Grandfather would want. I should send him and Tory a wire about all this, before they read about it in the Paris newspapers. You dress whilst I take care of that." She bent down to kiss his bristly cheek, whispering, "Don't ever get hurt again."

The duchess left, and Michael locked the door. "Your side will be tender for the next few weeks, but I'm sure you already know that. I noticed several old scars when I examined you."

"It's an occupational hazard," Paul said as the physician helped him to stand. "Is that bag for me?"

Emerson opened a brown leather valise, showing the earl a selection of clothing. "Lord Ailesleigh had it delivered from Westminster. Yours were stained and torn. It's a shame, for the shirt and waistcoat are probably ruined."

"Clothing," the earl muttered. "Clothing! Michael, is Reid about? If so, ask him to come in, please."

The earl had buttoned the new trousers and was pulling a pair of black braces over his shirt when the inspector knocked. Emerson unlocked the door and admitted the police detective.

"Edmund, what happened to the shooter?"

"He escaped during the panic, I'm afraid. We never found the driver or the hansom, but you saved Sergeant Littlefield's life, Paul.

He's in the room next door, recovering from a concussion. Two of my constables are here as well. Minor injuries, I'm happy to say."

"And the ravens?" Paul muttered. "Where did they come from?"

"Ravens? I don't know what you mean."

"The flock of birds that appeared at the same time as the runaway hansom. The ravens, Edmund."

"Paul, I saw nothing like that. Nothing. Emerson said you lost a lot of blood, perhaps, you imagined it as you lost consciousness."

"Yes, perhaps," said the earl, not the least bit convinced.

If I talked with an angel, then the ravens may have been supernatural.

We and the dead travel fast.

"Before he escaped, did you or any of your men get a look at the man's clothing?" asked Aubrey.

"Only slightly. They looked expensive."

"But ill-fitting. As if they were borrowed. Edmund, what if this shooter was hired by another and dressed to fit into a crowd of peers and reporters?"

"Yes, I suppose that might be true."

Like Beth, Paul had a remarkable memory, and he closed his eyes to recover the details of the shooter's appearance. "He was six feet tall. Walked with an odd gait, as if limping on one leg. Very thin. Sallow complexion. Grey or light blue eyes. I didn't see much of his hair, because of the hat, but I believe it was light-coloured. He shouted in German, but his accent was English and educated, for later, I heard him cry out to the reporters. He said 'Leave me alone. I didn't do it. It was Patterson! He's not dead!'"

Edmund smiled. "Your memory is without equal, Lord Aubrey."

Paul slipped a shoulder holster over the waistcoat. "Not quite. Charles and Beth both have such memories. We remember most everything we see and hear."

"You shouldn't wear that holster," Emerson told Aubrey. "It could irritate the bandage and open my fine stitching. You could switch sides, but if you wear it on the right, you'll have to fire with your left hand."

Reid laughed. "Our talented earl is ambidextrous, Michael. He shoots equally well with either hand."

"I'm sure that comes in handy to a spy," the physician noted. "No pun intended."

Stuart tried to return the smile, but a wave of pain stabbed his left side.

"That's going to smart like a son-of-a-gun. The less you move, the better," Emerson told him.

"I've been through it before. Thank you, Michael. Are you coming to the meeting at the London?"

"Yes, but I'll be delayed. I need to speak with Dr. Kessler about another matter first. Don't wait on me."

Reid picked up the earl's leather bag and followed him out the door. "Did either of you hear about the shooting at the London?"

Aubrey's face grew concerned. "There was another? When? Did anyone apprehend the shooter?"

"I don't know," said Reid. "I sent a team over, but I've not heard back yet. Thankfully, Treves said no one was injured."

Stuart sighed. "That's a mercy. What happened to Ailesleigh?"

"Who?" asked Edmund.

"A Cornish earl we've just met. He seems like an honest man, and he probably saved my life. I remember him moving close to Beth and me just before the shooting. Then later, as that hansom tried to run us down, he..." Aubrey stopped. Wheels inside his head turned upon the problem.

Can it be? No, surely not.

Paul shrugged it off, deciding to pursue the problem later. "I'm starved," he told the inspector. "Let's find a place to eat before we start for the London. Beth and I need food."

The earl left with Reid to find Elizabeth, and Michael turned the opposite direction in the corridor, heading towards the administration offices. He'd begun thinking through all he knew about Nathan Kessler. His Germanic name, his claims regarding fellowships and education, his peculiarities when it came to his wife's herbaceous plants in the solariums.

Nothing added up, but Emerson felt responsible. He'd only just learnt that Elizabeth hired Kessler, based in part on a recommendation, supposedly written by him. Michael had never met Kessler before and wanted to know why the so-called American had dared to implicate him in his scheme.

Emerson would find the mysterious cockerel had already flown the coop.

CHAPTER EIGHTEEN
Mirror World - A Midnight Visitor

Charles Sinclair was on his own in a strange castle. The duke had eaten most of the food on his tray: asparagus with garlic sauce, pheasant, truffles in a wine sauce, rosemary-seasoned carrots, roasted potatoes, and crusty French bread. He wondered how Theseus managed to secure so much fresh human food in an underground castle inhabited by members of the fallen realm. The enigmatic Fenwick had promised he could eat without fear, and so Charles had done just that.

After finishing a second glass of Drummond Reserve, the sleepy duke retired to the bedchamber, where he found a set of scarlet pyjamas laid out and ready for use.

He also found a short note:

> Sir – I must see to preparations for tomorrow evening's test, and so I shall be away for a short time. I have taken the liberty of placing a bar of the duchess's special soap beneath your pillow, and I laid out your pyjamas. I pray you sleep well, sir, with dreams of heaven and starlight.
>
> I shall endeavour to return to you soon, but a prayer to the One will bring me to you as quickly as lightning. I am ever at your service. – Fenwick

Charles smiled at the words 'at your service'. To think that a warrior angel, who stood before God Almighty, would serve him, a mere human, boggled the duke's mind. But then his mind was

225

worn out and weary. A good night's sleep would help him think more clearly.

He put on the night clothes, blew out the candle, and climbed into bed. Charles lay beneath the silk covers, staring at the underside of the tester's canopy, considering the regnal imagery painted upon it. C-R. Charles Rex. No, he could never accept being the actual King of England. To accept the position as secret and secondary was one thing, to assume it in public was quite another. Yet, Drina wanted him to take the throne. Indeed, she'd begged him, stating her son had no wish to become king, and that a Stuart-Plantagenet heir was the wish of the people and even Parliament.

No, he couldn't. Not unless the Lord God Almighty made it clear that it was HIS wish. Until such a time, Charles would remain in the shadows. What did the fallen realm hope to gain through his kingship? Why had Redwing and the Blackstone Society expended so much effort to push him towards taking a crown?

What did *they* know that *he* did not?

He lay awake for nearly an hour, and it became clear to Charles that he'd need to shut down his active brain, if he wanted to find sleep. He left the bed and put on a bathrobe, wondering what he might do to still his thoughts. His mind whirred with worries for his family and thoughts of kingship, but also the many statements Theseus had made.

Then, Charles remembered the piano. If he wished to untangle this conceptual Gordian knot, the mathematician in him required music.

Charles used the bedside candlestick to cross the darkened bed-chamber and enter the library next door. He could just make out a pair of silver candelabra, standing near the piano. He used the flame from his candle to light the candelabra and then sat before the instrument upon a tufted-leather stool. He placed his hands upon the cool ebony and ivory. The tactile sensation of the well-balanced keys felt familiar and reassuring.

Some of his earliest memories were made at a piano such as this. Now that he'd accessed most of his childhood, Charles remembered his mother playing Bach and Beethoven each morning. His father would lift him up to the bench so he could sit beside his mother, and she'd place his hands upon the middle section of keys to form the fingers into a C-major chord. Before long, he'd learnt to play other chords, then phrases, and finally an entire song by memory.

The first movement of Beethoven's *Moonlight*.

The duke began to play it now, recalling Angela Sinclair's soft blue eyes. He saw those same eyes in Adele's face. How might the world be different, if his younger sister hadn't been stolen from her cot as a baby? Would Adele still exist? Might Paul have married Charlotte and fathered Della anyway? Life choices with their infinite permutations, those what-if moments, the roads not taken, could drive a man mad, if he let them.

And how might his life have changed, if his father had lived? Seeing Robert Sinclair murdered had left the boy in Charles scarred and broken. His mother's choice to flee Rose House and then sail to Liverpool led to her death and to his loss of memory. Angela Sinclair would die in a mental asylum, asking everyone to find her lost son. Her free-will choice had parted them forever.

No, not forever, Mother, he whispered as the music filled his ears. *We'll meet again in heaven.*

With God's help, Charles had found his family again, but how might other choices have changed his life? Was all the heartache meant to be, or had God worked all the enemy's plots together for his purposes and according to his perfect foreknowledge and plans? He'd certainly looked after Charles in Liverpool that summer of 1860.

By then, his mother's fragile mind had thoroughly snapped, and God sent an angel in the guise of Anatole Romanov to rescue him. Unable to remember his own past, five-year-old Charles spent the next two years at Romanov's home.

He now remembered some of that time with Romanov.

The clearest memory was taking piano lessons.

He could already play simple pieces, but the prince taught him to memorise entire sonatas and concertos, instructing young Charles to let his long, nimble fingers play the notes with one part of his mind, whilst another part wandered far afield. That process had become a lifelong habit.

At university, he'd spent hundreds of pleasant hours playing Beethoven, Bach, Chopin, Liszt, and Mozart. Whilst his fingers were engaged, his mind solved advanced mathematical equations, considered Cartesian and Euclidian computations, pondered the nature of physics, electromagnetic radiation, and angles of incidence, or just life in general.

His passion for music soon drew the attention of Cambridge dons from other disciplines, and they urged him to abandon mathematics for musical performance or even musicology. But the solitary thinker preferred a quieter occupation; one that allowed him to ponder the deep mysteries of the world. Eventually, God would bring him to the attention of Robert Morehouse, an influential detective with London's Scotland Yard. And in 1879, the Lord would use this career to lead him to an investigation, where he'd meet a young girl named Elizabeth Stuart.

Now, years later, in an underground castle, the prisoner's talented fingers danced upon the keys with ease and familiarity, whilst his sharp mind escaped to another world. Was God working all of this together for some future good that Charles couldn't yet imagine? What road lay ahead for him? For Adele? For Beth and their children?

He left Beethoven's *Moonlight* in favour of Frédéric Chopin's *Piano Sonata, No. 1, Opus 4*. Charles enjoyed the mathematical precision of the repeated eighth and quarter-note motifs. The piano's keys were perfectly weighted and responded to his touch as if designed for his fingers alone. He began to smile in that lonely castle library, recalling the first time he'd played the sonata for his wife.

She'd listened quietly, her beautiful face alight with rapt attention, the small feet tucked beneath the hem of a yellow dress. A blue-and-white coverlet lay across her expanding lap. She'd been seven months pregnant at the time, and he'd come home from London to stay at Branham for one of their long weekends together. After learning from Kepelheim that her husband played, Elizabeth had a piano installed in the Branham study, and Charles would play song after song for her before they retired to bed. Now, with his eyes closed, the duke could smell his wife's fragrance and picture her smiling from a chair near the sunlit, balcony windows.

He'd performed this Chopin sonata in concert dozens of times, first at Harrow and later on at Cambridge. Perhaps it was due to Romanov's instruction, but even the most intricate, the most difficult compositions came easily to him. His eidetically wired brain made it simple to commit every note, every phrase, and even the composer's pedal instructions to memory, after just a few rehearsals.

Beth had a similarly designed brain, but insisted her playing lacked her husband's wonderful delicacy, and more importantly Sinclair's large hands, with fingers long enough to reach a thirteenth, which made it easier to form some of the required stretches.

Beth's small hands could barely manage an octave.

"Bravo, Captain!" she would shout as he'd strike the final phrase or chord. He'd rise and offer a formal bow, laughing as he did so.

"You should play at our charity concert this Christmas," she'd told him back in April. "If I agree to sing, will you play?"

"If my lady requests it," he'd whispered as he knelt beside her chair.

Had there been birds outside their windows that day? A family of sparrows, eagerly pecking at a wooden bowl of seeds? And beyond that balcony, perched upon a long oak branch, he'd spied a majestic white owl, sitting perfectly still and staring their way, as if keeping watch on their window.

"Even the birds enjoy Chopin," he'd told Elizabeth, saying nothing of the owl.

"Everyone loves Chopin, Captain," his wife had answered. "And you play his music so very beautifully. It's a wonder your dons didn't try to persuade you to read music rather than mathematics."

"The two are intricately entwined. Perhaps, the universe is built upon music," he'd suggested. "We read of morning stars singing together at the dawn of creation. Perhaps, the Almighty sang the world into existence."

"Or played upon an instrument," she'd added, taking his hand. "I hope our son has such hands and eyes," she told him that day. "I do so love your eyes, Charles. I always have. I wonder when I first saw them?"

"In '79, I should think. You said I looked lonely."

Beth had laughed with that sweet laughter that always soothed his soul. "Did I?" she had asked him. "I hope you didn't take offence."

"Of course not," he'd assured her and passed his free hand across her abdomen. One of the twins had kicked, and he felt certain it was Georgianna, reminding her father she'd be arriving soon and not to worry.

It was like touching the future.

"Back then, I'd no idea where that moment might lead," he told his wife. "I'm very glad you wrote to me last year, Beth, for I was lonely. So very lonely."

"And since?" she'd asked him.

"Not a single day. Not one."

Time stood still for them then, but those happy moments felt very far away as Charles played Chopin from his castle prison. Was Elizabeth safe? Did she know what had happened to him? Had the Lord sent some loyal angel to tell her where he was? Romanov, perhaps? Fenwick?

I wish you were here, little one.

He began the lighter *Menuetto* section of the sonata. The spritely notes brought a touch of gladness to his aching heart, and he imagined his wife's delicate laughter in the notes. The music brought a sense of peace. A blessed assurance.

Beth often sang a hymn with that title. *Blessed Assurance, Jesus Is Mine!*

Though she was blind, an American writer named Fanny Crosby had seen beyond her physical limitations to a greater truth, far beyond human sight, and her words could teach even a child about Christ's love.

He had to believe the Lord God would never burden Beth with needless agony. Charles knew how strong his wife could be, when needed. She might even be with Adele right now. At this very moment.

Charles also knew Paul would look after them all. The earl would never fail his family. And he could rely on James and Victoria; all the Stuart-Sinclair clan, including the stalwart and ever faithful Cornelius Baxter. All would keep his children and his little duchess safe until his return.

"I will return to you, Beth. I promise," he said aloud, as he reached the first measures of the *Larghetto.*

The languid nature of this movement concealed an unusual 5/4 time signature, a concept that produced mixed reactions in Chopin's original audience. The scandalously modern style had caused Charles's music instructor at Harrow to dub the piece an abject failure, not worth the paper it was written on. Somehow, that critique only made Charles love the sonata more, and it was the first piano piece he'd ever played for Adele. She also loved the strangely written movement, and often played it for the family after dinner.

Charles paused to take a breath, his long fingers suspended over the black-and-white keys as he thought of his precious daughter. Tears filled his eyes as he pictured her: Adele Marie Sinclair, the Watson to his Holmes, big sister to Robby and Georgianna, and the brightest penny in all the Empire.

The duke grew tired and so ended the piece. He closed the piano lid and rose from the bench, his heart aching from all the memories. He needed to sleep and forget that his family was far away. Forget he was a prisoner. He might even dream of his duchess. He whispered a quick thank you to the absent Fenwick for bringing the soap, for he knew the raspberry and vanilla scent would help to ease the pain.

Charles blew out the library candles and was walking towards the open doorway, when he heard a rustling sound coming from the bedchamber.

"Hello?" he called.

Charles picked up the small candlestick and entered the darkened bedchamber. He froze in his tracks, for the rustling sound came from within the deep shadows.

"Who's there?" he called into the darkness. "Speak! I know you're in here. Identify yourself!"

It might be Fenwick, but he didn't dare call the angel's name, for it might alert the others to his presence.

Charles took another step forward and moved the candle in a high arc to illuminate every corner. Nothing seemed unusual or disturbed. All was as it should be; that is, until the flickering amber glow fell upon the bed. The sheets had been moved. Someone or something was in there. Charles could see the outline of a body beneath the bed coverings. An intruder was lying upon the soft mattress, facing away from him.

Who would dare to enter his bed? Charles grew angry. Only one entity inside this castle would do such a thing.

"I know it's you. If you don't leave now, I shall call for the guards," he told the intruder.

The body turned towards him, and he wanted to throw the candlestick at it. He was right. Eluna von Siebenbürgen had made herself at home, like the housebreaker from *Aunt Friendly's Nursery*

Book. But unlike Goldilocks, the outline of Eluna's body beneath the silk sheet made it clear this housebreaker wore absolutely nothing at all.

"Get out before I throw you out!" he shouted angrily.

Eluna laughed and threw back the sheet to show off her assets. He was right. She wore nothing. Not one stitch. "Are you sure?" she asked him in a sultry voice.

"Now, I'm doubly sure," he told her with conviction. "Get out! I want nothing to do with you, witch!"

She laughed and sat up, stretching out her well-formed arms. "Witch? Oh, Charles, must you insult me?"

The duke threw a blanket across her nakedness. "I call you what you are. Must you insist on debasing yourself? I've told you again and again, I am not sleeping with you."

"I don't debase myself, as you so rudely put it," said the princess, leaving the bed to make herself easier to view. "Do you really intend to turn down this perfect body? Throughout history, men have given their last drop of blood to lie with me. Why is it you continue to spurn me? Is it my hair?"

The auburn strands transformed to dark hues, imitating his wife's raven hair.

"Stop it! It's not your hair, it's you! Get out!" he shouted, crossing to the door and banging on the wood. "Guards! Guards! I have an intruder! Show the princess back to her rooms at once!"

"Don't waste your breath, my darling king," she whispered, dancing closer. "I've ordered them to sit elsewhere until I call them. Theseus promised me a night with you, and I've come to claim that prize. If you refuse me, then you'll have to find another way to open the gates into the Maze. Oh, wait," she laughed, toying with his hair. "There is no other way! Only my lovely, seductive little moonlight will do the job, won't it? Sleep with me or risk everything."

"I've no wish to enter that place, Eluna, or Antoinette, or whatever name you use. Your charms are wasted on me. Leave now before I throw you out myself!"

"Ooh, does that mean you'd touch me?"

He threw a chair in her direction, but she dodged out of its reach. "You missed," she teased. "No other man has ever spurned me like this. All fall at my feet eventually, as will you, when you realise the Maze is your only path to freedom. And without me, those doors remain shut."

He picked up a nearby candlestick and threw it. Again, she avoided it. Eluna danced closer and curved her body into his, her hands running through the duke's curling hair. "My beautiful one, you think this challenge is a punishment, but crossing through the Maze will change you into something new. Seeing the clockwork that runs Time and History always does. Of course, if the Maze decides your blood is unworthy, it will devour you."

Charles stopped breathing. Her taunts had finally taken root. He pushed out of the unwanted embrace and asked, "How could a place devour anything? It's a maze, nothing more. A puzzle. I've solved labyrinths before, and they do not eat."

"The Time Maze is unlike any puzzle in the entirety of creation. Even the mighty Samael—the one who calls himself Anatole—would find himself trapped."

"Why do you mention him?" asked the duke, backing into a corner to keep away from her unwanted advances.

"You are so very sweet, my love. No, really, you are," she laughed. The mocking sounds emerged from deep within her throat like torrents of rushing water. "If you refuse me, you will never see your human wife again. The poor little duchess will wait endlessly like Penelope, forever weaving and destroying your death shroud in hopes you'll come home. But you won't be coming home. Poor little thing. If you like, I could let her know. Shall I do that? Shall I visit your *little one?*"

Charles stepped towards her, his voice dropping to a low, tense whisper. He wanted to kill the princess for the insolent words, but forced himself to calm. "Leave now, Eluna. Leave before I lose my temper completely. I will never take you to my bed. Not ever! If this challenge is so important to you and the others, then leave me to rest."

"And you wouldn't rest, if I stayed? Is that what you mean?" she asked, batting her thick eyelashes.

Sinclair started to answer, but thankfully, she'd already begun to dress. He shut his eyes, suddenly exhausted as though he'd run a hundred miles. All the relaxation, all the joy he'd found in the piano had vanished like warming snow.

"Poor lamb. I can see you're weary. Why else would you refuse me?" she reasoned. "Enjoy your sleep, my beautiful Charles. Dream of your dull human wife, if you wish. I'm going straight to Theseus and tell him the deal is off. You have refused me yet again, therefore I refuse to give him my beautiful, silver essence. No moonlight means no Maze. Thanks to your misguided pride, you will never return to your family."

Fearing he was now doomed to remain a prisoner, Charles nearly stopped her from leaving, but a voice spoke to him from the air to his right, as if a helpful angel stood nearby.

Let her go, Charles Robert. Just let her go.

"Do as you like, Eluna. If the Lord wants me to enter the Maze, then he will provide the light. I am in his hands," Charles boldly declared.

Eluna laughed loudly and so strangely, that she actually howled like a wolf. "That is very funny, my love! You make jokes at such a time as this. Bravo, Charles! Bravo! But your faith in the Hebrew God will lead to your doom, my beautiful one. Such foolishness always does. Enjoy these rooms and your piano, because you will be living here for the rest of your mortal life!"

These final words were shouted in that cold, wolf-like voice, and then Eluna slammed the door.

Finally alone, Charles nearly collapsed from the flood of warring emotions raging through his heart. He wondered if he might faint, but that same voice spoke again, and a firm hand took hold of his right arm.

"Now, now, sir, let's get you to bed. We cannot have you falling apart," said Fenwick gently. "The princess doesn't deserve even one of your thoughts."

"You've come back," Sinclair managed to say.

"And just in time, it seems. Now, lean on me, and we'll get you to bed."

The humble servant tucked the duke into the velvet quilts. Fenwick reached beneath the pillow, removed the bar of soap and handed it to his charge. Charles clutched at the scented soap and held it to his face, tears sliding down both cheeks.

"Thank you, Fenwick. Thank you! She's lying, isn't she? Eluna, I mean. Am I doomed to stay here forever?"

"Of course not, sir. The One is with you. As I've told you, sir, you are never alone. The One has a perfect plan. You must trust in him to work all things together for good."

"Was this a test, then? A test of me?"

"Not of you, sir. A test of her. The princess fails these tests again and again, I'm afraid. It makes me sad sometimes, knowing my family is torn apart, but the price of rebellion must be paid. Is there anything else you need, sir? Anything I might do for you before I blow out the candles?"

"Would you stay with me a little while?" asked the duke, suddenly feeling like a frightened boy again.

"I'd already planned to, sir. And may I say you play the piano beautifully? I've heard you play hundreds of times before, of course, but this is my first opportunity to thank you for it openly. Chopin's works shine when you play them, sir."

"That's kind of you to say, Fenwick. Or should I call you Hadraniel?"

"Fenwick is fine, sir. I've used many hundreds of names throughout history, but I rather like being Fenwick the servant. I may ask Lord Samael if I may use this guise again."

"You're far more than a servant, Mr. Fenwick."

"No, sir, that is precisely what I am. Serving is the highest calling. Even the Name served his disciples when he was on Earth. He calls upon each of us to serve in like manner. And by entering the Maze, you become a servant as well. Because it is the One's will. To obey the Creator is the highest service and the greatest joy, my very dear friend."

Charles smiled. "I'm honoured to be called your friend, Fenwick, and I feel the same. I'm very glad you're here. Goodnight."

"Goodnight, sir," the messenger answered as he began to blow out the candles. Afterward, Fenwick took a seat in a far corner, listening for the duke's breathing to become deep and regular. Once he knew Sinclair had fallen asleep, the warrior placed a hedge of protection around the bed and then inscribed fiery letters upon the windows, doors, and every possible point of entrance.

No one would disturb his friend this night.

No one.

CHAPTER NINETEEN
Real World - Montmore House

Forty-five minutes after leaving Montmore to find a doctor, Seth Holloway returned with someone from Paul Stuart's past, though the viscount had no way of knowing that. Dr. Lorena MacKey was a quietly beautiful woman, with upswept auburn hair, that Seth imagined might fall in thick locks down her back, when not restrained by pins. And her eyes were the greenest he'd ever seen, like clear emeralds.

But despite her rare beauty, Lorena MacKey knew medicine as well as any man. She arrived in Cordelia's bedchamber and introduced herself.

"Lady Aubrey, my name is Dr. MacKey, but you can call me Lorena. Or Rena, if it's easier. My friends call me that. Now, when did the pain begin?" she asked Cordelia.

"I'm not sure. An hour ago? Two?" said Delia from the bed. Her face was very pale, and it was clear to Lorena that her patient was afraid.

"Are you a friend?" MacKey asked Adele.

"Cordelia's married to my brother. My name's Adele."

This surprised MacKey. *This is Paul's sister. No, she's his daughter. Trent told me.* "I see. It's very nice to meet you, Lady Adele. You're the perfect person to help. Do you faint easily?"

Della shook her head. "Not at all. And I've helped look after other patients. Well, one patient, actually. My father."

Her father? Does she mean Paul?

"Wasn't your father the late Lord Aubrey?" asked MacKey carefully.

"Yes, but the Duke of Haimsbury's my father now. He wasn't my father then, you understand. Not when I acted as a nurse. He was unconscious then. Last year. He's adopted me now, because he loves me. It's all very complicated."

Lorena smiled. Charles Sinclair had a great heart. "I've met your father, and your brother as well. Both are fine men. You're very lucky."

As they talked, MacKey was laying out several medical instruments. One looked like an ear trumpet. Adele picked it up and examined it carefully. "What is this for?" she asked.

"It's called a Pinard Horn. It lets me hear the baby's heartbeat. Stethoscopes don't always manage it. I'll let you try it in a bit, if Lady Aubrey's all right with that."

She looked at her patient with concern. Cordelia Stuart had begun to pant, indicating pain. Perspiration covered her brow, and her eyes had a listless look to them.

"My lady, have your waters broken yet?"

"My what?" asked Delia weakly. "I don't know. Am I in labour?"

Mrs. Winstead stood nearby and offered the answer. "No, Doctor, they've not broken yet. And it seems to me this is too early. Might it be false labour?"

"It might, but we'll need to have a look to be certain. Lady Aubrey, I'm going to touch your abdomen. Is that all right?"

"Yes, of course."

MacKey drew back the bed coverings. "Adele, could you lock the door, please? We'll keep this next part just for us ladies, all right?"

Della complied and then returned to the bed. "May I give her some water?"

"Yes, that would be a good idea. And prepare a cool, damp cloth to wipe her face."

Lorena pressed down along her patient's midline, then palpated the upper and lower regions of her abdomen. Using the Pinard's Horn, she performed an auscultation, listening to the sound of the tapping. Afterward, she placed the horn over a specific area and listened again.

"Adele, if it's all right with your sister-in-law, you can listen, too."

Cordelia nodded a yes, and Della moved round the bed and did as Lorena instructed. She listened carefully, her blue eyes rounding. "Oh! It's the baby's heartbeat, isn't it? It's fast like a bird's. Is that normal?"

"Yes," answered MacKey. "Before they're born, babies' hearts beat very fast. As much as one-hundred-sixty beats per minute. I can tell a lot from the heartbeat. And most importantly, it tells me where the baby's head is presently."

Winstead's expression changed a tiny bit. She'd been a nurse for over three decades and learnt to avoid alarming a patient. "Has it turned?" she asked MacKey in an even voice.

MacKey shook her head. "No," she whispered. Then to Cordelia, she said, "Now, Lady Aubrey, I'm going to take a look more closely. May I do that? I'll need to get somewhat personal."

"I've grown used to it," Delia answered in a small voice. "It's easier with a woman."

"Which is why midwifery must continue," said MacKey. Winstead had already removed Cordelia's clothing, down to her chemise, and she helped lift the silk undergarment up over Cordelia's hips. The nurse then placed a pillow beneath them.

MacKey washed her hands in the connected bath and then used a Graves' Speculum to widen the vaginal opening and examine the cervix. Winstead and Shelton stood by quietly. Both women understood the gravity of the situation. If Lady Aubrey had begun to dilate, then halting labour could be very difficult. Finally, Dr. MacKey released the speculum and placed it into a towel.

"If you'd see to cleaning this, Mrs. Winstead? I can sterilise it when I return to St. Mary's."

"We have steam sterilisation trays, my lady. Anything you wish to clean, we can take care of, if you like."

"That's very helpful, Mrs. Winstead. Dr. MacAlpin's thorough, as always." MacKey palpated the abdomen again and listened using the horn before explaining. "Now, Lady Aubrey, this could prove to be a difficult. Are you brave?"

Cordelia had begun to pant again, her face showing signs of pain. "If my baby needs me to be. Am I in labour? Can someone send word to Paul?"

Adele wiped Delia's brow and said, "Dr. Holloway sent a telegram, and he rang Dr. Emerson's house. He has one of those new telephones."

"Am I in labour, Doctor?" she asked again.

"Not quite, which is good. You see, Lady Aubrey, your baby hasn't yet turned, which could give us a little trouble."

"Turned?" Cordelia asked. "I'm not sure what you mean."

"When babies are born, they generally emerge from the womb head-first," Lorena explained patiently. "That is a much easier way for them to leave the safety of your body. It's God's wonderful design. However, as with many other things in life, sometimes things don't happen exactly as we expect. Babies don't always turn their head towards the mother's cervix. If they're born feet first, it's called a breech. To prevent that, I'm going to try turning him."

Cordelia's eyes widened. "Turning him? How? Do you go into my womb?"

"No, I can perform the manoeuvre from the outside. But first, I want to relax your womb to keep it from reacting." She reached into her bag and withdrew a brown vial. "Mrs. Winstead, have you ever used cramp bark?"

Emily Winstead nodded. "Many times. How strong shall we brew it?"

"Use one quarter of the vial to two cups of boiling water. Let it steep for ten minutes. And bring honey and lemon with the teapot."

"Shelton, if you'd take care of that?" she asked the other woman.

"Right away, Mrs. Winstead. I'll bring it up shortly. Cook's got a pot of water boiling."

Lorena smiled. "I'll bet that was your idea, Mrs. Winstead. How long have you worked for Dr. MacAlpin?"

"More than ten years, my lady."

"Then you're the same woman he used to talk about. Henry certainly respects and depends on you, Mrs. Winstead."

"When did Lord Salperton ever speak of me to you, my lady?"

"At the Medical School for Women in Whitechapel. I took my degree there and then returned to teach. Dr. MacAlpin taught two courses on the brain, and he wanted me to specialise in alienism, but I preferred women's medicine and herbology. Dr. MacAlpin often referred to you as the woman who keeps him on track. I can see now why he said that."

Emily Winstead's chest puffed out, and she smiled. "He's kind to say it, and it's correct. Dr. MacAlpin's been like a son to me, my lady. He's a wonderful man, but can sometimes try a woman's patience."

Lorena laughed at this, her green eyes bright. "Oh, I know what you mean! He is a bit scatter-brained sometimes. And you needn't keep calling me 'my lady', Nurse Winstead. Doctor is fine, or just Lorena."

"That's kind of you, Doctor, but perhaps it's better here to keep to surnames. It's more professional."

"I'm sure you're right. Oh, good. Here's Shelton."

The stout nurse returned with a copper kettle and a china pot. She poured the hot tea into the warmed pot and set it on the nearest table. "Shall I pour the cup now?"

"Yes, please," she answered, then turned to Cordelia, "Lady Aubrey, we'll add honey and lemon to help with the bitterness. Drink as much as you can, then take a moment and finish the rest. Adele, could you assist her?"

Della prepared the teacup, adding a teaspoon of honey and lemon juice. She stirred in the honey until it melted thoroughly. "Here, Dee," she told her sister-in-law. "My little brother or sister is depending on you now. Drink as much as possible."

Cordelia took a sip and made a face. "It's very bitter. Could you add a bit more honey?"

"Yes, go ahead," Lorena told Adele.

With the tea sweeter, Lady Aubrey managed to comply and then, a moment or two later, finished the cup of cramp bark tea.

"How long will it take to work?" Della asked MacKey.

"Not long," said Lorena. "Shut your eyes for a few minutes, Lady Aubrey. Adele will read to you whilst we wash our hands."

She took the two nurses into the connected bath and closed the door. Lorena spoke softly. "I cannot guarantee this will work. The success rate for external cephalic version is about seventy percent. The mucus plug's still in place, but it seemed loose to me, and I found the area slightly bloody, which may be from the contractions. Also, the cervix is thinning. If we can successfully turn the baby, then I think she'll deliver in the next week or so. Has either of you ever turned a baby before?"

"I helped once," said Shelton, "but it was a long time ago."

"I've never done it, my lady—sorry, I mean, Dr. MacKey," said Winstead. "It's an old habit, ma'am. Many of the ladies here are from peerage families."

"My parents were very common," said Lorena. "All right. Let's all wash our hands well, and then I'll want to have all instruments ready for delivering a breech baby. If she goes into hard labour, we must prepare for the worst."

"What's the worst?" asked Shelton.

"Caesarian section and possible death of both the mother, and the child. Let's just pray it doesn't come to that."

CHAPTER TWENTY
Real World – Whitechapel Road

Two hours before Lorena took charge at Montmore House, the father of that unborn baby had just arrived with his Cousin Elizabeth at the London Hospital. Not surprisingly, Frederick Treves, the hospital's Chief Surgeon, insisted on examining the earl's wound and checking the bandage. Emerson's expert stitch work had helped, but because the patient refused to remain still, two stitches had broken. The gauze bandage required a quick change. Everyone agreed that Aubrey must have been watched over by a guardian angel, for the bullet passed through the oblique muscle but missed every organ and major vessel. At the end of the examination, Fred gave the earl a morphine injection for the pain and declared his patient 'good as new, or nearly so'.

Once done, Paul asked the duchess if she preferred to wait in the room next door to the lounge, where the circle members would soon gather.

"I'm content wherever you want me to be," she told him sweetly. "I don't want to be a bother."

"You're being conciliatory, because I'm injured, Beth, but you needn't be. Tell me your preference. In here or with us next door? You always join the meetings at Haimsbury House. Why not here?"

"I'm not being conciliatory, Paul. I'm very tired. Besides, you're carrying all our woes upon your shoulders. I insist you remove me from your mind."

"That is entirely impossible," he said as he stroked her cheek. "Whatever challenges God's allowing Charles to meet at this moment, he does so, knowing I'll watch after you. I'll always take care of you, Beth."

She kissed his hand. "You're so very good to me, Cousin, but I wish you'd go home and rest. An angel may have diverted that bullet, but it could be the first of many attacks."

"Do you remember the tree room at Briarcliff? How you'd pretend to be a princess, and I was your knight errant?"

"Of course, I do, but I'm no longer a child, and this isn't pretend. It's real. Quite horribly real."

He drew her close and kissed the top of her head. "A knight errant's sole purpose is to look after his princess. Even if she's grown up and married to another." He bowed and smiled, hoping to ease her mind.

Elizabeth understood that Paul needed to be chivalrous. How could he be a knight, if she refused his knightly deeds?

"I'm honoured to be your princess. You've done a splendid job protecting me. As always. Tell me, Sir Paul, where do you prefer I sit? In the meeting or in a nearby room?"

"I don't know, but you look a little feverish, Beth." He touched her forehead. "You're warm. Shall I have Fred take a look?"

"No, dear. I'm just worried. Nothing more."

"Then, you should rest. I can fetch you a book, if you want."

Beth smiled, touching his long hair affectionately. "Do you keep a book in your knight's bag, Sir Paul?"

This made him laugh, and he tried not to show the pain the contracted muscles caused. Beth notice the pain on his face, but acted as though she didn't. *The things men and women do to show their love for one another,* she thought.

"I fear my knight's bag is empty," said the Scotsman. "I'll see if Fred can find you a book. And I promise to keep the meeting as short as possible. We can't assume the shooting is an isolated event, so lock your door and send a nurse or porter, if you need me. I'm just one door away."

He kissed her cheek and left to find Treves, who brought Elizabeth a novel, saying his wife had enjoyed it. The Duchess of Branham obediently locked the door and drew the curtains to the window.

Though she couldn't see the street outside, the sounds of wheeled traffic and cries of costermongers on Whitechapel Road served as the backdrop for *The Woman In White* by Wilkie Collins: "This is the story of what a Woman's patience can endure, and what a Man's resolution can achieve," she read aloud.

Elizabeth smiled at the opening lines, for it echoed what had just happened twixt her and Aubrey. There was no man more resolute in all the world, none more true. She prayed the Lord would protect her cousin and also protect her equally resolute and ever-valiant husband.

Wherever Charles Sinclair was at that moment, he needed to know she prayed for him and waited.

Patiently.

Next door, in the surgeons' lounge, her resolute knight errant offered his thanks to Fred Treves.

"I appreciate your finding that book," Aubrey told the physician as they entered the lounge together. "Beth shows the world a brave face, but that business at the Haimsbury-Branham dredged up a great deal of fear inside her heart. It was just after the shooting at the christening last month, that Charles and Della disappeared. I'm sure she thinks another of her loved ones might vanish, and so I worry about her. The things we do for love."

"She's an extraordinary woman and worth all a man can offer," said Treves. "I've never met one braver, nor more selfless. Except for Lady Aubrey, of course. How is she? News of the shooting has surely reached Aubrey House. Is someone with her?"

"She's at Haimsbury House, actually. I find it simpler to watch over Delia and Beth, if they're in the same home. Lord Ailesleigh sent a telegram and even had a bag of clean clothes sent over for me. He's a thoughtful man. I wonder where he's gone?"

"Ailesleigh? Is that a new title?"

"It's actually very old. I knew Daniel's father. The 16th earl was also named Daniel. Like the Stuarts, the family use the names over and over."

"Typical for peers and kings. You might want to write your wife a letter, though. Hearing the story from a stranger gives her information, but little reassurance. Pregnant women can be emotionally erratic."

Paul sighed. "Delia's especially erratic, I'm afraid. I'll dash off a quick letter and send it with Granger."

Treves looked into the corridor. "Is Granger that red-haired bear?"

"A very good description," Paul answered, smiling. "He looks intimidating, but Hamish is a pussy cat with the ladies. Delia finds him very reassuring, as does Beth. It's like being protected by a great Scottish bull. Fred," he said, switching topics a little, "should we convert one of the rooms at Haimsbury House for medical care? For Delia, I mean."

"Shall I speak to Gehlen for you? He and I could provide you a list of equipment and medicines. It's always good to have the necessary items on hand in case of difficult births or the rare Caesarian. Most deliveries go like clockwork, but the unexpected must be anticipated."

"But is it really unexpected, if you expect it, sir?" asked Inspector Cornelius Baxter, who was just arriving. "That, my lord, has been the motto of the Branham staff since I joined as a page; and so it stands today. Expect the unexpected, I mean. Lord Aubrey, I heard about this morning. If there's anything I can do, you've only to ask."

"Inspector Baxter, you are most, most welcome!" exclaimed the earl happily. For the first time since the shooting, his face wore a genuine smile. "When did you return from France? I was told you left with my Uncle James."

"And so I did, my lord, but His Grace asked me to return and convey several new orders to you and the family. Esther and I arrived last night and had breakfast with the duchess and the Earl of Ailesleigh."

"You met our helpful Cornish earl?"

"I did, sir. He called at Haimsbury House at eight. I had only just arrived with Mrs. Baxter. She missed the twins whilst we were in France and wanted to go over as soon as she had dressed."

"Do I hear disapproval in your voice? Have you doubts about Ailesleigh?" asked the Scottish earl.

"I cannot say I disapprove, sir, but calling before ten simply isn't done unless there's an emergency. It's been a busy morning, sir. I had an errand to run in Fulham."

"Fulham?" said Aubrey. "At Montmore?"

"No, sir. I visited a lawyer on behalf of the duchess. It's in regards to some trunks that may belong to the late Lord Kesson."

"Well, you can tell me about it after the meeting, Cornelius. Do you know when Duke James is coming back?"

"Not exactly, my lord," said the former butler. "I'm to inform everyone of something your uncle is calling the St. Rosaline Abbey Mystery."

"If James calls it a mystery, then it must be extraordinary. Sadly, that's another story to tell later, but Baxter, I cannot say how it cheers me to have you here! Somehow, the world is now right again."

Treves stepped to the side of the doorway, allowing other members to enter. "It appears I'm in the way, Lord Aubrey. I'll get that list of medical supplies whilst it's on my mind and add a list of nurses as well, if you think that will help."

"Yes, thank you, Fred. As Captain Crenshaw is fond of saying, we have to circle the waggons."

The London's porters had organised the surgeons' lounge into a reasonable facsimile of the libraries where the inner circle meetings were often held. Four long tables were joined together to form a rectangle, and the men and women of London's membership began to fill the chairs.

Baxter kept the roll. Present that afternoon were: Sir Thomas Galton, Martin Kepelheim, Malcolm Risling, Sir Percy Smythe-Daniels, Inspector Edmund Reid, Chief Inspector Fred Abberline, Gerald Pennyweather, Matthew Laurence, Algernon Winters, Dr. Alan Callerson, Dr. Simon Allerton, Inspector Arthur France, Abraham Stoker, Dr. Elias Lieberman, Lady Louisa Bramstile, Dr. Diedra Kimberley, and many others. Soon, all forty-two chairs were filled, and Aubrey took control of the meeting.

The earl placed both hands on the back of the wooden chair, clenching the fingers to release the flow of tension from his back and shoulders into the wood. It wasn't the pain, but fear. Beth was the target.

How can I do this? How do I protect her?

To his surprise, Lady Louisa raised her hand. "I'm sure you had opening remarks prepared, Lord Aubrey, but may I speak first?"

"Yes, of course, Lady Louisa. The floor is yours."

"That's kind of you, Lord Aubrey, but I shouldn't require too much time. Sir Thomas has just told me about the shooting, and I wanted to offer thanks to God for preserving you and the duchess. I presume that's why you've called a full house with so little warning. I wanted to say that our fellowship is honoured to have you as its head during these troubled times. There are very few men in history to equal you."

She took her chair once more, and other members began to echo her sentiments, whilst a few asked 'what shooting?' and tried to glean additional information. Paul held up his hands for silence.

"Thank you, Lady Louisa. The Lord must have tapped on your shoulder, suggesting you deliver those encouraging words just now, for I don't feel at all qualified. Charles Sinclair is a natural leader and should be chairing today. He's designed for such authority. I'm happy to lead men into battle or teach them to spy, but chairing so lofty a group of deep thinkers gives me great pause. However, with Duke James in France, it's fallen to me to act as your chairman. Originally, I'd planned to meet with just a few ICI leaders, regarding transfer of William Wychwright tomorrow. We very seldom issue a mandatory full-house alert, but today's shooting left me no choice. What I say here today is to go no further. Do you all understand?"

He looked from one face to another, forcing every person to acknowledge the gravity of the situation.

"Good. Now, as Lady Louisa has said, this morning at the Haimsbury-Branham, a man who's yet to be identified opened fire on the duchess and myself."

Murmurs ran through the group, and Fred Abberline's hand went up. "Are you sayin' someone tried to kill you?"

"Yes, Chief Inspector, and though his aim missed with most shots, Emerson and Treves can attest to the wound I received. However, since I stand before you, the bullet failed to accomplish its work."

"And the duchess?" asked Stoker anxiously. "She is not with us. Please, sir, is she well?"

"She is, and I thank God for supernaturally protecting us both. The attacker fired at point blank range. By all accounts, we should both be dead. By God's grace, I stand here, and my beautiful cousin is unharmed and reading a book in the next room."

"And the man who did it?" asked Abberline.

"We apprehended him at the scene and were on our way to Leman Street, when a strange thing happened."

Paul paused, his mind flashing on the images of the mysterious coach, the black horse, the flock of ravens, a tall being of pure light, and then nothing—just waking in a bed at the HBH.

"Something happened that's beyond my ability to explain, if I'm honest. I'm sure Inspector Reid could offer another account, but to my recollection, a runaway hansom appeared as if by magic. Its speed was unnaturally fast, and it burst onto all of us so quickly, it seemed impossible to escape. I saw birds everywhere, then awoke at the HBH."

Reid stood. "I saw the hansom, Lord Aubrey. Unnatural is a good way to describe it, for I've never seen one move so quickly. We were all trying to get out of harm's way, but I'm sure I saw Lord Ailesleigh throw his arms round you just as the horse reached you. I saw no birds, and I cannot explain how either of you remain alive. The next I can remember is Ailesleigh ordering me to summon a maria to take you to the HBH. The shooter must have escaped during the panic."

"Did you see the weapon he used?" asked Percy Smyth-Daniels, who worked with armaments.

"A German prototype, I think," Paul answered. "A long barrel with an automatic feed system. Emerson recovered the bullet and mentioned it was a large caliber. Simon, could you talk with your contacts and ask if anyone's purchased a prototype handgun recently?"

Dr. Allerton nodded, making himself a note. "Of course. I'll begin with the German companies."

"Look to the Irish, too," said Abberline. "That fool at Special Branch is letting the whole lot run roughshod over London."

"We will, Fred," said Aubrey. "But I doubt it's the Brotherhood. The shooter shouted in German."

"What did he say?" asked Reid.

"Beth says it's a line from a poem called *Lenore*. He cried '*Wir und die Todten reiten schnell.*' It means we and the dead travel fast."

"That's a queer thing to say before you shoot someone," said Abberline.

Stoker wrote it down. "*Lenore?* Do you know the poet's name, Lord Aubrey?"

"I think she said Bürger. I'm sure the duchess would be happy to discuss it, Mr. Stoker."

"Yes, thank you. It's an intriguing quote."

The earl continued. "Now, another point about the man is his appearance. His clothing was expensive, but overly large. As if he'd lost weight recently or borrowed the clothes. His face had an emaciated look to it. Six feet tall. Greyish eyes. He wore a hat to hide his face, but I noticed strands of light hair beneath it. I thought him a reporter and watched as he work his way forward. I had an inexplicably cold dread of the man, and told Beth we should leave. Then the man called out the strange line from Bürger's poem and fired. Madness followed, and there were a great many reporters, which is odd, for the meeting wasn't published. I'd asked the hospital staff to say nothing about it to anyone. I wanted Beth to arrive in secret. And she took one of the old, unmarked coaches. So how did they know she was there?"

"More to the point," added Reid, "how did the shooter know? And did anyone know that you'd be there?"

Paul shrugged as he held his aching side. "When I was a boy, I asked God again and again, why he allowed Charles to die. As most of you know, Charles's father was murdered when he was five, and his mother took him to Castle Drummond. Had she remained there, none of this might have happened, but Aunt Angela fled the castle with my cousin and boarded a ship. Two years later, after much searching, their bodies were found in Ireland—or so we were told. Years later, we learnt this truth: Their ship docked in Liverpool, my aunt died in an asylum, and her son, unable to remember anything prior to age seven, grew up thinking he was adopted by an aunt and uncle. Because of this new direction and unaware of his peerage title, Charles chose a career that may have seemed an odd fit for a man who was actually the Marquess of Haimsbury; he became a policeman and then a detective. And he excelled at it! There are few who can match wits with my cousin. I've watched him work through dozens of difficult cases this past year. I say all this because I know what good policemen can do, my friends, and so with God's help, I know we'll uncover this shooter's tracks. And those tracks will lead us to the person or persons who hired him. No matter where he or she or they now sit. Even if it's inside *this room*."

In the room next door, Elizabeth set aside the book. She'd read *The Woman in White* before, and so after reading one chapter, decided to look through two packets of documents Lord Ailesleigh had given her after breakfast that morning. These were letters he'd found at the Regent's Park house.

On the outer envelope of each, he'd written a short note. On one, he wrote *Letters to Lord Kesson*, on the second, *Letters to Sir William Trent*.

She preferred to read those written to her father, but Beth wondered who might have written to the demonic baronet, William Trent.

She opened the second packet and withdrew the letters. Some were on fine paper with monograms, but two were on paper used by a far different segment of society: The British Army. After scanning through them, she left the quiet room and walked next door to knock on the surgeons' lounge. She could hear her cousin speaking, then his voice stopped. Two seconds later, Paul's face appeared in the open doorway.

"Princess, is everything all right?"

"Yes, but may I come in? I promise, I shan't stay long."

"Of course," he told her. "Come sit in my chair. I've been standing anyway."

"No, you should take the seat, Paul. You're injured."

He kissed her cheek. "I'm mending by the minute. Come, now. Sit in my chair."

She did as he asked, surprised to see how many members were in attendance. "Good afternoon, everyone. Forgive me for interrupting. I wonder if I might read something?"

"It isn't that novel, I hope?" Treves asked. "My wife enjoyed it, but I'm not sure it's to everyone's taste."

The duchess took the teasing with good grace. "No, Mr. Treves, it isn't," she said.

"What have you brought us, Princess?" asked the earl from behind the chair.

"It's a collection of six letters. I shan't read all of them to you, for I believe one will suffice to make my point. This morning, I received an unexpected call from Lord Daniel Porter, Earl of Ailesleigh. Inspector Baxter can confirm what I'm about to say."

The former butler nodded. "Of course, my lady. The gentleman called very early. Scarcely eight o'clock. He did so because a lawyer's firm had threatened to remove certain items from his Regent's Park home."

"A very strange reason to call on a duchess," said Dr. Kimberley. "Why on earth would he do such a thing? And what have all of us to do with this man's visit? Really, this seems a trifling matter. May we continue with the real reason we're here?"

Elizabeth's gaze fell upon the woman's face with such a cold expression that it shocked Diedra. The physician was accustomed to dominating other women, but Beth would have none of it. "*You*," she said with emphasis on the single word, "have a great deal to do with it. This membership needs to hear what Lord Ailesleigh brought to my attention. The lawyers in question act on behalf of the earl's late aunt. She left him a large house near Regent's Park, along with all its contents. However, her lawyers were given instructions to remove those contents tomorrow and make an inventory."

Sir Ralph Epperson, an influential baronet who advised the War Office, sat near the windows and was writing furiously. Elizabeth noticed the activity, but said nothing. Instead, she continued with her speech. "Because of the urgency regarding the house's contents, Lord Ailesleigh called upon me quite early."

"Why, Your Grace?" asked Abraham Stoker. "Was there something about the contents connected to you?"

"Yes," she told him. "Lord Ailesleigh was kind enough to bring samples of what he'd discovered in a cursory inspection. He'd found several unmarked trunks and broken open the locks to determine the owner's name. One was my late father, Lord Kesson."

Whispers coursed through the room, and Elizabeth noticed Sir Ralph passed his note to Dr. Kimberley.

"He found steamer trunks?" asked Aubrey. "Beth, did he also find three crates, used as sea cans?"

"Yes, he did," she told him. "All were used by my father to ship items back from India."

"That's incredible! James and I searched everywhere for those trunks and crates! How on earth did they find their way to a home near Regent's, Princess?"

"I believe this explains some of it," she told him. "Allow me to read you a letter that was posted to the Regent's Park address." She unfolded a one-page letter, typewritten on stationery used by the British Army.

Beth read:

The deed is done. I've given two 13s a new home. They're safely stored in our warehouse in Cairo. I've also left 'food' for them in six crates. When you arrive there on the 6th, speak to my man. Sievers will assist. I'm on assignment from the 5th onward. Someone must shoot these Musselmen, and no one is a better shot than I. Be sure the money is in my account by end of week.

Elizabeth handed the letter to her cousin. "The date on the letter is the second of May, 1888. I've intentionally left out the sender's name and that of the recipient, but I can tell you that both are known to this circle."

Then she opened a second letter and read:

My Darling,

I count the days until we're together again and intreat you to set aside that green-eyed redhead. She will be your end. Forgive my doubts. They're gone. All of them, and I've done all you asked and more.

Oh, how I miss you when you're away, Sweet William! Come back to London, please, and we shall while away the hours in my bed. If you want, I can even go to France and see to that small problem with HER. Give me names, and I shall see to it.

Please, explain, though. I know you want her to run to HIM, but why? Who is he really, and why does he matter? You keep hinting that there's more to this St. C. than meets the eye.

How can I help you defeat those dreadful Scots, if you don't trust me with all the information? Come soon and remove these last doubts, please!

Again, she handed the letter to Paul. "Now, I'll leave you to consider this information, and I shall return to reading the novel Mr. Treves was so kind to lend me." Beth stood to leave, but stopped at the door. "Two final observations before I leave you all. First, the letter 'M' is the thirteenth of the alphabet, making writing that number a very clumsy sort of code. The 'M' in question is no doubt a

Maxim gun, two of which went missing in Africa last year. The second observation is this: William Shakespeare crafted words like a tailor sews cloth, stitching together sounds and silences with perfect precision and beauty. There's a line from *Henry V*, which fits this situation. 'Treason and murder ever go together. As two yoke-devils sworn to either's purpose.' I believe there are traitors in this room, who thought murder might solve a problem. I'm here to tell them that it didn't. Thank you for listening."

She left quietly, followed by Aubrey, who turned to tell the shocked group, "A moment and I'll return."

Outside in the corridor, he pulled Elizabeth far away from the surgeons' lounge. He held up the letters she'd give him. "You're a daring lassie. Tell me, are there more of these?"

"Yes," she said, offering the envelope. "Four more. One from him. Three from her. It's clear she has an accomplice who's also a traitor. Be careful, Cousin. Adders slither beneath our circle of roses, and they've already tried to bite."

He kissed her hands. "You should be our leader, Beth. Your mind outshines all of ours combined."

"I'm glad to help. I love you, Sir Paul."

He kissed her hands and then her cheek. "And I love you, Princess. Always and forever."

She watched as he returned to the lounge and then waited long enough to make sure he'd not emerge again. Then, with every word of the letters branded in her eidetic memory, the duchess took a walk along the hospital's scrubbed hallways.

At first, she planned to find Joseph Merrick and say hello, perhaps play a game of chess or hear him recount tales of his friendship with Sinclair. She'd spent many days at the London the previous December, recovering from the Istseleniye Castle attack and fire. Stephen Blinkmire and the quick-thinking Ida Ross had saved Beth's life by taking her down a secret stairway to safety. The courageous Mr. Blinkmire had almost given his life that night, and Elizabeth rewarded him and all the Castle Company with permanent homes for as long as they wished. Blinkmire and Riga chose to live at Branham. Ida married Inspector Elbert Stanley, and the others had either remained at the Queen Anne Dower House or else continued as staff at one of Prince Anatole's many houses.

But Elizabeth had other memories of this hospital. Cordelia Wychwright, now Cordelia Stuart, was brought to the London after suffering a sexual assault in Whitechapel. Her attacker, Sir Albert Wendaway, had absconded to France and hadn't yet been found. Knowing her cousin, Beth sometimes wondered if Paul hadn't already found Wendaway, killed him, and dumped his body in the Seine. She didn't like thinking her chivalrous knight capable of such horrors, but the earl's temper sometimes ruled his head. He'd often spoken of taking revenge for his wife's physical and emotional injuries. Perhaps, he already had.

Vengeance is wrong, she thought as she walked. God would force Wendaway to pay for his deeds, according to his plans and timing. She prayed Paul had matured beyond such rashness, but understood his passion. Her beloved cousin wanted only to take care of those whom he loved.

After getting lost once and asking for directions, the duchess found Merrick's rooms on the second floor, but discovered he'd left half an hour earlier with a dermatologist named Henry Radcliffe Crocker, a colleague to Treves. Joseph wasn't expected back for at least two hours.

Disappointed that she'd lost the opportunity to visit with such a good friend, the duchess was about to climb down again, when she noticed a pair of policemen, standing beside a room near the far end of the hallway. Presently, the only patient to warrant police guards was William Wychwright. The young men were dressed in Metropolitan blue, their brass buttons gleaming, collar numbers brightly polished.

The peeress approached the men. "Good afternoon, gentlemen. You're both looking quite smart."

The policemen bowed their heads politely. The taller said, "Thank you, Your Grace. That's kind of you to say."

"I've seen photographs of the duke when he was a constable," she told them. "How handsome he looked! Your uniforms give a man a certain air of authority, like a warrior knight. I imagine your wives feel the same."

"Galway's not married," said the tall officer.

"I should think Constable Galway has many admirers," she replied. "And you are?"

"Siemens, ma'am. I've a pretty wife named Kitty. And Galway's not married 'cause he's spoiled for choice. That's the trouble," Siemens told her. "It's a pleasure to speak with you, my lady, but might I ask, what brings you down this way? Inspector Reid told us about the trouble at the HBH. You must be careful, Your Grace. We had a shooting here as well."

"Really?" she asked, though she'd already heard about it from one of the nurses.

"Aye, ma'am. Just a coincidence, I'm sure, but you ought to take care anyway, my lady."

"I feel quite safe with you gentlemen here. As to why I'm walking about, I'd hoped to talk with Mr. Merrick, but he's away presently. Lord Aubrey's conducting a meeting in the main floor surgeons' lounge, and I'm keeping myself occupied. This may sound unusual, but I thought I might show a bit of kindness to your prisoner by reading to him."

"That's thoughtful, my lady, but the baron's not to have any visitors," said Galway.

"Not even someone who only wishes to read? My cousin told me the baron's kept under sedation. When my husband was unconscious last year, our daughter read to him for hours and hours. Charles later said he'd heard some of it, and that it helped him to recover."

The two men whispered together for a moment, and Siemens told her, "Well, ma'am, seeing as the baron is asleep, there shouldn't be any harm in it. But keep away from the bed, my lady. Don't go too close."

"Isn't he bound to the bed? I believe my cousin mentioned that."

"He is, ma'am, but..."

"Constable Siemens, I'm hardly going to engage in anything dangerous. A bit of Christian charity might reveal some goodness in his heart. That's all."

"Yes, of course, my lady, but if he stirs even a twitch, you're to give us a shout. And keep away from the bed."

"I understand," she said carefully. "And I'll let my husband know of your devotion to duty."

"Is His Grace coming back to England soon, my lady?" asked Galway. Beth noticed his upper lip was shadowed by a light moustache. The lad couldn't be more than twenty.

"The duke hopes to be home very soon, I'm happy to say, but I cannot be certain when that will be. Politics and diplomacy take time, as I'm sure you're both aware. Now, I shan't keep you. I'll read a Chapter or two and then be on my way."

Siemens unlocked the door, and Elizabeth entered the dimly lit room. It had a single bed with an iron headboard painted green, a side table, a tall cabinet, a wardrobe, and two metal chairs, each painted white.

The prisoner, Baron William Wychwright, former army captain and aeronautic sharp-shooter, lay upon the mattress, beneath two green blankets. Over the blankets, she noticed three, white multi-layered braided cotton straps that crossed his chest and legs. These fastened to the bed rails by thick leather and brass buckles.

Wychwright's eyes were shut, and he breathed deeply and regularly. The duchess glanced at the bedside doctors' notes. Since deciding to establish a charity hospital, her interest in medicine and science had amplified, and she'd read dozens of books on patient care and surgical terminology. And so Elizabeth understood nearly everything written on the medical log.

She returned the chart to its rightful place near the cabinet and drew one of the chairs to the bed, sitting near the sleeping man. Wychwright looked small. Far less formidable than she'd imagined him. Was this the same man that conspired to have his own sister raped? The man who tried to assassinate Beth's husband and cousin? Who'd have slain her small children, given the chance?

Could he be involved in today's shooting?

Was he *really* asleep?

She opened the Wilkie Collins book, her eyes on the sleeping man's face. "Hello, Baron. Do you remember me? It's Elizabeth Sinclair," she told him. "I've come to read to you. My husband lay in a coma once, but he later said he could remember our daughter reading to him. Sherlock Holmes was her choice. I'm afraid all I have is a Wilkie Collins novel, but it's a very good story, about a young artist who falls in love with a fair-haired beauty whilst on the road to London. Shortly after, the woman vanishes, and he nearly goes mad trying to find her. Later on, he's hired to teach art to two sisters. One sister looks exactly like the woman in white; so much so, they might be twins. It's a mystery story, filled with villains and heroes. I'm sure someone of your abilities and reputation would find both themes thrilling."

Elizabeth's face remained impassive as she spoke, and she looked towards the door to make sure the constables weren't listening. The men were talking casually to one another, apparently assured of her safety.

She moved the chair a bit closer. "Which are you, Baron? Villain? Hero? Do you still have influence with Redwing?"

Wychwright's eyes neither twitched nor fluttered, but Beth felt certain he was awake and listening.

"Tis a pity about your mother," she told him. "She's denounced you, I mean. Connie is my cousin's mother-in-law, and he knows all about it. Your mother says you've disgraced the family, and she's petitioned the House of Lords to declare your younger brother, Ned, the new baron."

Several of his facial muscles contracted slightly. Beth moved closer still. "I know you hear me, Captain, so understand this. My Cousin Paul is the last person you want as an enemy. He is a *very* dangerous man. He pursues his prey relentlessly. He never stops. Some of his enemies have disappeared without leaving a single trace." The lashes of his upper lids moved slightly. "I imagine you'd like to strike me right now. A helpless woman is meat and drink to a man like you."

The eyelids creased and spasmed as innervation to the upper palpebral muscles caused them to contract. The lids popped open, and Wychwright stared at the duchess. The bloodshot eyes boiled with rage.

Most women would have drawn back in terror, but Elizabeth Sinclair had seen far worse sights. She smiled.

"I know what's going on inside your head, Captain. You want to choke the life out of me, but your hands are bound. You're powerless to act, just as your sister was once powerless." She paused, flashing a confident smile. "You know, I hadn't planned to come here today. In fact, I'd never even considered talking to you, but God's providence brought me your way. And so I thought I would offer you an education regarding my life. Sir William Trent brought horrors to me that make your petty crimes seem like child's play. I wonder where you and he met? Trent didn't serve with the military, nor was he a diplomat, yet you and he corresponded."

His eyes narrowed, but only gurgling came from his mouth.

"It's difficult to speak, when waking from strong doses of morphine, but be patient, Captain. I'm sure you'll find your voice and be able to confess how you stole two Maxim guns from the Army. I have proof of it, and I've given the letters to my cousin. Such indiscretion! Did you know Trent kept them? Probably to blackmail you later, but as he's dead, all that correspondence was waiting to be discovered. And now it has been. It's God's miracle, don't you think?"

She waited, intentionally allowing time for him to consider his position. The hands pushed up at the restraints.

"Those letters are just the icing sugar on a very interesting cake," she continued, holding the book so the constables would assume she was reading. "Most everyone knows my cousin has a vast network of spies that bring him information, but very few are aware of *my* network."

His eyes widened, and the unshaved jaw tightened.

"That surprises you, doesn't it? I'm sure it would surprise most everyone. I began to spin the first threads of my information web whilst living in France. If you watch closely and understand human nature, you can always find gentlemen who're happy to provide a peeress with answers in exchange for a career recommendation or small fee. Over the years, I've formed my own inner circle. There are diplomats, detectives, lawyers, estate agents, military men, postmen, butlers, bankers, clerks, and even schoolmasters. Over a hundred men and women write to me weekly. When I sit in my office at home, everyone assumes I'm creating menus for some large dinner party, or preparing a list of peers to invite to a gala. I'm just a woman, you see. I let them think that, Captain. The best stratagem is the one that no one expects, and no one expects me to engage in espionage. Yet, I do. And I shall continue to do so to protect those I love."

His hands clenched, and Beth reached out deliberately to touch them, knowing he was helpless to stop her.

"You have the scarred knuckles of a fighter, Captain Wychwright. Such traces of your past are obvious, but my spies have added to the store of information about you. You boxed for your unit, which explains the knuckles. You excelled as a marksman. You were awarded the Kabul to Kandahar Star as well as the Egypt Medal. On the surface, you're the epitome of British bravery, aren't you? But there is another side to your service."

His fingers formed into fists, that strained at the thick bands. The lips quivered against dry teeth. A guttural sort of groan emerged from his throat.

"Do you need water?" she dared to ask. "I'd be happy to offer some, but first let's consider your darker activities whilst with the army, shall we?"

She glanced again at the policemen. They'd begun to chat with a pretty nursing student, blissfully unaware of her conversation. "Two guards remain outside, Captain, and if you so much as raise your head, I shall cry out. Now, let's see about your service. I seem to recall one of my spies mentioning an incident regarding rifles and pistols. Then two Maxim guns disappeared, along with boxes of cartridges. Those are very expensive weapons, Captain. And deadly. I saw the Maxim demonstrated back in '84. Yes, I was quite young, but being a prominent duchess means I'm on almost every invitation list. The Maxim looked quite heavy, I thought. If a thief wanted to steal one, he'd require help, I should think. Who might that have been?"

The guttural groans slowly formed into words, not yet decipherable, but obviously threats.

"I appreciate your reaction, Captain, but it's in vain. I shan't allow you to harm me, so you really should just relax and listen. You see, I've spoken with your commanding officer about that theft, and he said you promised to retrieve the guns, but only after he'd received a report they'd been sold to the Mahdists.

"Now, being a woman, my head for politics and warfare is quite inadequate, isn't it? How could I know anything about the Sudan or the Mahdist campaign? Ah, but you see, I do. You always underestimate women, Captain. We sit quietly and listen. In my case, beginning at a very early age, I listened to my grandfather, my father, my uncle, and my cousin talk of politics and military matters. You might say I had a comprehensive course in warfare. So, yes, I'm quite familiar with the Mahdist uprising in the Sudan. England has lost many lives in that war, Captain. If I were a military man and found myself in a precarious position that connected me to theft and even treason, I might resign my commission and move back home to England at the first opportunity."

Drool ran down his chin as Wychwright finally spat out coherent words. "You!" he sputtered in a whisper. William hadn't used his vocal cords for many weeks. Despite the broken leg bones, he'd tried twice to escape the hospital, and Treves ordered him placed under chemical restraint in addition to the straps, and since that day, he received morphine round the clock.

The words "I'll kill you!" hissed through the dry vocal folds like wind through cracked wood.

"You'll kill me? I very much doubt that, Captain," Beth replied without a blink. "But leaving the army meant no income, and returning to England in a state of poverty wouldn't do, would it? A man like you needed the same authority here as when you were in the army, isn't that so? These letters from you to William Trent aren't the only letters that incriminate you. You really were indiscriminate, Captain. Perhaps, your hubris blinds you to the intelligence of others. I happen to know that you and your mother exchanged many letters prior to your father's death. Did the two of you plot with Redwing leaders?" She paused, a smile playing at her rosy lips. "You know, I received the most interesting visit the other day. Your old batman, Mr. Sievers, came to call on me."

"What?" he whispered. "You're lying."

"Why would I lie, when truth is sufficient to hang you, Captain? Sievers is out of work, now that you've been arrested, and he wondered if the duke might have a position available. He and I spent two hours talking, and I must say, the gentleman is a wealth of information. I'd already surmised a great deal about you, prior to that meeting, and I shared some of it with him. He is honest and loyal to his bones. Not loyal to you, Captain. He is loyal to England. Your behaviour troubled Sievers. He confirmed everything my spies had told me and added several other items to my list. For instance, last year, you received a visit from a man he described as a distinguished baronet. Not your friend, Sir Richard Treversham. But then, is he your friend? I don't think so. Not when the chips are down."

"You know nothing, woman," he mouthed.

"I know Treversham told the ICI that it was *you* who tried to rape Cordelia, not he. Sir Richard and his sister have both signed sworn statements to that effect, so I'm not sure you can call him friend any longer. But this other baronet I mentioned, the one who visited you in North Africa? You'd been corresponding with him for months, and thanks to my new friend's late aunt, I have six of those letters, typewritten by Sievers and signed by you. Sievers will confirm typing them, I'm sure. That conspiratorial baronet is quite dead now, but then I'm sure you know that. What you do not know, Captain, is that I watched him die. It was a horrible death. Trent screamed in a manner most unlike a human. More like an animal. He was shaken like a helpless leaf in a tempest, then thrown out a window. Do you know why he was killed?"

"I suppose you're going to tell me," he whispered.

"Of course, I am. He died because he tried to hurt me. That day, a divine protector came to my aid."

"Shall I fear you, then?" he asked huskily.

"You should fear God, Captain. Fear what happens to you after death, if you continue on this dark course. Redwing is not a road to power. It is a road to hell."

He smiled and spat out, "Hell is waiting for all of us. What matters is what role you'll play when you get there. You may be a duchess here, but you'll be nothing there! Nothing but food for my table!" These last threats emerged from the dry lips in an animalistic hiss, as if some demon spoke through him.

The duchess had heard demonic voices before and refused to be intimidated by it. Her voice was calm as she bent down low to whisper.

"Your beliefs are irrevocably skewed if you think that, *Demon*. God has already won the final victory, and he's prepared you a home in the Lake of Fire."

Beth pushed back the chair and stood. "I'll leave you now, Captain, both you and the demon inside you. It's clear that you're in need of an injection—for your pain, of course. I'll ask a nurse to see to that."

Then she leaned down low, her mouth just inches from his face. "And if you ever come near my family or any of my loved ones again, I shall have you dragged from this bed and thrown into the tunnels beneath Branham. Some of those passages are very deep and very dark, Captain. Some may even connect to Hell itself."

His eyes widened in shock.

Beth stepped back, then returned the chair to its proper place. Still holding the Collins book next to her jacket, she crossed to the doorway, saying, "It was lovely speaking to you, Captain. Don't force me to do it again. You won't like me when I'm angry."

As she left, she told the taller policeman, "I fear the book's content may have distressed the baron, Constable. You should call a nurse. I imagine he requires a morphine injection. Thank you both for your help."

And with that, Elizabeth Stuart Sinclair, primary peeress in the land, returned to the main floor, where she resumed reading *The Woman in White*.

CHAPTER TWENTY-ONE

The Circle Meeting Continues

"I'd planned to meet with just the core members today, regarding these missing corpses," Paul told the gathering, "but this attempt on our lives has forced me to call for a full house. I dread saying this, my friends, for this is the first time in many generations a circle member has spoken the word, but I have no choice but to speak it. The duchess has already hinted at it, but I must say the word aloud. Treason."

Every member began to look about, and whispers filled the room along with expressions of doubt, confusion, and shock. Paul raised his hands for silence, and the uproar died out. Every eye fixed upon the earl's face.

"Thank you," he continued. "All of us are vulnerable to the enemy's wiles, and though we endeavour to support one another and keep our focus on Christ, there is always a possibility that treachery might quietly seed itself into our ranks, like tares among wheat. I'm afraid that day is here."

More murmuring followed this, and Paul noticed two individuals whose expressions seemed less believable to his eye. He said nothing, but continued to address the group. "I wish this day had never arrived, but it has. I speak not only from suspicion, for I've suspected these members for a long time. Today, I have the confirmation. Someone hired this shooter to take aim at the duchess and myself. They failed in their goal, but left a mark."

Paul removed his coat, unbuckled the shoulder holster, and opened the Paisley waistcoat. He then unbuttoned three of his shirt's closures, revealing the top of bandage beneath. "This is that mark. The visible result of the attack. The bullet grazed my side, but might have killed me or my beautiful cousin, had the aim been truer. Had either one happened, I guarantee that the *full weight and power* of inner circle justice would have fallen upon the plotters' necks before the day was out. For those who aren't aware of it, whilst British law may only end a life by hanging, circle tradition is to behead those whose betrayal leads to death."

Some of the faces turned pale. The newer members discussed this revelation amongst themselves, including Arthur France and Abraham Stoker, who sat together.

"Beheading?" asked France. "Is that legal?"

Paul's face showed no hint of deception. "The Crown is aware of it, for the circle practises under ancient laws that supersede all others. We consider treasonous murder so grievous a sin that we exact the ultimate price for it. I do not say we *will* decapitate the traitors; only that we have the legal right to do so. Now, you may wonder if I know the names of these adders," he continued as he closed the shirt and put on the waistcoat. "The hospital meeting at the HBH had been planned since last Monday, but only a very few circle members were aware of it. The hospital administrators knew, of course. Some of our higher ranking ICI agents knew the duchess would be meeting her hospital staff and leaders this morning, and so it wasn't a complete surprise when a few reporters arrived at the hospital. However, no one knew of *my* plans to go there."

Paul paused and let this bit of information take root. Diedra Kimberley grew restless and tried to cover it by asking, "Surely, you cannot think any of us would inform the press? I detest those little cockroaches!"

The earl stared at the physician. "Of course, not. I should never think you'd call attention to your actions, Doctor."

She began to collect her handbag and a separate medical satchel. "If this meeting was called to catch-out treasonous members, then I suggest you name them. I have calls to make on women whose lives depend on punctuality."

"So that you may relieve them of the burden of unborn life?" the earl asked boldly.

Kimberley gasped. "What? I do not conduct abortions, Lord Aubrey. I patch up women who've suffered from another's botched work!"

She started for the door, but Paul ordered Galton to stop her. The room erupted into shouting and anger, giving Sir Ralph Epperson the necessary diversion to open a window and hop through it. By the time anyone noticed his absence, the unrepentant traitor had already hailed a hansom.

"You go nowhere, Dr. Kimberley," said Galton. "Lord Aubrey, what shall we do with her?"

Aubrey glared into the tall physician's grey eyes. "You have such skill in medicine, Dr. Kimberley. Why use that skill to murder? You pretend to heal, yet you'd take the life of an innocent? You are no better than Herod."

"I have told you, I don't perform abortions."

"Oh, but you do. And you work with an organisation called the Fourth Table, do you not?"

"Yes, what of it? Many London doctors attend Fourth Table meetings. It isn't illegal."

"Shall we all sit?" asked Kepelheim. "There's no need to interrogate Dr. Kimberley now, is there?"

The earl knew Martin well and had to assume he knew something Paul did not. *Trust your elders,* his father had said. *Don't assume grey hairs mean a grey mind. Wisdom rides on waves of silver, son. Remember that.*

"Very well. Dr. Kimberley, I suggest you go with Sir Thomas." Then to Galton, he whispered, "Take her to Loudain House and lock her in one of the smaller apartments. Make her comfortable, but guard her well until I can speak with her."

Galton did as ordered, joined by Percy Smythe-Daniels, and the door shut behind them. "Let's all sit, shall we?" Aubrey told the group. "I wish none of this had happened, but if Dr. Kimberley has conspired to betray us, then we must find out. I promise not to harm her. And the entire circle will vote on how to handle any sentence. Is that agreeable?"

Abberline's hand went up. Paul smiled, thinking again of his father's words about grey hair, for Fred Abberline's head boasted a great abundance of it. "Yes, Chief Inspector?" the earl asked.

"I don't mean to interrupt, laddy, but that tall fella who's been sittin' down this way is gone. Looks like he left through the window."

Aubrey counted the room. "You're right, Chief Inspector. There were forty-two here. Kimberley left with Sir Thomas and Percy.

That should leave thirty-nine. I count thirty-eight. Who's missing? Do you know his name?"

Fred Abberline grinned. "Nice to know I can help now and then. Never got a name. Real tall man. Slim build. Baldin' up top."

"Sir Ralph," muttered Algernon Winters, a chemist who worked with Drummond.

"Yes, I thought it might be Epperson," said Paul. "He and Dr. Kimberley were the only two others I told of my plans for this morning."

"Why tell them?" asked Lady Louisa. "Had you suspected them already?"

"Yes, and I sent them messages regarding today's core meeting but added that I'd be at the hospital with Beth. I even told them the exact moment that she and I would be there together. Every other person has been cleared. It had to be one or both of them that ordered the shooting."

"Or Captain Wychwright," suggested Kepelheim. "He's the first man Duke Charles would suspect, I should think. Has anyone monitored his visitors whilst in hospital?"

"Of course, we have," Paul answered. "After the las..."

The earl paled suddenly and became somewhat unsteady. Treves stepped over, as did Michael Emerson and Kepelheim. "You might be bleeding again," said Treves. "Paul, you really should lie down."

"It's just pain," said Aubrey, resuming his chair. "But to make you all happy, I'll sit. Does that suffice?"

"I can offer another morphine injection," suggested Treves.

"Not yet. Let's resume, shall we?"

The three men grudgingly stepped back to their seats, and Paul continued. "When we were attacked at Drummond Chapel in August, I took steps to ensure we'd never be under fire again, and yet two of our own have tried to remove Beth and myself from existence. Has my cousin's disappearance left us vulnerable? Did they wait to strike until both Charles and my uncle were away? And why? Why Beth? Was this some imagined plan to take control of her children?"

"This is the most dreadful of all possibilities," said Reggie Whitmore. "The circle's primary purpose is to protect those children, as well as Beth. But we cannot let the actions of these two lead us to suspect one another. That's exactly what the enemy wants. By design, members of this circle are interdependent. We rely upon one another, and we take our mandate from Christ, not a pack of devils."

Paul took a deep breath, trying not to react, but everyone could see the pain he suffered; emotional as well as physical. "I fear these two spiders have woven webs of deception with others," he told his friends. "Yesterday, I received a cable from America. There's an organisation there that parallels Redwing and Blackstone, but hopes to gain superiority over them both. Both Epperson and Kimberley have been communicating with this group through coded letters. Its base is Chicago, and it calls itself the White Council."

To everyone's surprise, Stoker's hand went up. "I've heard of this group, Lord Aubrey, but not in connexion with any nefarious goal. There's a literary foundation called the White Council. Do we speak of the same entity?"

"I'm not sure, Mr. Stoker," said the earl. "Kimberley's been using chemical abortifacients produced by an American chemical concern owned by the White Council. The company is called Sanguis. It was previously operated by Antonio Calabrese on behalf of Redwing, but Calabrese's gone missing, and the White Council have taken control. It's my belief that the Council's actually run by a powerful spirit entity, though I don't know which."

"And this Fourth Table you mentioned?" asked Abberline. "What the devil's that? Never heard of it."

Kepelheim's hand went up. Paul nodded, granting permission for the tailor to address the question. "Thank you, Lord Aubrey. This news has affected us all, I know, but we must proceed with renewed strength and purpose and lift up Christ as we protect the lines of the Plantagenet twins, no? Treason does not affect our core mandate. That remains unchanged. Now, as to this Fourth Table, Chief Inspector, there is a growing belief amongst some in medicine, that preborn children are not fully alive. For them, ending a non-living mass of blood and cells is just another surgical procedure. But all of us here take life very seriously. A child in the womb is as important as his mother or father." He paused. "We are agreed on this, no?"

Everyone nodded, and many of the men grew angry, for most were married and had sons and daughters. They considered abortion murder, pure and simple.

"You might wonder why I'd need to ask you such a question, but I fear abortion is about to become commonplace. Indeed, some would like to play God regarding *post*-born children; that is a child already living and breathing outside his mother's body. There are old Roman laws, called the Twelve Tables. These laws dictated the rights of all citizens. The Fourth Table refers to the rights of fathers, stating that a father may end the life of any child he considered unfit or deformed. This would be a *post*-term murder, my friends. Now, the international organisation that calls itself the Fourth Table wants to resurrect this idea. They want the legal right to destroy *any* life they deem unfit, be that life preborn or post. Duke Charles and I spoke of this in July, and he believes the group is responsible for the Embankment Killings; those bottles filled with pitiful infant bodies and bits of their butchered mothers that now wash up along the Thames here and the Seine in Paris."

The door opened, and a constable whispered something to the earl. Paul's shoulders drooped, and he lowered his head. "Thank you," he answered. After taking a deep breath, the earl made an announcement. "I've just heard Sir Ralph is dead. His body was found a few streets from here, shot through the head."

Shock ran through the group.

The Dowager Countess, Lady Louisa Bramstile stood. "This news is beyond tragic, but it is not your fault, Lord Aubrey! If Sir Ralph chose to betray us, then he's received God's justice. And that great and merciful God has removed the burden of punishment from your shoulders. We who remain must not allow this to divide us. That's what the enemy wants, you see. And it's clear that same enemy sees you and the duchess as impediments, which must be removed. Paul—and I hope you don't mind if I call you that," she said, her voice trembling a little. "Paul, I'm old and a bit stubborn, but you're young and vibrant and strong. I suppose I feel like a mother to you and Charles. I held him as a baby, mourned when we thought him dead, and rejoiced when he returned. And I've known you since you were a wee bairn at Briarcliff. I know the rootstock of the Stuarts and Sinclairs, and those roots are sturdy and strong! You've grown into a great, grand oak, Paul! Now, the winds have come to test you, but trust in those deep roots. Christ's Spirit is in you, Paul Stuart. You positively shine with it!"

The earl's eyes had begun to tear, and he wiped the grief and anguish away. "No other words could have cheered me more than those, Lady Louisa. Ah, but Charles always calls you Aunt Louisa. May I?"

"I should be pleased if you would," she smiled.

Aubrey wiped his eyes again, his dimples deepening as he, too, found a smile. "Then, thank you, Aunt. Now, we must all set aside our emotions; forget this heartache and move the original purpose of the meeting. Mr. Treves has lost two of his patients. Not living ones, but patients who've passed on. We all know the wave of missing dead now facing our city. That's why we're here. Yes, Risling? Your hand is raised," he called to his longtime friend.

Malcolm stood. "Let me look into the Epperson matter for you. I could take one or two men with me, if anyone's willing to volunteer."

"Thank you for offering, Malcolm. Chief Inspector Abberline? Inspector France? Would the two of you accompany Lord Malcolm? Considering the circumstances, this should be a joint Yard and ICI investigation. Edmund, do you mind remaining?"

Reid glanced up from a leather police book, filled with handwritten notes. "Not in the least. I've a number of things to report and would rather stay, if Fred can go."

"Happy to help Risling find his feet," Fred remarked as the three men gathered up their coats and walking sticks. "Cheer up, laddy. We've all had people we trust betray us. Most don't try to shoot us down, o' course; which is a plus, I suppose."

"Treachery often wears a smile," Paul told him. "And the wider the smile, the less you can trust it."

"One of your father's sayings," Kepelheim observed from a nearby chair. "Rob Stuart would be proud of you, Paul. No, he *is* proud of you. Your father's very much alive and standing with our Lord now, waiting for us to join him, isn't he?"

"He is, Martin, but speaking of our Lord, I've let the enemy distract me. I've neglected the most important part of our gatherings. Prayer. And with all this happening, I feel a particular need for it. Lady Louisa—no, let me make that *Aunt* Louisa, would you consider petitioning the throne on our behalf?"

"I'd be honoured, Paul, and I love being called Aunt by you," said the Dowager Countess. All stood, and Louisa moved round the table to stand beside Aubrey. "Gentlemen, let us go to God's throne and seek his answers to our worries."

Every head bowed, and Paul reached for Louisa's hand, pretending it was his late mother's and squeezing it tightly. Despite her advanced age, the elderly woman prayed with great power and authority.

"Father of all that is good and pure and honest and worthy and true, you created us and know us well; so very well, that you keep a tally of all the hairs upon our heads. You understand that we're fragile and prone to failure, but in you we may rise to greater things. I thank you for each and every member here today. Every one of these fellow warriors is a pearl of great price, my king; a rich and lustrous pearl upon your garment, a gem within your crown. But this value isn't earned by deeds done in our flesh, but because of deeds done in your Son's flesh. It is his blood that purifies us, his Spirit that fills us, his Light that makes us shine! All our worth comes from him. All our worth comes from you.

"Thank you so much, Lord God, for protecting Paul and Elizabeth this morning. When I think of what could have happened, it causes me to tremble. Yet, you foresaw it all and provided protection, though we could not see it. My Lord, the plots of humans and fallen angels are no mystery to you, but they often surprise us.

"It saddens me to hear of betrayal within our ranks, and we know it saddens you as well. Just as Judas betrayed you that night, so too have our companions betrayed us. And now, one has fallen into eternity and may even be damned. Still, from the dawning of the world, you knew it would happen, and yet allowed it, for your honour and glory. You work all things together for good, according to your purposes, and so I ask today that even this betrayal might work together, to honour you and bring about the triumph of good. And though we feel anger now, may we find it in our hearts to forgive, just as you have forgiven us.

"Be amongst us this day and protect us with your angels and the sweet presence of your Spirit. Protect our dear duchess, grant strength and courage to Paul, to his wife, and to his unborn child. And dear Saviour, bring our Charles back home. We know he is in your keeping, and we trust you to watch after him whilst he's away, but, please, Father God, bring him home! Bring him home to us. Now, may all our actions and conversation be honouring to you. We ask in the name of Christ, even our Saviour and King. Amen."

All members answered 'amen', and Paul pulled Louisa close, and with his head on her shoulder, it sounded as though he wept. "You shame me, dear and most beloved Aunt. Those are the words my own mother would have prayed, yet how far I've run from her sweet counsel! She loved God, just as you do. Forgive my foolish heart, dear Louisa! Forgive me, Lord in Heaven!"

She stroked his hair like a mother. "No man is better suited for this task, Paul Stuart." He raised his head, and she kissed the earl's stubbled cheek. "Be strong and of good courage. You are a very great man. All of us know it. And I am honoured to sit beneath your leadership."

She embraced him, and then Louisa Bramstile returned to her chair. Every eye was trained on the earl's face.

"Thank you for that, Aunt," he said. "A man's greatest strength comes from the prayers of women. Now, with God's blessing, we look once more to business. We've met many times since Charles was taken from us. We've heard Prince Anatole's assurances that God allowed the abduction for reasons yet to unfold, and so we must continue to trust in God's plans. Risling and his team will discern the facts regarding Sir Ralph, but no matter the cause, we must mourn the loss of two in our family. Sir Ralph is dead, and Dr. Kimberley will never sit with us again. I promise to do all in my power to show her mercy, for my gracious Aunt Louisa reminds me to forgive, even as we are forgiven.

"Now, I chose the London for our meeting, not only because of Baron Wychwright's impending transfer to ICI facilities, but because Mr. Treves has reported another of these mystifying abductions. As most of you know, there's been a storm of reports across the city regarding missing corpses and desecrated graves. Since the first report last December, the number of cases has skyrocketed.

"As the cases grew, Commissioner Monro despatched all available Metropolitan policeman to knock on doors, asking every man or woman if they'd suffered from the disappearance of a recently deceased husband, wife, child, or parent; or if they knew of someone who had. If the answer was yes, the policeman determined the condition the loved one was in at the time he or she vanished. Had they only just died? Had they been buried, and if so, for how long? I've asked Inspector Reid to compile all Monro's numbers into a list. Edmund, if you'd be good enough to give us your report?"

Reid stood. His thinning hair was slicked back with a bit of pomade to thicken it, and a pair of wire-rimmed reading spectacles rested upon the wide bridge of his nose. He opened the leather book.

"In total, our men have tallied over six-dozen such occurrences in less than a year, in places, ranging from Temple Park to Deptford. Commissioner Monro's also heard from the nearby counties, sir. These, too, are suffering funerary thefts. If you include all the neighbouring counties of Surry, Sussex, Kent, and Hampshire, then we have hundreds. We've interviewed undertakers, morticians, and bereavement service staff. The story's always the same. The dead simply vanish into the aether."

"Are the details like the story told by the man who drove Baron Wychwright's hearse?" asked Aubrey. "The one who spoke with my cousin and blamed the theft on a bird?"

"Yes, sir. Many of the reports mention birds, though we're careful never to suggest it. The mentions are voluntary. We're also seeing robberies from mausoleums. Thieves break in and leave empty tombs and open caskets, as though they want us to know. Someone in England is stealing the dead. The question is who and why?"

The earl turned to the London Hospital's chief surgeon. "Mr. Treves, if you'd tell us of your own experience?"

Frederick Treves was a well-dressed man of middle-age with a thick black moustache and a side-part to his wavy hair. He stood just shy of six-feet, but the surgeon looked shorter, due to a slight stoop caused by long hours bending over patients as he performed surgical procedures or taught anatomy classes to medical students. His voice was deep but troubled as he replied.

"Death is a constant watchman in any hospital setting, and so we keep a large morgue, equipped with pump-driven ammonia to refrigerate units that house the dead. For a very long time, our hospital was immune to these horrible crimes, but that changed two days ago. I sent word to Lord Aubrey as soon as we discovered the first theft, which is why he scheduled this meeting at our hospital. Since reporting the first to you two days ago, another has vanished. Just this morning. We think the shooting provided cover for the theft. This second missing body was that of a Whitechapel banker. He was an inveterate drinker who frequented the music halls. A fellow gambler didn't care for the man's cards and jabbed a knife into his ribs. We tried to save him, but failed. He'd lost far too much blood. We placed his body into the morgue three days ago, pending retrieval by his family, and this morning it vanished," said Treves sighing. "The first body, and the original reason I notified Lord Aubrey, is far more troubling. He'd come here, complaining of a severe pain in his right side, which we diagnosed as appendicitis. He'd let the malady go too long, and so I performed an emergency appendicectomy. Sadly, the infection was too advanced, and the organ had already burst. The man died on the table. It was a great blow to us all, for the gentleman was a reliable supporter of our endeavours at the London, particularly of our medical school. He knew of my research on appendicitis and insisted his wife bring him here. Once the funeral ends and the will is read, his widow has promised to fund a new teaching theatre in her husband's honour. However," the surgeon sighed, "the funeral may never take place, meaning his wife is bereaved of her final farewell. My friends, Sir Gaius Jordan's body has been stolen from our morgue."

Every person in the room gasped. Jordan invented many of the newest methods for building railways, and the 'Jordan Coupling' allowed cars to be connected and disconnected quickly by just one man. This and many other inventions had earned the industrialist widespread fame, a knighthood, and a very great fortune. Anyone passing by the Bank of England knew his home, for it stood opposite, in the heart of the City's financial district.

Paul spoke. "Mr. Treves, we commiserate with you and the London regarding this tragedy, but also with the families of both these missing men. And I promise that we'll bend the entire will of our organisation to solving it. I do wish Charles were here. He's a much better detective than I, but amongst our number, there are many who will help where I lack. Martin Kepelheim springs to mind," he said, smiling at the tailor. "Elbert Stanley is another, and Edmund Reid is considered the epitome of the detective's investigative art. To begin the formal investigation, the circle will need a list of all who've vanished; both in London and the surrounding counties. These bodies do not vanish into hidden realms, my friends. They must be stored somewhere. All vacant warehouses, shuttered estates, even abandoned hospitals must be considered."

"Jordan's disappearance has stunned everyone at the London," Treves told the earl and other members. "Lord Aubrey, with all that now besets your family, I hesitated to contact you, but Dr. Gehlen insisted upon it. Who would do this? And under our noses at that! The morgue is constantly manned. Is it some supernatural event? Might these bird stories have merit?"

Birds, thought Paul. *I saw birds. An angel.*

"Lord Aubrey?" asked Kepelheim. "Paul?"

"Forgive me. I'm all right. Mr. Treves, we all commiserate. Many of us have counselled families who've twice lost a loved one. First to death and then to theft. Duke Charles was there the morning the first incident happened, and he..."

The earl paused again, thinking of his missing cousin suddenly caused an emotional dam to burst. The shooting, the terrifying near-miss of the runaway coach, the cloud of supernatural birds, his fears for Beth, and the betrayal by longtime friends—it all wounded him, not just physically, but emotionally. Beth could have died, and one of their own may have hired the killer. It was a bitter pill to swallow, but swallow it he must.

"You need to rest, my lord," whispered Baxter, who walked over to help. "You may think this injury slight, but you mustn't take it for granted. Forgive me for saying, sir, for I shouldn't wish to sound impertinent, but this day's troubles only add to your grief at Duke Charles's absence."

"That is true," said Martin Kepelheim, who joined Baxter. "Paul, we all know how you long to be out there searching for Charles, and because you cannot, you throw your energies into whatever mystery arises. These missing bodies are important and no doubt form some part of the enemy's plans, but we cannot afford to lose you, also. Let us deal with all this. Take Beth home. Stay with her and Cordelia."

Paul shook his head, the long strands of hair moist with perspiration. The blood loss was clouding his ability to think. "I know what you're trying to say, Martin, and I certainly appreciate Baxter's opinion, as always. But how can I return to Westminster? You'd have me forget two of our trusted members have betrayed us? What else have they told our enemies? What else have they planned? We'll need a new code, Martin."

"Yes, I'd thought of that. We'll begin right away."

Anthony Gehlen raised a hand. "Paul, if it helps, I could see to Beth and Cordelia. As most of you know, my house is nearby, now that I've moved into Pencaitland Manor. Where is Beth? Shall I go check on her?" Fred Treves whispered something to his colleague, who nodded. "Ah, Fred tells me she's next door. I'll go over and say hello."

"Thank you, Anthony," said the earl.

Gehlen stopped just before leaving and said to Aubrey, "Paul, you should go home soon, or else plan on collapsing."

"I'll go as soon as the meeting's over," Paul promised.

Anthony left the members to discuss the missing corpses and the theft of Sir Gaius Jordan's body, which had thus far remained out of the press. He tried the room next door, but it was empty. He assumed the peeress was visiting one of the powder rooms and sought her out, but no one had seen her. Gehlen considered relaying the news to the earl, but decided to search the hospital before worrying Aubrey any further. Whilst passing through the reception lobby, the dark-haired physician encountered Lord Salperton, who was just arriving.

"I'm late as usual," Henry apologised breathlessly. My driver had to let me out several blocks away. Apparently, there's been some sort of murder or suicide nearby. The police are everywhere, and I think I saw Arthur France and Fred Abberline—they're an odd sort of pairing, don't you think? And Elbert Stanley joined them, just as I passed by. I feared the meeting might have dismissed already. Has it?"

Gehlen shook his fellow physician's hand warmly. "You might say we've had a bit of excitement, related to the crime scene. Paul will explain everything, I'm sure. The group's in the surgeons' lounge. Do you know where to find it?"

"I should hope so. I've been here enough times, to see Alex Collins and more recently to examine Baron Wychwright on behalf of the ICI. They want to know if he's fit to stand trial. Mentally, I mean."

"He's generally under morphia's wispy clouds these days," Gehlen told his friend. "Where's Seth Holloway? Everyone was ordered to come. No exceptions, or so my note said."

"I'm aware of that, but I asked Seth to remain at Montmore and keep our star guest company. Adele Sinclair, I mean. She's such a lovely girl and remarkably strong. Despite all that's happened, she's shown very few scars thus far. Visible scars, I mean."

"Do you think she bears hidden scars?"

"I'm sure she does, but only time will tell us how many and how deep they are. She's suffering troubling dreams, but that's not unusual for her age and experience. If the meeting's begun, shouldn't you be in the lounge with the others?"

"I'm looking for Duchess Elizabeth. She was supposed to be in the room next to ours, but she's gone missing."

Henry's brown eyes rounded. "Missing? Good heavens! Shouldn't we all be out looking for her?"

"Who's missing?" asked a woman's voice from Henry's elbow.

The two men turned to find the dark eyes of Elizabeth Sinclair watching them. Without giving it a thought, Henry drew her into a relieved embrace. "My dear friend! Where were you? Anthony just told me you'd gone missing, which sent me into all manner of dreadful thoughts!" Then, realising how the intimate embrace might appear to strangers, the viscount released her, adding, "What I meant to say is that I'm very happy to see you, Duchess. That's all."

"Apparently," Gehlen laughed.

"It's quite all right, Henry," the duchess assured him with a smile. "It's been a very long day, but seeing you always brings me strength. I'm sorry to worry you both. I'd gone to speak with Mrs. Chandler about staffing at the new hospital. I should have told someone. Did Anthony mention what happened at earlier?"

"No," Henry replied. "What happened?"

"Someone shot at us," she told him, her voice falling to a whisper. "It happened at the new hospital. I'm fine as you can see, but Paul was injured. He refuses to go home."

"Oh, my!" Salperton exclaimed. "But you're all right?"

"Yes, Henry, I'm well."

He placed a hand on her forehead. "I'm not so sure about that. You're warm, Beth, and your cheeks are flushed."

"It's the excitement. I'm sure it will return to normal once this has passed."

"Has someone checked your temperature?" asked Henry.

"Michael did," she told him. "Anthony was there. I'm sure he could tell you more, but I assure you, I'm fine."

"Despite that, I'm taking her home," said Anthony.

"Good idea," Henry answered. "Oh, shall I tell Della tonight's visit is postponed?"

"Yes, it might be best if both of us retire early tonight, but I don't want Adele to think Paul's injury is serious. Emerson called it a flesh wound. Nothing like last year's injury, praise God!"

"Last year's?" Henry asked.

"I'll tell you about it another time," said Beth, noticing heads turned in their direction. "And just so you know, Paul and I rest much more easily, knowing Della's in your care."

Henry blushed, and Anthony shrugged. "Lord Salperton gets all the ladies. He listens to your dreams and desires. I just deliver your children. It's the burden of the obstetrician, I suppose. Come with me, Beth. I'm to take you back to Westminster, and our heroic alienist must join the others in the lounge."

Henry smirked at the remark. "You should come see me about that jealous streak, Lord Pencaitland. I'm sure I can find a remedy for it."

They all laughed, and the viscount departed for the surgeons' lounge. Beth told Anthony, "I'm ready anytime you are." He helped her gather up a handbag and cloak from the room where she'd been reading. The duchess left a short note for her cousin and one for Treves, thanking him for lending her the novel.

They rode in Anthony's coach, a new two-passenger brougham, drawn by a pair of chestnut Oldenburg geldings.

"Thank you for keeping me company," Beth told Gehlen as they crossed the city. "It's probably best the window curtains are shut. Anyone seeing me with you might get the wrong idea."

"How so?" he asked.

"Some might say, 'There goes the Duchess of Branham with another man!'"

He smiled. "Trust me, no one would ever think that, Beth. Not where I'm concerned."

"Oh, but they would. You're a handsome gentleman, Lord Pencaitland. You joked with Henry, saying he gets all the ladies, but I find it hard to believe women aren't clamouring for your attention."

Anthony Gehlen was indeed a very handsome man. He had thick black hair, dark eyes, a firm jaw, and a fine physique. He dressed well and even before inheriting his title and lands, received a great deal of attention from female patients. Only now, at this very moment, did it occur to him, that he'd never felt even the slightest romantic hint from the duchess. Married women often threw them-

selves at him, but even when alone together, Beth never once behaved inappropriately. The duchess loved her husband as few men
were loved in this world. Elizabeth Sinclair was a true and faithful woman.

If only, I could find such a prize, he thought.

Beth was smiling at him, and the physician wondered if she'd
been reading his thoughts. "Am I amusing?" he asked.

"No, but interesting," she replied. "Of all my doctors, and I
have more than a dozen, you're the only one who seems lost, Anthony. Generally, doctors strut about the world as if they own it. You
walk as though the world has let you down. If you ever need to talk,
I'm a very good listener."

He reached for her gloved hand, saying, "Unlike some women,
you're a natural wife and mother. I think you'd be mother to all men,
given the chance. I know of no other woman like you, Elizabeth. I
admit that when I first met you, I assumed you were a flower that
might wither at the slightest heat or frost, but you're made of steel, I
think. Any other woman in your shoes would be weeping and taking
dose after dose of laudanum to dull the pain, but you press on, as
though every day will end in victory. How do you do that?"

"Really, I don't see myself that way," she told him. "And I press
on, because God is my guide and Shepherd. He leads me where he
thinks best, and I know he has a plan for Charles and our sons."

"Sons? Plural?"

"Oh, yes. We're to have six," she declared without blinking. "I
owe Charles five more, which leads to my question. Do you mind if
ask your medical opinion?"

"I'm your doctor and your friend, Elizabeth. You may ask anything of me."

Beth's cheeks pinked, and she glanced down at her hands.
"You're very generous, Anthony. It's just, when Michael examined
me, he thought he detected some signs I might be with child again.
Is that possible?"

"What signs?"

"He didn't say, actually."

"Were you and the duke intimate before he vanished?"

She nodded. "Yes, but only a few times. Michael pronounced
me recovered in late July and said we could resume our marriage, so
to speak. Charles returned to my bedchamber on the first of August.

He was taken on the eleventh, meaning we had less than a fortnight together. Surely, that isn't enough time, is it? Does, well," she continued, stumbling over how to say it. "Can a woman's fertility return so very quickly?"

He smiled. "I assume the marriage bed is happy?"

"Very," she said, blushing again.

"Had your monthly courses returned before then?"

"No. The bleeding after giving birth receded by the end of June, as you know, but I've not had any courses yet. Is that unusual?"

"Unusual, but not impossible. Have you been nauseous?"

"Sometimes, but only in the last few days. Might it be this Russian illness? I am slightly feverish. I was being a little deceitful with Henry, for I prefer no one worry about me."

"Still, we men worry, Beth. It's our nature to do so." He touched her forehead. "You're quite warm."

"Michael measured it at one hundred degrees."

He reached for his medical bag, withdrew a thermometer, and placed it beneath her tongue. She sat patiently whilst Anthony counted the time. After he removed the instrument, he examined it carefully. "It's now over a hundred and one. It might be the excitement, but you must go to bed right away when we're back at Haimsbury House. Now, tell me, are you sleeping well? Vomiting? Food cravings? Do smells seem different or bother you?"

"I sleep well enough, considering. When I dream about Charles, those are distressing. I always see him in a tunnel, like the ones I dreamt of as a girl. Paul says it's because of the tunnels beneath Branham; that I'm conflating Charles with Seth. I don't think he's right, though he means well. I've not vomited, but I do find some food less appealing the past few days. I may not always show it, for I keep busy. Nonetheless, my heart is weighed down with worry. Wouldn't that explain it?"

"Probably. May I come see you tomorrow?"

"Yes, of course. Thank you. My grandfather mentioned that you were installing a telephone at Pencaitland Manor. Is that true?"

"It's installed and working. I've been keeping an eye on Drummond House whilst James is in Paris. He's a very good neighbour. Instead of the usual gifts of wine, he sends Drummond whisky. I don't drink spirits, but my guests enjoy it."

"When Charles is back, we'll come visit and he can help you with that. Thank you, Anthony," she said. "I know Paul appreciates that you've brought me home. He needs to know I'm all right."

"As do we all," he said in a whisper. "We men look to you for solace, but such constant love takes a toll on you. I could prescribe a mild soporific, if you need one."

"We have laudanum, and Mrs. Baxter is a nurse. Oh, but would you look at Robby before you go?" she asked as the clarence turned off Queen Anne Walk towards Haimsbury Drive. "He's had slight fevers now and then. Esther says he may be teething already. He has a little bump on the top gum."

"I've seen other babies teethe at three months, so it's possible. I'll check both the children. Besides, I think of them as part of my extended family."

"When they're older, they can call you Uncle Anthony," she said, smiling.

"I'd like that."

After a few minutes, the brougham pulled into Haimsbury Circle, and once stopped, two footmen emerged from the magnificent mansion. One opened the coach door, whilst the other helped the duchess. "Welcome home, Your Grace," he said.

"Thank you. Is Mrs. Baxter still here?"

"She is, my lady. Shall I fetch her?"

"No, Dr. Gehlen and I will go see her together. Is she in the nursery?"

"I believe so, my lady. Dr. Gehlen, may I take your bag?"

"Thank you, no. I'm used to carrying it, and it has my medical supplies inside."

Anthony took Beth's arm, and they used the lift to access the nursery floor. Now that she was home, in her own private environment, the duchess allowed the exhaustion and fear to have its way. Whilst Anthony examined the twins, she put up her feet in the nursery's parlour.

"Esther, has my son's fever continued?" she asked her former housekeeper.

"It comes and goes, just like teething does, my lady. Mrs. Wilsham's of the same opinion. She's raised sons and been nanny to many a bairn. Did the telegrams reach you?"

"Telegrams? What do you mean?"

Esther hated mentioning it, for she could see the strain on the duchess's flushed face, but she didn't dare keep this news to herself. "The telegram was to Lord Aubrey, and it's from Lord Paynton at Montmore."

Exhausted, Beth's eyes had nearly shut, but now they popped back open. "Has something happened to Adele?"

"No, my lady, but to Lady Aubrey."

"What? Esther, how can Lady Aubrey have anything to do with Montmore House? She's in her apartment, most likely sleeping. Isn't she?"

"No, my lady, she's not. I only learnt of it after, but the countess took Lady Della's dog and went to Montmore."

"I don't understand. Why would Cordelia do that?"

"Ada said she wanted to get out of the house and stretch her legs. The girl said she tried to stop her, but Lady Aubrey was adamant about going."

"What's this to do with a telegram? Esther, what's happened?"

Mrs. Baxter shook her head. "The telegram said Lady Aubrey might be in labour and that Lord Aubrey had to come right away."

Beth jumped to her feet and crossed through the parlour into the largest of the nursery's bedchambers. "Anthony! Anthony, we have to leave for Montmore at once!"

Gehlen held Robby Sinclair in his arms, and he stared at the duchess. "Why? What's happened?"

"Lady Aubrey has foolishly gone there, and now she's in labour. We have to go there at once. Robby's not ill, is he?"

"No, just teething. He's growing into a healthy young boy. I'll leave instructions for the nurses, and I can go to Montmore. Beth, you should stay here."

"I'm going with you. Esther, please look to my children. And pray, Esther. Pray! The last thing my cousin needs today is to hear something's happened to Cordelia!"

CHAPTER TWENTY-TWO
Henry arrives at the meeting

Completely unaware of the telegrams flying round London, Henry MacAlpin entered the surgeons' lounge and greeted his fellow circle members.

"Forgive me, for being late. We encountered two possible crime scenes, if you can imagine it. One near here, which I'm told you know about. Sir Ralph Epperson, I understand. Dreadful thing. The other was just west of Waterloo Bridge. There were three of those police marias ahead of us, and a dozen constables were milling about the bridge and the surrounding area. Everything stopped until they'd completed their work, which made me so very late."

"Were they L-Division marias?" asked the earl.

"Yes, I suppose so. Does L stand for Lambeth? Well, I suppose it would, being that Lambeth begins with L. Is that how it works? No wait a moment," Henry blithered in typical fashion. "Hammersmith's T-Division, isn't it? And this is H, and we're in Whitechapel. So much for my alphabetical theory. It was probably Lambeth, then. Forgive me. My brain's a bit scattered today."

"Take a seat, Henry," Paul said, managing a smile. "Did Seth come with you?"

"Uh, well, no, actually," replied the viscount as he took the empty chair next to the Dowager Countess. "Good afternoon, Lady Louisa. Are you well? Yes? Good, so glad to hear it. No, Seth didn't come," he said, returning to Paul's question. "I know your message ordered every member to attend, but I hated to leave Della without one of us nearby. She finds Lord Paynton a great comfort."

"Is that so?" asked Kepelheim. "I've noticed Lady Della finds Count Riga's visits a comfort as well, though I rather doubt for the same reason."

Nearly all the members chuckled at this. Henry only smiled. "Yes, it's true. Our Dr. Holloway is an exceedingly handsome fellow, particularly to those ladies of a Jane Austen persuasion, no pun intended, I assure you. But Seth dearly loves Adele, in the same way each of us does," he added hastily. "And when required, Seth's quite a skilled marksman. Better than I am, should it come to that. Oh, that reminds me. I should have mentioned the house before I left," he muttered to himself.

"House? What house?" asked Aubrey.

"House?" repeated Henry, growing lost in thought.

"You said you should have mentioned a house to Lord Paynton," prompted the earl. "Which house is that?"

"Did I say that aloud? Yes, well, it's Hemsfield House."

"Hemsfield?" asked Aubrey. "Why should you have mentioned that house?"

"Because it's next door to me. Next door to Montmore, I mean. Which means it's next door to Adele, and she asked about it."

"Isn't Hemsfield House on Bedford Square?" asked Abraham Stoker. "It's the only white one in all those brownstones. Near Tavistock Mews."

"Yes, that's the one," said Aubrey. "Henry, how is this house near you named Hemsfield? Everyone knows the late earl boasted of his fashionable townhome, saying it was the finest on Bedford Square."

"Did he? I didn't really know the late earl, so I couldn't say," MacAlpin answered, his nut-brown eyes blinking. He rubbed at the left, as though something irritated the cornea, but continued speaking as he used a white handkerchief to remove the debris. "There, got it," he muttered with satisfaction and returned the kerchief to his pocket. "Sorry. The winds are kicking up, and a bit of dirt blew into my eyes."

"The house?" Paul prompted.

"Oh, the house! Yes. There's a Hemsfield House near me, you see, but the family abandoned it long ago. Shame really. It's a grand old place. My grandmother said it was the family's original London home, built when one of the viscounts was elevated to earl. I think for his part in the Seven Years' War against France."

The dark-haired alienist noticed a coffee urn on the buffet table and rose to pour himself a cup. He took a quick sip. "It's gone cold. That's what I get for being late."

"Henry, why is this house important?" Paul asked.

"Important?" asked the viscount, as he added two sugar cubes to the cold coffee and stirred it in. "Oh, the Hemsfield House! Of course, well, it's because of Adele. She slept poorly last night, and this morning, confessed to seeing shadowy movements in the third storey of that house, and so I offered to investigate. At this stage of her treatment, it's important to keep her mind calm. True to my word, before I left to come here, I called at the house and rang the bell. It's one of those abbey-style bells that clangs as though summoning a monk porter. And it's strange, for I had a very strong sense that someone did respond, only he never opened the door. I'm sure he lingered in the foyer the whole time I stood there. It's most peculiar behaviour for an empty house, don't you think?"

"Surely, you don't mean the house is haunted, Lord Salperton?" asked Lady Louisa.

Henry's mouth upturned into a quizzical grin, and he reached for the sugar bowl to add a third cube to his cup. "Haunted is a most intriguing word, don't you think? It implies habitation by unseen, post-mortem entities. Yet we of the inner circle deal with such matters every day, don't we? Yes, I sensed something on the other side of the door, and I'm certain that it, in turn, sensed me."

"And what do you think this entity decided to do, Lord Salperton?" asked Edward MacPherson.

"Obviously, it decided to remain invisible and uninviting," the alienist replied. "Adele senses something as well. We all know that ability is strong in the Stuart and Sinclair families. Is it a wonder she might have inherited it?"

Paul stared at the stack of reports. The idea of ghosts and missing bodies felt connected, but he couldn't work out how. Perhaps, the wound and blood loss prevented his mind from grasping it. *I wish Charles were here.* Then, he realised God had already sent him someone with 'eyes to see'.

Wir und die Todten reiten schnell.
We and the Dead travel fast.

"Henry, would you consider going back there with me?" asked the earl.

"To Hemsfield House? Yes, of course. If we can prove the house is really empty, it would ease Adele's mind. And the only way to do that is to go inside," said Henry firmly. "I spoke with Elizabeth before coming in just now, and she seemed quite tired. I believe you and she should postpone your evening visit to Della until you're recovered."

"Or Beth could rest, whilst you and I visit that house," the earl countered.

"Tonight? Is that wise? Gehlen said you've been injured, Paul," Henry objected. "Surely, you need to stay home as well? Besides, Cordelia must be terribly worried about you. The afternoon papers will undoubtedly splash the shooting across all their front pages."

"You're right. Tomorrow then," Paul decided. "I'll come with Beth, and she can sit with Della, whilst you and I call on Hemsfield's reclusive ghost."

"Might I join you?" asked Kepelheim. "I should like to see this ghost for myself."

"Of course. I'd value your input," said Paul. "Meet us at Hemsfield House at eight tomorrow evening. Not at Montmore. And come armed. Henry, is it north or south of your home?"

"Just north of it. Tall hedges border our gardens. Hemsfield's property is just the other side. Our upper floors share a line of sight."

"Reid, do you fancy a night of ghost-hunting?"

The inspector shook his head. "Ordinarily, I'd enjoy such an adventure with you, sir, but I'm up to my ears in cases, including this morning's shooting and now Epperson's death."

"I'll want a full report on both," Paul told him.

"I'd assumed as much," said Reid. "I imagine Abberline will stop by tonight and give me his account of Sir Ralph's presumed suicide. Is there ever an end to madness?"

"When Christ reigns," said MacPherson. "Only then."

The meeting then returned to the matter of the missing bodies. The possibility of resurrectionists in the manner of Burke and Hare was discussed, but Treves overruled it.

"It's true that in the past, medical schools and private researchers engaged in such ghoulish practices to obtain specimens, but the

Crown now provides ample numbers of suitable bodies from its prison populations, and sadly from Bedlam."

Henry sighed. "Bedlam. I deplore the way people are treated there."

"I agree," said Treves. "Paul, I've seen every donated body in our anatomy morgue, and nothing is amiss. None came to us from suspicious sources. We can open all the freezers, if you want, but I believe the missing bodies are taken for some other reason."

"I agree," said the earl, "but with the dead now vanishing from hospitals as well as funeral parlours and hearses, we must ask the obvious question. Is Redwing behind this? And if so, why do they steal the bodies? What can the recently dead provide that the living cannot?"

"I hesitate to mention this, my lord, but might the bodies provide a substrate for resurrection?" asked Stoker.

"A substrate for resurrection?" echoed Lady Louisa. "How? Surely, you don't think the dead can walk again, the way Lazarus did?"

"No, I'm not saying that, my lady," Stoker explained. "My friends, I realise I'm quite new to all this, but I've done a great deal of reading on the subject. Resurrection themes occur again and again in ancient texts. For instance, the Egyptian Book of the Dead gives instructions to the deceased for defeating the keeper of the Underworld."

"That would be Osiris," said MacPherson. "It's a shame Dr. Holloway isn't here. He's studied thanatology in depth."

"Thanatology?" asked Simon Allerton.

"The study of the dead," said Stoker. "I know because I've been researching it. The name is based on the Greek word for death. Thanatos."

"But death in this case is a personal name," MacPherson noted. "Thanatos is an entity."

"That's right," said Stoker. "Nearly every civilisation believes in the afterlife. Thanatos is one example of a psychopomp."

"A what?" asked Allerton.

"An usher to the underworld," said Dr. MacPherson. "When a man dies, his spirit continues. Christians believe he goes to Heaven or to Hell. The ancient pagans believed in a more active afterlife. Humans might become ghosts, and the souls of hybrids roamed the earth as good and evil *daemons*."

"Hybrids?" asked Lady Louisa. "Is that some unholy amalgamation of flesh? Like Mary Shelley's creature?"

"The hybrids were the comingled product of fallen angel and human women. Genesis Chapter six discusses it briefly."

Martin Kepelheim joined in the discussion. "Ah, yes, but the idea is more thoroughly examined in the book of Enoch."

"I've never heard of such a book. Is it in the Bible?" asked Callerson.

"No, but some argue it should have been. I've a good friend who's translating an Ethiopic copy into English. Robert Charles is his name. He's a fine man and an expert on ancient languages. He might be a candidate for the circle, actually. Shall I contact him?"

"Wait until Duke Charles is back for that, Martin. But if he has a copy of this text he might lend us, I'd love to read it," said Aubrey.

"Hybrids, thanatology, and the missing dead. It's all connected in some way," said Stoker. "It must be. Is it possible Redwing or another of these occult organisations wants to use an alchemical spell to re-energise dead flesh? You said the shooter shouted something from a German poem." He looked down at his notes, reading, "*Wir und die Todten reiten schnell.* Is that right?" Paul nodded. "This poem has meaning to the shooter. Why else quote it? We must read that poem in full, my friends, for it may help us to understand what's happening in our city."

Paul nodded. "Mr. Stoker, the Lord brought you to our cause just in time, it seems. Martin, if you'd find a copy of that poem? Does everyone read German?" Most nodded in the affirmative. "Good. We'll make that an assignment for Monday's regular meeting. What else do we know?"

Stoker raised his hand. "If I may, sir? There's a very strange group my friend Henry Irving is enamoured with. It's called the Golden Dawn, and their teachings include contacting the dead and trying to access entities they believe are ascended masters, but we would call them demons. I research such things for a new book I'm writing, but only to demonstrate the power of God over evil. Lord Aubrey, might these missing bodies provide the raw material for some horrid plan?"

"It's a very dark possibility, Mr. Stoker," the earl answered. "Our friend and colleague Inspector Elbert Stanley was part an

287

experiment to enhance men by injecting them with lupine characteristics."

"Lupine?" asked Louisa.

"Wolves, dearest Aunt. Man combined with wolf's blood in some way." He turned to MacAlpin, who was busily scratching out notes and passing them to Stoker. "Henry?"

"Yes?" the viscount muttered, glancing up from the paper. "Sorry. I was trying not to disturb you. I was writing this question, you see. Stoker's studying many of the same things Seth's working on, and I thought the two of them might collaborate."

"A very good idea," Aubrey agreed. "But I wonder if you'd like to collaborate with me? When we've finished here, I should like to call on Dr. Kepler at the Castor Institute. Henry, you accompanied Charles there last year. The two of you interviewed Alexander Collins. I believe he proved quite evasive, when pressed for answers about those lower levels."

"Evasive is an understatement!" exclaimed the viscount. "Alex Collins claimed there were no subterranean wards beneath Castor, yet I know for a fact, the building has at least four lower levels. I've seen the plans. Collins conveniently fell ill the very moment we insisted on a tour of those levels. Charles thought he was playacting, but we've since learnt the poor fellow suffered from a brain lesion. I believe you operated, Treves?"

"I did, but it was Dr. Gehlen who diagnosed the malady. I wish I could say surgery put an end to the seizures, but they persist. Or I assume they do."

"You assume?" asked Henry. "Why assume? Has he suffered another or not?"

"We've no idea. Dr. Collins was moved elsewhere; against my advice, I might add. He now resides at another clinic, operated by a Doctor..." he paused, searching his brain. "Do forgive me, Inspector Reid, do you recall the man's name? It's an unusual one. Foreign."

"Alphonse Theseus," answered Edmund. His voice held an edge to it. "The man showed up Leman Street, slick as you please, flashing paperwork from Secretary Matthews regarding Dr. Collins. We managed to put him off for a short time, but then the ICI leadership insisted we let Theseus have him!"

Aubrey answered the inspector with remarkable calm. "I understand, Edmund, but we've had this argument many times before. Charles and I made the final decision. Government matters are murky at best, and they sometimes interfere with our circle's primary mission, which is to battle Redwing and all its evil. The more we keep the Home Office out of our affairs, the better we're able to fulfill that mission. Giving them Collins seemed a small price to pay."

"Why shouldn't the Secretary be involved?" asked Salperton, who understood very little of Whitehall intrigues. "I mean, isn't the Intelligence Branch beneath the Home Secretary's aegis? I ask only because my education falters where high political office is concerned. Unless a minister sends me a family member for treatment, I seldom deal with any of them, which pleases me no end. Am I mistaken?"

"Generally, anything to do with Scotland Yard falls under the Home Secretary," Paul answered, "but when Charles agreed to head the Intelligence Branch, he insisted to Lord Salisbury and to Her Majesty, that he be given complete autonomy with no government interference."

"Then why cater to their whims?" asked Stoker. "Forgive the question, but government seems to me a theatre of masked players without a plot."

Aubrey laughed. "I've never heard a better description of Whitehall. Their plot is convoluted because there are far too many writers. Mr. Stoker, if you ever want advice, I can introduce you to Reggie Parsons."

"Parsons is invaluable," Salperton agreed. "But beware, if you have secrets. Reggie's rather like a truffle pig. He roots them out with gusto, which gives him an exhaustive script from which to write his own plots."

Paul smiled at this. "I think Reggie would consider that a compliment, Henry. Now, let's return to these missing bodies. Reid's made a list of all the cases and names with typed copies for everyone. Henry, would you take one to Seth?"

"Yes, certainly," Salperton replied as he received a set of six pages. "Good heavens! There must be over two hundred names here."

"Three hundred, fifty-three," Reid told the group. "That includes the neighbouring counties. Mr. Treves, you mentioned two missing bodies. One is Sir Gaius Jordan's, of course. If you'd give us the second name, we can each add it to our own copies."

"Yes, of course," Frederick answered, clearing his throat. "Unlike Sir Gaius, this fellow had no family. An immigrant, who arrived in London a few months ago and was renting rooms at Porter's, I believe. Dmitry Vrykolas."

"Vrykolas?" asked Aubrey. "Now, why does that name sound familiar? I'm sure of I've seen or heard it recently." He wrote it down. "Now regarding this list. Seven names are peers. One a peeress. All eight were members of Redwing, so that is where we must start. Charles was investigating a bereavement service on Wormwood in the City. His notes on the case haven't been located yet, but the duke always writes down every detail of his cases, so the notes are somewhere. Pennyweather and Sgt. Thicke are scouring the Queen Anne suite of offices. Thus far, nothing."

"They've vanished along with the bodies?" noted Salperton. "Seth will regret not coming today."

"I'm glad he stayed with Della," said Aubrey.

"Seth's made a huge difference to Della's treatment. He takes her for garden walks, and they read together. Sometimes, Adele plays the piano for him. She's become very fond of our dashing viscount."

"Then I praise God for him," said Paul. "Della is my first priority. She, Beth, and Cordelia rely upon our protection, and with this morning's shooting, it's become clear that we dare not relax our guard. The shooting," he mumbled to himself. Paul's face paled, and he shut his eyes.

"Sir?" asked Baxter. "Lord Aubrey, do you need water?"

"No, no, I'm all right, Baxter. Thank you. Wait, you can help. Would you send a cable to Duke James? I don't know if the duchess has already done so, but it's better to duplicate than neglect it. Let the duke know of the shooting, but emphasis that we're both well. I'll write him a letter and confirm that. Now, if there's no other business, we'll adjourn. Thank you all for coming on such short notice. We've dealt with two vipers in our nest. Let us pray there are no more."

Paul shook hands with the members as they left, but asked Henry to stay behind. "I have business here, and I wonder if you'd be interested in helping?"

"Me? I'd be honoured, but how can I help England's premier spy?" asked Salperton. "Do you need medical attention?"

"Not yet. The pain's bearable, and I've had worse. I plan to go back to Castor Institute and interview Dr. Kepler about their lower levels. I want to know if they're housing the dead."

"Oh, I'd not thought of that. Do you think they've begun a new experiment?"

"Anything's possible. Mr. Stoker, would you be interested in joining us?"

Abraham had been talking with Kepelheim. "I can think of nothing I'd enjoy more, sir."

"Good, we'll find my driver and leave right away."

As they crossed through the main lobby area, a nurse called for Aubrey. "Sir! My Lord! Sir, we have a telegram for you! From a Dr. Holloway!"

"Holloway?" asked Henry. "Has something happened at Montmore?"

The nurse approached with a sealed envelope. "I don't know, sir, but a courier arrived from Whitehall about five minutes ago. He said all of London's been trying to find you, and finally someone at the War Office knew about this meeting and sent the man here."

She handed Aubrey the message. Paul opened the envelope and read the note. "Our visit to Castor must wait, gentlemen. My wife's in labour at Montmore. It seems I'm about to become a father."

CHAPTER TWENTY-THREE
The Equinox Begins & Charles Enters the Time Maze

Charles slept deeply, not rising until nearly midday. Even then, Fenwick insisted he return to bed and try to sleep longer, explaining that Theseus wouldn't call for him until evening. The helpful messenger offered a glass of water, to which he added a drop of clear elixir, telling the duke it would cause drowsiness. Sinclair fell asleep within minutes, quickly reaching a restorative and dreamless sleep. Fenwick roused him at five and helped his friend to dress.

"You'll want to wear simple attire, sir. As you pass into the various rooms, as Theseus calls them, I'm told your clothing will adjust automatically to the new environment. Within the Maze itself, your original clothing will return. Does that make sense, sir?"

"Not really."

"Never fear, sir. I'm sure all will become clear once you're inside. Have you any other questions?"

Charles had just started to eat his final meal. He glanced up from the plate of braised lamb and dilled potatoes. "Will I survive, Mr. Fenwick?"

"I've been assured that you will, sir. If the only consequence of this test were to prove your blood to the fallen realm, the One would never ask it of you. There are lessons contained within the rooms that will serve you well in years to come. Remember, the One works all things together for good."

"To those who love him and are called, according to his purposes. Romans 8:28."

"That's right, sir, and you are called to a very great purpose, Duke Charles. Your future actions will change the world and prepare the way for the Son, whom we call the Name and Anointed One.

You and your children have been dedicated to this purpose, sir. It is a very great honour."

Charles set down the fork, his features thoughtful. "My wife had a dream—no, it was a vision. In June, when our twins were born."

"The duchess was called up to the throne, sir. It was no dream."

"You know this as fact?" he asked the angel.

"I was there, sir. That wonderful lady was given a glimpse into a future time, but as the One so often does, he used symbols to reveal that future."

"She saw six oaks and two willows," Charles whispered.

"Indeed she did, sir. The trees were set upon a great hill. And fiery, flying machines were trying to fell the trees. But then she saw a seventh oak rise up amongst them. Taller than the others, and together the trees withstood the attack."

"Yes," the duke marvelled. "Yes! She thought the oaks represented our sons."

"That's true, sir. And the willows are your daughters. Georgianna and the Lady Adele. Della's doing quite well, sir. I received word of her whilst you slept."

"She's well? Thank you, Lord! Thank you, Father God!" the human exclaimed. "And my wife? Did you hear anything of her?"

"Yes, sir. The enemy tried to stop your future purpose, but all is well."

"What do you mean, the enemy tried to stop it?"

Fenwick touched Sinclair's shoulder. "There was a spiritual skirmish at the Haimsbury-Branham Hospital, arranged by two traitors within your circle, but orchestrated by the malicious spirits who own them. Both the earl and your remarkable wife are well. Lord Aubrey is a great warrior, and he is taking charge on the field of battle. The One marshals his host and watches over the entirety of the war. Remember, your family are protected, sir. Nothing reaches them that the One does not allow. He works all human and spirit choices together, to bring about his perfect plans. And if it offers you comfort, know that Inspector Baxter has returned from France and also stands watch over all your family. He is a formidable man."

"He is indeed, Fenwick. Cornelius may no longer be young, but he can roar when needed. He's been in France?"

"With Duke James and Lady Victoria, sir. Yes."

"I imagine he and my uncle have enjoyed some interesting talks. Are they looking for me?"

"Everyone wonders about you, sir, but my fellow warrior, the one you call Anatole Romanov, advises the circle members and has reassured them of your soon return. Another matter took Duke James to France—again, sir, for the One's purposes. Have no fear."

Charles lifted his fork once more and took another bite. "Theseus serves fine food, considering his location. You're sure it isn't poisoned or otherwise suspicious?"

"It is blessed by the One, sir. And Dr. Theseus brings in the food twice daily from suppliers beyond the veil. He keeps a well-stocked larder. Oh, sir, I hear Dr. Theseus nearing the outer door. He's come to guide you to the entrance. I must leave you now. Be strong and of good courage, Charles Sinclair. I'll see you again soon, and remember, you are *never* alone."

The servant vanished, and one second later, a hand knocked on Charles's door.

The duke whispered a prayer: "Thank you for watching after my family, Lord; even those not yet born. Go with me now and help me to complete whatever challenges you set before me, according to your perfect will."

He put down the fork and answered the door. Theseus stood alone on the other side. The guards were gone.

"You'll want to take a warm jacket," the halfling told Charles. "The passages can be quite cold in some areas."

Sinclair wore tweed trousers and a matching waistcoat. The Sir John Bennet watch chain and acorn fob added gleam to the front; gold cufflinks did the same to his wrists. The only other jewellery was his wedding band. After donning a tweed travelling coat and making sure the scarlet sash was in his pocket, Charles returned to the main chamber.

"I'm ready," he announced.

Theseus smiled. "Yes, so you are. Come, then. You are about to make history, my friend."

Alphonse Theseus led Haimsbury back down into the castle's lower levels and through a large metal door, which he unlocked by speaking an incantation. The words sounded unwholesome to the duke's ears. The massive iron door opened of its own accord and swung back against the wall with a great ringing clang. Before them, yawned a corridor of utter darkness. A blast of frigid air hit their faces, along with the unpleasant smell of death and decay.

"No one's been down here for centuries," Theseus explained. "Not since the last traveller walked it."

"And he was?" asked the duke.

"A Transylvanian prince. As with you, the prince's blood traced back to ancient lines, and so he submitted to the test."

"And did he survive?" asked Sinclair as Theseus lit two lamps and handed one to the traveller.

"Yes. He emerged again into the human realm and became a member of Blackstone, who then granted him the title Comte de Saint Germain. Since then, he's taken other names as well."

"I thought Saint Germain was a myth."

"Some believe I am myth, yet here I stand."

"And was Saint Germain also a halfling? A demigod?"

"Not exactly," said Theseus vaguely. "Come, we must reach the other gate before the sun sets."

They proceeded down the long, twisting tunnel. The walls were made of smooth stones, cut into rectangles, and placed together without mortar. The edges of the silvery stones were so sharp and precisely fitted that Charles assumed the tunnel was recently made.

"I take it you created this passage?" suggested the duke.

"Not I," said Theseus. "The Ancients. The oldest gods, those who walked the Earth before Adam. Mankind has lost the secrets to such marvellous creations as this. Not only is the Maze beautifully constructed, but some of its rooms reach beyond Time itself. You'll understand very soon, assuming your blood is worthy."

"And if my blood is not, as you say, worthy?" asked Sinclair. "Will the Maze release me?"

Theseus laughed. "You ask the question as if the Maze were an entity, Charles. That is good! You begin to see with new eyes, my friend. But I believe in you. Let us not consider failure, eh?"

They walked for nearly quarter of an hour, seldom speaking, and Charles used the silence to offer up prayers to the true God, seeking his protection within these indifferent, pagan walls. If Theseus noticed the prayers, he said nothing. Occasionally, he would point out niches filled with strange linear statues that seemed modern in their aspect; as though the hand upon the clay strove to propel the god into a future time and place. With very few exceptions, the form was this: A slender arc, placed upon its curve with the points upward—rather like a crescent moon. The arc was then superimposed upon an eight-pointed star, which itself lay over an egg-shaped stone.

"What do these mean?" the duke asked.

"The figures? Votives to the Maze, left here by priests and petitioners long ago, when the world was young. There are many more inside. You'll notice each is different."

"Different? They all look the same to me."

Theseus used his lamp to illuminate one of the niches. "See here, on the circle? There are fine marks upon it. The lunar points align with the marks to depict a particular season of the year. I'm sure the mathematician in you would love to explore this area with your archaeologist friend, Charles. Dr. Holloway is a fine fellow, by the way. It was a blow when he chose to follow your God, rather than Blackstone. Also, I fear his father may no longer be one of our allies, but then he's no longer important to our efforts."

"Seth's choice to follow Christ came as a blow? Had you planned to use him in some way?"

"Yes, but we alter our plans as need arises. Now, regarding this niche. Notice the stars upon it. The points of the moon reveal the season, but the stars indicate the celestial year. You stand within a Time Maze, Charles. It is connected to all time, all space, and all possibilities."

"Does the lunar motif represent a moon god?"

Theseus laughed. "It represents triune iterations. The trinity is a constant theme with the Ancients and also with the Youngers. The eight-pointed star is the goddess. The lunar form represents the moon, but the crescent's points can also represent the horned one. Ah, but he's not as powerful as he'd like to think. Such an appetite he has! A God of Time that devours all."

Charles stared in amazement. "Are you saying these are statues of Kronos? He's a real entity?"

"Oh, yes. Kronos and his consort. Both are real, but inextricably linked to many others. They are a conglomeration of fallen criminals. Presently, they must rely upon one another in uneasy accord, for none is powerful enough to ascend the sides of the north on his own. That great throne entices all. Each climbs up, using others as foot and handholds. Kronos is one of the more powerful entities, and the Maze represents that power. Or perhaps, the Maze consumed

Kronos, the same way he consumed his own children. If we believe the old tales, that is."

They grew quiet again, continuing down the dark passage. Charles noticed the niches gave way to undecorated walls.

"You brought Eluna's light I presume?"

Theseus smiled. "If I hadn't, we'd be walking to our deaths. Any attempt to summon the gate without it leads to oblivion."

"You summon the gate?" asked the human.

Theseus held a small vial of shimmering light aloft. Its glow acted like a prism, causing a rainbow of colours to paint their faces. "You must summon forth the Keeper of the gate. He will consume the light. Fail to follow the rules, and the Keeper eats you."

"And this light will satisfy its appetite?" asked Charles, wondering if this were all a dream. *If only it were!*

"It will." The halfling held the vial near his face. The rainbow colours danced against his dark eyes. "It wasn't easy to obtain this light, Charles. I warned Eluna that you would reject her advances, no matter what face or body she might wear. Araqiel bet a fortune that you'd toss her out, and he's chosen to gloat over his great win. I fear Eluna didn't take it well. She tore through his face with both hands. He'll need a day or two to heal, and so neither has come to watch."

"She injured him? Really?"

"Oh, yes, Araqiel can be hurt. I believe one of your friends tore off his claw last December."

Charles smiled. "Mr. Blinkmire. He is quite strong."

"A man of faith might even say your giant friend was created with such strength for that very reason. We're nearly there. The gates are up ahead," he said, pointing into the darkness. "It's difficult to make out, but can you see them? There are carved pillars on either side of the doors. Only the rays of the equinoctial moon will open them."

"Why is that?" asked Sinclair. "Why that moon, I mean?"

"It's to do with the positions of the sun and moon when the doors were built. That's generally how these things work in the netherworld. It's difficult to discern in the darkness, but the pillars are set with gems that reveal the positions of the stars when they were put into place. Here, let me show you." He swung his lamp high, and the light revealed thousands of tiny sparks, glimmering from the two sides of the gateway. "Beautiful, aren't they? The ancient knowledge was far superior to that of man. Stand aside, now, and let me recite the words. Everything must be done according to the ancient laws."

They stood before a massive stone wall, broken only by a set of iron doors within a pillared frame. The gate stood mute and silent, with no hint of latch or handle, both doors shut up tight.

Theseus began to speak, intoning a rhythmic incantation in a foreign tongue. Charles would have recognised Greek or Latin. This was far different. Each syllable contained a mixture of traditional phonemes, mixed with guttural noises and harsh clicks that grated upon his ears.

Instinctively, the duke began to pray aloud. "Lord God Almighty, you know all that happens upon this earth. You know all that happens in the heavens and all that happens beneath the earth. I ask that you walk beside me now, please, and look after my family whilst I'm away. Help me to complete this task and return home to them, my King. Please, let me see my wife and children again."

If Theseus noticed the prayer, he said nothing of it. Charles fell silent, trusting in God as they waited for the doors to open.

But nothing happened.

The handsome demigod raised up the vial a second time, and repeated the strange incantation. The silver-blue light struck against a series of inscribed runes, illuminating each in turn, just as before. Theseus waited for several minutes, expecting the doors to open, but both remained shut.

He spoke the words a third time and shone the light upon the runes. And again, each rune glowed in turn, but the way remained shut.

"I don't understand. Eluna vowed upon her beauty that the light in this vial would open the doors," the physician complained. "She considers her beauty sacred and would never risk it. Tis a very strange thing. Perhaps, I misspoke some part of the incantation."

"Or perhaps, she's tricked you."

"No, I don't believe she would. Despite Eluna's claims to the contrary, she wants you to enter. She and all the fallen realm need you to walk the path and succeed, Charles. Eluna's promised your blood, which can only be satisfied if you reach the centre."

"My blood? What do you mean? What promise did she make?" he asked, growing angry.

"I cannot say."

"Cannot or will not?"

"Another limits what I may tell you now, but the answers lie behind these doors. I'm not to offer you anything more, I'm afraid. My hands are tied with very thick knots. Even the great Alexander couldn't cut through them."

"And if the doors refuse to open?"

"That is not an option. They *must* open. Otherwise, we are both consumed."

He performed the ritual a fourth time, shining the light upon the inscribed figures as he recited the strange words.

Nothing happened.

"I've said the words correctly. This should work! Perhaps, the precise time of the equinox hasn't yet arrived."

"Or she's tricked you," the human suggested again. "Regardless of what she might claim, Eluna is a devious witch and thinks only of her own plans. Why would you trust anything she says?"

Suddenly, Theseus began to laugh; a great throaty guffaw that exploded from his inner core, surprising his companion and echoing against the stone walls, like the laughter of a hundred voices.

"I cannot believe how stupid I am!" the halfling exclaimed. "Of course, the gateway isn't opening. I've made a very great blunder."

"With the light?"

"No, no, with the words! What I said is correct, but it is *you* who must hold the lamp and speak the words, Charles. Not I. You see, when I entered as a youth, I came alone and so twas I who recited the phrases as the light struck the runes. Later, Saint Germain did the same and succeeded. The walker must speak the incantation, not his guide. What a fool I've been!"

"I must speak them? No, I refuse to speak blasphemous words."

"But you must," Theseus insisted. "There is no other way. I shall speak them, and you repeat."

"I will not speak that heathen prayer!" Charles shouted as he took a step back. "If you want me to enter this hellish Maze, then you must find another way."

"But there is none," Theseus told him. "I am sorry, my friend, but that is how the doors work. The walker must recite the incantation, else they will not open. And our time to perform the rite ends soon. The equinox law is firm. If we fail, then we die."

"If that's God's will, then we die, but I refuse to speak that incantation."

Theseus sighed. "I understand, Charles, but if you do not enter, then your son will be taken captive. There is no alternative."

"My son?"

"Yes. He'll be brought here and kept until he is old enough to walk the path. Robby's blood is also compatible with the Maze."

Charles swallowed down the fear. He had no choice, but how could he speak words written by rebel angels?

"Father God, help me, please!" he prayed.

You are never alone, Charles, whispered a voice to his right. *Seek me.*

"Keep your light," the human declared, deciding to trust only in God. "Let me try another way."

"There is no other way," said Theseus.

"If I'm wrong, then we die," said Charles. He raised his hands and eyes upwards, as if looking into the very throne of heaven and prayed these words:

"Lord God Almighty, Creator of the heavens and the earth; ruler of all dominions, all realms, be they in heaven, on earth, or under the earth, I beseech you now to help me. I ask that your wonderful Spirit might make intercession for me, because, my King, I know not how to pray. I've no wish to do this task, but if you command me, then I follow you as a sheep follows a Shepherd. If you will open these doors, without any incantation or need for occult illumination, then I and all the spirits who watch will know that you have ordained it and caused them to open.

"David wrote that you take no pleasure in wicked things, nor does evil dwell within you. The foolish cannot stand in your sight; for you hate workers of iniquity. You destroy those who speak incantations and worship idols. And so in fear and trembling, I come to you and worship. You alone are ruler of things seen and unseen, and I ask you to open these doors and make straight my path.

"Lord, I am but a man, and my fear is very great, but you are greater. You spared not your own Son, but delivered him up as propitiation for our sins. For *my* sins, Lord. Jesus Christ shed his blood so that I might live. How then, could I refuse anything you might ask of me? St. Paul was blinded so that he might see the Truth. And though I feel blind and helpless, I'm persuaded that neither death, nor life, nor angels, nor principalities, nor powers, nor things present, nor things to come, nor height, nor depth, nor *any* creature that might present itself and claim dominion over me, shall *ever* separate me from your love! I know this, because that love rests upon Christ Jesus alone, who is my Lord and my King.

"When Elijah stood upon Mt. Carmel and faced the prophets of Baal, he prayed for a miracle; not for himself, but to open the eyes of those who watched, both human and spirit. You responded to that prayer with fire from heaven, and when the people saw it, they fell to their knees. And I'm sure, every rebel angel quaked with terror within their rocky tombs and in their chains.

"And so I ask this miracle, so that every eye in the fallen realm might see and know that you alone are sovereign. You are the one who opens and the one who shuts. You reveal the path with your light and your lamp. And one day, my Lord, you will open a door that no man can shut. Then all the redeemed will enter into your eternal rest. Hear me now, my Lord, El Shaddai, Mighty Jehovah, Prince of Peace, King of Kings, Creator and Ruler of All. If it is your will, open these doors, please. I ask all this in Christ the Redeemer's holy name. Amen."

The duke's head lowered. Tears of agony streaked down his face. He kept his head bent in reverence, still whispering prayers to the Lord, his hands clasped so tightly that his nails bloodied both palms.

One minute ticked by, but nothing happened.

A second minute passed, and still nothing.

As the third minute arrived, the stone floor beneath their feet began to tremble. The gemstone-studded walls shook and shuddered as if a great and heavy hand had taken hold of one end of the tunnel and tossed the entirety, to and fro, like a submissive stone whip. The shivering ceiling of the passageway threw off centuries of dust, causing pale spiders to scramble for cover. Every niche disgorged its pagan statue. The tunnel floor was littered with piles of crushed rubble, containing the cracked lunar arcs and all their starry constellations.

Then, the great iron doors, that so fiercely ignored Theseus and his pagan incantations, began to glow like tall chimneys of molten brass. Their brightness intensified to such a degree that both men had to look away to protect their eyes. A great heat engulfed the tunnel, like that of a fiery furnace, and Charles wondered if God had grown angry.

No, faithful servant of Jehovah, a soft voice whispered into his right ear. *Stand back, Charles Sinclair, and watch the One defeat Darkness with His ineffable Light!*

The iron metal glowed red hot. Charles thought it must surely melt, but only the occult runes melted away, and the rebellious symbols were replaced by the judgement of God:

Be it known to all who walk here:

ALMIGHTY YHVH

with his sore and great and strong sword
shall punish Leviathan, the piercing Serpent;
even Leviathan that crooked Serpent;
and he shall slay THE DRAGON
that is in the sea.

The doors cooled in an instant, but the newly inscribed words continued to glow and illuminate the tunnel with their brightness. God had answered the human's prayer of faith, confirming his promise to all mankind and vowing judgement to all the rebels who watched.

Within seconds, the heat had ceased, and Charles dared to reach out. At the very instant his fingers touched the metal, both doors flew open!

"Enter, Charles Robert Arthur Sinclair," spoke a deep voice from within the looming darkness. "Come and see the workings of Time and the fulfillment of a promise."

Theseus fell to his knees, trembling all over, and he feared to look up. Charles touched the halfling's shoulder and said, "The Lord God Almighty will keep his word, Alphonse. He will judge and condemn all who oppose him. Ask him to forgive you, before it's too late! You're part human. If your heart is truly contrite and you confess your sins, you may yet find redemption."

"No, Charles. It's too late for me. I am doomed along with the others," Theseus whispered, his head low. He glanced down at the impotent vial of light. "And she is doomed. But it won't stop them, Charles. They'll seek revenge."

"If so, then God will protect me," Charles declared. "And Eluna and all the rebels will understand just who the true King is! Not I, not any human, but Christ alone."

Suddenly, the light-filled vial in Theseus's hand burst apart, spilling the silvery liquid onto the cracked stone floor, where it disappeared into the fissures.

"I've chosen the wrong side," said the halfling.

"It may not be too late to repent. Seek him, Alphonse."

"It is too late. Go now. Your destiny lies ahead, and the True God smiles upon it."

And so it was, that Charles Robert Arthur Sinclair III, 1st Duke of Haimsbury, entered through the newly anointed doors, ready to face whatever challenges the Lord God Almighty would allow.

CHAPTER TWENTY-FOUR
Real World - Montmore House

It was nearly midnight. Cordelia Stuart's labour pains had finally subsided, and she slept soundly upon a bed in Henry MacAlpin's resident hospital. Nearby, in a small drawing room, her husband sat beside his cousin, where they talked quietly. Nearly everyone else had long since gone to bed. Anthony Gehlen slept on a sofa in the main floor drawing room. Lorena MacKey found a couch in Mrs. Winstead's parlour. The house was unusually quiet, and the two cousins watched the fire as they talked.

"Do you think she'll give birth soon?" Paul asked Elizabeth.

"That's a question for one of the doctors," she answered. "I've read that many women experience false labour a month or so before the child's due. Dr. John Braxton Hicks from St. Mary's wrote a monograph on it. He calls them prodromal pangs, as if the womb's preparing itself. What matters most is that Dr. MacKey turned the baby round, Paul, and stopped the contractions. A breech birth is very dangerous."

"Lorena saved my wife and son," Paul whispered as he put his arm round Beth's shoulders and drew her close. "God certainly works in mysterious ways. Think of how we met Lorena. Then, she was our enemy, our adversary. Now she's an ally. Even a friend."

Beth took a deep breath, her feet tucked beneath the hem of her dress. "I feel a bit ashamed, actually."

"Ashamed? Why?"

"For the way I've thought of Dr. MacKey. I felt she tried to manipulate you in Scotland, even cast spells on you."

"But the Lord stopped them. She's changed now, Beth, and she credits Charles with bringing her to Christ."

"Yes, I know," the duchess whispered. "That's the main reason I feel ashamed. Charles has been writing to Dr. MacKey regularly for months. And she writes to him."

The earl turned to look at her. "How do you know about that?"

"My own fears caused me to discover it," she admitted. "After Charles was taken, I suffered from terrible nightmares and fear. Despite Anatole's assurances that he was safe and undergoing a trial of some kind, I felt certain I could find him. I can't explain it, but I felt, and still feel, if I'm honest, that I'm to help him in some way."

"You are always honest, Princess."

"I try to be," she told him. "But in my desperation to find him, I boarded Charles's train. He keeps a desk there, and I thought the files might contain information about this Blackstone group or Araqiel. I'd overheard him talking with Kepelheim once about that puzzle chamber, and Charles told Martin that he kept three files in his desk on the *Captain Nemo* that contained many of his private investigations. He told Martin to read them, if anything should ever happen to him."

"He told me that as well," Paul said, "but with everything else, I didn't think to look. You found the files?"

"Yes, and I took them to Haimsbury House to read. Lorena's letters aren't personal or romantic, but the two of them clearly have a strong friendship. It made me feel as though I'd lost a part of him to her."

He kissed her hand. "Beth, it's possible to be friends with the opposite sex and remain chaste. You and I've become dearest friends, but we'd never behave romantically. Any affections we demonstrate come from true hearts. I love you very much, Princess, but not the way I love Cordelia. She's the queen of my heart. The centre of my world. Charles feels the same about you. He'd never betray your love."

"I know," she told him, "and that's why I feel ashamed. After talking with Lorena this evening, it's clear that she's found a new life in Christ. Charles is right to be her friend. We must all make room for her in our family."

"You're amazing."

"Hardly," she said. "How's your side? Shouldn't you be lying down?"

"The pain's tolerable. I've been injured far worse over the years."

"Have you? Paul, what was your first field assignment?" she asked. "If we're to keep watch, then tell me about the life you've led elsewhere."

"It's all quite boring, really. You don't want to hear about it."

"I do! All those adventures took you from your family, but you were serving God and our kingdom. Not just England's kingdom, darling, but also the heavenly kingdom. You're a true knight, Paul Stuart. Tell me."

The fire crackled and popped in the hearth, and the earl pulled her closer. "This feels very familiar, doesn't it? All those long nights when we'd talk. Very well, then. If I must entertain you whilst we wait, I'll tell you a story I've told no one else, save my parents. James knows, of course, for he was there. It's about the first time I ever trained in field work. It's not an easy story to tell, Princess, which is why I've kept it to myself. But it may offer insight into my life."

She snuggled close, her eyes on the fire. "I'm listening."

Paul took a deep breath, his eyes looking into the past. "It was in the winter months, after my eleventh birthday. Not yet Christmas. My father lived in Washington, serving as ambassador to the United States. I'd only just returned from visiting him, when James was called to Egypt."

"Called by whom?"

"The War Office, but also the inner circle. My father received information about one of Redwing's major suppliers of contraband, and he asked James to look into it. As regards England, Lord Derby was prime minister then, and he asked the circle to investigate Russian interference with the Suez Canal project. Adding to the intrigue, Charles de Lesseps had discovered an ancient Persian stela, which our government wanted to obtain. You might say, our mission was threefold. At the time, I was thrilled to embark on my first assignment. It never occurred to me there might be real danger."

Beth listened carefully as her cousin described his journey, her vivid imagination picturing every aspect, every risk.

"We arrived in Cairo on the fifteenth of December. I remember telling my uncle it was ten days till Christmas. He promised we'd be finished by then and would celebrate with Consul-General Stanton and his wife. We took rooms at Shepheard's Hotel. It was an overly opulent place, designed for English-speaking guests, but it attracted titled and wealthy clients from all over the world. Remember, I was eleven and wide-eyed. Everything dazzled me. I did my best to follow James's lead. If he expressed surprise or delight, so did I. If he remained aloof and quiet, I did the same.

"We'd been there for nearly three days, meeting over and over with the British Consul General and a representative of the French Rothschild family, regarding the canal project. That third night, James took me aside and said it was time to pursue our circle mission. The Redwing operative turned out to be the same Russian agent our government found irritating, so trapping him would satisfy two of our assignments. I remember James spent a great deal of time away from the hotel, and later I learnt he'd been organising circle agents into a special force, to keep watch on me."

"You? Why you? Was it because Grandfather had left you alone?"

"No, another agent watched me at the hotel. This network was to stand guard as I became bait for the Russian."

"No!" she exclaimed. "Grandfather would never put a child in danger."

"James felt this was the best way to trap the man, but he'd placed operatives into position in case things went awry; which they did."

"What happened?" she asked, clutching his hand tightly.

"The Russian's name was Maxim Morana and styled himself as a Grand Duke. I asked James if the title was real, and he said Morana was the great-grandson of a romantic liaison twixt Alexander II of Russia and Elżbieta Szydłowska of Poland."

"Is that another name for Elizabeth?"

"Yes, but she was of a far different moral compass than you, Princess. Morana was just over thirty and exceedingly handsome. Tall, muscular, dark-haired, with features that bordered on beautiful. Though married, he had a reputation as a lover of young boys."

"What?"

"Yes, dear. Sadly, that fetish is considered ordinary in some cultures. Egypt has entire businesses built on this trade. Morana ordered the boys through a local procurer, who usually brought him Egyptian boys. But James thought he might enjoy one from Scotland."

Beth's eyes rounded with shock. "You're not saying Grandpa wanted *you* to be that boy?"

"Yes, but James planned to rescue me long before anything happened." Paul grew quiet for a moment, his eyes on the flickering flames. "This is why I've never told anyone else. Nothing happened, you understand, nothing like that. But it nearly did. Even at eleven, I was quite tall for my age; much like Charles. I'd been working with swords and other weaponry for three years and developed a man's muscles. And though my body looked mature, I had no facial hair yet, and my voice hadn't changed. To a man like Morana, I was tempting and perfect. The boyish Apollo. He even called me that."

She squeezed his hand. "What happened?"

"James told me what to expect, but it still came as a shock. I was to meet the procurer in the lobby of the Shepheard. The man would come up to me and say 'It's a fine night for revels'. I was to answer, 'The bonny prince approves'. When the time came, we exchanged the code phrases, and this man, whose name was never given to me, led me to a gold-trimmed coach lined in velvet and silk. I prayed silently the entire time, whilst this man spoke to another in Arabic. I'd already begun to learn the language, and so I understood some of what they said. They talked of splitting the money they'd be paid for me. I was to be sold to Morana for five-hundred pounds sterling. It became clear that Redwing was smuggling more than armaments. They were trafficking boys. Honestly, Beth, I didn't know if I'd ever see James or my family again, but I tried to keep faith with God. If I'm honest, my faith wasn't as strong back then. I'd become a Christian at nine, led to the Lord by my father, but that faith had never been tested."

"Not until Egypt?"

"Not until then. The procurer drove me to an opium den in the eastern part of Cairo. The air inside the den was foul and thick. I could barely breathe, but I pretended not to notice. Morana was waiting in one of the private rooms. Brightly patterned Persian rugs covered the floor and walls, and there was a low table with embroidered silk cushions for reclining. He asked if I spoke English, and I told him yes. Then, he asked if I spoke any other languages. I told him I knew some Italian, French, and German, but left out that I had also studied Russian and Arabic. We conversed in French. Beth, Morano had that same look as these fallen angels. Like Grigor and Romanov. His hair was long, to the waist, and his eyes were that same icy blue. His face was handsome and clean-shaved. He stood nearly seven feet tall and claimed it was because of an inherited factor from Peter the Great. Do you understand now why I found it difficult to trust Anatole Romanov at first?"

She answered softly, "Yes, I do now. Why didn't you explain all this to Charles?"

He shook his head. "I couldn't, Beth. A man can't admit such things to another man. When James asked me later to tell him everything that happened, it was very difficult for me to be honest. Morano had bought me to be his sex slave. Remember, this was my first assignment, and I wanted to prove myself."

"He didn't... He didn't *hurt* you, did he?" she asked carefully, her hand in his.

"No, Princess, he didn't," he whispered. "James's men rescued me before it went too far. But Morano did ask me to undress. I cannot tell you how fervent were my prayers! But I trusted in my uncle and in the Lord to watch over me. I removed my shirt very slowly, praying someone would interrupt. He did touch me, but not intimately. Just my face and shoulders. Then, when he asked me to remove my trousers, like a miracle from heaven, three circle agents burst into the room! One was Tom Galton's father, another was Risling's. I was never so grateful for anything in my entire life. And it taught me a great lesson. Trust is a spiritual weapon. That shield of faith is offensive as well as defensive. It returns the enemy's darts and arrows back on them. Morano was arrested and extradited to England for slavery."

"Oh, my darling! How terrifying! Tell me, was he human?" she asked carefully.

Paul kissed her hand. "I don't know. Morano never faced justice."

"What? Why?"

"Somehow, all the paperwork was lost, and he was allowed to return to Kiev. But I'm sure he was one of the Watchers that MacPherson talks about."

"Did you tell your father about it?"

"I had to. James wrote to him. When Father returned to Scotland, I shared the story with him and Mother at the same time. I was grateful that I needn't tell it more than once."

She leaned into his arms. "Paul, you were so young! Not much older than Robby, when he rescued me in the Stone Realms. I know you don't believe I was there, but..."

"I do believe it, Beth. I've seen enough miracles now to know God works in ways, that are beyond our human senses and reasoning. You did travel to another realm, just as your unborn son did. It's unfathomable, yet it's true."

"He looked so much like Charles," she told him. "I imagine you had a similar look that night in Egypt. Innocent, well-formed, and beautiful in a masculine sort of way. If any man ever tried to enslave my son, I can't imagine what I'd do! To think my grandfather allowed that!"

"James trusted in God, and our actions removed that creature from Egypt. It was a temporary victory, but a victory nonetheless. I like to think my actions helped save other boys from being enslaved to such a master."

"Boys," she whispered. "Would you allow your son to take such a risk?"

He sighed. "I don't know. I suppose I'll have to see what God asks of me. Abraham was willing to sacrifice his son, but he trusted God to provide a substitute."

"Yes," she whispered. "Should we find a better place to sleep, Lord Aubrey?"

"A very good idea," he said, stretching. "I'll take the bedchamber sofa, to be close to my wife. If she's not entered labour tomorrow, then I may see if I can take her back to Haimsbury House."

"Another good idea," she said, standing. She helped him up, laughing as he pretended to be too heavy for her, and then the two cousins found beds—Paul on Delia's sofa, and Beth took a bed nearby. By half past one, both had fallen asleep. Elizabeth dreamt about Charles.

Paul dreamt of dragons with Russian eyes.

CHAPTER TWENTY-FIVE
The Time Maze

The deep darkness felt like a cloak of gloomy velvet, chilled by arctic ice. Charles Sinclair stood alone and still, calculating his bearings. The air in the tunnel was bitterly cold, and though he perceived no source of light, he was able to see, as if his pupils had miraculously widened to make use of any stray photon. Fenwick, his wise valet, had insisted he wear the tweed jacket plus an equally warm waistcoat.

"Thank you, Mr. Fenwick," the duke said aloud as he pulled the woolen collar up high against his neck. His long hair added warmth as well, and Charles thought of his cousin. Stuart often claimed the long thick mane helped on winter nights. Now, Charles understood that statement all too well.

The chamber was vast and seemingly endless, but near the far end of the telescoping madness, he perceived the lines of a tall door. Charles walked towards it, a journey that seemed to last for hours. No matter how many steps he took, the door never drew closer. Was there something in his way? Some invisible wall that held him in place, whilst his footsteps gave the impression of movement? A phantom hand, a beast, or barrier? He neither saw nor felt an obstruction, and yet one existed. Might the obstruction be Time itself? Was that four-letter English word more than a concept of linear progression? Could it be an entity?

"Now what?" Charles asked aloud. "How can I walk through a door, if I cannot reach it? If you've placed an impediment here for a reason, Lord, then please make it clear."

A tiny light flickered near the distant door, moving like an approaching candle in someone's hand. It drew nearer. Nearer. Nearer still. Charles could hear rhythmic footsteps, yet saw no one holding the candle. The light seemed to move of its own accord.

Then a voice called out of the flame.

"Hello, sir."

"Fenwick?" Charles gasped in relief. "Is that really you?"

"Of course it is, sir," the angel answered. "Oh, I see! No wonder you're confused, sir. I've forgotten to make myself visible."

A pop sounded, and Fenwick's lean face and laughing eyes materialised. "That's better."

"I'm very glad to see you!" exclaimed the human as he reached for the angel's hand.

"And I'm delighted to see you again, sir. Forgive me for being late. I intended to greet you at the start, but another detained me. That creature is now quite dead." He held a brass lamp, which he handed to Sinclair. "This will serve to light your footsteps, sir. If you lose it, have no fear. The lamp will appear again, whenever it's needed."

"A lamp," Charles said, his sea-blue eyes on the flickering glow. "The Lord is a lamp unto my feet and a light unto my path."

"He certainly is, sir. The One lights everything. Even in this cold darkness."

"What do I do now?" the human asked. "I've tried to reach that door, but something prevents me."

"Yes, sir. It's because the door is a false one that leads to a most disagreeable void. The barrier acts as your protector. Now, sir, allow me to lead you to the *true* beginning. Lift the lamp, sir."

Charles obeyed, and to his surprise, a second door appeared. The servant waved his right hand, and the doorway opened automatically. "This way, sir."

They passed into a second tunnel, lined on either side by lights that shimmered and moved.

"The lights are emitted by mirrors, sir."

"Mirrors?" asked Charles.

"Yes. The passageway may look familiar to you, Your Grace. You've been here before, in dreams. Did you bring the crimson sash, as I told you?"

"Yes," replied the human, producing the long scarf from his pocket. "It's here."

"Good. Keep it with you at all times. If it's in your pocket here, it will be with you in the various challenge rooms."

"I've a great many questions to ask, Fenwick. Or rather Hadraniel."

The angel smiled. "Either name is fine, sir. Hadraniel is a way of praising the One each time it is said, for it means Majesty of God. The humble name of Fenwick is a reminder that I must approach each moment with humility, for Fenwick evokes the earth. Places filled with fens and marshes. I've come to like the name. Ask your questions, and I shall happily answer those that I'm able."

"All of them?"

"All that time permits, sir."

"Time is the point, isn't it?" asked Sinclair. "Or so I'm told. Just what am I supposed to do in here? Theseus insisted the path would become obvious once I entered, but I still don't know which way to choose."

"Take heart, servant of the One. You will find your way through. The sash is connected to your helper. Think of her, and I shall make it so."

Every fear and question scrambled inside his mind, and Charles formed the image Elizabeth, the one person in all the world who gave him the greatest sense of calm, sense of purpose; the one person who filled him with the greatest courage.

The servant bowed low. "She will arrive shortly, sir. Have you other questions?"

"Will I survive?"

Fenwick touched the human's shoulder affectionately. "We talked of the duchess's brush with death in June. And of her vision. Six oaks and two willows. A mighty quiver, filled with true arrows, sir. Most are yet unborn. Yes, sir. You will survive, and in the coming decade, you and the duchess will raise up that small army of true arrows."

"Does this sash bring her here? Will she be safe ?"

"She is stronger than anyone knows, sir. Strong enough to bear many burdens and lighten many hearts."

"I need her, Fenwick. Of all the people in this world, Beth anchors me."

"That is how she sees you, sir. The two of you have been connected since long before Time began. Now, I must leave you, sir, and you must begin your journey."

"Don't go, Fenwick. Please!"

"I cannot stay, sir. This path is for your feet only, Charles Sinclair, but we'll meet again." Fenwick placed his hands upon Charles and prayed. "May the One light your way. May he bless you and keep you. May he make his wonderful face to shine upon you. And may he grant you perfect peace as you walk through this valley."

And so, with this one final blessing, the elohim vanished.

Moments passed. Charles remained still and silent, praying in whispers, wondering what he should do next. On the right and left, the dancing lights indicated the presence of black mirrors formed from volcanic rock. As before, a seemingly endless passage stretched out before him, narrowing into the distance.

He held onto the crimson sash, praying, "Lord, protect my wife, please. Keep her safe whilst I'm here, and show me the way, for I cannot see it."

Another moment passed, then something about the air changed. It felt lighter, less like a diseased miasma. And it grew considerably warmer. Music began to play. Softly at first, then slightly louder as though the breeze itself played the song with whispering fingers.

Moonlight, he realised, smiling. It was the song Beth loved so much, the one she'd played for her father on their final day together. Then, piercing through the plaintive piano notes, came a small voice.

"Who are you?"

Sinclair spun about. Before him, stood a child. She wore a blue night dress and carried a porcelain doll. The girl's long curls fell along each shoulder in ringlets of gleaming sable, and her dark eyes carried an innate light that instantly calmed the young duke's aching heart—as though she herself were the source of the music.

"Hello, little one," he said as he knelt.

"Who are you?" asked the girl.

He took the small hands in his own. "An old friend."

She smiled and touched his bearded face. "I've seen you before, but I can't remember where. Why are you in my dream?"

"Your dream?" he asked, his eyes sweeping over her sweet little face. Even as a child, Elizabeth's beauty had the power to mesmerise. Something about the eyes and her dimpled smile. Charles fought back tears. "Thank you, Lord," he whispered.

"Did God send you?" she asked. "Are you an angel?"

"No, little one, but you've given me wings just by being here."

"Where are we? I've been here before in my dreams, and I'm sure I know you," she said in her childlike voice. "I don't like this place. There are lots of faces, and they frighten me."

"Faces?" he repeated. "Beth, is this the dream room you once told your father about?"

"You know my name?"

"I do," he said. "Elizabeth Georgianna Victoria Regina Stuart."

She nodded. "How do you know about my dreams? Did Father tell you? Do you know him? Are you part of his circle?"

Rather than try to explain a concept even he didn't understand, Charles nodded a yes. "Lord Kesson is my cousin. Is this the place you once called 'too many faces'?"

Beth nodded again, but the smile disappeared. "They're everywhere. The faces, I mean. In the mirrors. Looking at me and calling for me to join them. Sometimes, they laugh at me. I don't like this place."

She pointed to the mirrored walls with her free hand, and as she did, the porcelain doll fell to the floor. Charles picked it up to examine it. He'd suspected it when she'd first appeared, but there could be no doubt now. This was the same, evil doll Beth had hated as a girl; the one bearing an eerie likeness to her.

William Trent gave her this doll. Might this toy be connected to her childhood nightmares?

"Is this your favourite dolly?" he asked. "Is that why you've brought it with you?"

Elizabeth shook her head. "No. I don't like her at all. I don't know why she's with me in my dreams. Father said she was lost, but she always comes back. I know it isn't right to say I hate anyone, but may I hate a doll?"

"Yes, I think you may use the word with this doll. She seems unworthy of love. Let's leave her on the floor, shall we?" Charles set the unnatural toy on the flagstones. He pointed to one of the glittering black mirrors. "I see lots of faces, too, but none are yours. What faces do you see?"

Elizabeth's dark eyes narrowed as she approached the nearest black glass. "I usually see mine, but I'm not there. I see your face, though. What's your name?"

"It's Charles," he told her.

"Charles," she whispered sweetly, as if singing. "I like that name very much. Why are you in my dream?"

"I'm not sure, actually. I think I'm supposed to find my way through these," he said, pointing towards the obsidian looking glass.

"Through the mirrors? Or through the faces?"

"Both, I think. Tell me, little one, if you had to choose where to begin, where would it be?"

Fenwick had said the sash connected him to Beth, and that she would be his guide. He'd expected to hear from his adult wife, or perhaps see her in a vision, but here she stood, not more than seven years old and already calming his heart.

Young Elizabeth touched his cheek, and the corners of her perfect little mouth lifted into a sweet smile. "I know where we've met! You're the one I call Captain, aren't you?"

"Captain? Yes, I suppose I am," he answered in amazement.

"You always call me that."

"And you always call me little one," she laughed. "Why?"

"Because you are my little one, and always will be."

She kissed his cheek. "I'm glad. That makes me feel safe. But you mustn't cry, Captain," she whispered. "God will show you the way."

The tears came anyway. They slid down both his cheeks and dropped onto her tiny fingers. Beth wiped his face and kissed both his hands. "Don't worry. This dream world is confusing, but I can help. And you'll find your way home."

"How can you be so sure?"

"Because you are the Captain, and you are honest and true. It's in your eyes. Honesty, I mean. They remind me of the sea."

"So you've said many times," he said, his heart soaring with joy. "Do you have any idea where I should start?"

"Oh, yes, I think I know. Come with me, Captain!"

She took his hand in hers, and the tiny girl walked the tall duke along the long dark corridor. He held the lamp high to light their way. And as they moved farther and farther into the darkness, the abandoned doll watched with envious eyes, the painted face turning angry. Once the humans vanished into the dimness, alone and unseen, the doll's porcelain head turned on its own, and it stood up on the leather-shod feet. A husky laugh left the painted Cupid's-bow mouth, and the enchanted toy passed through the nearest looking glass, then reappeared in the duchess's childhood playroom, as if by magic.

Which, of course, it was.

Far down the tunnel and through the next door, Charles walked on and on with Elizabeth, for the determined child refused to let her companion stop.

"The door's very hard to find, but we're close," she said as they turned to the right. This new corridor seemed even darker than the previous six, and Charles pulled her close protectively.

"Beth, are you sure this is the way? Might we be lost?"

"We're never lost, Captain. Not ever. There's whispering inside my head, telling me where to turn. It hasn't said to stop yet."

"Whispering?" he asked as they walked towards a section that had no light at all. "Beth, can you trust the whispers?"

"Oh, yes. The voice sounds quite correct and trustworthy."

He laughed to himself. Charles had learnt during the journey, that Beth had just celebrated her seventh birthday, and yet the size of her vocabulary constantly surprised him. She revealed a love of books and foreign languages, a growing taste for Italian and French opera, and a constant devotion towards her beloved Cousin Paul. Charles felt a tiny stab of guilt each time Elizabeth mentioned the earl, for a part of him still wondered if he'd stolen her from Paul.

"Here," she said at long last. "This is it."

They'd reached a dead-end, made of a smooth, non-reflective surface. Theseus had said the Maze consisted of passageways and side rooms. Each of the rooms contained a lesson from his past or possibly his future. He could walk into them and observe; sometimes interact. Generally, each room lay behind a black mirror. A few, Theseus warned him, were known as 'locked rooms', and contained alternative histories, created when he or someone else had made a different choice. Such alternative history rooms seldom opened, hence calling them 'locked'.

Which kind of room was this?

He reached out, feeling the familiar touch of woodgrain. "This cannot be right."

"It is right," Beth insisted. "The voice says it's exactly right. It isn't a mirror, Captain. It's a door. You just have to push."

Charles pressed gently on the cool wood. It yielded, and the movement inward startled him. A second later, a sudden cacophony of noise, like the blast of trumpets, consumed the quiet corridor. Both he and young Elizabeth stopped their ears with their hands.

"It's very loud!" she called over the din. "But I can still hear the voice in my head, Captain! You're to enter. It's a party!"

Charles listened carefully: music, conversation, glasses clinking—*servants and party guests?*

"You're right," he told her, lifting her up joyfully.

"No, the voice is right," she corrected him. "You must go in now."

He set her down and knelt before her, taking Beth's dimpled hands and kissing each soft palm. "May you enter with me? I rely on you, little one, for I've no idea what the rules are. And I've no wish to leave you."

"I know," she said in a very grown-up tone. "It's all right, Captain. You'll figure it out, and if you do grow lonely, you must think of me. I'll find you, no matter where you are. That's what the whispers say. Does that make sense to you?"

He drew her into an embrace, thinking of how this petite child would one day bear children of her own—*his* children. How in 1889, she would nearly die to give them life. And now she'd brought light and life and hope to him, when he'd feared all was lost.

"Thank you, little one," he whispered as he stroked her long curls. "Tell your father that you helped Charles Sinclair with a very difficult problem this night."

"I will," she promised. "But now I must go, Captain. I can hear birds singing near my window. Remember! Just think of me, and God will help me to find you!"

"I will, little one. I promise," he answered. Then, Elizabeth Stuart, one day to become Sinclair, vanished.

He stood and touched the wooden door. Charles pushed slightly. Through the small crack, he could hear the party noises. However, before crossing through, he released the door so he could pray, asking God to protect his future wife. Seven-year-old Beth had many heartaches ahead of her: Connor Stuart's tragic death in Scotland, her mother's marriage to a cruel and despicable man named William Trent, and then Trish's murder by that same man.

But that crime would lead to the moment when she first opened her eyes in a Columbia Road home and called him Captain Nemo.

Do I know you? You look familiar, Beth would say to him.

The marvels and mysteries of God, he thought. "Thank you, Lord."

Having finished the prayer, the former policeman took a deep, calming breath and pushed against the wooden door. He steeled himself for whatever surprises lay ahead.

It would be the beginning of a baffling and often terrifying journey, that would keep Charles Sinclair from his precious 'little one' for many weeks to come; finally returning in October, discovered by an improbable Irish giant named Stephen Blinkmire.

CHAPTER TWENTY-SIX
Real World – East End, London

The household of Montmore House rose and ate in shifts, having spent the long night keeping watch in turns. Cordelia's labour pains had stopped entirely; regardless, Gehlen and MacKey agreed that she should remain at Montmore and not be moved. Her womb needed time to recover from the fetal inversion, and Anthony worried his patient might go into labour during transport.

After a long post-breakfast discussion, Paul agreed to keep his wife with Henry until she'd given birth and recuperated. After all, the pleasant refuge was also a fully functioning hospital, with a modern surgical suite and every convenience. Just to be certain, Gehlen arranged to send over additional supplies.

Adele was delighted to have her friend and sister-in-law living with her fulltime. She told her brother that she and Lady Napper would keep watch over his wife, and Della asked to begin nursing classes with Mrs. Winstead.

"She'll be all right," she promised her brother. "We'll all look after her."

With Holloway also moving to Montmore and an experienced nursing staff, Paul felt certain his wife was in good hands.

He spoke with Lorena shortly after breakfast. They'd walked together in the garden and discussed their past. She apologised for the way she'd once behaved and thanked him for helping her to see Christ in his life. Paul cautioned Lorena not to grow too attached to Charles, but MacKey insisted she loved Charles as a brother, not in any romantic way.

Exhausted and still slightly feverish, Elizabeth decided to stay at Montmore for the day and rest. She also wanted to spend time with Adele, but keep an eye on Cordelia for her cousin. Paul left Captain Crenshaw at the house, in charge of three other agents, confident in his family's safety. With his family in good hands, Paul asked Henry if he'd still be willing to go with him to Castor and begin an investigation. The viscount eagerly answered yes.

It was half past noon by the time they reached Whitechapel, and Paul suggested stopping by the London to oversee the transfer of William Wychwright to the ICI's Loudain House. They arrived at Wychwright's room, and the earl spoke to the constables on duty.

"Has anyone from the ICI called in yet?"

It was Constable Bright that stood guard. "Not yet, my lord. Mr. Treves told us to expect your men at two o'clock, sir."

"Has the baron spoken?"

"He mutters now and again. He might've said somethin' when the duchess was readin' to him yesterday."

Stuart's eyes widened. "The duchess? Are you saying Duchess Elizabeth was here?"

"Yes, sir. Galway reported that Her Grace spent ten minutes or more with him, my lord, readin' a book. He might of woke up. The duchess called a nurse right after. Said he was in pain and needed morphine."

"Why did Constable Galway allow my cousin to enter this man's room? Baron Wychwright is dangerous. Only a few weeks ago, he tried to kill the duchess and her children! And yesterday morning, someone else tried the same—perhaps, funded by the baron's money!"

Bright chewed his lower lip. "Don't blame Harry either, sir. Neither of us was here here yesterday. John Siemens was the other man. Both are sick today with that new Russian illness."

"It's not your fault, Bright, but Inspector Reid will hear of this, as will Duke Charles when he returns. Now, keep watch on this door whilst Lord Salperton and I see if the prisoner's awake."

As they entered the dark hospital room, Aubrey thought Wychwright's eyelids snapped shut quickly, as though he'd been watching the exchange with the two constables. Paul lit the gas sconces and Henry pulled up a clipboard, which hung to the right of the door frame. He glanced through the doctors' notes and the staff entries left by nurses and male orderlies.

"He's on heavy doses of morphine," said Salperton. "I doubt he's conscious."

"Oh, he's conscious," Aubrey told his friend as he pulled a chair close to the bed. "You're awake, aren't you, William? Tell me, just what did my cousin have to say to you yesterday? If I find you've upset her in any way, you'll regret it."

MacAlpin checked Wychwright's vitals, noticing a slight fluctuation in the pulse each time the earl spoke. He grinned, telling the patient, "You should apply to Henry Irving at the Lyceum, Baron. You're quite an actor, but I believe you're awake. Alas, as with most of us, your heart gives you away. I wonder why the earl upsets you so?"

Paul glanced at his friend. "I knew you'd be useful, Henry. Are you saying I upset poor William? Now, why would that be true? Because his plan to kill me failed? Or because he failed to rape his own sister?"

Wychwright's bloodshot eyes popped open, and both arms strained against the bonds. "You contemptuous, elitist dog!" he shouted roughly. "I'll see you pay for your insolence, Aubrey. You and that harlot cousin of yours will regret crossing me," he hissed through dry vocal cords.

"Which cousin might that be?" Paul asked easily.

"She thinks she's queen of the world, but she's nothing but a pretty bit of skirt. A harlot and a damnable harpy!"

"Now, now, that's no way to talk about the premier peeress of the realm."

"She thinks herself so very smart," he whispered low, "but that woman will pay, I tell you. You'll both pay dearly."

"What's that?" asked Aubrey. "Did you just confess to yesterday's attempt on our lives? I believe you did, and I have a witness. Henry has a very good memory, and he's highly respected in the House of Lords. Shall I ask one of the constables to take it all down, so you can sign it? Shall I do that?"

Wychwright's face became a rictus of utter hatred. The pale moustache writhed as though separately possessed, and his upper lip trembled. "You will regret this, Aubrey!"

"I regret meeting you, but I do not regret arresting you," said Paul. "And in another hour, you'll be taken to a secure cell at Loudain House, where I'll have you all to myself. Remember our little dance there last year? We'll dance again, with no one to help and no way of escape."

"What?" he asked, doubt shadowing his face. "I don't know what you mean."

"Then, perhaps, your memory's impaired," the earl said flatly. "Henry, I'll need a full evaluation of the prisoner for ICI records, with something appropriate to keep him calm."

Salperton put on his best doctor's face and followed his friend's lead. "Happy to oblige. This chart indicates he's receiving morphine sulfate four times a day, but we could increase it, though he might become addicted, assuming he isn't already."

The baron looked at Salperton hopefully. "You're a doctor?"

"Oh, yes. Capable of diagnosing physical and mental ailments, as well as performing surgery. My instructors said I'm very good at cutting things out."

Paul laughed. "Well said, Henry."

"Thank you," the viscount answered happily. He was starting to enjoy working with the earl.

"Once you're in our custody, I intend to interrogate you to within an inch of your miserable life, William," said Aubrey. "Just what did you hope to gain by my death? Surely, you don't imagine yourself influencing my heir."

The crafty patient heard this and started to wonder. "Your heir? Has my niece or nephew been born? What month is this?"

"It's autumn, William. The twenty-second of September. You were brought here after your failed assassination attempt, remember? Your accomplice, Cecil Brandon, is in a dark cell at Newgate, by the way. You're in hospital here because of your injuries. Compound fractures of both legs, but you seem to be healing nicely. So, today, you come to my cells."

"But you talked of an heir? Is it a son?" Wychwright asked.

"Your sister hasn't given birth yet, but the Aubrey letter of patent is quite clear on who may inherit. A son who's reached twelve years of age. If I have no son, or if the boy's under twelve, then my secondary heir inherits or becomes my son's protector."

William paled. "Secondary heir? And who's that? Cordelia?"

"No. It's the nearest Stuart male, of course."

"James Stuart."

"No, not at all," said Aubrey. "It's my father's nephew, Charles Sinclair. If you'd done your research, you'd know he's my cousin twice over. Oh, but wait. You tried to kill *him* as well, didn't you? For a man who helped to plan army operations in Afghanistan and Africa, you're very sloppy with your plotting. Soon your only plot will be a bit of earth."

Suddenly, the insane man's eyes bulged, and his face flushed with utter rage. He strained against the bonds, his fingers tightened into a pair of fleshy claws. "You worm! You cannot keep me here! I have rights, Aubrey! I insist on seeing my lawyer! I'll have your title for this!"

Henry shook his head and made a note in the chart. "What a shame. This is a very sad case, Paul. The poor fellow's clearly suffering from an *idée fixe*. A type of obsession, I mean. It's a common mental derangement, that sometimes affects the body as well. I've seen cases like this destroy the heart and other organs, but the root lies in the brain. The baron would be much better off in a different sort of hospital. One accustomed to dealing with his particular compulsion and capable of healing his brain."

Paul stood. "Is that your professional opinion?"

"Oh, yes. Otherwise, he's quite likely to die in custody. The malady's very common in other countries. If left untreated, an idee fixe can lead to very dark thoughts and violent behaviour. The physician has to rule out physical causes, such as brain tumour, which would require surgery, of course. Sadly, with his current constitution, he's not likely to survive it."

William's jaw dropped, and his eyes grew still. The clawed hands relaxed into impotent gloves of flesh. "I have a brain tumour?"

"It's possible, but that could be good news. The law isn't likely to hold you responsible for notions rooted in a mental disorder. Now, your friend Mr. Brandon is another kettle of fish. He has no excuse beyond greed and a willingness to follow orders. It's providential your broken legs required hospitalisation, for it's allowed doctors time to assess your mental state. Not to worry now. I'll consult with Treves, and we'll get to the bottom of this."

Then, to add to the effect, Henry actually leaned down and patted the baron's hand as though he were a naughty school boy. Miraculously, the gesture seemed to calm Wychwright.

MacAlpin put his head into the corridor and called for a nurse. "Sister, come this way, please!"

A tall woman with fair hair and a white cap responded. She wore the insignia pin of a charge nurse. "Yes, sir?"

"I'll need a hypodermic syringe, a fresh no. 23 gauge needle, and a vial of morphine sulfate. Might those be nearby?"

"I can fetch them for you, sir. Have you the authority to administer it?"

"This is Dr. MacAlpin, Sister," said Aubrey. "His authority derives from mine. In Duke Charles's absence, I'm head of the ICI, and therefore in charge of this man's arrest."

"I see, sir. As to the morphine, syringe and needles, we've removed all supplies from the room, per Duke Charles's orders. He feared the patient might escape his confines and make use of them as weapons."

Paul smiled. "My cousin does think of everything."

"I keep the medicine nearby, though, Dr. MacAlpin. Give me a moment."

The sister returned speedily with the morphine and a hinged black box containing a clean syringe and the no. 23 needle. Henry expertly withdrew the liquid, forced air from the needle's tip, and then injected Wychwright's left arm. "There now. You'll be asleep again very soon, Baron. I promise to talk with Treves about the possibility of another option for you. Leave everything to me."

The two men remained until Wychwright fell asleep again. As they left, Paul spoke with the constables. "Sir Thomas Galton is due to arrive soon to take custody of the patient. In the interim, you're to remain at this door. Do not leave for any reason. And look sharp, gentlemen. Wychwright knows he's being transferred today. If he has accomplices, then today is when they'll strike."

It was half one by the time the two peers left the London, and the earl suggested they stop at a nearby pub called The Rose and Crown on Green Street. The men ordered bitter ales from the publican and carried them to a small table near the back, inside the pleasant confines of a warm snug. The fire smelled of hickory and applewood. Aubrey and Salperton took chairs opposite one another.

"Thank you for your help, Henry. Not just with Delia, but also with Adele. I know you're busy and want to get back, but with Charles gone, I could use a friend."

The alienist sipped the ale slowly, appreciating its aromatic, hoppy flavour. "My nurses are as capable as most doctors, when it comes to women giving birth. Gehlen promised to look in later, and Lorena was good enough to stay. Beth's in house as well. It's a veritable hen party, which makes us extraneous. What's on your mind, Cousin?"

The earl smiled. "I'm very glad we're cousins, Henry. I can't imagine life without family. How is Della doing?"

"Quite honestly, I'm amazed at her resilience. I'd like to say her speedy recovery is due to me, but I have to credit Seth with some of it, at least. Adele's quite taken with that devilishly handsome chap. They've even begun reading novels together."

"Do I hear a hint of jealousy?"

"No, not at all," the viscount argued, but only half-heartedly. "My greatest desire is for Della's happiness, but clearly you want that, too. Is she what's troubling you? I assure you, Della's in good hands with us, and Cordelia is safe as houses."

"I know, Henry. I know. There are other worries weighing upon my heart."

"Beth? Charles? Yesterday's attack?"

"The attack certainly didn't help," he answered, touching the bandaged side. "It's everything, I suppose. Henry, I know Anatole says Charles is all right, and that he must pass through some sort of test on his own, but I can't help thinking I should be with him. He and I were like brothers as children. The memories are vague, but I can remember part of our childhood together, even though I wasn't yet five, when he and Aunt Angela vanished. My poor mother took to bed for months over it! For those many months, I heard Charles's name over and over. With his return, our old relationship's become stronger than ever. He is like a true brother to me, Henry. In all ways, he's become my dearest friend in all the world. The thought of losing him is unbearable. It's like losing my own arm! I cannot think, I cannot sleep. But I mustn't let my fear show. Beth, Adele, and Cordelia look to me for strength."

"Paul, I've known you over twenty years," answered Salperton, "and you've always been prone to carry the world's woes. Those who don't know you assume you're indifferent, uncaring, and that you lack emotion. But the truth is you care too deeply. You have genuine empathy. You merely feign indifference to protect yourself.

I suppose empathy makes it easier to become other people in the world of spy craft, but in this case, you must let the world be the world. Don't assume its heartaches. My dear friend, your back is only so strong. If you don't release some of the weight, it will break."

"I'm aware of that," the earl admitted, "but my world's become so altered, I no longer know how to behave, Henry."

"For example?"

Paul took a sip of the ale. "Beth. She's changing into something new. I used to think of her as a delicate flower, a rare orchid that required constant care and tending to blossom."

"That's understandable," said Henry. "You and she were promised to one another since the day of her birth. I remember you spoke of her often at Oxford. She couldn't have been more than eight, when her father died. You both took that loss very hard."

The earl sighed. "And when Trish died, Beth was alone."

"Was she?" Henry asked. "Really alone, I mean? Beth's told me about her early meeting with Charles. It seems to me, that from her point of view, he became a fixture from that moment onwards. At least, in her thoughts."

"And in her heart," Paul agreed. "I used to be jealous of him, but now I understand. There's something about Charles that makes you feel safe, as if his shoulders are as wide as the sea. I miss him, Henry. My failure yesterday might have cost him a wife."

"Ah, now we get to the real issue," the alienist noted. "You feel as though Beth's become your sole responsibility again. Paul, she's stronger than you think. Besides, you have a lovely wife of your own to consider. And soon a son or daughter."

"A son, I'm told."

"You're told?" asked Henry.

"Long story, but the short version is an angel told me."

"Ah, I see. And for the record, I believe you. My mother used to see angels all the time, and Charles sees them now and again, and of course the circle is advised by one. Romanov's been very kind to Cordelia. When he and I last spoke, he advised me to keep a close watch on her. Tell me, Paul has she seen any further apparitions? Had any bad dreams?"

"Many, many bad dreams," Aubrey told him, "but I'd rather not get into them. Perhaps, when she's up to it, you might talk with her and make your own evaluation."

"I'll make it a priority. And look here, I know you must be annoyed with Cordelia for risking her health and possibly the baby's health just to deliver a dog, but I believe this is God's plan. Now, she can be with Adele, and the two of them can help one another. It will be a comfort to them both."

"You think God allowed this?" asked Paul.

"I do," said Henry. "Women need to be with other women when a child's on the way. They share their experiences, and I believe it's quite healthy."

A concertina player entered the pub and began to squeeze out James Bland's *O, Dem Golden Slippers*, followed by George Ware's *The Boy I Love Is Up in the Gallery*, sung by a pretty adolescent with flaming hair. Paul shut the door to the snug to keep out the music, for the entire pub sang along on each chorus.

"What do you mean?" he asked as he returned to the chair.

"I mean family is all important right now. Adele's not married, but she's at an age when babies and marriage play a role in her imagination. She, Elizabeth, and Delia can talk of children and childbirth and all manner of things. That sort of women's talk will help Della's mind to heal. Most of my resident patients are women, and they talk of female matters for hours on end. Actually, I find it rather enjoyable."

"So do I," Paul admitted. "All the more, because those pleasant discussions help to balance out Cordelia's darker moods."

"How are they dark? What causes them?"

Aubrey sighed. "She sees her dead father, flying outside the windows, or hiding in a closet. But also William, as she did at Christmas. He also flies near the window."

"She does know that William's at the London?"

"Yes, I've told her many times, but she says his spirit is still free to travel."

"Does she see them often, or is there some precipitating stressor?" asked Henry.

"Such as?"

"Hearing bad news, talking to her mother, reading letters, that sort of thing."

"If there is, I've not observed it. I fear my wife's mind is prone to wander without preamble. Sometimes, she even thinks she's sixteen."

"I've had patients with similar symptoms. It isn't hopeless, Paul, and..." Henry's comment stopped abruptly as the snug door opened to a pretty barmaid with auburn hair and green eyes. She couldn't be older than sixteen.

"I'm Becky. My sister Mary's the singer. What can I get you fine gents?"

"Mary has a lovely voice," said Paul, flashing a bright smile.

"Do you also sing, Becky?" asked Henry politely.

"No, sir. Mary's got the gift, not me. She wants to work on the stage, but actresses entertain after, if you understand. In private rooms. Mary's not that sort o' girl."

"And your dream?" the viscount enquired.

The girl blushed. "You'll think it strange, sir, but I'd like to be a doctor or surgeon."

"That's a very fine career," Paul told her. "There is definitely a place for physicians of your sex, dear lady. I applaud your dream. My cousin just opened a medical school and hospital near the Leman Street police station. They're accepting women."

"The HBH, sir? Wasn't there a shooting there yesterday? I don't know if I'd like bein' round guns. Dad keeps one behind the bar, but only cause o' the gangs. Would I need to use a gun, sir?"

"Not at all," the earl answered with another smile. "If you'll leave me your name, I could ask my cousin to send you more information. Have you completed any formal education? You're certainly well spoken for a Spitalfields lass."

"Oh, yes, sir. The Ragged School up on Church Lane, opposite George's Brewery. I attended eight years and got a certificate. My sister stopped after three and refuses to go back. Mary doesn't care much for school, sir."

Aubrey handed her his card, as did Henry.

Becky looked at both, her green eyes rounding. "You're telling the truth, aren't you, sir? About the HBH, I mean. You're the Earl of Aubrey, the duchess's cousin. And your friend is a viscount? It's a very great honour to make your acquaintance, sirs. Can I fetch you refills? Food? There's a nice chowder on today and roast beef, o' course. We have printed menus, if you want. The specials are the chowder, the beef, steak and kidney pie, shepherd's pie, and a ploughman's with ham, stilton, rye bread, pickles, deviled eggs, and apples."

"I'll take the ploughman and change my drink to Scottish ale," Aubrey told her.

"I'll have the same," said Henry. The girl shut the door as she left, and the alienist returned to the topic. "As I was saying, if Delia sometimes reverts to thinking she's sixteen, then there must be a precipitating factor and some past event that anchors it. Has she received news from old friends? Letters from her mother? Is she aware of William's imminent move to Westminster?"

"I keep newspapers away from her, but she does receive postcards from her mother. Now that you ask, Delia received a letter from an old friend a few days ago. I can't recall the girl's name, but it's someone who lived near them in Windermere. Henry, how am I to act, when she has these fantasies? Do I go along, or try to return her to reality?"

"A strange question, isn't it? I mean, what is reality?" asked the viscount thoughtfully. "Consider the concept for a moment, because it reaches into the very heart of madness. Is reality a material, objective presence? Or is it an intangible world inside our heads; a world that isn't quantifiable, but *feels* perfectly real to us? Della's started reading one of those Jane Austen novels right now with Seth. They each have a copy, and they act it out as if it's a play. He takes all the male roles, and she the women."

"Beth used to do that. Which novel is it?" asked the earl.

"The one with Darcy, I think."

"*Pride and Prejudice*," Paul told him. "Beth used to make me read the men to her women. She loved to imagine herself as Elizabeth Bennet. A part of Beth's always wanted to live simply, but I had to remind her that, outside the book, in reality, she lived like Darcy, not Miss Bennet."

"Ah, there's that word again. Reality. You see, I think that to Cordelia, and perhaps even to Adele right now, the world inside their heads is a safer place, and it's more real than this one."

"Why would seeing phantoms make Delia feel safe?"

"Madness skews our perception. Cordelia's accustomed to being mistreated by her family. Correct?"

"Yes."

"But you treat her very well, with respect and tenderness. She may see this positive affirmation as unfamiliar, she may even fear you could change any moment and become abusive. Remember, there were two attempts to force unwanted sexual advances upon her."

"Yes, but..."

"Allow me to finish," Henry insisted. "Cordelia's previous mistreatment from family and later these assailants, has caused a mental fracture, that leads her to think she deserves ill treatment, because she is to blame. She may even assume she's to blame for the sexual assaults. Guilt and shame go hand in hand with victims of force, Paul. I've seen it time and time again in my practice. But now, Delia's married to you, a wonderful, generous, and loving man, who treats her well. At first, this made her happy, but then that fractured part of her mind insisted on being noticed. She began to wonder how you could be so kind, and worry it might end suddenly."

"I'd never hurt her," Paul declared. "Never!"

"I know that, but the injured part of Delia's mind expects ill treatment eventually. It assumes you'll turn cruel, and so, she escapes to a place in her past that acts as a protective refuge. You've said her father treated her with kindness, perhaps he did something special for her at sixteen, and he flies outside her window as an angel, come to rescue her."

"Are you saying my wife wants to retreat from the real world? From me? That she isn't happy?"

"Oh, no, I'm not saying that at all!" exclaimed the alienist. "Cordelia's very happy being your wife. She's like Elizabeth Bennet, in a way, who's won her very own Darcy. Only, you're far more gallant and interesting than that boring chap in the book. My friend, Cordelia loves you deeply, and when she's part of what you and I call reality, she remembers there's a baby on the way and talks endlessly about names, clothing, schools, and taking her son or daughter for long walks. She wants to teach that child to ride and dance and sing; and to play the piano, or perhaps, the violin. She's told me how much she enjoys it when you play for her, by the way. Paul, your wife loves you with singular devotion."

He smiled. "I love her more than I ever thought possible, Henry. And we're going to have a son; so said the angel that talked to me last May. It was before Charles and I rode out to the lists at the tilt-yard. The messenger said this baby would be a son, and that he'd grow up to be influential in the world. It's a wonderful promise, but also a bit intimidating. What if I make a mistake? What if I fail him?"

"Stop thinking that way. Those 'what ifs' will drive you to madness, Paul. Besides, I can think of no one who'd make a better father. Be of good cheer, Cousin. God has a plan for all of us."

"Thank you, Henry. I value your counsel. When I think about the way you became part of the circle and our lives, it amazes me! I often quote Romans 8:28 to others, but now I'm seeing it play out in such a dramatic way. God truly does work all things together for good."

"Yes, and he quite often does it in ways we'd never expect," Salperton reminded his friend. "Now, I wonder if we might talk about Violet Stuart for a moment? Though, I suppose her real name is Susanna Morgan. Or is it Calabrese?"

"Calabrese's her birth name, or so Chicago's records say. I've a contact in Sicily who says Antonio Calabrese was originally Lorenzo Canicotti."

"Does it make a difference?"

"Only if you're running from the law. The Canicottis take their name from a town in Agrigento, where they're known for smuggling, running firearms, explosives, underage prostitutes, and all manner of contraband. They're also part of a culture that believes in the law of *vendetta*."

"Vendetta? A very curious word. What's that?"

"A sacred trust to avenge all grievances, eye for eye, tooth for tooth, limb for limb, life for life. Antonio Calabrese's father murdered six members of a rival smuggling ring in a neighbouring village. Since Garibaldi's conquest in 1860, Sicily belongs to Italy, and Italy's *Carabinieri* take a dim view of such gangs. They list Lorenzo Canicotti and most of his family as some of the most dangerous people in Italy."

"I take it these Carabinieri are a police force?"

"Yes, and it's one you wouldn't want to cross. The family are *personae non gratae* in America as well. The Chicago Police put Antonio Calabrese and his sons Enzo and Emilio, at the top of their most-wanted list."

"Enzo and Emilio are Violet's brothers?" asked Henry.

"Yes. They're wanted for murder in Sicily. And Chicago says they murdered four men from a rival family last month. They gunned them down in cold blood. Within hours, they'd fled Chicago for New York, boarded an Atlantic steamship, and arrived here soon after. I warned Violet about them, but she's not replied. Henry, if you ever see Violet, tell her to find me, and I'll protect her. She's in grave danger."

"I have seen her, Paul," Henry admitted. "That's why I brought her up."

"You've seen her? When?"

"The same morning Della was brought to Montmore."

"And you spoke to her?"

"Yes, of course, but only for a short time. Once Adele arrived, Violet left in a rush, and I've not seen her since. I thought I'd convinced her to live with us and study nursing with Mrs. Winstead. I offered her any apartment she wished, so long as she'd come back."

Paul's eyes filled with concern. "Please, tell me you're not in love with her."

"Of course, I'm not," the viscount argued halfheartedly.

"Henry, be very careful. The heart does what it will, but you mustn't become involved with Violet; not until this matter with her family is reconciled. If you won't think of yourself, then think of your patients! You'd be putting them at risk!"

"Including Cordelia and Adele," whispered the alienist. "Yes, of course. You're right. Since we're discussing it, I heard from the Italian police. One of their inspectors is coming here. I think it has to do with Violet's family."

"Leave it to me, Henry. When the inspector calls, just give him my address. I know how to deal with them."

"Yes, I will. Anatole says Violet's left England," the viscount added. "Do you know anything about that?"

"No, but I'll talk with him about it. Let me handle it, Henry. Promise me. These men are dangerous."

"Yes, yes, of course. I promise."

Becky returned with the ploughman meals, a selection of ham, Stilton and Cheddar cheeses, pears, apples, current jam, crusty rye bread, onions, tomatoes, and boiled eggs. "I asked my dad to add extra ham, sirs. We have lots, and it's a shame to let it go to waste."

"It all looks quite delicious. I wonder, have you any soup?" asked Henry.

"We do, m'lord. Oyster, potato, pea, an' a right nice beef stew."

"A very nice selection," the viscount remarked.

"We got a new cook, and he likes to make soups and stews. He says a man's heart needs soup for it to beat properly. He makes one he calls *borscht*. I'd never heard of it before. It's got carrots, potatoes, onions and beets. The cook adds sour cream to the top. It's Russian soup, I think."

Paul had been buttering the warm bread, and his head snapped to attention. "Did you say the cook is Russian?"

"That's right, m'lord. He's from the boat that caught fire a few months back. He doesn't speak much English yet, but he does a meat pie that pleases the regulars."

Paul set down his empty glass and stood, dropping several coins as payment. "Henry, you're welcome to stay here, but I want to visit this new cook."

The viscount drained his own glass and added several more coins to the tally. "Do forgive us, Becky. Duty calls. This should cover the tab plus something for your efforts. Call on the earl if you're serious about medical school. And I teach at the London School for Women. I'd be pleased to talk to you about it, anytime."

The two men hastened through a dense afternoon crowd, who were eating, drinking, and singing choruses of *Champagne Charlie*, *Glorious Beer,* and *Ask a Copper fer a Copper*. A few of the more boisterous raised a glass to the well-dressed men, and Paul had to chastise one man, who tried to pick his pocket. But both arrived at the bar intact and with their pocket watches present and accounted for. Paul spoke briefly with the landlord, who showed them through to a steamy kitchen at the back of the public house.

The earl introduced himself and Salperton to the cook in Russian. When he heard his own language, the sweaty cook became quite animated, even loquacious. Henry knew a little of the tongue from having cared for the granddaughter of a Russian diplomat, and he recognised words for 'ghost', 'fire', 'traitor', and 'ship'. The earl asked questions pertinent to inner circle investigations, particularly asking about the previous morning's attack. He heard Paul mention a *strelba*, meaning shooting, at the Haimsbury-Branham *bol'nitsa*, meaning hospital.

The earl ended with *spasibo mouy drug, vsego khoroshego*, meaning thank you, my friend, be well; and then he handed the man an ICI card and a five-pound note. After all this, Aubrey clapped Henry on the shoulder and led his befuddled friend out into the street.

"I take it something the cook said pleased you?" asked Henry.

"Indeed, it did," replied Aubrey, a spring in his step. "The girl was right. The cook worked aboard the *Podzhigatel*. That's the ship that caused the massive fire at St. Katherine's docks. You probably noticed scars on his face and forearms from the burns. He saw the man who started the fire, calling him a ghost and fallen angel. But he also referred to him as a demon that drinks men's blood, something he called a *vampir*."

"Vampire? Like the ones that work with Redwing?"

"Yes, and the cook got a good look at this vampire during earlier portions of the voyage."

"And?" asked Henry as they walked back towards the London.

"Very tall, he said. Nearly seven feet. Dark-haired with eyes as black as Hell. That's the phrase he used, Henry. Black as Hell. He said the demon could vanish into thin air and fly like a bat. It certainly doesn't sound like a human, does it?"

"Is it one of these Watchers, then?"

"I'm sure of it. And I believe I know which one, but I'd like to run my hunch past Romanov first. Only I have to find him today."

"Why the hurry?"

"Because this could affect James and Tory. The cook said a sister ship to the *Podzhigatel* left St. Petersburg the same day, bound for Calais. He believes another of the flying ghosts was on board."

"Another? Good heavens! Did he know the ship's name? Can we track it through Lloyd's?"

"Yes to both. The *Oboroten*."

Salperton shrugged his shoulders. "I fear my Russian's hardly sufficient. Should I know what it means?"

"*Podzhigatel* means 'firestarter', which implies a mission, and the vampire Watcher who started the dockside fire certainly achieved it. This second ship had a manifest listing numerous jewelled boxes, the size of large coffins or sarcophagi, similar to the one Blackstone discovered beneath Anjou Castle last year. Each of these coffins was to be loaded on a train at Calais for transport to Goussainville. Henry, that's the village close to Aunt Victoria's château."

"And there's some clue to this second ship's name?" asked Henry, dreading the answer.

"Yes," Aubrey said gravely. "*Oboroten* means werewolf."

At another pub, just a short walk away...

"More wine!" shouted a man at the end of the bar. "Make it a good bottle this time. I have money!"

Danny Gower had run the Hare and Hound public house since inheriting the popular establishment from his father six years earlier. He'd seen every type of man sitting at his bar: angry ones, fat ones, terrifying ones, peers, prophets, and many a sinner, but never had he seen such a man as this. He dressed well enough and had ample funds, but the thinning hair, hollow eyes, and sallow skin made him look a fright. He had all his teeth, but each was yellowed and stinking of rotten meat. His thin nose was severely swollen, and the skin beneath his eyes was black, as though he'd been punched by a very strong fist. The swollen nose caused his voice to sound muffled, and every 'r' became a 'w'. To make up for his stifled voice, the man's pale hands fidgeted like a fiddler's on a burning violin as he signalled over and over to the overworked barmaid. Danny feared the scarecrow might harm the girl, and so he stepped out from behind the taps and addressed the man directly.

"This here's a nice pub, sir. We don't treat our girls like they's whores. Iffin you wants that kind o' service, then hop yer carcass on out o' here and try the Empress, where they've got whores aplenty. The Red Wolf's good, too, sir. They's the sort o' rookeries your kind likes, I reckon. As fer me, I'm cuttin' you off, wiv nary a drop more, sir. Get out before I sends for one o' Mr. Reid's men to help you find the door."

Lionel Wentworth's bloodshot eyes turned into seething orbs of flame. "Reid? Reid!" the man cried, but it sounded more like 'Weid? Weid!' due to the swollen nose. "Who the devil is that? Give me ale or wine or whisky! Bwing it all! And sandwiches! And wed meat!" he cried, with every 'r' a 'w'.

"Inspector Edmund Reid runs H-Division, an' he's got plenty o' room in his cells, I reckon."

"Is that so? A cell? A wag and wubbish, *human cell?* Bah!" he laughed, a bit too loudly. "I'll have you know, I've been to Hell and back. Do you weally think a night in one of this man's cells would fwighten a man like me? Bwing me another ale and a bottle of wine! Beer, porter, anything, so long as it's wet and will get me dwunk! Else, I'll make holes in your chest the size of pennies!" He pulled back the elegantly cut coat and revealed a gleaming pistol.

"Gun or no, sir, this is your last warning. Leave now, or I'll send for a constable. And iffin you starts firing, then you better duck, cause I gotta shotgun behind the bar that'll put a hole in you the size o' yer head."

"Then do it!" Wentworth snarled. "Send for this man Weid. My fwiend and I shall meet him with sweet dewision and pellets of lead!"

"Friend, sir? You got no friends here."

"I'll have you know, my fwiend is an exceedingly importune, no that's not wight—an exceedingly *important* man," Lionel slurred, pointing to a vacant stool to his left. "Isn't that wight? You and I shall make the bizzies, bobbies, and buzzies of the Old Bill think twice before accosting Silver Spoons men, won't we, Pitt?"

The ghostly figure of Peter Patterson grinned back at Lionel, his dead eyeholes flittering with flies. "We could, except the policemen wouldn't see me, Worthy. Only you can see me, because you're special, remember? Look here, the police have your description, and we can't have you arrested again. We'll need to fix that nose."

"That man hit me, Pitt!" moaned Lionel, pointing to his damaged face.

The ghost touched the swollen nose, and instantly the break healed, and the bloody bruised area returned to normal; as if Granger's fist had never touched it. "There now. Good as new. The police will be looking for a man with a broken nose, won't they?"

Gower and several of his patrons stared at the loudmouth's miraculously repaired nose, and a few pushed their glasses away, assuming they were seeing things.

"The police?" asked Lionel, oblivious to Gower or the other customers. "I don't care about the police, Pitt. I have a gun!"

"Yes, yes, but don't talk about it and stop showing it to everyone. We don't want to draw attention to ourselves. Not yet. We've more to do first, Worthy. Now, let's abandon this establishment and find a place with softer voices. Ones that appreciate two such fine Cambridge lads, eh?"

"NO!" declared Wentworth, slamming the empty glass on the thick oak of the bar. "I will not budge. Not one inch. Not one centimeter until I've drunk my fill. You may go, if you want, but I am staying here!"

The landlord had endured enough and started towards the door to shout for a constable, but his efforts were wasted. The very second Danny Gower left the bar, the disruptive scarecrow began to shake all over and abruptly *yanked* himself out of the chair, then stumbled towards the door as though pushed by an invisible bouncer.

"This isn't the end, landlord! You'll be hearing from my father!" shouted Lionel as he pitched forward onto the dirty cobbles outside the door. "He's a QC, and he'll wrap you up so tightly in obscure laws that your own mother won't know you! He'll suck every last farthing from your pocket and give this place to me as compensatory, compos mentis, or compost something! He'll find a loophole *somewh...!*"

Lionel's final bit of nonsense was aborted by the invisible Mr. Patterson, who pulled at the human's arms and dragged him down the street. To those watching, the skeletal stranger seemed to dance and jiggle in a very peculiar fashion—an odd sight, even for Whitechapel.

"Don't waste your breath or your fine vocabulary," the ghost was telling Wentworth. "He doesn't see me, Lionel. No one sees me. I've told you this before, now shut your mouth! I've sprung you from one prison already; don't land yourself in another."

Danny Gower remained in the pub doorway, shouting for a constable, and Patterson's ghost hauled the scarecrow into a nearby cut-through to the next street.

"Quickly now, Worthy. We can't have the police arresting you again. They might hang you for attempted murder."

"Murder? I didn't murder anybody."

"No, but you did pull the trigger, didn't you?"

"I didn't want to. Your finger was on mine. You pulled it, not me!" shouted Wentworth.

"But they'll say it was you, Worthy, because I'm dead, remember? Now, follow me," he whispered into Lionel's left ear. "I know a place where you stay out of sight while you drink your fill."

"And food? Now that my nose is better, I could eat a horse. Not a real horse, but certainly a hearty serving of something meaty. How did you do that?"

"I'm magic, remember? I'm a ghost."

"I'm tired, Pitt."

"Then, you'll like this place. You can eat and drink your fill and then sleep it off in a clean bed."

"A clean bed? That sounds nice. I've not had a bed that wasn't filled with dirty straw since..."

"Since last December. Yes, yes, I know, Lionel. I've heard all about your woes. Come with me. You'll find rest at last."

They reached the next street, and the pair ran off towards the northeast, leaving Danny Gower to explain what had happened to Constable Davy Sunders, eldest son of Reid's surgeon, Dr. Thomas Sunders. The young policeman reported the matter, as well as the strange story of the healed broken nose, to his superior, who passed the strange tale to ICI liaison Inspector Elbert Stanley, who added the oddity to a list he kept regarding unusual activities in Whitechapel. Stanley took note of the pistol the customer had shown Gower, for it sounded identical to the prototype weapon used by the shooter at the HBH. Elbert also underlined the landlord's comment about the man's healed nose and how the customer talked to an 'invisible friend'.

As for the customer in question, Lionel Wentworth, fled towards Mile End, where he hailed a hansom. His course took him to Bethnel Green, then along Cambridge to Victoria Park, where he turned south again for several blocks until he reached a large campus of brightly lit buildings. In front of the largest building, a sign said: CASTOR INSTITUTE.

"We're here, Lionel," his invisible friend said.

"No. This is some kind of hospital," argued the human. "I don't need a hospital, I need a drink!"

"Food, whisky, and a soft bed await, Lionel. This isn't a hospital. It's your sanctuary. Dr. Kepler is an old friend."

"Kepler? I don't know any Kepler."

"But I do, now come along."

Lionel grudgingly left the coach and paid the driver from the funds he'd stolen from a fish stall the previous day. He stumbled towards the door, pushed by the invisible companion. Once through the main doors, he walked up to the receiving desk. A stout woman in a starched blue dress and white nurse's cap glanced up. "Yes, sir?"

"We need to see..." Lionel began. He paused, as if listening. "Sorry. I forgot. What I mean to say is, *I* need to see Dr. Kepler. Not *we*. Not at all. It isn't we. Certainly not. Please, tell the doctor that I—I'm Lionel Wentworth. Tell him I am here. He's expecting us—I mean, expecting *me*."

Lionel listened again, and then nodded to the unseen companion. "Yes, yes, all right. I will!" Then, he turned back to the woman. "Please, inform Dr. Kepler that I was brought here by my very good friend, Prince Saraqael."

The woman's plump face grew animated with mild surprise. "A prince brought you here? Really? And just where is this prince, sir?"

Lionel's eyes followed something unseen that passed through the doors without disturbing them. Two minutes ticked by, and then a very tall individual entered through the main doors.

The ghostly Patterson had transformed into something dazzling. He wore Romanian royal regalia: a high-collared, red silk caftan, stitched in gold embroidery that featured wolves and bats; and over this was a floor-length *shuby* or greatcoat, made of red silk and trimmed in sable. He wore no hat, allowing the waist length hair to dominate his spectacular appearance.

"I am Prince Saraqael ben Chosek," the elohim told the nurse. "My friend and I should like to see Dr. Kepler, dear lady."

The nurse looked as though she might faint. Her heart fluttered, as did her eyelashes. The middle-aged woman had never seen such a beautiful man in all her life.

"Yes, my lord, but he's in conference right now."

"Then ask him to leave it," Saraqael told her. "My friend requires attention. We've come a very long way. He is to be part of the lower-level unit. The one that I funded."

Suddenly, her eyes rounded. "Of course, Your Highness! Yes, yes! I'll fetch him at once. Please, take a seat, my lord, and I'll bring him to you."

She left, and the devilish prince laughed. "We needn't wait for her, my friend. I know where Kepler's hiding. He's not in conference, but engaging in a secret addiction, downstairs in the deep and the dark. We'll find our own way down, eh?"

Wentworth still saw the elohim as Peter Patterson's ghost, and the confused human nodded. "If you say so, Pitt. Why do you call yourself by this prince's name? I don't understand."

"You'll understand everything soon, Lionel. I'm about to introduce you to a man who'll remove all the old, weak blood from your body and make you into a strong warrior. Would you like that? Would you like to make Prince Araqiel pay for his ill treatment of you? Would you enjoy tearing Albus Flint's black eyes into bits?"

"I'd like to kill them both a thousand times over," Lionel whispered angrily as they crossed the main lobby towards the door to the lower levels.

"Then you'll need stronger arms than those. You'll do quite nicely as the Captain of my new army. And unlike the others, you're not starting as a corpse."

"A corpse?" asked the dull-witted human.

"Just do as I say, old chum. Silver Spoons men have a closely guarded secret, known only to the topmost members. It takes years to reach that high level, but I'm going to reveal that secret to you now. Won't that be fun?"

Saraqael snapped his fingers, and the door unlocked without out a key.

"What secret is that?" asked Lionel.

The door clanged shut, instantly locking behind them. Saraqael whistled a music hall tune as they walked together down a long, white-tiled hallway.

"What secret?" Lionel repeated as they passed through a second door and descended down four flights of stairs. "What's the secret, Pitt?"

The deceitful prince magically unlocked the door to the lowest level, where David Anderson, the former Mr. Thirteen, was once injected with foreign blood and chemicals, then subjected to spells and chants to alter his human nature into that of a dreadful wolf creature.

"What secret!!" shouted Wentworth as he tugged on the sleeve of his friend's ghost.

"The secret," Saraqael said as he led the human to an empty room, "is that the Spoons aren't run by humans at all."

"Not run by humans?" echoed the befuddled human. "What sort of nonsense is that? Of course, it's run by humans. We met them."

"It isn't nonsense, Lionel. I'm not human. And I'm not a ghost." Only then, did Wentworth see the dreadful bargain he'd struck. The ghost of Peter Patterson transformed into a a great beast, the gruesome creature known to those living in the Carpathian Mountains as *Striga*, king of all werewolves.

The massive wolf bent down and kissed Lionel's pale cheek, its breath warming the terrified human's sparse beard.

"You're very pretty," the wolf told him. "Now, sit boy. Sit and wait. Kepler will be here soon to begin your treatments. He's a little bit high on opium, but I'll help. It's time for you to grow up, Lionel."

"But you were Peter Patterson," moaned Lionel. "A ghost."

"I am whatever I wish to be, and you can have the same power," Saraqael told him. "We're Spoons men, right?"

"Yes, right," the human muttered.

"Well, did you know why the club's spoon is *silver?*"

"Because rich people use silver," Lionel answered.

"No. That's a lie, but members like to see themselves that way. No, my dear friend, I created the group when Trinity College was founded in 1546. I called my secretive group Silver Spoons because silver is poisonous. Not to me. The old trope that werewolves hate silver is a clever diversion that I whispered to poets and storytellers long ago. However, silver *is* poisonous to dragons like Araqiel and Raziel. I want both my brothers dead, Worthy, and you're going to help me do it by leading my army of the dead. I shall give you a great bow and all of your pretty arrows will be tipped in silver."

CHAPTER TWENTY-SEVEN
The Time Maze – Charles Enters the First Room

He'd been told to search for a mirror as the first passageway, but his guide, seven-year-old Elizabeth, had taken him to a wooden door, instead. She'd listened to a whispering voice and had no doubt at all, that this was to be his first challenge.

As he pushed through the door, Charles Sinclair stepped into a brightly lit party. Just as Fenwick promised, the tweed travelling suit became formal dress, white tie and waistcoat, beneath an elegant black cutaway. A footman offered a glass of white wine.

"Or do you prefer whisky, my lord?"

"No, thank you. Wine will do nicely," the duke replied, trying to sound perfectly natural.

Before him lay the grand foyer of Drummond House, crowded with gossips and gadabouts, dancers and debutantes. It was a very dense crowd of London's high society, whose numbers spilled into every drawing room, gallery, and parlour of the ducal house. Charles surveyed the area, trying to discern the reason for the unusually large gathering. James loved to host parties, but seldom invited all of London, except for very special occasions. He overheard snippets of conversation as he passed amongst the crowd, aiming for the staircase.

Years as a police detective had taught him to scan his surroundings quickly, and climbing up a few steps would offer a much better view and allow Sinclair time to quietly assess his situation.

The main floor was awash in wealthy and titled citizens of Westminster. Members of Parliament rubbed elbows with influential industrialists and businessmen; society ladies mixed together, whilst their husbands eyed younger beauties. Men boasted, women flirted, and from the balcony above, the music of a string quartet inspired dancers; whilst to his right, in the main floor music room, a skilled pianist offered a Chopin concerto.

Why had the doorway led him here, to this moment, to this party? Charles had no memory of any such celebration. Was this a moment in his future, or one of the so-called *locked rooms*, with an alternate version of his past?

According to Theseus, the Maze's primary purpose was to test a man's blood. If that man could reach the centre, the Keeper would then release him. It sounded simple enough, but Fenwick implied God Almighty, whom he called the One, had permitted this test for another reason: to teach him something. These various areas, or 'rooms', would impart information necessary for Sinclair's future task.

Theseus, the halfling physician, had also claimed, that if Charles's blood was as pure as the fallen realm believed, he might access the 'locked rooms' of the Maze. Fenwick told him these locked chambers were sealed and made inaccessible long ago, due to some past, free-will choice. For example, a decision to attend Harrow could seal a possible future, arising from Etonian friendships and experiences.

First he must determine which type of room this was: locked or unlocked? Had he just walked into an alternative life, or into the future?

A strident, high-pitched voice broke his concentration. Charles glanced down the steps to find a buxom woman in a gaudy purple dress, climbing to his position on the first landing. "Your Grace!" she squealed. "Whatever are you doing up here? Scanning the horizons? Tell, me, now, because I've been talking with several of my Parliamentarian friends, and we're all wondering what you plan to do about this horrid criminal. As you were close by, I volunteered to come up and ask."

"Ask?" he responded politely.

"Ask how we're all to act now, sir. I mean, it's one thing to have this sort of crime in the East End. They live in the sort of sordid squalour and pitiful penury that breeds crime, but this is Westminster. Why, it's simply unthinkable to have him strike here!"

Charles tried to imagine what criminal she meant, whilst wondering if he should reprove the woman for her thoughtless and derisive assumptions about the hardworking people of the East. The crimes he usually investigated were hardly the topics of drawing rooms or parties: the missing dead, tales of a woman in white clothing that lured children to their deaths, werewolves, vampires, golems, and of course, Jack the Ripper.

The plump woman in the glittering violet dress pressed harder, her face so close to his chest that he could feel her breath. "Duke Charles, you're usually so very open with your thoughts. Have you no opinion on that?"

"Forgive me," he said politely. "My mind was elsewhere. An opinion on what, dear lady? This crime you mention?"

He silently prayed the woman would explain.

"Yes, of course!" she exclaimed. "I've been talking to the other ladies, but also the men of Parliament that I mentioned. We're concerned about all the recent criminal activity in our own neighbourhoods. Such devilish practices! It curdles one's blood to think of it, and it's caused my two daughters, Belinda and Margaret Rose, many a sleepless night. You remember them, of course, Your Grace. From your last ball? Tell me, are you any closer to unmasking these devils? Pray, tell me you are, so I may calm my girls!"

"I should love to tell you in full, dear lady, but it's privileged information," he bluffed. "You understand how government works, particularly regarding something this sensitive."

The woman's heavily powdered face cracked into a smile. "Oh, my yes! My husband cannot get enough of your branch's secrets. They're like honey to the tongue, aren't they? Dear Edgar is such a spy, or he wishes he were. But your cousin is a real spy, isn't he, Your Grace? I wonder, is Lord Aubrey here this evening? I'd heard the marquess was attending, but no one's seen him yet."

Marquess? Paul's a marquess? And where is James? I need to find someone trustworthy to ask.

That someone came in the form of a familiar and very welcome face, with light grey eyes, a wide nose, and apple dumpling cheeks.

"Your Grace!" shouted his rescuer from the lower stair steps. Martin Kepelheim wriggled his way through a phalanx of MPs and middle-aged society women. The dapperly dressed tailor grinned with delight as he reached the befuddled duke.

"There's always a crowd whenever you host a party, Charles. But where is our beloved duchess? I do hope Elizabeth isn't unwell?"

All right. I must be hosting the party with James. And asking me about Beth means we're married. At least, that hasn't altered.

"You know my wife, Martin," he replied with deliberate vagueness. "I wonder if you have a moment? There's something I'd like to discuss with you."

Kepelheim's grey eyes lit up. "With me? Yes, yes, of course. If you'll excuse the interruption, Lady Maryville," he said to the inquisitive, powder-puff diva. "I overheard your question about that dreadful murder. This Songbird Killer keeps us all awake, doesn't he? But never fear, dear lady. Our most royal Commissioner of Intelligence has it all in hand." He turned back to Sinclair. "Now, Charles, I noticed your library is miraculously unoccupied for the moment. Shall we share some of your exquisite brandy?"

MY library? MY brandy? Is he saying that Drummond House is mine?

"Yes, of course," Charles replied. "Forgive me for abandoning you, Lady Maryville. I shall return momentarily. In the meantime, please, enjoy the party."

Haimsbury offered the woman a wink, and Maryville blushed coquettishly at the duke's dashing manner and charm. He followed Kepelheim to the guest library, which had mercifully drawn no attention, despite most other areas being crowded to the very walls.

Charles shut the door, dampening the noise. He took a deep breath to steel himself for what would, surely, be a difficult conversation. Kepelheim glanced at the handwritten labels on several crystal decanters set upon one of the sideboards.

"Anderson must have known you'd retreat in here. How very like your butler. He's given us a lovely selection of enticements. Oh, and here's Armagnac!" he exclaimed. "It's like brandy heaven, you know, but supplies are quite limited. Wherever did you find it?" The tailor filled a pair of snifters, offered one to Charles, and then joined his friend in a leather chair beside a cheerful fire.

"I hope you locked that door," Martin said with a wry grin. "Lady Maryville has a singular obsession with you, I've noticed. Our little duchess is remarkably tolerant when it comes to the advances of other women, but even she has limits. How is our darling Elizabeth these days? It's unusual for her to miss hostess duties, but then she's close to delivery, isn't she? Just one more month! Shall

I go up and look in? I noticed Anthony Gehlen somewhere nearby. I'm sure he'd be happy to see her."

Beth's eight months pregnant? Is this an alternate version of the first or a future second pregnancy? What year is it and why do I own this house?

Charles needed information. Working in such a deep dark hole required a candle of some sort, and thus far, he had none. Not even a stub of a candle!

"Martin, where's Paul tonight?" he asked the tailor, partly to gain intelligence, but primarily to deflect the question about Elizabeth.

"Ah, well, as you know well, our newly raised marquess has just returned from Egypt. He hoped to attend this evening, but I overheard him telling Lord Percy that he might be on the hunt, prowling about London in search of our oldest enemy, Redwing. Would that we might forget that devilish bird even exists!" The tailor's smile vanished and the grey eyes fixed upon the duke's face. "Charles, you're very serious suddenly. Is everything all right? You began this night with your usual aplomb and easy grace, laughing and even dancing now and then, but I sense something—oh, I don't know—unsettled in you now. I pray this report of another Songbird murder hasn't dismayed you. Is that why Beth hasn't come down?"

The duke tipped back the glass and drained the brandy in a single gulp. "I'll take another if you're pouring."

Kepelheim complied by bringing the decanter to the table and setting it twixt them. "I suppose that's answer enough. She's still angry, I take it?"

Charles shook his head. "I've no idea."

"Is there a way I might help? My darling Anna died twenty-two years ago, and our marriage lasted less than a year; therefore, my marital advice is decidedly limited, but I do know you, Charles. Something is very much wrong. What is it?"

Martin's a widower? There's no doubt now. This is an alternate history room.

The young duke stared into his friend's light-coloured eyes, which had always struck him as profoundly kind and intelligent. "Martin, you know me as well as anyone on this earth, I think. Do you find me changed?"

"Changed how?"

347

"My appearance? My behaviour? My memory?"

The tailor refreshed both their glasses, his silvering head tilted to one side. He sipped thoughtfully. "Changed? A very strange question to come from a man with the world at his feet. Charles, whatever is wrong?"

"If I said it's to do with time and an underground maze, would you think I've gone mad?"

Kepelheim's cheeks paled and his eyes widened. He set down the glass, his voice deeper and the tone decidedly serious. "It would. Now, tell me everything. Leave nothing out."

"I'll try, but you'll think me mad."

"I promise, I will not."

Charles took a deep breath. "What year is it?"

Kepelheim's bit his lower lip and the eyes rounded a little. "It is 1893. I see by your face you'd not expected that. What year did you think I'd say?"

"1889."

The tailor drained his glass and poured another. "Go on."

"Do you remember the clocks that used to sit on the mantels of my childhood bedchambers? One at Rose House and another here in London?" asked the duke.

"Do you mean the Arthur clocks?"

Sinclair nodded. "Arthur's Victory and Arthur's Defeat. I never knew the clocks had names until recently, and they looked the same to me. Do you remember which one stood at Haimsbury House?"

"I've no idea," Martin answered. "Your late father and I sometimes discussed those clocks, but he never liked them. Aren't they broken?"

"They were the last time I saw them," Charles said. "Paul sent one to a jeweller for repair last year. I imagine it's been returned to Haimsbury House by now." He paused for a moment, wondering how much to share. Martin Kepelheim had a unique way of deciphering information, and Charles often relied upon his counsel and his friendship. "Martin, where is Paul? Really. And why isn't James here?"

His friend's jaw dropped, and Charles heard the sharp intake of breath, revealing shock. Martin rose to his feet and paced back and forth several times before answering. After many such paces, he turned to stare at his host.

"Tell me just what you mean. You mentioned a time maze, and I admit that it took my breath away, when you said it. I've not heard you say anything like that since..." he stopped, a series of question marks rippling through his plump features.

"Since I was a boy?" asked the duke.

"Yes. When you were, perhaps, five or so. You used to talk about visiting other places and other times," Kepelheim continued. "You called these other worlds *locked rooms*, and they were found inside a Time Maze."

"I used that exact phrase?" Haimsbury asked the tailor. "A Time Maze and locked rooms?"

"Oh, yes. And you talked of seeing a little girl there, whom you'd sometimes meet inside the Rose House maze. Honestly, your mother assumed it nothing but a fertile imagination. However, your father had a very different reaction to your stories. They made him exceedingly angry; not at you, of course. I never once saw Robby Sinclair angry with you. No, I think his anger was rooted in fear."

"Did he ever discuss those fears with Beth's father? I know he and Connor were close."

"Indeed, the closest! Connor believed unseen entities were manipulating you both for some dark purpose. Do you remember a Rose House inner circle meeting, about a month before Connor was killed? I know you were just out of Oxford then, but..."

"Oxford?" the duke repeated. "Martin, I attended Cambridge."

Another series of questions visibly altered his friend's ageing eyes. Martin gulped down the third glass and then returned to the chair beside the duke. The tailor touched Sinclair's hand with great gentleness.

"Something has happened to you, my friend. You're like another man suddenly, and I cannot explain it. Can you?"

"I am not the man you know. I arrived here just moments ago, through a wooden door in the Time Maze. I've been here, in your 1893, for less than half an hour."

Martin grew pensive. He licked his lips several times, and then leaned close to whisper, "You must tell no one else what you've said here tonight, Charles. No one. Not even Aubrey. But for my part, I believe you. It isn't the first time, you've given me such information. Do you remember that peculiar, ornate mirror at Rose House? The one placed in your bedchamber, when you were small?"

"That mirror was in my mother's bedchamber, Martin. She had it moved there a month before Charlotte was born."

Kepelheim bit his lower lip, chewing on it thoughtfully. The tic meant the tailor felt great distress. Charles had a feeling he knew what worried his friend, and so he asked, "Martin, did Charlotte live or die in this timeline?"

Martin gulped. "So you know! Ah me, this is going to be a very great challenge to us all, I'm afraid. Elizabeth, in particular, given her history with these damnable puzzles. You say you went to Cambridge? That must have pleased your father. Robby always preferred it."

"I cannot say if he did or didn't. My father was killed on my fifth birthday."

His friend's countenance paled again. "Oh my! I wonder how many other things proceeded differently, and what choice drove us into our current path? But what of *our* Charles? If your experiences differ so much, then have you replaced him—or *become* him? How does it work?"

"I'm the wrong person to ask, and I wish I understood it," Sinclair answered, pouring them both refills. "There's a man I'd like to find who might know, if he's living in London now. Dr. Alphonse Theseus. He's in charge of this hellish experiment. He and the spirits behind Redwing and this Blackstone group..."

"Blackstone? You know about them? The Lords of the Black Stone? The Austrian organisation?"

"Yes, Martin, and they want proof of some unique property to my blood. The Time Maze is meant to provide that proof. As I pass through it, I'm to choose which mirror to enter, but Beth led me to a door instead."

"Beth? Is she also changed?"

"No, Beth the little girl. I think God sent her to me as a guide. Somehow, she's been involved in all this since childhood. Honestly, Martin, I'm as confused as you are. Perhaps, my blood isn't what they thought, and I'm failing miserably. But no matter what happens, I do know this: God Almighty wants me here, in this timeline, at this moment, for his reasons. I'm to learn something here. And where is James? Why did Mrs. Maryville call me the host?"

"Charles, James is..." he stopped before saying the final word. "Forgive me. I'm very sorry to tell you this, Charles. Not only are you the 1st Duke of Haimsbury, but you became the 11th Duke of Drummond last year."

"What?" mouthed the traveller in shock. The thought of James Stuart dying slammed a brick of cold reality into Sinclair's mind. Was James Stuart just as mortal as other men? Would he die one day, and the whole world mourn?

"I cannot picture my uncle dying, Martin. He's active, robust, and healthy. And what of Adele? Does she exist here? And what of my children?"

"Our sweet Della is at Maisie Churchill's home this evening," the tailor replied gently. "Master Winston is hosting a get-together for a small group of friends and cousins. You and Beth have four healthy children. The four-year-old twins, Charles Robert and Elizabeth Georgianna, three-year-old Jamie, and young Connor, who's sixteen months. Elizabeth's seven months along with your fifth. She says it's another son. Our beautiful Princess has been acting strangely lately, possibly due to these Songbird murders. It might also be due to that incident with Lorena MacKey."

"MacKey?" Charles asked. "What loyalties does Lorena serve here? Is she still with Redwing, or has she found Christ?"

The other man's eyes widened. "Redwing? What? Charles, you *are* a different man, aren't you? My friend, you've known Lorena MacKey for over twenty years! Your mother found her, remember?"

"No, Martin, I don't. I know nothing about it," the traveller reminded his friend.

"Oh yes, of course," the tailor observed with a sigh. "Well, your dear mother founded a charity that helps young girls to avoid or leave prostitution, and she discovered Lorena selling violets near Christ Church. The girl was just nine and newly orphaned, and with the sort of basic education those Ragged Schools provide. She showed high intelligence and a talent for science. Angela brought her home, intending to install her as a maid-in-training, but you took an interest in the girl. Lorena was born the same year Charlotte died, and you became a sort of, surrogate elder brother. Recognising your affection for the girl, your father made her his ward. When he passed away and you became marquess, you took over her education and sponsored Lorena's medical training at the School for Women, which your father endowed."

"I put her through medical school?"

"Oh, yes, and she's become a very fine doctor. She works at St. Mary's and has a private practice in Paddington. I've always admired Lorena. Sadly, she and Beth don't always get on."

"Not a surprise," Charles muttered. "Martin, when did my father die?"

"Twelve years ago, and your mother passed two years after, from grief. After Charlotte died, she was never strong."

"And when did Charlotte die?" asked Charles.

"The poor thing was just one day old."

"As with my experience. Is Adele Paul's child?"

Martin nodded. "She is, though very few know it. Beth learnt only last year, and it nearly broke their relationship."

"Are she and Paul close here? Who was given responsibility for Beth when she was born?" he asked, slowly making sense of the differences twixt this reality and his own.

"Why, you were, of course! Charles, can your life have so few reference points that coincide?"

"It seems not. Perhaps, my task here is to discover when this world diverged from my own."

"Yes, I believe I understand, but what of *our* Charles?" the tailor asked again. "Where is he?"

"I'm not sure, but Dr. Theseus might know."

"Theseus?"

"An alienist who's more alien than his patients realise, but wait! There's another with far greater wisdom," he added, an idea forming in his head. "Has a man named Prince Anatole Romanov ever visited anyone from the circle?"

"If you mean that arrogant Russian, the answer is no! He is a notorious leader in Redwing, Charles. Why would you even mention that foul name in connexion with our wonderful circle?"

"Because Anatole's more than he seems, Martin. Once this party's done, I intend to call at his home."

"Impossible. No one knows where he lives. You'd think as a Russian advisor to our government, he'd live at Chesham House. Not so, nor does he keep an office there. The circle's been trying to find his secret residence for years. We might ask Tom Galton. He's been working on it."

"I can find Romanov."

"How?"

"By going to Fulham."

Kepelheim sighed. "Fulham? Ah, very well, but wait until to-morrow. This party isn't likely to end for hours yet, and Beth will want you here with her." The tailor's face twisted into lines of worry. "Charles, you are married to Beth in your world, I hope? Tell me that such a foundational truth hasn't altered!"

"We are very happily married, Martin. We have the twins. Robby and Georgianna. Remember, it's only 1889. We've just been married a year. Will this Beth be like my own, I wonder?"

"I cannot say, assuming I've not gone mad," said Kepelheim, his face turned serious. "What you ask me to believe is quite difficult, Charles. But I cannot imagine our dear one being anything but gentle and true-hearted. Beth's sweet love anchors us all."

"Then, she is the same," said Charles, smiling.

A knock interrupted, and the tailor crossed to the door and opened it slightly. Charles could hear him speaking to a man on the other side. Finally, he turned, saying, "All this talk of theoretical worlds must abate, my friend. We are wanted. Or rather you are. The Songbird Killer has struck again, and this time, it's very close to home. Queen Anne House."

CHAPTER TWENTY-EIGHT
Real World - Castor Institute

When Henry MacAlpin and Paul Stuart entered the brightly lit lobby of the posh mental asylum called the Castor, they had no way of knowing Lionel Wentworth and Saraqael had arrived just one hour earlier. Henry had been here once before with Charles Sinclair, when they'd interviewed the previous director, Dr. Alexander Collins. But the evasive alienist suffered an epileptic seizure, which Sinclair presumed was feigned. Since that day, Collins had undergone trepanation of the temporal skull to ease pressure on the brain. The procedure was a great success, according to Frederick Treves. After several weeks of political bickering, led by Henry Matthews and Dr. Alphonse Theseus, Collins was moved from the London to Castor's twin institute, the Pollux in Fulham, and he remained there to this day.

As they reached the registration area, Stuart called to a pleasant-looking nurse, whose cap and badge indicated her senior status. "Sister, I wonder if you might help us?"

The charge nurse left a conversation with a middle-aged patient and crossed to the earl. "Yes, sir?"

As always, Paul carried both his ICI and IB warrant cards in his pocket, but decided to try a charm offensive first. "Might Dr. Kepler be in residence this afternoon? I'd hoped to speak to him about a relative of mine. It's a very sad case, and it's confused my entire family. That's why I've brought my friend, Dr. MacAlpin, to help me understand the medical language. I fear the time's come to consider an alternative to home care."

The nurse smiled congenially. She assumed Paul was a wealthy aristocrat with a mad sister, wife, or cousin. "May I tell the doctor who calls, sir?"

"I'm Lord Aubrey," announced the peer with a slight bow.

"Of course! I thought you looked familiar, sir. You and your cousin are quite the newspaper celebrities," she said with a little curtsy. "We're all very sorry for the business at the Haimsbury-Branham yesterday, my lord."

"Did you read about it, or has someone told you?"

"Why, it's in *The Star*, sir."

"Have you a copy nearby? I've not had time to read any news today," Aubrey explained.

"Yes, my lord. *The Times* described it as a wild west show. Are you all right, sir? Both papers said you were injured."

"A slight scratch," he told her, touching his side.

"And the duchess?"

"Unharmed, but as you can imagine, she was somewhat shaken. She remains at home today."

"That's wise," she said. "Do you have an appointment, Lord Aubrey?"

"No, and I apologise for not setting one, but as my friend was already with me today, and our errands took us through your neighbourhood, I decided to take a chance. I fear this family matter is becoming more than I can handle safely. Is he available?"

The nurse touched the earl's gloved hand. She was middle-aged and wore a wedding band. Paul took the gesture as one of commiseration and kindness. A motherly sort of act.

"I'm very sorry, my lord. You and your family continue to suffer, don't you? But you, the duchess, and Duke Charles have many friends in the East, sir. Will His Grace be coming home soon?"

"The duke's business should conclude soon, but may also lead to other matters elsewhere. Such is the nature of Crown affairs, I'm afraid," he said, emphasising the word 'crown'.

The nurse smiled. "It is a heavy weight, that crown, but His Grace would carry it well, I believe. Now, if you and Dr. MacAlpin will take a seat in the lounge, I'll let Dr. Kepler know you're here," she said, indicating a comfortably furnished parlour. "A porter will bring you refreshments."

"Sister, I wonder, might you have a telephone room?"

The woman smiled in that same, motherly manner. "We do, my lord. Just installed a fortnight ago for emergencies. Not many hospitals have them yet. Do you need to use it, sir?"

"If I may. With such gloomy reports in the papers, I'd like to reassure my wife again. She's nearing the time to give birth, and I don't want her distressed."

"A child? How wonderful for you both, my lord. Of course. Come this way."

She led him through the receiving office to a smaller room equipped with a telegraph and a black and gold candlestick Belle device. He lifted the earpiece and a woman's voice answered.

"How may I connect you today?"

"Aubrey House," he told her.

"Of course, sir. May I give them your name, sir?"

"It's Lord Aubrey."

"Right away, my lord," she said in a business-like manner. Several clicks followed, then a final click, and Paul heard his butler answer, 'Aubrey House', to which the operator announced the earl as the caller. Immediately, Bailey took the call, and his master began to speak.

"Bailey, I'm with Lord Salperton at Castor Institute. Has anyone called from Montmore House?"

"Yes, sir. Duchess Elizabeth came by and collected some books and clothing for Lady Aubrey. Her Grace said that all is well there, and that the countess is sleeping peacefully."

"That's a great relief. Lord Salperton has no telephone installed yet, so if you'd be kind enough to send word to the duchess that we're delayed in the East?"

"I'll despatch a footman at once, sir. Will you be overnighting at Montmore again this evening?"

"Yes, Bailey. And I may be there a few nights. Send word to Lester and Pennyweather at Queen Anne and to Mr. Miles at Haimsbury. Let them know of our plans. Did the duchess intend to stay at Montmore tonight?"

"Her ladyship didn't say, sir. Do you need clothing, sir?"

"A case with a week's worth of clothes would be appreciated. Thank you, Bailey. Forward all my post to Montmore for the present."

"Very good, sir. We'll take care of everything."

"Have the decorators begun?"

"They have, sir. Shall I ask them to place the project on pause for the present?"

Paul thought a moment. With the shooting, perhaps having strangers in the house, even those who'd been cleared by circle background checks, might prove dangerous. "Yes, Bailey, put the project on hold until further notice. Thank you. I'll ring again tomorrow."

"Please, let Lady Delia know that we're all praying for her, and for all the family, sir."

"I will. Thank you, Bailey. Goodbye."

Aubrey returned the earpiece into the cradle. By the time he found Henry again, the alienist had begun a conversation with an elderly man with silver hair. The man reminded Paul of Martin Kepelheim.

The earl found a chair and began to jot down notes to himself in circle code. Item one: Talk to Martin about D. Kimberley. Item two: Have N. Kessler investigated. Item three: Send word to Branham about the shooting. Item four: Talk with War Office about missing Maxims.

Seeing Paul was back, Henry excused himself and joined his friend in the next chair. Noticing the odd symbols, he asked, "Is that your code?"

"I rarely write in plain English. I could teach it to you."

"I'd like that. It could prove useful when writing medical notes. Who invented it?"

"I'm not sure who created the first code, but the circle's used ciphers since the beginning. We alter them regularly. I suppose we'll need to update it again now."

"Why?"

Paul realised Henry knew nothing of Kimberley and Epperson's treason. "We've been infiltrated," was all he had to say. "I'll explain later."

"I see, and I shall remind you about that. So, when was the first code created?" asked Henry.

"Probably the fifteenth century, but Martin's found evidence of a previously formed inner circle that reaches back to the first century." The earl twisted his spine a bit in an attempt to ease the pain in his side. MacAlpin noticed.

"I should check those bandages once we're done here. I could ask to use one of the examination rooms, if you need it."

"I'm fine, Henry."

"That's a typical answer for you, but when we're done here, I intend to have a look at the bandages."

"And that's typical for you," Paul countered with a grin. He set down the pencil and shut the book. "Does Montmore receive daily newspapers? Adele and Cordelia know about the shooting, but I'd prefer they didn't read salacious stories about it."

"All newspapers go directly to my office, which is kept locked. None of the residents see them. I only allow books and older periodicals. Most news is far too distressing, particularly the crime reports."

"That's a relief," Paul said. "Has Della said anything about Charles?"

Henry kept one eye on the lobby doors whilst answering in a whisper. "I never question her directly about the abduction, you understand. Della suffers from retrograde amnesia, caused by the trauma she suffered. As far as Charles is concerned, she believes our cover story, that he's travelling. I suppose, in a very real way, he is."

"Have you thought any more about hypnosis?"

"I just don't know if her mind can handle hypnosis, Paul. Allow me to pursue a gentler therapy for now. Sometimes, severe trauma leaves memory gaps that never heal, because the trauma is too horrific to remember. Elizabeth has similar memory gaps and still suffers from dark dreams."

"I'm all too familiar with that phenomenon and those nightmares. The 'too many faces' and 'wolf' dreams in particular. Are you saying Della could suffer for the rest of her life? Henry, is this a spiritual matter? Might it be..." The question was left unfinished, for the nurse had returned. "We'll talk more later."

The nurse cleared her throat. "Dr. Kepler will see you now, Lord Aubrey. And he's most excited to learn Dr. MacAlpin is with you. If you'll follow me, sirs?"

The stout woman led the two men through the lobby, past a series of pleasant-looking patient wards, and then up a flight of marble steps. She used one of her many keys to open a half-windowed door, which took them into a wide corridor, with black and white floors and walls painted with pastoral frescoes, featuring the god Pan and his female followers.

SHARON K. GILBERT

"This is the Hemsfield Ward, sir. It was originally underwritten by an endowment from a Romanian prince, and then generously funded by the late Lord Hemsfield, God rest his soul. The caveat placed upon that donation is that we named the ward for him."

"And this Romanian prince didn't complain?" asked MacAlpin.

"No, sir, he knew Lord Hemsfield well and agreed to the stipulation. Lady Hemsfield also believes in our work, and considers this her late husband's legacy. The ward is specially designed and furnished to make our more aristocratic guests feel at home. We've spared no expense to do so, my lord. Guests may live in the same elegance and comfort they enjoy in their own homes. Most fail to discern any difference and believe themselves still at home. I know your family member will find it quite comfortable, Lord Aubrey. Dr. Kepler's office is just down here, sir."

The spacious patient apartments might easily blend into any West-End townhome. The suites were decorated as French or Roman villas with rich fabrics, expensive wallcoverings, and expensive furnishings. Most included a large parlour with a separate dining area, a bedchamber, and privy rooms for bathing and dressing.

To his surprise, Aubrey recognised one of the inhabitants; Miss Gemma Rosalind Finchley, whom he and Charles encountered at the H-Division booking desk the previous year. She'd been in the company of a vile, pugilistic procurer with bad teeth and a stained suit. Gemma's legal guardian was her elder brother, the current earl. Had Lord Finchley installed his only sister in this privileged and very expensive madhouse for some special reason? Was she mentally ill?

"Excuse me, Sister," he asked the nurse. "Isn't that Gemma Finchley?"

"It is, sir. Do you know the lady?"

"We were childhood friends. May I speak with her?"

The nurse smiled patiently, not wishing to alienate such a high-ranking peer, particularly one so close to Charles Sinclair. "I'm sure she'd enjoy talking with a friend, but Miss Finchley's mind is somewhat delicate, my lord. She suffered a terrible assault last year that left her prone to nervous prostration and ideation. Her mind is fragile."

"I see. Thank you," Paul replied, whispering a prayer for God's guidance in the matter. "If you'd ask Dr. Kepler's permission, I'd appreciate it, Sister."

"I will, sir."

They continued past Gemma's rooms, all the way to the end of the brightly lit corridor, where a charming sitting room and adjoining office welcomed them. "Dr. Kepler?" called the nurse into the office. "Lord Aubrey and Dr. MacAlpin are here."

"Thank you, Sister MacCallum. You may leave us now," replied a diminutive man in wire-rimmed spectacles. He left the office and crossed to the door to greet his guests. "It's an honour and very great privilege to meet you, Lord Aubrey. And Lord Salperton as well, eh? This is a banner day, indeed! Do come through, gentlemen. This way."

They passed through the sitting room to a large office, where several leather chairs awaited their pleasure, not far from Kepler's large desk. "Take a seat, gentlemen. The chairs were delivered yesterday from a furniture maker in Holland. They're framed in ash and covered in dyed lambskin that's conditioned with a secret combination of exotic oils until the leather feels like a woman's soft cheek against your arms and back. I find myself wanting to sit all day, for it is heavenly. You'll want the name of the manufacturer, I'm sure."

Paul chose a red chair, whilst Henry sat in its matching neighbour. Kepler's chair was dyed with a deep, golden yellow stain, and the arched back rose up high into a carved winged-sun emblem. Stylised lions formed the ornate arms, but the legs were oxen hooves.

It looked very much like a throne.

MacAlpin smiled, for his colleague was clearly compensating for some perceived insufficiency. Henry had an Austrian friend, whom he'd met in Paris, who'd have thought the chair significant. *I must write to Sigmund and mention it*, he thought.

"Welcome to Castor, gentlemen. How may I help you?" asked the Lilliputian alienist from his sun-king throne.

"Thank you for seeing us without an appointment, Dr. Kepler. I'm sure you're a busy man," Paul began. "Your nurse may have mentioned my concern for a relative. I pray you won't take offence, but I've actually come to seek your advice on a police matter."

Kepler's face grew hard. "Police?"

"Not actually the police, *per se*, nonetheless, one of law enforcement." Paul removed the Intelligence Branch warrant card and showed it to his host. "The IB is relatively new, and whilst we confer with Scotland Yard on many investigations, our authority supersedes theirs. Now, my question will sound unusual, but I assure you, this is no idle curiosity. Last year, several women were attacked and two were slain, not far from here at Victoria Park. Do you remember the case?"

"Yes, of course, I do, Lord Aubrey. A most horrible thing it was, too. As you're aware, Victoria Park is but a short walk from Castor. Why, we use it for exercise therapy! Imagine our horror when these crimes occurred. Our patients became most excited by it."

"Excited?" the earl asked.

"Not in the colloquial usage of the word, but a medical one, sir," Kepler explained. "Excitation is a negative, nervous condition and can prove detrimental to those with a sensitive disposition. I'm sure Lord Salperton understands."

"Dr. Kepler's right, Paul," said Henry. "An unstable person can become a danger to himself and others, when hearing of nearby murders and other violent crimes. Excitation in this case isn't an emotional response, but a dangerous compulsion for self-harm, and sometimes, for harming others. It can cause an otherwise complacent person to emulate and imitate those crimes. The afflicted patient might even believe himself the killer."

"Exactly as you say, Lord Salperton. It can be quite detrimental," Kepler continued in that high-pitched, regal tone. "Why do you mention these crimes, Lord Aubrey? Has the murderer struck again? We've heard nothing of it here. Your own recent experience at the Haimsbury-Branham is known to us, of course. I'm relieved to see you're unharmed."

"Thank you," said the earl. "Dr. Kepler, I ask about the Victoria case, because similar crimes persist in this part of London. I'm sure you're aware of the stories told by East-End children regarding a Lady in White, who tries to lure them into the Thames or the River Lea. But also stories of animalistic behaviour and even transformed physicality."

"Lord Aubrey, I hope you're not falling for these Jewish fables," their bespectacled host said. "Wolfmen and monstrous golems are hardly real, sir. These tales are spread abroad to protect the real offenders, who are humans, sir. Nothing but troubled humans, bent on performing evil deeds for selfish or deluded purposes."

Henry jumped in at this point. "Troubled humans, Dr. Kepler? Might their troubles be inflicted upon them?"

"What do you mean?" asked Kepler suspiciously.

"Last year, I came here with Duke Charles, and we discussed these matters with your predecessor, Alexander Collins. We asked him specifically about a former patient, listed as Mr. Thirteen."

"Thirteen? A very strange name."

"Oh, it's not a name, sir, but a cruel, dispassionately assigned number. It's the sort of thing a researcher might do with a rat or other experimental animal. I've met and tended to Mr. Thirteen, and his injuries were profound and exceedingly cruel. The man was grossly mistreated."

"A most unfortunate gentleman," Kepler noted from the throne, his hands steepled.

"Yes, but God has smiled on him, you see," said Lord Salperton. "Not only has the man recovered, he is now gainfully employed in a peerage home. During his recovery, the former inmate told me some very troubling things regarding this institution."

"Our institution?" Kepler asked, his tone hinting at annoyance.

"Yours, sir," Henry said without batting an eye. "During my previous visit, I asked politely to view the lower levels and was denied. Dr. Kepler, I must now insist on seeing them. If you refuse, I shall take the matter to the Royal College. They hold a very dim view of secretive, illegal human experimentation."

"We've broken no laws, Doctor. If this gentleman lived beneath our care, then he came here willingly, or else was judged to be mad by two or more qualified physicians. We always follow the law, sir."

"If that's true, then your paperwork would identify him, and therefore support that statement."

"Lord Salperton, I'm aware of your considerable influence with the Royal College, and I'm aware of all current regulations regarding the ethical treatment of mental patients. Truly, sir, as a fellow explorer of the mind, I respect and admire you. Ours is not a timid journey, nor is it for the faint of heart. Lord Aubrey's reputation at gathering intelligence on behalf of the Crown is legendary, but I suggest the mind is a far more dangerous field of endeavour than spy craft. Yet, we who serve in those deep mental labyrinths are seldom rewarded, are we? Even those whose methods lead to advancements in the human condition are often misunderstood. Mary Shelley's book is called fiction, but I tell you such science exists, and one day, I shall be lauded for my great work!"

As he uttered these last statements, Kepler's small face became a mask of rapturous exultation, and Salperton began to wonder if Kepler weren't as mad as his inmates. If so, then he and Paul had to proceed with caution.

"I couldn't have said it better," Henry chose to reply. "Your work sounds very important, even groundbreaking. I should love to observe and learn from your methods, Dr. Kepler. Forgive me for being so brusque earlier. I'd assumed you would be as uncooperative as Dr. Collins was last year. Clearly, I've misjudged you."

"Many do," the other said, smiling like a god. "Genius is seldom appreciated during one's own lifetime. I shall happily show you the lower levels, Lord Salperton, but I fear such a tour must wait for another day. It's late, and I've an appointment in an hour at the palace. And tomorrow, I leave for France. I'm meeting with Dr. Charcot and his colleagues in Paris. I believe you studied with him, Dr. MacAlpin."

"Yes, I spent half a year with Charcot."

"Then you'll be interested to learn, I'm giving a lecture on the nature of hypnosis and its value to science. I plan to return next Thursday week and would find your company quite enjoyable. May we arrange to meet then?"

Henry started to object, but Paul stood and offered the delusional Lilliputian a firm handshake. "That's most accommodating of you, Dr. Kepler. We'll set an appointment with your receiving office. But before we go, I wonder, if I might speak to Lady Gemma for a moment? Perhaps, you and Dr. Salperton could confer on that *other matter* whilst I do so?"

"Other matter?" asked Salperton.

"The missing patients," Aubrey replied. "Particularly any who've disappeared from Dr. Kepler's morgue. As part of our survey."

"Oh, oh that! Yes, of course," Henry said as he caught on.

Kepler appeared content, but warned the earl, "You'll find Miss Finchley somewhat easily agitated, Lord Aubrey. Do be careful not to mention anything distressful. Yesterday's shooting, for instance. Or any of these horrid crimes."

"I won't," said Paul as he left Henry on his own and returned to the corridor.

When he arrived at Gemma's apartment, he knocked on the glassed door. She'd been reading and glanced up, a pair of spectacles aiding her vision. Her mouth dropped open at seeing a familiar face, and she snatched off the eyeglasses. "Is that? No it can't be! Lord Aubrey? Can that be you?"

"It is," he said. "May I come in?"

"Oh, yes, yes! Please, do!" she said excitedly. "But why are you here? I hope no one's ill. Did my brother Andrew send you?"

"Not at all. I've come on other matters. Might I sit?"

She removed a stack of magazines from the closest chair and brushed the green velvet seat. "Will this do?"

"Perfectly," he said with a bright smile. "How are you, Gemma? I saw your brother two weeks ago at Whitehall. He didn't mention you were ill."

"That's because I'm not ill. Not really," she muttered. "It's quite embarrassing, really. Andrew thinks I'm... Oh, how shall I say it? He thinks my brain isn't as sound as it should be. He might be right. I'm sure I saw him, but Andrew says I couldn't have. After all, David's dead, isn't he?"

"David?" asked the earl. "Which David might that be?"

"I probably shouldn't call him by his Christian name, but he was always so kind to me. Whenever Andrew grew angry, David would intervene on my behalf. He was always so very chivalrous."

"Intervene? Gemma, is your brother violent?"

"Oh, no! I shouldn't have said anything," she whispered quickly. "I'm sure Andrew has good cause for his anger. I can be quite trying at times. I'm well past the proper age to marry. I'm almost thirty, and I've become a burden to him. David understood that. He once saw Andrew, when he was very angry, and he stood up to him, *for me*. I'm sure you'd have done the same. You're so very chivalrous, Lord Aubrey."

"You used to call me Paul," he whispered. "We've known one another for a long time, Gemma."

"Yes, of course. Paul." Her dark eyes cast about the room nervously, as though trying to find the right words that were hiding somewhere inside her damaged mind. "Paul, have you seen him?"

"Have I seen Andrew?"

"Oh, no. Not Andrew! I mean David, of course. He used to come visit me at Tarling House, whenever Andrew was away on business. I'd sometimes visit him at the Exchange. He was forced to close his office last year. Still, we often met there. David kept a key to it, you see. It was quite thrilling!"

"Darling, what David are we discussing?" asked the earl patiently.

Gemma smiled as she reached across to stroke his long hair. "Darling," she whispered. "You used to call me that when we'd dance, didn't you? Darling. If only you'd asked me to marry you back then, Paul. I'd probably not be here now, would I? Perhaps, David will come to get me. Do you think he might?"

He took her hand, noticing its coolness. "I remember those military dances and the debutante balls. I remember your debut, Gemma. You were radiant, darling. Your auburn hair shone like molten copper beneath the Tarling House chandeliers, and we laughed and laughed, didn't we?"

"You took me out to the gardens. We danced and watched the stars."

"We did."

"And you stole a kiss."

"I stole several, remember? Your skin was soft and smelled like summer lilacs. You've always been very special to me, Gemma. I hope you know that."

"Ah, but then you started travelling all the time, to this country or that. I wrote, but seldom heard back." She sighed. "We cannot alter the past, can we, darling Paul?"

"No, dear, we can't," he said, his heart breaking to see her so very changed. He sometimes saw that same sadness in his wife's face. "You're still very beautiful, Gemma."

"David always said so," she answered wistfully, her attention wandering. "Poor, poor David. Why did they murder him in such a way, Paul? He still bears those marks, you know. On his throat and hands."

Suddenly, Aubrey realised what David the woman meant. Was it even possible? "Gemma, are you talking about the late Baron Wychwright?"

"Of course, I am!" she exclaimed, a wild look to her eyes. "Who else would I mean? I know David is a married man, but..."

"*Was*, Gemma. *Was* a married man. David Wychwright is dead."

"Everyone says that, but is he really? I mean, just what is death? Is it the end or a new beginning? I do see him, Paul. He comes here to see me. Late at night, after all the nurses and orderlies have left. We have such lovely talks, and he tells me all sorts of things. Lately, he talks about Lord Haimsbury. Oh, wait. It's Duke Charles now, isn't it?"

He still held her hand, and Paul had to force himself to remain calm. *Don't frighten her. Let her talk.* "Duke Charles?" he asked. "What about him?"

"Charles is so very nice! Handsome and generous, just like you, but then the two of you are cousins, aren't you? He reminds me of you a little."

"Elizabeth says the same," Paul told her.

"The duke was very kindhearted towards me last year. At that place," she whispered. "You know the one. With the policemen everywhere."

"The Leman Street police station?"

"That's the place. I was so embarrassed to be there! But then the two of you came in, and the duke punched that awful man on the jaw and knocked him to the floor! He did hit him, didn't he? I'm not imagining that? Dr. Kepler says I imagine a great many things."

"No, darling, you didn't imagine it. Charles hit him with a very powerful punch. I'm sorry you had to endure such an ordeal," he said, still holding her hand.

"Yes," she whispered with a deep sigh, "but it's all over now, and David explained what happened. With your cousin, I mean."

"What did David say about my cousin?"

"Who?"

"Duke Charles. You said that you and David sometimes talk about him," Paul prompted.

"Oh, we do! The duke's in a sort of underworld, David said. Inside a great labyrinth or maze or some such thing. It didn't make any sense to me, but David assures me that there is such a place. Paul, isn't there a maze at Branham? Might the duke be there? I was reading this article in *The Gazette* that says he's in America. Now, why would any true Englishman go to America? I heard there are pigs and cattle running about the streets, and red Indians scalping everyone! I shouldn't think any sensible person would go there."

"Did David say anything else about this maze?" asked the earl, trying to keep her focused.

"Not much. I could ask him the next time he visits. He doesn't visit me every night, but he's here quite often. Dr. Kepler might know about the maze. He asks me about David, too. And about Duke Charles. Do you think I should tell him about Adele?"

Paul gasped, his blue eyes widening. "What about Adele?"

"She's your sister, isn't she? David said she was taken to a place with a very silly name. Sin? Or Sen? Or perhaps, Sense? I can't remember, but he said she'd be coming back. Has she come back?"

"My sister's just fine, Gemma," he replied, not wishing to reveal too much. "She's staying with a friend. You said Dr. Kepler asked about my cousin. What does he ask?"

"He mostly asks me what David says about him. About Duke Charles, I mean. Charles is so handsome! He looks a bit like you. Did I already say that?"

"Yes, dear. What else does he ask?"

"Who? David?"

"No, dear. What does Dr. Kepler ask?"

"Oh, well, he sometimes mentions someone named Theseus."

"Theseus?"

"I think I'm right. Theseus. Isn't he one of those Greek demigods? I remember reading about him at finishing school. You don't think Charles will have to fight a Minotaur, do you? If he's in a labyrinth, there might be all manner of beasts inside it."

"You're sure Dr. Kepler asked about a labyrinth?"

"Oh, yes. And sometimes, my brother is with him. They both ask about Charles. Is he going to be the next king?"

"I don't know," Paul answered carefully. *Why would Kepler want to know all this? And is Andrew Finchley part of a new plot?*

She noticed a porter in the corridor and became nervous. "We're watched, Paul. That man's not human."

Paul glanced at the window. The apartment had two, large curtained windows that allowed nurses to see into the parlours. "Why isn't he human?"

"I can't say why, but I can see his true form," Gemma told him. "He's actually a walking bat. Oh, he's very ugly." She leaned forward, her hand on his, and she whispered, "Talk to Alexander Collins. He knows all about David."

Paul stared at her. She seemed sincere, but was she mad? "I'll do that," he told her. "Gemma, may I visit you again?"

"Oh, yes, I'd like that," she said. "I don't get many visitors, except for David, of course. And that other one. I'd never met him before, but he is quite handsome. There's something odd about him, though. I'm not sure he's human either."

"Who?"

"What?" she asked, her face grown blank.

"Who is this other man you mentioned? The handsome one?"

"I'm not sure. Is there one? I wonder if he's the fellow who came here after I took my nap? He was so very beautiful, but came with an odious person named Wentworth. Such awful breath! It made my eyes water. He laughed like a madman and looked like a well-dressed scarecrow. Do you know, he claimed that he shot someone yesterday, but then he didn't have a gun, did he? He talked to me for a while, then Dr. Kepler took him away, I'm very glad to say. I'd have liked for the other one to stay though."

"Wentworth?" Paul echoed.

"Who?"

"The thin man. Did you hear his Christian name? Might it be Lionel?"

"It may have been. At first, that other one looked a little like some of the strange animals they keep downstairs, then he changed into the most beautiful, angelic creature. David says there are angels who call themselves princes. Perhaps, this man is one."

"A prince?"

"Perhaps. He was tall and so very beautiful. Such long, dark hair. He kissed me. Not on the mouth, but on the cheek. His breath was lovely."

"Did he give a name?" asked Paul.

"Who?"

"The prince."

"No, he didn't. I could ask David. Poor David! He has the most heartless wife. Honestly, I could tear that woman apart sometimes!"

"So could I," muttered the earl. "She's my mother-in-law."

"Lady Wychwright? Oh, you poor man. I'm very sorry," she said sweetly, kissing his hand. "Be careful, Paul! The bat's watching us. You mustn't stay any longer. He'll tell on us. And I should probably sleep anyway. I'm very tired suddenly."

He kissed her forehead and gave her pale hands a little squeeze. "I'll come back soon. And if there's a way, I'll get you out of here, Gemma. I promise."

"But would David be able to find me, if I leave?"

"I'm sure he would. Be safe, dear. You're in my prayers. If you ever need anything or anyone, send word to me at Aubrey House. My butler will know how to find me."

The earl kissed her cheek and then left, his heart heavy at his friend's condition, but trying to sort through their strange conversation. Was she really seeing David Wychwright? Certainly not. Then again, the late baron's body went missing in May. Perhaps, Gemma conversed with a dark spirit that used the baron's form to gain her confidence. Is that how this 'David' knew about Charles? And why are Kepler and Andrew Finchley so interested in her visions?

When he reached the reception area, Paul found Salperton talking with Sister MacCallum. Both wore smiles.

"Capital place!" Henry was saying to the woman. "I shall have to employ all these modern ideas at Montmore. You and your staff are performing medical miracles, Sister MacCallum. Thank you again for the tour. And, please, let Dr. Kepler know we'll visit again after he returns from Paris."

"I will, my lord, and we'll be pleased to add the appointment to his diary, sir."

He joined Paul, and the two peers left the institute. Inside the coach, the earl related his story. "I'm sure Gemma is being used somehow," he told Henry after finishing the tale. "She imagines seeing David Wychwright, of all things."

"Cordelia's late father? Now, that is strange. I have a resident patient who insists her late husband shares the apartment with her. But I also have six non-resident patients who say they've conversed with people who've recently died. Paul, what on earth is happening?"

"I'm not sure, but Gemma claims the dead baron told her about Charles. He said he's in a maze of some kind. I hate to leave London, but I think I should visit Branham to see if there's anything amiss in the maze there. Do you think Cordelia might go into labour in the next day or two?"

"There's no way to divine that. Anthony thinks she's stable for now, but he doesn't want to risk anything by moving her. If you really must go, I'll make a point of staying close, and Lorena said she'd remain at Montmore, if we ask. I got the impression there's a troubled history twixt you two, but she's a very capable doctor, Paul."

"Yes, she is." Aubrey reached for the bandaged side, his eyes pinched together with pain. "Sometimes, I feel as if the world is collapsing."

"Or perhaps you are," said Salperton. "Let's go back to Montmore and take a look at your wound, and whilst we're about it, we can talk this out. Don't make any decision about Branham yet. Give it some thought. Since I've known you, Paul, you incline towards acting first, thinking later. Perhaps, you might do the opposite today?"

The earl managed a smile. "You give very sound counsel, Henry. Why didn't I appreciate that in school? Yes, let's enjoy an evening with our ladies and forget about dark matters for a few hours."

"We might even get Seth and Adele to act out some Austen for us."

"Oh, that's just what I need," Paul laughed. "Very well. Jane Austen it is. Wherever Charles is now, I pray he's finding the world a saner place."

CHAPTER TWENTY-NINE
Time Maze - Queen Anne House

It was long past one o'clock in the morning, when Martin Kepelheim joined his friend to visit the crime scene at Queen Anne House. He and Duke Charles sat inside a black brougham for the short ride from Drummond House to Queen Anne, and Martin used the time to fill Charles in on the crimes of the Songbird Killer.

"The first murder took place one year ago, and there've been eleven since. One every month. This death breaks that pattern."

"How so?" asked the duke.

"Because, there was another just two nights ago, also in Westminster, which is why everyone was discussing it at the party this evening. All the other murders occurred in the outer boroughs; most in the East, and all the victims are singers or actresses. There is, however, a theory that the victims were somewhat free with their charms. In a professional capacity, if you get my meaning. Though, it is only conjecture."

"Yes, I understand. Martin, what sort of life have I led?"

"Forgive me, Charles, but it's very strange to hear you ask such a question, and I continue to wonder where our Charles might have gone, or worse, if either you or I have simply gone mad! But I shall tell you about yourself, as mad as that might be. You attended Eton, and then..."

"Harrow. I went to Harrow."

"What? No, Charles, you and Paul chose Eton to remain together."

"Paul went to Eton, and I went to Harrow, but go on."

Kepelheim took a deep breath. "Well, regardless of the school, you excelled at every lesson. Then, as now, you and Paul were often called the Scottish twins."

"Why? I was born in England."

"Yes, I know, but Rose House is near the edge of that division, not far from Hadrian's Wall, and besides, your mother was a Scot, as were most of your ancestors."

"Excepting those who were French."

"Yes," the tailor smiled, "excepting those. Now, at Oxford, you and Paul..."

"Cambridge, remember? I studied at Cambridge."

"Not here, Charles. You're asking me about your life here. And this Charles chose Oxford; again, to remain close to your cousin."

"Forgive me. Continue, please."

"Yes, well, you chose foreign languages and mathematics, whilst Paul read history and languages, emphasising Russian and Greek. As before, you both excelled and took top place in all your tripos. You and Paul were once again called the Scottish twins, and every eligible young lady in the kingdom followed you about like adoring lambs. You both completed university after just three years, and then Paul left for Russia, whilst you took a posting to the Sûreté in Paris. You always had a methodical approach to the world, and your father thought you might enjoy criminal investigation. Once you returned home, you and Paul again formed a duo, but after a while, you drifted apart and nearly came to blows."

"Over what?" asked Charles.

"Elizabeth. Even though she was promised to you long ago, Paul had fallen in love with her, you see. Your own attitude towards the duchess was more pragmatic back then. In all honesty, I think you were in love with someone else, but you've always been a man of honour, and so you proposed to Beth when she turned sixteen."

"I was in love with someone else? Impossible! I cannot imagine that."

"Oh, I can, for you and I talked about it, long into the wee hours of many nights, my friend. Oh, those long talks! How they would go and on, but only because it tore at your heart so very much."

"Who was this other woman?"

Martin took a deep breath. "Why, Lorena, of course."

"No, I find that impossible to credit. Beth's my heart and soul, Martin. How could I love someone else with her in my life? You might as well ask the sun to stop rising!"

"And yet you did love another," sighed his friend. "For her part, Beth loved you with singular devotion from a very early age. I think you set the wedding date so very early, because you worried Lorena might do something to dissuade you. She'd become somewhat forceful, let us say. And so, you and Elizabeth wed in '86, one day after her eighteenth birthday. In just two months, she learnt she was with child, and since then, you've shown her the true love and attention she deserves. It's rather like a romance novel, Charles, for you fell in love with your own wife. Few men can make such a statement."

"And what of Lorena?"

"Ah, Dr. MacKey set up a practice at St. Mary's, to make sure she was close. She still works in Whitechapel, of course. She teaches at the London and the Women's Medical School and helps out at the Eastern Dispensary."

"My life's entirely different here."

"Is it? Then, perhaps your task is to discover where it first diverged. Or you're simply overwrought, and your mind's weary."

"The divergence had to be long ago, for my real life was far different, Martin," Charles explained. "I had no idea of my peerage roots. I only learnt my true identity as a Sinclair in October of '88. Beth and I married shortly after. It's a long tale, but we met when she was about eleven, and we slowly fell in love with one another. We married last year. By that, I mean last year *to me*, in 1888."

Martin smiled. "The two of you are so very close now, and Beth's faith in you never falters. However, I fear your sponsorship of MacKey still causes friction. Not so much from Beth's side as from the doctor's. I fear Lorena's becoming somewhat unstable in her obsession."

The coach pulled to a stop on the mansion's east side. A police constable met them and opened the door. Beside the young man, walked a man whom Charles had known for a very long time. Robert Morehouse, his murdered friend.

"Commissioner, it's good of you to come at such an hour," Morehouse said as Charles left the coach. "The body's round the side of the house. Near the entrance to the kitchens."

Charles and Martin followed Morehouse and the constable past a Grecian-style pavilion, through rows of formal plantings and statuary, then around the east-wing corner, to a long avenue of herbs and berry bushes. Here, a gravel and brick walkway led them past budding fruit trees and bare willows. Charles recognised the servants' entrance, where a dozen policemen and several plain-clothes detectives milled about drinking hot cocoa and coffee. He could see several kitchen maids beyond the sparkling windows; and the butler John Miles was sitting beside the cook, Mrs. Hilda Smith. She looked pale and confused in her nightcap and bathrobe, but it was reassuring to find both of Elizabeth's faithful servants in this world as well.

"Tell me, Martin, is Baxter in London or at Branham?"

"Baxter?" asked the tailor. "Is he a peer?"

"Cornelius Baxter," Charles clarified. "You don't know him?"

"Oh, wait, there was an underbutler named Baxter. He worked at Branham long ago. I believe Beth's mother dismissed him during one of her many tirades. When Connor was posted overseas, Trish's temper could ignite into a volcano at the merest glance. Beth might know what happened to him," he said as they reached the body. "Oh, my," Martin whispered, at seeing the body. "This fiend stops at nothing. Chief Inspector Morehouse, it's a shame we have to meet again over so wretched a deed."

"I prefer to meet over a plate of good English beef, Mr. Kepelheim." Morehouse turned to Sinclair, "We've tried to leave the scene alone, sir, but the kitchen staff had already trampled the area by the time we arrived. Does the duchess know about this?"

Robert Morehouse stood an inch taller than Sinclair. As usual, he smoked a briarwood pipe, its smoke filling the air with a sweet tobacco scent. The silvery smoke swirled round the policeman's dark hair like a grey halo. Charles found the image reassuring and familiar. He sorely missed his former commanding officer, but was this version also embedded with Redwing, as his friend had once been?

"I've not told her about it yet, no," he told Morehouse.

"With these newfangled telephone devices, she'll know soon enough," Morehouse said flatly. "The world's getting far too mechanical, if you ask me."

"Who found the body?" Sinclair asked, turning to the work.

"A night watchman. Tom Jefferies. The lad's inside now. He's badly shaken up," said Morehouse. "We're all hoping you can offer some insight that our police detectives lack, Your Grace."

The duke bent down to examine the remains. "Do we have a name?"

"Pamina Soubret. She's a singer at the Lyceum."

The same young singer who was killed by Sir William Trent and his hellish friends last year, thought Sinclair. *Is Trent here—lurking about somewhere in this reality?*

"And her eyes? Have we located those?"

"They were in her hands, sir. We removed them for examination."

"Why? Surely, that's your surgeon's job."

"Blame me, Your Grace," said a slender man with a meagre moustache. "I wanted to photograph them,"

Charles could hardly believe his eyes. "Is your name O'Brien?"

"Yes, sir. We worked together once before, but I'm honoured you'd remember, Your Grace."

Michael O'Brien is a police photographer? What a strange incongruence!

"Why would you photograph her eyes separately? Surely, you don't give credence to this fabled notion that a killer's image is recorded on the eyes?"

"There's been some modest success with that, Your Grace, but actually I wanted to record the optical nerve tissue, to see whether it was torn or cut, sir. But I also photographed them whilst still inside her hands, where the killer put them. I try to be thorough, sir."

Martin had stepped back to allow his friend to work unhindered. "You're an American?" he asked O'Brien.

"That's right, sir. From Chicago."

Charles had always thought Michael O'Brien hailed from New York or Boston, based on his accent. He'd have to look into the matter once he returned to the real world and home.

"Has anything else been moved or tampered with, other than her eyes?" he asked.

"No, sir," Morehouse answered. "Just the eyes."

Charles found it strange to be called 'sir' by Robert Morehouse, but he had to behave as though everything were normal.

Concentrate! Back to work.

Pamina Soubret had been brutally ravaged, as if by an animal. Her eyes were torn out, as well as the tongue; and her abdomen ripped open. She wore the clothing of a boy, rather than a dress: dark blue trousers, black braces, a white cotton shirt, and a red waistcoat. She wore no overcoat. Her hair was pulled into a tight chignon on the top of her head, and a blood-spattered cap lay nearby, nestled in a patch of newly sprouted flowers.

"She was killed elsewhere and then left here," Sinclair told Morehouse. "Was she appearing in a playhouse nearby?"

"The Lyceum. We sent a constable to the theatre, and fetched a playbill. The owner, Mr. Henry Irving, was still about, and he gave us her name."

"How did you know to go to the Lyceum?" asked Charles.

A constable spoke up. "Me, sir. I saw the lady there last week. She was singin' in a rehearsal."

"Did you know her prior to that, Constable?"

"Just a bit, sir. Not personally. Only to watch her sing, sir."

Charles sighed. The boy looked young; no more than twenty. "What's your name, son?"

"John Pebble, sir."

"Mr. Pebble, you must recuse yourself from the investigation and take a seat elsewhere for now. Someone will interview you later. Do you understand?"

The boy gulped. "Am I a suspect, Your Grace?"

"Not yet, but we have to rule it out. Go inside and have a cup of coffee, son. Tell Mrs. Smith I sent you."

The lad left, and Sinclair glanced up at Morehouse. "What else has the boy said?"

"No more than her name and what the playbill says. The girl was performing in a Mozart opera. *The Marriage of Figaro.*"

"Then her character was Cherubino," Kepelheim declared. "It's Count Almaviva's page."

"Why would a female singer play a page?" asked Morehouse.

"It's known as a trouser role. A boy page would have a high voice, you see, and since children cannot sing difficult operatic arias, a young woman plays the part. The opera's all about madness; or rather the appearance of madness. Almaviva insists on taking his *droit de seigneur* with one of the maids."

"He insists on taking his what?" asked Morehouse.

Sinclair had the answer. "Feudal lords used to believe they had the right to bed any servant girl on her wedding night, before she slept with her new husband. *Droit de seigneur* is French for lord's right. Today, we'd call it rape."

"But she's dressed as a boy," said Montmore. "Is that how maid servants used to dress?"

"No," said Kepelheim, "our victim played the page, but if she's like the others, the Songbird Killer had his way with her first. It's rather like the count's intent, only this time with a girl playing a boy."

"This Songbird Killer rapes them first?" asked Sinclair, wishing he'd said nothing, for every head turned his way. "Forgive me. I'm tired. What I meant to ask is, might the killer know his victims? Perhaps, he coerces the girl into bed, then kills her to stop her from reporting it. He might use chloroform or opiates to induce a euphoric state of implied consent. Do we have blood tests from the autopsies?"

"No one's ordered any," said Morehouse in an odd tone. "I'll have A-Division's men take a look, though. Earlier, you said she was moved here, sir. How can you tell that? The nearby shrubbery and grass look disturbed, as though he worked here, and there's blood all about."

"But notice her face," said Charles. "It's white as snow. I doubt there's enough blood in her veins to fill a thimble. All the blood on her clothing has oxidised, yet the blood on the ground has not. That blood was placed here as misdirection. Rather like stage-craft."

Martin smiled appreciatively. "Leave it to our expert to notice such things."

The duke remained on site for nearly an hour, talking with the man who discovered the body as well as Smith and Miles. Finally, as Westminster's clocks struck three, he and the tailor climbed back into the coach and headed towards Drummond House.

The party was long since over, with but one or two stragglers. Charles said goodnight to Kepelheim and climbed up to the master apartment. He told his valet to go to bed and then crept carefully into the bedchamber, trying not to wake the duchess. It felt strange to sleep here. He'd had many wonderful conversations with James Stuart in this apartment, sharing Drummond Reserve and listening to the duke's tales. The apartment seemed void and lifeless now. *How can James die?* It felt wrong, as though the Maze taunted him.

He began to undress. As with many master apartments in peerage homes, this one was situated at a corner and included multiple living areas: duke and duchess bedchambers, a spacious bath and robing rooms, a parlour, office, and library. He crossed through a robing room into the bath to wash his face.

The porcelain basin sat atop a walnut table trimmed in gold. Above the basin, hung a bright mirror, flanked by electric sconces. For the first time since arriving in this challenging 'locked room', Charles was able to examine his face. There were a few, additional age lines round the eyes. His hair was cut short, and the black beard trimmed into a *pike-devant*, or Van Dyke style. The now familiar scar on his right jaw (left by last year's explosion on Columbia Road) was missing. He felt at the back of his head. There should be a scar just above his neck from the same explosion; that scar was also missing.

Apparently, everything changes when I enter a new room of this Maze. Not just clothing; my physical appearance, too.

Then, he remembered Fenwick's promise. Charles reached into the right trouser pocket, exhaling with gratitude, for his fingers touched the silk of the red sash. Withdrawing it, he kissed the fabric, thinking of seven-year-old Elizabeth, who'd helped him find his way. He thought of the woman that child would become. She was his true wife, which begged the question: was the woman in the next bedroom his Beth, or someone else's?

"Charles?" called a soft voice. "Darling, did you go out?"

He had to talk to her, but would she be the same? Assessing a murder victim was tragic, but familiar ground. Trying to glean truth from a world not his own, was quite another.

Charles returned the sash to his pocket. He took a deep breath to steel his nerves and then crossed through to the duchess's bedchamber.

Immediately, he could smell it: raspberry and vanilla, the simple fragrance that represented his Elizabeth. The only light in the room was the dwindling fire, and he noticed a chill in the air.

"Have you been out?" she asked as he reached the bed. "Sit with me, Charles. Please. Tell me about your night."

He helped her to sit up, noticing the rounded abdomen of advanced pregnancy. She wore a lace-trimmed peignoir, which also smelled of raspberry and vanilla. Her wedding rings were the same.

The Pink Princess diamond surrounded by white diamonds. *At least, some things haven't altered.*

"I had to visit a crime scene," he told her.

"Was it him again? The Songbird Killer?"

"Yes. Darling, you're going to hear this or read it in tomorrow morning's newspapers, so let me tell you. The woman's body was discovered at Queen Anne House."

Her mouth opened a little, and her eyes widened. "Is everyone there all right? Was the victim one of our maids?"

"No, dear. And everyone's all right. Mrs. Smith was a little shaken up, as were the kitchen maids. The groom that found her as well. Morehouse and his men will likely be there until morning."

"Who was the victim?"

"A singer from the Lyceum. Beth, you should sleep."

"I can't, Charles. Actually, I haven't slept much at all. Did you talk with Paul tonight?"

"No, dear. I didn't see him."

"But he told me he was going to speak to you. Charles, he wants to explain. Please, tell me you'll let him do that."

"Explain what?" he asked, noticing she shivered. "It's cold in here. Shall I add some wood to the fire?"

"Not yet, but I'd take another blanket or quilt."

Two were folded at the foot of the bed, and he drew them both up over her body. "Better?"

"It would be warmer with you beside me."

Martin said she's nearly eight months pregnant. It's doubtful we're intimate now. "If you like."

She was holding his hand and gazing at it, turning it over and over. "Do you ever sense that the world is wrong, Charles?"

"How might the world be wrong?" he asked in amazement.

"I'm not sure. It feels empty somehow. As though all the air is escaping. As if everything is but a shadow without true substance." She reached up and touched his shoulder. "Do you think I might be seeing things again? Perhaps, the strain twixt you and Paul has caused some shadowy strain in me. You needn't answer me, Charles. I'm talking nonsense."

"Not at all," he said. "Beth, what strain is there betwixt Paul and me?"

"Is it possible I'm dreaming now?"

"I don't think so," he said, lying beside her, still fully clothed. He propped himself up on his left elbow, so he could look at her face. "Why do you ask that?"

"You're different. I can see you, but there's another you beneath. As though one is superimposed on another. For a moment, I thought I saw long hair, and your beard was full."

What? Could Elizabeth see his true self? Was it possible she had the ability to see beyond the Maze's games?

"Look carefully, darling. Look at my face." He drew her hand up. "Feel the jawline. Tell me what you sense."

Her soft fingertips traced his entire jaw, and then she felt along the shoulders again, and round to the back of his head.

"Well?" he asked.

"Shall I tell you the truth? Charles, my mind may be wandering—as it used to do. Are you afraid of that?"

"Not at all. Tell me honestly, little one."

Her eyes widened, and there was a sharp intake of breath. "You never call me that—but, the other you—the man in the Maze does. Are you making fun of me now?"

"No, darling! Not at all! I've called you little one for as long as I can remember. Since I first met you."

"The day I was born? That's when you met me, Charles. Father gave me to you and told you to look after me."

"Did he? Are you sure about that?"

Her hands grew cold, and she pulled the quilts up over them. "Don't ask me to talk about it."

"Little one, you may speak the truth. Tell me."

"I'm not sure about anything. I made the mistake of telling Paul, and he told Lorena. Did she say something to you?"

"I've not spoken to her, Beth. Darling, if I said my father died when I was five, and that I first met you in 1879, what would you say?"

Another sharp intake of breath, and then her brows furrowed as the duchess pondered his statement. "Can that be *true?* Paul says I dreamt it all, and Lorena thinks I should be placed into care at some asylum."

"I'd never allow that. Never. What did they say, Beth? And why did Paul and I argue? Was it about your memory?"

"You don't know?"

"Darling, if I told you that I'm not part of this world, what would you say?" he asked her gently, her hand in his. "If I said I only arrived here last night, would you think I'd gone mad and needed an asylum?"

"Am I dreaming now?"

"No, little one, you're not."

She breathed quickly, as if in pain. "Beth, are you all right?"

She smiled. "No, darling. Your son kicks again and wants to be born. Just one month more, darling."

He placed a hand on her round abdomen. The kicks were strong and came from two spots. "Do you know how many sons we'll have?" he asked.

"Six. Six strong oaks on a great hill."

"And two willows," he added for her. "And flying machines are all round?"

"Trying to kill the trees, yes!" she exclaimed. "You never believed me before. Charles, I..."

"You call me by another name in our true lives, little one. Do you remember it?"

She stared at him as if he were a completely new person. "Your hair's long now. Curling past your neck. You were injured on our wedding night."

"Yes."

"The night *he* died. Sir William."

"Trent. Yes."

"Captain Nemo," she whispered. "I call you Captain."

He kissed her hands. "Yes, little one! Yes! I'm your Captain."

"Charles, come home!" she cried suddenly. "I think I'm dreaming. Come home, please! We need you!"

He kissed her mouth, his senses filling with memories of their first night of lovemaking. She stroked his cheek. "Find me, Captain. Find the way home."

Her eyes closed, and the breathing became regular. Had she been asleep this entire time? Was he talking with his true wife as she also slept?

Charles stayed beside her in the large bed until the sun grew bright. Elizabeth snuggled in close.

Did his Elizabeth form some kind of nexus with this false world? The Maze wanted to test him, but *was it also testing her?*

How?

He had to escape—not only for himself. But for his little one. And for the sake of all the future oaks on that hill.

CHAPTER THIRTY
Time Maze – A Trip to Istseleniye Castle

Charles awoke next to Beth, her arm draped across his chest. How could it be true? Was his own, true Elizabeth really here with him? Perhaps, whilst in a dream elsewhere? There was no time to chase theories now. He had to determine the reason why the Maze had directed him into this false version of reality. To do that, he needed to speak to someone outside of time.

As Charles left the bed, he noticed several photographs set about the room. Most were of him with their children. In this version of the world, Robby and Georgianna were three year old, and a recent photograph showed them both, sitting on his knee. Robby was the spitting image of his father. Charles wondered if Albert might have looked the same at that age, had he lived. And Georgianna could have passed for a three-year-old version of her mother. He longed to visit the nursery and see them, but this world wasn't his home. He had to find a way back to his real children. His world.

He crept from the duchess's bedchamber and crossed through to his and dressed quickly, trying to keep as quiet as possible, so as not to wake his little one. She needed the rest, and though this wasn't his Beth fully, he couldn't help loving her.

The fog was particularly thick that morning, a dense grey miasma that made the journey through the West-End streets seem cold and surreal. He stopped to collect Kepelheim at his home on Wilton Crescent in Belgravia. The tailor hadn't yet eaten, nor had Charles, and so they enjoyed breakfast at a tea room specialising in the full Scottish: fried eggs, bacon, sausage, beans, tomato, mushrooms, tattie scones, and of course, haggis. Charles chose to forgo the latter but asked for Fearn Abbey sheep cheese and an additional scone.

Filled and ready for the day, the men climbed back into the Drummond coach, and Martin asked, "Where now? I assume we're not returning to your home, though I'd prefer it. Charles, are you certain seeing this man is wise?"

"I pray the Lord will allow me to see him," the duke told his friend. "Truthfully, Martin, I'm still trying to figure out why I'm here. Romanov may be allowed to answer it."

"Allowed by whom? Redwing?"

"By a much higher authority than that."

"Higher? Is this a philosophical question?"

"No, Martin, it's a practical one. I want to get back to my own reality and to my real wife."

"Are you saying Beth isn't real to you?"

"She's very much like my own Elizabeth, but she isn't mine. Not fully. We talked for a while when I returned to the house, and though I can't explain it, I think she's connected to my Elizabeth somehow. Beth sometimes dreams about the Time Maze. She calls it the 'too many faces' room. Perhaps she's with me in her dreams."

"Charles, none of that makes sense."

"I'm sure you think I'm losing touch with reality, but that's exactly what's happened."

Kepelheim shook his head. "And our current destination will help you to resolve all this?"

Charles sighed. "I don't know. I hope so. Martin, I've no idea how to proceed. I'm here without a map or guide. Theseus insisted it would all become clear to me once I entered the Maze, but thus far, nothing is clear. It's like trying to find my way through London's thickest fog."

"Perhaps, talking to someone would help," Martin suggested. "A professional, I mean. I've a friend who's very good about such things. And he's discreet."

"I also have a friend who's good at that. Also a professional," Sinclair answered as the coach passed by Margravene Manor cemetery.

"There it is!" shouted the duke as he tapped the roof with his hand.

"Charles, that's just a ruin," said Martin, for he could see only a run-down estate, where a Medieval castle once stood.

"Trust me. It's here," said the duke.

The driver turned the horses towards a narrow lane that ran beside the abandoned castle. Charles didn't wait for the groom to open his door. As soon as the coach stopped, he jumped out and ran up to the crumbling stone gates.

Kepelheim followed, carrying the duke's hat and coat. "Take these, Charles. It may be March, but winter's breath blows round us still. Please, put on the coat and hat before you freeze. You're becoming as nonchalant as your cousin about outerwear."

Charles did as ordered, but only to pacify his friend.

"Much better," Martin said as he made sure the coat was properly buttoned. "I should lengthen these sleeves a bit. Now, why've we stopped here?"

"Anatole lives here."

"Here? In this pile of rubble? No, Charles, that's impossible. Let's return to the coach and go visit my friend. Or even yours, if you prefer."

"I'm not mentally unstable, Martin. This is where he lives."

"Does he live beneath it all? In some hiding place?"

"He lives in the castle."

"Ah, I see," said Martin. "One might have thought the prince rich enough to afford a nicer place to live."

"This pile of rubble is an illusion," Charles answered. "You'll see what I mean shortly, assuming he's here. I'm not even sure that I can get inside. Henry had a devil of a time finding the path through the gates last year."

"Whatever do you mean?" asked Martin. "No one lives in this dilapidated hovel, except for a few bats and rats. Come, Charles, let's go home. I'll send for my friend, and we'll all have a nice chat."

"Have faith, Martin," said Charles, his eyes on Kepelheim's. "Faith is a very powerful weapon. Did you know the word faith appears in the Bible two-hundred and thirty-one times? All but two of those are in the New Testament. Jesus uses the word *faith* over and over. Beth told me that. My Beth. She and I were reading together one evening, and I mentioned my fears about a case the ICI was investigating."

"ICI?" asked Martin.

"Inner Circle Intelligence. Paul and I head it together. Beth said that faith fights fear, and then she mentioned how many times it's found in the Bible. She'd underlined it every time it occurred and counted them. Faith is part of our armour, Martin. It protects us from the enemy's assaults. The Apostle Paul prayed for the church at Thessalonica, that their faith might made perfect. What if all this is to strengthen and perfect *my faith?* What if the Maze is more than a testing ground? What if it's also a training ground?"

"And this pile of rubble will help with that?"

"It might, assuming the gates will let me through."

Kepelheim had begun to worry deeply about his friend, and he took the duke's arm, trying to lead him from the ruined gates. "Come, please, Charles. Let's go home."

"That house is not my home, Martin! James Stuart is alive. He is Duke of Drummond, not I. This whole locked room is about testing my faith in God, Martin."

"And exploring this ruin is part of that test?" asked Kepelheim. "Is this why you've dragged me to the very end of the city?"

"Sometimes, faith requires looking beyond our natural sight, Martin. Romanov's castle exists in a hidden realm. It's a refuge. A place of healing. In fact, its name Istseleniye means *healing* in Russian."

"Nonsense. Romanov would never live in such a place, nor would it be a place of healing! His tastes run to the exotic and very expensive and poisonous, I'm sure. He's rumoured to live near Marlborough House, though no one's ever found the exact location."

"He may keep a home there that's also beyond our sight. Not everything is as it seems at first glance. Have faith, Martin. Have faith!"

The duke removed his gloves. He reached out with his bare hand and touched one of the strange symbols on the pillar. A mild current of electricity ran from the rock into his hand, and the symbol began to glow. The frigid air round the two men warmed, and the dense fog parted. "Thank you, Lord," Charles whispered. Then to Kepelheim, he said, "I believe the prince just invited us in. You're about to see with new eyes, my friend."

Grudgingly, Martin followed Charles through the gate. At first, very little altered, save the air, which slowly grew warmer, carrying sweet scents that promised summer blooms and green grass. Several more steps forward, and the mist vanished, revealing a dazzling garden, filled with ripening fruit and colourful flowers. A fountain bubbled nearby, and turtle doves flew overhead.

At the heart of the impossible garden, stood the most beautiful castle Martin had ever seen. It looked as though the builders had only just finished it. Every stone, every timber, every roof tile, and every window sparkled and gleamed with dazzling newness. Even the trees seemed newly born, as though created solely for their enjoyment. Each impossible tree contained ripe fruit, as well as colourful blossoms upon its plentiful branches, offering fragrance to soothe the mind and food to fill the belly. The cobbled pathway curved gently to the right, through berry-laden hedges and graceful willows. The songs of every kind of bird filled their ears with music so glorious, it seemed straight out of heaven.

As they neared the main entrance, the men passed by a golden coach, presently being cleaned by a servant with thick black hair, parted down the centre. The servant bowed as Charles walked past. When the duke stepped onto the slate floor of the entry, the huge doors opened wide, and a man in black-and-red livery stepped out to greet them.

"Good morning, Duke Charles. Mr. Kepelheim," he said, bowing. "The prince is expecting you. This way, sirs."

The visitors entered, and Vasily, the prince's imposing looking butler, led them into the same drawing room where Elizabeth Sinclair had once enjoyed musical evenings with Stephen Blinkmire and Count Viktor Riga. Whilst he and Martin waited, the duke assessed the extraordinary room's Russian-style furnishings, fabrics, and wall coverings. He'd never seen the interior of the castle before; indeed he'd never enjoyed the unspoilt grounds, observed the unbroken battlements, or smelled the orange blossoms; for on that fateful night last December, when Henry led them through the gates to bring him news of Beth, all they found was a burnt-out ruin. He'd never seen Istseleniye Castle's splendour or felt its mysterious power.

His *faith* had opened the gate.

No wonder Elizabeth had loved this place so.

"Are we to speak to a wizard?" asked Martin. "If Romanov can conjure up this castle from ruins, what other unholy spells might he cast? Don't listen to him, Charles, please! He'll try to beguile you."

Before the duke could answer, the doors opened, and a familiar voice greeted them with, *"Dobroye utro, dzhentel'meny.* Good morning, gentlemen. The day is magnificent, no? Change is in the air. Now, tell me, what brings the esteemed Duke of Haimsbury and his tailor to my door this beautiful day?"

"He's the Duke of Drummond," said Kepelheim.

"No, he is Duke of Haimsbury. James Stuart is Duke of Drummond."

Martin laughed. "See, Charles? Apparently, your wizard cannot even keep up with peerage matters! No doubt, he is too busy conjuring up spells for Redwing."

"That's enough, Martin," Charles warned his friend. "I need to talk to him, please. Forgive him, Your Highness," the duke told Romanov. He shook the Russian's hand, finding it warm, friendly, almost brotherly. "We apologise for dropping by without warning, but we have need of your counsel and trust you have the answers we seek."

"Ah, yes, I see," said Romanov, glancing at Kepelheim. "I shall be pleased to offer counsel, Duke Charles, but only one of you trusts me."

"And why should I trust you?" Martin snapped. "You may bear a noble title, sir, but your actions are hardly that."

"My actions?" asked the Russian. "What actions do you mean?"

"Give me a book of paper, and I shall fill it!"

"I could give you a library of books to fill, Mr. Kepelheim, but you'd find every entry contained a misconception."

"How dare you!"

"Enough!" Charles interrupted. "Please, may we set this argument aside for now? This Martin Kepelheim doesn't know who you really are, Anatole."

"And this prince is the same no matter the place or time," Martin grumbled. "Charles, we should go before this one bewitches you."

"He is not a wizard, Martin. Please, if you cannot trust him, then trust me, all right?" He turned to Romanov. "Anatole, I believe this castle is outside the confines of the Maze and its locked rooms and mirrors. If my hope is true, then help me."

"Shall we all sit?" the other replied cordially. The visitors took chairs near the fire, and Anatole sat opposite the large windows. "Tell me, Charles, what is your impression of these locked rooms and mirror worlds?"

"Pay no heed to his question," Martin interrupted. "We're leaving."

"No, we're not," Sinclair told him firmly. "Anatole, I'm inside a locked room now, and I think the Lord allows it so I might learn some great lesson, but how do I know when I've learnt it? Beth once told me this castle existed outside time. And so I prayed God would allow me to find it."

"Yet, you brought a man with you who doubts. I wonder why the gates allowed him in?"

"Clearly, you allowed us both in to perform some trick!" the tailor interrupted again. "Charles, let's go. Romanov isn't to be trusted, and this phantom castle is proof of his occult abilities. Come with me, please!"

"He fears for you, Charles. Is it not a comfort to know our dear Martin Kepelheim is ever true?"

"Don't pretend to know me, sir," the tailor warned.

"The good tailor thinks me an enemy. Do you think me an enemy, Charles?"

"Of course, not," the duke answered. "I assume this castle exists outside of the Maze's tricks. Am I breaking the rules by coming here?"

"I'm sure Theseus and my rebel brothers would say that you are, but their opinions have no weight. However, the fact that the veiled gates opened to you, shows me the One approves of your visit. Shall we have tea?"

As if silently summoned, Vasily and a similarly liveried footman entered. Each pushed a rolling cart, set with a chased silver samovar, sugar, tea, and tea glasses with their silver filigree holders. A tiered stand held hearty sandwiches made from yeast rolls, filled with tender beef and pungent cheeses. There were ripe orange sections, crusted in vanilla-flavoured sugar; pecan and apple tarts; frosted raisin cakes; candied cherries dipped in chocolate; and a silver bowl of salted nuts.

The servants poured the tea and arranged the food on a marble-topped ebony table, carved into the shape of a roaring lion.

"I find these *piroshkis* particularly delightful," the Russian told them with a handsome smile. "The filling includes mushrooms and garlic, along with the beef and cheese."

"That's kind of you, Anatole, but Martin and I ate just before we arrived here."

"Did you?" the angel asked with a tiny smile. "Are you certain of that fact?"

To his very great surprise, Charles felt hungry, very hungry, as if his stomach hadn't been filled for years. He looked at his friend, and Martin had already added two piroshkis to a plate.

"Mr. Kepelheim is wise. Eat, Charles," Romanov advised him. "What happens in this house happens for a reason, and it brings healing. That is why it is called Istseleniye House. When you leave here, no matter how much you eat, you will not feel overfed. So enjoy. And if you like desserts, the sugared oranges are particularly good. The Duchess Elizabeth enjoyed them often, when she was here."

"She still talks about the food and has our cooks make Russian tea cakes and sugared fruit for all our guests now," Charles replied. "No milk for my tea. Thank you."

The servants completed their tasks and left the room, closing the doors.

"No milk? I thought you enjoyed 'a splash' as you English say," opened Romanov. "Or are you adopting a new persona for this world?"

Sinclair laughed. "I'd hoped you might notice that small change. Yes, I generally add milk, but not today."

"Mr. Kepelheim, what do you think of your friend? Has he altered in any way?"

"I cannot say, Your Highness. I begin to think I'm in my bed and dreaming all this. And I'm sure you know, our circle members place no faith in you."

"I appreciate your honesty, but faith is the point," the prince replied with a handsome smile. "Charles can explain my apparent duplicity to you at a later time, but I imagine there are other things on his mind just now. The One allows your visit, so what would you ask me, my friend?"

Sinclair took a sip of the tea. "What can you tell me about Alphonse Theseus?"

"Ah, the very interesting Dr. Theseus. He is a strange fellow, don't you think?" the Russian said as he stirred sugar into his tea. "His fellow conspirators call him the halfling. They think to insult him by this, but Theseus wears the label with a fierce kind of pride."

"Does he really see himself as superior?" asked Sinclair.

"Oh, yes. Theseus believes he rises above humans and above all the elohim. The Creator never meant for such mixtures to occur, you understand. When Semjâzâ and his rebel followers left the upper realms and descended to Mount Hermon, a tidal wave of miscegenations followed, and the rest is, as you say, history. But histories become confused when passing through the Time Maze. Theseus was forced to pass through its turnings and complications as a young hybrid to prove his worth, and it altered him forever. He believes this alteration makes him greater, wiser, and even more powerful than the elohim. He is wrong."

"Theseus? Surely you cannot mean the mythological being," Kepelheim objected.

"Of course, I do. The word myth does not mean untruth, Mr. Kepelheim. It merely refers to heroic epics, accounts of actions performed by the gods and demigods."

"Gods? Plural?" asked the tailor.

"Do not play coy with me, Mr. Kepelheim," warned Romanov. "I know you much better than you realise, and your storehouse of ancient knowledge is deep. With multiple layers and hidden meanings."

Charles had a feeling the angel was speaking in code. Why? *Is it meant for me? Or for Martin?*

"The gods are just fallen angels," the duke told his friend. "Go on, Your Highness. You were explaining about Theseus."

"He is a demigod," the prince replied, "but he lives quietly now and goes by Alphonse Theseus. Despite this outward appearance of diminution, he is still the proud halfling that founded Athens."

"Myth! Nothing but myth!"

"Duke Charles is well aware of the truths behind the myths, Mr. Kepelheim, and this version of the Stuart-Sinclair inner circle is only now beginning to discern them."

"This version, sir?" asked Kepelheim. "There is only one."

"There are many, when considering the concept of fractured chronology."

Martin stirred three sugars into his tea. "Poetic Russian nonsense."

"It is neither poetic nor is it Russian, Mr. Kepelheim, but the consequence of rebellion and free-will choices. Allow me to introduce a metaphor. Think of time as a mirror. A hammer blow would cause it to shatter, yes?"

"I suppose so."

"But if you place a sharp icepick at just the right spot, then tap with the tiniest pressure, you could create a web of fine lines, radiating outwards like a spider's web. There would be no brutal shattering of the glass. Instead, you would have hundreds of individual mirrors, that all belong to the original mirror. Free will is similar. If you choose to go left at Piccadilly, your journey continues on that line. If, however, you go right, then your feet take you in an entirely different direction."

"I don't understand," said the tailor. "Perhaps, my brain is too small, or more likely, this is nothing but Redwing lies."

The prince took no offence. "I appreciate your candor, Mr. Kepelheim, but the physics of Creation are not up for debate, nor are they dependent upon any interpretation by Redwing members. Allow me to try another way to explain it. As we know, Charles studied mathematics at Cambridge."

Martin interrupted. "Oxford."

"No, Cambridge," the Russian repeated. "Trinity College. He took firsts in all the tripos and graduated in three years with honours."

"Yes, but those honours were earned at Oxford," the tailor insisted. "I should know. I visited him there often enough."

"Are you certain of that? Or does this mirror shard make it *seem* you did? Reflections are not reality, Mr. Kepelheim."

"Is there no end to your mirror metaphors?" asked Kepelheim, whose rising vocal pitch revealed his frustration level.

"My dear Mr. Kepelheim, I use that metaphor because mirrors form the very heart of this test, as Charles knows all too well," said Anatole. "But to put this in mathematical terms, let us consider an equation that requires calculating the sum of a man's life, written as x. The equation consists of all variables that combine to form a life on the left of the equal sign, and the x, representing the man's life, on the right."

"Yes, and?" asked Martin.

"And the equation must be solved with an infinite number of variables on the left but just one constant to divide them."

"That's impossible!" declared the tailor. "An infinite number? You're being intentionally obscure. Any Oxford student would declare such an equation a fool's errand."

"Cambridge," the prince countered with a wink at Charles.

"Have we all gone mad?" shouted Kepelheim, wiping sweat from his brow with a handkerchief.

"I did study at Cambridge, Martin," the duke said softly. "And I agree with Anatole regarding that sort of equation. I assume the one constant is God, for only he is the same yesterday, today, and forever."

The angel smiled. "You were always a fine student, Charles Robert." He turned to the tailor. "Mr. Kepelheim, there is but one capital T *Truth*. Only one version of God's reality; that which he has worked together for good. Yet, the duke now traverses a deep Maze that presents infinite options within dazzling mirrors; tempting shards of reflected truth, to enter and discover."

"I'm very confused now, Your Highness. If all these mirrors, all these variations are lies, then how is Charles here? How am I here?"

"You are a shadow within a reflection, Mr. Kepelheim. Nothing more. Charles has stepped into a shadow of himself."

"That is preposterous!" shouted the outraged tailor. "I'm obviously real. The coach that brought us to your gates is real. London is real. You are mad as a hatter, but I'm even madder, to sit here and listen to it. Charles, let's leave this phantom castle!"

"I tell you that the One is allowing Charles to enter into these shadowy shards for his purposes, Mr. Kepelheim. Charles not only looks into a darkling glass, he has stepped *through it*."

"Very well. If so, then has he stepped *into* God's singular truth, or out of it?" asked the tailor. "Scripture says God is everywhere. If God is Truth, then how is this place a lie?"

"God is Truth, but lies still exist. And I did not say this shard is a lie, but a shadow," the prince answered. "Have you never dreamt of another version of your life, Mr. Kepelheim? A version where you might be older, younger, thinner, fatter, richer, poorer, married, or not married?"

"Yes, of course, I have. Everyone's had such dreams, but they are only dreams, Your Highness. Nothing more."

"*Only* dreams?" asked the elohim patiently. "Do not discount the power of dreams, Mr. Kepelheim. Does not the One speak through dreams? To Joseph, to pharaoh, to Jacob? Have you read Job? The One speaks to men in dreams, in visions of the night, in slumberings upon the bed. The One, whom you English call God whispers secrets into the minds of men and reveals his great plans through dreams."

"Even Satan knows the scriptures, but he fails to see their merit and does not believe," said the tailor.

"Oh, he believes, Mr. Kepelheim. He believes it all, but that adversary is convinced that he, along with those of his own inner circle, can circumvent God's final judgement. They are all wrong."

"Am I to trust you, then? Knowledge of the Bible's truths does not equate to belief unto salvation, sir."

Anatole smiled. "And if I told you that Charles has dreamt dreams and endured hardships sent by God, to prepare him for a great future? That he will perform a pivotal role regarding the fulfillment of prophecy? Would you think that a marvel, Mr. Kepelheim? Or would you call that a lie as well?"

The tailor grew silent, his eyes on the duke. "I've no doubt my friend will play a great role in the future, just as he does even now. But you imply he is at the whim of Redwing's plots; that he wanders through a shadowy, mirror-shard world like some puppet. The Charles Sinclair I know would *never* be a puppet, I tell you. Never!"

If Martin Kepelheim had been a knight with a sword, he would have drawn it, but as his only weapon that morning was a butter knife, he brandished it bravely at their host. "I do not trust you, Romanov, nor will I ever!"

"Martin, if your faith in me is that strong, then heed my words. I believe the prince," said Sinclair, taking the tailor's knife and setting it back on the table. "Everything he says is true. If you care for me and my family, please let him speak. I've come here for advice, not to debate."

The prince waved his hand, and every one of their knives turned into a spoon. "There. Let us put an end to enmity."

Martin began to grumble into his plate of raisin cake.

"Yours is a difficult path, Charles Robert," said Romanov, ignoring the tailor. "Take heart. You will find its end soon. Your entry into this locked room, as Theseus calls it, has already convinced the fallen realm that your blood is true, but your journey is not yet over. The One brought you here to learn and grow in your faith. He allows the test to continue, and he allows the Maze to lure you into its traps."

"You say that as if the labyrinth were alive."

"It is," the angel answered without hesitation. "It is alive with suspicion, anger, deceit, and hatred. All these come from the Keeper. You must face him before the end."

"Then, I may return home?" asked Charles. "My wife needs me."

"The *world* needs you, Charles Robert," declared the angel.

"Anatole, is Elizabeth connected to this test?"

Romanov gazed at the duke, his icy eyes gleaming. "An interesting question. How might she be connected?"

"I'm not sure, but perhaps in dreams."

"And?"

"Beth often dreams of a place that sounds very much like the Time Maze. Does she travel in her dreams?"

"Ah, a very interesting word."

"Dreams?" asked the duke.

"Travel," said Anatole. The tailor muttered something about nonsense, but the prince ignored it and continued. "Humans presume that travel indicates physical movement from one place to another, but travelling is also possible in the spirit. I have already explained that the One sometimes speaks to his children through dreams, but here is a question: does the One come to you, or do you travel to the One?"

Charles considered this for a moment whilst sipping the tea. "Numerous prophets and disciples talked of being 'in the spirit', so I imagine we travel to God."

"Thus, a man can travel without using his body, correct?"

"Are you saying we choose to travel, or that we're made to travel?"

Anatole refilled his cup and added sugar and lemon. "Presently, there are some who call themselves spiritualists, who teach a concept they call *astral travel*. They teach a self-willed departure of the spirit from the physical body. Most in this movement are charlatans, but a few use dark arts to open forbidden portals. Their travels are real. As you're aware, reality consists of multiple layers or dimensions. This castle is invisible to most eyes, but Henry MacAlpin can see it; as can you. The gates opened to you, Charles—but not because you spoke an incantation. It was because you asked the One to open them; the same way you prayed to the One to open the Maze."

Charles smiled. "God opened those doors in a most spectacular way."

"Yes. Sometimes, our Creator speaks with thunder, sometimes with the softest whisper. But remember, he holds the true keys. Spiritualists use false keys to force the portals open. Like one of your housebreakers, they think themselves clever, but this leaves them open to manipulation by the enemy."

"And is Beth allowed to take dream journeys? Or is that doll involved? Does it force the portals open and drag Elizabeth through?"

"The doll is evil. William Trent used occult science and spells to design it. Do you remember the small bag of tiny bones that hangs from its neck?"

"I'd forgotten about that, but yes. Strangely, after we recovered the doll from the tunnels last year, it disappeared again."

"A demon took it. I watched him steal the doll when your family were celebrating Christmas. I sought permission to destroy the doll, but the One has another use for it—as he works all things together for good."

"What use?" asked Charles.

Anatole smiled. "He's not yet told me, but I trust my General. Therefore, I await his orders regarding the doll."

"Doll? What doll?" asked Kepelheim. "What are you talking about?"

"It's a likeness of Elizabeth, down to the tiniest details," the duke explained. "Bisque face, hair that looks real."

"The hair is real, and some is from a dead child," said Anatole. "As are those bones. Not the same child, but both are related to the duchess. Her own hair is mixed into the scalp, and some of her skin cells were mixed into the clay that forms the bisque face. That doll is similar to a pagan statue and provides a physical form for a demon. That is why Elizabeth dislikes the doll so much."

"Why was she carrying it, then? If she dislikes it, how did it become part of her dream?" asked the duke.

"The doll's influence is quite strong. Or rather the demon's is. She feels connected to it because of the bones."

"Does she know the bones are there?" asked Charles.

"No. Not at all, and you mustn't tell her."

"Wait, you said the bones and hair came from children related to Beth. Who were they?"

Charles had a very great dread of this answer, for he'd begun to reason out the answer. Romanov waited, remaining silent to allow his friend to follow those thoughts and give voice to his suspicion.

"Tell me Trent didn't dig up Beth's dead elder brothers!" Charles cried out at last. "Tell me he wasn't that fiendish!"

"He was and is. A demon inhabited the body of Sir William Trent. And yes, he used the aborted sons' hair and bones to fashion the doll."

Suddenly, Charles wanted to lash out, or else vomit. Anger rose up in his spirit and bile into the back of his throat. "How can anyone be so cruel?"

"Demons have no limits to their cruelty, Charles, nor do some humans. Elizabeth knows nothing of her elder brothers. If you decide to tell her one day, be gentle. Talk with Inspector Baxter about the doll."

"Yes, I will," muttered the duke.

Anatole reached over and placed a hand on the duke's forearm. The angel shut his eyes and whispered a prayer in a heavenly language. In response, warmth and strength spread throughout the human's spirit and body. Anatole continued to whisper, then after several minutes, he opened his eyes. "The One would tell you this, Charles Robert. The doll will come into Elizabeth's life once more, in the spring. Look for it, and when you see it, use scripture. Speak the Word, and the demon will flee."

"What scripture?"

"When the time comes, you will know. The Spirit will bring it to your thoughts."

"And what of the doll?"

"Give it to the brown owl. He will destroy it."

"Owls? Cursed dolls?" asked Kepelheim. "This is all mumbo-jumbo nonsense and proves you're a wizard! Charles, I beg you to come with me, please."

"I'm staying, Martin. Thank you," he told the angel. "And Beth? How is she connected to this? Is it solely because of the doll?"

"Not at all. The One connected the two of you before Time began. Even now, Elizabeth dreams, and whilst dreaming, she connects to you—both as a child and as an adult. The enemy knows this and tries to hurt her through your journey, but trust in the One and in the Son, whose blood covers you both and all your children. And remember, the One has permitted this challenge to prepare you for a very great future, all according to his plans. Shortly, you will leave this mirror shard, but not before your heart is broken. Afterward, you will proceed through the remaining challenges with greater speed. Each will teach you a lesson about yourself and your true past. Finally, you'll be shown a vision of your future. The One allows this to strengthen your resolve and encourage you for a great purpose. No one in the fallen realm will see this vision. It is for you alone. They must remain blind to the One's plans."

"I think I understand," Charles whispered. "God will lead me home?"

"Yes, but you must defeat the Keeper first."

The duke grew silent, considering the gravity of the angel's words. "Very well, then. If God chooses to show me a vision, then I pray only to be worthy of that choice. His power is mighty and his plan perfect. When the great prophet Isaiah was called up to heaven, he saw the very throne of God. In that place of judgement and power, he heard God's plans discussed and was asked, whom shall I send, and who will go for us? And though I'm imperfect and feel incapable, you say that God wants me to follow this path and endure this test. To this I can only say, here I am, Lord. Send me. I submit to your plans. And if God chooses to slay me, then I submit to even that."

The angel gazed upon the human with great compassion. "As one of your elder brothers, Charles, I must tell you that your light shines very brightly!"

"Anatole, if my light shines at all, then it is only the reflection of the Saviour. Elder brother?"

"Of course!" Romanov exclaimed. "All who accept the sacrifice of the Son are our brothers; those prodigals whom the Shepherd leads home. You were created to replace the fallen rebels in the great council, and the One stands ready to place a signet ring upon your hand and a crown upon your head. For now, what more would you ask of me, little brother?"

Charles laughed. "Now, that is something I never imagined you saying. But, yes, since you're speaking plainly, tell me, what is the purpose of that strange chamber at the centre of my home?"

"Ah, it is strange room, no? That chamber is all that remains of an ancient temple that stood at the fork of the Thames and the Tyburn. The Iceni tribe worshipped a goddess there. She's used a thousand names or more. Rhiannon, Epona, the Morrigan, Ishtar, Venus, Inanna, even Hekate. In 47 A.D., the Romans ransacked the temple. The soldiers stopped, shortly before reaching the mirror chamber, because the goddess appeared to them and promised to protect Londinium if they would worship her. She called herself Epona, a goddess of horses and war. The trick worked, for that chamber stands even now. It contains the oracle's mirror."

"The black mirror that forms part of the door?"

"Yes. You passed through it as a child."

"I remember now," Charles whispered. "That's the real reason I was trying to find the mirror the morning my father was killed. But what is the writing? Why is it there?"

"That temple is connected to the Time Maze. I placed the marks upon the walls many ages ago, to prevent the Keeper from escaping. The black mirror leads into the Maze, you see."

"How is this Keeper involved with a temple to a goddess?"

"They are both part of an otherworld kingdom, ruled by a greater evil. Your cousin, Paul Stuart, nearly fell into that abyss, but you and Henry saved him. However, the goddess marked him, meaning she will try again to lure him inside. I have offered my help to the earl. He is a somewhat stubborn Scotsman."

Martin stared at the duke, his grey eyes moving across his friend's face and form, as if looking for subtle differences. "I feel as if I'm falling through a vortex of madness! The Red Queen will come in soon, I'm sure, and call for my head. All this talk of temples and goddesses, cursed dolls and mazes. You, sir, are a mad prince, and this is not the Charles Sinclair I know."

"No, I'm not," Charles said in a measured, compassionate tone. "Look at me carefully. Concentrate and let your mind relax. Really look."

"Very well, but only to prove you wrong." The tailor took a sip of tea and then shut his eyes for a moment. When he opened them again, he did as Charles asked. He stared at the duke for a very long time. Finally, his eyes rounded, and shock ran through the man's features. "It cannot be! No, I refuse to see this!" he exclaimed, placing his hands over his eyes. "You're too tall, and your hair's long. No, this is some mad vision!"

Charles reached for his friend's hand. "Martin, you are not mad. I am just over six-three, according to your own measurement, and my hair is long. My beard is full. You make most of my clothing, and you were never married; though you do court a fine woman named Calhoun."

"Iris Calhoun?" the tailor mouthed, barely breathing from shock.

"Yes, Iris Calhoun. She's quite lovely, and you've said you hope to marry her one day."

"Iris is very charming," the other whispered. "Marriage to her? That would be nice."

"I attended Harrow and then Cambridge," Charles continued, looking into his friend's eyes. "I also performed several piano concerts at the college chapel, which were well received."

"You play the piano?"

"Yes. As to my childhood, my father died when I was five, and my mother died shortly after. I grew up thinking I was the adopted son of Edna and Elijah Burke. I served with London's Metropolitan Police and Scotland Yard for thirteen years, which led to my first meeting with Elizabeth in 1879. We married in November of 1888, and we have three-month old twins, a boy and a girl. I am Duke of Haimsbury, not Drummond, for James Stuart still lives, praise God! This version of my life is just a shard in a metaphorical mirror."

Romanov smiled at his pupil. "I should like to take credit for that metaphor, Charles, but it's actually yours. Whilst you lived with me as a boy, we discussed the One's promise to work all things together for good. You said it might be like a mirror, quoting St. Paul's first letter to the Corinthians, regarding the looking glass."

"I remember that," said the duke wistfully. "You asked if free-will choices might cause cracks to form upon that glass, producing shards of reflected life."

Romanov smiled again, his light blue eyes sparkling. "We'd been discussing the nature of Chaos, and you wisely suggested such an enemy might break our free-will mirror, but God, being all-powerful and all-knowing, could find every shard and transform them into a single mirror again. You were scarcely six years old."

"And you spent every moment challenging my beliefs and sharpening my mind. Were you preparing me for the Maze?"

"Yes, Charles Robert. I was. But also for what comes after the Maze."

Kepelheim had grown quiet again and stared at his hands.

"Mr. Kepelheim, you are still troubled, I think," said Romanov.

"Am I real or just a shadow on a shard of glass?" the tailor asked, his voice almost childlike.

"Charles, what do you think?" the angel asked the duke.

Sinclair took a deep breath, his mind focusing on the problem. "If you want the truth, then I think all of this is a shadow. A reflection of possibility, but only that. The question is why does the fallen realm want me to believe this is a true but alternate version of my life?"

"And why would God bring you to this particular shard of mirror?" Kepelheim voiced. "And why did you decide to confide in me?"

Romanov answered the tailor's question. "You begin to understand, Mr. Kepelheim. And Charles confided in you, because he trusts you. Even as a dream figure, your mind and personality are strong, for you dispute your role and argue with Charles and with me. I've known few men with such conviction, Mr. Kepelheim. If you were you a building, you could withstand any gale, any shaking of the earth. All the mountains would fall before you did, sir."

"Ah, I'd prefer to be a library, if I may choose the metaphor," the tailor quipped. "But still, it's good to know Charles trusts me."

"And because of that strength, I knew you'd help me," Charles told his friend. "Even though you argue with me. Martin, you've been my closest confidant ever since I was a boy, and after I learnt my true identity, you became the rock to which I tether my line."

The tailor smiled at last, his grey eyes glistening. "Ah, my very dear friend, there is no greater compliment. But where do we go from here? Are you to dream something new?"

"I'm not sure. How do I leave this mirror shard, Anatole?"

"As the Maze is not strictly a physical place, you must wait for your guide."

"But Beth led me here."

"Yes. And the little duchess was led by a whispering voice, remember?" asked the prince. "Both you and she have walked the corridors of the Maze many times as children. She calls it the 'too many faces' dream world. You also dreamt of it, when you were young. You called it the dragon world. You and she sit at the heart of the fractured mirror—a fracture that commenced the moment you stepped through the Maze's doors."

"Are you suggesting that God heals a fracture *before* it was created?" Charles shook his head. "It's exceedingly complex. I understand the theoretical concept, Anatole, but as with an equation with one constant, I could neither write nor solve it."

"Nor could I, Charles. Like you, my brethren and I are created beings. We are finite. Only the One is all-knowing and all-powerful," said the prince.

"Amen," said Sinclair. "If I require a guide to leave this shard, should I talk to Beth again?"

"Yes, but you may also talk with the Elizabeth of this shard. She knows, but only when she is dreaming," the prince answered plainly.

"And Adele? Is she safe?"

"Yes, the Lady Della is safe, but she needs her father to find total healing. And she will see you again! Your future is bright, Charles Sinclair. You and your sons will one day fulfill prophecy and change the world. Go now and find the centre. I shall meet you there."

As soon as the final word finished, the mysterious angelic prince vanished. The beautiful drawing room, the castle, the servants, the impossible gardens with fruit and flower, the coach, and every cobble in the courtyard returned to their previous ruined state.

Kepelheim looked as though he might faint.

Charles seemed unfazed by the prince's behaviour. "Come, Martin, we've work to do."

CHAPTER THIRTY-ONE
Real World – Montmore House

The sun had long since set by the time Paul Stuart and Henry MacAlpin returned to the asylum. As promised, Paul's butler had personally delivered a packed bag and extra weaponry to Montmore, and he'd even unpacked it all in the second bedchamber of Cordelia's apartment. Elizabeth took a one-room suite near Adele on the north side of the house. And Seth had also moved into the large home and now occupied a small bedroom near Henry.

Shortly before supper, Paul passed by Elizabeth in the corridor. "Sorry about all this," he said.

"Sorry about what, darling? Impending fatherhood?"

"No, of course not. I mean my wife's rash decision to come here. It's forced all of us to crowd into Henry's house. I'm sure it's an inconvenience."

"Nonsense," she said sweetly. "Babies seldom respect our timetables, Paul. They know only their own schedules. He'll be born, when he's ready to be born. And besides, it might be God's will that Delia's here right now."

"Do you really think so?"

"Let's assume it is and allow him to work his will upon it all, shall we?" She reached up on tiptoe to kiss his cheek. "You'll want to shave soon, Cousin. Newborn skin is very tender, and I imagine Cordelia appreciates a less prickly face for kissing. She was just waking when I passed through. Go see your wife."

The earl kissed Beth's cheek in return and then entered the apartment. Whilst he and Henry were away, Elizabeth and the nurses had been busy. They'd stocked the room with Cordelia's clothing, medicine, and even her special pillow and bath soap. The bedside table had a large photograph of the couple, taken on their wedding day last December, along with Paul's Bible, inherited from his grandmother.

Delia was just sitting up, and he stepped over quickly to help with her pillows. "Thank you," she whispered.

"Any more contractions?" Paul asked as he sat on the bed's edge.

"None. Dr. MacKey came by a little while ago. She offered to stay here at Montmore, if I wanted, but I wasn't sure."

"Do you feel comfortable with her?"

"Yes, Paul, I do. Somehow it's easier to talk to another woman. Did Dr. MacAlpin come back with you?"

"He did. I think he's downstairs talking to Adele."

"Della's said some very odd things," Cordelia told him. "Paul, did you see my brother today? Is he still at the London?"

"My men took William to Loudain House this afternoon."

"What about my mother? Did she leave me again? Have the two of you quarrelled?"

The question startled the earl. Could Delia have forgotten about her mother's remarriage? "Your mother's still on her wedding trip, remember? She and Lord Brackamore are touring the Continent and then sailing to Cairo. I doubt they'll return before Christmas."

"Oh, yes. I'd forgotten," she sighed. "Christmas will be too late, I think." She reached for his hand. "Paul, am I dying?"

"No, dearest, not at all. And I think you're very brave. Did it hurt when Dr. MacKey inverted the baby?"

"A little, yes. Beth nearly died after giving birth, didn't she? Do all women bleed that much?"

"You'll bleed a little, but don't be afraid, *mo bhean*. God is with you."

"Will you be here, too? I overheard Mrs. Winstead say this room's too small for a lot of people. She said you'd have to remain outside. That only medical people could be here with me. Charles was with Beth when she delivered the twins. Can't you be here, too?"

"I'll be right by your side, dearest. Just as Charles was with Beth. Now, would you eat something? There are delicious smells coming up from the kitchen."

"Could you bring it up here?"

"Of course. Henry has no lift, which means you're to remain on this floor until after your recovery."

"Might you stay up here and eat with me? I don't want to be alone, Paul. I'm afraid. I wish I hadn't come here now. I should have stayed at Haimsbury House."

"What frightens you, *mo bhean?*"

"Everything," she whispered. "I hate being alone."

"You're not alone, darling. Even if I'm away, Della and Beth will be here. And Henry. You like Henry, don't you?"

"Yes, but not the *others*. Not the... not the dead ones."

She'd been so lucid, so tethered to reality that her departure to the old visions startled the earl, but he managed to keep his expression neutral as he asked, "What dead ones, darling?"

"Father's out there, but also another. A monstrous thing with sharp teeth. Please, don't leave me alone, Paul."

"I won't. I promise."

"Be careful in the gardens. They walk in the gardens, you know. Mrs. Emmerdale knows about them. Ask her."

"I will, dear. I promise."

"You do believe me, don't you? I saw them, Paul. Father and that other. A great wolf man."

This caught his attention. "Wolf man?"

"He carries a cane with a wolf's head on it. He's terrifying, with sharp teeth and red eyes! But there are many others, and they walk in the garden next door."

"Not Henry's garden?"

"No. Henry's garden is peaceful, but you can see the other garden from his, and also through my windows. They walk up there, too. On the top floor of the other house."

"Hemsfield House?"

"I don't know what it's called."

"I'll go check it out right away, darling. Do you trust me?"

"Yes," she whispered, her hands trembling. "Do you believe in premonitions?"

Another switch in topic. Or was it? "Yes, sometimes, if they're from God."

"I don't know if it's from God or not," she sighed. "I saw you, Paul. You were bleeding. Shot. I thought you might be... That you might be dead."

She began to cry, and he pulled her close, stroking her thick hair. "Did someone tell you about yesterday morning?"

"No. Why? Did something happen? Is that why you were delayed in Whitechapel?"

"Did you see a newspaper today or yesterday?"

"No, why? What happened? Has Charles come back? Is that what happened?" she asked anxiously.

"I wish he had, but no, he hasn't. He's still..."

"In America, right?"

"Yes, that's right, darling. He's travelling for the Crown. Now, look at me, Delia. Do I look ill? Do I seem harmed in any way?"

"No. You look fine."

"Then I've survived whatever premonition you had." He removed the waistcoat and shirt to show the bandage beneath. "I've promised to be honest with you, which is why I'm doing this. See the bandage? Yesterday morning, someone fired a pistol into a crowd, and one of the bullets struck my side."

Her eyes widened. "But you're all right?"

"Yes, dear, I'm just fine. Delia, I've been shot dozens of times over the years. That's why I have so many scars."

"Like the one on your left shoulder?" she asked as she touched the year-old scar. "When did that happen?"

"Last October. A man shot me whilst Charles, Beth, and I were on a train for Branham. Darling, men shoot at me quite often, and I'm usually able to avoid being hit, but a bullet will find its mark now and then. Leaving marks on me. God keeps me going, though. Trust in him, if you ever doubt. I'm in his mighty hands."

Someone knocked on the outer door. "Give me a minute!" the earl called as he hastily dressed. "All right. Come in."

Esther Alcorn Baxter's friendly face appeared in the door as it opened, accompanied by her bear of a husband. "Good evening, sir," said Esther. "Neil and I brought a few things for her ladyship."

"Mrs. Baxter, it is very good to see you," the earl said happily. "Inspector, I'd hoped to see you again this evening. Might our wives talk whilst we discuss other matters?"

"My very inclination, sir," said the detective. He placed a large basket on the nearest table and kissed his wife's cheek. "Let me know if you need anything. Lord Aubrey and I will be a while, I imagine."

"Take your time," Esther told her husband. "Women need time to talk, too. Lord Aubrey, we saw Lady Adele on our way in. She asked us to tell you supper's at eight with a piano recital and dramatic reading to follow."

Paul smiled. The idea of hearing Della play the piano or read aloud always made him happy. *If only Charles were here to enjoy it.*

Once the men had gone, Esther began to unpack the items from the basket. "I understand you had a bit of a scare yesterday."

"I was so very foolish, Mrs. Baxter. It's a wonder I didn't kill my baby."

"Now, no more talk like that. And you promised to call me Esther, remember?" said the elder woman. "Besides, wanting to visit Adele isn't so foolish. I'm sure she's pleased as punch to see her Napper again."

"Yes, she is. And the dog's happy to see Adele. I'm very confused about it, though. Did Adele leave for a little while? I sometimes feel as if I'm dreaming."

"Is that so? I sometimes wonder the same thing," Esther told her patiently. "What happens in your dreams, my lady?"

"I see things," Cordelia answered. "Sometimes, I see my father. He tells me the strangest things. He said Charles isn't in America. Is that true?"

"Duke Charles is working very hard," Esther answered vaguely. "Now, I brought some of your favourite perfumes and soaps for your bath. There's even some rose petals from the Queen Anne gardens. The bushes are nearly at the end of their season, and this will be the last, I imagine. The white petals have such a lovely scent to them."

"That's very kind of you. Esther, how will I know I'm in true labour, if yesterday was false?"

"Oh, you'll know, my lady. For one, your waters will break."

"Waters?"

Mrs. Baxter set the basket aside. "Has Dr. Gehlen told you nothing of what to expect, Lady Aubrey?"

"Please, call me Delia. Lady Aubrey's so very formal."

"That's kind of you, Lady Delia. Did Dr. Gehlen explain the process to you?"

"He may have, but I haven't a very good memory."

She sat beside the countess and took her hand. "You have a very fine memory. It's just some folks have told you otherwise. Lord Aubrey believes in you, and he loves you, doesn't he?"

"Yes. He does. I don't know why he does, but..."

"No buts, now. The earl loves you. No doubts."

She smiled. "Paul is very good to me."

"And you're good to him, and good for him, too. I've never seen the earl happier or more content, my lady. Now, I've brought a book with me that might help you to understand what's happening to your body. The book's filled with information about the last weeks of pregnancy and even has hand-coloured illustrations. Shall we have a look together?"

The young woman smiled. "That would make me so very happy! I want to do this right, Esther. I want to bring Paul's son into the world without hurting him. I could have hurt him yesterday, and I don't want to do anything wrong again."

"Then, we'll have a look through the book. And after, I'll see about bringing you something to eat. Are you hungry?"

"Not really. Thirsty, though."

Esther poured a large glass of water and gave it to Delia, then she drew a large book from the basket. It was two inches thick with a stiff leather cover. Inside, entire passages were underlined, and many of the pages were dog-eared.

"I used this book when I studied nursing, many years ago," the elder woman explained. "From the time I was six, I was raised at Branham, and the old duke sent me up to Edinburgh to take a nursing course, when I was eighteen. I loved being in Scotland again. I'd not lived there since I was a girl, though I'd visited relatives now and then. I lived in Edinburgh for an entire year. It was a grand time!"

"When was that?" asked the countess.

"Before the Crimean War. It was like the old duke knew I'd be needed. I met my first husband in Scotland. Amos Alcorn. He was a doctor. Did you know that?"

"No," said Delia, fascinated to hear the woman's story. "What happened to him?"

"Amos and I weren't on the battlefield, not usually. We mainly served at a British hospital, constructed inside the Selimiye Barracks of Constantinople. Thousands of wounded were sent back there for treatment. We spent most of the time treating infections caused by field surgeries. Many of the men had lost eyes, arms, or legs. Then, in early '55, cholera started running through the city, including the hospital, and it struck Amos. He died within days, a shell of his former self."

"How awful!" exclaimed Cordelia, reaching for Esther's hand. "I'm very sorry."

Esther sighed deeply. "Thank you, my lady. It was hard, but I kept working to avoid thinking about it. Thankfully, the war didn't give me much idle time. Then, one day, in August of that same year, Duke James knocked on my door and told me the war was over. I knew the duke from his visits to Branham, and he saw to my transport back to England. Once I was home again, Mr. Baxter, my childhood friend, was there, and he listened to all my sorrows. I suppose our marriage was a long time coming."

Cordelia squeezed Esther's hand. "You're so very nice, Mrs. Baxter. I'm glad you found someone who loves you so well."

"And you have, too, my lady. Lord Aubrey loves you with a singular passion, I think. Now, let's see what this book has to say about signs of impending labour."

Downstairs, Paul Stuart had convened a small circle meeting in Henry's library. Cornelius Baxter shut the doors and then joined the others at the table. Present that evening, according to the record kept by Baxter, were Lord Aubrey, Duchess Elizabeth, Lord Salperton, Lord Paynton, Captain Crenshaw, and of course, Inspector Baxter. This small fellowship gathered round an oval table with Paul twixt Baxter and his Cousin Elizabeth.

"Before we speak, my dear friends, we should pray. Beth would you like to lead us?"

She shook her head. "I'd prefer it, if one of you fine men would pray. I always love hearing men pray. Do you mind?"

"Not at all, Princess. Baxter, could you take us to the throne?"

"I'd be honoured, sir. May we all bow our heads?" Everyone complied, and the former butler's deep voice filled their ears. "Dearest Saviour, we come to you this evening to seek your face and your guidance. We thank you for allowing us to meet freely, without fear of reprisal or retribution from any human authority. We thank you, that we may speak our minds to you in prayer, knowing you understand our frailties and our weaknesses; for you walked this earth as a human, lived a perfect life, offered up your blood as our substitute on the Cross, and praise your mighty name, you did not remain dead! If you had, Lord, we'd have no cause for joy, no reason for hope, no promise of eternal life. In light of what you gave on our behalf, offering up our thanks is a very small thing.

"When King David was delivered out of the hand of Saul, he gave thanks. 'Blessed be the Rock', he proclaimed. And referring to that wonderful Rock, he said in Psalm eighteen: 'he delivered me, for he delighted in me.' And again, said, 'For thou wilt light my candle, the Lord my God will enlighten my darkness. For by thee, I have run through a troop, by my God I have leapt over a wall.'

"Miracle upon mighty miracle, dear Lord, that is what you performed then, and it's what you continue to perform in our midst today. David knew that his rescue came at your hands. And we must remember that any victory this circle enjoys comes only, because you provide the shield and the sword!

"I begin to age, my Lord. But as my eyes dim, my heart sees more clearly. Yesterday morning, plans were set into motion that were meant to take the life of one or more members at this table. Lord Aubrey was injured, and though he claims the wound is slight, every one of us knows the path of that bullet might have killed him, had it not been for your divine interference. You shielded him, sir. You protected him.

"We also know that one of those bullets might have struck our precious duchess, yet you became her shield, Lord. You turned back the enemy's darts, and you saved her. We can never thank you enough for that, my Lord! Never!"

Baxter stopped, his voice breaking as he wiped tears from his eyes, for the thought of losing Duchess Elizabeth had struck him very hard. She sat in the next chair, and the duchess squeezed his hand.

"Life is precious, Father," he whispered as he squeezed hers in return. "So very precious. Thank you. And now, if I may, allow me to offer up these few petitions. Our number is diminished by the lack of our beloved leader, Duke Charles. Though we do not know his location, you know it, and so we trust you to watch after him and bring our duke home. Be his light and lamp in dark places, help him to run through a troop and leap over a wall! Be his shield and his sword, my King! Be his light!

"We also ask you to keep watch on our loved ones, wherever they may be. Duke James and Lady Victoria in France; Duchess Elizabeth, Lady Adele, and Lady Aubrey here. Help our young Della to heal, and if it is your will, may she remember all that happened.

Be with our Lady Aubrey and help her to deliver this baby safely. New babies are miracles, my Lord. Precious little miracles, wrapped in flesh. May this child remind us of your Son, for as we love him, let us remember that you loved your own just as much—nay, more! And yet you offered him up for our sins.

"Lastly, Father, I ask that you be with our duchess. My lady seldom complains, but I know she worries. Bring her the comfort that only your Holy Spirit can supply. And reveal to us, the faltering men of her life, how best we might bring her aid. Now, my Lord, we ask that you lead our conversation so that it might honour you. In Jesus the Christ's name we ask all these things. Amen."

"Well done, Neil," said Aubrey as they raised their heads. "Very well done. I'm sure the Lord looks forward to hearing all your prayers."

"As I look forward to hearing from him, sir. We'd all be lost without Christ."

The earl opened a small book, where he kept notes about cases and various thoughts. This was separate from his personal journal, which was currently locked in a safe at Queen Anne House. He thumbed the book open to a section near the middle.

"My friends," he began, "just as our Mr. Baxter said, yesterday, we beheld a miracle. Captain Crenshaw, I know that you've been in touch with your fellow agents. Could you offer a report regarding the current status of the shooting's aftermath?"

The Texan remained seated, but he also opened a small book, made of hand-tooled cowhide, overwrought with the letters ICI inscribed within a circle. "Lemme just say I sure appreciate the inspector's prayer. Ole Baxter lets it rip when we meet on our own, sir. I reckon God's up there smilin' right about now. Now, to business. Me an' Sir Thomas had a long talk today, so what I'm tellin' y'all includes his actions, too. We had four agents that spread out across the neighbourhoods round the HBH—I reckon it's okay, me callin' it that, Yer Grace?" Beth nodded, and the agent continued. "Thanks, ma'am. Now, what we learned from all them interviews is this. The shooter didn't talk too much, but a woman name o' Rose Flaherty struck up a conversation with him. She bein' a professional woman, you might say, an' she give this description. I'll just read it out, the way she told it to Agent Summers, sir. 'Six foot. Gold sort o' hair what needs washin'. Greyish sort o' eyes. Well spoke, like a gentleman. Nice clothes, real smart. Baggy, though, like they was someone else's. Had a limp an' bad breath.'"

Paul stared at the Texan. "I saw the same, and the hair and eyes are right. As is the height. Go on, Captain."

"Yessir. All the witnesses agreed 'bout his appearance. This here Rose is the only one talked to him, though. Here's the rest o' her testimony: 'He didn't say much, but when I asked if he wanted a girl, he said he had lots o' girls waitin' for him. Said his friend could get 'em. An' he seemed real interested in the duchess. Kept askin' if anyone knew her.' That's the end of Miss Rose's report, sir. However, I conducted an interview with Dr. Kessler. Now, he's a right interestin' fella, sir. I reckon the duchess already knows this, Kessler's got a bad reputation with the Pinkertons."

Beth's eyes widened. "What do you mean by bad reputation, Captain Crenshaw?"

"I mean, ma'am, Kessler's involved with a group called the Fourth Table. It's one o' them philosophical circles that thinks there's too many people in the world, and they figure the best way to stop it is to control who has children. Folks that's poor, drunkards, feeble-minded, they call them inferior stock. Like they's breedin' cattle."

Henry MacAlpin raised his hand. "If I may? I'm aware of this philosophy. It goes by many names, depending on the country, but the basic aim is the same. Eugenics, as Francis Galton calls it. Purifying humanity's basic design, or if you're an esoteric philosopher, returning it to a former, semi-divine or even divine form. These groups set the bar very high when describing true human beings. Anyone who doesn't reach that bar is deemed inferior and must be controlled or culled. As you say, Captain, like cattle."

"Controlled? Culled?" the duchess asked. "Are you saying Dr. Kessler believes in this cruel philosophy? That he sees the people of Whitechapel as inferior?"

"Accordin' to the Pinkertons, ma'am, he does," said Crenshaw. "I got a cable from New York yesterday afternoon 'bout Kessler, and he don't come off too well. His qualifications are real. He's studied all over the world, but in each place, he comes up against the law and moves on."

"Why?" asked Aubrey.

"He performs abortions, sir. He also uses surgery to sterilise women."

Elizabeth's face paled considerably, and her hands were clenched in anger. "How could I be so fooled?"

Paul took her hand and whispered, "He fooled us all, Princess. I had my New York agents check him out, but it seems we should have turned to Captain Crenshaw. His Pinkerton contacts know more than my own."

"But I should have interviewed him in person," Beth said. "Instead, I allowed his letters and recommendations to make my decision. Praise God, we haven't opened the hospital yet! Perhaps, God allowed this shooting to open our eyes to Kessler's motives. Might that be it?"

"It might," the earl answered carefully. "This Fourth Table group has members in London as well. Dr. Kimberley for one."

Crenshaw turned the page in his book. "And there's lots more, sir. When you told me 'bout this Kimberley person, I put out the word to all my old contacts. You'll remember how we met, sir? I was guardin' Lewis Merriweather's old place over on Wormwood in the City."

"I remember, Captain. You should have stopped Duke Charles and myself, but you allowed us through."

"I never liked Merriweather none, nor Urquhart neither. I can tell you, they sometimes met with the full Redwing club. In a big ol' room in the basement. After you an' the duke was there, I took a hard look at what Redwing was teachin', an' I didn't care for it. Not one bit. I got hired as a gun, nothin' more. Nobody told me they was workin' with devils, sir. Me? Now, I love the Lord. Always have. Got saved in church when I was six. But you talk about how God might of allowed the shootin' to shine the light on this Fourth Table? Well, God allowed you and Duke Charles to come into my life, so I could see his light shinin' on Redwing's black feathers. I quit that same day an' got down on my knees. God sure works through mysterious ways, sir."

"He certainly does, Captain Crenshaw!" agreed Baxter with a satisfied nod towards the American.

"There's more 'bout this Kessler, Lord Aubrey," continued Crenshaw. "Just an hour ago, I got a cable back from an old friend in Paris. He thinks Kessler lived there under the assumed name o' George Dupuis. My man's sendin' us a photograph, but the description matches Kessler. This Dupuis fella experimented on..." He paused, looking at the duchess. "I'm real sorry, ma'am, but he used electricity on aborted babies, tryin' to see if he could bring 'em back to life."

Beth's already pale cheeks whitened to snow, and she lowered her head. "Oh, I cannot believe this! I apologise for my weakness, gentlemen, but I'm the one who brought this devil to London!"

"He fooled all of us," said Paul, "but never fear, darling. God has used this shooting to heal our blindness regarding Kessler's twisted beliefs." He looked to the captain. "Send word to your men and have them round up Kessler immediately. Detain him on a charge of infant murder and say we have extradition papers from New York and Paris. I'll wire my police friends and see if we might make that statement true. I do not want that man loose in London."

Henry raised his hand. "Captain, did you find any other information regarding this Paris experiment? Duke Charles had been investigating a series of murders involving young women and fetuses, all of them washed up along the Embankment or some other shore of the Thames. And I seem to recall his mentioning similar events along the Seine."

"I'll get on it, sir. Bill Grimes is my old pal in France. He's a former Ranger, too. If it happened, he'll track it down. I reckon Lord Aubrey's got more men he can put on it as well."

"We'll find the truth of it, Captain," said the earl.

Beth remained pale but tried to listen to the others. Diedra Kimberley was discussed. After questioning, she'd denied any participation in the shooting. She insisted the late Sir Ralph Epperson had plotted the deed alone and even bragged of it. The purpose was to kill Duchess Elizabeth.

"Paul, please tell me you won't kill her," Elizabeth said to her cousin. "We're better than that."

"She is a traitor, Beth, and she wanted you dead. It's circle law to execute those who betray our trust."

"And you'd send her to Hell? Is that what Christ would want us to do? Couldn't you find a legal reason to incarcerate her? Isn't it better to keep her under lock and key and learn her reasons for betraying us? In doing so, we might have a chance to bring her back to God's light!"

"Assuming she ever saw it," muttered Baxter. "My lady, I applaud your compassion, but if Dr. Kimberley performed abortions or plotted an assassination, then she has broken England's law, not just those of the circle. That makes her subject to Crown prosecution."

"She still needs salvation," said the duchess, standing. "Forgive me, gentlemen, I cannot stay. All this gives me a headache, and I'm very sleepy suddenly."

Elizabeth left the table with Paul following close behind. As they reached the door, a piercing scream shattered the silence. Everyone rushed into the corridor and then up the stairs towards the voice. The screaming filled the entire house—a hair-raising wail like that of a child.

The earl reached the source of the scream first. Not a child, but Cordelia. She and Adele stood before the bedchamber windows, both of them shouting about someone or something in the upper floors of the house beyond.

"What is it?" Paul breathlessly asked his wife as he threw his arms round her middle. "Darling, what's wrong?"

The countess mumbled, as though she were in a state of extreme agitation, but Adele answered. "Paul, don't you see it?" she asked. "There! In the second window! The wolf! There's a gigantic wolf!!"

Aubrey followed her pointing finger and stared, wide-eyed, into the darkened windows of Hemsfield House. Sure enough, a great shadow moved from window to window in one of the apartments. It undulated in a way that indicated it walked on all fours, but then it stood upright. A flash brightened for a second, as if someone in the other house lit a match. The light was fleeting, but it was enough.

Adele hadn't exaggerated. Not only did Paul see a huge black wolf. He also saw the humans standing round it. And one of them looked very much like the late Baron David Wychwright.

CHAPTER THIRTY-TWO

Time Maze – Drummond House

"Before we do anything else, I need to see Elizabeth," Charles told his friend Kepelheim. "I have to know if she's connected to the real Beth."

"Is that supposed to make sense to me?" asked Martin as he followed the duke into the house. "I am but a mirror shard mentality, after all."

"Perhaps, you are, but I'm not sure that Elizabeth is," said the traveller as he dashed through the Drummond House foyer towards the main staircase. He'd reached the bottom of the steps, when a woman called to him.

"Charles," she said. "Please, it isn't my fault."

The voice belonged to Lorena MacKey. Or rather the mirror shard version of the woman he knew as Lorena. Here, she was raised as his father's ward. Martin had warned Charles that this Lorena had a marked fondness for him. Not as an adopted sister loves a brother, but as a lover.

"I didn't mean for it to happen," Lorena told him. "Paul kissed me, not the other way round. No matter what he's told you."

"What? Lorena, I don't know what you mean."

The duke's skin tingled as if something dark were about to happen. It was that old sensation of approaching spiritual wickedness. Did it come from MacKey, or some other direction?

Suddenly, Charles remembered Romanov's warning that he'd suffer heartbreak before he could leave this mirror shard room. What sort of heartbreak? Fear heightened the tingle along his hands and the back of his neck.

Something's coming. Something awful.

"You do understand, don't you?" asked MacKey as she drew close enough to take the duke's hands. "Charles, whatever Paul's said, it's a lie. You believe me, don't you?" she whispered, her lips coming closer and closer.

The duke stepped back. He tried to remove himself from her advance by climbing the stairs, but he wasn't quick enough. Lorena's mouth found his, and she forced him into an unwanted kiss. The tingling began to scream as her lips found his—warm, wanton, as though her skin were coated in some horrid aphrodisiac.

That briefest of seconds dragged out into internal hours, and he thought of the real Lorena MacKey, the former Redwing witch, who'd worked with William Trent to cast a spell on him and Elizabeth last year. He pushed the woman away. The deceitful kiss made him want to wretch, but his rejection came half a second too late.

"Charles, what are you doing?" he heard Elizabeth say from the top of the staircase. Then, she took a step, just one step with her dainty foot in the air. One step towards disaster. The hem of her dressing gown caught on the heel of her shoe, and everything else happened in slow motion.

Her head pitched forward.

There was a flash of yellow silk and white lace, billowing like a cloud round her body.

Then the dreadful scream as Beth rolled forward, headfirst, down the stairs.

Charles raced to catch her, but she tumbled so very quickly, no one could have stopped it.

Then, voices. Shouting. 'Ring Dr. Gehlen!' 'Fetch Mrs. Campbell!' 'Find a cushion!' 'No, sir, let me!'

And on, and on, and on until it all became a blur in the duke's head.

"Elizabeth?" he was saying, wondering if he dared to lift her head.

Lorena MacKey, the cause of the accident, was by his side.

"You mustn't move her, Charles. She might have broken her neck or back. Here, let me examine her first."

Charles had no choice. He had to move aside and allow the medical professional to work, but obeying her command boiled inside him like molten anger.

"Beth, can you talk?" he asked as he watched helplessly.

Her eyes opened, but the duchess said nothing. She stared up at the high ceiling as MacKey performed a survey of bones and systems. Finally, after an eternity, Lorena looked up. "Nothing's broken, except her left ankle. We can move her, but do it carefully. Mr. Kepelheim, if you'd open the doors to the lift, then Mr. Anderson can take her upstairs."

"No! No one else touches her! I'll carry her upstairs myself," Charles declared to all. He very gingerly placed his hands beneath her upper back and thighs to lift the pregnant duchess into his arms.

Her eyes remained open, and she whispered, "Captain."

Tears rained down his cheeks as Charles carried Beth to the elevator. She felt warm and fragile. *She's so close to delivery,* he thought. *But this is a mirror shard. This is just a shadow. It's something the Maze wants me to believe.*

"Or is it something God wants me to know?" he said to himself as they reached the master apartment.

"What?" asked Kepelheim, who trailed close behind. "Charles, I don't know if you noticed, but she's... She's bleeding."

He laid her upon the mattress, and Charles came away with stained hands. Martin was right. The duchess was bleeding.

The housekeeper, Edith Campbell, arrived carrying a large medical bag. Charles was pushed back against the corner. Martin took his forearm.

"We should wait in the parlour, Charles."

"No. I'm staying."

"Let Campbell and MacKey do their jobs. We're just in the way. Beth will be all right. A broken ankle, remember? That's a miracle, considering her fall."

"She's losing the baby," Charles said, his hands gone numb with tingling. "She's miscarrying."

It's 1893. Is this my future? Is it a shadow of a possible future? Is it a warning?

The duke lost all track of time. Someone had rung Anthony Gehlen's telephone next door. By God's mercy, the doctor was home and arrived with amazing speed. Now, he and Lorena worked together. An hour passed, then another. Charles watched as a tiny body was gathered up into a towel. Then, a few minutes later, a second smaller body followed that one.

Twins?

Anthony whispered to Mrs. Campbell, who nodded and took the bodies to the bath. A few minutes later, Charles saw her reenter the bedchamber. She whispered to Gehlen, who joined the housekeeper in the bath. More time passed. Then a plaintive cry pierced the quiet air. And a second echoed it one moment later. Charles felt like an unwanted observer to his own life. Three, four, sometimes five people hovered round the duchess.

Finally, the bath chamber opened again. Anthony Gehlen came over, saying, "You have twin sons, Charles. Born a month early, but miraculously alive. I've given orders for them to be wrapped in foil and cotton blankets. We'll need a wet nurse right away. I'm afraid the duchess is in no condition to provide anything. In fact, Charles, I cannot even guarantee she'll live."

"What?" he managed to ask. "Is it blood loss? She can take mine. We can perform a transfusion."

"Charles, there isn't enough blood in your entire body to do that," Gehlen told him. "The twins are identical, so only one placenta pulled away, but that isn't the only source of blood. Beth has internal injuries from the fall. Without opening her up, we can only guess what vessels are torn. You need to say your goodbyes."

Charles stood there, frozen, unable to think. Time passed, and Romanov's words echoed in his thoughts. His heart must be broken before he could leave here. Now, he knew what evil he'd dreaded: Losing his beloved wife.

Mrs. Campbell tapped him on the shoulder. "We've made the bed nice now, sir. All fresh. Go talk to her. She's asked for you."

Charles approached the bed, and everyone else moved aside. Elizabeth's eyes were partially open, and she reached out with a pale hand.

"My darling husband. Come to me."

No one else spoke. Every tongue was stilled in reverence. Campbell's maids had removed all the soiled linen and remade the bed with scented sheets and dressed the duchess in her finest bedclothes. Perfumed lace covered her shoulders, as though she already wore a shroud and waited for the angels to carry her to Heaven.

Charles thought he might collapse.

"Would you ask the others to leave, please?" asked Elizabeth.

Everyone else, including MacKey, left the room without speaking another word. The door shut, and the air grew still, as if every molecule of matter stood silent, holding its breath.

"I'm sorry to leave you this way," Elizabeth began. "Have you seen them? Our tiny boys? Forgive me, Charles. Forgive my foolishness. They mustn't die because of me."

"They won't," he assured her, kissing the pale hand. "It's all right. We'll look after them."

"It's just, seeing Lorena kiss you that way..."

"You needn't explain, little one."

She smiled, a new light entering her eyes. "Oh, Captain! How I long to hear you call me that! I miss you so much! Come home, please!"

"Home? Beth, is it really you? Little one?"

"I'm here, Captain, but also far away. Sleeping, I think."

"Where?" he asked her.

"Why does it hurt? My body feels so heavy, but also empty. Where am I?"

"You're all right, little one. I love you. I love you so much!" He began to weep with his head against her breast. The failing heart was beating slower and slower.

"Don't weep, Captain," she whispered as she stroked his hair. She was using up precious breaths, and he couldn't allow it.

"Please, Beth, rest. Just sleep a little."

"I'm sleeping now, but this body will pass," she said, her face radiant. "I have to tell you something first. Charles, it's about... About..." Her heartbeat grew erratic, and she gasped for air. Beth's cool fingers squeezed his as though searching for strength.

"Don't talk, please!" he begged as teardrops fell onto her gown.

"No, I... I must," she whispered, her voice barely audible. "Come closer. Listen to me."

"I'm here, little one. I'm listening."

"Little one," she echoed with a bright smile. "My Captain. You must leave this place. Find your way home. Find the centre and come home to me."

"Beth, tell me what you know."

"God is with you, Captain," she told him. "Listen. The music will guide you. Promise you'll come home. We need you. Georgie needs you. Robby cries for you. We all do!"

Her hands grew weaker, barely grasping his now, and the eyelids closed.

"Little one? Darling, are you there? Are you sleeping?"

"Yes," she whispered.

Her eyes opened again, the pupils large, irises dark as midnight. Beth's thick lashes were covered in tears, like iridescent pearls on long strands of black velvet. *How can any earthly creature be so beautiful?* he wondered. What had he ever done to deserve such love?

"Captain?" she called weakly.

"I'm here, little one."

"I see her," she said, pointing to the fireplace. "Look there! She's waiting for you."

He turned, expecting to find a maid or Mrs. Campbell.

Instead, he saw Beth. The child Beth. She wore a different nightgown now, but no longer carried the porcelain doll.

"Do you see her?" asked his dying wife. "I think she's... She's myself, isn't she? I remember this dream. I remember helping you through the Maze. Follow her, Captain. She'll lead you to the music. Follow the music."

"Beth, don't go!"

"We'll meet again soon, darling husband. Please, tell Lorena that I understand her love for you."

"I will."

"Kiss me, Captain. This isn't goodbye. Follow the music and come home to me."

He kissed her lips. They were cool, for the heart could no longer beat with enough force to circulate blood efficiently.

"I love you, little one."

"And I love you, Captain. Go now. Go with God, for he is never far from you. And remember, my darling husband. You are never alone."

Her slender fingers fell limp in his hand, and the eyelids shut. The chest rose and fell twice more, and then stilled. He watched for many minutes; expecting the lungs to fill again, the heart to send an electric order to its chambers.

The room was filled with raspberry and vanilla.

The child version of Elizabeth walked to his side and touched the grieving husband's hand. "We have to go, Captain. Come, we must follow the music back to the Maze."

He had no will to leave, but the girl's reassuring touch brought him peace. "Yes, we must," he answered.

Charles bent down to take one last kiss, then left this dead, but still achingly beautiful, mirror-shard wife and followed little Beth, the dreaming child.

She led him down a back staircase. They passed servants, Lorena and Gehlen, Kepelheim, and many others, but no one noticed. They'd become ghosts within a mirror-shard world.

"Where are we going?" he asked the child.

"You'll see," she said.

The foyer's lamps were dim, and Charles could hear the weeping and wailing of mourners. He glanced towards the upper level, thinking of his wife.

No, this Beth wasn't his wife. His little one still waited.

Come home, she'd said with her final breath.

"In here," the child Elizabeth said, leading him into the western drawing room. It was here, in this same room, where he'd come with his late wife, Amelia Winstone St. Clair, and they'd talked with James, Paul's father, and of course Paul. Amelia had giggled—actually giggled!—she was so joyful to be welcomed into such a high peerage home as this.

"Over here," Beth said, sitting on a sofa near the window that overlooked St. James's Park. "Do you remember now?"

The streets beyond Drummond House were shrouded in fog and night. "Remember what, little one?"

"The first time."

He knelt before her, confused and uncertain. "What first time, Beth?"

"Everything began here. Not at Leman Street. It all began in this room, when you took my hand. Do you remember? You never took her hand here, not that way. You were never St. Clair, always Sinclair. Don't you see? Everything that the enemy meant for evil, God has allowed for good."

"I'm not following. Beth, is any of this real?"

"It's real to you, and that's what matters." She wiped the tears from his eyes, and kissed his cheek. "You and I had to meet that way. It formed something in me, and also in you. A bond that's hard as steel, yet soft and resilient, like the scarlet sash in your pocket. That strength is passed to all our children."

She kissed his cheek, those dark brown eyes filled with more trust, more love than any ocean could ever hold. "It's time to go, Captain."

The child led him into the foyer, both of them still just ghosts to the mourning servants and family who'd begun to gather. The front entry door stood open, admitting various neighbours and family. Charles saw Paul Stuart run past him, anguish written on his face.

"Don't worry. That isn't the real Paul, Captain. None of this world is real," she told him. "It's just a dream. Come now."

The door was ajar, and she led him out to the porch, down the steps, and into the night. The cold air began to warm, and then he saw nothing but light and mirrors.

The locked room's wooden door shut behind them, never to open again.

CHAPTER THIRTY-THREE
Real World – Montmore House

It took nearly half an hour to convince Cordelia her dead father wasn't trying to reach her with a message. Paul told the others to go down without him, and he remained with his wife until she'd fallen asleep. When he joined the others, he found a surprise waiting for him on the main floor. Lorena MacKey had called and learnt about the countess's fears. After speaking with Henry, the former Redwing operative decided to stay at Montmore another night.

The meeting never reconvened. Captain Crenshaw's men stood guard outdoors once again and they spread out across the grounds to watch for possible intruders.

With the house returned to a semblance of normality, Paul took Lorena by the arm and led her into the west garden area, where a large sunroom offered protection from the night's cold. He lit a fire in the hearth. Beth stopped in to ask if she should join them. "For propriety's sake," she'd whispered to the earl. He noticed how weary his cousin looked and suggested she might enjoy spending time with Adele.

"If you prefer that, but I'm happy to stay out here and talk. Mrs. Baxter's watching over Delia. All is well, Cousin."

"I thought you might need to rest, Beth. It's been a very busy two days, and I know the things Crenshaw told us upset you."

"Yes, but we mustn't dwell on the past. We have to trust God to work something wonderful from all this."

He pulled her close, whispering, "And he'll bring Charles back home to us. For now, we put one foot in front of the next and follow Christ. Right, Princess?"

"Yes, Sir Paul. That's right."

"That's my brave lassie. Go enjoy Miss Bunting's piano playing and tell Della I'll join you soon. I want to talk with Lorena for a bit."

"All right," Elizabeth finally agreed. She shut the doors to the sunroom and Paul chose a chair far enough away from MacKey to avoid suspicion.

"I don't bite," the doctor told him.

"No, but rumours do. I'd rather no one begin one about us."

"Yet you embrace the duchess openly?"

"She's my cousin and looks to me for encouragement and protection. I've treated her that way since she was small."

Lorena removed her glasses and polished the lenses with a handkerchief. "Sorry. I still revert to old habits sometimes. I'm sure it's been difficult for you; looking after Beth in Charles's absence."

"More than you can imagine, but he'll soon be home. Has Romanov offered any hints regarding my cousin's welfare?"

"No," Lorena answered. "Anatole's very circumspect. But now that I know more about him, I can understand why he's so vague sometimes. I used to think he was being intentionally obtuse, waiting for me to achieve a new level of understanding."

"I'm sure he still does that," Aubrey countered. "I have come to trust in him, but it's clear that he only reveals what God allows. I suppose I should be grateful we're told as much as we are."

"Is that why you asked to talk with me? To learn more about Anatole?"

"No," Paul answered, his eyes on the men patrolling the grounds. "I need to ask you about Redwing."

She moved slightly in the seat, as if suddenly uncomfortable. "You still don't trust me?"

"On the contrary, I've come to trust you as much as I trust anyone who serves in our circle. You've been very helpful during all this, Lorena. I can't imagine what might have happened with my wife, if you'd not been here." He paused to assess her reaction. "Does that bother you? My mention of a wife?"

She laughed. "It shouldn't, but it does sting a bit. There was a time when I genuinely liked you. Romantically, I mean. Now I like you as a friend. Back then, Sir William ordered me to lure you away from Beth, but I came to admire your smile and honesty. If only I'd been honest with you. Honest with myself. I don't feel jealousy exactly. It's envy, I think. What woman doesn't want what Cordelia has? I don't mean your title, Paul. I mean an honest, loving husband. We all want security, to be protected, and even adored a little. Delia has all that with you."

"And Beth has it with Charles."

Her expression grew more serious. "Yes, she does. Admittedly, there was a time when I felt fierce stabs of jealousy about the duchess, but I've come to admire her. I mean that. I really like her, Paul. She's doing a wonderful work in Whitechapel. When I studied at the School for Women, I worked with dispossessed women and orphaned children. Very few rich people give such people a passing thought. Oh, they may contribute to charities or even serve on a board, but few would speak to them on the street or offer them food from their own hands. I've seen Elizabeth do both. I was with her in late July, shortly after she and Charles returned to London. She asked me to meet her at the new hospital and discuss a future position. Honestly, it surprised me. I'd been writing to Charles for months, sending a letter every few days, and he'd said Elizabeth might ask to meet with me, but when her letter arrived at Anatole's home, I nearly fell off my chair! She was open and quite generous with her praise."

"Why would that surprise you?" asked Paul.

"Because I'm a threat."

"How?"

She smiled. "At first, because of you and my affiliation with Redwing, but later because of Charles. I was once in love with him."

"And now?" he asked.

"Now, I'm content to live a simple life and practise medicine. Tell me, is that why you wanted to talk with me? Because of Charles?"

He shook his head. "No. I used to suspect your reasons for writing to Charles, but I trust him."

"And me?"

He smiled, showing those deep dimples that made ladies swoon. "Yes, Lorena, I've come to trust you as well. What I want to discuss is something called the Fourth Table. Do you know anything about it?"

Her green eyes widened. "How do you know about them? They keep their heads very low and try not to be noticed."

"They keep low, because their activities are illegal."

"In part, yes, but there are other reasons they keep a low profile. Why do you ask?"

"I've just learnt that Dr. Kessler's a member."

"Nathan Kessler? That's troubling. I haven't spent much time around him, of course, but he struck me as competent. Somewhat snooty regarding women and lower classes. His father's a wealthy banker in New York, but his roots are Austrian. The Kesslers come from the *hochgeboren*."

"The high-born?"

"Yes. They're Habsburg lineage to the bone. His wife is cousin to the late Prince Rudolf, and Nathan's related to Prince Leopold of Bavaria. Surely, you knew that?"

"No, and if Beth's aware, she hasn't said."

"I can tell you one thing about Kessler," Lorena continued. "If he's joined the Fourth Table because of membership in other dark clubs, then he supports Blackstone not Redwing. Redwing's hated in Austria."

"And what about New York? Redwing has branches there, too."

"It has branches almost everywhere, but some are weaker than others. In Austria, Blackstone is king."

"And the Fourth Table?"

"Are you familiar with the ideas of Thomas Malthus?"

"Of course. He believed the world has an upper limit. That our arable land can only feed so many people. He claimed helping the poor leads to economic crisis, because it encourages idleness."

"Yes," she said. "And Malthusian groups want to reduce the number of poor and change laws and social systems that encourage lower-class procreation. The Fourth Table emerged from this wicked wellspring. They use the Twelve Tables of Roman law as a guide. The Fourth Table of Rome listed the rights of the *pater familias*, which included killing any children the father deemed deformed or unfit. Members of the Fourth Table see poverty as a type of deformity, and believe mankind cannot achieve Utopia, if the deformed and unfit remain; so they sterilise women and abort children."

"How dare they?" he asked, his hands tensing. "Every person has a right to life. Every person. And each has a right to enjoy life through decent living conditions. That's what Beth wants to offer them. Yet, Kessler would use his position to begin such a devilish campaign? No, I will not have it!"

He began to pace back and forth, his eyes glancing now and then at the guards outside. "Do you think Kessler feared Beth might discover his true motives?"

"He might have. I know she told him she planned to hire me to teach medicine there."

"I'm sure that went over well with Kessler."

"Do you really believe he's involved in the murder attempt?" she asked.

"I don't know," he said, crossing to a door that led to the gardens. Aubrey pushed it open. "Leyton!" he shouted to a lean gentleman near the gardener's cottage. Kevin Leyton had been speaking to a fellow guard, a middle-aged man named John Preston. Both answered the earl's command.

"Yes, sir," Leyton said as they neared the door. "Is something amiss, my lord?"

"How many are out here at present?"

"Eight, sir. Preston and I watch to the west. Tilson and Morrow are to the east. Priest and Packard are east. Houghton and that new man, Somerset, watch the north."

"Is Crenshaw still here?"

"I believe he left to follow your orders about some doctor named Kessler, sir."

"I need to alter those orders. Ask Somerset to take your place here. I want you to find Crenshaw and give him new orders. I'll write them down, so there's no question. Meet me at the front of the house."

"Very good, my lord."

Paul shut the door, and Lorena was standing. "You're planning to arrest him, aren't you?" she asked.

"I'd already asked Crenshaw to arrest Kessler. Now I want every Redwing member brought in for questioning. I'm sick of being reactive. Charles told me before he vanished that we needed to get off our back-foot position and start hauling Redwing in. It's time I started doing just that."

"What of Diedra Kimberley?" asked MacKey. "She's also a Fourth Table member."

"So I've become aware. I'm also sure she had something to do with the attempt on our lives."

Lorena followed the earl through the house to the foyer. Aubrey composed a short letter to Crenshaw and then met Leyton at the door. "Give this to Captain Crenshaw personally. Send me word as soon as it's done."

The man left, and Paul retired to a nearby room to think. Lorena stayed with him. "There's more on your mind."

"Am I getting this wrong again? Since Charles left, I feel as if I'm missing an arm; or worse, missing a part of my brain."

"Paul, you're doing all you can, but brains require food and relaxation to function correctly. Come with me," she said, taking his arm. "Let's eat and then enjoy an hour of music."

Dinner was served at eight, with a delicious assortment of meats and sides, followed by chocolate torte with almond butter-cream icing. Adele ate two slices, her face alight with joy at having her family with her at Montmore. Music commenced at nine, beginning with three selections from Adele, two Beethoven and one by Mozart; followed by Gillian Bunting, who returned to her favourite composer, Frédéric Chopin.

Bunting played for half an hour, and most assumed she'd relinquish the seat, but instead, the young woman chose to start a new piece, Chopin's *Piano Sonata No. 3*. The B minor composition had a quick opening that required dexterity and concentration, but was still simpler than many of his other compositions. Elizabeth had memorised the sonata long ago and noticed a few mistakes; but overall, Bunting played with proficiency and delicacy.

Most in the room listened politely. Mr. Gosberg stifled yawns. Ewan MacNee said nothing, his hand on a small butter knife, which he'd concealed in his pocket at dinner. Mrs. Emmerdale leafed through old magazines and occasionally spoke to an invisible companion; her long dead husband, whom she believed lived with her.

Della sat nearby and noticed Emmerdale saying her brother's name with regularity. She switched to a different chair that was closer to Emmerdale and strained to hear the whispered words. Apparently, the woman was asking her unseen husband why the earl had taken a sudden interest in 'that harlot from Redwing'.

Adele was about to interrupt, when a very strange thing happened. Pamela Emmerdale suddenly leapt to her feet and blurted out a phrase that chilled Paul's bones.

"Wir und die Todten reiten schnell!"

At that same instant, like a monstrous serpent from the depths of Night, *Chaos* took control of the room, and everything seemed to flip upside down. Emmerdale pushed past Seth Holloway with such force, that the small woman knocked the tall viscount to the floor. Before running up the stairs, she turned to look at the assembled group, shouting, "The Dead will take over the world, and Charles Sinclair will never leave the Maze. Never!"

Beth and Adele jumped up in shock. Henry, who was busy helping Holloway to his feet, tried to soothe them both.

"She's just spouting nonsense. Please, pay no heed to her words, ladies. She doesn't know what she's saying."

Chaos whispered again, and Gillian Bunting pounded the piano to get attention. "Listen to me! I am playing Chopin!"

Simultaneously, Mr. Gosberg overturned a table in a highly unusual fit of anger.

Ewan MacNee began to scream Queen Victoria's name over and over, and he rushed at Adele, his eyes turned wild, the butter knife held high in his left hand.

Both Henry and Seth tackled MacNee, and Holloway took a slight wound to the upper arm for his trouble.

Della screamed from terror, and Elizabeth pulled her close.

The knife attack would be the last thing Adele Sinclair later recalled from that night, for one second after Seth and Henry tumbled to the floor on top of MacNee, she suffered a severe seizure.

Adele Marie Sinclair would lie in a feverish state for many days.

CHAPTER THIRTY-FOUR
Time Maze – The Second Challenge

Charles leaned heavily against the cool stone of the Maze's corridor. He'd made it back to some semblance of the real world, but how many challenges lay before him? Romanov had said he must find the centre, just as with the hedge maze, but how? And what final test awaited him there?

The glittering light from a nearby mirror flickered against his pale face, illuminating the sea-blue eyes, but those eyes were filled with fear. Young Beth drew close, her hand in his, offering strength and reassurance.

To think, a child could soothe my soul just now. Oh, Beth! What wonderful miracle bound us together?

"You mustn't rest too long," the child told him. There are creatures in here that eat living things."

"Living things?" he said, his stomach knotting. He'd just held his dying wife. It felt tragically real. But was it? Had she been real? Was this child version of her real? And would he find his true wife alive, when he finally escaped?

"How do you know about these creatures, Beth?" he asked, needing to hear her voice again.

"I've dreamt of this place many times, Captain. The creatures eat rats and mice and bats, too, but they cannot hurt me, for I'm just a dream. You're real, just like the mice. You're alive and awake, Captain, and I prefer you'd remain that way." She offered a sweet smile and kissed the back of his hand. "Come, Captain. I hear the music."

She pulled his arm, and he followed like a duckling follows after its mother. Charles wondered just who here was the adult. "What music?" he asked.

"Don't you hear it?"

"No, I hear only our footsteps. Beth, if there are dangerous creatures hereabout, then let me carry you."

"You may if you wish, but they won't hurt me."

"Because you're a dream?"

She nodded. "But also because I haven't got the dolly. If I'm carrying her, the monsters are allowed to find me. I really don't like that doll, Captain. I'm very glad you threw it away. If I try to leave her, she always comes back, but you've banished her, I think."

"I'm glad, little one," he answered. "Wait. I think I hear it now. Is it Beethoven's *Moonlight?*"

"That's right. Oh, I'm beginning to wake up. I hear my father calling. You'll be fine now, Captain. Just follow the music."

He bent down and drew her close, holding her small body like a drowning man might hold a bit of driftwood or a friendly buoy. "I wish you didn't have to go."

"So do I, but I must," she said. "I don't know where you're going next, but it might be one the mirrors. You've proven you can open the locked doors. I doubt he'll ask you to do it again."

"He?"

"The Maze Keeper. You'll meet him soon, and once you do, then, the Lord will bring you back to me," she said, her smile deepening.

"Then I'll truly be home," he whispered, his eyes filled with tears. "For you are my home, Beth. You always have been."

Elizabeth kissed him and backed away, releasing his hand. "I love you, Captain. Follow the music."

"I will, little one. I'll be fine."

She faded from view, leaving her distraught, future husband alone.

Charles walked for nearly an hour through the long, mirror-lined hallway, noticing how the design curved, almost like a gigantic series of circles. The walls varied from one section to another, as if different builders created them. The music drew him to the left, where he entered yet another section with a unique structure.

This corridor's ceiling was higher than its predecessor and the facing stones were highly polished and regularly shaped, their rectangles uniform and set without mortar. It reminded him of the tunnels beneath Lion Hall, that Seth Holloway described as a 'transformation chamber'. Each stone was painted with colourful imagery, depicting tall figures with multiple sets of wings, walking amidst smaller ones with no wings. He assumed the wingless walkers were humans, and the winged giants were some type of elohim. These used whips and lightning rods to force the small humans onward.

Farther on, he encountered pictures of great mountain ranges, capped in painted snow. Below them, lay broad valleys covered in stone monuments that looked like doorways, or perhaps tables. Amongst these, rose high stepped pyramids; to the east, slithered serpentine formations that resembled horned dragons. Emerging from the tallest of the stepped pyramids were two sparkling rivers painted blue and studded with lapis lazuli.

"Who built this place? Why go to all this trouble just to test a man's blood? It's madness," he muttered.

The music led him through yet another bend, this time to the right. The painted stones were replaced by a maze of black mirrors, that drew him into a circular path, spiralling to the left. The corridors were formed from sheets of volcanic glass. Suddenly, the lantern Fenwick had given him at the beginning appeared in his hand. Its light glinted upon the obsidian surfaces so that he sometimes saw himself, but other times revealed scenes of life, as though he watched through a window.

Was that the goal here? To locate one precise point of entry in two endless walls of glass?

Follow the music, Beth had said. But where along here did the music originate? It seemed to come from everywhere.

He walked slowly, listening carefully to each part of the endless obsidian walls, pausing now and then to put his ear to the cool glass. Once, his face started to pass through a portal, and he quickly pulled back. The music had stopped abruptly. It was the wrong place to enter.

Charles prayed silently, asking for guidance and the protection of his family. As if in answer, the piano grew louder, coming from several feet ahead. Its dolorous notes led the duke around a long curve that veered to the left. The new passage ended at a blank wall.

"Now what?" he asked, his hand automatically reaching for the scarlet sash in his pocket. Realising what he'd done, he quickly returned the cloth ribbon to the pocket. If using this meant Beth would appear, he'd find his way alone. He didn't dare bring her here again.

Charles had a strong sense of danger and feared the creatures she'd mentioned might be somewhere nearby.

"Confused?" asked a sultry voice.

Charles spun round, but could see no one.

"I'm here," the voice said again. "Shall we play?"

A woman.

"Play?" he repeated. "As the dragon likes to play, or is this a musical question? Shall I play the piano? Is that it? I thought your brother was the one who enjoyed such juvenile pursuits."

The woman laughed huskily. "You're always so entertaining, my darling. Congratulations on unlocking the first door. I always knew your blood was worthy. You, my dear Charles, are a giant amongst men."

"I want only to be a *good* man. I care nothing about being a giant or even a king," he answered.

"Really? I think you enjoy these games, Charles Rex. Come find me and we'll play some more."

The music stopped, and Charles leaned against the dressed stone of the dead-end wall.

"Father God, I'm at a loss, and I see no way out. Help me now, please. My heart grows weary, and I begin to lose hope. I cannot, nay, I *will* not summon little Elizabeth to me again. There's danger here. I can feel it." He paused, remembering his brave wife and how much she loved to recite the twenty-third Psalm. "The Lord is my Shepherd," he whispered, thinking of Beth's soft voice. "You are here, aren't you, Lord? No matter where I go, you are there, standing beside me; leading me onward. Forgive my doubt, Lord. You are the good Shepherd, and I want for nothing. I rejoice when you lead me beside the still waters, but if I really trust you, then I must be content, when you take me through darkened paths. Therefore, I ask you to lead me now. Though the path may lead to tunnels darker and deeper than this, I will trust in you, my King and Shepherd. Lead me now, please, and I shall rejoice in it."

A sweet breeze swept past his face, and he heard a voice whisper, "Enter now and see what might have been."

A fiery door appeared upon the wall, and the duke took a deep breath. "I follow, my Lord. Lead on."

Charles passed through the fire unscathed, trusting God to clear the path and protect him, no matter what. *If I die, then it's because God allows it,* he reasoned.

But what place was this?

He could still hear the piano music, playing from somewhere nearby; but amongst the music, he discerned voices, merry sounds of mirth and joy. As before, his attire changed to fit the new environment, this time to a charcoal grey ensemble with a subtle check of shimmering silver thread. He wore a ring on his left hand that bore the Haimsbury coat of arms; a pocket watch of silver with an inscribed initial 'H', presumably for Haimsbury, and the lion-headed fob was set with diamonds for eyes. He opened the watch, finding an inscription: *To my son on his eighteenth birthday. With greatest affection – Father.*

But wait. Fenwick had promised he'd keep a few precious items with him, no matter what area he entered: Beth's scarlet sash, his wedding ring, and the Sir John Bennett watch Beth had inscribed last year. *Fenwick wouldn't lie.* Trusting in the angel's word, Charles reached into his right trouser pocket and found the scarlet sash, wrapped round the Sir John Bennett watch and his wedding ring. Beth's tokens had remained. *Thank you, Lord!*

"Sir?" asked a footman in red-and-gold livery. Only now, did Charles realise he stood on the landing of a staircase; one he immediately recognised.

"Branham," he whispered, smiling.

"Branham? Yes, my lord. Do you wish to speak to the duchess? Shall I let my lady know you've come down, sir?"

Charles felt different, as though his body had changed along with the suit of clothing. "Yes, thank you," he answered automatically. "Tell me, young man, are the morning papers in one of the morning rooms?"

"Of course, sir. We've taken them all to the Lion, sir. As always. And may I say how very good it is to have you back, Lord Haimsbury?"

"You may indeed. It's very good to be back."

The uneasy traveller knew the way to the eastern drawing room known as the Lion, but decided to wander about the main level first, to gauge how this Branham Hall might differ. He noted the familiar Christmas decorations. A team of footmen bustled about the foyer, hanging garlands, bows, bells, berries, and fragrant boughs, just as he'd seen them do last year, when Queen Victoria had come to visit.

Charles began to reason through his current situation. The servant called him Lord Haimsbury, not Your Grace. He wore the Haimsbury signet, and yet he'd never seen this particular suit before, nor had he seen the watch. For a moment, he considered the possibility that it might be an heirloom, given to another version of Charles by his father. Had the Lord led him to another alternate reality? Had he broken through a second 'locked room' door?

"Good morning, Charles," a welcome voice called from the Lion Room. "In here, son. Come join me."

He followed the cheerful Scottish invitation into a room he knew should have white panelled wainscoting, and yet the wood was stained a deep mahogany red. The inset of each panel bore a trio of golden lions, painted in the traditional *passant* position of Plantagenet heraldry. The blue walls above were filled with paintings of past dukes and duchesses. And over the white fireplace, hung a portrait of the current duchess with a four-year-old child on her lap. Connor Stuart stood behind the chair, holding his beautiful daughter's small hand.

"You still dreaming, son?" asked James.

"Probably, sir," Charles answered, relieved to see his uncle alive and well. The very thought of James Stuart dying had hit him almost as hard as losing another version of Elizabeth. The weary traveller crossed to Drummond's chair and took the vigorous Scotsman's hand, allowing that familiar, strong grip to reenforce Stuart's actual presence and remind Charles that the 10th Duke of Drummond was tough as steel.

"It's very good to see you, Uncle," said the grateful nephew.

"And you as well, son," said Drummond, "though you look a might pale. Cambridge treating you all right?"

"Yes, sir. I just need sleep."

"As do we all."

"All? Where's everyone else?"

"Connor left just before you came down. He might be looking for Trish."

Connor's alive? But I'm here. This is another alternate world, then. "Where's Trish gone?"

"Who can say? She took off in one of her huffs, like she does every holiday."

"If Beth awake yet?"

"I'm told she's sleeping in. Poor lassie had bad dreams again last night. There's coffee on the long table, if you've a mind for some. You look as if you had a rough night as well, Charles. What time did you get in?"

"I've no idea," Sinclair answered honestly. Seeing the coffee and croissants, his stomach began to growl. He realised he'd not eaten since Romanov's castle. "I'll tuck into some pastries, if I may."

"That's why Baxter brought them. So how's Cambridge?" asked Drummond.

At least Baxter's about somewhere, thought Charles gratefully. He poured a cup of coffee and placed two warm croissants and an eclair on a gilded, red-and-white china plate. After adding cream and two sugars to the coffee, he took the chair opposite his uncle. "Cambridge, sir? It's well enough," he answered vaguely.

"A short answer. You keep as close to the vest as your spy cousin," laughed his uncle with a proud glance. "Aren't you giving another concert next month? Tory and I might come, if that's all right."

"I'd love that, sir," Charles said. "How is my aunt?"

"Feisty as ever. So feisty, she plans to ask Trish to let Beth spend a few months with her in Paris. That's not likely to go down well, but my sister can be persistent."

"Is there a specific reason, or does Tory just want to enjoy my little cousin's company?"

"Primarily for the company. Tory's feeling lonely, I think. And Connor wants Beth to improve her French. Immersion in the culture's the best way to do that. We did the same with you and Paul, remember? Oh, and speaking of that, your cousin sent a telegram. He should arrive in about an hour, assuming his train's running on time. Have you seen the papers?"

"Not yet."

"Here, then," said the duke, handing his nephew several morning editions. "Look at *The Times* first. The front page headline says it all."

Sinclair took the paper, discovering two important clues: One, the present date was 23rd December, 1875. Two, a murder had just occurred. The headline announced in tall type:

ANOTHER SONGBIRD
DEAD IN WHITECHAPEL
Death Toll Rises to Four with
Grisly Discovery of Music Hall Queen
Polly Bryant Near St. Katherine's Docks

"Whitechapel? Who's investigating?" Charles asked.

"Henderson's put together a force of six detectives, headed by an experienced man named Isaac Thrawl."

"Experienced how, sir? With crime in general or with serial murder?"

James refilled his coffee cup from a silver server. "I thought you'd be interested. Do you think it's one man or several committing them?"

"I'd have to look at the case notes, sir. If the police need any assistance, I'd be pleased to help. Do you know if Lord Aubrey might have any influence with them?"

"I should think so. Your Uncle Rob knows Commissioner Henderson well, and they even get along, which is a miracle. Are you considering a new career, son? I thought you planned to follow your father into politics."

"I made a study of serial crimes and their methodology—as part of a statistics course," he bluffed. "I found it interesting."

"Is that so? Well, if anyone can arrange it, Rob Stuart's your man."

"Is Lord Aubrey about?"

"Outside, I think, having a stroll. My sister's still upstairs, with your mother, no doubt. Twins, eh?"

This caused Charles to smile. The thought of seeing his mother, this side of heaven, caused him so much joy that he stood without thinking. "I might take a quick stroll as well."

"You've hardly eaten, son. Sit back down."

"A walk will increase my appetite, sir. Save the plate."

"Very well, but when Kepelheim shows up, he's likely to steal your eclair."

"I'll take that chance, sir."

"Enjoy the walk, but don't be long. The sky portends snow and lots of it. And if you see Baxter, tell him to add two more places to luncheon. Martin's bringing a friend."

"I will, sir."

Sinclair left the Lion Room but dashed upstairs first, anxious to visit his mother. He found a footman near the ballroom landing, who offered the confused traveller directions. Apparently, his mother had taken rooms near her sister in the east wing. Charles asked the servant which east wing, and the servant looked confused.

"There's only one east, sir," he told the young peer.

"Of course, there is," Charles replied, hoping the servant didn't wonder if the guest had gone mad. "And my room? I always get turned round here."

The busy footman smiled. Three strands of garland hung from his arms. "You're sharing the King Charles apartment with Lord Marlbury, sir. The viscount just arrived."

"That's right. Sorry. My brain's still waking up, I suppose. Thank you."

Charles knew the King Charles apartment very well. After he'd married Elizabeth, he discovered four large apartments that were shuttered at Branham. The King Henry, King James, King Richard, and King Charles. Of these four, named for the kings that once used them, only the Richard and Henry were now redecorated and open for use. They planned to redecorate the James and Charles next year, and Beth asked if they might move their master to the King Charles; a fitting apartment she thought, and it was closer to the new, much larger nursery.

He decided to retreat to the apartment first, if only to check his face in the mirror. *The King Charles*, mused the traveller as he walked to see his mother. Two previous English monarchs used that name. The first was beheaded. The second ruled during the London Fire, the Great Plague, and the birth of England's two main political factions, Tories and Whigs, but still managed to keep his head. The 'Charles' regnal name certainly had a troublesome past.

It took several minutes to reach the apartment door, and he discovered a pair of housemaids loitering nearby. They were young, with scrubbed cheeks, bright eyes, and ringlets of blonde or strawberry hair peeking from beneath their caps.

"Good morning, ladies."

The maids giggled and answered in unison with a little curtsy, "Mornin', my lord."

Charles returned their smiles and then entered the apartment. He crossed through the parlour to one of three spacious bedchambers. The walls were fitted with panelled white wainscoting, and above, the walls were painted a light blue. As with most of the first floor apartments, the ceiling was twenty-five feet high. Lighting came from a dazzling, Venetian gasolier that hung from the ceiling's centre. Each wall had matching sconces, also fed by gas pipes.

This was the corner bedchamber of the southwest wing, and silver-blue chintz draperies accented six tall windows. A spectacular, golden tester bed, trimmed in blue-and-white toile, dominated the space. The windows on the west opened to a grand balcony that overlooked Queen's Lake, and even its railings were bedecked with Christmas greenery.

The door to a connecting bath stood ajar. Charles crossed through to find a mirror. A porcelain bowl formed a sink, filled from a golden tap, which sat atop an oak dressing table, painted with Plantagenet lions and *fleur de lis*. Over the bowl, hung a large oval mirror of the very best Venetian glass, giving the viewer a clear and perfect reflection.

He stared at himself, running a hand across the younger face. His suit was smartly cut, and the cravat and shirting expensive and hand-tailored. The dark hair was cut slightly shorter than in real life, curling one inch below the starched wing collar. His jawline was shaved smooth with a hint of overnight shadowing. He was twenty years old, certainly leaner, but his height seemed wrong. He glanced down at the shoes, noticing his heels were quite low.

Am I taller?

"Enjoying your good looks, Cousin?" asked a welcome voice. He'd only seen Paul Stuart for the briefest moment in the previous challenge, as the Scotsman raced past him at Drummond House to pay last respects to the dead Elizabeth Sinclair. His cousin hadn't seen him, for he and the child version of Elizabeth walked past as ghosts, heading back into the Maze.

Seeing Paul again lightened the weary traveller's heart. He turned to greet Aubrey—or more correctly, the Viscount Marlbury, as his father was still living.

"It's time you got here," Charles said casually.

The two men embraced, and Sinclair felt relief, knowing their friendship was a constant, no matter the timeline. "How were the rails?" he asked his cousin.

"Busy, just as one expects this time of year. All of Parliament are deserting London for their country homes. Christmas makes even politicians stop to enjoy life again. Is Kepelheim here yet? Father wants to convene a meeting."

"I'm told he'll be here for luncheon and is bringing a friend. No name was offered."

"That'll be Henry," Paul told his cousin. "Remember Salperton, the Earl of Lasberington's son? He used to visit Rose House, when we were children. He's spent the last year in Edinburgh, studying medicine. He's planning to be an alienist, if you can imagine it."

"Yes, I remember Henry. He's what? A year older than us?" he said, glad to know the reliable Lord Salperton would join them.

"Yes, and smart as a whip."

Charles hoped Martin would serve as confidant here as well, but might Paul believe his tale? Could his cousin and best friend be relied upon to trust in so great a story as time travel and an underground maze?

"Have you seen our Princess this morning?" called Marlbury from the next bedchamber. He was opening cases and unpacking suits, shirts, shoes, and pistols.

Charles joined him, reaching down to examine one of the guns. "This is a nasty bit of business. Another prototype?"

"Of course. This one's from the Mauser Company in Germany. It feeds the shells through automatically. I've found it useful. And Beth? Have you seen her yet?"

"Still sleeping. I'm told she had bad dreams."

"Those again? I'm sorry to hear that. I should talk with her about it, if there's a good moment."

"Paul, did you see this morning's papers? There's been a fourth Songbird killing."

"That's why we're meeting today," the viscount replied as he stowed the shirts and linen into drawers. "Father thinks the murderer's a member of Redwing."

"A human member?"

Paul stopped what he was doing, his hand on a folded shirt. "Are you suggesting it might be an inhuman member?"

"I'm saying the evil spirits advising the group could be sowing seeds of fear. I'd like to see the case files. James thought your father might put in a word for me with Scotland Yard."

"I can do that," Paul answered. "Commissioner Henderson owes me a favour. I helped the Met with a little problem last year. I'd planned to send a telegram to London anyway. My men got word of another murder at three o'clock this morning. Very close to Queen Anne."

"I don't like that," Charles said, thinking of the Lyceum girl's body on Queen Anne grounds in the previous mirror-shard challenge. "Should I go to London right away? It's two days till Christmas. I don't think Trish and Connor would mind."

"My father's probably already considering it. He was speaking to Sir Henry Howard near the reflecting pond as my coach came through the drive. Howard's in the Home Office."

"Does Connor know about this morning's murder?"

"Yes, but be gentle with our cousin, Charles. He and Trish are going through another of their bad patches. I fear this could be a difficult Christmas for our little princess."

"I can go find her," Charles answered. "You finish unpacking."

Paul smiled. "She's your future bride and your responsibility, Cousin. But tell her we'll go riding later, and I'll race her. The circle meeting doesn't start till five. If it doesn't snow, we'll have time for fun."

Charles left the apartment, passing by the same two housemaids, who giggled once again and curtsied.

"Ladies, do you know if Lady Anjou's awake?"

"I heard one of the other maids talking about it, my lord," replied the taller girl.

"She's awake and wrapping a gift, I believe," said the other. "For her father. It's to be a secret, though, my lord."

"I shan't spoil it," he promised. "Is her nursery still on the northeast corner of the second floor?"

"Yes, my lord."

"Thank you. Have a lovely day."

Charles left the maids, and as he walked, he remembered the first time he'd taken this winding journey to Beth's nursery. It was the previous October, on the sixth. Elizabeth had arrived, unannounced and unaccompanied, at the H-Division police station during a street riot. Seeing her without an escort had terrified him, causing Charles to realise how much he'd come to love her.

She'd brought him the first 'Saucy Jack' letter, written in red ink. Realising she was in danger, spurred Charles to remove Beth from London; and so with Paul's help, they boarded the Aubrey train and rushed to Branham. They met with a skirmish en route, and Paul was shot by one of William Trent's men.

Charles met Martin Kepelheim during that fateful journey, forming a lasting friendship he cherished to this day. It was Martin who led him to Beth's nursery. He'd wondered then, why Patricia Stuart would place her only child in rooms so very far from the master apartment. But as he learnt more about the willful duchess, Charles discovered she'd been a very poor mother. However, Trish Stuart redeemed herself in the end, and gave her life to save her daughter.

He'd reached the nursery apartment. The main door stood open. He could hear Elizabeth, talking with her nanny.

Charles knocked. "May I come in?" The pitter-patter of small shoes upon thick carpet was his answer, followed by a very warm hug.

"Happy Christmas, Cousin Charles!" young Elizabeth cried happily as he lifted her up. "Are you going to be in the photograph, too? Nanny says I'm not to go outside yet, for it might spoil my new dress. When did you get here? Is Cousin Paul here, too? Did he come with you?"

If it's December, 1875, then Beth is seven and a half, he thought. In the real-world timeline, this would be the final Christmas with her father. Would that same, dreadful murder happen in this mirror-shard world? And how long was he to be trapped here? One day? Two? Longer?

"You're very far away," he heard her say. "You're not dreaming, are you?"

"No, dear, I'm not," he said after kissing her rosy cheek. "Paul's unpacking, and I arrived last night, long after you'd gone to bed. How's my future bride this lovely morning? Did you sleep well?"

"I'm much better, now that you're here," she told him.

"I heard you had a nightmare last night."

"A small one," she whispered, "but you're here to watch over me now. Shall I show you what I've made for Father? It's by my bed."

"Yes, of course." He set her down, and Beth took his hand to pull him through the parlour, past the playroom and library, and into her bedchamber.

"Mrs. Wilson!" she called to the nanny. "I'm going to shut the door. We're talking secrets!"

Beth closed the door, then drew him to the window. "See there?" she asked, pointing towards two rows of marble statues near the maze entrance. "He was there again last night. He called to me and said you were coming. How did he know that?"

Charles saw that she pointed to the statue of the first duke. "Do you mean the Shadow Man?" he asked, recalling that the real-world Elizabeth had seen the same thing.

She nodded.

"This Shadow Man told you I was coming? But you already knew that, darling."

"Yes, but did you come through a maze? He said you'd come here from a maze. Did you? Was he right?"

How could she know that? "That's a very strange thing for him to say. Might you have dreamt it?"

"No, I did dream about you, but it was different. In the dream, you and I were in the maze together. There was music playing. I don't remember much other than that. But when I awoke, someone was whistling below my window. It was the Shadow Man, and he was standing right there, by that statue, whistling the song."

"And he told you I was coming?"

"Yes," she told him. "He said you'd come through a special door. He said the music would bring you here. What does he mean, Cousin?"

"I'm not sure," he managed to answer. How could she know about the music and the maze? Was this Elizabeth also connected to the real-world version, like the previous Beth? He wished Fenwick were here to solve the riddle, but perhaps that was *his* job.

"Please, don't tell anyone," the child pleaded. "Especially not Mother. She thinks I've imagined him, but he's real. He's horribly real, and I don't like him."

"Did he say anything else?"

"He said you'd be confused and might need my help. Are you confused? If you are, I'll help," she said, her small hands against his face. "I'll always be here to help, if you need it."

"Thank you, little one," he told her, kissing each palm.

Was this Shadow Man part of the Time Maze? They'd all assumed the creature was Raziel, a Watcher who'd escaped from the Mt. Hermon stone in '71, but might there be more than one fallen angel playing this horrid game?

"Does the Shadow Man ever enter the hedge maze?" he asked her.

"Yes," she answered. "Once, I saw him coming out of it. I don't like the hedge maze, Cousin. There are wolves inside it, and they try to bite me."

"Real wolves?"

She nodded. "I think they're real. They have red eyes, and they're very big."

He drew her into his arms. "I'll protect you, little one. I promise. Beth, where's your mother?"

"I'm not sure. Downstairs, I suppose, getting ready for the photograph. I'm late, but I wanted to wrap Father's gift first. Mother's not happy with him, and I thought the gift might cheer him up. They argued all day yesterday and were still shouting after supper. I was helping to hang garland with Mr. Baxter, and we both heard it."

"Ah, Baxter," said Sinclair. "He's a remarkable man, isn't he?"

"Mr. Baxter's my friend," she said.

"And mine, too. If you're ready to go down, we can walk together. I need to stop and say hello to my mother first, but I'm sure she'd love to see you. Have you spoken with her yet?"

"Of course, I have, silly. Aunt Angela's staying next to Auntie Tory's apartment. She misses Uncle Robby—I mean, you father. So do I."

"As do we all, sweet Cousin."

She pulled him down and kissed his cheek. "I'm glad you're here. I always feel safe, whenever you're with me." They started to leave, but then she suddenly stopped near the main door. "Father's gift! Stay here. I shan't be long."

Beth dashed back into the bedchamber, her small feet flying beneath the velvet skirt. He followed and watched her take a silk-wrapped box from one of her closets, but then, without warning, the box dropped from her hands.

"Princess, what is it?"

Her eyes had gone still and glassy, her pale face towards the window. "It's the Shadow Man," she whispered. "He's standing there, just inside the maze, looking at me. He says our world is wrong. He called it..."

He bent down, her hands in his own. She trembled. "What did he call it, little one?"

"A mirror shard."

Elizabeth grew unsteady, and he feared the girl might faint. Charles retrieved the fallen gift and then lifted her up again, talking to her sweetly, as though nothing strange had happened. "We'll visit my mother later, all right? Let's take this lovely present and put it beneath the family tree. Do you think I can carry you all the way down two flights of stairs without getting tired? You're getting heavier and very grown up, you know. Soon, you'll be wearing a wedding dress, and I shall have a special morning suit tailored, won't I? For our wedding day. Isn't that right?"

She said nothing, her eyes fixed on the window. Charles turned to look one last time into the statuary park. A large orb of multi-coloured light shimmered near the entrance, its contours similar to that of a tall shadowy man—with wings.

CHAPTER THIRTY-FIVE
Real World – Montmore House

It was the fifteenth of October. Ten days had passed, and Adele final-ly awoke from her strange fever. Though she had no knowledge of it, she'd been tended by a revolving team of doctors, including Ge-hlen, MacKey, Emerson, and Henry MacAlpin. Elizabeth and Seth took turns reading to Della. Holloway demonstrated deep concern for the adolescent. He and Beth spoke often during the long vigil, and the viscount found himself considering Adele Sinclair as a fu-ture wife. Elizabeth suggested Seth speak to Charles about it, once the duke returned and had time to rest.

The distinguished committee of medical experts feared Della might have contracted the new influenza, for she remained feverish throughout. Henry insisted the eruption of chaos in the music room had triggered an underlying negative condition, rooted in the trauma of her abduction experience. But in the slight chance Adele's seizure was caused by the Russian disease, Henry moved Della to an apart-ment farther from Cordelia.

Paul's butler responded by sending enough clothing to last the earl a month. And since having all the ladies beneath one roof made it easier to watch over them, Paul asked Beth to move to Montmore as well. And so Henry's new cook began preparing meals for a very full house.

Della had awakened the previous day, and Henry stopped by at eleven o'clock to evaluate her recovery. Beth was sleeping in the next bedchamber, and so he knocked softly before entering Adele's room.

"Am I intruding, lovely lady?" he asked before entering. Della was awake and gazing into a small hand mirror.

"Not at all," she said, her tone startlingly grown-up. "I've been thinking and hoped you'd come by."

"Thinking about what?" he asked, pulling a chair close to her dressing table. "I like your hair that way. Did Adelaide braid it, or was it Beth?"

"I did," said Adele. "Does it really look all right? I can't tell about the back."

"It's beautiful. As are you."

She blushed prettily. "Adelaide's gone back to Haimsbury House, but Ada MacKenzie arrives today to act as lady's maid to me and to Cordelia. Mrs. Baxter looks after Mother."

"I'm pleased to hear it. Not because you need someone else to braid your hair, you understand. You clearly have great skill, but because I enjoy hearing women laugh and talk. It's very pleasant, I find. What did you want to ask me?"

"Ah, that," she said, setting the mirror aside. "It's about the date."

"Date?"

"Yes. I asked Mrs. Winstead to tell me what day it is, and she said it's the fifteenth. That cannot be right, can it?"

He reached for her hands, speaking softly. "It can, actually. That's why Adelaide went back to Haimsbury House. Della, you were in a feverish state for ten long days. I doubt you remember any of it, for you spent most of it in an unconscious state. Do you remember your father's coma last year?"

"How could I forget?" she asked. "I was so very afraid he'd die, and I didn't know if I could live without him. Dr. Emerson said I should read to him, and so I read a Sherlock Holmes story to him. *A Study in Scarlet.* I had to read it to him again after he awoke. Was I in a coma?"

"Strictly speaking, no, but very nearly so," Henry explained. "And you had many people reading to you. Della, you are much beloved by all of us."

"Really?" she asked, her eyes on his face. "By everyone?"

"Every one of us, yes. Seth spent a great deal of time at your bedside. And you had four doctors looking after you. And entire team of professionals! We were very worried, if you must know. Now, as your primary doctor, I have to ask you some questions, but before I do, is there anything else you want to ask me?"

She thought about this for several minutes. "Is my dog still here?"

"She is. I think Napper's doing just that. Napping, I mean. She's been keeping Lady Aubrey company. I think your doggy's become quite protective of the countess."

"Napper's very perceptive. Has Dee had her baby yet?"

"Not yet, but Dr. Gehlen and Dr. MacKey call twice a day and consult together on it. They believe Delia's getting very close."

Adele smiled and asked, "Might she have it on the twenty-fourth? That's Paul's birthday. Georgianna was born on our father's birthday. The tenth of June. Wouldn't it be lovely if Paul's baby were born on his birthday?"

"That would simplify celebrations, wouldn't it?" Henry replied with an endearing grin. "Now, may I ask a few questions?"

"Oh, yes. Please, do."

"First of all," he began as he opened his medical notes, "what is the very last thing you remember?"

Her nose crinkled up as she struggled to recall. Henry thought the expression quite attractive, for it drew attention to her high cheekbones and soft blue eyes. "I'm not sure," she answered. "I remember Mr. MacNee with something in his hand, but I also remember seeing a brown owl. And when I shut my eyes, I cannot see anything else, for some reason. Just a brown owl with spectacles."

"A very strange picture. Is the owl wearing anything else?"

"No. But I think he can talk. Shall I write it down in my dream journal?"

"Yes, I think so. Any headaches today?" he asked, feeling her pulse. Her fever had reduced considerably, and the rhythm of her heart was solid and regularly spaced. Henry decided to take a gamble and mention the house next door. "Did I tell you I knocked at that old house?"

"Which?"

"Hemsfield House. The one just north of here. You could see it from your former rooms."

His fingers remained on her radial pulse, and as he expected, the rhythm quickened.

"You went to the house?" she asked. "What happened?"

"I rang the bell several times and waited long enough for a servant or cleaner to answer, but my efforts received no attention. Not a soul answered."

Her cheeks paled a little. "Not a soul. Isn't that a strange way to put it? Does everyone have a soul, Dr. MacAlpin?"

"I rather think they do," he answered. "Why wouldn't they?"

"What if God didn't create them?"

Her pulse grew quicker, and he feared sending her into a second shock. "Let's talk of something less philosophical, shall we?"

"Is it a philosophical question, or might it be a religious one? I see you're worried about me, but I'm strong. Really, I am."

"I know you are, dear, but you gave us all a fright with your fever."

"I'm sorry," she said with a sigh. "I miss my father, Henry. Are you certain he's in America? I've the most horrible feeling he's somewhere else that's dark and frightening."

"Why would it be dark and frightening?"

"Because it's filled with monst...!"

She stopped in the middle of the word monsters, but the look of terror in her eyes was enough for MacAlpin to end the questions.

"Here now, I think you should lie back down for a little while. I'll send Ada up as soon as she arrives. For now, it's very important that you remain quiet for an hour or so. Are you hungry?"

"A little."

"I'll have Mrs. Merchant prepare something easy to digest. You've been a long time without food."

"I'm very sorry for frightening you," she told him.

"It's quite all right, dear. If you promise to rest, I'll send up the food along with a friend."

"Who is that?"

"Lord Paynton. He's been terribly worried."

"The dream about the trees," she whispered to herself.

"What?"

"The dream about the woodcutter. Did you read it in my diary?"

"Yes, did you have it again?"

"No," Della told him, "but I think the owl was telling me about the trees. I remember more of the dream now. And I think I know what I saw in the house next door. Not trees, of course, nor a brown owl, but I saw the woodsman. He was ugly and beautiful, both at the same time, and he whispered to me. He said my father..." She stopped, and her entire body trembled—somewhat like it had before her collapse.

"You mustn't think of it, Adele, please," he said, placing his hand on hers. "Try to think of good things."

"He said my father's lost in a great maze, and the woodsman said he'd make sure Father never got out. Then, he laughed at me, Henry! And I didn't dream it, I saw it! I think the woodman's in the house. The house isn't empty at all!" She clutched at his hands, squeezing them with her own. "Don't go back there. Promise you won't go inside! It's filled with evil. I know it!"

"I promise to keep out for now, but you mustn't think about it, Adele, or else you'll relapse. Shall I prepare some laudanum?"

"No," she whispered as he held her close. "I don't like the taste. I'd like to see my brother, though."

"I'll send him up right away," Henry said, kissing her forehead.

"Don't go into that house, Henry. It's full of dead things. I think the woodsman is some great lord of the dead. The dead travel very fast, and they'll take you with them."

CHAPTER THIRTY-SIX
Time Maze - Christmas 1875

Charles Sinclair descended the grand, Branham Hall staircase holding his future wife's small hand. That summer, in the real world of 1889, he'd read a newly published novel called *A Connecticut Yankee in King Arthur's Court*, given to him by the author, Samuel Clemens, also known as Mark Twain. At the time, Charles thought the book well-written but a bit fanciful. The notion that a blow on the head might transport a man into a distant past, not to mention an entirely different continent, was patently absurd. Still, as a mathematician, he recognised patterns within creation that implied inner workings, similar to the complications or gears of a watch. Theoretically, if one could access and reorder those universal gears, even reverse their motion, where and when might you travel? He doubted God would ever allow such things, but he couldn't deny his current situation. The very Creator who'd spoken those gears and complications into existence had allowed Charles to make an impossible journey to a mirror-shard version of the past.

But was he actually here, or might these scenes by playing out inside his mind? Did it matter? No, not if God had purposed it for his reasons. Even dreams had their purposes. And so, he continued to move forward through the Maze, not to please the fallen realm who'd tricked him, but to please God.

Charles and young Beth reached the bottom step, just as a tall, well-dressed gentleman with black hair and dark eyes emerged from the red drawing room.

"You're late," he told them in a Scottish voice. "Shall we blame your cousin for this, Princess?"

"Cousin Charles is never late, Father," she said very seriously. "He is ever and always on time."

Connor Stuart had a handsome, mobile face that always looked as though it wanted to laugh. Charles imagined James had looked this way in his thirties; with a muscled physique, broad shoulders, long legs, and a trim waist. Connor Stuart's dark hair was shoulder-length and tucked behind the ears. Charles had only seen paintings and photographs of Beth's father, but no facsimile conveyed the mirth in the man's eyes, nor could it offer insight into the Scotsman's complex mind.

Connor bent to embrace his daughter, tickling her sides. Beth giggled and grabbed at his large hands. "We must be quite serious today, Father! The photographer won't want us smiling or laughing."

"She's very bossy for a wee lass, isn't she, Charles? Best we go in then, Princess. Your mother's been asking after you, and we mustn't give her cause for complaint. Good to see you, Charles," he told Sinclair. "You and Paul arrived just in time for the Christmas photograph. I know it's a chore, but these family times are important to record, and it certainly beats sitting for a painting, doesn't it, Princess? What's this on your ear? A smudge of coal dust? Have you been helping the chars with their fires again, lassie?"

"What smudge?" the girl asked, touching both ears.

Connor examined the smudge in the light of the chandelier. "Oh, it's just a bit of charcoal," he laughed. "Were you drawing pictures of your horses again?"

"No."

"What's your subject matter then?"

She whispered. "I was drawing the Shadow Man."

"The Shadow Man?" he repeated, glancing at Charles. "You drew him? Charles, did she show you this drawing?"

"I'm afraid not, but she did mention seeing him again."

"Beth, you mustn't tell your mother," Connor said firmly. "She's already cross, and I don't want her shouting at you."

Elizabeth's chin dropped, and she squeezed Charles's hand. "Mother tore up the last drawing she found."

"You've drawn him before?" asked Connor.

Beth nodded. "Yes, sir. The pictures are in my desk. And he's real, Father. Cousin Charles believes me."

"So do I, darlin' girl. When did you see this creature?"

"Early this morning," she confessed, her voice trembling. "The moon was still high, and I couldn't sleep. He was standing by Duke Henry's statue. He's often out there."

"Princess, when you say he's often out there, do you mean every night?"

She shook her head. "Not every night, but most. He's never there when the moon fades. And he doesn't always talk to me."

"He talks? What does this creature say?"

"May we speak of it later? I promise to tell you everything after Mother goes to bed. But only if Cousin Charles is with me. Will you, Cousin?"

Sinclair knelt down and kissed her hand. "If you ask it, I shall be there anytime, anywhere, little one."

The pet name caused her to smile. "You sometimes call me that in the Maze."

"In the what?" he asked, stunned at the comment. "Inside the hedge maze?"

"No. The Maze inside my dreams—the one with the mirrors. Shall we take the picture now? Oh, but first I have to put this present under the tree!"

Elizabeth scampered off, carrying the wrapped box.

"She's a stubborn one," Connor told Sinclair. "And she'll likely be a stubborn wife at times, but a good one, I'll wager."

"Elizabeth will be the best wife of all time, sir," said Sinclair softly.

The two men followed Beth's path into the red drawing room, where a warm fire burnt within a tall, marble hearth. White panelling brightened the lower third of each wall, whilst above, the red plaster held paintings that told the histories of the Branham duchy: knights on horseback, ladies in Tudor dress; scenes of battles, coronations, and marriages. Over the fireplace, hung the room's most prominent oil painting of a youthful, flaxen-haired woman, standing beside the sea. On either side were portraits of Duke George Linnhe and his French wife Catherine du Bonnier.

The young woman of the central portrait now waited beside a beautifully decorated Douglas Fir. Patricia Regina Charlotte Linnhe Stuart, Duchess of Branham, measured nearly five-foot and nine inches tall, but the heels of her Italian leather shoes added three additional inches, causing the woman to tower over her petite, seven-year-old daughter. At six-foot-five and a smidge, James Connor Robert Ian Campbell Stuart, 17th Earl of Kesson, was a good match for a woman of such stature. One might imagine the two peers as well-suited and happy, but that morning, the duchess's sullen mood had the power to make her tall husband visibly shrink, as though trying to vanish from his wife's piercing gaze.

"As usual, you're late," she told father and daughter. "Mr. Kaplan was most precise with his request. We were to gather no later than nine o'clock. It is now quarter past, Connor. Is this your fault or Elizabeth's?"

"It's probably mine," Charles interrupted as he entered the drawing room.

"No, it isn't," Connor told his wife, his eyes on Sinclair. "But fifteen minutes is hardly a tragedy." He reached for her waist, as any husband might, trying to show tenderness. "Kaplan was still setting up when I arrived. This will be a fine portrait, my darling. You'll see. A Christmas portrait to remember. Isn't that right, Princess?" he asked his only child.

"Do stop calling her Princess!" the duchess shouted as she wrenched free of Connor's embrace.

"Why?" Sinclair dared to ask. "I call her Princess, as does Paul. And James does as well. Has it become a crime?"

Hearing the guest's remark, Trish's tone softened markedly, and she smiled. "No, but it gives the wrong impression, Charles, and besides, I prefer Elizabeth remain out of that inner circle nonsense."

"Nonsense?" muttered Connor. "How is keeping our families safe nonsense?"

"The circle is medieval and totally unnecessary," Trish countered. "Do back me up on this, Charles. This business is what gives Beth nightmares."

"Her nightmares arise from elsewhere," Charles told the angry duchess.

"If you say so," Patricia muttered, dismissively. "Have Angie and Abigail come down yet? Has Tory? I've not seen any of them this morning. Charles, do you know if your mother plans to be in the photograph?"

"I've not spoken to her this morning," he said, hoping it were true.

"Aunt Abbie's not feeling well, and Uncle Robert's gone out with my father," said Connor. "I believe they're checking to see if the reflecting pool has frozen over. You know Dad. If he can't shoot pheasant on Boxing Day, then he'll want to ice skate."

"Oh, I know your father all too well," Trish complained. "And I doubt Abbie's really ill. She's just unsociable. I cannot understand why she and Robert come all the way from Briarcliff, if they don't intend to spend any time with us."

"It isn't intended as a snub," said Connor to his wife. "Briarcliff's a long way from Glasgow, meaning Rob seldom sees my father, and Abbie has very little chance to visit with her sisters."

"You'd think she'd make more of an effort after almost losing Angie."

"Cousin Charles, is your mother sick? Shall we send for Dr. Price?" asked Beth innocently.

"No, little one, my mother's fine," he said, wondering what Patricia could mean.

Beth sighed. "I wish I had a brother or sister."

Patricia's fierce countenance softened slightly. "Being an only child means more love, doesn't it?"

"Yes, only..." the girl started to say, but stopped when she noticed her mother's light blue eyes turning angry again. "What I mean is, I'm very happy to have such a nice home and lots of friends like Mrs. Alcorn and Mr. Baxter. We're all very lucky, aren't we, Cousin Charles?"

"Let's find everyone and get this photograph taken," said Patricia, who felt a headache coming on. "Mr. Kaplan, are you ready?"

"Yes, Your Grace. The cameras are set and the plates prepared."

"I can look for Grandfather and Uncle Robert," said Beth, heading towards the doorway to escape her mother's temper.

"Not on your own!" her father called.

"I'll take her," volunteered Sinclair.

"Thank you, Charles. That's very thoughtful," Trish said in a sugary sweet voice.

"It's nothing," he said. "We enjoy doing things together, don't we?" Elizabeth nodded. "Then, we must find warm coats. It looks very chilly out there." Charles turned to Patricia and added, "We won't be long, I promise. Just give us a shout when the photographer's ready to begin."

Charles and young Beth left the house by way of the wide south portico that led into the formal gardens. They walked together towards the Hall's reflecting pool, a magnificent arrow of blue, that led visitors from the Lion Gates to the greatest estate in all of Kent.

"Mother's not really angry. She's just sad," Elizabeth told him as they approached the northern edge of the pond. "Can married people stop loving each other?"

"Not if they're truly in love. Would you ever stop loving me?" he asked.

"Never," she said, smiling up at him. "Not ever."

Charles thought of his first wife, Amelia Winstone St. Clair. At first, she seemed to love him, but then quickly lost interest. Had she willfully strayed, or did he push her away? Was Harold Lowry's charm the cause, or was it his fault for refusing to become a lawyer?

Despite the pain, God spun all those lonely moments into a golden future.

"You're very far away, Captain," Beth said.

He opened his mouth to apologise, but then suddenly realised she'd called him *Captain.*

"Captain? Why would you call me that?" he asked.

"Don't you like it? It's from a novel. Father used to read it to me to help with my French. Captain Nemo is the main character. I think you're quite heroic."

"I'm glad you think so, little one," he said, noticing two tall men farther on, strolling through the entry gardens. "What book is it?"

"*Vingt mille lieues sous les mers,*" she replied, perfectly pronouncing the French. "By Jules Verne. Father said it was a great adventure book, and hearing the French would help me with the language. Perhaps, I could read it to you?"

"*Oui! J'aimerais beaucoup ça,*" he replied. "*Tu parles très bien la langue, ma petite.*"

She laughed. "I think I understood most of that. And you speak the language very well, too, *mon Capitaine.*"

"Do you call me Captain because I'm heroic?"

"Yes, and because you always seem a little sad," she told him, moving a bit closer. "As though you think you're all alone—like Captain Nemo. But you're not alone, Cousin Charles. I'll always be there for you, and I shan't ever stop loving you. Not for one fraction of the tiniest moment."

He stopped and dropped to one knee. "No one has ever shown me more love or devotion, Princess. Shall I propose to you now?"

All humour left her face, and she leaned in close to whisper, "I'd like that, but first, you must finish the Maze."

He drew back, shocked at her words. "Why would you say that?"

"Because it's what the Shadow Man told me. He said you were working very hard to find your way through. Then I had a dream that we walked past all the many faces together, and I helped you find your way. I shall always help you, Captain. Always."

Her simple promise caught him by surprise, and Sinclair's eyes filled with tears. "You love me far more than I deserve."

"Not true," she said, looking quite serious. "You deserve only the finest, purest love; for that is what you give. Oh, hello, Uncle Robert," she said, glancing at two approaching men.

"Hello, Princess," called Lord Aubrey. "I see you have a gallant knight as escort this morning."

"He's my very own Captain. That's a reference to a book," she explained.

"I see. I'm glad you made it, Charles," said Lord Aubrey. "I assume you're discussing politics with the real expert in the family. Are we late for the portrait?"

Sinclair stood and shook his uncle's hand. "It's always an honour, sir. I'm very glad you and Aunt Abigail made it down this year. Is she unwell?"

"You know my wife. She's been prone to illness and delicate since Paul was born, but she rallies when needed. Beth, are you getting taller?" he asked, lifting her into an embrace. "Oh, and heavier, too, it seems! Or is it this new coat that's heavy? Are the pockets filled with gold treasure?"

Beth giggled as he tickled her cheeks. "No treasure, Uncle Robert. Just lots of love."

He smiled at the sweet comment. "That's the best treasure of all. And I suppose most of that love belongs to our Charles? Well, that's only fair. Let's go inside, shall we?" He continued to carry her, walking beside Charles and Duke James.

"How's your mother, son?" Drummond asked his nephew.

It struck the time traveller that he'd not yet visited his own mother. He wondered how she'd sound and look. "I'm told she's quite well," he bluffed. "Mother's rooming near Tory."

"Those two were always thick as thieves," James said. "Once we're done with this photograph, let's find Paul, and then the four of us can spend a few minutes in the library."

"You're going to talk about inner circle things, aren't you?" asked the child.

"We might," James answered with a friendly wink. "Would you like to join us, Princess?"

"Not today," she said in a very grown-up voice.

"Your future husband will lead the group one day," said Aubrey. "Will you join the circle then?"

"Only if he needs me. And he'll be a fine leader. The Captain can do anything. Don't you agree, Uncle Robert?"

"She's quite astute, our girl," said Drummond, laughing. "Aye, but don't mention the meeting to your mother, Beth."

"I won't. Will Father join you?"

"He might."

"Is that Mr. Baxter on the porch steps?" asked Charles, glad to see the butler's imposing figure.

"It looks like he's holding a bit of paper," said Aubrey.

"Might be a telegram," said James.

"Shall I see what it is?" asked Elizabeth. "I can run very fast."

Aubrey set her on the gravel. "Show us your speed, then. Go see what Baxter has, Princess. Run now!"

The girl hastened along the ornamented walkway, past the main fountain, and up to the portico. She spoke to Baxter and called back to the men. "It is a telegram! From London!"

James smiled. "It's probably from Drina. She mentioned visiting for Christmas."

"As in Auntie Drina?" asked Charles.

"Is there another?" laughed Drummond.

"Wonderful. I look forward to seeing her again," answered the younger man with conviction.

They reached the portico several minutes after Beth, and as he stepped onto the porch, Charles reached for the butler's hand to shake it. "Good morning, Baxter. It's always good to see you," he said to the impressively dressed servant.

Younger by fourteen years, Baxter's hair was far less grey, and his face had fewer lines, but the dark brown eyes carried the same intelligence and mirth. It was reassuring to know that, no matter the timeline, no matter the mirror shard, some things never changed.

"A very good morning to you as well, my lord," he told Haimsbury. "I trust you slept soundly?"

"Like a top," Charles assured him, though he'd not slept here at all, just appeared an hour earlier.

Robert Stuart took the telegram and read it quickly. "I'm afraid it's not from Drina, but the Prime Minister. It looks as though our Christmas could be cut short."

Baxter took Elizabeth's hand. "Lady Anjou, shall we return to the house?"

"We should find my father, Mr. Baxter."

"Of course, my lady. Come with me."

As the group entered the foyer, they encountered a rush of decorating activity. The foyer tree had arrived, and a dozen footmen were setting up ladders and unpacking large boxes, to begin trimming its glorious branches.

Oblivious to the activity, Patricia stood near the magnificent staircase, arguing with Paul Stuart. From the first floor landing above, Victoria watched the intriguing commotion with another woman. Charles's heart leapt at seeing her, for it was his mother: alive, healthy, and looking exceedingly more beautiful than any of her portraits.

"Excuse me," he told his uncles. "I just need to wish my mother a good morning."

The time traveller wriggled his way through the jostling crowd of footmen. Each bowed his head as he passed.

"Excuse me," Charles said politely. "Pardon me."

As he neared the staircase, Trish Stuart threw up her hands and began to shout. "Fine! I've had enough of all of you! Take the photograph without me. I've a headache. If my husband asks, I shall be upstairs with a migraine."

The duchess hastened up the steps and pushed past Tory and Angela without speaking.

Charles spoke to Paul as he reached the steps. "Trouble?"

The left side of his cousin's face was red; the look of a man who's just been slapped. "More trouble than you know. I'd avoid the master wing for now, Cousin. There's a fierce storm blowing."

"I'll batten down the hatches, but if you want to talk, I'm here."

"It's nothing a little time won't heal," answered Stuart, rubbing his cheek.

"Once we've taken the portrait, your father wants to convene a meeting in the library. Do you mind asking the photographer to wait a little while? I want to have a quick word with my mother."

Paul sighed. "Yes, go ahead. I'll keep Beth company."

Stuart left to find the child, whilst Charles climbed up to the landing. *What do I say to a woman I barely remember?*

Angela Sinclair was smaller than Charles had imagined. He'd always pictured his mother tall and willowy like Victoria, but she was no taller than Elizabeth and slightly plump. He wondered if her twin sister, Abigail, had a similar physique. Angela's eyes were blue with hints of turquoise, and her hair an auburnish sort of light brown with streaks of grey amongst the thick strands.

Overwhelmed by emotion, Charles pulled her into a tight embrace. "I cannot believe it's you!" he heard himself say as tears wet his cheeks. "My own beautiful mother. How I've longed to hold you like this!"

Victoria stood nearby, watching with measured consideration. "I'm here as well, Nephew," she said in her usual droll tone. "Do I, also, merit so loving a hug, or do Trinity's seniors find aunts extraneous now?"

Charles responded by pulling Tory over and making it a family embrace, grateful to have such a miraculous moment and wishing it could last for years.

"Charles, are you all right?" his mother asked once he'd finally released them. "You're not ill, I hope?"

"No, Mother," he said, kissing her dimpled hands. "Your son is very healthy, but also exceedingly happy. Sometimes, the Lord uses ways unimaginable to bring us joy."

"I've no idea what you mean, but I'm very glad you came down from Cambridge," she told him. "You look thin."

"I'm hardly that," he said, kissing her cheek. "Happy Christmas, Mother. And may every day be blessed for you. I love you very, very much."

Angela smiled. "Tory, it's a shame you never married, for few things bring more joy than hearing a child say he loves you. Come now, Charles, let's say hello to Abigail. She's under the weather and asks for you."

Charles stepped back to have a good look at Victoria. Her hair hadn't yet greyed, and the dark locks were fashioned into a long braid. She wore riding breeches and boots.

"I take it you plan to visit the stables?"

"Are you detecting, Charley Bob? Yes, after much coaxing, I've convinced your mother to see this new stallion of Connor's. His name is Paladin. Such a magnificent animal, which is a miracle, for he nearly died last year. He's now the fastest horse in the county. Beth's already mastered him, if you can imagine that tiny girl astride a tall stallion."

"I can imagine it," he told his aunt. "Mother, we're about to take the photograph, and then I've promised to meet with my uncles in the library. Might we postpone visiting Aunt Abigail until afterwards?"

"Oh, yes, of course. Circle meetings always take precedence. You'd have made your father proud, Charles."

"Nothing would please me more," he whispered, kissing her cheek.

"I'll pose for a portrait, but I'm skipping the meeting," said Victoria. "I'm sure I know what it's about, and my input isn't needed. If he'll let me, I plan to take Paladin round the lake before it snows."

"You'll find his gait smooth and steady," said Charles, recalling his and Beth's daring ride from St. Arilda's Abbey to Parker's Clearing to reach Edmund Reid's hot air balloon. "I've never ridden a horse more reliable or sure-footed."

"You've ridden Paladin?" Tory asked in surprise. "You must have a miraculous way with animals, Charles. The creature snorts and stamps anytime Paul or James comes near him. I'd always assumed he prefers women."

Charles had spoken without thinking, so he changed the subject to divert his inquisitive aunt's further questions. "The photographer's waiting, ladies. Shall we? I'll visit Aunt Abbie later."

He offered one arm to his mother, the other to his aunt, and together the three descended to the main floor and then through to the red room.

Assembling the Stuart-Sinclair clan took another ten minutes, with some murmuring about Trish's glaring absence. The photographer took fifteen plates, and then switched to a stereo camera, exposing another ten plates. Finally, after nearly half an hour, he declared that year's session complete and began to pack up his equipment.

Elizabeth decided to accompany Victoria and Angela to the stables, telling them she'd taught Paladin several tricks. The men convened in the Hall's private library. Baxter delivered coffee, tea, and a selection of breakfast dishes, and then quietly retreated to perform other duties.

Robert Stuart sat at the head, with Duke James on his left, Paul on his right, and Charles sat at the opposite end of the rectangular table. Connor declined to attend, deciding instead to escort Beth and his aunts.

"With my son absent, we can say a few things I'd ordinarily leave alone," James began as he stirred cream into a cup of strong coffee. "I'm sure you can imagine what I'm about to say."

Paul looked like a guilty man caught in a trap. "I can imagine it, sir. I fear Trish isn't well, and I do not refer to her migraines. She's begun to talk about Ian again, and..." he paused, looking at his father, "and she's blaming you, sir."

Robert Stuart had a serenity about him that seemed almost otherworldly. Even at sixty-one, his blue eyes remained clear, and the boyishly handsome face youthful. "I'm accustomed to being Patricia's target," he told his son. "Just stay clear of her for now."

"Why would she blame you, sir?" Charles asked his uncle.

"She thinks I prevented her from marrying Ian, but that's not true." Then Robert looked to his son. "Paul, we couldn't help but notice your argument. Did Connor see any of that exchange?"

"I don't think so, but it wasn't my fault, sir, I assure you. And I'd watch my back, if I were you, Charles."

"Why?" asked Sinclair, trying to learn as much as he could about the situation. *Why am I here? Why did God open this particular mirror shard?*

"Charles?" the duke interrupted, tearing the traveller from his thoughts.

"Sorry, sir. I was just trying to reason out why Trish might argue with any of us. Surely, she's content with life. She has a great title, beautiful estates, and a perfect family."

"I don't know if you're aware, Charles," said Robert Stuart, "but you look a great deal like my late son. Ian had the same basic facial features and physique. It's not surprising, as I'm your uncle twice over; your grandmother being my elder sister. The Stuart traits are very pronounced in you. Patricia was fiercely obsessed with Ian. She told my wife that he'd promised to marry her at Gretna Green. Ian's sudden death ended those plans. But the truth is far different. My son was already betrothed to another, and Trish knew this. I fear the duchess has been prone to invention for years."

"You're saying Patricia and Ian weren't in love?" asked Charles.

"She was, but Ian was not. We warned Connor to be careful, but the lad was head over heels."

James sighed and stared into his cup. "I wish my son could find the same happiness you've found with Abigail, Rob."

"As do I, James," the earl answered sadly, "but no matter what we may wish, words alone cannot fix a marriage." He addressed this last comment directly at Paul.

"I wasn't trying to fix anything," the younger Stuart argued. "Trish said things that were entirely inappropriate. Not about Connor or me, or even you, Father; but about Charles."

"What did she say?" asked James.

Paul wished he'd said nothing. "It doesn't matter. I was in error. Shall we get to the reason we're here? I assume it's to do with these murders in London."

"The so-called Songbird Killings?" asked Charles. "Paul mentioned there'd been another early this morning. In the West End near Whitehall. Uncle Robert, is that why Prime Minister Disraeli sent word?"

"I fear it is," said Lord Aubrey. "He's asking the circle to investigate the matter. Assuming we'd be discussing this, I took the liberty of bringing all records regarding the crimes. No one outside the circle can know these details, gentlemen. Some are quite shocking."

Charles felt at home now, in his proper element. Police work was familiar, no matter the era or mirror-shard reality. "May I see them, sir?"

"Yes, of course." Robert handed him a box file marked 'S.B.K.' and embossed with the circle's unique emblem, a P crossed by an S.

Charles opened the file and began to examine the documents. As a seasoned policeman, he'd seen thousands of such records and was able to ascertain the pertinent facts quickly. "They're strangled, then disemboweled," he said. "All under twenty. All singers. No, wait. Alice Graham wasn't."

"No?" asked Drummond. "What was her occupation?"

"Prostitute, though the entry obscures that fact. However, if you read closely, you'll see a fellow claiming to be her brother, said Miss Graham performed nightly at the Tower Hamlets Club. That isn't a music hall, but a notorious rookery. Though the women perform, they do not sing."

"Charles, how on earth do you know that?" asked Lord Aubrey. "

"Let's just say I have some experience."

"With prostitutes?" both uncles asked in unison.

"No, not that way, sirs. I've..." he paused, wondering how to explain himself without opening the Time Maze topic, which would lead to a trove of other questions. "I've been studying maps of London along with newspaper accounts. It's become a hobby of mine. Solving crime is similar to solving mathematical equations, and I thought it might help me with circle investigations."

James began to laugh and lifted his cup in a sort of toast. "Here's to you, son. As Beth's future husband, you'll lead this group one day. It's good to learn your nose has left maths and music long enough to study real-world matters. So, tell us about this rookery. Do you think it's a departure from the murderer's pattern?"

Charles thumbed through the other pages; the women's physical details and family information. Most were on their own, either unmarried or divorced. However, he noticed a detail on a Westminster victim that surprised him. "Sirs, did either of you see the witness statement on Theresa Coleman? She was killed two months ago near St. James's Park."

"I remember that case," Paul interjected. "She sang at the Lyceum and also at a music hall near Kennington Oval. What witness statement do you mean? Her manager's?"

"No, that of an audience member. She was killed shortly after the final curtain, in a storage area off the fly-space. But unlike all the others, Coleman's eyes were removed and then placed inside her hands. The witness spoke to Detective Brown, saying, 'The poor girl sang like a lark in the mornin'. Such pretty eyes she had, too. Shame about those.'"

"This audience member said that?" Paul asked. "How could he know about the eyes?"

"Exactly," Charles told his cousin. "Why would he mention the eyes, and how could he have known? According to his own statement, he sat in the cheap seats, because he'd bought a late ticket. The Lyceum is a very long hall, and unless he brought opera glasses, he couldn't have seen her eyes. Either he knew the girl, or else he knew her killer. But he certainly knew details of the crime that were never published."

"That's a leap of logic, son," Lord Aubrey told his nephew. "I can see why you might be suspicious, but perhaps he did know her. Personally and previously."

"Meaning she also serviced men," Paul noted. "Are all the victims working girls, then?"

"It's a theory we need to explore," Drummond said as he loaded up a plate with eggs and salted kippers. "Rob and I were discussing taking his train up to London to investigate this personally. I hate leaving the Hall, as it's possible the queen may wish to come down."

"Why not send Paul and me, sir? We could overnight at my home," Charles said, referring to Haimsbury House, which he assumed was open and functioning in this world.

"A very good idea," Paul's father replied. "Martin's coming down in an hour or so. He's using our second train, which gives you a lift back. We'll keep the first train here at Branham for emergencies."

"Then, it's settled," said Drummond. "It's probably best if you both stay out from under Trish's sensitive feet till her migraine's over. My son may love that woman, but sometimes, I really wish he'd married someone else."

"Then, we'd not have our Beth," said Robert Stuart.

Baxter knocked on the closed door, calling, "Sirs, might I come in?"

"Of course, Mr. B. Come in," replied the duke.

The butler entered, then shut the door immediately. "I'm to say the little marchioness has returned and must speak with Lord Haimsbury at once. She said to tell you it's about a maze, sir."

Charles stood at once. "Let me talk to Beth and then we'll make plans for London."

As he left the room to find Elizabeth, he could hear the other men talking about his surprising abilities at criminal detection. Smiling at this, Sinclair passed through the busy footmen and followed Baxter.

Beth was in the red room, sitting beside the family tree. "Oh, you're here," she said, wiping her eyes. She'd been crying, and he wondered what might have caused it. "

Thank you, Mr. Baxter," Charles told his friend. "I'll take it from here."

The butler shut the doors, leaving the two cousins alone.

"What's caused all these tears? I thought you went to the stables with Aunt Tory and your father?" Charles asked as he sat on the floor next to her.

"I changed my mind. I'm being silly, I know," she sniffed, "but I'm afraid, and I don't know why."

He pulled her close, his fingers running through her long, raven curls. "Afraid? Might you have even the tiniest idea what caused these fears? You can tell me anything, you know. I will always believe you, little one. Always."

"Even if I told you about whispers? Mother says people who hear voices are mad. She said she might send me away if I talk about it."

This shocked Charles. What kind of mother was Patricia Stuart to even suggest such a thing?

"No one is going to send you away, little one. If you hear voices, then someone must be talking. What do the whispers say? What do you hear?"

She leaned in close, clutching at his arms for protection. "I think they're ghosts."

"Are they? When did you hear these ghosts? Was it just now?"

She nodded. "I waited until Father left with Auntie Tory and Aunt Angie, and then I came in here. I was watching Mr. Kaplan pack up his things, and after he left, and I was alone, I saw them."

"You saw ghosts?"

Beth's entire body trembled in his arms. "Yes. The ghosts said you're from somewhere else. That you're a traveller, walking through some sort of maze, and that this is a test. The Shadow Man talked about a maze, too."

"Are these ghosts women or men, darling?"

"Both. First a woman, then a man. It's very confusing. Is Mother right? Am I going mad, Captain?"

"No, darling. If you are, then so am I. Did these strange ghosts tell you anything else?"

She nodded. "The woman said I should take you to the old stone circle. That you'll know why."

A man and a woman? Might these ghosts be Eluna with her mad brother? Charles had no idea why either of them would tell this beautiful, sensitive child to go to such a pagan site.

"Do you think we should go?" he asked her.

"I don't want to," she said, clutching his arms. "I'm sorry to interrupt your meeting. Were you helping Grandfather and Uncle Robert?"

"I was. And Paul's with them, too."

"Mother's very angry with Paul."

"Why? I thought your mother liked Paul."

"They fight almost every time he visits. He came down last month from Oxford, and she threw plates and cups at him after we finished supper. You can ask Mr. Baxter. One of the plates shattered behind his head and cut his left ear. It bled and bled. Mother felt terrible and tried to make up for it, but Paul was terribly angry and left right after. She's very different when Father's away."

"How often is your father gone?" he asked, realising at once that the Charles Sinclair of this world should already know the answer.

Beth took no note of it. "Far too much. He only just got back from India a few days ago, and he's to leave again next week for Constantinople."

"I'm sure he'd much rather be here," he said. "But let's not think about any of that now, all right? What do you say we visit those stones together? Perhaps, the voice is sending us on a Christmas adventure."

He stood and reached down for her hand.

"Are you sure?" she asked.

"Very sure. After we visit the stones, we'll walk to the stables to see Paladin. Perhaps, we'll ride him together."

"I'd like that," she said, brightening at last. "I think Auntie Tory's riding him today. We may have to wait."

"I'm sure we can find something to do whilst waiting."

It was then that Charles noticed a set of eyes in the room that he'd missed entirely during the photographic session. Beneath the Christmas tree, placed upright, dressed in the same clothing it had worn every other time, was the porcelain doll. Instinctively, he picked up Elizabeth, for he always felt a sense of dread whenever the doll appeared. It was an evil doll, perhaps even a possessed one. He wondered if the doll were the real source of the voices she'd heard.

"Is that a new dolly?" he asked her.

"Mother's friend gave it to me, but I don't like it. I asked her to give it back, but she insists it must always be in the house."

"Did you bring it down here and set it near the tree so it could celebrate with us?"

She shook her head, the dark curls bouncing in the chandelier's glow. "No. And it wasn't here when the photographs were made. I'd have noticed, Captain. It wasn't here."

"Perhaps, someone else brought it down, thinking you might want to have it with you. Never mind, darling. We'll deal with the doll later." He carried her back to the foyer, signalling to Baxter. "Could you bring the marchioness's coat?"

"Of course, Lord Haimsbury. Also, Duchess Patricia asked if she might speak with you. Upstairs."

Beth clutched him tightly. "Don't go," she whispered.

"Please, tell the duchess that I'll see her shortly, Mr. Baxter. This dear lady and I plan to take a short walk first. Beth, have you eaten yet?"

"I had some toast and tea in the nursery. I'm not hungry."

"Neither am I," he said. He helped her with the coat and made sure her boots were tightly buckled, and then carried Elizabeth through a labyrinth of interior rooms, into the solarium, and then out to the north gardens. As they walked, the cold December breeze tousled his long hair, and Elizabeth touched his cheek.

"What's this scar?" she asked.

"Scar?"

"I don't remember it. I hope Mother didn't throw china at you as well."

He reached up with his free hand, to the spot she'd indicated. The raised scar tissue ran along his jawline for half an inch. He knew it well, but hadn't expected it to be on his face here. He reached behind his head, finding the deeper scar left by the iron post on the night of his wedding to Beth.

Now, why are these here?

"The scar's from fencing," he said, finding it the easiest explanation. "At school."

"Oh," she said, kissing the scar lightly. "Did it hurt?"

"I can't remember, honestly," he said, which was true regarding the explosion. He had no memory at all of the fire on Columbia Road, nor of the injury which kept him in a coma for many days. "Tell me about this friend who gave you the doll. Do I know her?"

"Not her. Him. It's a man who sometimes visits, but only when Father's away."

"Is that so? Do you remember this friend's name?"

"It's Sir William. I don't like him at all."

Trent! Why did this demonic fiend appear so often? Was this what he was meant to learn here? Is this why the mirror shard opened? *Father God, what am I to do? Do I stay here and protect her? If Trent has already achieved some hold on Patricia, then this Beth will be tortured by the brute!*

They'd reached the edge of the northeast gardens. From here, a gravel path led to the kitchen gardens and beyond those to the stables. Beth once told him the proximity to the gardens made it easier to transfer the ever-abundant horse manure to feed the plants. They crossed through an arched willow gate, covered in withered jasmine vines. A footpath would lead them to the ancient circle of stones, some five hundred yards away.

His long silence worried the child. "Are you angry with me, Captain? I'm sorry. I probably shouldn't have said anything about Sir William. Please, don't tell my father."

"No, darling, I'm not angry, and I shan't say a word. But I should like to meet this Sir William person. Do you know where he lives?"

"I think it's somewhere near Regent's Park. Mother once told our driver to take her there, and when she came home, she was wearing a new sapphire brooch. She said it was a gift from Sir William."

"Did she mention the street to the driver? Did she ever go there whilst you were with her?"

Beth's smile vanished. "Once. Don't ask me about it."

He knelt down and kissed her hands. "I won't let anyone hurt you."

She pulled into his arms. "I know. The house overlooks the park. It has lots of other houses round it, but it's the tallest one. Four storeys. White with a black door."

"You're very observant," he said proudly as they resumed their walk. After several minutes, they reached a clearing near a stand of oak trees. The ancient stone circle dominated the landscape. A large raven sat atop the King Stone. The bird stared at Charles. It had yellow eyes.

"We're here, little one," said Haimsbury. "Do you know where inside the circle we're to go? Did these whispers explain what we're to do?"

"No, but may I wait here? This place frightens me a little."

"Why?"

"It feels wrong. Like... Like monsters are hiding inside."

"Monsters like the Shadow Man?"

"Yes," she whispered.

"Shall I go inside?"

She nodded. "Be careful, Captain."

"Will you pray for me?" he asked sweetly, noticing the tears in her eyes.

"I always pray for you, Charles."

No child version of Beth had never called him Charles. Cousin Charles once or twice, but never just Charles. Not even the real version, whom he'd met after finding her mother's mangled body on Commercial Road in Whitechapel in 1879. Four years from now, a passing prostitute would discover Patricia Stuart's body, the porcelain skin bloody, and the sky-blue eyes dead and empty.

Suddenly, Charles felt pity for the willful duchess. Why had she asked to talk to him? Was all of this some twisted sort of trick? He felt uneasy about the whole thing and wondered if they shouldn't return to the house.

He touched Beth's cheek, which was wet with tears. There was such trust in those dark eyes, such boundless love! Was it any wonder he'd loved her from the very start?

But what and when was their real beginning? In Whitechapel? Somewhere inside the hedge maze? He'd begun to see time far differently. Perhaps, God had connected them before the beginning of Time. Even before he said, 'Let there be light!'.

"Shall we go back, or should I go into the stones?"

"The whispers say you must go in," she told him.

He kissed her hands. "Very well, then, but I'll be right back."

Elizabeth threw her small arms round his neck as though she feared she'd never see him again. As though she were saying goodbye. "I love you, Captain," she told him in a manner so grown-up, so mature that it startled Charles.

"You own my heart, little one. You always have." He kissed her cheek and then both hands. "I'll see you soon."

Leaving her behind, he walked towards the circle's centre. Charles turned just before reaching the largest stone, called the King's Stone by villagers. Beth blew him a kiss and waved. Charles smiled, then turned once more.

After taking three short strides, he disappeared.

CHAPTER THIRTY-SEVEN
Time Maze – Charles begins the final journey

One minute, Charles had been at Branham Hall of 1875, next he'd stepped into a house, and all was dark. He could feel carpet beneath his feet, and smell the welcome scent of baking bread.

But whose house was it? And when?

Was it even his proper world?

He touched the scarlet sash in his pocket, grateful to find it. He checked the jacket. The Sir John Bennett was tucked safely in the breast pocket, and his wedding ring remained on his left hand. Having these tokens, gave him a sense of hope; a connexion to Elizabeth and HOME.

Thank you, Lord.

"Are you lost again?" asked a small voice.

Charles turned about, and a tiny light flamed up. A candle. The yellow light illuminated the girl's dark eyes and perfect mouth.

"Beth?" he asked.

"Of course, Captain."

"But I just left you," he whispered, his breathing quickening. Every bit of blood flow threatened to leave his brain, and Charles thought he might faint.

Her small fingers touched his, and a lightning bolt of strength surged up his arm. He opened his eyes. Behind Elizabeth stood a tall figure that seemed lit from within by a bright and brilliant orb.

"I've brought a friend," she told him. "He's been whispering to me, and now he wants to talk to you, Captain."

"Who are you?" the traveller asked the bright figure.

"Don't you recognise me, sir?" asked the other. "Oh, do forgive me! I've forgotten to assume the proper form again."

The brilliant figure's outline rippled and seemed to melt into something new. Charles wondered if he had fainted and now hallucinated some new vision or entered a mirror.

"There now," the other said as he solidified into a familiar face and body. "As I say, it's my fault. I'd just come from delivering a message elsewhere and neglected to assume the appropriate guise."

"Fenwick?" asked Charles. "It's you? Am I dreaming?"

Beth sat upon a chair and helped her future husband into one next to it. "He needs water," she told the angelic servant.

"Of course, he does," said Fenwick, who instantly produced a glass of clear, pure water. "This will strengthen you, sir. You're very nearly there. To the centre, I mean."

Sinclair drank the entire glass, which tasted like sweet nectar. "What happened to the other Elizabeth? I was at Branham. I entered that circle, and then I was here. What happened to her?"

"Yes, sir. It is confusing, but that is how the Maze sometimes works."

"No, she needs me! I left her alone by that pagan circle!"

"So you think, Your Grace, but you were never really there. The locked rooms are drawn from your own memories and given a twist to overwhelm your senses. They're nothing but shadows of reflections. Didn't Prince Anatole explain it to you?"

"Yes, but..." Charles sighed, his brain aching as well as his heart. "I just want to go home."

The child Beth took his hand. "Soon you'll be rescued, Captain. Take heart and trust in the Lord. He's always been here with you."

Fenwick smiled. "You're nearly done, sir. This is Rose House, and you're to enter the hedge maze. Once inside, another will guide you."

Beth left her chair and stood on tiptoe to kiss his cheek. "I'll see you soon, Captain. Trust in God."

She left the small room and shut the door.

"What now?" Charles asked the servant.

"I'll take you outside to the hedge maze, but you shouldn't have any trouble. Just walk towards the centre, as you did many times as a boy. The turnings may be a little different than you remember, but your guide is inside."

"Very well. Fenwick?"

"Yes, sir?" asked the kind-hearted angel.

"Will you pray for me? I'm growing very tired and confused. I just want all this to be over."

"I've been praying for you all along, sir. As are all my loyal brothers. The One can see all times and all choices. He's always known what you would experience and how you would respond, but my brothers and I cannot see these things. Your courage is far greater than I imagined it to be, sir! Take heart, for it is nearly done. However, the final challenges are the most difficult."

"If God leads me, then I shall follow," said the duke. "Take me to the maze."

When they stepped outside, the sun shone with crystal beauty upon trees filled with golds, reds, and oranges. "It's autumn," said Charles.

"It is, sir. It's mid-October."

"Am I still in the mirror world?"

"Yes, sir. It looks exactly like God's true world, because it is, in a way. You see, humans cannot see beyond a certain set of dimensions. The fallen realm live in a dimension outside human perception. It is why, whilst in the Rose House and Branham mazes, you would sometimes vanish as a boy. Sometimes, you'd meet up with the little duchess."

"As I did last year?"

"That's right, sir."

"Why can I see this world?"

"The One has allowed it. The fallen realm think your blood is special because of them, but the One works through you, for his reasons and plans. You will one day change the world, sir. You and your sons."

"My sons," said the duke, smiling. He took a deep breath. "I had to watch my wife die, Fenwick. In that first mirror-shard world. Beth died in my arms."

"Yes, sir. I am sorry, Your Grace, but it didn't really happen. The genuine duchess is very much alive and waiting for you to come home."

"And we'll have more sons?"

"Yes, sir. Five more sons. Your guide is waiting, sir."

"Who is it?"

"You'll see. I'm not to say."

"Thank you, Fenwick. Will I see you again?"

"You will, sir. May the One's blessings keep you safe. We're all praying for you. I'm always praying for you."

They walked together several more steps, through a garden that had seen better days. If this place revealed the true condition of Rose House, then Charles needed to hire someone to renovate the estate and grounds.

The hedge maze which had so fascinated him as a boy stood about two hundred yards to the west. The smell of the yews brought back a flood of old memories, and he smiled, picturing a boyish Paul Stuart, trailing along behind him. The two of them would run and play in the maze's many turns, pretending to be pirates or knights or even their fathers.

Now, the long-neglected hedges took on a menacing look. Before going inside, Charles decided to stop and pray; to gather up his courage. He found a ragstone bench nearby. He sat upon it and began to filter through everything he'd seen and experienced thus far. What did the Lord want him to learn from all this? Was it that he could count on Beth no matter what? He already knew he could. Or might it be that she was strong and eager to help? He'd discouraged her inclusion in circle meetings, but only because of previous physical reactions. She'd suffered a terrifying seizure in Scotland, according to Duke James and Paul.

What had young Beth told him about William Trent? That he lived in a white home with a black door. It stood four storeys high, taller than its neighbours and overlooked Regent's Park. If Trent had lived in such a place, the house should be simple to find. He sifted through the many dozens of conversations he'd enjoyed—or not enjoyed, depending on the topic—and one stood out: the meeting with Paul's father regarding the Songbird Killings. In fact, now that he thought about it, each of these experiences included some reference to that group of murders. They'd happened in '74 and '75 in the real world. He'd need to see Scotland Yard's records, but also those kept by the inner circle. Might the names of the victims be important? All were singers, yet some appeared to be prostitutes as well. But all included a victim from the Lyceum. And two victims were discovered near Queen Anne. One in the mirror-shard world; one in the real world back in '74. Once he made it home, he'd comb through Scotland Yard's records and see if the victims' names were the same. Somewhere inside those files was the connexion to all this.

Energised by the idea of returning to good, honest police work helped motivate the duke to push on towards the final challenge. After rising from the bench, Charles stopped at the entrance, knelt down, and prayed.

"Father of all times, all worlds, all that is past, future, and present, I come to you now seeking strength and courage. The world of men has no need of heroes. Not in the classical sense of the word. Halflings like Theseus have no special place in history, for they pale when compared to your Son, Christ Jesus, who is my King and Saviour. The Son who is also you, my Lord. You. Only your blood is special, for it alone provides payment for all of mankind's sin! It provided payment for my sin. Your journey alone was special, for you lived a sinless life and then carried my sins upon your back, as you carried that cross to Calvary.

"Why am I here, my Lord? Not to prove any intrinsic value to my life or to my blood, no, that is what the fallen think, but they're wrong. I am here in this place to please you, my Lord. I am here, because you have ordained it, for reasons yet unfathomable to me. But it matters not if I can plumb those depths. A sheep does not question the Shepherd. You are my Shepherd, and so I follow where you lead. If you lead me to green pastures, then I shall sing and enjoy the bounty; if you take me beside still waters, then I shall drink to my fill, knowing you keep watch whilst I enjoy the clear water. Even if you lead me into the valley of the Shadow of Death, I will not fear, for you are with me! You carry a rod and staff that terrifies the fallen and protects me, and so even then, I may walk in safety.

"And so, my King, whatever awaits me, be it green pastures, refreshing water, or even the terrors of Death, I go willingly and trustingly. I ask only that you watch after my family and, if it be your will, lead me home to them. In Christ the Good Shepherd's name I ask all these things. Amen."

The duke rose from his knees and took a deep breath. Then, he stepped into the great hedge maze.

Charles had memorised the pattern to the Rose House maze as a child, but this version was far different. At first, he thought it might be a mirror image of the real one, for this was the mirror world, after all; but trying to follow a backwards inner map also failed. Ages seemed to pass. He'd walked through so many turns now, that he'd lost count, and the former sunshine had long since sailed away and left a gloomy night in its wake. The night had no moon, causing him to stumble once or twice, and finally Charles met a dead-end.

Such traps at the real Rose House, as with its twin maze at Branham, contained opportunities to sit and rest. Generally, these included one or two benches, urns of blooming plants, and even statuary. This one was similar, only the statue was of a tall figure with a man's body and a pig's head. The animal head had unsettling eyes, barely visible in the fierce darkness, but Charles imagined them red and roving.

He sat down on the trap's hard bench, ignoring the hybrid statue's gaze. "Now what, Lord?" he asked. The night's gloom mixed with a heavy change in the air; indication of an oncoming storm off to the east. He had no umbrella, no hat, just his travelling suit and the scarlet sash that connected him to Beth. He withdrew the red ribbon from his pocket and kissed it. "I'll be home soon, little one. I promise."

Thunder rolled in the dark heavens, followed by a fierce flash of lightning. The pig-headed statue seemed to moan as if responding to the advancing storm. Charles began to think of Beth, dying in the other reality of the first locked room. We all are mortal, and so all must die, but he'd never imagined that she might precede him in death.

What if she dies in the real world? Is that what God wants me to learn?

"Forgive me, Lord," he prayed aloud. "I'm letting this gloom enter my heart, but you still lead me, don't you? And though I cannot see the end, I know that you do, and so I trust you, my King. Be my Shepherd, now, and lead me, please, for I've no guide in this dark place. I thought I knew the way through, but nothing here is familiar."

The lightning flashed as if answering, and a large brown hare hopped into view. Hares were generally nocturnal, but what might this one be? Was it natural? Was it a friend or a foe? Charles left the bench and approached the hare with caution, bending down to take a look at its calm face. Rather than run from the human, the hare looked back, its intense gaze fixed directly on Sinclair's face. Lightning flashed again, and the rabbit's almond-shaped eyes performed an impossible trick, changing from amber brown to a very familiar *icy blue.*

Without warning, the blue-eyed hare bounded away, its paws digging into the white and grey gravel. The ocular effect had so startled the duke that it took him another second to recover, but then he dashed after the hare, for he knew this animal was leading him towards an answer.

"Thank you, Lord!" he sang out as he ran.

The hare's legs were quick and muscular, taking the sharp turns with a leaning motion. Charles ran as quickly as his long legs could manage, praying as he rushed after his guide, so fixed upon the purpose that he failed to notice the first drops of rain had begun to fall. The night had no moon, and the human shouldn't have been well-sighted enough to perceive the rabbit's movements, yet he could and did. The hare led him through a set of complex calculations, as if coursing along the outer edges of gears set within a watch. They curved this way and that, sometimes doubling back, but Charles kept pace with his guide.

The early drizzle had become a downpour by the time he reached the centre. As with the Rose House and Branham mazes, the centre of the labyrinth contained a great fountain. At Branham, the fountain took the form of an angel with a sword. At Rose House, the figures were unicorns and lions.

But here, inside the Time Maze, the fountain featured seven, human-like figures, each with a different animal head. The heads faced outward, their hands joined, and behind their backs were long wings.

The blue-eyed hare stopped at the base of the fountain and stood up on its hind legs, its front paws outstretched as if to challenge the anthropomorphic animals.

A brown hare rampant, though Charles with respect. Then, the downpour stopped with one final rush of wind. A flash of lightning illuminated the fountain. The seven heads turned, each one looked down at the hare. The courageous brown hare remained on its back legs, and the icy eyes seemed to flash a series of warnings.

Charles walked round the fountain, wondering if this were a doorway. At Branham, he'd discovered a hidden portal near the fountain's base. He bent to speak to the hare. The animal remained upright and looked directly into the human's eyes.

"I think that you're no natural rabbit," Charles said to the animal. "Are you from the Lord? Did Christ Jesus send you?"

The rabbit's impossible eyes blinked several times, and its paws remained in the rampant position, as if it were ready to battle the unsettling statues. Lightning flashed again, and the wind stopped. The air became still. And then, to the duke's utter shock and amazement, the brown hare *spoke*.

"Cross into the fountain. The winged statues will try to stop you, but you are protected, Charles Robert. The final journey awaits on the other side. Keep your wits about you, for the final challenge has caused madness to others. And always remember, my dear friend, you are never alone."

"Thank you," Charles told the hare. "But thanks be to God most of all."

He stepped towards the fountain's centre, and just before he passed through the portal, he thought he saw the hare transform into a magnificent white owl.

CHAPTER THIRTY-EIGHT
Time Maze – Charles Nears the End

Charles had entered a very familiar landscape. His clothing had changed once again: a shooting jacket and riding boots. He checked his waistcoat. The gold Sir John Bennett was there.

What world is this? he wondered.

"Now that is the question," spoke a man's voice. "Oh, yes, I can hear your thoughts. And there are no blue-eyed bunnies here. You're on your own now."

Charles could see no one. He'd emerged from the first maze into the centre of another. The figures on the fountain had changed. The base contained rows of humans engaged in debauched, sexual behaviour, whilst the statues above were gods and goddesses of ancient lore. Some had wings, but all gazed down upon the lower order humans as though approving the sex rites. The topmost god was horned, and a fountainhead spewed forth from his shoulders, the waters were red, like blood.

"Like it?" asked a tall man, stepping through one of the yews. "I find the figures inspirational and the blood fountain truly energising, don't you? Most refreshing!"

Sinclair offered no reply, for he knew the creature wanted him to react with fear. *Be my Shepherd, Lord!* The demonic entity had materialised from out of the greenery, without so much as bending any of the tangled branches. The yew hedge now served as backdrop for the very same creature the young Elizabeth had drawn over and over. The Shadow Man. He was exceedingly tall, red-eyed, with a body formed from black smoke, a broad belt decorated with human skulls circled his waist, and emerging from his back were great leathery wings, like those of a bat.

"I've watched you with great anticipation, old friend. I must say you're even more impressive in person," said the Shadow Man as he reached out to shake the duke's hand. The hand had six fingers and long nails like talons. Charles refused the handshake.

"Where is this? Where am I now?" he asked the creature.

"Isn't it obvious? You've reached my home, of course. Or rather the outer edges of my land. You're getting closer and closer to my *sanctum sanctorum*, King Charles."

"I am no king, and your language is blasphemous," the human replied. "You dare to mock God's holy of holies?"

"Not at all," the other argued. "I pay tribute to it, but in my own, particular style. These rings of yew form my outer gardens. Did you know that the Branham and Rose House mazes are modeled after my royal garden? But my fountain has no rampant lions, no loyal angels. Bah! Who needs such weak, impotent things, eh? I find these scenes much more interesting. It represents what your Dr. MacPherson calls the first incursion. We call it the Treaty of the Mount."

"Treaty? A pact amongst devils, you mean," said Sinclair.

"Devils? Don't insult me, Charles. Do you know the root of devils is Greek? That silly halfling Theseus would know, of course. Such a fool! It's *diaballein*, meaning to throw or reach across. Do I look as if I'm throwing or reaching? Hardly. I've no need to reach. You've come to me of your own free will. See here?" he continued, his six-fingered hands upon the base. "Behind the top figure? Of course, the horned one is a secret. I can't reveal his identity to you—not yet—but he's an old, old dragon. The Dragon of dragons, you might say. Please him, and you'll become king of the world."

"I've no wish to be king of anything."

"Then why accept this shadow king position in England? Lovely title, by the way. Shadow King."

"What is your name?"

"That would be telling," said the Shadow.

"And *when* is it? I've crossed through different realms and different times. I assume this is just another of those maddening mirror-shard rooms."

"Not at all," the other answered. "There's no need for mirrors now that you've found your way here. I'll admit to surprise that you made it. After you entered two locked rooms in a row, I decided to try a further test. And so I whispered to the child and gave her instructions. She's a pretty little thing. Those were the first words you spoke about her, inside Robert Morehouse's office."

Charles ignored the bait. "You whispered to her? Then, you knew that entering the stone circle would bring me here?"

"Actually, no. Honestly, I had no idea where it might take you. It might have killed you, or vaulted you through a whirlwind of time, back to the days when humans were sacrificed to Herne the Hunter in that same stone circle."

"If I'm so important to your plans, then why risk my life?" asked Sinclair.

He smiled. "Clever boy. You're right. I wouldn't have. You are far too valuable. I lied."

"Who are you? What is your name?"

"You've already guessed it," the stranger countered, walking close enough to breathe its hot breath upon the duke's face. "I'm the Shadow Man."

"Raziel Grigor?"

"You're insulting me again, Charles. Grigor is a problem child and nothing more. Honestly, I was glad when Samael threw him into that stone. And leaving him on the Mount of the Treaty was a very nice touch. When Alexander's men came through, I made sure they noticed the stone and scratched the old words on it. The words of the Oath. No, Raziel's impersonated me a few times, but I soon put a stop to that. I told Araqiel how to cast him into a new prison. Only this time, it's a pretty jewelled box."

"Araqiel, the brainless dragon?" asked Sinclair.

"Yes, he is a bit brainless, isn't he? Eluna's the true power there. However, you should keep an eye on Saraqael. He's very bright and very tricky. Even I can't control him. You play chess, or course?"

"Yes."

"Are you familiar with a lovely old opening called the King's Gambit?"

"Yes, why?"

"Because you're living it. The Otherworld isn't a single united realm. We bicker and make war, much like humans."

"Why is that chess opening important?"

"Because I intend to win this match, which is why I chose you."

"I presume that I'm your pawn, and you're the king?"

The Shadow smiled. "Of course."

"And the other side in this match? Is it God?"

"Your 'God' has nothing to do with this," the Shadow insisted. "He doesn't really care what happens to you. I could destroy you, and he'd not even blink."

"You're wrong."

"Am I? Charles, you're a deep thinker. Let me offer a lesson in logic. The heavens and the earth are part of a massive, multi-dimensional clockwork. The wheels and gears grind on and on, throughout endless millennia, never altering."

"And the clockmaker in this metaphor?"

"Gone. Absent. No longer interested. I admit that the One spoke it all into existence, but as with many clockmakers, he's bored with all of it. He's moved on to other things."

"How is this metaphor related to chess?"

"When my friends and I decided to help mankind, the absent clockmaker grew angry and banished us into a hidden realm. All we want to do is return this rusting clockwork to its original, beautiful form. We're repairing it."

"That's a lie."

"No, it's the truth," the other whispered as he moved closer. "These many factions of human rule must end. If we could find the right human to rule, one that all the Otherworld tribes can agree on, then the gears will shine like gold again! Isn't that worth risking one's king in an opening move?"

Charles turned to look into the creature's red eyes. "The king? I thought I was a pawn, and you were king."

"Did I say that? No, you've always been the king—the greatest risk of all. I had to know if your blood is pure enough and ancient enough. And so it is. After all, you made it here."

"If I'm king, then who are you? You claim this is the outer garden to your home, but it's still the Time Maze, correct?"

"Of course."

"Then, if this is your home, and I'm nearing the centre, you must be the Maze's Keeper. The Minotaur of Theseus."

A volatile eruption of harsh laughter burst from the Shadow Man's red lips; a cruel laugh that caused the ground to tremble. "You think me some hybrid's pet? No, Charles. No. I'm far more than that."

"Which is?"

"Meet me in the centre, and we'll discuss it," the creature said. "I'm tempted to tell you now, but first you must pass one final test."

"That's not for you to decide, Creature," Charles declared boldly, his shoulders straightening. "And I am neither your pawn nor your king. God is my Shepherd and my Redeemer. HE is King! If I remain in your trap, it is because he wishes it. Not you!"

The other's crimson eyes glittered, and a set of nictitating membranes blinked sideways. "My but you're brave! You and I are going to make beautiful music together."

The nine-foot tall creature turned to leave.

"And Beth?" Charles asked.

"Which one? The little girl you just left, the dead one in your first challenge, or the one who awaits your return?"

"How are there multiples?"

"You already guessed the answer. You tell me."

"There's only one," Charles told the Shadow. "One Beth who feels it all. One true reality."

The creature smiled. "Well said. One flesh and blood wife. One real world. You are clever."

"And my final test?"

"Ah, now the great Samael would never answer you, not without twisting it into a riddle. He's a sly one."

"Do you mean Anatole Romanov?"

"Don't feign ignorance, Charles. You've known his true identity for a very long time. Now, come find me in the centre, and we'll talk for days and days and *days*."

"How do I get there?" asked the human.

"Ask your blood. Inside those royal veins, flows a metaphysical key that will lead you." The creature smiled once more and then dematerialised back into the hedge.

Charles knelt down and with head bowed, began to pray. "Why show me all this, Lord?" he asked aloud, the breeze in his hair. "Am I part of some cosmic chess match, or a soldier in a long war? I trust in your guidance, my Shepherd. Help me now, I beg you! Take me home!"

The light wind brought the sweet, familiar scent of raspberry and vanilla—and music.

Not the music of bees and birds, but real music, he realised. Music! Was the Lord leading him, or did another hand play the keys? The sound was faint but real; definitely piano music, just as before in the tunnels. He reached into his right pocket, touching the scarlet sash. Charles shut his eyes and prayed, "Father, I ask you to protect my wife and children. Protect Adele. And, if it be your will, show me the way home."

The music grew louder. He followed it along the gravel-floored corridors of evergreen. Charles could hear singing, high-pitched and sweet, and as he turned the next corner, he saw her. Little Beth Stuart, dressed in a long red nightgown. She looked up, her eyes round and dark. "You're nearly done, but this part will be very hard for you, Captain."

He fell to his knees, and the girl took his hand.

"Hello, little one. No dolly this time?"

"She's gone," said the girl. "Father said she was lost."

"That's probably best," he answered. "Tell me, little one, why will this part be hard?"

"I'm not sure. It's just what the angels tell me, but you'll be all right, Captain. Remember to follow the music. And be careful of the Shadow. He'll try to trick you."

The child began to fade as before, calling as she vanished, "Follow the music, Captain. And remember, you're never alone."

CHAPTER THIRTY-NINE
Time Maze – Utter Darkness

The yew hedges led Charles back into a rock-hewn dungeon, with increasingly lower ceilings. He could hardly breathe in the dank chamber, and his stomach growled for lack of food. When had he last eaten? A small breakfast at Branham, just before the circle meeting. Then Beth had called for him.

Elizabeth had been his touchstone all along, and his arms ached to hold her; not the child, but the woman. His real, warm, wonderful wife.

Follow the music. Little Beth's instructions echoed like a sweet, comforting refrain inside his weary heart, bringing light to the discomfiting darkness. The exhausted duke had never felt so alone. He entered a new corridor and stopped to rest, leaning against the cold stone. He could feel his heartbeat, the muscular contractions of the atrial and ventricular chambers playing the repetitive tempo of life.

Place one foot in front of the other. Keep moving.

Charles began to walk again, passing through the cramped darkness into a broader section of the labyrinth. The air grew warm, moist, fresher than anywhere else within the passages. Usually, the tunnels stank of mould and disuse. But warmth and moisture drew in other creatures, too. Sometimes, he'd see shadowy figures, like large scuttling rats, following behind. Charles wondered what they might eat—demon, dragon, *human*?

After a time, one of the creatures lunged forward, its long teeth bared. The ugly snout flattened against an invisible force, just inches from Sinclair's eyes. The bruised beast ran off, snarling and spitting angrily, into the endless darkness.

His eyes had grown used to the low light now. Every twenty feet or so, a torch flickered against its iron housing. Charles soon realised that each of these flanked portals contained a black mirror that displayed scenes from his own life: His birth, Beth's birth, but also his son Albert's birth and death. And there were happy scenes of himself and Paul as children, playing inside the ruins of Pendragon Castle. He'd even watched as Paul's brother Ian was thrown to his death on the rocks below Briarcliff Castle.

Lorena MacKey often appeared in these strange mirror plays; like a pawn in a chess match. Charles felt that he owed her something, friendship at the very least, but also a sense of family and support. He wanted Lorena to find happiness, and he found himself praying for her safety and continued growth in Christ.

Slowly, he realised something had changed—not just the air. There was a palpable silence. The music had stopped. Had he turned the wrong way? Were the displays of his past meant to confuse him into becoming lost? He strained to hear the piano, but heard only the scratching of tunnel rats' claws.

"Now, what?" he asked aloud. "Father, I've failed you. I've failed my family. Lead me now, please!"

That same sweet breeze that blew through the tunnel earlier returned. He heard a voice inside it, whispering, as if the soft wind were an exhale.

"You're not alone, Charles Sinclair," it said. "You are never alone."

"Thank you, Lord!" Charles cried out. He began to weep, his back against the cold stone. "Please, be my guide."

Far down the midnight-hued passage, arising from within its inky depths, came the slow, low notes of the piano. The duke held his breath and strained to hear more.

The piano played again, as if a ghostly left hand struck deep, insistent C-sharp minor notes; throaty, mournful chords, held in long, anguished cries of *sostenuto* suffering. Then the right hand commenced with triplets; as if bringing aid and comfort to the weary notes of the left.

Charles began to smile. He knew this melody. The tones brought happy memories and hope, for he'd heard Elizabeth play the piece many times, and he'd performed the sonata at Cambridge during his final recital.

"Beethoven's *Moonlight*," the duke whispered. "The opening movement."

He stepped past the nearest torch, ignoring a tempting scene of family bliss playing upon the black portal. He moved farther and deeper into the gloomy darkness, praying the music meant a miracle.

"The Lord is my Shepherd. I shall not want," he said aloud as he walked past more torches, their flames providing a seemingly endless line of tempting mirrors and family scenes. "He makes me to lie down in green pastures. He leads me beside still waters."

The music grew louder, and he could see a wall ahead, looming closer and closer with each step. Was it a dead-end? A door?

"He restores my soul."

He'd reached the wall and could see upon its surface a shadowy reflection. Not a wall at all, but another mirror.

Was this a portal or a trap?

"Yea, though I walk through the valley of the shadow of death, I will fear no evil. For though art with me. Thy rod and thy staff, they comfort me."

The duke took a deep breath; steeling himself against the possibility he might be walking to his death.

"I love you, little one. If this choice goes awry, I'll meet you at our Saviour's throne."

He placed his right hand upon the cold, metallic surface—and pushed.

On the other side of the mirror, Charles discovered himself in yet another maze of endless corridors; this time, made of scarlet and black marble with fiery streaks cutting through the surface; as though struck by lightning. Surprisingly, the wall felt cool, and he was able to lean upon it. His stomach cramped from hunger.

The music continued to summon him onwards, and he followed the piano through dozens of turns, left, then right, straight, then left again. Gradually, the marble walls yielded to something softer, more organic. The corridors became alleyways, and the floor stone cobbles, tufted here and there with bits of dead grass. Street lamps provided an ambient glow to the new surroundings, and city sounds met his ears. Horse-drawn carriages, costermonger calls to roll up and buy, women of the evening shouting prices of two bob, raucous laughter and men swearing as they crowded near a tavern door. This was London, without a doubt. He could smell grease and sweat and manure. But no one took notice of him. Charles passed through their midst like a ghost.

Onwards the music drew him, another turn to the left. The smoke, smells, and soot of London vanished like a dream, and Charles emerged into a lush panorama. Above his head, a round moon sailed upon a sea of stars. And still, the music played on, urging him forwards, but to what?

"Thou preparest a table before me, in the presence of mine enemies. Thou anointest my head with oil," the duke spoke in challenge to the indifferent moon above him. The orb sailed on, but the ground below became dark moors with softly mounded knolls, bisected by a narrow path that led towards a rocky hill. A howling chorus of night creatures, bats, badgers, and foxes, tried to drown out the piano.

And from somewhere beyond the hill, came the chilling howl...

...of a wolf.

Charles thought of the massive grey with red eyes that chased their carriage as he rushed Beth to safety on the night their twins were conceived. Matthew Laurence and his fellow riders had shot most of the pack, but the grey leader had vanished only because of dawn.

William Trent. Dead now and burning in Hell.

But if he's a demon, what then?

Did it matter? No. Whatever happened here, whether he survived or not, the young duke knew with all his being, that God would work it together for good—somehow.

The dirt pathway crested at the top of a steep hillock, and once atop its height, Charles beheld a great castle, off in the distance. Its French-style spires rose high into the mist. A rush of relief ran through his bones; a familiar sense of kinship, for this was Castle Drummond, family seat of royal dukes for over four centuries.

The music commenced anew, drowning out the wolves, and Charles turned towards the castle, dreading what this portion of the maze had to teach him.

As with all other experiences within the tortuous maze, the passing of time paralleled that of a dream. One moment, Charles stood upon the rise of a hill, walking towards the eastern gate of Drummond Castle, five or more miles away—then, in a flash!—he'd arrived at the edge of the courtyard's circular gravel park.

And all the while, the music played on.

The hypnotic music intensified the dreamlike sensation and the impossible time leaps were disorienting. Charles forced himself to focus.

You're never alone, he could hear Fenwick say, as though the valet walked by his side.

Captain, you are never alone, young Elizabeth's sweet voice whispered into his right ear.

Charles smiled, and grateful tears formed at the corners of his aching eyes. He could feel a strengthening breeze upon his face, as though an angel had touched him.

"Thy rod and thy staff, they are a comfort to me, O Lord!" he quoted, continuing the psalm. "Even the lessons taught here in this endless prison are allowed by you, my King! Thank you!" he shouted in triumph. "Demon of this Maze, you will not weaken my faith in the Almighty! I do not walk this labyrinth because you command it, but because the Lord is using it for HIS purposes! And I am never alone! Not for one step, not one breath!"

As if in answer, the music suddenly stopped.

Far to his right, the wolf's voice cried out.

And the castle's front door opened.

CHAPTER FORTY
Time Maze – A Dreadful Past

For hours, days, weeks—nay, for time unknown, Charles Sinclair had endured a series of confusing, often terrifying moments of real and imagined histories. He'd seen boyhood versions of himself chased by winged monsters, beheld the duel that ended his father's life, and then watched his dying father speak to his mother, who then fled with him from their home. He'd revisited the moment when, at four-and-a-half, he'd seen a demonic shadow steal his baby sister, who'd later become Cozette du Barroux, mother to Adele Stuart Sinclair.

Charles witnessed his very first meeting with five-year-old Elizabeth Stuart, when she suddenly appeared in the Rose House maze, a yew construction identical to that of Branham Hall. Beth had called him 'Captain Nemo' even then, the name she'd chosen, based on a character in a Jules Verne novel. Though born thirteen years apart, by some strange tangling of time, he'd known her since he was a boy, and she'd known him since she was a girl. They had passed through portals of doubt into the past and the future, tying the unbreakable knot of scarlet thread that ran from her heart to his.

Were all these historical panoramas true? Might some be fanciful lies, created to confuse him? He'd suspected the designer behind the cruel Time Maze of twisting truth, just as he twisted the turnings and tunnels. Perhaps, all this took place in his mind, whilst he dreamt upon a bed somewhere. He'd visited the Stone Realms whilst in a coma. Might not Theseus and his companions have placed him into some similar state and inflicted these visions upon him?

But why? What value did it bring to the fallen realm, or to Theseus? Might it be meant as a reminder of something long ago forgotten?

I am but king among the dead.

No, I'm not a king. God has a purpose, and that is why I'm here. Not to please the rebels, but to please their Creator!

That much I DO know!

He'd reached the entrance to his uncle's home. To his shock, no men stood guard. It was highly unusual for the Duke of Drummond to break so basic a rule. Whilst watching from the gate, Sinclair had seen the great doors to the castle open, and so expected to see a servant or groundsman emerge, ready to take up his post.

But it wasn't a man who left the castle on that cold, dark autumn night. It was a child.

Elizabeth Georgianna Stuart.

The music returned, and time slowed, its pace matching the rhythm of the mournful song.

Moonlight. Why hadn't he realised it sooner? The moon and wolves went hand in hand, like some supernatural alliance of night. Moonlight.

"Beth! No, wait!" he shouted, the cry lost in the rising mist.

The child paid no heed, her eyes turned northwards where the gardens merged with a thick copse of fir trees, and thence to Drummond Moors. She walked as though in a trance, following some siren song. Perhaps, she heard the same music, for its source lay beyond the trees, and she moved towards it with unhalting purpose.

Charles pounded on the castle doors to alert a butler, a footman, anyone who might help. He turned to watch Beth's progress, but she'd moved impossibly fast and was already at the woods' edge about to disappear into their dark embrace.

He ran to stop her, for Charles knew exactly what moment in time the Maze now forced him to watch.

It was the night of the Wolf.

The night Connor Stuart was fatally mauled whilst saving his daughter.

Sinclair raced along the garden path, and his long legs soon outpaced Beth's small ones. As he caught up to her, he called, "Beth, stop! Please, Beth, stop! Princess, please!"

She paused for a moment, her dark head turned towards him as if listening. But then another voice called from within the unfriendly woods, and the words chilled the duke to his very marrow.

"Come to me, Sweet Child!" called the liar. "Come to me! I am waiting! Your friend awaits! We shall travel, Sweet Girl! We'll see ships and shores and sail upon moonlight! Come to me!"

Charles knew that voice. He'd heard it hundreds of times as a child and later as a man. Not the voice of William Trent.

The voice of...

...a dragon.

Hello, boy. Let's play, it snarled.

The *Moonlight Sonata* played on and on, without mercy, and Charles was forced to watch the sickening attack. No matter how much he shouted, Elizabeth never saw him. Everything slowed to match the dirge's time signature, and the tableau of death commenced in full.

Behind him, Charles could hear a man shouting, and he turned to look, dreading what he would see. He'd guessed rightly. It was Connor Stuart, running to rescue his daughter, though in this dreamscape, his legs seemed locked in lead weights.

Elizabeth had reached a rocky hillock, overlooking a deep crevasse. She stood upon the pinnacle, her trusting face turned downwards, as though contemplating the sheer drop. She didn't see the preternatural wolf's approach. Its hackles formed a black stripe down its muscled back, and the massive paws could cover a man's face with ease. The animal's shoulder would reach his own, thought Charles.

That wolf could eat Beth in one bite.

He shouted again, but she didn't hear. He tried to run, but the effort was wasted, for his legs were frozen to the spot. The Maze was forcing him to watch in silence as the murder played out.

Elizabeth turned, her dark brown eyes rounding in fear as, for the first time, she beheld the beast. The gargantuan wolf stood still as death, the shoulder blades as thick as ploughshares, the red eyes fixed upon the innocent child. Connor Stuart neared his daughter's position, but the music refused to allow him to reach her. Not yet. His legs moved slowly, and the Scotsman screamed in agony. His precious daughter was about to die.

Beth was oblivious to the peril, for she lifted her right hand and reached out towards the beast.

Connor was nearly there, drawn and directed by the music of *Moonlight*, a sonata written by a man who would later lose all hearing. The first movement of this genius work seemed to inhabit two worlds, that of the living and the dead.

Moonlight. The last song Beth had ever played for her father. Charles remembered the story of this night:

Beth had played the first movement for her father, and then she'd gone to bed. Connor joined an inner circle meeting in his father's sound-proof library. But an inner whisper, most likely that of an angel, prompted the young father to leave the meeting suddenly to check on his child. Seeing her gone from the bed, another voice told him to look out the window, for Beth would sometimes walk in her sleep. There she was, on the north lawn, heading towards the hill. Connor ran from the house to stop her.

Now, Charles could see other men rushing towards the night's inevitable ending. *Moonlight* floated upon every molecule of the air now, accompanying the dreadful, slow-motion vista of violence and futility.

Elizabeth reached out for the wolf, unmoving, still dreaming. But the wolf remained still. The two were locked in a strange equality of resignation and recognition. Was that why Beth reached out? Had she known the creature's purpose? Had she seen the wolf before?

Yes. In the centre of the Branham maze, one year earlier.

Onward ran the other men: Robert Stuart, his twenty-one-year-old son Paul Stuart, and the ever valiant James Stuart, Beth's grandfather. These were proud, House of Stuart men, descended from kings and princes.

And every one was willing to die to save a child.

Charles longed to help, but his feet refused to move. No matter how much effort he expended, his shouts went unheard, and his flailing arms unseen.

Time slowed to a desperately drawn-out crawl, for the hands upon the piano deliberately dragged out each new chord with a maddening sort of hatred.

Charles watched in horror as Beth's small mouth slowly formed into a piercing scream.

The wolf responded by opening its jaws, each sharp tooth dripping with thick, glistening saliva.

Then, time sprang forward with a snap! Connor reached the cliff. His arm muscles bulged as he used every ounce of strength to drag the wolf by the tail and free his daughter.

The beast howled and leapt upon the sacrificial father.

Beth tried to interfere, but her leg became entangled with one of the wolf's lower teeth.

To save his child, Connor tore at the animal's shoulders and forced it to fall once more upon him.

Shots rang out, echoing against the rocky summit. The Stuart men fired volley after volley at the mass of grey fur, limbs, and blood.

From his position, Charles could see every action, as though reading an illustrated page of history. In a way, it was a replay of the night Beth faced the wolf in '88. She'd placed herself in jeopardy, to save the sleepwalking Adele.

Beth had only done what her father had done.

Robert Stuart reached Beth first, and he pulled her into an embrace. The child had lost consciousness. Paul arrived next. His father handed Beth to him, and Paul carried her to a safe distance.

Guns blazed again, and James shot the wolf over and over, until it finally broke off the attack. Then, losing its balance, the beast fell into the great crevasse and disappeared into its dark depths.

The fallen Connor Stuart was covered in blood from head to foot. Charles watched James and several servants carry the dying earl back to the castle.

Only then, did the music stop.

But his feet still refused to move, and so Charles watched the men until they receded beyond the rise of the moor and into the dark woods, bound for the castle beyond.

CHAPTER FORTY-ONE
Time Maze – Castle Drummond

Charles stood beside a window inside Connor Stuart's bedchamber. He knew the room well, for he'd stayed here in October of '88, the pivotal year when his entire life had taken a new path. At that time, he'd worn the late earl's dressing gown and found the key to an unread diary, filled with coded information about him.

After the wolf attack, he'd followed James, Paul, and Robert back from the crevasse and now stood beside a deathbed. No one seemed to notice his presence, allowing Charles to move easily about the room. A team of professionals worked furiously to stop the flow of blood from the earl's many wounds. The medical team were the castle's housekeeper, Mrs. MacAnder, and two physicians: Reggie Whitmore, a trusted and longtime circle member, who stood as tall as his patient; and the second would one day betray them all, Solomon Lemuel.

Charles had learnt a lot during his walk through the Time Maze, and one of the portals had revealed some of Lemuel's background. Not only had the disgusting man performed sterilisation procedures on trusting women; his cousin, Crispin Favor was the charlatan who'd killed Sinclair's first son by injecting a deadly agent into Albert's bloodstream. Charles had assumed Favor was yet another version of William Trent, for that is what he'd been told, but the portal implied differently.

Once he returned to the true world, the duke intended to open an ICI investigation into this hellish team of cousins and their medical malpractice. If Crispin Favor still breathed, he'd find him and make sure he hanged.

Charles kept a close eye on Lemuel's actions, wondering if the traitor might also have caused Connor Stuart's death. Both doctors busily stitched up the wounds and dressed them with ointments and linen. Connor remained conscious long enough to ask about Beth. After hearing his daughter was injured but alive, the brave Scot fell into a swoon.

Why had the Shadow Man brought Charles here? Why had God allowed it? What was he to learn? Something else about Lemuel? Something about Connor?

Deciding to look in on Beth, the young duke left Lord Kesson's apartment and crossed to the room she had used last October. Finding the door open, he entered and discovered a third medical man, methodically working along with a team of two nurses.

Duke James sat nearby, alternately weeping and praying.

To his surprise, Martin Kepelheim entered the room as a third assistant to the doctor, a man Charles recognised as circle member Dr. Simon Abel. Elizabeth was unconscious. Abel had laid the child on her right side, to allow access to the leg wound. The wolf had ripped through the skin and exposed the gastrocnemius muscle of the left calf. Abel incised a long opening, from the back of her knee to just above the ankle, so he might examine the vascular region. Two veins were severed mid-calf, and a third slightly nicked. He placed a tourniquet on her thigh, to stop the flow of blood temporarily.

"We must work quickly," Abel explained to the nurses. "We dare not risk the tourniquet any longer than five minutes."

He stitched the veins back together with amazing skill and speed, then repaired the third vein. After just four minutes, the surgeon released the tourniquet. Everyone held a collective breath as they waited to see if the repaired blood vessels would leak. Moments passed, and the calf muscle pinked with colour. The sutures held. Then, Abel stitched the entire wound closed. The first hurdle in Beth's long recovery had been cleared.

"All right, now we must replace the lost blood. Lord Marlbury?" he said, looking at Paul Stuart. "I cannot say how much the child will need, but you're a strapping fellow. This shouldn't require more than you're capable of providing."

Paul removed his waistcoat and rolled up his sleeve. Martin Kepelheim had already inserted the needle and tubing into the young man's arm. It was a strange replay of last year, when Stuart was shot and required blood. Then, Beth had told Charles the story of this very moment.

Without Paul's blood, little Beth Stuart would have died.

The flexible rubber tube crossed from the Scotsman's left arm to the extended right of his unconscious cousin. Unlike her father, Elizabeth hadn't said anything, and her eyes remained shut. Her face was exceedingly pale. Had Charles not known the successful outcome of the operation, he'd have fallen to his knees right then and there, to plead with God for the sweet child's life.

Paul gave me his blood when I fell in Scotland, Beth had told him on his first night at Branham Hall. *If he hadn't, I would have died.* To this day, Elizabeth's left calf bore a thin scar to mark the event, but had faded so much, that it was barely noticeable.

Unaware that his long-lost Cousin Charles stood watching an arm's length away, or what the future held, Paul Stuart asked, "Martin, will she live?"

"I fear, the leg was badly mangled," the tailor answered in a whisper, "but because of our circle meeting, we have Dr. Abel with us. We must thank God for it! Simon is the finest vascular surgeon in the kingdom. Isn't that so, Mrs. Complin?"

The auburn-haired nurse nodded silently for she was counting respirations and listening to Beth's heart using a Cammann stethoscope. "I believe he's the greatest surgeon in all the world, sir," she replied after completing the task.

The blood tube remained filled as it crossed to Beth's veins, and Paul lay back against the armchair, his eyes closing. Mrs. Complin checked the young man's heart. "You mustn't give too much, Lord Marlbury."

"I'm fine," Paul answered, his eyes still shut. "Keep going."

"Doctor, perhaps I should fetch another gentleman to provide blood. Lord Marlbury is looking somewhat fatigued, sir."

"I need you here, Mrs. Complin. Martin, could you do that for us, please?" asked Simon, who then turned back to the nurse. "Also, I may need another box of sutures. They're in my bag."

"I'll get them," Kepelheim offered, allowing the nurse to remain by the child's bed. He searched through a large black medical case, and then returned with a metal box of catgut. "You'll have to show me that vascular technique when our worries are past, Simon. I'll go downstairs now and find more men who can donate."

As Kepelheim passed through the doorway, he actually brushed against Charles's arm without noticing him, but for some strange reason the duke could feel the tailor's arm against his own. He wanted to offer his blood for Beth, but knew it was impossible. This had happened long ago, and he was little more than a ghost from her future.

The piano music commenced anew, alerting the traveller to a possible change in his journey. Charles had no wish to leave Beth's chamber, and so lingered as long as he dared.

James anxiously kissed his granddaughter's pale hand. "Oh, Lord, why? Why take my son and his precious girl, both of them on one night?"

Paul's father passed by Charles; again the traveller could feel the man's arm against his own, but Robert Stuart noticed nothing.

"James," said Aubrey, "you should go sit with Connor. I'll look after Beth."

"Yes, yes," muttered Drummond. "Has he said anything more?"

"Not much. He woke a little while ago and asked about Charles, for some reason."

"Charles? *Our* Charles?" asked the duke. "Why would he ask for him? The lad's been dead for sixteen years."

"His exact words were difficult to discern, but I heard him say the name Charles clearly."

"Poor Charles and Angela. How many more must we lose, Rob? Connor's my heart, my legacy. And if Beth dies, then..."

"She won't die, James. We won't allow it," the earl told his friend. "Go sit with him now. I'll stay with Beth." He looked to the doctor. "Simon, do you need another donor? I can give. If Paul's blood works, then surely mine will."

"Your son's given more than is wise."

"I'm fine, Father," Paul insisted. "I'd give my last drop for this girl. I should have run faster. Better the wolf take me than her. My precious, precious Beth!"

"Paul?" whispered a small voice.

As if roused by her brave cousin's words, Elizabeth's eyes had opened. She blinked several times, and then touched her forehead with her right hand. "What's happened? Why is everyone in my room?"

Paul kissed her cheek. Not wishing to alarm her, he said, "We finished our meeting, and now we're all making our way to our own rooms. Father thought he heard you call out."

Aubrey stepped forward. "Two servings of chocolate cake seem to have caused a bad dream, I think. Forgive us for disturbing you, Princess. Go back to sleep now."

Charles smiled in amazement. Elizabeth remembered nothing of the attack. She would have asked about her father right away, if she remembered the wolf. He wondered what angel had removed Beth's memories, but Charles had an inkling who it might be. He'd not seen much of Anatole Romanov in the Maze, but he felt sure the warrior angel had trod each level with him. Romanov, and quite likely many others, including the ever-faithful Fenwick.

"I am never alone," he whispered, assuming no one would hear.

But Elizabeth must have, for she asked, "What? Who's there?"

"Where, Princess?" asked Paul's father.

"By the door. Can't you hear him?"

Aubrey looked, seeing only several groundsmen who'd been rounded up by Kepelheim as blood donors. "There? That's just Mr. Jones, dear. He's come to take that fading heliotrope plant of yours and give it a good repotting. Remember how you mentioned it to me yesterday?"

This explanation seemed to satisfy her, and she nodded, yawning. "That's right. Is that man a gardener, too?"

"Who, Beth?" asked Paul. "Do you mean Mr. Gower? You know him, dear."

"No. The other one. Who is he?" She paused, her eyes focusing on Sinclair. And then she smiled. Beth's dark irises sparkled in the soft glow of the gas lamps and candles.

"Captain Nemo," she said in a clear voice.

Charles gasped. *She can see me!*

"Does she mean the character in that novel?" asked Kepelheim. "The one by the Frenchman?"

"Yes, I suppose so," Aubrey answered. "Shall we fetch the Verne book for you, Princess? Shall I read it to you?"

She shook her head. "Can't you see him? There, by the door. It's the Captain. He's here."

Charles smiled at her. "Hello, little one."

"You always call me that," she answered.

"And I always will," the grateful traveller promised.

Paul's father looked towards the doorway. "Does she see someone we cannot?"

"It's the laudanum," Abel told them matter-of-factly.

"I don't think so," answered Aubrey.

The earl walked to the doorway, standing close enough to reach out and touch his long-lost nephew. But to the human, living in 1876, spiritual insight did not equal physical sight. "I can't see him, Beth. Is it an angel?"

"No, Uncle Robert. It's the Captain. But he has to leave now. He has to follow the music."

Charles's breath caught in his throat. "How can you know that, little one?"

She smiled. "I hear it, Captain. It's *Moonlight*."

He started to ask her how she knew, but was stopped when a small hand touched his. Charles glanced down to find his miraculous guide smiling up at him.

"It's time to go, Captain," the child Beth said.

"Can they see you?" he asked.

"No," his small guide answered, "and neither can she—the other Beth, I mean."

"How is that possible? How can there be two of you?"

"I'm not sure, but God can do anything, and he has all of it under control."

"So he does," agreed her companion as they left the upper floor and descended the staircase to the main level. "Do you know where I'm to go next?"

"No," she admitted, "but the music grows louder through there."

Elizabeth pointed towards the anterooms that led to the dining hall, breakfast room, and a rather splendid drawing room—and beyond, to the duke's private library.

"He's waiting for you, Captain," she said. "Remember to follow the music."

He knelt before her, tears glistening in his sea-blue eyes. "Must you go? I've come to depend on you, little one. Will I see you again?"

She touched his face, the tiny fingers wiping the tears. "Not here, no. But when you find the centre, then you'll find your way home. I'll be waiting for you."

He kissed her hands. "I shall miss you, little one. Are you dreaming now?"

She nodded, the movement causing her dark curls to bounce. "Yes. Thank you for being my friend, Captain. I love you very, very much."

"And I love you, little one. Very, very much."

She laughed in that same musical giggle that always caused his heart to skip a beat. "Don't be afraid, Captain. The Lord is ever with you. Remember. You are never alone."

With that final word, his faithful guide's image faded; the same way Georgianna's had done after she'd led him through the Stone Realms.

"How like our daughter you are, my love," he said as he stood alone. "Thank you for loving me, Beth. God willing, I'll see you soon."

The music grew louder, reminding him of his mission. Taking a deep breath, Charles turned the handle to the duke's library. It should have been locked, but it yielded to his touch.

Charles stepped into a room filled with an eerie darkness and *Moonlight*.

CHAPTER FORTY-TWO

Time Maze - Charles Reaches the Centre

"Hello?" called the duke as he entered the darkened library. Beethoven's piano music played from every corner, making it impossible to discover the source. Charles knew there was no piano in the library, but one played nonetheless. "Hello?"

The music's mournful tones seemed alive, and it occurred to Charles he might no longer be at Drummond Castle. Though the room had no light source, he'd begun to see unusually shaped shadows.

"*Mondscheinsonate*," a deep voice announced from far away. "I find the music inspirational, don't you?"

"I suppose it can be," replied Sinclair, trying to locate the speaker.

"It's not the original title, though. Beethoven named it the rather uninspiring 'Piano Sonata Number 14'. Dull, isn't it? His instructions, however, offer insight into Ludwig's mind. *Sonata quasi una fantasia*."

"Sonata in the manner of a fantasy," Charles translated. "I'm aware of the piece's history."

"Of course, you are!" the voice laughed, still playing the sonata's first movement. "You performed it at your recital, didn't you? The piano is a mathematical instrument, after all. Tick tock goes the clock—numbers, numbers, numbers. I do love the way your mind works, Charles Robert."

"You have me at a disadvantage," the visitor told his invisible host. "It's clear you're familiar with me, but I've yet to see you. Have you a face?"

The music stopped.

"Of course, I have a face. One that you've seen many times, Charles Robert, though you've forgotten it. Here, let me help with your vision. Let there be lights!" he commanded.

Instantly, a rainbow of brilliant hues revealed a cavernous space within the darkness. A hundred black mirrors bounced prisms from one to the other, as if each were alive.

"Is that better?" asked the magician.

Charles could still see no one, though the room had certainly revealed itself. "I fear my eyes are blind to your face. Is it in one of these mirrors?"

The mystery man laughed, and the music commenced anew. "You're not really looking, Charles Robert. And yes, like silvery moonlight on rippling water, I'm in one of the mirrors."

The duke examined the baffling maze of mirrors, trying to discover where the room ended and the looking glass walls began. "Are you Theseus?" he asked, hoping the man's reply might aid his search.

"Alphonse Theseus? Really, Charles, I ask you, what sort of name is that for a demigod? And the very idea of taking a Christian name is detestable. I wonder why he feels the need to fit into the human world?"

"I think he finds humans interesting," Charles answered.

"Oh, I agree with that. Humans are delightfully interesting. You're spontaneous whilst at the same time, as predictable as last evening's news. Speaking of news, the London papers are having a devil of a time figuring out how to write up that disappearing act of yours."

"Mine? I didn't vanish, not of my own accord anyway. Someone else made that happen."

"Your duchess handles the reporters with great style, though, I must say. She never falls for their tricks. There are few women like her. And I speak from experience."

The source of the voice still baffled Charles. He remained still, listening carefully. The silence continued for over a minute.

"No comment?" the being asked. "For a man known for his elegant speeches, you're certainly keeping your light hidden under a bushel. Lovely turn of phrase."

Rather than play the creature's game, Charles lowered his head and began to pray. As he whispered petitions to the Lord, the mirrors began to shine with an altogether different light. The bouncing prisms separated, each mirror projecting its own single colour.

Charles thanked the Lord for answering.

"Think yourself clever, do you?" the other asked him. The voice came from just one mirror now. Charles stepped towards it. Unlike its brothers, this mirror's internal light shimmered and pulsed with regularity, like a heartbeat.

A cool breeze caressed his face, and a voice whispered into his right ear: *You are not alone, Charles Sinclair. You are never alone.*

Charles stepped into the pulsing mirror.

"So you found me at last," the voice laughed. "Now, where were we regarding Beethoven?"

Charles had emerged into another mirrored space, only this one included a piano. And sitting at the piano was a man. Or rather the semblance of a man. He wore dark clothing that smoked along the limbs and shoulders; as though the black threads waved in the air and danced to the music. The costume was from a bygone century, German or Austrian in style. In Europe, the outer coat would have been made from wool, but the fabric of the stranger's coat hadn't the proper sheen for true wool. Instead, it seemed to absorb light, and the eighteenth-century style helped Charles to pinpoint the era.

Stepping closer, he could see the man's waistcoat, or *stomacher* as the Germans called them. It was made of rich red brocade, embroidered in gold and black thread, depicting a double-headed eagle. No. It was something else.

A multi-headed *Dragon.*

"I knew Beethoven quite well," the creature continued to brag. "He and I spoke often about this composition. I commissioned it, you see. As a gift for one of my countless lovers. Of course, he and I argued over the *allegretto.* It's far too sugary for my tastes. But the final movement, the *presto agitato,* now that speaks of urgency and despair, doesn't it? You played it at Cambridge, but were never satisfied with your performance, were you, Charles? But I thought your interpretation quite satisfactory, even inspired."

"How would you know that?" asked the human.

"I was there that night, sitting beside a fat woman named Gantry in the front row. We applauded with resounding appreciation. That's why I used the sonata as your key point, you might say. Oh, how the choice angered Eluna! *Moonlight* without moonlight, you might say."

"Clever, I suppose," Charles replied. He walked round the gleaming black grand piano, trying to get a good look at his opponent. "I might have played with more conviction and speed in some sections. The *alberti bass* sequences nearly exhausted my left hand. It began to cramp near the end."

"Yes, I noticed that, but no one else did. Do have a seat, Charles. I've anticipated this moment for a very long time."

An overstuffed wingback suddenly appeared. Beside it, stood a table filled with a variety of tempting food, including a carafe of red wine and a decanter of an amber liquid that looked like whisky.

"It's Drummond Reserve," his piano-playing host told him. "Naturally, the wine is a Tuscan *sangiovese*. Jupiter's Blood. Rather fitting, don't you think?"

Charles could see the creature clearly now, and he judged every detail as his host left the piano bench and took an identical chair opposite his guest. He was tall, but not unnaturally so. After all, Stephen Blinkmire stood a whisper below eight feet; an unusual height, to be sure, but not impossible. Originally, he thought the man had multiple heads, but these had now merged into a singular head of fine quality. His hair was golden and fell in soft ringlets to the middle of his back. The eyes were a light blue with flecks of amber yellow, as though reflecting sunlight. His facial features were like those of a marble god: A straight, finely balanced nose, a sensual mouth. The upper lip was shaved smooth to match the bare cheeks. The middle of the chin bore a soft cleft. Strong, expressive brows arched over the remarkable eyes and nose. The man would be called beautiful by women; not a feminine beauty, but one that tempted women into bed whilst inciting men to jealousy. Even high-society ladies would do almost anything to spend a night in such a man's arms; many had and still did.

"I didn't catch your name," the duke opened as his host poured the wine into a pair of stemmed glasses.

"That's because I didn't offer it. Tedious of me, isn't it?" he said, smiling. "I know how much it annoyed you that Uriens refused to tell you his. I do detest that insolent crow, don't you?"

"Most would agree. How is it you know me?"

"Ah, now that is a question that requires a very long time to answer. Have you the time? Oh, yes, I suppose you do," the creature laughed. "After all, this is a Time Maze."

"Does time here pass differently from real time?"

"But what is *real*, my friend? Reality for one is but fantasy for another. Hence, my choice of *Moonlight*. Beethoven's instructions, remember? Played as though in a fantasy. You loved this piece when you were a boy, Charles. You had a gift for playing. Such long fingers for one so young! You can thank me for those."

"I thank God for the design of my body and my soul."

The other smiled as he dipped a finger in the wine and touched it to his lips. "Jupiter's blood is so satisfying! Like bottling vengeance. Those Tuscans are very clever."

Despite a raging thirst and hunger, Charles had no intention of eating or drinking. He didn't trust the creature. Instead, he silently prayed for the strength to endure whatever length of time this hellish game would last.

"You're missing a rare treat, Charles Robert. Or rather Charley Bob, as your aunt called you. I imagine she's more formal these days."

"You imagine?" Sinclair asked, mouth widening into a half smile. "Then you're not omniscient. That must be irritating."

"You've no idea!" the other laughed in answer. "I knew you'd be fun. But not just an amusing companion, no, no; you're far too complex for that. There are countless depths unfathomed in you, Charles Sinclair. No sounding could ever discover the bottom of your soul. To begin, I'll tell you my story. Which, in turn, will lead to yours. Does that seem fair?"

Charles nodded.

"You're circumspect. I admire that," the being answered with a smirk and a shake of his golden ringlets. "First of all, telling you my name would lead you nowhere. I've so many of them. Allow me to offer the one name with which you're most familiar."

Sinclair took a breath and held it—waiting for the revelation. The other smiled and took a deep breath of his own.

Finally, after many minutes of silence, he said in a declarative voice, "I am Legion."

"Legion?" asked Sinclair. "That's rather anticlimactic, isn't it? You're boasting to be a Roman regiment?"

"Hardly."

"A gaggle of demons, then."

"Dull, dull, dull. Try again. Think beyond the obvious."

The duke searched his memory for any books he'd read regarding Roman legions. "Etymologically speaking, *legion* is Greek, but borrowed from the Latin *legionem* and *legere*, meaning to gather together. Are you saying you are a gathering of something else? Not demons. Fallen angels?"

"You're getting warmer. Keep trying," he told his guest. "Try the wine, Charles. I've not poisoned it. And the bread is fresh. I'm afraid it does have leavening, though. I hope that doesn't disappoint a man as pious as you."

"I'm hardly pious, and I prefer to avoid eating. I don't trust you," Sinclair returned. He looked at his opponent for some time, wheels in his head turning. This being thought himself clever, and yet he wanted Charles to guess correctly. Somehow, his pride demanded it.

He wants me to succeed. Why? What investment does this creature have in me?

Theseus had navigated the Time Maze and found the exit. His reward was to become a demigod. The food on the table was an imitation of Christ's final meal with his disciples. Wine and bread—only this bread had leavening in it.

In other words, this meal celebrated sin and embraced it.

"No blood wine? Surely, you're thirsty?" asked the other. "The blood is the life, after all."

"Do you mean my blood?" asked Charles.

The other's face opened in surprise. "Yes, yes! Go on."

"My blood is somehow the life. Not a sacrificial life, but a life you seek. A life you need."

"Yes. Oh, you are so very close."

"You call yourself Legion, not because you are one of many, but because you are many in one. You've taken a legion's worth of identities and used another legion's worth of blood for some dark purpose. But what is it?"

Legion leapt to his feet excitedly, like a child who's been given a new toy. "What is it indeed? Charles, my friend, you are so close, it's blinding! The answer's been staring you in the face."

The duke blinked, trying to clear his vision, but his eyes saw truly: Legion's form began to ripple like water. That familiar tingling sensation ran along his hands and fingers, and his head began to throb. He'd come to recognise this coupling of sensations as God, trying to get his attention. As if the Lord heightened his senses in preparation for a shock.

And the shock came in a hurry. With a rushing of wind. With flashes of light and peals of thunder.

He expected the golden-haired piano player to shift into the popular image of Jupiter. After all, he'd chosen Jupiter's Blood as a substitute for the true blood of Christ for his hellish mockery of communion.

But instead of the Roman storm god, another face appeared. And it made Charles want to vomit.

The new god was the perfect reflection of himself.

Sinclair stared into the face of a man with his eyes, his nose, beard, hair, build; even the same suit of clothes; as though the reflection had come to life.

"Am I supposed to be frightened?" he asked the false Charles. "Amazed? Dismayed? Is there a particular emotional response you prefer, or do I just applaud?"

The 'Charles' version of Legion sighed. "I'd hoped for something, oh I don't know, more spectacular, I suppose. To be honest, I'm a bit disappointed in you."

"Is this a first?" Charles asked, inwardly praying, for he was frightened, amazed, and dismayed all at once. He had no intention of admitting it to this vile creature.

But the being said he'd waited a long time for this moment. Meaning there was more to come.

"And your story?" the human prompted. "You promised to regale me with your own mythology."

The Charles creature resumed his seat, a twisted smirk upon his face. "Mythology! Now that is droll. I knew I'd like you. I'm sure you feel every emotion you deny, yet you remain outwardly calm. Those are kingly qualities, indeed. Even godly."

"I've no desire to become a king or a god."

"Don't you? Why do you think it was so easy for me to reproduce you, right down to whether you dress right or left? By the way, that manly aspect to your physicality is another of my gifts."

"Silence!" Sinclair shouted, surprising himself. "You forget scripture, Creature."

"Creature? That's rather insulting, and what scripture do you mean? I know them far better than you."

"Psalm 82. 'I have said, ye are gods; and all of you are children of the Most High. But ye shall die like men, and fall like any of the princes!'"

Legion blinked. "Ouch! Touché, Charles. Well done. Yes, that scripture is problematic, but we're working on a loophole."

"There is no loophole to God's holy word," the human answered angrily.

Legion smiled again. "Feeling a bit edgy? Yes, that would be the Kronos Web's effect."

"Kronos Web?" Sinclair asked, feeling light-headed suddenly.

"Yes. Mankind's forgotten one of the meanings to the old god's name. Time and how it eats everything. It's why the Maze is so very disconcerting. Rather like a spinning wheel of intentions, possibilities, and failures. You've seen the power of this spinning wheel, Charles. The Maze is a marvellous machine, rather like a living timepiece that feeds on human emotion, and your long journey's given me the energy to become this. To become you."

Legion strutted round the room proudly. "Never fear. I've no plans to impersonate you in the real world. Why should I? I have every confidence that you'll do the work for me, my friend."

Sinclair ignored the impersonator, choosing instead to pray the words of Psalm 91 in his mind: *I will say of the Lord, He is my refuge and my fortress: my God; in Him will I trust. Surely, he shall deliver me from the snare of the fowler and the noisome pestilence.*

"You're thinking again," Legion interrupted. "Whilst I admire the intricacies of that handsome brain of yours, using it to petition the One is futile. He doesn't hear you here. That tyrant doesn't even know this place exists."

"That's where you're wrong," the duke challenged the pretender. "Sheol is naked before God, and Abaddon has no covering. Job 26:6."

"Nice one," Legion volleyed in return. "'Like sheep they are appointed for Sheol; Death shall be their shepherd,'" he quoted. "Psalm 49:14. If Death's allowed to be your shepherd, then it reveals just how little the One values his second sons.'"

"If you believe that, then why stop at verse fourteen? 'But God shall ransom my soul from the power of Sheol, for He will receive me.'"

"Yes, yes, yes. Selah and all that," Legion countered as he returned to his original appearance and tossed his golden mane. "Ah, much better. I enjoy being you briefly, but most women prefer me as I really am. Does the duchess prefer your new look?" he asked, changing the topic to a personal attack. "The longer hair, I mean? The full beard? If I didn't know better, I'd say you're trying to look more like the earl. Her ever faithful Scottish knight."

This hit the tender part of the duke's human heart. He still experienced doubts in the wee hours of the morning; when Beth slept peacefully, and bad dreams awakened him. At such an hour, Charles would reflect upon his failures—the way he and Beth conceived their twins being uppermost on that list.

"Paul Stuart should have married her, Charles," said Legion. "And if he had, she'd be safe now. Safe from us, I mean. It's always been you that we valued the most. But since you decided to steal her from him, we combined your seed with hers to make twins. It's the doubly sweet icing on a very delicious cake, you might say. Robby Sinclair is going to make a magnificently malleable king one day, and he carries your blood with a beautiful purity. That Scotland ritual certainly bore fruit."

The exhausted duke nearly fell into Legion's clever trap, but a gentle breeze caressed his cheek, and Charles could sense the presence of Truth. That presence whispered a verse, and the duke repeated it. "For he shall give his angels charge over thee," he quoted from Psalm 91, "to keep thee in all thy ways. They shall bear thee up in their hands, lest thou dash thy foot against a stone.'"

"That old chestnut? You have to do better than that, Charley Bob," said Legion. "Even Satan couldn't make that one stick."

Suddenly, a blinding light burst through, from every mirror, and Charles feared he'd somehow given power to the creature, for the entire chamber began to resonate with a deep throaty hum.

"No! I will not allow it!" shouted Legion, as he pulled a sword from the air and started towards Sinclair. "I'll kill him first!"

Charles had no weapon, and he shut his eyes and prayed. "Yea, though I walk through the valley of the Shadow of Death, I will fear no evil," he spoke aloud. "Thy rod and thy staff, they comfort me."

Legion's sword burst apart just as he swung it, and the creature's lips curled into a sneer. His sunlit-blue eyes turned to crimson flame and he began to scream and curse at the pulsing light. "Unfair, unfair! No, no, no! You are not allowed here! Go away, go away!"

The blinding light brightened further, gleaming from every looking glass, dividing into fractions within fractions within endless fractions of light, then coalescing back into the original beams.

Charles opened his eyes and stared at the strange interplay of beautiful light against the ever-deepening Shadow of Darkness. "For he shall give his angels charge over thee," he cried out, quoting Psalm 91 again. "They shall bear thee up with their hands, lest thou dash thy foot against a stone."

"Stop saying that!" cried Legion as he cowered near the piano, trying to cover himself with a shroud of gloom and night.

The mirrors shattered, and a great voice shook the walls. "Thou shalt tread on the lion and the adder," cried a voice. "The young lion and THE DRAGON shalt thou trample under foot!"

The horrid Shadow King that called itself Legion screamed as it began to diminish and fade, as though the light had broken its ability to retain its form.

"And because he hath set his love upon me," the voice continued as a figure emerged from the light, "therefore will I deliver him. I will set him on high, because he hath known my name. He shall call upon me, and I will answer him. I will be with him in trouble. I will deliver him, and honour him. With long life will I satisfy him, and show him my salvation."

The figure grew brighter and brighter, like that of a hundred suns—and finally, Legion was gone, banished by the light.

Alone now and trembling, the duke nearly collapsed; but the figure of light reached out and lifted the human up and helped him to one of the chairs. At first, Charles couldn't discern anything other than a blinding amorphous light.

But then a firm hand touched his eyes, and he perceived not one, but two shining entities. Both stood ten feet tall or more, their perfect bodies adorned with gems and glittering gold, as though each brilliant jewel formed a part of their skin. Their hair was white as snow, and their faces like lightning.

"My Lord and my God," the duke confessed as he fell to his knees.

One of the entities placed a hand on his shoulder. "Give thanks and praise to the One, Charles Sinclair. Only HE is worthy of praise."

"I am but a man," the duke whispered.

"You are my friend," said the bright angel as it transformed into Fenwick. "Fear not. You are not alone. My brother and I have aided you many times during this trial."

The painful brightness of the second being's attire and skin faded now, and his height adjusted to a bit beyond six and a half feet. "Hello, Charles Robert," he spoke in his usual Russian accent.

"Anatole. Fenwick. Am I dreaming? Have I died?"

"No, Charles Robert," said Romanov. "It is done. You have finished the course. Come, there is one final task, and then we shall take you home."

"Another task? I have no strength, Anatole. Please, I cannot even stand."

Romanov bent down, his hands placed upon the human's arms in fellowship. "You have seen many moments from history. Some are true, some are lies. Now, let us show you a future moment. The goal towards which all this leads."

"The future?" asked Sinclair. "Am I dreaming?"

"In a way," said Fenwick. "All will be explained soon. Now, take my hand, and we'll show you the end of your life."

"The end?"

"Or the beginning," said Romanov.

Charles felt himself lifted up. The room fell away beneath his feet, and he was taken out of the Maze.

The duke felt wind upon his face, and the noise of war machines. Plagues and famine and the march of many nations. He looked down into a haze and saw a great hill, taller than any other in the world. Upon it, grew six oaks, flanked by two delicate willows. The air filled with smoke and lightning, and a thousand flying machines zoomed round the trees like a hoard of angry flies. The machines spewed fire and belched black smoke, trying to fell the trees and destroy their roots.

Then a seventh oak grew up amongst the others, its strong branches spreading outwards, the roots reaching deep into the ground. One by one, the flying machines fell and each was pulled down into the Earth.

The seventh oak sheltered the smaller trees with its crown. Finally, another tree sprung up from amongst the others. It was a fig. This tree grew and grew and grew, protected by the oaks and willows, until the fig filled all the earth.

The vision ended, and Charles found himself standing inside the Branham maze.

"Did you understand the vision?" asked Romanov.

"I'm not sure. Was that my wife's dream?"

"It is not a dream, Charles, but a true vision of the future; a future that the fallen realm seek to prevent."

"And the trees?"

"The six oaks are your sons. You are the seventh great oak. The willows are Adele and Georgianna. You and your children will help plant the fig. You will protect it, water it, and nourish it until its true owner returns."

Charles felt dizzy, overwhelmed, achingly tired.

"And the fig is?"

"Israel."

That single word sounded like a peal of thunder; a pronouncement of stone and steel.

"Israel?" echoed Charles.

"Yes. As shadow king of England, you will help to fulfill a great prophecy. The enemy wants to stop the fig from rising. But they cannot win. The One has already won the victory through the Cross."

"Why have you brought me here?" he asked. "This is Branham, isn't it? What year is it?"

"It is six weeks after you left," said Anatole. "You'll require sleep and rest to recover. The trial has taken a great toll upon your body and your mind."

"I feel as though I could sleep for years," said Charles. "It's autumn?"

Anatole placed his fingers upon the human's forehead. "Forget," he whispered. "Remember these things only when the time comes. For now, you must sleep."

Sinclair slumped into the soft grass near the central fountain, his eyes closed.

Fenwick felt for the human's pulse. "Is he all right?"

"He is weakened, but will recover fully soon. For now, you and I must return to the Time Maze and make sure the Keeper remains inside."

The lesser angel stared at his superior. "Do you mean he might escape?"

Prince Samael gazed upon his friend with eyes filled with wisdom and experience. "I've fought him many times before, my friend, and he is tricky. He planted the dark roots of these human organisations, Blackstone, Redwing, the White Council, and countless others, long ago. In ages past, years without number. He plays a very long game."

"Is his name really Legion?" asked Hadraniel.

"What do you think?" asked the elder elohim.

"I'm not sure. It's what the demons said to the Son, when he asked their name."

"Had you noticed it is the only time the Son asked a demon for a name?"

Hadraniel's face filled with questions. "No. Why is that?"

"Nothing in the scriptures is incidental, Hadra. Even the *lack* of information is intentional. Remember that. Now, you go to London, whilst I whisper to our friend Stephen Blinkmire to take a walk in the maze. Our duke needs rescue. He will require many days of rest, but once he's recovered, the next battle will commence."

"The next battle, sir?"

"Yes, my friend. We go to war against the Dead."

COMING FOR CHRISTMAS 2021
TWO KNIGHTS DEFENCE

ABOUT THE AUTHOR

Science, writing, opera, and geopolitics are just a few of the many 'hats' worn by Sharon K. Gilbert. She has been married to Sky-WatchTV host and fellow writer Derek P. Gilbert for nearly twenty years, and during that time, helped to raise a brilliant and beautiful stepdaughter, Nicole Gilbert.

The Gilberts have shared their talents and insights for over a decade with the pioneering Christian podcasts, *PID Radio, Gilbert House Fellowship,* and *View from the Bunker.* In addition to co-hosting SkyWatchTV's flagship interview program and *SciFriday* each week, Sharon also hosts *SkyWatch Women* and *SkyWatch Women One-on-One.* She and Derek speak several times each year at conferences, where they love to discuss news and prophecy with viewers, listeners, and readers.

Sharon's been following and studying Bible prophecy for over fifty years, and she often says that she's only scratched the surface. When not immersed in study, a writing project, or scouring the Internet for the latest science news, you can usually find her relaxing in the garden with their faithful hound, Sam T. Dachshund.

Learn more about Sharon and *The Redwing Saga* at her websites: www.sharonkgilbert.com and www.theredwingsaga.com

OTHER BOOKS BY SHARON K. GILBERT

- *Veneration: Unveiling the Ancient Realms of Demonic Kings and Satan's Battle Plan for Armageddon* (non-fiction, co-authored with Derek P. Gilbert)
- *Giants, God, and Dragons* (non-fiction, co-authored with Derek P. Gilbert)
- *Ebola and the Fourth Horseman of the Apocalypse* (non-fiction)
- *Blood Lies: Book One of The Redwing Saga* (fiction)
- *Blood Rites: Book Two of The Redwing Saga* (fiction)
- *The Blood Is the Life: Book Three of The Redwing Saga* (fiction)
- *Realms of Stone: Book Four of The Redwing Saga* (fiction)
- *Realms of Fire: Book Five of The Redwing Saga* (fiction)
- *Winds of Evil* (fiction)
- *Signs and Wonders* (fiction)
- *The Armageddon Strain* (fiction)

CONTRIBUTING AUTHOR
- *God's Ghostbusters* (non-fiction)
- *Blood on the Altar* (non-fiction)
- *Pandemonium's Engine* (non-fiction)
- *I Predict* (non-fiction)
- *When Once We Were a Nation* (non-fiction)
- *The Milieu: Welcome to the Transhuman Resistance* (non-fiction)